WHEN YOU WISH UPON A STAR

A TWISTED TALE NOVEL

ELIZABETH LIM

AUTUMN
PUBLISHING

Published in 2024
First published in the UK by Autumn Publishing
An imprint of Igloo Books Ltd
Cottage Farm, NN6 0BJ, UK
Owned by Bonnier Books
Sveavägen 56, Stockholm, Sweden
www.igloobooks.com

1024 001
2 4 6 8 10 9 7 5 3 1
ISBN 978-1-83795-966-2
Sold as part of a set, not for resale

Cover illustrated by Giuseppe Di Maio

Printed and manufactured in China

WHEN YOU WISH UPON A STAR

A TWISTED TALE NOVEL

For my sister, Victoria,
for the love, the music, and the laughs

–E.L.

PROLOGUE

The Blue Fairy wasn't supposed to listen to wishes tonight, and especially not wishes from the sleepy little town of Pariva. But there came a twinge in her heart as she flew across the low-roofed houses and narrow cobbled roads, and her conscience begged her not to ignore it.

It was well into the evening, and many of the houses were dark, their inhabitants gone to bed. Candlelight lit only a handful of windows, and the Blue Fairy saw eager faces peek out of the open frames. Adults and children alike cried into the empty streets, "Look up! The Wishing Star is bright tonight!"

And so it was. It shone so brilliantly that its light eclipsed the stars around it, and even the moon.

"Hurry, hurry!" the Blue Fairy heard a girl cry. "It'll

be gone if we don't hurry up and make a wish! I've always wanted to see the Wishing Star. Finally, it's here!"

With a smile, the Blue Fairy descended upon the roof of Pariva's old bell tower, her silver slippers landing on the cracked clay tiles with the gentlest tinkle. The bell tower was empty, but even if it hadn't been, no one could see her. She was invisible, as all her kind could be when they wanted. Such allowed her to go about her business and perform the necessary duties without being seen.

Now more than ever, she was grateful for that ability. Oh, she knew it was silly to feel that way. After all, there wasn't anyone in Pariva who would have recognised her even if they could see her. And yet, that twinge in her heart sharpened.

Pariva was a small village, unimportant enough that it rarely appeared on any maps of Esperia. Bordered by mountains and sea, it seemed untouched by time. The school looked the same as she remembered; so did the market and Mangia Road – a block of eating establishments that included the locally famous Belmagio bakery – and cypress and laurel and pine trees still surrounded the local square, where the villagers came out to gossip or play chess or even sing together.

Had it really been forty years since she had returned? It seemed like only yesterday that she'd strolled down Pariva's narrow streets, carrying a sack of pine nuts to her parents' bakery or stopping by the docks to watch the fishing boats sail across the glittering sea.

Back then, she'd been a daughter, a sister, a friend. A mere slip of a young woman. Home had been a humble two-storey house on Constanza Street, with a door as yellow as daffodils and cobblestoned stairs that led into a small courtyard in the back. Her father had kept a garden of herbs; he was always frustrated by how the mint grew wild when what he truly wanted to grow was basil.

The herbs went into the bread that her parents sold at their bakery. Papa crafted the savoury loaves and Mamma the sweet ones, along with almond cakes drizzled with lemon glaze, chocolate biscuits with hazelnut pralines and her famous cinnamon cookies. The magic the Blue Fairy had grown up with was sugar shimmering on her fingertips and flour dusting her hair like snow. It was her older brother, Niccolo, coaxing their finicky oven into working again, and Mamma listening for the crackle of a golden-brown crust just before her bread sang. It was her little sister Ilaria's tongue turning green after she ate too many pistachio cakes. Most of all, magic was the smile on Mamma's, Papa's, Niccolo's and Ilaria's faces when they brought home the bakery's leftover chocolate cake and sank their forks into a sumptuous, moist slice.

After dinner, the Blue Fairy and her siblings made music together in the Blue Room. Its walls were bluer than the midsummer sky, and the windows arched like rainbows. It'd been her favourite room in the house.

The memories made the Blue Fairy's heart light and heavy all at once. Instinctively, her gaze fell upon her old house. It was still there, the door a faded yellow and the roof in need of repair. No one was at the window making a wish upon the star.

With a deep breath, she turned away from her childhood home and concentrated on the rest of the town. Still standing on the roof of the bell tower, she leant forwards and touched the end of her wand to her ear so she might hear the wishes being made below:

"Oh, Wishing Star, please help my little Maria do well in school."

"Dear Wishing Star, I'd like for my Baci to have a whole litter of puppies. Nine of them, that look just like him – all healthy and happy, of course."

"I wish for my shop to have more success."

So on, the wishes went.

Several of them caught her interest, but the Blue Fairy couldn't answer them. Pariva was not a town where she was permitted to grant wishes. Another fairy would listen to the hearts of those who spoke tonight and would heed the pleas of those they deemed worthy.

A white dove appeared at her side, settling its wings as it landed on her shoulder. It made a gentle purr, urging her to leave.

"Don't worry, my friend," she replied. "I know what time it is."

She'd already overstayed the hour, and she'd be missed if she lingered any longer. "Farewell, dear Pariva," she murmured. She raised her wand, preparing to depart – when one last wish caught her ears.

"Starlight, star bright, first star I see tonight…"

Quickly the Blue Fairy drew a circle with her wand, creating a magical window through which she could observe the speaker more closely. He was an old man kneeling upon his bed, with a spry black kitten at his side while he gazed wistfully up at the stars. His voice was not one she knew, but the sound of it – with its gentle inflections and earnest way – was familiar.

"I wish I may, I wish I might," he continued, "have the wish I wish tonight."

His name rushed back to her in a breath.

Geppetto.

Forty years had turned his hair entirely white and aged

his face beyond recognition. But his kind blue eyes and even his nose, round and slightly ruddy, were the same.

Geppetto turned to his pet, a young prince of a cat with sleek black fur and white paws. "Figaro, you know what I wish?"

Figaro shook his head.

"I wish that my little Pinocchio might be a real boy. Wouldn't that be nice? Just think!"

Geppetto's smile was warm and bright, but the Blue Fairy had always had a gift for seeing into one's heart. She could sense the loneliness lurking behind his eyes; he had no company but for his cat and the goldfish in his workshop – no wife, no son or daughter, no siblings. Pariva's children delighted in the toys he made, but their laughter filled only his days. His evenings were almost entirely empty.

Still smiling at the idea of having a son, Geppetto tucked himself back into bed. Within minutes, he was sound asleep.

The Wishing Star faded from the sky, and the Blue Fairy started to lower her wand. It was time to return home. Another fairy would see to it that Pariva's wish-seekers were well taken care of, she told herself.

Yet she couldn't go.

Seeing Geppetto had released in the Blue Fairy a flood of emotions – compassion, pity and a flicker of guilt – and she paused in her step. Her gaze fell upon the wooden puppet sitting in Geppetto's workshop. Her chest squeezed. She knew she ought to leave. She wasn't supposed to be there at all, honestly, but she couldn't bring herself to go.

Her dove tilted its head inquisitively, and the Blue Fairy made a tentative smile.

"Well, why not?" she said to the bird. "No one will know."

Before she might think better of it, she waved her wand and became a soft beam of starlight, travelling swiftly into Geppetto's home.

She entered through an open window and waited until Geppetto and his cat, Figaro, were fast asleep before she unfolded from the light.

There she stood, in the middle of Geppetto's workshop. She'd visited before, so long ago it felt like a dream. The walls were the same; the low ceiling and the long wooden table to the side, cluttered with tools and pots of paints and brushes and sketches, too, but she would not have recognised it otherwise.

Toys sat on every shelf: wooden horses with legs that wobbled and elephants with flopping ears, tiny families in boats that sang when they were wound up from the side. There were clocks, too. Clocks whose hands pointed at stars, clocks where angels standing on clouds trumpeted the hour, clocks with bunnies and sheep running out of a barn when the time struck noon and six. Ships with red-dyed sails hung from the ceiling, and toy soldiers watched over the workshop from a high shelf just below the ceiling.

So much had changed, but the smells were familiar: pine wood and paint and gentle smoke from the hearth and snuffed wax candles. Geppetto had always loved working with wood, and the Blue Fairy's heart warmed to know that after all these years, that hadn't changed.

"You were true to your word," she murmured, taking in the dancing couples and music boxes. "Your promise to bring joy to all those around you."

A cricket hopped onto one of Geppetto's shelves and settled into an open matchbox. The Blue Fairy smiled to herself. Even it felt welcomed in this cosy little workshop.

She paused then before Pinocchio, the wooden boy Geppetto had spoken of in his wish. The puppet was leaning against the wall, newly finished and paint still drying.

He was tenderly crafted, simple compared to some of the other toys in the room. But the care in every detail, from the soles of his brown shoes to the gentle lift in his eyebrows, made the Blue Fairy want to reach out and hug the young toy. He was Geppetto's masterpiece.

There was a certain mischief to his round eyes, and his

innocent smile had echoes of Geppetto's own. Had he been a real boy, he could have passed for the old toymaker's son.

A real boy.

The Blue Fairy inhaled a deep breath. It was not within her power to grant such a wish. But her conscience would never forgive her if she left now. If she ignored the pain emanating from this noble man who had brought more than his fair share of love to the world – who could bring even more, if given the chance.

The first lesson she had learnt as a fairy was to follow her conscience. To let it guide her.

"Good Geppetto," she murmured, "you have given so much happiness to others. You deserve to have your wish come true."

Magic gathered in her wand, sparks glimmering from the star at its tip. She pointed it at Pinocchio's feathered hat. "Little puppet made of pine," she said, "wake."

A silvery crown of starlight burst from her wand, shimmering across Pinocchio's body.

"The gift of life is thine," said the Blue Fairy.

The light swelled until it encompassed all of Pinocchio. Then, once it faded, Pinocchio wriggled to life, sitting up on his own. He rubbed his eyes and looked around before fluttering his hands.

"I can move!" he exclaimed in astonishment. The

young puppet covered his mouth with his hands, his wide eyes blinking as if he didn't know where the sound had come from. "I can talk!"

The Blue Fairy chuckled as Pinocchio rose unsteadily to his feet.

"I can walk." He took a few steps before he fell down onto the table once more.

"Yes, Pinocchio," said the Blue Fairy kindly. "I've given you life."

"Why?"

"Because tonight, Geppetto wished for a real boy."

"Am I a real boy?"

The Blue Fairy paused, not wishing to dampen his happiness with the truth, but she wouldn't lie to him. She chose her next words carefully. "No, Pinocchio. To make Geppetto's wish come true will be entirely up to you."

"Up to me?" Pinocchio echoed.

"Prove yourself brave, truthful and unselfish, and someday you will be a real boy."

"A real boy!"

The Blue Fairy smiled, ignoring the wave of unease rising to her chest. She couldn't bring herself to tell the young puppet that she might not be able to grant Geppetto's wish in earnest. Turning Pinocchio into a living, breathing wooden boy in itself had been no simple feat, and it would surely come with consequences. And Pinocchio becoming a *real* little boy would be another matter entirely. But whatever the cost, she would bear it – and she would see his journey through.

I will find a way, she thought. *Geppetto deserves this happiness. And Pinocchio deserves to be real.*

She looked around, trying to figure out a way to quell the worry that still nagged at her. Even with a good father such as Geppetto, a wooden boy was bound to find himself in trouble. Especially one as new to life as Pinocchio.

A conscience. Pinocchio would need a conscience.

The Blue Fairy eyed the workshop and spied the humble cricket who had been eavesdropping on their conversation. She had a soft spot for crickets. Doves, too.

Pinocchio would need help – why not a cricket?

This one would do fine, the Blue Fairy knew in her heart. After a pleasant introduction, she knighted 'Sir Jiminy' to be Pinocchio's official conscience.

Then she renewed her attention on Pinocchio. "Remember, be a good boy. And let your conscience guide you."

As Pinocchio and the cricket waved farewell, the Blue Fairy exited Geppetto's workshop in the same soft beam of starlight with which she'd come. But she lingered outside Geppetto's house, listening to Jiminy warn Pinocchio about the world's temptations.

The cricket chirped about learning right from wrong, and taught Pinocchio how to whistle when he needed Jiminy's help.

She chuckled, and the unease in her heart faded. Pinocchio would be just fine.

Now all she had to do was find a way to fulfil the whole wish. Surely her fellow fairies would be sympathetic to Geppetto's cause. She'd bring it up with them as soon as she could, at the next monthly meeting on the Wishing Star.

She shot onto the rooftop of Geppetto's workshop, reassuming her fairy form to take one last look at her old friend's home. She didn't know when she'd have another chance to come back. Then she spun, about to make for the Wishing Star that had disappeared behind the night, and a shadow fell over her.

"Still making promises you know you can't keep," mused a woman from behind. "Some things never change."

The Blue Fairy recognised the intruder immediately. Slowly she turned, and as her eyes met the Scarlet Fairy's, her famous poise and serenity faltered, and her lips parted with disbelief.

"Speechless, I see," said the Scarlet Fairy. She lowered her arm, letting the slender red wand in her hand click against the roof. A round ruby sparkled at its head, bright as fresh blood. "Well, it *has* been a long time."

"So it has." The Blue Fairy tried to search the Scarlet Fairy's face for signs of regret or remorse. For any feeling at all.

It shouldn't have surprised her that she found nothing.

She raised her chin, refusing to let the Scarlet Fairy's appearance ruffle her. "I do intend to keep my promise to Pinocchio."

"And make him a real boy? Pray tell, how?"

"He is a good lad. I'm certain the other fairies will see so, too. They'll find that Geppetto deserves some happiness, and Pinocchio will be a worthy addition to the world. They will grant me permission to give Geppetto his wish."

"But what if Pinocchio *isn't* worthy?" The Scarlet Fairy lowered her lashes. "You assume he'll be unselfish, brave and truthful, but…"

"But what?"

"But he's a puppet." The Scarlet Fairy toyed with a strand of her dark hair, as if she were twisting the strings of a marionette. She paused meaningfully. "He has no *heart*."

Suddenly understanding what the Scarlet Fairy meant to do, the Blue Fairy's pulse quickened in alarm. "Please. Don't—"

"Interfere?" the Scarlet Fairy said with a laugh. "But that's my duty. My *responsibility*. How ironic, Chiara, that after all these years, it's *you* who should falter from your responsibility. Then again, I shouldn't be surprised. You aren't as loyal as you make everyone think."

The Blue Fairy flinched, both at the insult and at the sound of her birth name. "Now, that isn't true—"

"Once your hopeless little fairies see what a wicked boy Pinocchio is," the Scarlet Fairy went on, ignoring her, "you'll have to turn him back into a pile of wood. How sad old Geppetto will be then."

"You wouldn't!"

The Scarlet Fairy's lips curved into the ghost of a smile Chiara had once known and loved, except it was all wrong. There was no cheer in it, no warmth. No mischief. It was cold enough to freeze the Lyre Sea.

Forty years had wedged a world between them.

The Blue Fairy half closed her eyes, missing the days when the Scarlet Fairy spoke to her without vitriol, and she replied with dread. "Unless what?"

"Unless we make a wager," mused the Scarlet Fairy. "Or are you too good and righteous to partake in a harmless little bet?"

"Coming from you, I doubt very much that it will be harmless."

"It could be very beneficial for your dear Pinocchio," the Scarlet Fairy said. Before Chiara could respond, she went on, "If you win, I won't tell the fairies about what you've done here tonight, and I'll even help you turn Pinocchio into a real boy."

Surprise made the Blue Fairy look up. "You'd help me?"

"*If* you win," confirmed the Scarlet Fairy. "But if you lose…"

Chiara went silent, knowing that the price would be high. She'd been caught in a trap, and she knew it. If she left now to tell the others, the Scarlet Fairy would embroil poor Pinocchio into an awful plot, and everyone on the Wishing Star would unanimously vote that Chiara lift her spell. There would be a good chance she'd lose her wand and wings and be cast out from the fairies forever.

How did we become like this? she wanted to ask aloud. *Can we go back to the way things were?*

But she already knew what the Scarlet Fairy's answer would be.

Hiding her disappointment, the Blue Fairy eyed her companion coolly. "Name your terms, sister."

CHAPTER ONE

Forty years earlier

Ask anyone in Pariva, and they would have agreed that Chiara Belmagio was the kindest, warmest girl in town. Her patience, especially, was legendary. Then again, anyone who had grown up with a sister like Ilaria Belmagio – local prima donna in both voice *and* demeanour – and still considered her to be their best friend had to be nothing short of an angel.

Chiara was newly eighteen, having celebrated her birthday a month earlier, in June, and she was the middle child of Anna and Alberto Belmagio, beloved owners of Pariva's only bakery. In short, she had modest ability on the harpsichord, favoured blackberry jam over chocolate and loved to read outside under her family's lemon tree, where she often helped children with their arithmetic homework and nurtured nests of young doves.

Like her neighbours, she knew each name and face of the 387 people in Pariva, but unlike most, she took the time to make anyone she encountered smile, even grumpy Mr Tommaso – who was a *challenge*. And she took pleasure in it.

When people wanted to talk, she listened. That was how she learnt of the dreams and hopes of everyone in town. Many dreamt of leaving Pariva, some to seek fame and fortune, others to find adventure or even romance. But never once did Chiara ever desire to leave her hometown. Never once did she covet such things as fine dresses or invitations to grand parties in Vallan. Still, that didn't mean she was without dreams.

Hers was a simple one, compared to her sister's of becoming an opera singer or her brother's to master their parents' rye bread and serve it to the king one day. A silly one, Ilaria would say, if she knew.

But Chiara never spoke of her dream. Unlike most folks in town, she never looked out for the Wishing Star to wish that it might come true – she was too practical to believe in miracles that came from wands or wishes, and she certainly didn't believe in fairies. She didn't believe in magic, either, at least not the sort of magic in the stories her papa had told her and her siblings when they were little, about fairy godmothers who could turn pumpkins into carriages and magic wands that could change stones into diamonds.

The magic she believed in was of a different sort. The sort that cheered a pall of melancholy, that fed a hungry belly, that warmed a cold heart. She believed in kindness, in compassion and in sharing what fortune she had – with those who needed it.

Ironic, of course. For little did she know it, but Chiara Belmagio was about to meet a fairy.

It was a blistering August morning. Too hot even for Chiara, who typically loved the sun. She was outside in the garden, pruning violets and bluebells to take to the bakery. She liked giving flowers to their customers; it always made them happy.

"Mamma and Papa sent a messenger," called her older brother, Niccolo, from the back door. Careful to stay under the shade of the roof, the young man had one foot out in the garden, and one foot remaining in the house. "You've the day off. No one's buying bread in this heat."

Chiara bunched the flowers into a bouquet and rubbed her hands on her aprons. "Are Mamma and Papa coming home, then?"

"They're going over to Mr and Mrs Bruno's after they

sell off Papa's sandwiches. Bet they'll be there all afternoon playing cards." Niccolo turned back for the kitchen. "I made juice. Orange and lemon. Come inside before Ilaria drinks your share."

Ten more minutes outside under the torturous sun, and Chiara decided to take her brother up on his offer. She was parched. Her scalp burned, and her skin was so warm she felt almost feverish. As she retreated into the house, she doffed her hat and wiped the perspiration that pooled at her temples. Her fair blonde hair clung to her temples, and the blue ribbon she always tied around her head was practically drenched.

The promised glass of juice awaited her in the kitchen, and she drank quickly, savouring the tartness of orange and lemon on her tongue. "Ily?" she called, entering the hall. "Nico?"

Beyond the kitchen, in the Blue Room where her family gathered while not eating, she heard her siblings. Sixteen-year-old Ilaria, primarily, wheedling their brother to take out the boat. Chiara stopped just outside the door, not wanting to interrupt.

"Will you stop being such a slug, Niccolo, and take pity on your poor, favourite sister for once? All I'm asking for is just an hour at sea. You always love taking out the boat—"

"I don't think I've ever called you my favourite sister,"

replied Niccolo, turning the page of his book. His dark brown hair fell over his eyes. "That honour belongs to Chia."

Ilaria ignored the insult. "The house is a furnace. If I stay here any longer, I'll perish."

"Then go outside for a walk."

"Outside isn't much better. You know how sensitive my skin is on days like this. I'll peel and burn – I need fresh sea air."

"Fresh sea air is still under the sun, sister," Niccolo pointed out. He dipped his head back into his book. "I told you, the water's dangerous. There's talk of a giant whale in the sea. It's already capsized four fishing boats."

"Giant whales." Ilaria rolled her eyes. "I bet if they were mermaids you'd be clamouring to go for a sail. Even if their siren song made us crash against the rocks."

"There are no mermaids. Only a whale."

"So you say." Ilaria leant against the chipped blue wallpaper, the back of her hand to her forehead. Chia knew the look well – the prelude to a dramatic swoon. At the age of seven – when Ilaria first decided she would become a world-famous opera singer – she'd begun practising the art of swooning. By now she was a master.

Unfortunately for her, Nico wouldn't fall for her tricks.

"You kill me, brother," Ilaria said, going ahead with the swoon anyway. "I shall die of heat and suffocation."

"Go ahead. Usually it's consumption, lovesickness or utter boredom that are going to kill you. Heat and suffocation should be amusing. Are you going to sing a twenty-minute aria now as you die?"

Ily glared. "I sense a mockery being made of me."

"You make it too easy."

With a scowl, Chia's sister folded her knees under her skirts and began to slump gracefully down against the wall. In about three seconds, she would wilt into a well-posed puddle on their grandmother's knotted rug.

One, Chiara counted.

Ilaria fanned herself with her hand.

Two.

Ilaria tugged at her collar.

Three.

Ilaria collapsed with an elegant thud. A beat later, Niccolo lowered his book and rose from his seat, walking leisurely to his sister's side. "No song this time?" he teased.

When she didn't reply, he dropped his book squarely on her stomach, and her eyes snapped open.

"Why you – you could have broken my rib!"

"Hardly," said Niccolo dryly, retrieving his book, which was small enough to fit in his pocket. "You've cried wolf far too many times, little sister. Did you really think I'd believe you?"

Ilaria rolled up, twisted towards the mirror vainly, and touched up her crumpled hair. "You'll regret this when I'm famous."

"Your death scenes are already famous – in this house."

Chiara chuckled, giving away her presence just outside the room. Niccolo glanced over his shoulder, and his frown released into a smile. "See, even Chia agrees. Maybe she can accompany your swan song on the harpsichord."

Ily threw up her arms and appealed to her sister. "Every day, he mocks me. How am I related to this uncultured boor!"

"It might be wise not to call our brother an uncultured boor," said Chia evenly. "Especially when you're trying to ask a favour of him."

"Ignoramus, then," amended Ilaria without a hint of contrition. "Chia, I have to get out of here." Her dark green eyes rounded with a plea. "Please, help me?"

Chiara pursed her lips as she studied her sister. Side by side, she and Ily didn't look much like sisters, and their temperaments too were as different as night and day. Chiara was bright like the meaning of her name, with sun-kissed golden hair – the colour of uncooked pasta, Nico liked to tease – that curled at her shoulders, and eyes as blue as the jays that perched along their roofs come spring. She was kind and patient and warm, while the only angelic thing about Ilaria was her voice. Mischief and cunning made the younger Belmagio daughter's green eyes glitter, and she shared the same dark chocolate hair as Niccolo and their mother. But what both girls did share was the heart-shaped blush on their cheeks when they were happy, the way their heads tilted to the left when they were quizzical, and the way they sighed – as Chiara did now, with resignation.

Why not, her heart told her. After all, like Niccolo said, the bakery was closed and didn't need flowers, her parents were playing cards with friends – and most of all, it would make Ily happy. Chia loved seeing her sister happy.

But how to convince Niccolo to take them out?

"Think of my voice, my future!" Ily went on. "It hurts just to breathe, the air is so thick."

"Smell this, then," said Chiara, passing her sister a small bouquet of the flowers she'd plucked outside. She made a curtsy. "For the prima donna of Pariva."

"Are you sure you want to encourage that ego of hers?" said Niccolo.

Chiara knew what she was doing. While Ily sniffed the flowers, Chiara seated herself at the harpsichord and coaxed out the opening chords to her sister's favourite aria, 'The Nightingale'. As she predicted, Ilaria couldn't resist joining in on the music. Without even realising it, Ilaria started singing the first stanza, which mimicked a lost nightingale chirping as it searched for its home.

Music always cast a spell over the Belmagio household and eased away any discord between the siblings. The three had spent many afternoons in their youth making music together, Niccolo joining on his violin. By the time Ily had sung through the whole song, even Niccolo had forgotten his irritation at Ily and was clapping. Just as Chia knew he would.

Chiara joined in on the applause. "You see?" she said to her sister. "A little heat has no chance against a voice as powerful as yours. Which means when your auditions come around, they'll be a breeze."

Ilaria grinned. "Only because *you're* at the keys, Chia."

"Well, I'm not going anywhere. I'll be your accompanist as long as you need me." Chiara paused, turning slowly towards Niccolo as she flexed her fingers. "Though now *I* am a bit warm."

It was true. Sitting at the harpsichord by the window had made Chiara's skin heat. She raised her glass of juice for one last sip. "If Niccolo won't come, maybe *I'll* take the boat out for some fresh air."

Ilaria gasped in delight. "You're a bona fide saint." She hugged Chiara. "Thank you, thank you!"

"You can't take the boat out by yourselves!" Niccolo exclaimed.

"Why not? If you won't go…"

Their brother grimaced and tugged on his collar, the way he did when he was about to give in to something. "I told Ily already I don't think it's safe—"

"Because of the whale?" Ily snorted. "Who'd you hear this from, the sailors on the docks? You really believe there's a giant beast large enough to swallow entire houses?"

Niccolo flinched. "Monstro. Everyone says he's real."

"Then maybe we should look for him." Ilaria knew better than anyone how to pull her brother's strings – when she put her mind to it. How to pull anyone's strings, really. That was her talent. "Unless… you're afraid."

"Afraid?" Niccolo spluttered, though from the way his shoulders tensed, it was obvious that he was. "*I'm* not afraid of a big fish. I'm afraid of putting my two sisters in danger."

"You talk as if we're delicate lilies wilting under the sun," said Ilaria. "We're—"

"Grateful for your worry, Nico," Chiara interrupted. "How about we only go for an hour, and stay close to the coast? If the water starts to become too rough, we'll come back straight away." She cast her sister a meaningful look. "Ilaria will even help row."

Niccolo gave Ily a narrow look. "I'll have to see it to believe it."

"It's a promise," said Ilaria, making a crossing motion over her heart. "Honest."

Niccolo sniffed. But he was tempted; Chiara could tell by the way he tilted his head, considering. "I guess there's no harm so long as we keep in sight of the coast," he said slowly. "I'll bring my telescope in case there's a Monstro sighting."

Ilaria let out a triumphant squeal and pushed Chiara towards the stairs. "Hurry and get your hat, Chia. Can you pack some sandwiches, too?"

"And pistachio cookies?"

Ilaria winked. "You read my mind."

Simple as that, Chiara's plans were changed. Fate had stepped in and ordained that she should go sailing with her siblings.

It was to be a decision that would change everything.

CHAPTER TWO

Geppetto blamed the heat for muddying his senses, and for making him slip out of the workshop in the middle of the afternoon for a row around the coast. It wasn't like him to take off to the sea, especially in his father's cherished but mouldy shrimping boat.

At least he wasn't the only one with the idea. Back at the docks, Niccolo Belmagio was untethering their family boat while his sisters, Chiara and Ilaria, hopped inside.

"Looks like they're going for a sail, too," Geppetto murmured. Had he waited twenty minutes, he might have got to say hello to them.

He laughed at himself. "Even if you had," he admonished, "you'd be too shy to speak with them. To make friends." Oh, Niccolo had always been pleasant to him; they were the same age – nineteen years old – and had gone to school together, and there was no one kinder than Chiara, but Ilaria… Ilaria probably didn't even know he existed.

Geppetto's laugh died in his throat. He could never admit aloud, not even to himself, that it was Ilaria he wanted to speak to. Well, it was Ilaria he wanted to *hear.* Her voice, round and resonant with a singer's richness, was his favourite sound in the world. It was music to his ears, and simply thinking of it made a clumsy smile spread across his face. Without realising it, Geppetto started humming.

The sound filled the silence between his oar strokes, and finally he succumbed to the ache in his arms and set the oars aside for a moment's rest. He was a competent enough sailor, thanks to the frequent trips to sea he and his papa used to take before his mother had passed away two years earlier. What he wasn't – was a rebel.

Taking the shrimping boat out without permission, leaving in the middle of the day when there was still work to be done – it had to be the heat that had stolen his senses. He could hardly believe what he'd done. He'd regretted it the moment he'd jumped into the boat.

But the current was strong, and when he tried to turn back, it pushed him the other direction – into the wide and open sea. He glanced back, watching his hometown shrink against the horizon.

He took an uneasy breath. "I guess I should just enjoy it."

Folding his arms behind his head, Geppetto leant against the side of his boat and gazed at the sky, marvelling at how far and blue it unfolded. When was the last time he'd just stared at the clouds? All day and evening, he worked as Pariva's sole luthier, repairing instruments. Papa's fingers had become swollen with age, so he increasingly relied on Geppetto to keep the workshop running. And Geppetto did, dutifully.

He didn't have the courage to refuse.

Nor did he have the courage to open the trove of dreams he kept stowed in his heart. Secret dreams, like the one that had led him out to sea today.

"That's all they will ever be," he murmured to himself as he watched the sea. A ripple disrupted the still water. "Dreams. Papa will never understand."

The ripple ballooned, and Geppetto thought he glimpsed the flash of a black tail far in the distance. He sat up, the rush of fear in his gut telling him he should pick up his oars right away and row back towards shore.

But then the breeze picked up and a gull squawked and he realised how silly he was being on this perfect day.

"It's probably just a seal," he said, laughing at himself. "Don't be such a coward, Geppetto."

With a sigh, he picked out the pencil he had tucked behind his ear and fumbled for the sketchbook he'd brought. He might not have the courage to tell his father about his dreams, but he certainly wouldn't run away from a seal. Still humming to himself, he flipped past sketches – a father and son hiking the base of Mount Cecilia, an old woman feeding pigeons along the old fountain in the middle of Pariva's town square, a young couple strolling around the bell tower at dusk – until he found a fresh new page. In a series of crisp, confident lines, he drew a seal's tail, and he readied his pencil for more as the ripples grow closer and stronger.

Everything seemed to go perfectly still.

Then the water beneath his boat suddenly lifted, and the sea turned black as night. Geppetto stopped humming, but it was too late.

Two wrathful green eyes lifted out of the sea.

And Geppetto found himself face to face with a monster.

CHAPTER THREE

"Fine," Niccolo finally conceded, when the Belmagio siblings had made it out to sea. "This was a good idea."

"Didn't I tell you so?" said Ilaria as she basked in both Niccolo's compliment and in the breeze. She tugged at the red ribbon in her braid and let her hair fly loose. "This is how summer should be spent. Much better than having to be in Mrs Tappa's shop selling hats to old fuddy-duddies. Or chopping pistachios with Mamma right next to the oven. Why so quiet, Chia?"

Chiara smiled. "I'm enjoying the view."

And what a beautiful view it was. Mountains to the north, with a clear vista of Mount Cecilia – its snowcapped peak so high Chiara couldn't tell it from the clouds – and endless blue sea to the south. The weather was perfect there, the day's heat muted by the generous breeze from the water and the sun's glare mellowed by the shadows from the mountains.

"We should've brought cards," complained Ilaria, who couldn't stay still for longer than a few minutes. She picked up Nico's telescope. "How about a game? One minute each with the spyglass, two rounds. Whoever sees the biggest fish is the winner, and losers swim one lap around the boat?"

"I don't think you want to be taking a dive in that dress, Ily," Niccolo retorted. "Besides, your head's so full of air you might float away – and what would happen then?"

Ily punched their brother in the arm.

Nico nearly dropped his oar. "Hey!"

"It could be fun," Chiara said, mediating. "Though let's not have winners and losers, shall we?" She took the telescope from Ily and turned it to the water, taking in the wrinkles in the otherwise still sea. Strange; they seemed to be getting stronger, and the water darker. Squinting to take a closer look, she followed their trail all the way to the curve of the earth beyond the sea. On the edge of her lens, an enormous black tail cut through the water.

With a gasp, she shot up to her feet. "A whale!" she cried.

"You can't win already," Ily muttered, not grasping the danger.

But Niccolo's eyes widened, and he seized the telescope to look. "Stars Almighty, it's Monstro!"

"I want to see," said Ilaria, grabbing at the telescope. But no sooner did she speak than Monstro reappeared, his tail lashing out of the sea like a mighty whip. As it hurled down, waves rolled across the sea so far that even the Belmagios could feel the creature's power.

"Have you ever seen anything so enormous?" Niccolo was flush with adrenaline. "Just the size of his tail – it's bigger than all of us combined."

"We've got to get a closer look," Ilaria urged.

"Are you sure that's a good idea?" said Chiara, holding her hat as a sudden wind gathered.

"When will we get this chance again?" Ily needled Niccolo. "Come on, just a little closer. We're miles away as it is."

Their brother didn't need the encouragement. He was already steering the boat in Monstro's direction.

"We're getting awfully far from the coast," cautioned Chiara. "Remember what the sailors said… that Monstro is—"

Before she could finish her words, the wind disappeared. The waves flattened, and the water went still as it had been before. Too still.

"He's gone," Ilaria breathed, shooting up to her knees

for a better look. Indeed, the whale was nowhere to be seen. She slapped the side of the boat. "Look what you did, Chia. We missed him!" As her balance faltered, she sat back down with a moan. "All that for nothing. I think I'm getting seasick."

"Rest," Chiara said, moving to the side so her sister could lift her legs. While Ily lay down, she propped her arms on the edge of the boat. The water was as blue as before, as if nothing had happened. Bluer than the sky, really, and the cornflowers and bluebells that Mrs Vaci sold in her chocolate shop. Chiara's favourite colour.

Chiara dipped her fingers into the sea, letting them skate across the water as Niccolo took a break from rowing. It was still warm, but the air had cooled. The ripples that she created were black – like the dark water earlier. Was she the only one who noticed that?

The hairs on the back of her neck bristled, and her stomach churned with dread. Something wasn't right. There was evil in the air; in the sea, too. She didn't know how she knew, but she could feel it. She clenched the telescope and scanned the horizon.

To her far left drifted the remains of a boat. Planks of wood floated among a trawl net and a plain white sail.

There, amid the debris, flailed a pair of human arms. "Help! Help!"

Chiara gasped. "There's someone out there!"

"Someone out where?" Ilaria echoed. "I don't see anyone."

Chiara wasn't listening. She kicked off her shoes. Every second marked the difference between life and death, and she had none to waste. Her knees buckled at the sight of the waves ahead, some thrashing so powerfully they sounded like thunder. There it was again: that cold prickly feeling in her stomach.

Danger. Wrath. Fear.

It should have made her hesitate, but Chiara sensed something else beyond the darkness that gathered in the sea. Her heart had always been sensitive to the needs of others, and what she felt now was so familiar that her entire being latched to it like a magnet.

Hope. It was feeble and dying, like a candle being held against the wind. Still fighting, but without much longer until it became nothing.

I'm coming, she thought to it.

She dived off the boat.

CHAPTER FOUR

The water was the perfect temperature for a dip, but that was quite possibly the last thing on Chiara's mind as she swam. The currents were against her, trying to push her back towards her brother and sister, so she kicked harder, ignoring their shouts and screams.

"Chia, come back!"

"Chia!"

The water and wind swallowed Nico's and Ily's cries, and soon Chiara was utterly alone. Never before had the world been so silent yet deafeningly loud. Water thrashed and roared in her ears, yet amid it all, she could hear her heart thumping in her chest, her breath growing shallower.

A cracked piece of wood coasted past her, travelling at

alarming speed. It nearly crashed into her head, and Chiara swerved only at the last second.

Go back, her body screamed at her. If she went on, there was a high chance she would get caught in the tides and drown.

"Help!" cried the young man again. "Help!"

There's a chance you'll die, her conscience agreed, *but there's also a chance you might save him. If you give up now, there will be no chance for the boy. Only death.*

That was all the convincing she needed. She threw aside her fears and pushed even harder. Salt stung her eyes, and seawater choked her throat and burned up to her nose. The pain quickly became unbearable, yet as the water roared in her ears, Chiara had only one thought.

Faster. She had to swim faster.

Keep a steady rhythm, she told herself. *Don't panic.*

But Chiara was only human, and she was nothing compared to the sea. Soon she could feel herself losing against the tides, and for every kick forwards, the sea pushed her back five strokes. She was losing him. She was losing herself, too.

Chiara blinked, struggling against the seawater brutally flushing her eyes. They instinctively closed, leaving her in the dark. Her legs at least kept kicking, but her muscles were on fire, and her strength was near the end of its reserves.

Over there, came a voice in her ear. It wasn't hers; it was a woman's voice that she didn't recognise. *Just a little more. You can do this, Chiara Belmagio. Keep fighting.*

The voice sounded like a friend. Chiara trusted it, and its intensity gave her the strength to force her eyes open. Sunlight painted her world white before granting her sight again; another blink, and she saw him.

The young man who had shouted for help. He looked unconscious, and his arms were wrapped precariously over a floating log.

With all that she had left, Chiara swam until she reached him.

He was from her village; that she knew right away. The luthier's son. Not someone she often saw in the town square, but were she not half-drowned, his name would have come to her immediately.

She struggled to keep his head above the water. His moustache was soaked, and his skin was so cold she couldn't tell whether he was alive. "Stay with me," she said hoarsely. "You're going to be all right."

It felt like a lie, even though she didn't mean it as one.

What now? she thought desperately. She couldn't swim him all the way back to Niccolo's boat. Even if she wanted to try, she couldn't see it; she knew her brother and sister were looking for her, and she couldn't risk swimming in the wrong direction. And there was no way for her to try to revive him while they floated in the sea, one fierce wave away from death.

The seconds ticked, each an era. Now that she wasn't swimming, the water felt colder than it had earlier. Chiara's teeth chattered uncontrollably. She was hot and cold at the same time, her muscles weeping as she cycled her legs to stay afloat. *Focus,* she told herself as she bobbed out of the water, shouting for help.

She might have cried when she spied Niccolo and Ilaria. Even her sister was rowing, for the first time in her life – a fact made obvious when, in the excitement of finding Chiara, she stopped and accidentally dropped the oar in the sea.

"T-t-take him first," Chia said, pushing the luthier's son into Niccolo's arms.

She waited until he was safely aboard before accepting Ilaria's outstretched arms.

"Don't you ever do that again!" Ily cried, hugging her fiercely. "I thought you died."

"C-c-careful," Chia tried to tease, but her voice came out as a series of hacking coughs, "you… you might get your favourite dress wet."

"At least you'll be alive to help me wash it."

Chiara would have laughed if she could, but she was exhausted. She let her head fall back against the boat, hardly able to move. She was still shuddering, and her teeth still chattered violently.

"Drink some water," urged Ily. "Here, take my—"

"Give… to him," Chiara rasped, pointing at the luthier's son. Niccolo was pumping the young man's chest in vain.

Ilaria twisted; she'd forgotten the half-drowned young man. "He's not even awake. Nico's helping him. I want to be with you."

Chiara choked. "Ily…"

"All right, all right." Ilaria angled back towards the luthier's son and took his chin, sweeping aside his moustache. "Hey, don't die on my watch, all right? I'd never hear the end of it from Nico and Chia."

As she dribbled fresh water through his lips, the young man's eyes fluttered. "My word," he murmured, half-consciously. "A fairy! The most beautiful fairy I've ever seen in my life."

Ilaria giggled at Chia. "I like this one. Even half-dead, he knows beauty when he sees it."

Consciousness returned to the young man, and his eyes went round. "Oh, my!" he cried, springing upright. His body was a step behind his mind and wasn't quite ready to rise yet – resulting in his breaking into a fit of coughs.

As he spluttered, seawater dribbled from his sleeves and splashed onto Ily's skirt.

"Watch it!" Ily moaned, holding up the outer layer of her skirt against the sun. "It's all wrinkled."

Niccolo yanked Ilaria behind him and caught the young luthier before he teetered off the boat. "Easy, easy," he said. "Breathe in, out."

"Here, have more water," Chiara offered. She crawled to the young man's side, covering his hand with hers. Thank heavens it was a warm day. Already some colour was returning to his cheeks.

"Thank you," he said, catching his breath. "Thank you."

"You're old Mr Tommaso's son!" said Niccolo at last. "Geppetto."

"Yes, yes, I am," said Geppetto dazedly. "And you are?" He squinted in Nico's direction and his fingers went to his nose, where his missing spectacles left two reddish imprints. He scrabbled about the boat, searching, and explained, "I can't see much without my glasses. I must have lost them."

"I would bet that you lost them," said Niccolo, laughing. "You nearly drowned. But better that we fished you out and not your glasses, wouldn't you say?"

"Niccolo Belmagio!" Geppetto cried, recognising him at last. "I thought it was you getting onto your boat earlier. It's a good thing you saw me. I'm indebted to you."

"Thank my sister, not me. Chia's the one who saved you."

Dipping his head, Geppetto turned to her and practically bowed at her feet. "Thank you, Chiara. If not for you, well…"

"Call me Chia," she said. "All my friends do."

"Chia," repeated Geppetto. Just then, the boat tilted over a rough current, and Geppetto stumbled over a trawl net. As he struggled to regain his balance, he grabbed Ilaria's arm – then immediately recoiled.

"Awful sorry, Miss Ilaria." Geppetto reached for an imaginary hat on his head before remembering he didn't have one. He repeated, "Awful sorry."

"Sorry won't make my dress dry," Ilaria lamented.

"We save a fellow, and all you care about is how wrinkled your dress gets." Niccolo clucked his tongue at his youngest sister. "To think, Geppetto thought you were a fairy. He must really not be able to see without his glasses."

"Hush, you." Ilaria slapped Niccolo's arm. "He said I'm a fairy because he thought I'm pretty." She leant closer to Geppetto and batted her lashes. "Don't you?"

"Well, I… I…" Geppetto averted his eyes to the bottom of the boat. "Yes, Miss Ilaria."

"See?" Ilaria tilted her head triumphantly. "Though

come to think of it, we never got around to introducing *my* name."

It was true, and Chiara hid a smile. Young Geppetto's face had gone from being seasick pale to tomato red.

There came a tender ping in Chia's heart. *He likes her*, she realised.

That ping in her heart turned into a warm buzz. She was familiar with the feeling, even though she couldn't pin down what it was. But when she listened to it, often good things happened. Like saving Geppetto. And right now, it was telling her that the young man and Ilaria would be wonderful for each other.

I agree, Chiara thought. On the other hand, Ilaria had lived her whole life in Pariva and probably had never known Geppetto existed before today.

I'll have to help change that.

"Pariva's a small town," said Chia helpfully. "It's really Ily you should be thanking, Geppetto. If she hadn't asked us to come out today, we wouldn't have found you."

"Thank you truly," said Geppetto to Ilaria. "And I'm sorry about the dress."

"I was going to wear it to my audition in Nerio," Ilaria said coyly. She crossed her arms, pretending to be displeased. "Now it'll have to be pressed again."

Niccolo rolled his eyes. "If you knew you needed that

dress for an audition, why wear it out to sea in the first place?"

"Are you accusing me of lying?"

"It wouldn't be anything new."

"Why, you—"

"Ily," Chia interrupted, "I'll help you press your dress before your audition. It'll look as good as new."

With a harrumph directed to Niccolo, Ilaria sat beside her sister. "I hope so."

"I'm terribly sorry," said Geppetto again, looking more distressed about Ily's dress than he had been about nearly drowning. "If I could afford it, I would offer to buy you a new one… Miss Ilaria, you have such a beautiful voice, I would never forgive myself if I hampered your efforts towards… towards…"

"Becoming the most famous prima donna in Esperia," Ilaria finished for him. She leant forwards with interest. "You've heard me sing before?"

"A few times last summer," he confessed. "Ms Rocco's house is next door to my father's workshop—"

Ily gasped. "You've eavesdropped on my singing lessons?"

"I couldn't help it," Geppetto said bashfully. "I like opera."

"You do?" That made Ilaria's face light up, and she

stuck out her tongue at Niccolo. "See? Someone here likes opera."

Niccolo rolled his eyes and resumed rowing.

Hastily, Geppetto picked up a spare oar to help. As he cut into the water, he asked Ilaria, "Will you sing again this summer?"

"Unlikely," she replied, evening out the folds in her skirt before she placed her hands primly on her lap and crossed her ankles. "Mamma says it isn't ladylike to sing out in public. And ever since that tavern opened, she thinks it's less safe."

"I hadn't thought about that."

"That's enough, Ily," said Niccolo between breaths. "You can seize the conversation later. We haven't asked what happened to this poor fellow."

"No, no, it's all right," Geppetto insisted.

But Niccolo went on, "How did you end up capsizing your boat?"

Geppetto inhaled. "I don't even know what happened. I was looking at seals, then it wasn't a seal. It was a monster. A—"

"Whale," said Niccolo. "Monstro."

"Monstro?" Geppetto repeated, confused. "What's that?"

"You haven't heard the stories?" Niccolo sighed. "Oh,

Geppetto, you really need to get out of your father's workshop more. And not just to listen to my sister sing."

Impressive, how quickly Geppetto's face turned red again. Chiara supposed it was good for his circulation.

With a smile, she passed him one of the sandwiches she had packed while Geppetto and Ilaria defended the importance of listening to opera, and her brother resumed rowing them all back to Pariva.

Everything was well, and as the new friends sailed back towards Pariva, no one noticed the sinister clouds of magic that oozed out of the distant sea.

CHAPTER FIVE

Ilaria saw the fairy first. It was past nine o'clock, and she was late to Mrs Tappa's for her morning shift, but the old lady was probably still asleep in her bed above the shop. Besides, Ily was the prettiest girl in town, and she modelled Mrs Tappa's hats every time she went out. The lady would never fire her.

Rather than hurry, she strolled into the garden and crouched beside Mamma's prized rosebush. After snipping three of the loveliest roses, she plucked a bright red bud from the bush and plaited them all into the hat she'd borrowed from Mrs Tappa's display.

The hat was an ugly thing, woven of brown straw the colour of horse dung. But the roses would help, and a sprig of rosemary from Papa's herb garden, too, to make it smell nice.

"With any luck, this will sell today," Ily said to herself,

admiring how she'd made over the hideous hat. The more hats she sold, the more money she'd make, and she was aching for a new dress. She hadn't had one in over a year, and she couldn't bear the thought of going to auditions in Nerio and Vallan in one of her chocolate-stained gowns and torn gloves.

Vallan, especially. An audition in the capital was the final round, and she'd get to sing for her idol, Maria Linda. She had to make an impression from head to toe.

But I'm getting ahead of myself, she thought with a sigh. *I haven't had a lesson in over a year since Ms Rocco died.*

As she admired her reflection in the window, a soft bloom of light floated behind her, gliding along the roof of the Belmagio residence. Ilaria ducked behind the rosebush, but her eyes followed the light. It was a shimmery violet she had never seen before, and when she looked hard enough she could almost make out tiny wings fluttering within. About half the size of her fist, it was too large to be a firefly, but no bird could emit such a powerful light.

Her heart leapt as she realised.

A fairy!

She held in a squeal of excitement. What was a fairy doing here? Maybe she'd heard the wishes Ilaria had made, night after night when she stared out her window searching for the Wishing Star. Maybe she was here to finally make Ily's dreams come true.

The light slipped through an open window into the house, and certainty welled in Ily's chest. Unable to contain her excitement any longer, she raced inside, quietly tiptoeing up the stairs after the fairy.

When she was halfway up the stairs, Ily rose to her toes. The fairy was hovering in front of her doorknob, its light fanning over the bronze handle. Like magic, the door creaked open, and Ily hastened up another two stairs.

Until the fairy left her room and swooped up the stairs into the attic. To Chia's room.

Ily halted in her step. *Chia's room?*

Her sister didn't believe in fairies. Her sister didn't believe in magic.

What could a fairy possibly want with Chia?

The corners of her lips tugged down into a frown, and Ilaria turned back downstairs. She should get to work. Mrs Tappa liked her, but at this rate, she'd be half an hour late. Even for her, that was beyond the pale.

And yet… how would she be able to concentrate on work if all she could think about was why a fairy was visiting her sister?

Throwing aside her cares, Ilaria crept up the stairs to

Chia's room in the attic and pressed her ear to her sister's door.

Sure enough, she heard the fairy's voice. It was a rich and resonant alto, but she could hardly make out what the fairy was saying. Soft bells muffled her voice – as well as Chia's. As if they knew Ilaria was eavesdropping.

With a grumble, Ilaria lifted her ear from the door. By now she was burning with curiosity and wanted nothing more than to waltz inside, pretending she didn't know Chiara had a visitor. If it'd been anyone else except a fairy inside, she would have. But she had respect for fairies. The stories warned that while they were kind and generous and fair, if you offended them, they wouldn't hesitate to teach you a lesson. Like her mother, in a way.

Mamma would have made an excellent fairy.

Ilaria knelt by the door and peered into the keyhole. Her view was a partial one, but she could see Chia speaking to a lady dressed in purple from hat to shoes. Correction: a lady dressed in purple from hat to shoes, *with wings*! Wings that cast silvery reflections on the wooden parquet, wings that sparkled like a slice of moonlight upon the sea. Wings that made the fairy's feet barely touch the ground.

That confirmed everything: Ily couldn't hold back any longer. "Chia!" she cried out, pushing into her sister's room.

There was no one inside. Chia and the fairy had disappeared.

Ilaria clambered to the window, but there was no sign of them outside. She hurried down the stairs to the kitchen, the Blue Room, the parlour. No one there, either.

She combed a hand through her hair, baffled.

Letting out a loud sigh, Ilaria grabbed her hat from where she'd left it by the rosebushes. She ought to start for Mrs Tappa's shop in the square, but maybe – just maybe – she ought to wait at home a little longer.

Wherever Chia and the fairy had gone, she'd find out soon enough. Her sister never kept secrets from her.

Chia would tell her everything. She always did.

CHAPTER SIX

"Still don't believe in fairies?" said the Violet Fairy as she and Chiara emerged in the middle of Pariva's market square.

Chiara drew a startled breath. She whirled, taking in the familiar sight of Mangia Road. There was Mamma and Papa's bakery in the north-east corner, where she was due in minutes to deliver an account of their finances and spend the rest of the day helping Papa make sandwiches. And there was Mr and Mrs Vaci's chocolate shop, the local fishmonger, and the market, where clusters of tomatoes hung on bright green vines across a rusty yellow wagon. A pocket of children ran around the fountain, likely playing truant from class.

"How…"

"Magic, Chiara," the Violet Fairy replied. "Obviously.

Come, time's more precious than magic, and you're standing about as if you've inhaled a whiff of stardust." The fairy chuckled. "You did, in actuality, and I'm pleased you aren't heaving. That's an important requirement for a fairy-to-be."

Chiara hardly heard a word. She was in a daze, unable to believe that the woman before her – the Violet Fairy, she'd called herself – was actually, well… a fairy!

But how else could she explain everything? Only minutes before, a beam of purple light had sieved under the door into her room. Chiara hadn't thought anything of it until the light swelled, radiating from floor to ceiling. Then *poof!* A woman about Chiara's height materialised, with cropped brown hair that curled below her ears, full ruddy cheeks and chestnut eyes that shone when she spoke. She'd called herself the Violet Fairy, and she'd waved her stick in the air with a flourish.

And here they were, in the middle of Pariva's main square.

Chiara fumbled at the thin shawl over her shoulders. She was sure she'd left it at home; same with the wicker basket under her arm – the very one she carried when she went out on her errands. At her side, the Violet Fairy chuckled at her astonishment.

None of the folks bustling by seemed to notice them suddenly appear. Normally, the nosier townspeople would have stopped to ask whether the Violet Fairy was visiting from Elph or Nerio. Yet no one gave her a second glance.

That surprised Chia more than anything.

"They only see you," said the fairy as if reading her mind. "So try not to move your lips too much while you're talking, or else they'll think you're mumbling to yourself."

Chiara stared as the townspeople cheerfully waved at her.

"It *is* magic," she breathed. "You really are a fairy."

"Not so loudly." Mischief twinkled in the fairy's eyes. She leant closer, "Your neighbours are what made you believe, not the travelling light or the magic wand?"

"Everyone knows everyone's business in Pariva," said Chiara sensibly.

"Well, no one else knows mine." The fairy guided her down the cobblestone path towards the pasture. "I prefer it that way. The fewer distractions, the better." The Violet Fairy gestured casually at the statue of three fairies in the centre of the square. Simona, one of Ilaria's friends, was there asking the statue when the next Wishing Star would appear in the sky.

"You see? I'd like us to have a conversation without being interrupted."

Fair enough. Chiara inhaled, finally getting her bearings.

She had so many questions. "Why me, of everyone here? Are you my fairy godmother?"

"Do you have a wish you wanted to make?"

The question made Chiara's gaze flit to the ground. "No," she replied. "Not for myself, anyway."

"Then I'm not your fairy godmother." A chuckle. "I will say, it's unusual for someone who doesn't believe in magic to get an invitation, but I'd argue that not believing isn't necessarily a bad thing. You're a practical girl, and you like to get things done yourself. We could use more of that."

"An invitation?" Chiara echoed, remembering what she had called her earlier – a *fairy-to-be*. "From… the fairies?"

"Yes, indeed." The fairy waved her hand dismissively. "I'm assuming you've changed your mind about us existing. It's fortunate I've observed before what a bright girl you are. Otherwise I'd be having doubts right now."

The gibe was honest but good-natured, and Chiara smiled. "We don't see much magic in Pariva."

"So I've learned," huffed the fairy. They'd arrived at Pine Grove, a pasture behind Pariva's local school. It was a quieter part of town, at least until the school bell rang and the children ran towards the fields to play. Chiara had spent many afternoons sitting on the grass, naming the cows and sheep that grazed there. Beyond was a grove of pine trees where she occasionally spotted Geppetto gathering wood for his projects.

The fairy guided Chiara under one of the trees and patted her arm. "I suppose I should properly introduce myself. I am Agata the Violet, a member of Esperia's oldest school of fairies. We listen to wishes made in good faith, and we guard the love, hope and wonder in the hearts of all. You may call me simply Agata."

"Agata." Chiara dipped, making a curtsy out of habit. "I'm pleased to make your acquaintance."

"This isn't the first time we've met." Agata winked, and when next she spoke, her voice became resonant, echoing as if it bounced off a hundred walls. "Do you remember me, *Chiara Belmagio*?"

Chiara gasped. "It was you! You spoke to me when I was rescuing Geppetto."

"I was going to save the lad myself," replied Agata, "until you came out of nowhere. And you needed no magic to answer his calls." The fairy's voice turned sombre. "You were close to perishing yourself, Chiara. You knew that before you leapt, but still you went on."

"I couldn't let him die."

"You'd be surprised how many would," said Agata. "But I knew you wouldn't give up. I've been watching you long since before you saved Geppetto."

"Watching me?"

"You have a talent for seeing into people's hearts," the fairy explained, "and for helping them."

"I'd hardly call it a talent," Chiara said. "I've lived in Pariva all my life. Almost everyone here is my friend, and I care about them."

"So you do," Agata agreed. "But you went beyond what most people who care would do. When Mrs Cousins' husband died, you visited her every day for three months so she wouldn't be lonely. You played cards with her and helped her plant a tulip garden. You even found her a stray kitten to keep her company."

"That wasn't much—"

"When Mr Vaci's wife came down with fever, you made broth for her until she got better. You feed the pigeons by the fountain with leftover bread from your parents' bakery – the ducks by Pine Grove pond, too – and you tutored little Clarence and Lila with their arithmetic until they got high marks at school."

"Those were hardly good deeds," said Chiara. "I did them because—"

"Because it's your calling," Agata finished for her. "You get a feeling in your gut when you see someone who's sad or lonely or in trouble. You listen to that feeling, and it shows you how to heal their hurt – how to bring joy."

Chiara stared. No one knew about that, not even Ilaria.

They had stopped walking, and Chiara found she couldn't say anything. "How…?"

"Because I feel it, too," replied Agata. "Everywhere I go, and before I was a fairy, too. Let me guess… you can sense other people's happiness and unhappiness."

Chiara nodded slowly. Then she remembered, and added, "On the day I saved Geppetto, I thought I sensed something."

"What did you feel?"

Chiara frowned, remembering. "The water… it felt cold. Inside it, I felt… wrath and danger… evil."

"That was Monstro," confirmed Agata. "His strength is overwhelming, even for a seasoned fairy such as myself. Yet even while near him, you could still sense Geppetto's hope. That's how you found him – and saved him."

Chiara's knees went weak, and she could hardly breathe. "Yes, I suppose it is."

"You have great empathy, Chiara. And a powerful conscience. It guides you, doesn't it?"

Was Agata talking about the hum in her heart? "It's nothing special."

"Even so, not everyone is so in tune with theirs that they listen to it. You are, and that's what led me to find you," said Agata.

"I… I don't even believe in magic. I mean, I didn't – until now."

"Listen, the wisest fairy turns to magic only as a last resort. That is why I have reason to believe, Chiara Belmagio, that you would make an excellent fairy."

A laugh bubbled in her throat. "Me, a fairy? I don't think so. Like you said, fairies are wise, and I barely know what I'm doing with my life. I wouldn't know how to grant wishes."

"Experience and age have no correlation to the strength of one's heart," said Agata. "Your whole life, you've shown courage, compassion and kindness."

"There are plenty of others who are kinder than I am, and braver, too."

"Perhaps that is true," said Agata, looking pleased that Chiara was uncertain. "But fate did not lead me to their doors. They led me to yours." The Violet Fairy paused. "I've already proposed your name to my council, and we unanimously agreed to invite you to trial with us. Should you complete your training, we would grant you wings and a wand – should you wish it."

Chiara was stunned. "You *are* serious."

"I don't lie, Chiara Belmagio," said Agata.

"What… what would I even do?" asked Chia. "What do fairies do?"

"A good question. Most know us for granting wishes, but that is only a fraction of our responsibilities." Agata inhaled. "The world can be a dark place, dear. Our greatest role is to guide the light wherever we can. It is no trivial task, I assure you, and few are suited for it. But I hope you'll try."

Chiara said nothing. Usually she depended on her heart to tell her what to do, on that tingle in her gut to guide her. But here, in this moment that could change her entire life, any guidance was absent. "I don't know what to say," she admitted. "That's not the answer I'm supposed to give, is it?"

To her surprise, Agata chuckled. "If you had jumped at the chance to wield a magic wand and fly on fairy wings, then you wouldn't have been the young woman I thought you were." Then her expression changed. Her brown eyes filled, but Chiara couldn't tell what had stirred their sadness. "Life as a fairy is more than the ability to conjure magic or wear sparkles and fly on beams of starlight. Far more. It's the chance to make hearts full and make the world a slightly better place."

"If fairies are able to do such wonderful things and bring joy," observed Chiara quietly, "then why do you sound upset?"

"Our job *is* wonderful," Agata admitted. "But it is not

without its costs, sacrifices. I'll explain more at the end of your training… should you come trial with us."

The older woman could sense Chiara's scepticism. "Think on it, please, Chiara. I will visit you again in a week for your answer. Until then, I ask that you speak of my invitation to no one. Not your parents, your brother, even your sister. There is wisdom in caution, and humans have fickle memories – especially when it comes to fairies. We'll tell them together about the trial if you should choose to do it. But I wouldn't want a stray comment now to influence your decision. Will you promise?"

Chiara hesitated. In her mind, she was certain she already knew her answer. Grand as Agata's invitation sounded, she couldn't leave her family.

She waited for that warm hum in her chest to affirm her decision, but it was absent. She was on her own.

"Think on it," repeated Agata, this time with a small smile – as if she knew.

Chiara supposed a week of consideration wouldn't hurt. "All right, I promise."

"Good. Until next time, then."

Agata vanished in a fan of light, leaving Chia alone once more.

Her mind wheeling back and forth between disbelief

and excitement, Chia raced home, forgetting for the first time in her life that she was expected at the bakery for work.

Ilaria pounced on her as soon as she returned home. "Where have you been?"

Chia had to bite her cheek so she wouldn't tell Ily everything. No one would appreciate Agata's visit more than her sister, who loved fairy tales and believed in fairy godmothers and wishes that would come true.

But Chia had made a promise.

"What's wrong, Chia? Cat caught your tongue?"

"No." Chiara fumbled. She wasn't good at lying, so she settled for what was technically the truth. "I… I forgot the ledger for Mamma and Papa."

"That's unlike you. Did something happen?"

"Nothing important." Chia hastily slipped past her sister and headed up to her room. Any other day, she would have heard the disappointment in Ily's voice and tried to set things right.

But not today.

And so, Ilaria stood alone on the stairs, gripping the railing as her chest tightened. It was to be the first crack in her heart.

CHAPTER SEVEN

A week crawled by, and there was not a peep from Chiara about her meeting with the fairy.

Ilaria went back and forth from being frustrated to being charitable. Every chance she got, she plopped in front of her sister and gave her ample opportunity to bring it up. "Do you think there'll be a Wishing Star tonight?" she asked casually one morning. And, "You know, I'm really starting to love the colour purple. I should wear more of it."

But Chiara never took the bait. She merely replied, "The Wishing Star, tonight? I don't know, Ily. Maybe." And: "Purple is a lovely colour. I think it'd suit you beautifully." Then she returned her gaze to the blocks of dark chocolate she was chopping to make Mamma's famous chocolate-hazelnut spread and completely missed the scowl that Ilaria sent her way. "Your lunch is on the table, Ily. If you want cookies, they'll be ready at the bakery before noon."

"If you want cookies, they'll be ready at the bakery before noon," Ily mimicked under her breath. "Always so prim, always so responsible. You're my sister, Chia, not my mother."

Resentment made Ilaria scowl, and she tore away from the kitchen, not bothering to ask if Chia needed help. On the way to work, she breezed past Geppetto, picking up fallen tree branches in Pine Grove. When he saw her, he fumbled with the bundle in his arms so he could wave, but she pretended not to notice. These past few weeks, he'd stopped by the bakery every other day to chat with Chiara and Niccolo – they spoke about dull and dreary things, like the ships Monstro had recently sunk and whether the tomatoes in Pariva were in bloom. Every time, Geppetto glanced at her as if he wanted to say hello – just as he was then – but Ily couldn't be bothered. Any friend of Chia's was not a friend of hers.

She arrived at the hat shop ten minutes early, a miracle that unfortunately bore no witness since old Mrs Tappa was still asleep upstairs. Annoyed that her effort was for nothing, Ilaria went straight to the mannequin in the front of the shop and yanked at the hat's pale blue ribbon.

Chiara's favourite colour, same as the ribbon she tied around her head every day.

Just seeing it sent Ily a sharp stab of resentment. She wasn't used to being angry at Chia; she couldn't even remember the last time they'd had a disagreement.

But then again, Chia *never* kept secrets from her. What could the fairy have said to her that she wouldn't immediately tell?

Ily thought hard as she tossed the blue ribbon over her shoulder and replaced it with a tight red bow. Chia didn't believe in fairies, so there was no chance that she'd made a wish and the fairy had come to grant it. Or was there?

It was the only answer she could come up with. As for why Chia wouldn't tell Ily…

Maybe she made a wish for me, Ily thought, some of her resentment washing away in shame. Knowing Chia, she'd never wish anything for herself.

Could she have wished for Ily to go to Vallan? To study with the great Maria Linda and become the most sought-after prima donna in Esperia?

Don't be stupid, she told herself. *Chia wouldn't wish that. She'd waste her wish on something for everyone, like a good tomato harvest or a cure for the pox.*

Besides, Chiara was acting like she had a secret.

One she didn't *want* to share, was keeping from her on purpose.

The shop door rattled, and Ily nearly jumped to see Chia herself poke inside, swinging her basket. "You forgot your lunch," said her sister. Her cheerful tone made Ily cross her arms. "Are you eating with Nico and me today?"

Ily acknowledged Chia with the barest flick of her eyes. "I'm having lunch with Simona."

"Simona?" Chia held her basket still as she stepped inside. "Are you sure? I saw her a minute ago with Pietro. They're riding to Elph for the day."

Ilaria gritted her teeth. Just her luck that Simona would lunch with her beau. The traitor.

"Is everything all right, Ily? You seem upset."

"What would I be upset about?" Ily repositioned the hat on a mannequin and pretended to fiddle with some pins and flowers. "I've been busy is all. Gia Fusco ordered half a dozen caps for her husband and a dozen hats for herself." An outrageous lie, but she'd already spun it and couldn't stop: "I'll be working non-stop for the next few days just fulfilling her order."

"I see," said Chia. "Shall I bring you cookies, then? We're making the cinnamon ones today. Your favourite."

As if Ilaria didn't know what her own favourite cookies were. "Don't bother. I'm cutting down on sweets."

"They'll be fresh out of the oven."

Curse Chiara for knowing her too well, and bringing her weakness for cookies into their argument. Ilaria waved her sister away. "Have to practise. Since Ms Rocco died, I have no one to help prepare me or take lessons from… and my audition's only a month away."

Chiara's shoulders fell. "Gosh, it's only a month from now?" Her face softened. "I'm sorry, I haven't been helping."

"I haven't asked you to. Besides, you've been busy with… who knows what." It was a shameless punch at her sister, and from the way Chiara's face folded, Ilaria knew she'd made a hit.

"Let's practise together tonight. We'll put on a concert for Mamma and Papa after dinner."

"I won't be home till late," Ilaria blurted before she knew what she was saying. "I'm going to… to see Ms Rocco's niece. She said I could use her harpsichord to practise my new aria. Hers is much better than ours."

"I could come with you," Chia offered.

"Her niece wants to play for me," Ily lied. Janissa Rocco was an awful player who attacked the keys as if her fingers were knives, but she didn't think Chiara knew that.

"All right, then," said Chiara, swallowing. "We'll see you when you get home."

At long last, Chia left, and Ilaria bit down hard on

her lip. The pain helped keep her from running after her sister.

Pride had always been her weakness.

Dusk couldn't come soon enough, and Ilaria leant her head against the wall, praying for the clock to hurry up and strike six. She pressed her palm against the window and looked outside. Mrs Tappa's shop was close enough to the bakery that she could see her parents cleaning up the shopfront and preparing to go home.

As Pariva's bell tower chimed six o'clock, her mother glided out with the day's aprons and cloths tucked under her arm to wash at home.

Ily swore her mother had the eyes of an owl. Mrs Belmagio instantly caught Ily watching from her shop window and frowned in consternation. An understandable reaction: usually, by this time, Ily would have left work to see her friends or gallivant about town with her latest admirer.

A quick jaunt across the street, and Mamma arrived at Mrs Tappa's shop.

"You're working late, darling," she greeted Ily. "Chia told me you were going to Janissa Rocco's to practise?"

Ily pretended to uncuff her sleeve. "I'm about to leave."

Mamma paused, and for a moment, Ily was certain she could detect the falsehood. After all, Mamma always liked to tell her: *A lie keeps growing and growing until it's as plain as the nose on your face.*

But no such lecture came from her mother today.

"You've been working so hard lately," Mamma said instead, which only made the ache in Ily's chest sharpen. She helped Ily with her sleeve, then touched Ily's cheek. Mother and daughter had the same dark chocolate hair, though only Chia had inherited Mamma's curls. "Try to be home before dinner, all right? Until then…"

Mamma dipped into her pocket for a small pouch. Ily smelt cinnamon right away, with a lace of chocolate.

"Cookies?" she breathed.

"Your favourites. Saved them for you."

Ily couldn't resist them again. She clasped the pouch, warming her palms with the treats. There were only two people she ever felt guilty about lying to. Chia and her mother.

Ily wanted to keep silent, but another lie slipped out. "I'll try."

"I'll see you at dinner, then," Mrs Belmagio said. "You're going to do wonderfully at that audition."

"Will you come with me?"

"I thought you'd asked Simona or Beatrice – or Chia." A pause. "Is everything all right with you two?"

"Of course it is," Ily lied.

Mamma cocked her head. "You sure?"

"I'm sure."

"You won't be embarrassed to have your mamma with you?"

"Never."

That pleased Mrs Belmagio, and her cheeks glowed. "I suppose that your father can manage half a day without me." She chuckled as Mr Belmagio stepped out of the bakery, still absent-mindedly wearing his baker's apron and hat before he remembered to leave them back inside.

Ily wanted to hug her mother. She wanted to sink into her arms and cry and have Mamma end the fight she was having with Chia. She wanted Mamma to make everything better again. But she wasn't a girl of seven any more. She was almost seventeen – a young woman. So she placed the cookies in her pocket, and said in her evenest voice: "Thank you, Mamma."

Once her parents disappeared from the square, Ilaria slid out of Mrs Tappa's shop and strolled across the street. No one in Pariva ever locked their door, so all Ily had to do was turn the knob, and she was inside her parents' bakery. The smell of yeast and unbaked bread tickled her nose, and a rush of warmth from the ovens – still cooling – swelled to her cheeks.

"Anyone here? Nico?" She waited. "Chia?"

No answer.

The tension she carried in her shoulders released, and she glided past the counter through the half shutter doors into the kitchen. The ovens still emanated heat, and sweat prickled on Ilaria's skin. She didn't mind. She'd spent her childhood within these walls, tossing flour at Niccolo and pouring extra chocolate into Mamma's cakes while Chia kneaded bread with Papa.

The racks by the wall were empty, but crumbs sprinkled the floor, and there was a cake pan left on the counter where Mamma displayed the sweets of the day. The day before had been almond cake with blackberry – Chia's favourite. That day, cinnamon as well as pistachio cookies, the latter perfectly round and pale green, topped with plump pine nuts.

Ily nibbled on one of her cookies as she went up to the south-facing brick wall. She counted the bricks and tapped on one just off the centre of the wall, then wriggled it loose. Behind was where Mamma and Papa stored their profits for the week, if there were any.

Five meagre oros, sitting on a cracked plate, awaited her.

Ily sighed and placed the brick back. Then she noted the fresh lilies on the counter, the basket of lemons under the table. No one in Pariva was wealthy, and Mamma and Papa often let their customers pay with goods like flowers or fish or salt instead of money. Before she'd taken her job at the hat shop, Ilaria herself had only had three dresses, most of them so worn Chia had helped patch the seams.

"When I'm famous, Mamma and Papa won't have to work any more," said Ilaria to herself. "They'll have a house on the fanciest street in Vallan, right across from mine. And all of my dresses will have lace on the sleeves and on the collars."

With that, she tucked herself into the back of the kitchen and stood in front of a pan to see her reflection. A girl holding a foolish grudge against her sister stared back at her.

"I can't go home now," she told her reflection. "I already said to Mamma and Chia that I'm at Janissa Rocco's practising."

The girl in the pan made a righteous face at her. *Then tell them the truth. That you're bored, and you don't want to spend the next three hours holed up in the kitchen. Go home and eat and make up with Chia.*

"No," Ilaria refused, stubborn as ever. She tossed the pan under a table and settled herself in a corner. Her stomach growled, and she didn't feel like singing. But she wouldn't let go of her pride.

At least she had cookies.

It was well past the Belmagio dinnertime when Ily finally came out of her hiding place in the bakery and hurried home. She felt like an interloper as she turned onto

Constanza Street, practising her lies under her breath. She only hoped there was still food left. Mamma would have saved her a plate. Chia, too.

But as she doubled her pace towards home's yellow door, she heard voices from the window.

"Are you sure this is what you want, my dove?" Mamma was asking.

"I meant to say no," Chia responded, "but something in my heart told me I was making a mistake. So I have decided to do the trial."

Ilaria froze. *What trial?*

"We'll take good care of your daughter," someone with a lilting voice said.

Who is that?

A rush of wind stole away the response from her parents, and Ily hurriedly barged into the house before she missed the rest of the conversation.

She was already too late.

Her mother and father were rising from their respective chairs in the parlour, and Chia was rushing upstairs to her room. Only Niccolo was still sitting. Something smelt a lot like hot chocolate.

Hot chocolate was a special-occasion drink. It was Ilaria's favourite… though Mamma always resisted making it during the summer.

"What's going on?" asked Ilaria. "I can't tell whether someone died or we inherited a fortune."

Mr Belmagio set down his mug. His eyes were glazed, like the sugar he worked with all day. "You missed her."

"Missed who?"

"The fairy."

Ilaria's heart skipped. "The fairy?"

"She said she had to leave. We waited for you as long as we could." Mrs Belmagio pushed Ily's red mug in her direction. "Your cocoa's gone cold."

It *was* hot chocolate. Usually a treat in the Belmagio house. It meant there was cause for celebration, or a need for comforting. Or both.

"Have you eaten?"

Ily shook her head numbly, forgetting to lie.

"I'll get you something—"

"No," interrupted Ily. Nico and Papa were avoiding her gaze. As if they'd been stricken by news. Only Mamma would tell her the truth. "Will you tell me what's going on?"

Mrs Belmagio stirred her hot chocolate slowly. "Your sister's been asked to join the fairies."

That was quite possibly the last thing Ily had expected. "What?"

"It's an invitation." Mrs Belmagio held her mug

unsteadily. "For Chia to study under her at the Wishing Star. Chia's asked for our blessing."

Ily's pulse spiked. Chia, leaving to become a fairy? She couldn't make sense of it. "What a ridiculous invitation. Of course you said no, didn't you, Mamma?"

At her mother's silence, Ilaria's stomach sank. "Didn't you, Mamma?"

"It's a wonderful invitation. And my children are old enough to make their own decisions," replied Mrs Belmagio as Chia returned to the parlour and appeared in the door-frame.

"I said yes," her sister replied softly. "I'll leave home in two weeks to study with the Violet Fairy."

"You're leaving us?" Ily couldn't believe it. "In two weeks?" She whirled, bombarded by emotions she couldn't control. "Mamma, Papa…"

"We've given Chia our blessing," Mrs Belmagio said. Her father nodded.

"Chiara being invited to join their ranks is a stupendous honour."

So already her sister was no longer Chia but *Chiara*.

"Well, she doesn't have *my* blessing!" spluttered Ilaria.

"Ily!"

"No one told me anything. No one asked me anything."

Chia swallowed hard. "Ily, I'm sorry. I wanted to tell you, but I promised—"

Ily didn't want to hear another word. She raced up the stairs and slammed the door. She threw her quilt over her head, but even then she could hear Chiara's footsteps. They landed just outside her door.

"Ily? Please."

"Let her be," said Niccolo in a low voice. No doubt he thought she couldn't hear through the door. "She'll feel better about it tomorrow."

He was wrong. Ilaria wouldn't feel better about it. Not tomorrow. Not ever.

A pang of disappointment squeezed Ily's chest as the footsteps departed. But Chia came back, alone, a few minutes later. She knocked.

"Go away," said Ily spitefully.

Almost always, Chia listened. But she didn't today, and she came inside.

Her sister had brought an assortment of cookies – cinnamon and pistachio and chocolate ones, too, on a dish with a fresh glass of milk. She held out the plate as if it were an olive branch, but that only irritated Ily further.

"Ily," began Chiara, "I don't want you to be angry with me."

"Who said I was angry?"

"I've known you all your life, ever since you were a baby in nappies and wouldn't stop sucking on your toes. I know when you're unhappy."

"I didn't suck on my toes," she retorted. "That's disgusting."

"Babies aren't disgusting. They're adorable."

"Of course you would say that." Ilaria shut her curtains with one yank. "I've been angry for a week and you didn't even notice."

Chia settled the plate on Ily's desk. She hung her head, looking sincerely contrite.

"Don't give me that look," said Ily. "You always think pastries or music will make things all better. Not this time. I saw you with her. I knew you were keeping something from me."

"Ily. I'm sorry. I wanted to tell you, truly I did. But I promised I'd keep everything a secret until I'd decided."

Ily threw up her arms. "How can you make a promise to a complete stranger – over your own sister? How can you leave me?"

"I haven't promised to leave," said Chia softly. "It's just a trial for me to see if I like it, and for them to see if they like me."

"You didn't even think about my audition," said Ilaria sourly. She wanted to push as much guilt onto Chiara's plate as she could. "If you're leaving in two weeks, you'll miss it."

"I'll help you prepare," Chia promised. "I'll bake you cinnamon cookies every day before then, too – for luck."

"I won't be able to fit into my dress, then!"

"I'll sew you a new one." Chia paused. "I need to take this chance, Ily. There's…"

"What?"

Chia chewed on her lower lip. "Sometimes I get this feeling." She touched her heart. "It's like a hum or a buzz, and when I listen to it, it tells me whether something is good or bad. Agata says that it's what led me to her."

"What is it, a fairy sense?" It sounded so silly and nonsensical Ily couldn't help laughing. Who would've thought her sister, who as of a month before didn't believe in fairies or magic, would be talking to her about inner voices and gut feelings? "Not everything's good or bad, Chia. You can't rely on some fairy voice to tell you what to do."

"It isn't a fairy voice…" Chia bit her lip. "It's hard to explain. But… I can't help feeling like I need to try to understand it. To go with the fairies, at least for a little while. For myself." She looked up at Ily, as if for approval. "It's only a trial. I won't be gone forever."

Ily's laugh died. All these years, Chia had been at her side, helping her prepare for her auditions and giving all she could to help Ily follow her dreams. How could she be so selfish as to deny Chia the same opportunity? Still, she couldn't help voicing her fear: "What if you decide to stay with them?"

"I'd miss you too much to do that," said Chia gently. "And this—" Without warning, Chia threw a pillow at Ilaria's face.

"Hey!" Ilaria retaliated, and within moments, the two sisters were laughing and fighting at the same time.

"All right, all right," cried Chia when Ily hoarded all the pillows to throw. "Truce!"

Ily grabbed her sister's hand and they fell backwards onto the bed, stretching their arms high as they caught their breath.

"What if I really do make it to the Madrigal Conservatory?" Ilaria whispered. "And you become a fairy? Will we still have moments like this?"

"Of course we will."

Chiara meant it with all her heart, and the last traces of Ily's fears and anger faded until they were forgotten.

Neither sister could know that this time, it was Chia's words that were a lie.

CHAPTER EIGHT

In the middle of Pariva's main square was a statue called the Three Fairies. It had been there ever since Geppetto could remember, and from what he knew, since his father's and grandfather's and great-grandfather's times, too.

The children in town liked to touch the fairies' stone wings for luck before their exams, and plenty of Pariva's residents – adults and children alike – often stopped before the statue to ask, "Will there be a Wishing Star tonight?" According to local legend, if a bird landed on one of the fairies within a count of ten, that meant yes.

Geppetto had never approached the Three Fairies with the question before, but for the first time in years, he caught himself *wanting* to.

Three fairies. One was an elderly lady, one a middle-aged

gentleman and the third a younger woman – about Ilaria's age. They were all smiling serenely, their wands pointed towards the sky – as if a reminder to make a wish. To *believe*.

Their names, their homes and their pasts were mysteries. Geppetto didn't even know if they were real people, let alone whether they were from Pariva.

"Maybe Chia will find out," he mused aloud.

Chiara Belmagio's invitation to become a fairy was the talk of the town. Mrs Belmagio had spoken of it to only a few confidantes, but such news could not be contained for long. Within a day, it had spread across the town, and no one could hide their excitement.

Imagine, a fairy from Pariva!

Geppetto wasn't surprised at all that Chiara had been chosen. She'd always had a knack for bringing happiness into people's lives. After she had rescued him from drowning, she'd gone out of her way to befriend him, and he looked forward to when she and her brother visited his shop. Niccolo would tease him about never going out, and Chiara would ask him questions about the lutherie business and recount stories that she had read recently. Their company made the long, lonely hours pass quickly.

The only person he could imagine not being pleased about the news was Ilaria. The sisters were so close. Often when he walked down Constanza Street, taking the long path towards the sea, he could hear the sisters making music together.

He'd hum along, for he recognised every tune. But lately, the Belmagio house had been quiet.

With a sigh, Geppetto sidestepped away from the Three Fairies. There was a crowd of children behind him waiting to approach the statue, and he smiled as they flocked around the fairies.

"I'd like a new toy, please," Bella Vaci told the statue dolefully. "My brother Gus just got a new cat, and it scratched my doll. I'd love a new one."

Geppetto couldn't help listening. From his pocket, he took out a wooden shepherdess and sheep he had carved and painted. When no one was looking, he placed them on a bench near the statue, then started back for home.

Before he left the square entirely, Geppetto glanced over his shoulder. Just as he'd hoped, young Bella had spotted the figurines and picked them up in delight.

"Look!" she cried to her brother Gus. "It's a shepherdess. A sheep, too! See, I told you fairies were real." She held them close. "Thank you, fairies!"

"Let me see," said Gus, reaching out for the toys. When his sister passed them to him, he started running off. "Can't catch me now!"

While the siblings squealed, Geppetto chuckled to himself. He loved watching the children in town. How happy and free they were. Unburdened by responsibility or the worries that there wouldn't be enough food on the table for dinner, or by the reality that not all dreams came true. He knew this wasn't true for all of them, but at least when they played together in the park, they seemed happy. He missed that carefree joy, and he couldn't remember the last time he'd laughed. Really laughed.

He'd grown up without brothers or sisters, and he'd always wished for someone to call his dearest friend – or at least someone other than his distant father to keep him company. But finances were tight, and there was work and cooking to be done, so Papa insisted he come home straight after school instead of getting to know his classmates, like Niccolo Belmagio.

By the time Geppetto's work was done, the hour was late, so he passed his precious spare minutes before bed whittling toys out of spare wood for the village children. But even that displeased his papa.

"That wood's for making violins," Papa said crossly. "Not for carving silly trinkets."

"The piece is too small to make any parts," reasoned Geppetto. "It's just a toy, Papa. The children are so happy when they find my toys around Pariva. They make the funniest

stories with their imaginations. Matilde pretended the wooden cow could jump to the moon—"

"Imagination doesn't feed the belly." His father cut him off. "You want to talk about children? When I was half your size, I was already earning my keep in the house. Now, if I catch you wasting firewood to make useless baubles, you'll go without dinner, understood?"

Geppetto gulped. "Yes, sir."

Mr Tommaso was a stern parent, but Geppetto didn't resent him. After all, it was thanks to his father's training that he was able to craft the toys he so loved to make. However he could, he saw to it that the children of Pariva had toys to play with. That they could be happy.

And maybe one day, his own child might be happy.

Geppetto slowed in his step, trying to bury the secret longing that rose in him: his wish that one day, he might have children of his own. He'd raise them differently than his father had raised him. Oh, he knew his father was strict because he wanted the best for him, and that it had been difficult to raise Geppetto alone after his mother had died. But a child needed love to bloom, and Geppetto would have so much love to give.

"Geppetto, Geppetto!" called a young voice behind him. It was Bella Vaci. "Did you make this?"

She held up the wooden shepherdess and sheep.

Geppetto couldn't lie. "Yes."

"You left them for me to find, didn't you?" The girl's eyes rounded with gratitude. "Thank you, Mr Geppetto. I thought it was from the fairies at first, but that you made it – is even better. Thank you!"

Geppetto was tongue-tied, and before he could think of something to say, Bella made a shy curtsy and ran off to join her brother. While she ran, she bumped into a young lady – Ilaria Belmagio!

Out of instinct, Geppetto ducked behind a tree. Usually Ilaria was flanked by her friends Simona and Beatrice, but she was alone today.

She approached the Three Fairies, and Geppetto wished he had the courage to say hello.

Why, hello, Ilaria, he'd imagined greeting her a thousand times. *What brings you here? Are you looking out for a Wishing Star?*

Yes, Geppetto.

It wasn't couth to ask anyone what they wished for, but in Geppetto's daydreams, Ilaria always told him. *I've been wishing to become a singer. Chiara and I have been practising for ages. One day, I want us to put on a concert for all of Pariva, maybe even start a music school.*

And Geppetto would compliment her on what a wonderful idea that was, and they would stroll together for the rest of the afternoon, chatting about their favourite songs and all the wonderful emotions that music made them feel.

But in reality, Ilaria barely even stopped in front of the statue. She passed it without so much as a glance and headed towards Mrs Tappa's hat shop.

How sad she looked. She tried to hide it, but her steps had a heaviness about them, and her hands no longer conducted an imaginary song as she walked.

He might not have had Chiara's gift for cheering people up, and the sisters' business was none of his – but he cared about the two of them. Chiara and Ilaria were born best friends.

If there was anything he could do to cheer Ilaria up and help the two sisters reconcile, he had to try. But what could he do?

Geppetto stopped humming.

"That's it," he cried aloud. "That's it!"

He hurried home, his steps light from the joy of a brilliant idea.

CHAPTER NINE

Too soon, Chiara's last day in Pariva arrived.

She lay in bed longer than usual, letting her head sink into the pillow she'd slept on every night since she could remember, and inhaling the faded warmth of the quilt her grandmother had sewn for her when she was born. Sunlight stung her eyes, and for the first time, it hurt.

How could a heart feel so light and heavy at the same time? She couldn't separate one feeling from the other, the heavy sadness and the great hope.

Clouds scattered the sky, and she smelt the possibility of rain. A typical September morning in Pariva – except it wasn't at all.

Chiara dressed and tiptoed down from the attic, careful to avoid the squeaky corners on the steps. She hesitated as she passed Ily's room. In the two weeks since Agata had last come, she and Ily had an unspoken pact not to mention when she'd have to leave for the trial. But the day had come.

Chia's hand rose, her fingers closing to shape a fist. She wanted to knock on her sister's door, yet at the last second she withdrew. Best not to waken Ily; she was always grumpy in the morning.

Downstairs, Niccolo was drinking coffee in the kitchen, and a smear of milky foam coated his thin moustache. Under his arm was his violin, and he strummed its strings idly until he saw her.

"Saints and miracles," he said brightly. "Everyone's up before you."

"Morning," echoed Chiara. A platter of yesterday's pastries awaited her on the table, bordered by a frame of fresh berries and apples. A far more sumptuous breakfast than they usually enjoyed. "Where are Mamma and Pap—"

"They left. Errands for the bakery."

Chiara raised an eyebrow. "On a Sunday?"

Everything was closed on Sundays.

Niccolo shrugged and tugged the end of his moustache – his tell that he was lying. Chia didn't pursue the truth; she wasn't surprised her parents were up to something on her last day home. "You said Ily's awake?"

"The other miracle of the morning. She's in the Blue Room warming up her voice – or, given the silence, just staring at herself in the mirror."

Chia started, but Niccolo grabbed her sleeve and held out his violin. "Wait," he said. "Chia, I need some help. My G and A strings snapped this morning. Could you get me new ones?"

"Don't you have extra strings? I could have sworn I bought you some last week—"

"I've misplaced them," Niccolo said abruptly. "I need new ones. The sooner the better. I have a chamber music rehearsal with Abramo after lunch, and – here, take my violin to Geppetto."

"Won't you come with me?" Chiara asked as she carefully placed Nico's violin into its case. "It'd be nice to say hello to Geppetto."

"Mamma needs me to rake leaves from the yard," replied her brother. "The old oak across the street's started to shed, and she's worried the leaves will fly over and smother her precious rosebushes. And Papa's basil. Why don't you ask Ily? Or don't. If she comes with you, he'll be so distracted he might accidentally saw my instrument in half."

"Very funny," said Chia, though it wasn't that far-fetched a notion. Poor Geppetto was hopelessly infatuated with Ilaria. Whenever she visited, he always found some way to bring up Ilaria. He would say her name as if it were a song, taking extra time with each syllable.

In spite of Chiara's urging, not once had Ily visited him. Maybe today she'd finally come.

Ilaria was sitting at the harpsichord, warming up her voice with a series of hissing and grunting noises, then a stretch of verbalising nonsense syllables. Every time she struck a chord on the harpsichord, she made a face.

Their instrument was an old one, with three keys missing and dubious tuning on the highest notes. "When I'm famous, we'll have a real harpsichord," Ily liked to say. "A pianoforte, too, since that seems to be the future."

This morning, she didn't complain about the harpsichord's condition. Instead, she cast Chia the barest of glances and said, "Don't you ever wear anything other than blue?"

"It's my favourite colour. Just like yours is red."

"I don't wear red every day."

"Red is too ostentatious for daily wear," Chia quoted their mother.

Ily smirked. "If that's Mamma's reasoning, maybe I ought to wear it more. Who knows? Maybe I'll offend the right people and get sent away from Pariva."

Chiara gave her sister a stern look, then decided it best

to change the subject. "Niccolo needs me to get new strings for his violin." She paused. "Do you want to come along?"

"To the luthier's?" Ilaria sequenced her warm-up a step higher.

"You've never come with us to say hi to Geppetto."

"He's *your* friend, not mine. Besides, he falls apart every time he looks at me." Ilaria scoffed. "He might break Niccolo's violin while he's at it."

"Only because he likes you. You should give him a chance. He's far nicer than the other boys you—"

"Nice is what you say to describe a wallpaper colour, not a boy. I'm yawning, Chia – it's a good thing you're not a salesperson. Now I've got to practise. My audition's next week."

Ily resumed her scales, but when she'd reached her highest note, Chiara scooted next to her on the bench.

"You could use a friend while I'm away. A real friend, not like Simona and Beatrice."

"What's wrong with Simona and Beatrice?"

"You know what I mean," said Chia. "Let Geppetto be a friend – at least until I'm back."

"*If* you come back." Ilaria's fingers flattened against the harpsichord keys. "Two weeks went by faster than I thought it would. We didn't even get to go sailing again. Or run through the fields like we said we would. Or spend the day in Elph looking at dresses..."

Ilaria's voice trailed, and she reached behind the harpsichord to open the window. The smell of lemons flooded inside. It came from the tree just outside the Blue Room, and Chia inhaled, relishing yet another smell of her childhood. She paused, unsure how to answer her sister.

"Anyway, hurry up and get out of here," said Ily, pushing her aside. "It's almost noon, and Mamma and Papa want you out of the house."

"Why?"

Ilaria gave her a dull glare. "I'm not going to be the one to ruin today. Just go." She rolled her eyes and uttered what she knew would make Chiara eager to leave. "Tell Geppetto I said hello."

That made Chiara smile. "Will do."

Chia hurried into the marketplace. All the shops were closed since it was Sunday, but she still savoured the familiar sights of summer tomatoes on display and sprigs of lavender for sale and the smell of stinky cheeses drifting out of the market's cracked window. At the far end of the market, beyond the schoolhouse and a few more streets down, was Geppetto's workshop.

Chiara slowed, mindful of every stone under her foot,

every pigeon that flew over her head, every tree that she passed.

The shops were closed, but the townspeople descended upon her almost as if they'd been waiting for her. "There's our Chia! Shouldn't you be at home with your family?"

She raised her brother's violin. "Niccolo sent me off on an errand."

"Inconsiderate of him," Mrs Ricci said. "You're leaving to become a fairy tomorrow."

There it was again, that wash of excitement and sadness. Chiara couldn't untangle the two. "I'm leaving to apprentice under a fairy," she corrected gently. "We don't know whether I become one in the end."

"I'd eat my rubber tree if you didn't," huffed Mrs Ricci. Mrs Valmont appeared at her side and nodded fervently.

"You're the goodest girl I've ever known, Chiara Belmagio. Everyone is going to miss you. We are so proud of you."

"There's nothing to be proud of," said Chiara. "Honestly, I—"

More people were gathering around her. "Don't be so humble, dear. Let yourself beam."

"Yes, be proud! We know so little about fairies and their mysterious ways. To think, the next one is our very own Chiara!"

"Take this," said Mrs Ricci, tucking a generous sack of olives and chestnuts into her basket. "A taste of Pariva will keep the homesickness at bay. You will think fondly of us and visit, won't you?"

"There's plenty of wishes to be granted here," chimed in Mrs Valmont's son.

Chiara smiled, because she didn't know what to say. She reached for her money purse.

"Don't you even think about paying," exclaimed Mrs Ricci. "It's our gift to you. Watch over our little town."

"I'll do my best, ma'am," said Chiara, meaning it. She made a small curtsy. "Thank you for the olives. And the chestnuts."

Mrs Ricci was only the beginning. Everywhere she turned, townspeople stopped her, filling her basket with wares from their shops and gardens.

"I know what you did for my darling Giulia," said Mr Passel, stopping Chiara before the fountain in the town square. "I know you meant to keep it secret, but you've helped rekindle her love for painting. She's happy again."

"Art brings her joy," said Chiara simply. "It was nothing."

Mr Passel nodded. "What will we do without you, Chiara?"

So on it went for the next hour. Chia loved seeing her neighbours and friends, but she had a feeling they were trying to postpone her journey. The way Mrs Vaci, carrying sacks of chocolates, hurried off in the opposite direction of her house, and Mrs Valmont with a bushel of flowers, only added to her suspicion. Were Mamma and Papa planning a party for her?

That would explain Niccolo trying to get her out of the house. Ily, too.

Testing her theory, Chia finally deviated from the market for the path around the square. The townspeople waved as she left, and when she turned back they were all hurrying about their business – definitely odd for Sunday.

With a shrug, she continued down the hill towards the old part of Pariva. It was a longer path that went past the dodgier sections of town, but there was a road ahead that would cut straight back towards Geppetto's home.

"Well, well, if it isn't Pariva's very own fairy," drawled a man loitering outside the Red Lobster Inn, the local tavern. She'd never seen him before. A tail of uneven grey hair curled behind his back, and his words were slurred even though it wasn't quite noon. In his hands was a bottle of pungent ale.

The sort of man Mamma called 'unsavoury'.

He tipped his hat in her direction. "Good morning, Chiara Belmagio."

Chiara slowed. Were Ilaria here, she'd have made some

tart remark and nudged Chia to move along. But that tingly feeling in her heart bade her be kind to everyone, even this unsavoury-looking man.

"Good morning," she responded.

Encouraged by her greeting, the drunkard grinned at her. "Hear there's a party in your honour tonight. Am I invited?"

"If there is, it's my parents' party," replied Chiara truthfully. "I don't know much about it."

"A surprise party, then?" The man covered his mouth with his hand. "I suppose I ruined the surprise. Dear me."

"It's all right. I already—"

"You'll be granting wishes as a fairy," interrupted the man, looking up from his hat. His bloodshot eyes were fixed on her. "Won't you?"

"To the brave, the unselfish and the truthful," she replied, quoting what the Violet Fairy had told her. "If you have such qualities, your wish upon a Wishing Star will be heard."

"Oh, you'd best hear *my* wishes, little Chiara, or I'll be paying your family a visit!" He flashed a set of bright white teeth. "That pretty sister of yours, especially."

Chiara tensed all over. "It'd be wise not to threaten my family," she warned.

"What will you do, turn me into a toad?"

"If you deserve it," she said.

He sniggered. "You don't have it in you."

She wouldn't be cowed, and she gave him her most dauntless stare, holding it for good measure before turning on her heel. The man simply laughed and laughed, the sound bubbling in her ears as she hurried in the opposite direction.

All of her trembled, and she crossed her arms over her body and held herself still. It should have come as no surprise that there would be people who would try to take advantage of her. But to have a complete stranger threaten her and her family left her unsettled.

It won't scare me away, she thought, easing away the fear icing her heart. *The world's not a perfect place, and if I become a fairy, I'll have the chance to make it better.*

She picked up her nerve and continued on her way, trying to focus on how good it'd be to see Geppetto.

CHAPTER TEN

Geppetto was humming to himself. It was a habit of his to make music when he was happy, and he was happiest when he was working on one of his secret projects. A music box, this time. His most ambitious project yet.

He'd only just finished designing it, after two weeks of studying the mechanics of how to construct one. He didn't have any money to buy supplies, so he had built everything from scratch. Thus far he'd constructed a rough cylinder, which was meant to fit into the box just above a metal comb. The plan was that as the cylinder rolled, the comb would tickle the nodes on its surface, and each would produce a pitch that was part of the song he'd selected.

That song, of course, was the Nightingale Aria. Its melody was simple enough for even him to sing, and so memorable that it always took hours to get out of his head. It was a popular tune these days, about a young bird that had lost her way and kept singing until she found her way back home again. Geppetto took the box onto his palm, carefully etching the beginnings of what would become a nightingale carved onto the lid. Then he would paint it, and maybe, if he summoned the courage, he would give it to—

There came a knock on the door, and, worried it was his father, Geppetto hastily threw a cloth over the music box. Then he remembered – his father was upstairs playing his guitar.

"Silly me," he mumbled with a laugh as he opened the door. "Now who could it be?"

Chiara Belmagio stood at the threshold, carrying her brother's violin and a basket loaded with wares from town.

"Why, Chiara!"

"Greetings, Geppetto. Is the shop open?"

Out of habit, Geppetto looked behind her – hoping that he might see Ilaria Belmagio, too. But no younger sister came.

"Yes, yes, we're always open," replied Geppetto. He put on his apron and gestured for her to come inside. "What does Niccolo need this time?"

"He says two of the strings snapped. I think he just

wants me out of the house." Chiara opened the case so Geppetto could take a look. "I don't mind – I meant to stop by anyway."

"Hmm." Geppetto turned, reaching for the cupboard where he kept extra violin strings. As he opened the doors, a small wooden figurine tumbled off its shelf. Chiara bent to pick it up.

"Did you make this?" she said, admiring the thumb-sized cat. "It's beautiful." She rose and noticed the row of similar such creatures Geppetto had carved, sitting carefully behind the box of violin strings.

"They're just chunks of wood," he said hastily. "Nothing special."

"How long do they take you to carve?"

"A few hours, if they're small. A week for a larger piece."

Chiara studied the figurine on her palm. Recognising it, "This is little Gus's new cat," she said. "You even captured her forked tail."

Geppetto shrugged shyly. "I thought little Gus might like it."

"He'll adore it. Will you give it to him?"

"Maybe," said Geppetto. "After it's painted."

Chiara passed him back the cat, watching as he tenderly returned it to its place in the cupboard. When he faced her again, her expression had turned pensive.

"You should open a shop, Geppetto. A toy shop. I can already imagine what joy you'd bring to the children."

"A toy shop?" Geppetto pretended he'd never dreamt of such a thing. "Oh, no, no. There's no future for a toy maker here."

"Is that you speaking," said Chiara softly, "or your father?"

It astounded him how easily she saw into his heart. No one had said that to him before. Was that why the fairies had come to her, because she could read his dreams and the fears that hindered them?

Geppetto found he couldn't reply. But his actions were telling enough. Without meaning to, he stole a glance upstairs, flinching when the sound of his father's guitar playing came to a halt.

As he fixed his attention on Niccolo's violin, Chiara lowered her voice. "It's what you love," she said. "I can see it in the way you beam about your work, and the way you handle your creations. You don't feel that love when you're repairing violins and guitars."

Geppetto forced a laugh. "Not everyone is meant to do what they love," he said woodenly, as if he'd rehearsed the words to himself a hundred times. He mustered a smile and spread his arms to show his father's workshop. "This is close enough."

Before Chiara could reply, footsteps thudded down the stairs. "Which of the Belmagio girls are you?" growled Geppetto's father. "The fairy or the diva?"

"Papa," said Geppetto, his cheeks growing hot. Papa was in a mood, thanks to the weather. As autumn approached, it was getting colder, and that made his joints ache and his guitar playing clumsy. He didn't like any reminders that he couldn't play or work as well as he used to.

"Papa," said Geppetto again, "she's a customer."

"The fairy, then," Tommaso said. "The whole village is in a frenzy, getting ready for your party."

"Father!" Geppetto said. "It was supposed to be a—"

"It's all right," said Chiara politely. "I already knew." She gave his father a winsome smile that he did not deserve. "Will you be attending, sir?"

"Parties are for gossips and nags," replied Tommaso, "and freeloaders. My son and I don't keep such company." He harrumphed at the goods in her basket. "Besides, it seems like you've gifts aplenty, Ms Belmagio. What could my humble shop offer a future fairy?"

"You misunderstand, sir," said Chiara. "I don't want any gift—"

"I don't care how you meant it," replied Tommaso. "I suppose your parents will be well looked after, now that their girl's going to be a fairy – but not everyone in this town is thriving."

To her credit, Chiara barely flinched. "Mr Tommaso," she said warmly, "your son is my friend, and he would be my honoured guest tonight. Without him, I might never have met the fairies."

"Geppetto's too poor to have friends. And too busy." His father started for the door and wagged a finger at Geppetto. "Don't you be giving her the strings free just because she saved you!"

Chiara glanced at Geppetto, who wouldn't meet her eyes. Like a turtle, he shrank into his shell and did not know what to say.

This was what he had feared every time Chiara and Niccolo visited. This was always why he insisted they leave the workshop and go for a walk downtown. It wasn't only because of the creaks in the floor, the broken panelling or crack in the windows, or that he had nothing to serve his friends, or even that he was forced to charge the Belmagios for his services even when Chiara had saved his life.

It was because he was afraid Papa would come barging down – as he just had – and frighten away his friends.

"Well, there you have his answer," Geppetto mumbled,

staring at his cat figurine as his father made for the door. "No party for me."

"I'm sure he'll change his mind if I—"

"No, he won't."

Chiara's brows furrowed determinedly, and she started after his father just out the door. "There will be cake," she called. "A table full of cake. Chocolate, so I've heard. No one bakes a better chocolate cake than my mamma."

Geppetto's father donned his hat, bright yellow with a blue band. By now he could have been well down the street, but he stopped midstep. Though he didn't turn around, he was listening.

"Even if you don't come, you must try some," said Chiara brightly. "I'll ask my mamma to save you and Geppetto an extra-large slice… though, to be honest, it's best when it's fresh."

The old man let out a grunt, finally whirling to face Chiara. "You trying to bribe me with cake, Belmagio?"

"I would never bribe," said Chiara truthfully. "I'll ask my sister to bring you a slice tomorrow."

"Your sister?" Geppetto's father grunted. "I don't want your sister stepping foot in my workshop, what with those giggling geese she's always with. Gossips, the lot of them."

"Then maybe Geppetto can fetch it tonight," said Chiara. "He can simply stop by."

Geppetto stared at his hands. There was no way his father would fall for this.

"No," said his papa, after too long a pause. Stars above stars, he was actually hesitating. "The whole town will wonder why he didn't bring a gift. Gossips like Becca Vaci and Gretel Valmont will notice."

"Then he *will* bring me a gift," said Chiara.

Now Geppetto spoke up, low and quick. "Chia, we can't—"

"I'd like a wood carving," she interrupted, turning to him. "A figurine, like the one you made of Gus's cat."

"You want a stupid trinket?" Geppetto's father scoffed.

"They're not stupid trinkets. They're beautiful. I'd love one to treasure when I'm with the fairies."

Geppetto's father shook his head as he fastened the top button of his coat.

"Please, Mr Tommaso," said Chiara. "It would mean a great deal to me."

A grumble. "All right," said Geppetto's father, to his son's astonishment. The old man softened. "The boy's only young once, I suppose, and a party's how I met his mother. If he finishes his work along with your gift in time, he can go. I'll come, too, to make sure he's back before nine o'clock. I won't have him in the company of this town's carousers."

"I understand, sir," Chiara agreed.

The old man's face went stern again, and he let out a harrumph – clearly to have the last word – then left the workshop.

Once his father was gone, Geppetto leapt off his bench. He was shaking. "How did you…" He gaped. "He said I can go!"

"All I did was ask nicely," said Chiara, grinning, "and remember that your father loves cake. Baked goods always help turn things around."

Chiara bit her lip as soon as the words came out, and Geppetto couldn't help noticing that her smile faltered. But he wasn't brave enough to ask her about it.

"My stars," he said, hands still trembling as he packed Niccolo's violin back in its case. "The whole town will be there. Maybe I shouldn't go. I'm not much fun at parties. I never know what to say."

"Niccolo and I would love for you to come. You always know what to say around us." Chiara paused. "And Ilaria will be there."

Geppetto hated himself for how his breath hitched.

If Chiara noticed, she hid it very well. "Come for the music, Geppetto. Come for the food and the company. Come because it's my last night in Pariva."

That made Geppetto look up. He blinked, pushing his glasses up the bridge of his nose. "You're really leaving?"

"It isn't called a farewell party for no reason," said Chiara, her eyes filling with mirth. "I'm leaving tomorrow morning with the Violet Fairy."

"I didn't realise it was so soon." Geppetto remembered then that she had asked for a figurine. "What shall I carve you?"

Chiara thought for a moment. "A dove," she said finally. "It's what my mamma and papa used to call me when I was little – because I'd bring peace between Ily and Nico." The nickname made her smile. "And it's my favourite bird."

"A dove," Geppetto repeated, nodding. He raked his fingers through his black hair. "That's simple enough. I should finish it by tonight."

"So you'll come?"

"You're not going to leave until I agree."

"Promise?" She teased, "You can't break a promise, you know, especially not to a potential future fairy."

"Yes, yes." Geppetto nodded. "I promise."

"Good." She tucked Niccolo's violin case under her arm and picked up her basket. "The party starts at seven."

CHAPTER ELEVEN

The Belmagios gave up trying to keep Chiara's party a surprise. A good thing, because by seven o'clock there had to have been at least two hundred people – half the town – crammed onto their property. Guests spilled onto the road, many of them in line to view the long table set up in the courtyard: Mrs Belmagio's famous dessert spread.

The tower of cookies was high enough to touch the lanterns Mr Belmagio had hung on the trees, and everyone clapped appreciatively when Mrs Belmagio and Mrs Vaci brought in a five-tiered chocolate cake, meticulously decorated with plump crimson cherries and hazelnut frosting. Each layer was shaped like a scalloped bowl, meant to resemble the fountain in Pariva's central square, and topped with a generous sprinkling of bluebell petals.

But what made Chiara tear up were the cards pressed carefully into the cake, each on a sliced piece of cork – messages from every friend, neighbour, child and elder she had ever known.

We'll miss you. May you spread your light and make all of Esperia bright.

Good luck with the fairies. They'd be fools not to take you in.

And so on it went.

Chiara held the cards to her heart. She hugged the children at her side, who had been reading over her shoulder, squeezing each of them affectionately. She turned to her parents and kissed them on the cheeks. "How lucky I am to have you, Mamma, Papa. Thank you." She faced the waiting guests. "And how lucky I am to have been born in Pariva."

"Don't forget to watch over us when you're a fairy!" Mr Sette shouted.

"Of course she will."

"That's our Chia!"

Chiara pursed her lips. She knew they all meant well, but she couldn't help feeling a twinge of uncertainty. She was only leaving on a trial; her heart told her she owed herself a chance to see what becoming a fairy would be like, but she hadn't made up her mind about what would happen afterwards.

What could she tell them without letting everyone down?

"*If* I become a fairy," she said, "I'll do my best to make you all proud."

"Now, let's eat!" her mother cried, wiping at the tears that slipped from her eyes. "Cake for everyone!"

At the announcement, Niccolo and his string quartet filled the merry courtyard with songs, most of which were serenades to woo Sofia Farrio, the young lady he'd started seeing. Mrs Belmagio wove around the house, chatting with the guests and making sure everyone's plate was full, while Mr Belmagio ushered people to dance and drink and eat cake. The house and the courtyard buzzed with laughter, with fond memories of Chiara, with everyone having a marvellous time. Even Mr Tommaso, who had made a surprise appearance with his son. The stern luthier was helping himself to the promised piece of chocolate cake.

While everyone celebrated, Chiara couldn't shake the feeling in her gut that someone here was far from happy. Someone was miserable.

She spun slowly, holding an invisible compass that guided her.

That was when she found her sister.

Ilaria was parked beside Papa's herb garden with Simona and Beatrice, eating cake. Every few seconds, she threw her head back and laughed, and her face settled into an overly wide smile. Her actress's smile, Chia knew. It only showed her upper teeth. When Ily was genuinely happy, you could see the bottom teeth, too. Her eyes kept drifting off to the side as if she'd rather be anywhere but there.

I need to talk to her, Chia thought.

Squeezing her way through the crowds towards her sister was a herculean effort. Every two steps, someone stopped Chia to congratulate her, and out of courtesy, she couldn't cut the conversation short. By the time she made it to her sister, Simona and Beatrice had already finished their slices of cake.

"What do you mean, you don't know whether she's going to join the fairies?" Simona asked, licking the frosting from her fork. "When she comes back, she'll be a fully-fledged one, won't she?"

"She'll be able to grant wishes then," Beatrice added. "I wonder, will we still need to wish on the Wishing Star if we have our very own fairy?"

Simona rolled her eyes. "I know what *you'd* wish for – for Niccolo to finally notice you. Well, you'll have to wish him away from Sofia."

"I wouldn't waste a wish on that." Beatrice's cheeks flushed with anger. "Not everyone's as shameless as you and Ily."

"Ily's kissed half the town," said Simona. "I've only kissed Pietro."

Simona passed her plate to the waiting young man

and ordered him to fetch her another slice. Then she turned to Ily. "*You* must be happy. All your dreams are going to come true."

"What do you mean?" asked Ily thinly.

"Why even bother applying to the conservatory when your sister's going to be a fairy? One tap of her wand, and you'll be rich and famous."

"I didn't spend years studying and practising for my sister to make me famous," said Ily. "I can do it on my own."

"You think so? Let's face it, your voice is pretty, but it's the sort of pretty that's for peddling extra money on the street and lulling babies to sleep."

"And getting boys to kiss you," added Beatrice with a giggle.

Ily glared.

"It doesn't strike the ear as diva material," Simona went on. "On top of that, you're not even a good actress. Last time I saw an opera, Maria Linda made me sob – she was divine."

Ily's fists clenched at her sides.

"Luckily, now you have Chia."

"Your future's all sorted," Beatrice agreed. In spite of what she'd said, Beatrice was just as shameless as Simona, and she tugged on Ily's hand, wheedling: "I can't think of the last time a fairy's visited Pariva, and I look out for the Wishing Star every night. Help a friend, Ily. We've been like sisters ever since we were born. Do you think—"

"No," said Ily coldly. "I don't know if she'll be able to grant your wishes." Ily eyed Chia's approach. "Why don't you ask her yourself?"

Her friends whirled, finding Chiara behind them. It was an awkward situation to arrive in, but Chiara deflected the girls with a pleasant wave and asked, "May I borrow my sister for a minute?"

"It's your party, Chia," said Simona, her words honeyed in a way Chia had never heard directed at her. "You can do whatever you'd like."

"Thank you." Chiara steered Ily into the house. It was crowded inside, too, but not as badly as in the courtyard. "You all right?" she asked her sister as they hiked up the stairs. Piles and piles of gifts covered the staircase.

"It's a like a funeral," muttered Ily, overhearing someone praise Chiara's kindness. "Except you're not dead. Everyone saying all these wonderful things about you, everyone toasting your memory. Doesn't it bother you?"

"A little," admitted Chiara. "But the party's more for Mamma and Papa than for me. Agata didn't tell us what will happen if I decide to become a fairy after I finish my training. Whether I'll get to live at home again and see you often… or…" Her voice trailed, and she didn't want to think about the alternatives.

"It'll be different when you come back," said Ily.

"What do you mean?"

"Everyone loves you. They always have. But now they want you to love them, too." Ily glanced at the mound of fruit baskets and wrapped sliced meats and homemade soaps and candles that had taken over the staircase. "In case they want something from you."

"Not everyone is that mercenary."

"We'll see."

Often it amazed Chiara how different she and Ily were. She tried to see the goodness in people, whereas her sister was far more cynical. *We balance each other, I suppose*.

She reached for Ily's hand. "I heard what Simona and Beatrice said. You don't need friends like that."

"Then who will be my friend?" said Ily. "You? You're not even going to be here."

"I'll always be your sister," said Chia. She dusted a crumb from Ily's collar. "Now chin up. What would a Belmagio party be without a concert? Let's not let your practising go to waste."

"I don't feel like singing," mumbled Ilaria.

That didn't sound like her stubborn younger sister.

Ily thrived on attention; she'd practically been born giving concerts. "Is it because of what Simona said?" asked Chia. "Don't listen to her. You've a beautiful voice, Ily. A showstopper voice. Would I lie to you?"

"You can't lie," Ily scoffed. "Even if your life depended on it."

"See?"

Her sister released a woeful sigh. "No one wants to hear me sing tonight. This is your party, not mine."

"I can think of one person who's here for you, not me."

Ily crossed her arms. "Who?"

"Come with me." Chia guided her sister downstairs to the Blue Room. Inside were dozens of Mamma and Papa's friends. But standing in the corner, studying the design of the lyre music stand, was Geppetto.

Ilaria's shoulders went tight under Chiara's hands. "No, Chia. I already told you, I—"

"He's our friend, Ily. I'm not asking you to marry him, for goodness sake. But you never talk to him."

Her sister cast her a glare. "Because he literally turns into a tomato every time he's within three feet of me. Maybe I'm the one who's becoming a fairy."

That got a laugh out of both sisters, and Ilaria finally relented. "All right, but only to show you I'm right."

Right she was. Geppetto practically tripped over the

music stand at the sight of Ilaria, and his ears turned bright red.

"Find the music stand fascinating, Mr Geppetto?" said Ilaria, sending a sidelong I-told-you-so glance at Chiara.

"Oh. Um. Yes. The engravings on the cedar are quite special. It must have been in your family for a long time."

"Our great-grandmother was an accomplished violinist—" supplied Chiara.

"Much better than Niccolo," Ilaria added.

"—and it was a gift to her."

"Well, it's beautifully preserved," Geppetto said, straightening. He backed up until his heels hit the wall. "And… and this has been a wonderful party."

"Our family owes its fortune to you," said Ilaria dryly. "If you hadn't almost drowned, the fairies would never have noticed Chia."

"Ilaria!" Chiara exclaimed. "That's an entirely inappropriate thing to say."

"No, no," Geppetto insisted. "I think the fairies would have chosen Chiara even if I hadn't fallen off my boat. It's fate."

"I don't believe in fate," replied Ilaria, crossing her arms.

"Perhaps you should," said Geppetto. "Fate watches over all of us. She's the reason we're here tonight."

Ilaria arched a dark eyebrow. "I never would have taken you for a dreamer. What dreams would a luthier's son have?"

He reddened, stammering. "I…"

"I thought so. There's not much potential for dreaming in a dusty old workshop."

"Oh, no. There's an art to lutherie. Making an instrument the very best it can be is a craft."

"You talk as if the instruments are alive."

"They are – when they're played," Geppetto said seriously. "I guess that makes the voice the most natural instrument of all."

The creases on Ilaria's brow smoothed. "I suppose so," she allowed, softening.

Her sister was charmed, Chiara could tell, and she backed away a little to give the two some space to talk.

Geppetto and Ily had much in common. They were both secret dreamers who shared a deep love for music. Yes, Ily was reckless and headstrong, but Geppetto… Geppetto was endlessly patient and caring. They would balance each other beautifully. In her heart, Chiara knew they would find their way.

But it helped to give a nudge.

"Speaking of which," she cut in, "Ily's agreed to sing. How about the Nightingale Aria? It happens to be both your favourite."

Before Ily could question Geppetto whether that was true, Chia towed her to the centre of the room, where an audience was already beginning to congregate. While Ilaria gathered her poise, Chiara settled on the harpsichord bench and rested her fingers on her opening notes. The ivory keys had begun to yellow with age, but their sound was full and joyous.

She glanced at her sister, taking a breath to cue that she'd begin.

The second Ilaria released her voice, the chatter ceased. People eating cake in the hallway ambled into the chamber to listen, and someone opened the windows so guests outside in the courtyard could hear, too.

"The nightingale waits for a song to go along," Ily sang.

It was a bittersweet aria, whose story Ilaria had mastered sharing with not only her voice, but also with the expressions on her face, the movements of her arms and the carefully choreographed blocking she performed as she crossed one side of the room to the other. Yet tonight, something was off. Her tone carried more melancholy than usual, and the tempo she led was a beat slower than when they'd practised. Chia doubted anyone would notice. Ily's pride was in her coloratura, and every moment was still magnificent – each note in the impressive cascades attacked with vim and beauty – as if she were truly a bird chirping. But behind the technical difficulties of the piece, Ily managed to show her musicality and bring emotion to her voice; that was what cast a spell over everyone who listened.

"Brava!" the guests cheered when the song was over. Applause made the walls vibrate, and Chiara remained at her instrument while her sister curtsied and bowed.

Usually after a performance, the children raced up to Ily and tugged on her skirt adoringly. "Will you sing more for us, Miss Ilaria?" they would ask. "How does your voice go so high? You sound like a bird! Sing another one!"

But tonight, Ily ignored the children as they went up to her. Her mind was on something else, and as she slipped out of the room, the children turned instead to Chiara. They peppered her with questions about the Wishing Star, about wands and wings and other things Chiara couldn't answer. A reminder of how little she knew about the future she was about to undertake.

"I don't know," she replied, to question after question. While she indulged her curious admirers, she kept an eye out for Ily.

Her sister did not return to the Blue Room, and Chiara was getting up to find her – when Geppetto came up to her at the harpsichord.

He smiled at the children and shyly offered them a few little toys from his right pocket: the small figurines Chiara had spotted in his cabinet. The cat with the forked tail, a wooden tiger and even an elephant.

The children gasped with delight and ran off to play with their new toys.

And as Geppetto approached Chiara, he reached into his left pocket. "I put this on the stairs at first, but it's so small I worried you wouldn't see it." He plucked out a wooden dove and presented it to her bashfully. "I didn't get a chance to paint it, but—"

"It's perfect," said Chiara, cupping her hands to accept the gift. She held the dove on her palm and marvelled at how lifelike it looked with its smooth rounded wings and gentle beak. "If I have a window on the Wishing Star, I'll set it on the sill."

That made Geppetto beam. "Imagine that. Something I've made, on a fairy's windowsill."

"I'm not a fairy yet."

"You will be," he said. "Everyone's proud of you, even my papa – though he'd never admit it. Having a fairy come from Pariva, well… it's a great honour."

Everyone said that, and Chiara's shoulders fell. "Not everyone is happy," she murmured.

Geppetto furrowed his brow, then guessed: "Ilaria?"

"Is it that obvious?"

"No. But she… she sounded different tonight."

Of course Geppetto had noticed.

"Will you talk to her?" Chiara asked.

"Me?" Geppetto said. Without looking, he aimed his hands for his pockets but missed completely. He stared at them as if he'd been betrayed. "I don't know. She doesn't seem to like me much."

"That's not true," said Chiara softly. "I have a feeling you two are destined to be friends. She'll like you very much once she gets to know you."

Geppetto's blue eyes flew up. "You think so?" He cleared his throat. "I mean… I don't…"

"She could use a friend when I'm not here. A true friend."

Geppetto looked down at his hands again. "I seem to forget how to speak when I'm around her."

"She's nicer than she acts," Chiara encouraged. "Will you be a friend to her – as a favour to me?" When still Geppetto hesitated, Chiara knew she needed the two to come together. She played her very last card, smiling: "I did save you."

A gentleman like Geppetto couldn't refuse. "All right."

"Why don't you go look for her now? She's been in the kitchen a while and everyone's waiting to hear her sing more."

"My father…"

"Don't worry about your father." Chia glanced at Mr Tommaso, who was embroiled in a hearty argument with Mr Vaci. "I doubt he'll be ready to leave."

Geppetto drew a deep breath, as if gathering his courage. Then he nodded.

"Don't forget to take a slice of cake for him."

CHAPTER TWELVE

It wasn't like Ilaria to slip away during the middle of a party, but she wasn't in the mood to celebrate. She hadn't even been in the mood to sing, but she hadn't wanted to make a scene in front of half the town.

She'd done her best to be charming: she'd smiled, she'd danced, she'd piled her friends' plates with cookies and echoed her sister's praises. But the moment her part on 'stage' was finished, she made for the wings. After all, no one had asked her for an encore, and aside from a guest or two offering half-hearted praise for her singing, no one cared about her performance. Even the knots of young men who usually clamoured for her attention ignored her. All anyone was talking about was Chia.

Alone and forgotten, Ily fled into the kitchen, kicking out the guests loitering inside.

Once alone, she blew out the candle and sank onto a stool, listening to the forks tinkle against plates in the courtyard, to Nico's string quartet playing in the Blue Room. Chia was still there, probably surrounded by a den of admirers. Ily could pick out her voice through any din; it was rich and warm – with a lilt that instantly made people love her.

But honestly, if everyone loved Chiara so very much, why celebrate her leaving?

That morning, Ily had accepted the idea of losing her sister. Accepted the idea of having her world turned upside down and losing her best friend.

What had been wrong with her?

Mrs Belmagio tapped on the kitchen window from outside. "Ily? Mrs Vaci said she saw you inside. Ily?"

Reluctantly, Ilaria got up and cracked opened the window, music and chatter from outside spilling into her quiet refuge. "There you are," said her mother. "We're serving coffee now. Bring some sugar out, please. Cream, too."

How can you smile, Mamma? she wanted to ask. *How can you laugh and dance and entertain half the town when tonight is our last night with Chia?*

She could already hear what Mamma would say: *Because*

what can we do, Ily, other than show her how much we love her?

Ilaria pasted on her brightest smile. "Yes, Mamma, I'll bring them out right away." But as soon as her mother disappeared into the crowds again, Ily closed the window and dashed out the front door as fast as she could.

No one would look for her. Not Simona or Beatrice or Niccolo. Not even Chia.

Summer evenings in Pariva were brisk, and Ilaria ran to keep from shivering, making for the sea. It was quite a walk, and by the time she reached the shore, the lights of Pariva were a faint blur against the dark of night.

Wind tousled her dark hair, and she undid the chignon at her nape, letting her long locks fly loose. She glanced behind her, but no one had come.

Of course no one had come. The only person who'd paid her any attention tonight was Geppetto. It'd been sweet of him to talk to her, to actually listen to her while everyone else was fawning over her sister.

Are you actually warming up to Geppetto? she asked herself. *It's his fault the fairies noticed Chiara. If he hadn't been out sailing that day, if he hadn't been foolish enough to chase after Monstro, then… then…*

Her hands squeezed into fists at her sides. Then she wouldn't lose her sister.

Ilaria sighed, knowing it was hopeless to wish she could change the past. She crouched, picking up a handful of pebbles and flinging them angrily into the sea. The water was so dark she might as well have been tossing them into oblivion, but she heard the rocks' splash. Then a louder splash.

Frightened, she stood and took a step back. Shadows had gathered in the water, tracing as far as she could see. "Monstro?" she whispered.

"I'm not Monstro, my dear," responded a woman's voice, low and rich and faraway – it came impossibly from the sea. The voice drew nearer. "But he's a friend. Asleep now, though he'll awaken soon enough."

Ilaria gasped and jumped away from the water. She staggered to turn back for the road, but curiosity nagged her to stay. Putting on her grandest tone to mask her fear, she demanded: "Who are you?"

The water washed up, almost touching her toes. It was a shade of green under the moonlight, something she had never seen before. "Just a passer-by."

"You're lying," said Ilaria. A chill raced down her spine. "*What* are you?"

"I'm embraced by the forgotten, the unwanted, the unworthy. That's how you've been feeling lately, haven't you – Ilaria?"

Forgotten. Unwanted. Unworthy.

As Ilaria repeated the words silently, they left a bitter taste on her tongue. Forgotten, yes. Unwanted? Sometimes, when her mother scolded her for being lazy and vain, for shirking her duties at the bakery and at the hat shop.

Unworthy?

She gritted her teeth. Every night she looked out for a Wishing Star, and she practised hours and hours every day, sometimes until her voice went hoarse.

A shameful thought, which seemed to have been kept deep beneath the fears of losing her sister, suddenly reared its ugly head: why had the fairies never come to her? Why had they gone to Chia – who had no passions, who had no dreams? Was it because Ilaria was somehow *unworthy* of their attention?

All anyone ever did was praise Chiara. Love Chiara.

Even Mamma and Papa preferred Chia, though they never admitted it. All anyone could talk about was Chia.

"How have I ended up with two girls so different from each other?" Papa had said once. "Ily wants the whole world, while you, Chia – you want absolutely nothing."

He'd glanced at Ily, at the bright red ribbons in her hair, the extra lace on her sleeves that she'd painstakingly sewn herself. As if she had no substance compared to her sister. As if she'd been made of dreams that would never come true.

"You've been a shadow to your sister all your life," said the mysterious voice. "Why do you tolerate it?"

The secret spring of envy buried inside her bubbled up. There was nothing special about Chiara. Feeding a few ducks and helping an old woman or two carry their groceries had amounted to a gift far grander than she deserved. Ilaria would have rescued Geppetto from drowning if she'd had the chance.

She'd simply never been given the opportunity to prove herself.

I'll become a famous singer, she told herself. *I'll become the greatest prima donna in the land.*

It was easy telling herself that when she had the loveliest voice in Pariva, but what if she wasn't good enough for Vallan? There were a thousand girls in the capital just as talented as she – maybe even more so. A true star was supposed to shine no matter where she was. Deep down, she feared everyone was right. That all her dream would ever be… was a dream.

How was it fair that at the same time, Chiara would get to be a fairy? Everyone knew that fairies lived as long as they wanted and stayed young forever. She'd never have to worry about greying hairs or wrinkles or sagging skin – or her voice losing strength over time. All while Ilaria would age and die, then be forgotten.

"It isn't fair, is it?" the woman whispered, as if reading her mind.

Ily threw a rock at the shadow, but it did not flicker and ripple as the water did. The rock disappeared into the darkness as if consumed.

Spooked, she grabbed another rock and reeled away from the sea. "Geppetto!" she said, spying a silhouette behind the trees. "Heavens, Geppetto. You scared me! Why aren't you still at the party?"

He looked flustered. "I… I, um… I…"

"The docks aren't on the way home for you." She eyed him suspiciously. "Were you following me?"

"No! No."

He was a terrible liar.

"Yes," he confessed. "Your sister was worried about you, so I went to go find you. But when you weren't in the house…"

Suddenly the rock in her hand felt heavy, and she let it go. It tumbled down, falling against the pebbles on the shore. "I just needed some air," she lied.

"You didn't even bring a jacket," he said, doffing his. "Please."

"What a gentleman you are, Geppetto," said Ilaria. "Now won't *you* be cold?"

He was wearing only a shirt and a vest.

"I can still work if I catch cold," he said, scratching at his moustache sheepishly. "But you won't be able to sing."

Ilaria's eyes drifted into the sea, where the shadow had spoken to her. It was gone now, but she wondered whether she'd imagined it. She pushed the thought out of her mind and reached into her pockets.

"I forgot my cloak, but I did steal some cookies from the party. Almond and pistachio. Would you like some?"

Geppetto accepted an almond cookie. "The view's better from here," he said, guiding them towards a bench further down along the docks.

"Shouldn't you be at home?" said Ilaria, plopping onto the bench. "I've never seen you at any other parties. A good boy like you… your papa won't like that you're out with me."

"Papa's bark is worse than his bite," Geppetto replied. "Besides, he's still at the party. Chiara talked him into letting me come."

Oh. Ily immediately soured. "All good things are always thanks to Chiara."

Geppetto didn't catch the sarcasm in her tone.

"It's lucky she came by," agreed Geppetto. "Cakes are Papa's weakness. Boats, too… but I guess thanks to me, ours is gone." He hung his head. "As soon as I can afford the wood, I'll build him a new one."

"You know how to build a boat?" Ily asked.

"Papa taught me when I was young. He's good with construction… he says it's not so different from making instruments. It used to keep his mind off Mamma."

Ilaria remembered that Geppetto had lost his mother many years ago. Everyone had gone to her funeral, though she hardly remembered the occasion – or the lady.

"I'm sorry," she said.

Geppetto stared off into the sea. "He wasn't always the way he is now. Working at the shop was his greatest joy, and he used to travel across Esperia to sell his instruments. But now every other town has a luthier, and business… business is failing." He gave a wan smile. "I'm sorry, I must be boring you."

"Have you told Chiara?" asked Ily. "She's going to be a fairy. She could help."

"Oh, no. I couldn't."

"You haven't told her?" When Geppetto shook his head, Ily felt a rush of pleasure. It pleased her that Geppetto had confided in her and not Chia. "Maybe you should travel more. Sell violins, like your father used to. There are plenty of music schools in Vallan."

"Like the Madrigal Conservatory. That's where you want to study, I heard."

Ilaria tilted her head. "You've been asking about me?"

Even in the dark, she saw Geppetto's cheeks turn red. "I… I didn't say that."

"I think you have," Ily teased. "You're the only one who noticed I left. You followed me all the way here."

"I was worried about you. You… you sounded different tonight. Sadder. Maybe I imagined it. I don't think anyone else noticed."

"But you did." Ily paused. "You said you used to listen to my lessons with Ms Rocco."

"I couldn't help it," he replied shyly. "Her house isn't far from mine."

Yes, Ilaria knew that. That was how she'd first spied Geppetto, working away diligently at his father's shop.

Ms Rocco was the closest Pariva had ever had to a local celebrity. For over twenty years, she had sung in the Accordo, Vallan's opera house, as a member of the chorus. After she retired, she returned to Pariva.

It had taken Ilaria weeks to convince Ms Rocco to give her lessons. She'd badgered the old lady until finally she caved, and Ilaria had taken a job at Pariva's hat shop – which she loathed – just to pay for her lessons. They'd been her favourite hours of the day, half focused on training her voice and learning the masterpieces by Esperia's composers, and half filled with stories about the lady's youth in the capital, and what it'd been like to sing in the greatest opera house in the world.

"You must go to Vallan," Ms Rocco had urged her. "You aren't meant for a place like this, full of milkmaids and fishmongers."

"My family is here."

Ms Rocco wrinkled her nose. "Do you want to work in the hat shop forever, Ily? Listen to me so you won't end up with my fate. You have the voice to go far, my dear, but there will be others who wish to bring you down. Do not let them. Follow your dream, no matter what you have to do."

Ily had wondered what Ms Rocco had meant by the warning not to end up like her, but she'd never asked. Then her dear teacher had passed away, and there were no more lessons. Still, Ilaria kept her job selling hats so that she might afford tuition at the Madrigal Conservatory. If she got in, anyway. Her first audition was next week in Nerio. If she passed that one, she would advance to Vallan – and meet Maria Linda.

"She left me all her music," murmured Ilaria, thinking of her treasured cabinet at home, filled with a lifetime's worth of songs she studied whenever she had a moment. "Said it'd be a waste if I didn't use my talent to become great."

"Then you will."

Typically, Ilaria would have raised her chin haughtily and said, *Of course I will.* But maybe it was the melancholy rising to her chest, or the solemn way that Geppetto looked at her, truly believing in her music, that humbled her.

"I don't know," said Ilaria, voicing her uncertainties. "Maybe it's a silly dream. A reverie, like they say in the city. A pastime." She didn't give Geppetto a chance to speak. "She told me I need to pick a new name. Ilaria is too… country bumpkin."

"I like the name Ilaria," disagreed Geppetto. "It's lovely."

"Lovely isn't suitable for a prima donna," said Ily with a huff. "Lovely is how you describe a babbling brook or lace that goes on a hat. You don't describe a shining star as lovely. A shining star is magnificent. I want to be magnificent."

"What name will you choose?"

"I already have one." She leant close enough to smell almond on his breath. "Do you want to hear?"

Under the lamplight, Ily could only make out a hint of how intensely Geppetto was flushing. "Y-y-yes."

She whispered, in her most dramatic voice: "Cleo del Mar."

The words steamed into the cold air, and Ilaria lifted herself, drawing some space between them as she waited for Geppetto's reaction.

"Cleo," repeated Geppetto, tugging nervously at his collar. "That's a… that's a fine name."

"The name for a prima donna," Ilaria said, puffing up with pride that he approved.

"It is." A long pause. "But I still think Ilaria suits you better."

What did he know? "Maybe here," said Ilaria, displeased. "But I'd be a fool if I wanted to stay. There's nothing for me here. Only donkeys and sheep." She scoffed. "Not even the wolves come to Pariva."

Poor Geppetto had gone speechless. He opened and closed his mouth, trying to come up with something to say, but Ily took pity on him and let out a sigh.

She said, softly, "Knowing my luck, I'll be stuck here forever."

"That wouldn't be so bad. Would it?"

"It'd be the worst fate ever. Never getting to see past the mountains or what's on the other side of the Lyre Sea."

"But you'd be near your family. And—"

"And what, Geppetto?" Ilaria recognised the lift in his voice. Coyly, she said, "Why, would you miss me?"

It was quite impressive how red Geppetto instantly turned. He blinked and stammered and mumbled, all while looking as though he wished the sea would swallow him whole. "Oh, um… who wouldn't miss you, Miss Ilaria? I mean…"

"If you call me *Miss* Ilaria one more time, Geppetto, I'll push you into the sea. And unlike my sister, I won't dive in after you."

"Oh." Geppetto's lips rounded, and he nodded, taking the threat seriously. "Yes, *Ilaria*."

"That's better." Ilaria hid a smile. Who would have thought she'd find strait-laced young Geppetto charming? But there was something about the way he listened to her, as if every sound she uttered were gold.

She liked it. More than that, she liked her effect on him. He was obviously in love with her, but it wasn't like the puppy love that the other boys in town showered her with. After a few weeks at her beck and call, they always tired of her. Ily had a feeling Geppetto was different.

Inching closer to him on the bench, she threaded her arm through his. The way Geppetto's spine went straight, she worried it was about to snap. Yet then he drew a deep breath, and he asked, "So what's your favourite opera?"

Ily grinned. Now that was something she could talk about for hours. And for hours they did, until the world grew so still that even the sea made no sound.

"I can't believe you've never heard an orchestra before," Ilaria exclaimed. "And you call yourself a luthier?"

"Tickets are expensive," replied Geppetto. "Besides, hardly any orchestras ever come to Pariva."

"Wait until you hear one," breathed Ily. "One violin sounds nothing like twenty. And with the flutes and oboes and horns – you'll feel like you're in heaven!" She clasped her hands, remembering how amazing it sounded. "I've only heard one once, when Mamma and Papa took me. It was a long time ago. I'll take you to a concert one day."

She blushed, realising suddenly what she'd proposed. A meeting as such was usually only for young men and women who were courting.

"Maybe my first concert will be yours," said Geppetto quickly, noticing her stricken silence. "Miss Ilaria Belmagio and the orchestra of—"

"No," said Ilaria. "We'll go together." She smiled. "It'll be a grand time."

He smiled back, and Ilaria felt the most unexpected flutter in her stomach when Geppetto looked at her.

"Oh, my," Geppetto said, glancing at his pocket watch. "It's almost midnight! My papa and your parents must be—"

"Asleep by now," Ily finished for him. "Will you walk me home?"

Geppetto extended his arm for her to take, and she took it.

CHAPTER THIRTEEN

The torchlight along Constanza Street flickered, but the road was empty. Mamma and Papa's guests had gone home, and all that remained of Chia's party was a smear of chocolate on the fence and a lone pink glove that had fallen into a bush.

As Geppetto accompanied Ily to her door, the awkward tension she'd helped him forget the last few hours resurfaced in the worried grimace on his face. His expression gave everything away: what did he do now? Did he stay to ensure she entered safely; did he say he'd see her again soon; did he dare reach for her hand and hold it, as he'd been wanting to all night?

Ilaria was tired, but not too tired to shine her most winning smile at the poor young luthier. "It was a pleasure getting to know you better, Geppetto."

"Um. You… you too, Miss… I mean, *Ilaria.*"

Still smiling, she tipped up her chin and half closed her eyes. "Goodnight," she murmured.

Unfortunately, Geppetto didn't understand her games at all, and he merely tipped his hat nervously. "Goodnight."

He turned back for the road, and Ilaria stared after him, blinking with disbelief. Then she shook her head and laughed to herself. Only Geppetto would miss the opportunity to kiss her goodnight.

What he did do, though, was wave to her from the end of the road. It was a shy wave, but his smile was as wide as his entire face, and it warmed Ily in spite of the night's chill. As did the sight of him quickly whirling to hurry home, muttering something about his papa being angry that he was so late.

Sand and seawater squeaked out of Ilaria's shoes as she entered her home. The party was long since over. All the guests were gone, and not a candle was lit. In the darkness, she toed off her shoes and leant them against a wall to dry. Then, as she made her way into the hall, a shadow darted out from the parlour.

Fear iced Ilaria's stomach. She thought of the strange voice she'd heard at the beach tonight. Had she followed Ilaria home?

Without thinking twice, she picked up the closest thing

to her: the lyre music stand, placed in the hallway right outside the Blue Room. The intruder *should* have dashed out of the back door in the kitchen and jumped over the fence. But he was greedy and refused to give up the heavy sack over his back. Ilaria charged and whacked him as hard as she could on the back.

He thumped against the wall and dropped, silverware clattering out of his sack – Ily's own pillowcase, stuffed with gifts that their neighbours and friends had brought to Chia's party.

Rage filled Ilaria, and she set down the music stand, breathing hard. Then she knelt and studied the thief's face by the moonlight. She didn't know him, which meant he had to be from out of town. When he grunted in pain, she gave a hard kick to his ribs. "You… you scoundrel. Get out of here, you thief. Get out before I—"

"Ily?" Chiara whispered from the stairs. Her sister crept down from her room, holding a lone candle. "Ily, I heard a crash. What—"

Chiara saw the body on the floor, and the anxious crease on her brow turned into shock.

"He was stealing your presents," said Ily, waving a tired hand at the thief. Chia held her candle over his face. Grey hair and a poorly cropped beard. "Doesn't look like he's from Pariva. Do you know him?"

Her sister actually shuddered. "I saw him by the tavern today."

"Just our luck," Ily grumbled. She dusted her hands and grabbed the man's feet, lugging him out of the door. "He's unconscious. Help me get him out of here."

"You're going to put him on the street?"

"We're definitely not putting him on the daybed," retorted Ilaria; she knew exactly what Chiara was thinking. "He tried to rob us!"

Together, they hauled the thief onto the roadside, and Ily dusted her hands as if she'd just dealt with an enormous rat. "I'm guessing this isn't how you thought you'd spend your last night in Pariva."

"It certainly will be memorable."

Chiara knelt and took out her handkerchief, using it to wipe a smear of blood off the man's forehead where Ily had struck him. Under their neighbour's wan lantern light, Ily was proud to see that a hideous bruise was already forming.

Her sister, on the other hand, loosened the shawl from her shoulders and placed it over the thief.

"For this crook?"

"Have some compassion, Ily. It's a cold night."

Ily rolled her eyes as Chia got up to go back in the house. When her sister wasn't looking, Ilaria yanked the shawl back. Then she followed Chiara inside and locked the door.

—

Ilaria let out a yawn as she entered her room to sleep. She was certain she'd left her bed unmade, but the wrinkles in her blanket had been smoothed, and her pillows were neatly fluffed. Mamma had stopped making her bed ages ago, and had all but given up censuring Ilaria for her messiness. Ilaria crossed her arms at Chiara. "I don't need you to make my bed."

"I was waiting for you to come back."

"Why?" Ilaria muttered. "Mamma and Papa didn't care enough to stay awake."

"Where were you?" asked Chiara, choosing to ignore her sarcasm. "I was worried."

"I went for a walk by the sea."

"Alone?"

"Certainly not with you." Ilaria didn't regret the barb even when her sister flinched. She wanted it to hurt. She needed Chia to hurt.

"Doesn't matter." Ily jumped onto her bed, instantly creating a ripple of wrinkles. "No one missed me."

"I did."

Chia's voice was soft, and as her candle flickered, illuminating her face, Ilaria saw that her cheeks were wet. Had she been crying?

Regret pricked at her, but Ily pushed it aside. She crossed her arms and turned away from her sister.

"If you care about me so much, then don't go tomorrow," Ilaria said. It was a test she knew Chia would fail. Still, she dared to hope. "Don't leave with the fairies."

Don't leave me, she almost added.

The mattress dipped under Chia's weight as she sat on the edge. She said, quietly, "How does music make you feel?"

A flash of irritation rose in Ily's chest. "What does that have to do with anything?"

"Just answer."

Ilaria grabbed a pillow and hugged it close. It had been a long night, and she was too tired to be petulant, so she answered, "It makes me feel alive."

"That's how helping people makes me feel."

"It's not the same. Helping people isn't a… a…"

"A job?"

"You're not a doctor, Chia. You're not saving lives."

"In their own way, fairies do save lives," responded Chiara. "Doctors heal the body. Fairies look after the heart."

Ilaria hugged her pillow tighter. She didn't want to understand. She didn't want to listen.

Chia scooted into the centre of the bed and pried the pillow from her sister. "It sounds silly, but there's always been this feeling I get – inside me – when someone's unhappy. It makes me unhappy, too, until I help them feel better."

"That's nonsense."

"Is it?"

Chia was serious, which made Ily frown. "You're saying you can feel how I'm feeling? Like, you can read my mind?"

"I can't read your mind. I can just sense that you're unhappy… with me."

Ilaria snorted. "Didn't seem to work for you that week when you were keeping secrets from me."

"I'm not very good at it yet," said Chiara. "And it helps when I'm focused."

"So what is your fairy sense telling you about me now?"

Chia pursed her lips, the way she always did when she was about to say a truth Ilaria wouldn't like. "Right now you're angry. You wish you could come with me."

At that, Ilaria finally let go of the pillow. "I *am* jealous," she admitted. "You get to leave Pariva and see the world. While I'm stuck here."

"Stuck here?" Chiara chuckled. "Next year, you'll be in Vallan studying with Maria Linda, the most celebrated prima donna in Esperia. Before long, you'll be gracing Accordo and the world's greatest opera houses." She tucked a stray brown lock behind her sister's ear. "You're destined for an amazing adventure, Ily. I can't wait to see how far you'll go."

Ilaria jerked her head away and twirled her hair back in place. But when she spoke, her words had only a trace of their earlier bitterness. "You *were* the best accompanist I've had. Pity I'll have to find someone else."

"Yes." Chia poked her arm. "Too bad Geppetto doesn't play the harpsichord. He found you at the sea, I'm guessing. That's why you're back so late."

Ilaria threw her pillow at Chia. "I should have known you sent him after me! You're sneakier than I took you for."

Chia caught the pillow. "I thought you two would get along." She winked. "It's my special fairy sense again."

"Your special fairy sense," Ily repeated. The corner of her mouth twitched, and a smile peeked out of her frown despite herself. "He was nice. He walked me home."

"See?"

"See what?" Ilaria crossed her arms. "I'm not going to marry him. He wants to stay in Pariva forever. I'm getting out of here the first chance I get."

"I'm not trying to play matchmaker," Chiara said, laughing. "I only want you and Geppetto to be friends. You'll need friends who will stay by you through good times and bad. Geppetto would do that for you. He's a good person."

"Unlike Simona and Beatrice."

"Simona and Beatrice don't always have your best

intentions at heart. I heard what they said about your singing, Ily. It was unkind, and untrue."

"What if they're right, though?" Ily said, voicing her fears. "What if I *do* need your help? Hundreds of girls will be applying to study with Maria Linda." She sighed. "Girls who've grown up seeing operas at the Accordo and can afford acting and singing lessons. Girls who can play both ingénue and vixen and have four-octave ranges. Girls who can reach a high F without straining."

"Worrying about your competition will make you neither a better singer nor a happier one," said Chiara. "Focus on yourself. Which reminds me." She reached into her pocket for her money pouch, neatly tied with a blue bow. She placed it on Ily's lap. "Here, open it. This should help you buy that new dress you've been longing for and help you settle into a new place in Vallan."

Ily stared at her sister, then into the bag. There had to be a hundred oros inside, over a year's worth of savings.

"Chia!" Ilaria breathed, tongue-tied. "You can't – how did you…"

"I saved a little every day from my shifts working at the bakery, and Mamma let me sell some of her flowers. It's hardly enough for life in the big city, but it should help you get started."

Ily swallowed hard, so moved she could hardly speak.

Chia tucked the loose strand of brown hair back behind Ilaria's ear. "It doesn't matter whether I'm gone for one month or one decade. I'll miss everything about Pariva. I'll even miss the smelly fish street on the way to our old school. I'll miss Niccolo and Mamma and Papa. Our mornings playing music together. Most of all, I'll miss you."

I'll miss you, too, Ilaria started to say, but then she noticed that a star had risen above the moon out the window.

"Look!" she cried, pointing outside. "Is that a Wishing Star?"

Chiara squinted. "I think so."

Ilaria pulled her sister towards the window, planting their elbows on the sill. "Let's make a wish. You're still allowed to, right? You're not a fairy yet."

"I think so."

The sisters knelt side by side, and Ilaria mouthed a silent wish.

"What did you ask for?" Chiara asked.

Ilaria grinned. "You should know that if I tell you, it won't come true." She scooted to her sister's side, leaning her head on Chiara's shoulder the way she had when they were children. "You'll just have to wait and find out – like everyone else."

CHAPTER FOURTEEN

The Belmagio household was an uneasy balance of laughter and sorrow as the family nibbled on leftover cake, made light-hearted digs at Ilaria's walk with Geppetto, and danced around the topic of Chia's departure.

"Robbers tried to take our silverware," Ily recounted. She embroidered the truth with some extra details: "They had knives on them, and they were taller than bears! You should have seen their faces when I thwacked them on the head with the music stand."

"So that explains why it's cracked," said Niccolo. "Maybe Mr Tommaso can repair it. You wouldn't mind a visit to Geppetto, I hear."

Ily glared while Mr Belmagio chuckled at his children.

Mrs Belmagio was not in the mood for humour. "You're not eating, Chia," she observed.

"It's rather early for such a feast," replied Chiara.

"Nonsense. Here, you didn't take any of the almond cookies." Mrs Belmagio plucked her own cookies, toast and sliced meats and piled them onto Chiara's plate. "I packed you extra bread and cookies in your bag, too. There should be enough for a good week. Who knows what kind of food fairies eat, or if they have to eat at all! But don't forget your meals, my dove. Three meals a day will keep your energy up and bring you sweet dreams."

"I know, Mamma," said Chia softly. "Thank you."

At last Mrs Belmagio set down her jam knife, her napkin trembling as she dabbed at her eyes and sniffed. "My sweet, sweet girl. If it doesn't work out with the fairies, you come straight back, understood? You're always welcome home. All my children are. Remember that." Mrs Belmagio smiled her pinched, sad smile – the one that told Chiara that her mother was secretly hoping she wouldn't find her place among the fairies, but felt awful about it.

"It isn't farewell," Chia said, setting down her fork. "It's only a trial for a few months. I'll be back."

"I know," replied her mother. Her voice quavered. "But it's the last time you'll be my Chia, my little dove that I raised for eighteen years. Whether or not you take up a wand, you'll be different the next time we see you. And we'll be different to you."

Mr Belmagio had been quiet during breakfast, but now his spectacles fogged. He wiped them on the bottom of his shirt, a habit Mrs Belmagio always fussed about but overlooked now.

"This is not a path I could have predicted, Chia, but it is the path that has chosen you. No matter where it takes you, remember, home will be here."

"I will, Papa," Chia whispered.

It was nearly time, and the Belmagios gathered in the Blue Room, their hearts never more sad and anxious and proud to hear the clock chime.

Tears pooled in her parents' eyes, and Chiara was crying, too. She turned to Niccolo. "Take care of Mamma and Papa while I'm away. Make sure Papa doesn't lose his reading glasses – they're usually on top of his writing desk. And help Mamma warm her milk: simmer for six minutes."

"I will," promised her brother.

"Be good to Ily," said Chiara to her brother, hating how her words sounded so permanent and formal. "Don't fight too much."

Last was Ilaria, and a lump formed in Chia's throat. Without saying anything, the two sisters hugged each other.

Then Ily blurted, "How long will you be gone exactly? Will you write us?"

Chiara didn't know the answer, and Ily never got a response, because Agata had appeared. The older woman leant against the clock as if she'd been there all along.

"The Violet Fairy!" Mr and Mrs Belmagio exclaimed, bowing in respect.

"No, no, none of that," said Agata, motioning for them to get up. "I'm not a queen. Not even a lady."

She lifted herself from the clock. "As for your question, Ilaria – correspondence between the fairy realm and Esperia is not encouraged."

"Why not?" Ily asked.

Mrs Belmagio sent a warning look at her younger daughter, but Agata didn't mind the question. "Over the years, we've found that it is best for our initiates to focus on their lessons rather than have one foot at home and one foot in the fairy realm. Chiara will have until the winter to complete her training – five months."

"Five months means she'll be back by my birthday," said Ilaria, making the calculations aloud. "What happens after that?"

"Then she will have a week at home to make up her mind. Either Chiara becomes a fully-fledged fairy, or she returns home to the life she led before."

"What happens if she stays—"

Mrs Belmagio took Ilaria's arm, urging her to be quiet. For once Ily obeyed, but her face twisted into a frown.

"All will be explained in due time," Agata promised. She turned to Chia. "You've packed?"

"Yes," was all Chiara could say.

"If you are ready, will you come with me?"

If I'm ready. Chia wasn't sure she'd ever be ready. It was the heaviest step she ever took to reach Agata's side. She pivoted slowly so she could face her parents, her brother, her sister. "Goodbye," she mouthed, so quietly the sound barely came out.

Agata waved her wand in a gentle arc, and a soft silvery light enveloped them.

"Don't forget us!" Ily called after her. "Don't forget to come back for my birthday."

Chia's throat tightened, and as she nodded, she felt the weight in her stomach anchoring her to home. In a flash, she left behind the only life she had ever known.

They were flying! Chiara could hardly believe it, but the rush in her stomach did not lie. The clouds were closer than she'd ever seen before – they drifted by in a stream of white that she could reach out and touch. When she looked down, her home was a yellow dot against a cluster of brown and red roofs, a patchwork of fields and pastures, a pool of sea and then a lining of mountains. All too soon, the town she'd known all her life became smaller and smaller until it was smaller than her thumbnail, and then it disappeared altogether.

They pierced the clouds and made deep into the sky. This was where the light became a gauzy cloak over Chiara's vision, and she had to close her eyes.

The rush in her stomach returned, accelerating as they soared higher and higher. But when Chiara finally opened her eyes again, it was over.

Her feet touched upon ground, and a cloud of silvery dust bloomed up to her waist. Her clothes shimmered, and the chequered cotton dress she was wearing became an elegant white gown with a silver cord around the waist.

"Your apprentice gown," explained Agata. She gestured ahead. "Welcome to the Wishing Star."

Before her was a village not unlike Pariva, only every cottage was a different colour: rose, violet, mahogany, marigold. Burgundy, magenta and pearl. Even the flowers in the gardens matched the colours of the houses, and trees made of gold and copper and silver lined the shimmering streets. In the centre was a house made of crystal, its windows stained with hearts of every colour in the town.

As soon as her gaze fell upon the house, its door opened,

and over a dozen fairies filed outside, each wearing a warm smile.

"Welcome, Chiara," greeted the first fairy. Chia recognised her immediately as one of the Three Fairies in the centre of Pariva.

In real life, she was a head shorter than Chiara, but the presence she carried – emanating pride and kindness and courage – made her seem like the tallest person Chiara had ever met. She wore entirely gold, from the bells on her slippers to the gilded leaves sprinkled against her grey ringlets. "We've been looking forward to welcoming you. I am Mirabella the Gold, the mother fairy of sorts, but really just the longest serving on the Wishing Star. You'll find that being a fairy isn't too different from being a girl in Pariva. You'll live in a cottage where you eat and sleep, and you'll find companionship among your fellow fairies."

Mirabella gestured at the others behind her. "For now, you might find it easier to remember our titles rather than our names. I am the Golden Fairy." She curtsied, and the fairies behind her introduced themselves one by one – the Rose Fairy, the Orange Fairy, the Silver Fairy and so on it went. "Your title you will choose after you complete your training with the Violet Fairy. Do you have any questions?"

Chiara had hundreds of questions, but she settled for the one that nagged at her the loudest. A glance at all the fairies showed her a troupe of men and women from all around Esperia, and of varying ages. Yet all of them had an ancientness about their eyes, as if they'd been on the Wishing Star for many, many years.

"How long does one serve as a fairy?" she asked.

"While you reside on the Wishing Star, time shall pass differently for you," replied Mirabella. "You will serve as long as you wish."

A vague response that only half answered her question. Yet judging from the firmness of Mirabella's tone, Chiara wouldn't get more explanation from the head fairy. At least not right now.

"And each fairy is represented by a colour?" Chiara asked.

"My favourite colour was always violet," Agata said, "and Mirabella's gold. They started off as nicknames, but they seem to have stuck."

Peri, the Orange Fairy, stepped forwards and offered her a friendly grin. "Blue is available, in case you were wondering. Agata told us it's your favourite. We sense the colour's been waiting for you."

Chiara was touched. "Thank you."

Peri picked up the hoard of books floating at his side and his smile widened. "If you have any other questions, always feel free to find me in the Archives. Though I doubt there will be much I can answer that Agata cannot. Along with Mirabella, she's one of the oldest fairies on the Wishing Star. She's trained many of us, myself included. You'll be in capable hands."

"Thank you," said Chiara.

Peri smiled amiably. "I was in your shoes once. Nervous, and uncertain what would happen. I'll warn you that our duties are many, and the work can be heavy and non-stop, but nothing will make your heart fuller than to see the changes you will make on each life."

The words did warm Chiara, and she smiled back.

"A wonderful welcome." Mirabella clapped. "The rest of us must depart for Esperia, but Agata will give you a tour of the Wishing Star. We look forward to getting to know you, Chiara Belmagio."

One by one, the fairies wished her well on her first day. Then they lifted their wands, identical silver rods with pointed stars at the tip, and disappeared. Leaving Agata and Chiara alone on the Wishing Star.

"Well, short and sweet as always," her mentor remarked. "You'll find we don't waste time around here. One of my favourite things about being a fairy." Agata snapped her fingers, and every lamp along the road lit.

Chiara stared in wonderment, but Agata had already begun strolling down the starlit road. "Hurry, hurry," the

Violet Fairy trilled. "We have much material to cover, and I have to show you to your house."

My house?

Chia dashed after the Violet Fairy, marvelling at how each step on the silvery road emitted a note from her favourite song.

"Our tour will be short," said Agata, "because there isn't that much to see. We spend most of our time in Esperia doing fieldwork – responding to distress calls and granting wishes. Your time on the Wishing Star will be either to rest, eat, research, or consult your fellow fairies." Agata pointed at the crystal building in the centre of the Wishing Star. It looked like a modest castle, with two towers on either side and spires that changed colour every time Chiara blinked.

"That's the Star Centre," said Agata. "When the bell on the tallest spire chimes, it's a call for an official meeting. It's where we meet for official business, and where you may access the Archives. I myself go every morning – the Archives hold records of what every fairy has done during their tenure, and it's where you may research should you have questions about any person in Esperia.

"Once you have your wand, you'll be able to ring that bell on the top spire there."

Chiara looked up, spying a crystal bell that hung suspended over the rest of the building.

"Chime once if you need guidance from a fellow fairy. Chime thrice if you're in a pickle, and every fairy available will find you no matter where they are."

"What sort of emergencies might a fairy encounter?" Chiara asked.

"Now that is a question best answered while on the job," said Agata. "But I'll say that we are not without enemies, Chiara. Oh, don't look so agitated. Come, let's continue on with happier things. Look, there's Mirabella's Wishing Well."

"Wishing Well?"

"Every fairy has one on their cottage grounds," explained Agata, circling Mirabella's. She motioned for Chiara to come closer. "From it, you may see wishes that are being made in Esperia." Agata pointed her wand at the sparkling waters within. "How high its waters flow reveal how much magic you currently have on Earth. Magic is limited, you see. It buds from bravery, kindness and nobleness of heart. So the more we spread hope, the more magic we have to continue our work. It's a rather sympathetic cycle, I like to think. Just take care not to overexert yourself."

They moved on towards a cottage behind a brook of pink water and trees with marbled leaves and star-shaped fruit. Chiara couldn't stop staring at the otherworldly garden, so much that she barely paid attention as Agata approached an empty field to their right.

"This will be your new home," the Violet Fairy said, waving at the lot.

"My home?" Chiara blinked. "But it's…"

Agata's mouth twitched with humour, and from behind her back, she waved her wand in a grand circle. Before Chiara's eyes, a cottage sprang from the ground, with a pale blue door and windows with painted doves.

"Oh, my!" Chia exclaimed.

Inside, the cottage was sparsely furnished, with four wooden chairs covered in blue cotton cushions, a table with hearts carved along the edges, an oven that smelt like chocolate and cherries, and a harpsichord in the corner by the window. But it was everything Chiara could have dreamt of. A home of her own.

"This spot is one of my favourites," Agata narrated. "Absolutely lovely. Look there, you've a view of the Silver Brook, and in the mornings the moon crickets sing most beautifully."

Chiara inhaled. All the smells she had loved most from home – the wild grass, the pine cones from the trees, the fresh loaves Papa baked before dawn, the musty parchment from Ily's music paper. They flooded her nostrils all at once, as if she'd brought them with her.

"It's perfect," said Chiara, clasping her hands. "It looks like it's straight out of Pariva."

"I had a feeling you might say that," Agata said. She spotted a patch of dust on one of the chairs and swept it clean with her finger. "I designed it to remind you of home, but I set down only the basics. Whatever doesn't suit you, change it as you wish. You'll have plenty of time to spruce up the place however you like, and we have all tastes here." She gestured to the right, where the Pearl Fairy had designed a house that greatly resembled a clamshell. "You'll want something of your own. Trust me.

"While you're on the Wishing Star, you needn't worry about budgeting your magic. It's different from Esperia. Here, all you need do is ask, and what you've requested will come. Same with your meals, unless you prefer to cook yourself. Once we're in Esperia, it'll be a different story. You won't have magic until I give you your wand. Until then, the dust will do."

"The dust?" Chiara repeated.

"Stardust, of course." Agata chuckled. "It's the stuff of hope and dreams and joy. The whole house is made of it, and some goes into our magic, too. Go on, try it. Ask for something."

"I… I wish for a cup of juice, please," said Chiara slowly. She wasn't sure to whom to address her request. "Orange, with a hint of lemon, like Niccolo makes."

To her astonishment, a cup of juice appeared in her hand.

"Stars, Chia. You haven't conjured a ghost." Agata laughed as Chia jumped, startled. "Try it."

Taking a breath to calm herself, Chiara tipped the cup to her lips. "Tart and sweet." Her eyes misted, and she had to set the juice down on a table before she dropped it. "Just like my brother makes. It's delicious."

"Of course it is."

The cup suddenly weighed like lead, and Chiara couldn't take another sip. She'd only been gone from home a few hours, and already she missed her family fiercely.

Agata touched her shoulder. "It'll get easier, Chia. Every day.

"Are you ready for your first lesson, or do you want to rest and finish unpacking?"

Chiara had forgotten about the bundle of belongings she'd brought with her. She didn't have much: some sheet music, the quilt her grandmother had made her long ago, a few small paintings, the dove Geppetto had carved her and the food her mother had packed.

"I'm ready to learn."

The Violet Fairy led her to a door with a silver knob shaped like a star.

The door led to Chiara's Wishing Well in the garden. As soon as she came near, a pale blue light fanned from the well, and in the light emerged a map of Esperia.

"Once you receive your wand," said Agata, "this map will show you the areas that you have been assigned to observe. But for now…" She clapped, and thousands of golden dots appeared on the map.

"What are those?"

"A gold light indicates people who've made a wish recently. Your duty will be to listen to each one, and to deem whether or not they are worthy of our attention and magic."

"There are so many!"

Agata chuckled. "The life of a fairy is a busy one."

Chia folded her arms over the lip of the well, studying the gold lights. "How will I know whether a wish is worthy of my attention?"

"That is tricky," Agata admitted. "There are many kinds of wishes: selfless ones, selfish ones and all the sorts in between. You'll hear people asking all the time to become richer, cleverer or more beautiful. You'll hear couples wishing to have a child, widowers wishing to find love again and children wishing that their parents' business would improve. All of them, we listen to, but we tend to listen most closely to the wishes that come from the heart."

"Then we grant their wish," said Chiara.

"To an extent," allowed Agata. "You'll find it's best not to grant someone's wish in its entirety. Take your sister, for instance. Ilaria. She wants to be a famous opera singer, doesn't she?"

It shouldn't have surprised Chiara that the Violet Fairy knew. "Yes."

"Has she asked you to help her on that journey?"

"No."

That seemed to surprise Agata. "Well, she might in the future. And if she does… firstly, it cannot be you, Chiara. Fairies are not permitted to consider the wishes of anyone they used to know. Secondly, if another fairy *were* to help her, it wouldn't be by granting her fame or even admission into the conservatory. That would be unfair, you see. We would simply give her the tools to use what she already has – her voice, her charm, her ambition – to the highest of her ability."

"What sort of tools?"

"A train ticket to Vallan, for instance," said Agata sensibly. "A coat so she wouldn't catch cold during the winter months; mittens and a hat, too. Perhaps a bottle that never runs out of water, for a touch of magic. Singers need to stay hydrated, or so I'm told."

Ily would have wrinkled her nose and said, *That's all?* Chiara merely blinked. "A train ticket and winter clothes?"

"What, did you think we'd give her a ballgown covered in rubies and have butterflies fly out of her sleeves whenever she sings?" Laughing, Agata shook her head. "You've been reading too many fairy tales. Those stories are fluff made for the romantics. We mostly give a nudge in the right direction." She paused. "But every now and then, we do encounter a situation that deserves special attention. That would be when you consult with your fellow fairies."

"I see," mused Chiara. "What about wishes we don't listen to?"

"We listen to every wish, but we *never* respond to wishes that intend ill harm towards another. Those are wicked, and we do not pay them any heed."

"Why listen to them, then?"

Agata's voice went tight. "Because there are other fairies, who dwell in the arena of evil. And it is our duty to undo as much of the damage that they cause as possible."

Upon Chia's look of confusion, Agata went on, "We call them the Heartless. They're led by Amorale the Grey and Larissa the Green. They and their kind specialise in fostering wickedness and envy, wrath and hatred. They take the seeds of a malevolent thought and plant it in a human's heart, nurturing it until the heart turns rotten."

Chiara did not like the sound of Amorale and Larissa. "Why would they do that?"

"Excellent question," Agata said, leaning forwards. "Just as we fairies gain power from the joy we bring, the Heartless gain strength from the misery they sow. Once we begin our lessons, you'll find it can be challenging to encourage people to be kind to one another, or to bring joy when there's pain, sadness. In those cases, it's far easier to do the opposite, to plant seeds of misunderstanding and cause people to be angry and cruel to one another."

Agata grimaced. "Larissa and Amorale were two of us, but once they found it was easier to gain power by preying upon weathered hearts… they formed the Heartless."

"Hearts that are bitter or angry or in grief are the most vulnerable," Chiara said, understanding.

"Yes, and that's not even the worst of it. After they've heaped misery upon someone's life, they'll offer to take their pain away. But there's always a cost, and rare is it the case that anyone can pay."

"It's a game to them," Chiara murmured.

"Indeed, and those who lose become shadows of their former selves… and their misery fuels the Heartless's future ploys. It's a vicious cycle, but fortunately, most of their work can be undone."

"Most," Chiara repeated.

Agata's tone darkened. "On rare occasion, Larissa and

Amorale offer someone the chance to be like them. But to prove themselves, they must destroy their hearts – for good. That's why they're called—"

"The Heartless," Chiara realised in horror.

"Once done, the damage is irreversible." Agata stared into the well. After a sigh, she clapped once, and the map floating above the Wishing Well shuttered.

The Violet Fairy regarded Chiara. "I told you that granting wishes is only a small part of what we do. I believe that the people who need us most are those who are vulnerable to the Heartless's influence. It doesn't mean they are bad – or wicked, even. After all, most people crave something they cannot have: fame, money, power… but these temptations are often a gateway to attracting the Heartless's attention."

"How can we help them?" Chiara asked.

"For a start, we help them listen to their conscience."

Conscience. Agata had used that word before, when they'd first met.

"I mentioned before that you have a strong sense of empathy, Chiara. It keeps you attuned to how others are feeling and gives you your compassion. Something all potential fairies must exhibit, for it is our empathy that keeps us from being cold and merciless like the Heartless.

"But what I also noted was that you have a powerful

conscience as well, Chiara. Empathy without a conscience is like living with only half a heart. Your conscience is what motivates you to act. It is our compass, guiding us in the direction of doing what's right.

"Unfortunately, not everyone chooses to follow theirs. We fairies try to give a nudge in the right direction, but we can only do so much. No magic can make someone's mind up for them, and we have no control over a person's will.

"Which brings me to you, Chiara. You must know – becoming a fairy will require certain sacrifices that you may not be willing to make." Agata's smile turned tight. "At the end of your training, I will explain fully. Once I do, you will have one week to decide whether you wish to stay with us. When that time comes, there is no right or wrong answer. No good or bad decision. Listen to your heart, and make your decision without any regrets. Understood?"

"Yes."

But as Agata continued with the lesson, Chiara's thoughts were full of wishes and questions and broken hearts.

CHAPTER FIFTEEN

Lessons with the Violet Fairy were nothing like going to school and learning from books and reciting sums and figures. Every day, Chiara shadowed the Violet Fairy across Esperia, learning first-hand what it meant to attend to the wishes of the brave, the truthful and the selfless. They helped reunite a father and son lost in the forest by dropping a ball of twine that would lead them to each other. They showed a young woman how to brew a soup that might help her and her husband conceive a child. They helped a young man with no family find employment in town as a cook.

Chiara loved every moment of it.

She especially loved learning to use the magic in her Wishing Well. When she approached it, within its waters would appear a map of all Esperia, with countless bright lights dotting the land.

"Each one represents a person's heart," Agata explained. "See the different colours? White symbolises people currently contented. Blue, people with wishes or needs to be attended."

"What about red?" asked Chiara.

"Red lights are causes for immediate attention."

A pang of worry struck Chiara, and though Agata couldn't read her mind, the older woman could certainly sense her concern. "You miss your family, don't you? Especially your sister. Why don't you ask to see them?"

Chiara spoke into the Wishing Well. "Will you show me my family – the Belmagios in Pariva?"

Almost immediately, a tall wave of water rose from the well, and her home town emerged on the map. A watery outline of her family's house appeared along Constanza Street, and to Chiara's great relief, the four lights within were bright and white.

Mamma, Papa, Niccolo – and Ilaria. They were all happy.

That cheered Chiara, but the Violet Fairy's face had gone sombre.

"What is it?" Chiara asked.

"Nothing," said Agata, before she quickly amended, "Nothing that I won't explain in due time." She smiled warmly. "Your family will be fine, Chiara. You have nothing to worry about."

The Violet Fairy's sombre mood had vanished, but Chiara still ached with curiosity. She had a feeling whatever Agata was keeping from her had to do with the sacrifice she was supposed to make. Her mind had been reeling about it for days, trying to imagine what it could be.

In the silence that followed, Chiara observed the lights around her home. Niccolo's was the most radiant, which she sensed meant his courtship with Sofia was going well. Mamma's and Papa's, too, were clear, which warmed Chiara's heart to see. But Ily's – Ily's had been bright an instant ago, yet it made the barest flicker now – from white to blue.

Chiara frowned and leant forwards to get a closer look. But Ily's light went steady once more. "Agata, did you see that—?"

The Violet Fairy waved over the map, bringing Chiara's home closer into view. But as she focused the corner of Pariva on Ilaria, a faint speck of red appeared along the edges of the Lyre Sea.

Agata gasped.

"It's Monstro," she exclaimed. "Come, we must ring for the others. This might be our chance to deal with him once and for all!"

Within an hour, the Wishing Fairies had cornered the great and terrible Monstro in the Lyre Sea. On their way there, Agata had explained that he was no ordinary whale, but a monster born of the cruel wishes the Heartless had granted. Then the fairies jumped to their task while Chia observed. It impressed her how efficiently they worked together. Peri and two other fairies immediately set to rescuing the fishermen who had encountered Monstro, and sent them sailing home safely on a raft.

The rest of the fairies concentrated on restraining the whale.

"All together now," Agata cried to her colleagues as magic sizzled from their wands. Their powers braided into a thick ring of light that encircled the beast, trapping him so he could not escape.

As the only one without a wand or wings, Chiara stayed on a floating cloud that Agata had conjured for her. She leant over the edge of the cloud, watching intently as Monstro struggled against the fairies.

"He's teeming with anger and the need to wreak havoc,"

said Peri, catching his breath on Chiara's cloud after he sent away the fishermen's raft. "It makes him an incredible source of power for the Heartless."

"What do you mean, a source of power?"

"That's how Monstro grew so large to begin with. Ever since the Heartless created him, he's been full of wrath and hunger. The more he devoured, the larger he became. The fear he inspires benefits the Heartless, you see, for they're able to wield it as power."

"The same way we wield hope," Chiara murmured, remembering Agata's lessons.

The whale was powerful, that was no question. Even against twenty fairies, he held his own. The battle would be close.

As the braids of magic intensified and wrapped around him, Monstro leapt up from the sea, jaws wide.

Chiara's instincts were on fire. Seconds before Monstro would have devoured her mentor, she jumped off her cloud. "Agata!" she cried, pushing the Violet Fairy out of harm's way.

"That was close," Agata muttered, catching her protégé by the arms so they stayed afloat. "Thank you, my dear."

One after another, Monstro attacked the fairies.

"It seems twenty of us aren't enough," Agata told Chiara. "Will you help?"

"Can I?"

Agata nodded. "Hold my wand with me, and think of your fondest dreams. We want to put Monstro to sleep – ideally, for a long, long time."

A tingle shot up Chiara's spine as she grabbed one end of Agata's wand. Power coursed through her and out the wand, joining with the other fairies' magic.

What was more, as she held Agata's wand, she could *feel* the fear and awesome wrath coming from Monstro. It was a taste of wild power, so intense and strong she felt she could do anything with it.

Now she understood why Monstro was so valuable to the Heartless. His wrath was never-ending, and it took little effort for her to sense that his wells of strength were immense.

Chiara pushed Monstro's power aside and focused on Agata's instructions. She was supposed to wield the wand while thinking of her fondest dreams. She thought about all the mornings she had spent with Ily, making music together, making messes in their parents' bakery kitchen, tossing pistachio cookies and chocolate cakes at each other.

Was it her imagination, or did a stream of pale blue magic course out of Agata's wand? She couldn't tell, but it didn't matter.

Monstro's cold green eyes began to close. The fairies' spell was working!

It felt like forever before Chiara could be sure, but at last, the whale went still. He was asleep, and he sank deep into the sea until Chiara couldn't see him at all.

The fairies all let out a jubilant cheer.

"It's done!" Mirabella exclaimed. "Finally! Let's all return to the Wishing Star. We have much to celebrate today."

Even Agata let out a whoop of joy. "Well done, Chiara. You helped us."

"Only a little."

"More than a little." Agata hid a smile, and Chiara wondered if she'd seen that hint of blue that had shot out from her wand. "It'll be a blow to the Heartless when they learn that Monstro is missing and that his fury has been silenced."

Agata turned to leave with the other fairies, but Chiara still had questions. "What if they find him?" she asked.

"They will eventually," said Agata through her teeth. "But let's hope that's quite some time from now."

"Peri said that Monstro is a source of power for the Heartless."

"Sneaking in a lesson, are we?" Agata smiled at her fondly. "Yes, he's their most precious creation. But it's thanks to you that we've been able to track him. I would never have guessed his den would be so close to Pariva."

Chiara lowered her voice. "I felt his power, when I took hold of your wand. It was… unlike anything I've ever experienced. That ruthlessness and hunger… there was so much, I…"

As her voice trailed, Agata touched Chiara's arm. "I'm glad you had a taste of what the Heartless can do. It'll serve you well in the future… but as your mentor, I must caution you not to get too close."

"I won't."

"There will be days when we have to make difficult decisions – whom to help with our magic, and who to trust will be fine without it. Our powers are finite and have limits, Chiara. One of the reasons those limits are put into place is so we do not stray towards the path of the Heartless. A young fairy not too different from yourself made that error many years ago. He was trying to help an old woman who had fallen sick, but he'd run out of magic and there was no time to seek more, so he thought he could borrow some of the Heartless's power."

"What happened to him?"

"As you know, we have strict rules about our interactions with the Heartless. His wand was taken away, and he was sent home. Banished from the Wishing Star forever."

Chiara swallowed hard. "But his intentions were good."

"They were, but rules are rules, Chiara. Put in place for a reason, especially since you know how the Heartless themselves came to be. We must be careful."

Agata chuckled at Chiara's anxious expression. "Don't worry, it won't happen to you – if you do end up joining us. Now come on. If we don't head home soon, all the celebration cake will be gone. And it's got blackberry jam, which I hear you love." She stifled a yawn. "After that, all of us fairies will need a nice long nap ourselves. You'll have to excuse us all for being in a kerfuffle the next few days. That slumber spell's a strong one, and it's drained most of us. I suspect even I won't make it through today's celebration."

Agata extended a hand, but before taking it, Chiara glanced down at the Lyre Sea, taking in the slow ripples that swept across the water.

Something about the banished fairy's story had unsettled her. Chiara had never had trouble following rules. She'd never had trouble sorting whether decisions were right or wrong. After all, even Ily liked to tease her about it:

Not everything's good or bad, Chia, Ily had said to her. *You can't rely on some fairy voice to tell you what to do.*

But what if, one day, good intentions led her to make a decision that the fairies didn't agree with?

Look at you, thinking about this when you haven't even decided to become a fairy yet. Chiara laughed silently at herself. *Worry about it if and when the time comes.*

Shrugging off her concern, she took Agata's hand. As the two flew back to the Wishing Star, a last ripple brushed across the Lyre Sea.

Then the water went still.

CHAPTER SIXTEEN

Geppetto whistled as he put on his hat, doffed his apron, and strolled to the Belmagio Bakery to pick up lunch. Usually, he could afford only a small cookie or a slice of bread rather than a full lunch. But today, he was going to buy an entire sandwich. Coffee, too.

Why was he in such a jolly mood?

Because of the music box he'd been making for Ilaria. After weeks – no, months – of tinkering with it whenever he could, he'd mostly finished carving and smoothing out the exterior of the box. But he'd had trouble making it, well, musical.

Setting the melody of the Nightingale Aria into the box had been the bulk of his difficulty, but last night, he'd managed to inscribe the first two notes. A promising breakthrough. If his progress continued at this rate, he might even finish it before Ilaria's birthday, two short months away.

Still whistling to himself, he approached the main part of Pariva. Autumn was here, and crisp golden leaves showered down from the trees, landing on Geppetto's hat and shoulders.

As he swept them off his shoulder, he cast a glance at Mrs Tappa's hat shop. Ilaria was inside, tying ribbons around the latest designs. When she saw him, a bright smile touched her face, and she waved.

For once, Geppetto wasn't shy about waving back. And when she poked her head out of the door, shouting, "Geppetto!" his smile widened and he went to greet her in person.

"Heading to the bakery?" she said. "Let me guess, another square of shortbread?"

"A sandwich today," said Geppetto.

"Ah. You're branching out. What's the occasion?"

Geppetto felt himself growing taller. "Can't say. It's a surprise."

Ily raised an eyebrow. "A surprise?"

"You'll see… in a few months."

"A few months?" Ilaria tilted her head. "Will Chiara be back in time to witness this surprise?"

Ily's voice had the faintest strain as she spoke her sister's name. In the weeks since Chiara had left, Geppetto noticed that Ilaria tried to bring her up whenever she could in a conversation. Those were the moments he could tell just how much she missed her sister.

"I would expect so," Geppetto said, not knowing how else to answer. "She did promise to be back in time for your birthday, didn't she?"

"This surprise is related to my birthday? Now my curiosity is piqued, Geppetto."

Geppetto's eyes widened. "No… no… that's not what I meant."

Ily laughed. She clearly enjoyed tormenting him. "At least give me a clue."

He shook his head.

"What about…" Ily ducked inside the shop and returned with a young yellow rose. "What about for this?"

Geppetto took the rose, almost dropping it because his hands had mutinously begun to tremble.

"Now, will you give me a hint?"

"It… it… it sings," Geppetto stumbled. "Or at least, it will."

Ily offered her most winning smile. "Then I'm sure I'll like it, whatever it is. After all, I trust my friend's taste in music." She started back into the shop. "Have a fine day, Geppetto."

"You, too."

The shop door closed, and Geppetto could have done a little dance in the middle of Pariva's square for joy. Ilaria Belmagio had called him her friend!

He twirled the little rose in his hand, then opened his innermost pocket to store it carefully inside. There, inside his coat, the rose would go wherever he went.

And he was certain he would treasure it forever.

CHAPTER SEVENTEEN

One might think that since Monstro had been found, cast into a deep slumber, and safely hidden from the Heartless, the fairies of the Wishing Star might take a break from their hard work. But on the contrary, there was little time for rest. The next day, Chiara's lessons resumed.

"With Monstro asleep, the Heartless will be endeavouring to find a new source of power," said Agata. "No doubt they're already spread across Esperia trying to make mischief and misery. That means no time for rest! Off we go."

Chiara was ready. "I saw a few red lights by the south-east coast. Is that where we're headed?"

"My, you are a bright pupil," said Agata with an approving hum. "I had a feeling you'd be. Yes, that's where we'll start. Come now; they'll be quick visits and won't require too much magic – or talking."

By then, it was no surprise to Chiara that Agata turned to magic only as a last resort, and rarely did she physically manifest before those she was helping – but Chia hadn't thought to ask until today: "Why don't you like talking to those you help?"

"Precious minutes are wasted with idle chit-chat," Agata explained, holding onto Chiara's arm as they flew. "It's better to remain unseen. Fewer questions that way. People are always astounded to see you, and ask if you're real or if you're their fairy godmother, and all that. It gets tiresome after a while, trust me."

Chiara flushed. She had asked the same questions.

"But sometimes our visits do require some face time," Agata went on. "Take our next wishers, for instance." She held her wand horizontally, and it became a scroll listing the names and locations of the people they were to visit today. "Rosa Leo – the Heartless turned her fiancé into a bear a few days ago. We ought to go see her."

Agata waved her wand, and the two popped into the Hallowed Woods, the largest forest in Esperia. Chia had never been before, but every tree was grey, with leaves shaped like curved daggers.

"Now where is that girl?" muttered Agata, picking up

her skirt to cross a muddy puddle. She pointed her wand at a nearby tree, which had been slashed by a bear claw. "She and the bear are supposed to be right here."

Chia shivered as her breath steamed into the air. She whirled, taking in the desolate woods. Everything was grey, and even Agata's usually vibrant purple cloak looked drabber. "It feels like despair," she murmured.

"You're picking up on the bear's sentiments. Poor thing." Agata tapped her wand on another tree. "Let's hope we break his curse before dark."

"Will the Heartless be back for him?"

"Unlikely," replied Agata. "They gleaned all the misery and despair they needed from the pair already. More likely they'll go back to Vallan or the like."

"Why Vallan?"

"The Heartless prefer big cities where there are more people to prey on, and a missing soul here and there can easily go unnoticed."

Chiara didn't like the sound of that. Ilaria wanted to live in Vallan; she'd have to warn her.

"Ah, there you are," said Agata, approaching a young woman riding a great brown bear. When Rosa saw Agata and Chia, she raised the stick in her hand fearfully.

"There, there," said Agata, putting away her wand. "There's no need to be frightened. We're fairies here to help you, not harm you. The Heartless turned your fiancé into a bear, yes? Not to worry, his curse is quite breakable."

"It is?" Rosa Leo nearly collapsed with relief. The stick dropped from her hand, and she slid off the bear's back. "Thank the stars, you heard my pleas. I thought for sure that no one would."

"A little patience will go a long way, my dear," said Agata. She held out a handkerchief. "Now don't you two ever take a shortcut through these woods again."

Rosa Leo nodded, and the bear let out an affirmative growl.

"Brilliant. My apprentice will give you the instructions on how to break the curse."

Rosa took the handkerchief and wiped at her eyes. Then she looked at Chiara expectantly.

"Hello, Rosa," Chiara said warmly. She dipped her head at the bear beside Rosa. "And Mr Bear." She touched the journal she kept in her pocket – every morning, she reviewed the wishers she and Agata would visit and cross-referenced their requests with similar ones that had been made before. She'd been up since dawn looking up the way to break a bear curse. Agata assured her that such spells and their remedies were like recipes and would become second nature to her given time and experience.

"Climb to the top of Mount Reve and take nine leaves

from the crooked tree that grows there," said Chiara from memory. Reading off her notes wouldn't instil confidence in Rosa or her ursine betrothed. "Brew a tea from the tree and have him drink it. By the morn, he will be born again."

"Oh, thank you!" cried Rosa. "I'll do that. Thank you."

"This cloak will keep you warm," offered Agata, waving her wand. A velvet cloak fitted over the girl's shoulders. "The weather's getting cold, and the climb to the mountain will be an arduous one. Take care. And here, a bottle of tea that will never run out."

Chiara hid a smile, recognising the very items Agata had hypothetically offered to give her sister. So practical.

As the young woman gushed with thanks, Agata took Chiara by the arm, and outwardly they vanished in a flash of light. But really, they simply became invisible once again.

"I think you've got the hang of the wish-granting business," whispered Agata. "I'll leave you in charge of writing up the shard this time. "

"Shard?"

"Every time we come to Esperia on business, we make a record of the magic we used and the people we visited. Oh, you know what I'm talking about. Peri tells me you've been spending all your free time in the Archives, reading shards."

"Oh, the reports!" Chiara said.

"We call them shards, affectionately. One of the more

bureaucratic and painful parts of being a fairy," said Agata cheerfully. "But now that you're my apprentice, I can take a break from them." The Violet Fairy winked. "Take care not to spend *too* much time in the Archives, Chiara, or Peri will have *you* become the Archives manager within the year."

The Violet Fairy dusted her hands. "Now that all that's been taken care of, we'll finally take lunch—"

Just then, Agata's wand chimed. Once. Twice. Thrice.

An emergency.

"Mirabella needs help," Agata said, drawing furious loops with her wand. Within the circle, the Golden Fairy appeared, looking alarmed. "Just as I feared, a death curse. Quickly, Chia, take my hand. She isn't far."

Usually Agata gave Chia a chance to catch her breath before the two flew off in a beam of starlight, but not this time. It was an emergency.

They followed the sound of Mirabella's wand to the other side of the Hallowed Woods, where, beside a narrow snaking brook, awaited the Golden Fairy – and a girl who'd been turned to a tree. Her legs were roots, already deeply entrenched into the earth, and her arms branched out towards the sky, her cotton sleeves transforming into crisp green leaves. Her hair and face had already turned into wood, and all that was left were two eyes, a nose and a mouth. But within minutes, they too would be gone.

It was the most horrible thing Chiara had ever seen.

"Agata, Chiara! Help!"

Sparks flew from Mirabella's wand; the Golden Fairy wielded it with both hands, as if she were lifting a boulder, not a slender stick of magic.

For once, Agata didn't explain the situation. She rushed to Mirabella's side and pointed her wand at the girl. A violet rush of magic burst from Agata's wand, braiding with Mirabella's golden power.

Chiara didn't know what she could do. She didn't have a wand yet, so she went up to the girl. Fear clouded her pale brown eyes, and Chiara reached for what remained of her cheek. She touched it, wishing she could do more than sense someone's emotions and could lend the girl courage. "Don't be afraid," she said gently. "Mirabella and Agata are here. They'll break your curse. I promise."

"Will you stay with me until they do?" said the girl, sounding very young.

"Of course. I'll be right here."

The gold and violet light from Mirabella's and Agata's wands twined together into a cord that wrapped around the tree, slowly extracting the Heartless's curse. Little by little, the branches turned into arms, the bark into smooth, freckled skin and the leaves into curled, unkempt hair.

The girl fainted into Chiara's arms. She was human again.

As Chiara laid her gently on her lap, Mirabella wiped sweat from her brow and collapsed herself.

"Despicable," she said. "Absolutely despicable."

"The Heartless?" asked Chiara.

"Who else?" said Agata through her teeth. "There was a time they wouldn't attempt such death curses, but they're growing bolder. Cleverer, too. This sort of spell takes more than one fairy to break. A minute or two later, and it'd have been too late. This girl would have been a tree… forever."

Chiara brushed a leaf from the girl's forehead. "How long until she wakes up?"

"It could be hours," said Mirabella. "Seems like her horse ran off, and it's a good hour's walk until she reaches home."

"We can't send her through the woods alone," Agata said.

"Quite right." Letting out a tired grunt, Mirabella stood to survey the area, then crouched and collected a handful of pebbles. Using her wand, she stacked them until she created the shape of a man. Then she took a step back and touched her wand to Agata's.

"Little stones at once combine," began Mirabella. "Until the stroke of nine, awake; the gift of life is thine."

Chiara watched in awe as sparks of life glittered across the pebbles, and they burst to life, wobbling on uneven legs.

"Escort the young lady home to her family," Mirabella instructed the tower of stones.

It spread its arms in agreement, for it could not nod without its head falling off. Then, obediently, it lifted the young lady and carried her home.

"Watch out for foxes and wolves!" Agata called after them.

Chiara followed the pair with her eyes until they disappeared into the forest. Then she turned to Mirabella in amazement. "You gave life to a pile of stones!"

Mirabella chuckled. "Magic can do wondrous things, my dear. As I'm sure Agata has shown you."

"What will happen to the stones at nine?"

"They'll become as they were again. But that should be plenty of time for the poor girl to return home to her worried mother and father." Mirabella yawned, and Agata quickly followed. Both of the elder fairies had dark circles under their eyes that hadn't been there minutes before.

"It takes powerful magic to undo the wickedness of the

Heartless," said Agata, reading the questions on Chiara's face. "Mirabella and I will be fine after some rest."

"I wish I could help," said Chiara.

"You will, in time," Mirabella assured her. "But for now, consider yourself lucky you haven't come across a Heartless."

"She's come across Monstro," said Agata. "Many would say he's worse."

Chiara shuddered, remembering how all the fairies had battled the great whale and finally cast a slumber spell over him.

"Have the Heartless found out?"

"Of course," replied Agata. "They're already searching for him."

"It'll take them a while," Mirabella added. "Though it's best to be on your guard. Amorale must already be planning her revenge." She eyed Agata. "Larissa, too."

Chiara swallowed hard. Something in her gut told her that she wouldn't have to wait long before meeting one of the Heartless.

CHAPTER EIGHTEEN

A week later, in the middle of the night, a domed tent appeared outside the bustling town of Miurin. No one noticed it, for a dense fog shrouded all the town and did not clear until the morning.

A dense fog with the slightest hint of green, not that anyone would notice. Anyone, that was, except the fairies.

Chiara and Agata arrived to investigate, cloaked by an invisibility spell. Mist curled about the tent, leaving tracks of dew over its wide burgundy stripes. Agata pointed at the mist with her wand.

"See the trace of green in the air?" she murmured to Chia. "That's not natural, I can tell you that. The Heartless leave a trail wherever they go."

The mist hissed at the Violet Fairy viciously, but it

didn't dare come near. Instead it stretched towards Chiara, growing claws that brushed against her cheek.

Such a bright heart, it whispered into the crevices of her mind. *Full of hope and strength and courage.*

Chia recoiled, but she wasn't afraid, and she only dug her heels into the moist grass to steady her balance. "It's hungry," she observed as the mist crawled down her face and past her neck.

"It's trying to seep into your thoughts and into your heart," said Agata. "It latches on to fear, anger and greed. To envy and hate and anything that causes pain – and grows it inside one's heart. Green is Larissa's colour. Go on, greet her."

Larissa, Chiara spoke in her mind, greeting the Heartless's mist. *Agata's told me about you.*

Naturally she has. Larissa snickered. *What a fairy you'll make, so kind and fair and… gullible. Having second thoughts yet? No, I take it from your bright little heart that you've yet to see the darkness I weave. Aren't you curious about your family? Your poor, darling sister in particular. Would you like to see how miserable you've made your dearest Ily?*

Chiara's blood chilled. Yes, she did want to know how Ily was faring. Every day, she wondered about her family. She wanted to know that they were well, to ask the Wishing

Well for a glimpse of her sister. But Agata had discouraged using the Wishing Well to check on her family again, at least until her training was over. Agata had promised to let her know if anything terrible was happening. Chiara wouldn't break that trust. Especially not for a liar like Larissa.

Begone, said Chiara.

Ah, there it is. That prick of doubt. So you do *worry about your sister. I thought so.* The mist curled up at the ends, like a faceless smile. *Why don't you ask your mentor what price you'll have to pay to become a fairy?*

Chiara inhaled. *I'll find out when Agata deems me ready. Now begone.*

As you wish. Have fun with Remo. He's been drinking my poison ever since he was young. He rather likes it.

Who's Rem—

Before Chiara could finish her question, the mist flew out of her in a rush, dissolving before her eyes. Then, suddenly, the air was clear.

Agata was watching her curiously. "Larissa spoke to you."

Chiara nodded.

"She warned you of the sacrifice you'll have to make to become a fairy?"

Chiara stared at the ground. "Yes."

"Don't you want to know what it is?"

"You said you'd tell me when I was ready."

A sad smile touched Agata's mouth. "So I will, Chiara. So I will. Come now. Our mission today shan't be an easy one."

Ignoring the twinge in her chest, Chiara followed Agata around the tent until they approached the front. There, they found a young boy pasting posters along the side of the tent, and on the wagon parked against a tree. Thanks to Agata's spell, he couldn't see Chiara or the Violet Fairy, or the green mist that flew behind him.

Chiara approached the posters. They illustrated a man posing in an extravagant blue coat, with purple tassels and a gaudy gold buckle. On his shoulders were six monkeys in matching blue capes and hats.

Remo the Extraordinary Showman, read the flyer. *Dancing monkeys and singing crickets. Feast your eyes on something incredible.*

"Remo's a depraved soul if ever I knew one," Agata remarked with disgust. "The Heartless got to him long ago. Thankfully there's still hope for his sons. Vito is the elder, and Stromboli is the younger. I want you to speak to them."

"All right," agreed Chia nervously. "But what will I say?"

"Listen to your conscience," said Agata, gesturing at her heart. "It'll guide you. Go on, Chia. You can do this."

Taking a deep breath, Chiara turned her attention to the young boy who'd been putting up posters along the tent: Vito, Remo's older son. He certainly didn't look wicked, and if anything, a cloud of melancholy hung about him, casting over his heavy steps and the downward slope of his shoulders.

She'd start with him.

He'd finished with the posters and entered the wagon by the tree. Still invisible, Chiara followed quietly, but she wasn't prepared for the sight that awaited her inside the wagon.

A large wooden cage hung from the ceiling, five thin-limbed monkeys crammed inside.

Vito hurriedly opened the cage door, letting them out. "Don't make too much noise," he warned them. "Papa's nearby."

As the monkeys ran and jumped about the wagon happily, Vito reached into his knapsack for a bunch of bananas. He peeled them deftly, one for each monkey – and an additional banana.

"Where's Odi?" he asked.

The monkeys grunted and pointed behind them at the tent.

Vito gritted his teeth. "Stromboli has him?"

One of the monkeys nodded.

This did not make Vito happy. "Hurry, eat, eat."

While most of the monkeys nibbled on their bananas, the youngest, smallest one crept for the door. Vito stopped him, blocking the door with his body.

"I wish I could let you go," he said, falling onto his knees. He stroked the young monkey's head affectionately. "I really do. But Papa has Odi…" His voice trailed. "He'd be furious… and when he's furious…" Vito chewed on his lower lip.

Chiara's heart tightened. Anyone could see the terror on young Vito's face. Just what had Remo done to him?

In the near distance, coins jangled inside the domed tent. Vito's shoulders instantly tensed. "Papa's coming. Quick, back into the cage."

"Vito!" Remo roared for his son. "Vito, get back here! And bring the crickets!"

Hurriedly, Vito locked the monkeys back into their cage. "I'll try to get you all extra food tonight after the show." He swallowed. "One day, I'll set you free. I promise."

Then he grabbed a box labelled SINGING CRICKETS and stumbled out of the wagon.

Chiara followed him into the domed tent, where Remo the Showman was pasting on a black moustache and combing his wig in front of a long mirror. Behind him, his younger son, Stromboli, counted coins from their last show.

The resemblance between Stromboli and Remo was strong – same thick eyebrows, deep-set eyes and pronounced jaw. The same glittering greed in their laugh.

The sixth monkey squirmed under Stromboli's heel, and the boy stepped hard on its tail, making it screech in pain.

"Shut up, I'm counting," Stromboli said, flicking coins into a pile. "Ah, here it is!" He plucked out a gold band from the sack of profits. "There's the ring I told you about, Papa! Look, I slipped it off a lady's finger." He snickered, and green mist curled about his fingers. "She didn't even notice."

"Well done, my boy." Remo chewed on the ring, then made an approving whistle. He patted Stromboli's head. "Tonight we'll have to work even harder. That includes you, too, Odi." Remo pointed at the monkey. "I expect this pile to double, or else you and your brothers aren't getting food for a week!"

The monkey squirmed out of Stromboli's grip and raced out of the tent, but he didn't get far. Remo and Stromboli had bound his arms with string. Stromboli yanked, and the monkey flew back, screaming.

"Look, Papa, he's a puppet!" Stromboli howled with laughter as he forced the monkey's arms behind his back.

"That's enough," Vito cried, rushing to Odi's aid. "You're hurting him!"

"Hurting him?" Remo threw up his arms. "I'll show you what hurt is."

The showman thrashed his son's face with the back of his hand. The impact made Vito stagger back.

"Don't think I don't know what you've been doing, feeding the animals behind my back." Remo raised a ringed hand and shook a banana at his son. "Maybe I should make you go without food, too! Then that would teach you some respect!"

Vito cowered in the corner. "Yes… yes, Papa. I'm sorry, Papa."

"Sorry, Papa, yes, Papa," Remo mimicked cruelly. "How do I have such a spineless boy?"

"A sheep!" Stromboli taunted. "Vito's a sheep."

Remo cackled. "And we are wolves."

"Stop that!" Chiara cried, stepping out of Agata's invisibility spell. She pulled on Remo's coat from behind before he struck his son again.

Remo whirled on her. "The tent is closed. Can't you read?" he growled.

When he saw her, he relaxed. "Ah, it's a fairy. It's been a while since one of you has come. I'm flattered you haven't forgotten about the majestic Remo." He puffed out his chest and put on his wig. "Have you come to grant my wish at last?"

Chiara was starting to understand why Agata chose to remain invisible for most of her visits, showing herself only when necessary. She loathed the way Remo was looking at her, clearly calculating what he could get out of their encounter.

"I have not come to grant wishes," she said as calmly as she could. "I have come to give you a chance to redeem yourself. Return the money you and Stromboli have stolen, free the animals you have in your captivity and treat Vito with respect."

Remo blinked at her as if she'd spoken in a foreign language. Then he guffawed, the sound booming across the cavernous tent. "Ah, I see, you must be new. No wand. No wings. In that case, our business is done. I have a show to prepare for." He put on his wig, adjusting the black hair in front of the mirror. "Come, Stromboli."

"We aren't finished," said Chiara, an edge to her voice.

"Will you punish me? I think not. Ho, ho!" Remo laughed. "I know your kind. You won't use your magic to punish me. You don't even have magic yet."

A wand suddenly appeared in Chiara's hand. Agata's wand. *Thank you,* she gestured with a glance up, knowing that the elder fairy was watching her.

Stromboli's eyes lit, and he tugged on her skirt. "I want a wish!" he said. "I want a wish!"

"Let the monkey go," said Chiara to the boy. "Let him go free."

Stromboli kicked the monkey away. As it scampered to Vito's side fearfully, Stromboli turned back to Chiara. "There, I let him go. Now give me my wish."

She shook her head. "Wishes aren't transactions, paid for doing something that's right. You should act with kindness for your own sake as much as for the sake of others."

"What a load of baloney," said Stromboli, yanking angrily on her skirt. "You lied!"

Chiara stepped back. "I did not. I never said I would grant you a wish."

"You'll be sorry!" Stromboli wagged a finger at her. "Papa! Did you hear what she did?"

"Yes, yes, I heard." Remo stroked his false moustache. "It seems Ms Fairy has much to learn, doesn't she?" Chiara had no idea what the father and son were scheming, but she was immediately on her guard.

Cackling with delight, Stromboli gambolled towards the box of crickets Vito had brought. He shook it. Hard.

While the crickets slammed against the wooden walls, Stromboli parted the lid and plucked one of the poor creatures up by the wings. The cricket was as large as his tiny fist, and he cupped it with both hands so it couldn't escape. The cricket chirped in distress.

"You seem like the caring sort, Ms Fairy," Stromboli said in a singsong voice. "So I'm going to try again."

His voice turned into a growl: "Give me a wish, fairy." He raised his hands threateningly. "Or I'll smash this cricket into smithereens."

Chiara could hardly believe such wickedness from a young boy. "Don't do that, Stromboli."

"Or what? You'll teach me a lesson?"

Ever patient, Chiara knelt beside the boy. "I'd like to teach you to listen to your conscience. It's a voice inside your heart that tells you right from wrong. Do you hear it?"

"Conscience? What rubbish are you spewing, fairy?

She glanced at Vito, who had put his hand on his chest and was frowning as if trying to listen. At least her words were reaching *someone.*

"Will you let the cricket go?" she said to Stromboli, offering him one last chance. "And promise not to hurt it again? You ought to treat others the way you wish to be treated, Stromboli."

Stromboli blinked, and like his brother, he put his hand over his heart. He sniffed. "Oh, I understand now. Of course I promise, Ms Fairy."

Chiara almost let out a sigh of relief. "Very good, Stromboli. I'm glad you—"

A sneer came over the young boy's face. Without

warning, he dropped the cricket and pushed Chiara as hard as he could, snatching her wand, and then ran across the tent.

"Look, Papa, I've got her wand!" Stromboli flaunted it over his head. "Make me rich. I wish to be rich. Rich as a king!"

Chiara rose to her feet, shaking her head at the boy as the cricket raced to Vito for safety. She wasn't hurt, and she wasn't angry; she only regretted that she'd had to become involved so impulsively, without having had more time to consider how she might approach Vito and Stromboli.

So what was she to do? Instead of heeding her advice to listen to his conscience, Stromboli had tricked her. Lied to her.

The first way you begin to lose yourself is with a lie, Mamma had taught her. *A lie keeps growing and growing until it's as plain as the nose on your face.*

"Mamma's wise words," Chiara murmured to herself. "If only they would help Stromboli, too."

As soon as she uttered the command, the wand in Stromboli's hand began to glow. The boy laughed and laughed, thinking gold was about to rain from the ceiling and that his wish would soon come true.

But the magic gathered around his nose… which began to grow.

"Papa!" he screamed, coming to a halt.

Remo seized his stool, raising it high and threateningly. "What are you doing to my son?"

"Teaching him something that you would also do well to learn," Chiara replied. Outwardly, she maintained her composure, but her heart raced as she witnessed the wand's power. *Let it be temporary*, she commanded it silently. "You will treat others the way you wish to be treated. And a lie will not get you what you want."

"Get out of here, you witch!"

"Very well." Chiara started to lift her wand.

"Wait," Stromboli cried. "Turn my nose back!"

"No," said Remo. "We don't beg. We don't bargain." He whirled to face Chiara. "This fairy's heart is as weak as a bird's. She'll do anything to save even a cricket's life."

Stromboli sneered. "What do you care about a stupid cricket? It's going to get eaten soon enough, anyway. Or stepped on."

Remo grabbed his elder son. "You want to prove yourself to me, Vito? Smash the cricket. Show the fairy who's king around here. Go on!"

Vito cringed and cowered in fear of his father. "I…"

"Do it! You weak sap, do it now!"

The cricket made a pleading chirp.

Chiara lowered her wand. "You don't have to do that, Vito," she told him warmly. She knelt beside him. "Have courage. There's strength in you. When you're unsure of what to do, follow the voice in your heart: your conscience. It will guide you."

"I… I can't kill it," Vito stammered. He gave the cricket to Chiara.

"Why, you treacherous…" Remo raised his hand to strike his son, but Chiara intervened – such that when he grabbed Vito's arm, his sleeve was hot as a burning poker.

He jumped up in pain.

"You must never strike your sons again," she warned Remo firmly, "and you must teach them not to lie."

"You mean not to be like me?" Remo's sneer was identical to his younger son's. "Even if I did all those things, beautiful fairy, blood is thick. My boys will end up like me no matter what anyone teaches them."

"We'll see," Chiara said.

She had hope for Vito, but to be honest, she was troubled about Stromboli. From what she'd seen, his father rewarded him for cruelty and taught him that acts of kindness were weak and worthy of punishment. She wanted to help him further, but she didn't know how. Agata had taught her how to bring out the good in people's hearts and show them to trust their conscience, but not everyone's goodness could be unearthed after one or two visits. How did she guide someone like Stromboli?

Hiding her uneasiness, she winked at Vito, then scooped up the box of crickets and tapped her wand on the box. Instantly the crickets were free; the monkeys in the cage, too. As the former flew out of the tent and the latter scampered to freedom, she, too, made her exit.

Only after Remo had painted over his posters to announce that the night's show was cancelled did Stromboli's nose return to what it had been before.

"You did well," congratulated Agata.

"Was I too harsh?"

"No, but however did you come up with the idea to make Stromboli's nose grow longer?" said Agata. "You're smiling. You have a story. Do tell."

Chiara smiled wanly, thinking of the memory that had popped into her head while she'd held the wand. "Well, it's just that when my mamma caught us lying, she'd say, 'A lie keeps growing and growing until it's as plain as the nose on your face'."

"Oh, I love it!" Agata exclaimed. "Sometimes one has to be tough to get a message across, as you were with

Stromboli. Show the profound effect the truth – and untruths – have on the world."

Chiara sighed. "I worry about Stromboli, Agata. He's just a child. One visit from a fairy surely will not undo the lessons his father has taught him. You saw the way Remo goaded him." She pursed her lips. It'd be naïve to think that freeing the monkeys and crickets would lead Remo to choose a more honest profession, or that he might suddenly change overnight and decide to become a good father. Chiara's shoulders fell. She no longer felt like she'd done well at all. She felt like she'd failed. "Is there some way we can help them choose a different path? The boys, especially?"

"I will speak to Mirabella about it," said Agata. "Perhaps we can have one of the senior fairies keep an eye on the two boys."

Chiara nodded. "Vito will need help finding his way, if he ever leaves home. And Stromboli…" Her voice trailed off. "If the Heartless came to Remo, they will certainly be after Stromboli, too. I saw green mist about him. It didn't follow him everywhere, like it did with Remo, but—"

"I won't forget about Stromboli," Agata promised. "There is one thing you must learn, Chiara, and this is not about Remo's boys, but about humans in general. No two hearts are the same. And the same heart might look very different depending on the day. Humans have thousands of choices all of the time. They do not always get it right, and sometimes they do not wish to. There will be days when our work seems futile, days when we'll encounter people who act without a sense of right or wrong. We can only provide guidance and help those who want to be helped. We cannot force our ways, even on someone like Remo."

"Larissa mentioned that she'd been visiting Remo for years. Is that why he's so…"

"Heartless? It certainly helps." Agata sighed uneasily. "I should have known that Larissa would be here today. Did she say anything about a new apprentice?"

"No."

"It's only a matter of time, then," mused Agata. "She'll be looking, now that I have you. If I were to guess, Larissa already has her sights on someone to pit you against. They're always recruiting people to their side; Larissa and Amorale are obsessed with not being outnumbered by us."

"All the people they recruit… do they take their hearts?"

"Only the ones who become fairies like them," Agata replied. "That fate is, fortunately, reserved for a select few."

She touched Chiara's shoulder. "Don't look so worried, Chiara. I won't lie – we can't save everyone from the Heartless. Sometimes we are too late, or sometimes their hearts are too far gone rotten. But it makes a world of difference to those we can help. I'd say that's what makes our job so difficult, and so fulfilling."

"After today, I see what you mean," Chiara replied. Not being able to help Stromboli and Remo left an unsettled feeling in her gut. She could only hope that a more experienced fairy would help Stromboli – before Larissa's influence found him, too.

A new apprentice. Agata's words haunted her. That would mean a Heartless devoted to interfering with Chiara's work.

Chiara couldn't help wondering whom Larissa was trying to recruit.

CHAPTER NINETEEN

"Ilaria!" cried Mrs Belmagio. "Mail for you."

Ilaria flew down the stairs. This was it: the letter she'd been waiting weeks for.

She reached for the letter with shaking fingers and nearly tore the envelope in half instead of opening it. The paper was thick and creamy and smelt like hope. She held it to her chest, then shook her head. "You read it for me, Mamma. I don't dare."

"My hands stink of yeast. You sure you want that all over your mail?"

"Yes. If it's bad news, I'll burn it."

Mrs Belmagio chuckled at her daughter. "Let's read it together."

Holding her breath, Ilaria unfolded the letter. Her head had started spinning, and she had to fix her eyes to the paper to read properly: "Dear Miss Belmagio, it is our profound pleasure to inform you that—" Ilaria didn't need to go on. She let out a screech that frightened off the jays perched outside the kitchen and immediately raced up the stairs to shout out the news.

"I've advanced!" she cried. She clambered up to the third floor, taking two steps at a time to the attic—

"Chia, Chia! You'll never guess – I've advanced to the audition in Vallan! I'm going to sing for Maria Lin—"

As she burst through the door, she stopped mid-sentence. In her excitement, she'd forgotten. Her sister wasn't there any more.

All at once, Ilaria deflated. She kicked at the door. "Stupid me," she muttered.

Three months. It'd been three months that Chiara's room in the attic had been empty. Still, the sun shone brightest in her room, and everything was left the way it'd been before. The neat stacks of books, the ribbons hanging on a hook across her mirror, the picture Ilaria had drawn of the two sisters when they were little girls.

Swallowing the lump that had formed in her throat, Ilaria held the letter to her chest and closed the door.

—

Ily didn't want to share the good news with her friends, but Simona's father was the postmaster of Pariva, which meant she knew everyone's business.

"Heard you got a letter today," said Simona. Her so-called friend was waiting outside Mrs Tappa's hat shop for Ily to open up. Beatrice was there, too, and the two followed Ily into the shop like unwanted shadows.

"Are you going to tell what it is?"

Ily ignored her friends. The only reason she even consorted with Simona and Beatrice any more was because, now that Chia was gone, Ily had no other choices in female companionship her age. Still, all Simona and Beatrice liked to do was gossip and speak ill of others, even of each other when one wasn't around.

But bad company was better than no company, wasn't it?

Ily ignored the pang of loneliness that sharpened in her chest. Niccolo had started seeing Sofia Farrio, the miller's daughter, which meant he was head over heels and even less fun than usual to talk to, and Mamma and Papa were busy with the bakery. Beatrice and Simona were weak replacements for her brother and her parents, but it was better than talking to the wooden mannequins that stood in front of the shop window.

Or so Ily told herself.

"It was a letter from the Madrigal Conservatory," boasted Ily. "I'm going to Vallan."

"Really?" Beatrice's eyes widened. "When?"

"Tuesday. It's going to be wonderful. I haven't gone to the city in years."

"Think of all the new boys you can flirt with," said Beatrice enviously. "Maybe I should come with you."

"Niccolo's taking me," Ilaria lied quickly. "Sofia, too. They're inseparable these days."

Beatrice's expression soured. Ily knew that was exactly what she hadn't wanted to hear.

"You'll need something new to wear," Simona said, clearly envious. "Your old dresses will be out of fashion in Vallan, but something in vogue will be expensive. Maybe Chiara can send you a new one."

Not even Simona's backhanded insult could ruin her mood. "I already have a new dress," Ily said giddily. "Mamma went with me to have it made in Nerio last week."

Thanks to the money Chiara had given her, Ily had toured Nerio's garment district and treated herself to the loveliest red gown.

Even if I don't make the Vallan round, she'd told herself, *it'll be something beautiful to have and look at.*

But as it'd turned out, she *was* going to Vallan!

Ily's smile widened. "It's got lace on the sleeves and

rosettes along the neckline. Wait until you see it." She reached for a hat on display. "Mrs Tappa's even letting me borrow a hat for the occasion. The red velvet one that's worth a small fortune."

Beatrice made a humming sound, which Ily knew meant she was searching for something else to poke at. Her so-called friends were like hens; Ily only wished she could throw them some feed to make them go away or lock them up in a pen like real chickens.

"I'm glad for you, Ily – about Vallan… but I thought the letter would be from Chia." Simona clicked her tongue. "It's been three months, hasn't it? Papa says there hasn't been any word from her."

Leave it to Simona to find the one way to storm in on her good mood. Ily raised her chin high. "Why would a fairy write letters when she has magic? She can send messages over beams of starlight or have butterflies bring gifts from the Wishing Star."

"Has she?" said Beatrice. "Or has she forgotten about you?"

"Watch yourself, Beatrice. My sister would never forget about me."

"I'm only asking because of what *my* papa said."

"What did your papa say?"

"That she won't be the same." Beatrice cast Ily a pitying

smile. "Don't you know? There's a girl from Benoita who became a fairy, what, twenty years ago? Hardly anyone even remembers her." Beatrice leant closer conspiratorially. "They say the fairies cast a spell over the family. Over the whole town. They either make you think she's dead, or they make you forget her completely."

A chill bristled down the back of Ilaria's neck, but she ignored it and pretended to huff with disdain. "I've never heard this before. Where did your papa hear this rubbish?"

"He was a librarian in Benoita for twelve years," Beatrice replied. "He heard things."

"The books talk?" Ilaria snorted.

A glare from Beatrice. "I think it makes sense. Why else don't we remember anything about the fairies? All we know is they once were human. Don't you think someone would have tried to ask by now?"

Ily said nothing. She had no good answer for that. During her short meeting with Agata, the fairy had been unresponsive to nearly all her questions. Chia, too, had been secretive.

Simona flipped her hair over her shoulder. "I guess we'll all find out when Chia's back. She *is* coming back, isn't she?"

"For my birthday," said Ilaria, hoping the extra air she pumped into her voice would hide her uncertainty. Her birthday was in a month, and she knew that Chiara wasn't supposed to write, but still – every day she didn't hear from her sister, she worried that Chiara had lost track of time and had forgotten.

Stop worrying, Ilaria thought, tying the ribbon on her hat a little too tightly. *Next you'll be believing those stupid tall tales Beatrice made up because she's jealous that we have a fairy in the family. She's always been jealous of Chia and me because she and her sister don't get along.*

Taking a deep, calming breath, she set aside the hat and drummed her fingers on the table. "Why don't you two watch the shop for a while?"

"Us?" Beatrice exclaimed. "It's not our job to—"

"I'm going to ask Mamma for some cake," Ilaria lied. "I'll bring you each a slice."

Simona smacked her lips. "The blood orange one with chocolate?"

Ilaria sweetened her tone. "Of course."

"I don't want anything," said Beatrice, crossing her arms. Ever since Niccolo had turned his affections to Sofia Farrio, she refused to even talk about him, let alone patronise the bakery where he worked.

"Don't take too long," called Simona after her. "What will we do if there's a customer?"

Ily pretended not to hear and flitted out the door. She

needed air. Needed to get away from the same old faces, the same old clock tower with its spindly arms, the same old crooked welcome sign in front of the flower shop and the same old smells of lemon and cheese and grass and pine.

She hadn't had a good practice session in days, and she needed to get in shape before her audition. She certainly couldn't practise in the shop with Beatrice and Simona there. They talked over her singing and made unwanted commentary, and when she took her music outside, former beaus came by to flirt and other townspeople constantly interrupted her songs with greetings and questions about Chiara. Well-intentioned, but irksome, all the same.

I'll make for the pastures, she thought. She'd climb one of the low hills to the top – the way she used to with Chiara – then sing and sing. Rare was the errant eavesdropper, and the birds would make a finer audience than anyone in Pariva.

Anyone, that was, except Geppetto.

As soon as she thought about him, her gaze found the young luthier as if she'd conjured him – wandering the middle of the town square.

He pushed his wind-tossed black hair – in dire need of a trim – out of his eyes. Her stomach fluttered as he ambled through the square, carrying two long loaves of bread under each arm and nearly bumping into Mr Vaci in the middle of the road. Ily smothered a laugh at the sight.

How strange. She'd never thought shy Geppetto handsome before. He certainly didn't have the strapping build of the young men she was used to flirting with, or the chiselled jaw and dark, mysterious eyes that infatuated most girls her age. But there was something sweet about him. Something sincere, too.

Sweet and sincere? She laughed at herself. *You must be lonely, Ily.*

Still, unlike Simona and Beatrice, at least he didn't try to provoke her with every other sentence. Everything about him was straightforward and honest; she could even tell from the way he fidgeted with his hat and how his feet pointed towards Mrs Tappa's door that the hat shop was where he was heading – so Ilaria intercepted him with a tap from behind.

"It's a fine afternoon to shop for hats, isn't it, Geppetto?"

To say he was startled was an understatement. He jumped, and practically tripped over one of the uneven cobblestones under his shoe.

"I… I was going to see you, actually."

"Me?" Ilaria pretended to be surprised.

Geppetto spoke in a flustered rush, "I… I heard that

you advanced to the final round of auditions at the Madrigal Conservatory. And I… I wanted to… to…"

"Who told you that?" Ilaria asked, genuinely surprised.

"Uh. Um. Your mother?"

"You don't know?"

Ilaria liked how pink his ears turned. It was adorable.

"Yes, I do. It was your mother, Mrs Belmagio. She said that I ought to…"

"To congratulate me?"

A deep breath. "Yes."

"That's very sweet," said Ilaria, meaning it. "Thank you, Geppetto."

Maybe she really did have a magic power. There Geppetto went again, his face turning redder than a tomato. Ilaria had to smother a giggle. She couldn't help being amused – and even charmed.

"I'm on break from work," she said. "Walk with me."

"Oh, no, I couldn't. I have to get back to—"

"A short walk," interrupted Ilaria. "Come on, Geppetto. It'll be too cold for strolls soon."

Geppetto relented, and Ilaria couldn't walk fast enough. Only when the bell tower ringing eleven o'clock was but a faint chime in the distance did she slow down. She glanced at Geppetto, still at her side but falling a step or two behind.

He was trying hard not to sound out of breath as he wiped his face with a handkerchief.

She forged up a low hill where dozens of pine trees grew. "Hurry, we're almost there!"

"Where?" Geppetto called.

"Here," said Ilaria, fanning out her skirt before she plopped under the shade of a tall old pine tree on the top of the hill. "My favourite spot in Pariva."

That was a lie; she didn't have a favourite spot. But at least here, she could see more of the world than anywhere else in this sleepy little town. She could make out the corners of Elph touching Mount Cecilia, and when she stretched her gaze far, she imagined the iron spires of Vallan beyond the clouds.

Geppetto tumbled down beside her and wiped at his forehead again. He folded his handkerchief before returning it to his pocket. "Some would say the journey is the best part," he said belatedly.

"Not me," replied Ilaria. "I want to get to where I'm going as fast as I can."

"Like Vallan?" said Geppetto pensively. He leant against the tree and watched the clouds. "What will you sing for your audition?"

"They asked for one song," said Ily, sinking onto the grass. She didn't care if she stained her dress. It *was* old, as Simona had pointed out, and the pink stripes had faded until they looked practically white. "You have one guess."

Geppetto considered. "The Nightingale Aria?"

"It does seem to be a crowd pleaser. And it's my favourite."

"Mine, too. Are you nervous?"

Ilaria hesitated. "Yes," she confessed. "It'll be the most important day of my life. Five minutes that can change everything."

"I thought you didn't believe in fate."

Was he teasing her? Ilaria couldn't tell behind the twinkle in his eye. She hugged her knees to her chest. "I believe we make our own choices, and we shape whatever future may come."

"But sometimes, out of the blue, something might happen."

"Like what? Chiara becoming a fairy?" Ilaria scoffed. "She could have said no."

"She could have," Geppetto agreed. "But I think it was always her secret longing to help people. It brings her joy unlike anything else."

How could Geppetto, who had only known Chiara for a few months, see more clearly into her heart than Ilaria?

Ilaria bit down on her lip. "That's what she told me before she left."

"Don't you have a secret longing?"

Ilaria thought of the wish she'd made on the Wishing Star. She thought of her music, and how wonderful it would feel to hear her voice echo across the walls of Esperia's grand opera houses, to become a prima donna and sing with an orchestra. To see stars shine in the eyes of everyone she met, and have fresh roses and flowers tossed at her feet wherever she walked. To have grown men and women swoon whenever she blew them kisses.

"Of course I do," she said.

"Music," said Geppetto, reading the lift in her expression. "I can hear it in your voice when you sing. You love music."

"It makes me feel alive," she said, repeating what she'd told Chia. "When I sing, I'm no longer Ilaria Belmagio. I'm a princess or a revolutionary, I'm a milkmaid who's just had her heart broken – or a fairy who's lost her wand."

"Or a nightingale who's been found by a lost boy."

"Figaro," Ilaria said, naming the character. "Together, they help each other find their way home. I've always liked that story."

"Me too. It's one of the happier operas. I always cry when they're sad."

"I didn't take you for a weeper," Ilaria teased. "Or a dreamer."

"I listen to too much opera, I guess. Blame my father. He doesn't seem like the sentimental sort, but he is."

There weren't many other boys in Pariva who loved opera. Plenty listened. It was hard not to, given that the melodies spread across Esperia, carried on the wings of good gossip. It was just that most of the other boys spent their evenings at the Red Lobster Inn or playing cards. Even Niccolo had been playing his violin less these days.

She kicked at the dirt and the grass. Before Geppetto could respond, she said, "What is *your* secret longing?"

Geppetto took a deep breath. In his quietest voice, he professed, "I want to make toys."

That surprised Ilaria. "Toys?"

The light in his eyes sparkled. "Toys for every child in Pariva. Toys that delight the heart and tickle the fancy. Toys they can pass to their children and their children's children."

"But what about your father's shop? I thought you loved music, too."

"I do. But repairing guitars and violins… that's my father's passion, not mine. They bring their own kind of special joy to the children." Geppetto stared at his hands. "Papa won't be pleased when he finds out."

"He doesn't know?"

Geppetto hung his head. "I haven't been brave enough to tell him. But I will, soon."

Ilaria could sense Chiara's handiwork in this. She didn't know how she knew, but she did. It irked her, just the tiniest bit.

"I want to make my own music, my own way," Geppetto went on. "Clocks and singing boxes and dolls and puppets."

"And you want children of your own, I'm guessing."

It was impressive how instantly Geppetto's face turned red. "Who… who doesn't love children?" he stammered. "They are the future. They have their whole world in front of them, and they're free to dream."

Ilaria couldn't agree. To be stuck in Pariva for the rest of her life, living a street away from her parents, bouncing children on her knees… such thoughts did not bring her joy.

Geppetto was eager to change the topic. He cleared his throat and said, "Have you hired a carriage to Vallan?"

She nodded. "Niccolo helped me. Mr Muscado is bringing me in Monday morning."

"Is Niccolo coming with you?"

"Niccolo won't come, because he's still working." She shrugged. "I don't mind. He doesn't like the city anyway."

"What about your parents?"

She tried to hide her disappointment, but Geppetto saw the flicker of discontent that crossed her face.

"They can't come," he realised.

"I asked," said Ilaria miserably, "but it's an entire day's

trip. Mamma and Papa can't leave. Oh, it's not because they don't want to, or they can't afford to, but the whole town depends on the bakery… and Niccolo won't come, because it's Sofia's birthday—"

"So you'll be going alone?"

Ilaria tipped her chin up, mustering enthusiasm. "It'll be a great adventure."

"The audition is the most important event of your life," said Geppetto. "You shouldn't be alone." He bit on his cheek, then sucked in his breath. "Would your parents… would they allow me to accompany you?"

Ilaria's eyes widened. "You would do that for me? It's a whole day's trip, Geppetto."

"I don't have much work right now," said Geppetto, raking his hand through his hair. He wasn't a good liar. "Business has been slow."

"Would your father be angry? I know he relies on you to—"

"He'll understand," Geppetto assured her.

Would he? Ilaria wondered. Mr Tommaso certainly wouldn't understand his son spending a day escorting Ilaria Belmagio – of all girls – to Vallan. She knew her reputation.

"I wouldn't miss being there for you," said Geppetto, his voice shaking. But his meaning was firm. "I'll pick up some chocolates for Papa and work extra hard these next few days. It'll be all right."

Ilaria was touched. A rush of warmth overcame her heart, and without thinking, she reached for Geppetto's hand and laced her fingers in his. "Thank you," she said.

She'd nearly forgotten she'd come to the hill to practise.

Summoning the song inside her, she parted her lips to free the first note, a *la.* She'd never sung with an orchestra before, but in her mind, she imagined violins sustaining the tender chord of the nightingale, and flutes fluttering an impression of wings and wind. Once their introduction was finished, she began her song in earnest.

Geppetto listened. Not once did he yawn or pull out a book to read, and she knew from his expression that her song moved him.

One true listener is worth a hundred idle ones, Chia used to say when Ily declared she wanted to sing before thousands in the Accordo Opera House.

For once, Ily agreed. And as Geppetto listened to her practise for her audition for the rest of day, she didn't think once about what an awful place Pariva was.

CHAPTER TWENTY

It was a morning of disasters. Ilaria tore a button off her dress and couldn't find it, so she had to sew on a new one that didn't match, and the carriage she had spent three months saving for was little more than a hay wagon – pulled by donkeys, no less. Not even horses!

"Nothing can be done, Ms Ilaria," said Mr Muscado, observing her disappointment. "There was a crack on the front carriage wheel. Wouldn't be safe to take it out."

"I paid twenty oros for a carriage—" Ily spluttered. "I'm not going to take a wagon!"

"Then I wish you luck finding another ride at this hour," said Mr Muscado sharply.

"You're a swindler."

"Your brother hired me to take you safely to Vallan by

noon. Doesn't matter if it's in a wagon or a carriage pulled by horses or sheep. You'll get there on time."

There was an edge to Mr Muscado's tone, and Geppetto touched Ilaria's arm, urging her to accept.

She gritted her teeth. It was a good thing Geppetto was with her. If he hadn't come, she would have thrown a fit right there and then. But when Geppetto offered his arm to help her climb aboard, she put on an air of nonchalance – for his sake.

The ride was rough; the donkeys kicked up dust from the road, which dirtied Ilaria's hair and clogged her throat. And the smell! She knew by the end of the four hours she would smell like straw and hay, if not dung.

It was so awful she wanted to cry. She couldn't stomach the idea of arriving in Vallan caked in dust. Worst yet, nausea crawled up to her throat thanks to the bumpy roads and thick air. How would she sing at her best like this?

"A game of cards?" Geppetto offered, trying to distract her from her misery.

She shook her head and reached into her satchel. Out came six sheets of parchment – the music to the Nightingale Aria – but Geppetto frowned.

"You've sung the aria a thousand times," he said gently. "You don't need to sing it again. Let your mind and voice rest."

"How can I rest when I'm practically choking on dust?"

"Look," he said. "We can't even see Pariva any more. When was the last time you journeyed so far from home?"

She swallowed. "Three years ago. Chia and I came to Vallan to see our first concert together. There was a famous duo I'd wanted to see – a soprano, and her sister at the harpsichord." Ily's voice went low with longing. "They performed together across Esperia. I always thought that might be Chia and me one day."

Geppetto's shoulders fell. His lips were parted, and he was clearly trying to find some way to comfort her. "What an adventure you'll have today," he said at last. "No matter what happens, it'll be something worth remembering."

She couldn't quite summon Geppetto's optimism, but she did smile. "I hope so."

"I know so."

Ilaria inched closer to him, revelling in how her nearness made Geppetto lean nervously against the edge of the wagon. If he moved any more to the left, he'd fall out.

Then he reached into his coat pocket. "For luck," Geppetto said, passing her a small box wrapped in newspaper that had been carefully painted red, her favourite colour.

Ily looked up at him. "A present? But my birthday isn't until next month."

"I know. I meant it as a birthday present, but I finished

it early. Last night. Thought I'd bring it in case you needed a smile, and it looks like you do."

That did make Ilaria smile. She loved presents.

She undid the paper, not even minding when some of the red paint smudged her fingertips. Geppetto's gift was a heart-shaped box, its dark wood intricately carved with a nightingale on a tree bough, the leaves etched with a vibrant yellow paint.

"It's beautiful," she breathed. "Did you make this? I'll put all my jewellery inside. It's perfect!"

"It's a music box, actually." The young man blushed. "Here, you'll see. Let me help you wind it up."

Geppetto wound the crank on the side of the box, and a song tinkled like little bells. Ilaria recognised the tune immediately.

"It's my aria!" She stared at him in amazement. "How did you do that?"

"I read a bunch of books," he said shyly, "and took apart my mother's old music box. Papa would have killed me if I hadn't put it back together, so I found a way."

"I'm glad you did."

He ventured, "It doesn't sound as pretty as you do."

It was Ilaria's turn to blush. Mostly because she knew he meant it. She held the music box close. "Thank you, Geppetto. I'll treasure it always."

She played the music box over and over until her fears subsided and her worries fell to the back of her head. This time, when she moved closer, Geppetto went still. She leant on his shoulder and closed her eyes, letting her mind drift to the music of Geppetto's steady breathing and the tinkle of her favourite song.

"Ily, Ily!" Geppetto shook her awake. "We've arrived."

Ilaria jolted, and instantly sprang up. They were in Vallan!

Ilaria forgot about her shame over arriving on a cart. She forgot about the dust in her curls and how her throat tickled when she breathed in. Before her, only a hundred steps away, was the city.

She practically ran, and poor Geppetto had to sprint to catch up with her.

"We're late," he said, though Ilaria was hardly listening. "Mr Muscado will be waiting for us to take us home—"

"Do you see that, Geppetto?" she breathed as she looked up.

Geppetto craned his neck. "What are you looking at?"

"The sky," she exclaimed. "I can hardly see it. The buildings – there're so many of them. And they're so close together. It's marvellous, isn't it?"

"Ily, did you hear me? We're running—"

She darted down the street. There was a restaurant on every corner, and how fashionably the men and ladies dressed! She adjusted her hat and brushed invisible dirt off the ruffles along her neck. How fine she'd thought her dress when she'd bought it in Nerio. Here it looked like an old frock twenty years out of date. No one had rosettes on their waist, and it seemed that ruffles were only for grandmothers or babies.

Still, everywhere she turned, there were sights that dazzled and mesmerised her. Acrobats in the middle of the streets, surrounded by a crowd tossing coins and flowers at the performers; opera singers in masks who sang along the street corners.

"You've ten minutes… t-to reach the c-conservatory," said Geppetto between breaths.

"Ten minutes!" Ilaria exclaimed. She hiked up her skirt. "Why didn't you tell me?"

"It's this way."

Together they dashed down the streets. Ilaria had no idea where she was going, but Geppetto had studied a map of Vallan while she'd napped, and he led her on turn after turn until she saw it.

The Madrigal Conservatory.

It occupied its own block on the street, with the names of Esperia's great composers carved into the white stone facade, just under the roof. The very sight stole away Ilaria's breath. It was the grandest building she had ever seen.

There was only a minute until she was expected, and she hastily patted at her perspiring temples and tried to iron out the wrinkles on her dress.

"No need for that," said Geppetto. "You'll dazzle them with your voice." He offered her the last of his water.

While Ilaria drank deeply, Geppetto sat on a bench beside a lamppost.

"I'm a bit too dusty from the road to accompany you into a place like the conservatory," he said sheepishly. "I'll wait for you out here."

Ilaria wanted to tell him that she wanted him there with her, but she didn't want to make him feel out of place. "Don't you want to explore the city while you wait?" she asked. "It might be a while."

"A scoop of ice cream costs half an oro here," replied Geppetto sensibly. He took out his half-eaten sandwich from his bag. "I'll wind up penniless simply from walking around."

Ilaria laughed. It wasn't meant to be a joke, but she found it funny anyway.

She licked her lips and returned his canteen to him. "Thank you."

"You are the music, Ilaria. Show them that, and there is no way you can fail."

The words warmed her. She leant forwards and kissed Geppetto on the cheek.

Without looking back to see his reaction, she straightened her posture and strode into the conservatory. The school's interior was even grander, with lush burgundy carpets and a winding staircase with marble railings. She could practically smell music being made; the walls were the same colour as parchment, embellished with gilded symbols that looked like clefs.

After a few minutes, she was taken into a narrow hall on the second floor. There, another girl was already waiting. She had perfect golden curls, a spotless white dress with lace so delicate it looked knitted by spiders, and dainty silk shoes with embroidered roses on the sides and an elegant heel that gave her extra height. A matching parasol rested at her side, and as Ilaria approached, a fragrance tickled her nostrils. The girl smelt like… like flowers from Mamma's garden.

No one in Pariva indulged in an extravagance such as perfume. Ilaria hadn't even thought of it! But suddenly she became all too aware of the sweat prickling under her arms and the odour that followed. She grew conscious of the loose button on her bodice, the dust stains on the ruffles over her shoulders – only noticeable if you looked closely, as this girl seemed to be doing from behind a curtain of thick black lashes.

"Are you Ilaria?" said the young lady, her voice far too honeyed to be sincere. "I'm Carlotta. Carlotta Linda."

Ily's eyebrows flew up.

"Yes, Maria Linda's niece." Carlotta bowed her head demurely. "They're waiting for you inside."

"Oh. Thank you." Ily hurried towards the door opposite Carlotta. In her haste, she didn't watch her step, and Carlotta's parasol shot out of nowhere.

Ilaria tripped and fell flat on her face.

"Oh, I'm sorry!" Carlotta said, extending a hand to help her up.

Were she Chiara, Ily would have gratefully accepted the hand. But Ily knew the face of a devil when she saw one.

"You tripped me!" she cried.

"Pardon?" Carlotta tilted her head. "I was sitting. My parasol must have fallen."

Ily gritted her teeth as she leant against the wall to get up. *Don't make a scene,* she told herself. Her dress was fine; she wasn't hurt. She'd go in for her audition as if nothing had happened.

She had started to pivot for the door when Carlotta plucked a piece of straw from her skirt. She flicked it to the ground, giggling. "Figures you came here by wagon, Ily Bumpkin. Break a leg."

Ilaria's shoulders squared. She shot Carlotta a glare that usually unsteadied even the most resolute of souls, but Carlotta didn't even flinch. She put on a smug simper as if she knew something that Ilaria did not.

Ily whirled away, but inside, her heart was hammering, and she felt suddenly light-headed, her stomach whooshing as though she had eaten something disagreeable.

Stop it, she rebuked herself. *You can't let a silly girl ruin this.*

She had imagined this moment a thousand times. Walking confidently into the room, where a mahogany harpsichord, a ceiling-high arched window, and a bookshelf of music awaited.

Aglow with energy, she'd sing her best. Her voice would be velvet, and every note would be smoother than the chocolate Mamma spread onto their toast.

But in reality, she could hardly speak. Maria Linda was there, seated beside an elderly gentleman with a grey velvet coat and brass-buckled shoes: the conservatory director, Maestro Lully.

All Ilaria could focus on was Maria Linda. Her idol.

The diva was as beautiful as Ilaria had heard, with raven black hair plaited into a long braid at her side, and pearls as large as marbles dangling from her ears. While her white gown had a scandalously low neckline, the fur stole over her shoulders added just the right touch of modesty. Even the way her gown fell, into a satin silk pool at her feet, looked luxurious. The entire effect was a picture of glamour and elegance; she looked like a goddess, the goddess of music.

"Ilaria Belmagio?" said Maria Linda.

"That's me," Ilaria replied, almost trilling in her excitement.

Maria Linda barely looked up. She fluttered a hand at the harpsichordist. "Start at the recitative."

The accompaniment began without any warning, giving Ilaria only a second to compose herself and step into character. She was a bird, a lonely nightingale that had lost her way, but she'd come across a kind young man, Figaro, who was also lost in the forest. She would appeal to him to help her go home.

Maria Linda closed her eyes, listening with a far-off expression.

Excitement bubbled to Ilaria's toes. She didn't expect to learn the results of her audition immediately after singing, but from the notes Maestro Lully was furiously scribbling into his book, she knew she was making an impression.

"That will be all."

Maestro Lully waved his notebook, and the accompanist

abruptly stopped playing. Ilaria didn't understand what was happening, so she kept singing, certain it was a test to see how she sounded unaccompanied.

"I said, that will be all."

Lully's tone was sharp this time, and Ilaria's song died in her throat. She couldn't move. She blinked, certain she had misheard. "That'll be all? I hardly finished the recitative. I haven't even begun the aria—"

"Had you arrived on time, you would have been allowed to sing more."

Anger burned in Ilaria's chest. "Do you know what it took for me to get here?"

"We judge on the quality of your voice, Ms Belmagio, not the hardships you face getting to your audition on time."

"But I've practised—"

"For months? Years?" Maria Linda spoke this time, and she uncrossed her ankles. "Yes, and you are not alone in that. You are a fine actress, I'll give you that, and your voice is lovely. But a star is far more than that. How many languages do you speak?"

"One," said Ilaria, pursing her lips. "But I can sing proficiently in five—"

"Who was your teacher?"

"Ms Rocco."

"Rocco?" Maria Linda frowned. "I'm not familiar with the name."

"Valeria Rocco," Ily supplied. "She sang in the Vallan Opera for years before she retired."

"She was an *alternate* for the chorus," corrected Maestro Lully. "I remember the name. Quite a scandal at the opera… she was dismissed for coming to rehearsals drunk."

Shame heated Ilaria's cheeks. Ms Rocco had enjoyed the occasional drink, but… Ily swallowed. "Please, let me try again."

"When you are onstage, they will not let you *try again*," said Maria Linda. She stood and circled Ilaria, her heels clicking against the wooden floor as she walked.

"You're a lovely girl with a lovely voice, Ms Belmagio, and you have a decent ear as well as a fine sense of drama. But that's all it is. Lovely. A prima donna cannot afford to be lovely. She must make the stars themselves bow down when she enters."

Maria Linda leant in as if she had an invisible monocle with which to scrutinise Ilaria's clothes. Then her nose made a disdainful wrinkle. "Yes. Yes. It is as I say. Your unfortunate ensemble can be rectified with a visit to a proper clothier and your deplorable pronunciation are things that can be worked on and trained, but your presence? The

Nightingale Aria is about more than a bird who is lost in the forest. The nightingale is angry, she is miserable, she is in pain. It is a song of transformation, of transcendence. You see, when her melody returns, it transcends into something new. She finds love amid despair and wretched loneliness; it is this new transformation, this change in her song, that allows her to finally find her way home. It is meant to make the listener weep and feel joy at the same time. I sensed none of that spark from you."

Maestro Lully nodded in complete agreement. "I couldn't have said it better." He set down his book of notes. "We thank you graciously for your time, Ms Belmagio, but unfortunately the conservatory is not a fit for your efforts. You may go."

You may go.

In three words, Ily's thirteen-year-long dream came to an end.

Her world spun, and she didn't remember storming out. But in the next dizzying minute, she was outside in the narrow hall once more, the heat of tears held back blurring her eyes.

To make things worse, Carlotta held out a handkerchief. "The washroom is that way." She pointed. "First left and down the hall."

Any other time, Ilaria would have snapped that she

didn't need directions to the washroom and that she was fine. But the tears were already starting to fall, and she would *not* cry in front of Carlotta Linda.

She ran into the washroom and leant against the wall, slumping down until she was on the ground. Years of dreaming – of practising until she sang even in her sleep, of walking miles to the next town where a new aria might be sung, of training her ear until she could transcribe a melody after hearing it only once – all of it had distilled into a few minutes in a dimly lit room.

She pounded her fists against the wall, furious at herself, angry at Maria Linda and Maestro Lully.

She *was* the nightingale. Lost and miserable and in pain. But she'd find her way home. She'd *make* her way home.

"I'll march right back there and make them accept me," Ilaria determined. "I won't give up."

Determined to snatch back the fate she knew she deserved, Ilaria inhaled a shaky breath and strode back towards the audition room.

But she didn't get very far. Even one hall down, she could hear someone singing from the room. Carlotta Linda.

Carlotta's voice was a light and airy soprano, completely unexpected and different from her speaking voice. The aria she'd chosen was a difficult one, a showstopper requiring a four-octave range and difficult leaps that were barely supported by the harmony in the harpsichord's accompaniment. Yet Carlotta glided through the song fluidly, masterfully.

Every note was wrought with passion and emotion, and even if Ilaria hadn't understood a single word that Carlotta sung, she wouldn't have been able to wrest her ears away.

There she stood, her palm pressed to the door, half-miserable, half-riveted. Spellbound. If she'd thought Maria Linda had made a mistake about her, she didn't any more.

Carlotta had it all: the voice, the presence, the power.

Ily's knees went weak with realisation. Maria Linda hadn't tried to be cruel; she had simply conveyed the truth. Ily wasn't good enough.

Tears welled around the rims of Ily's eyes.

I won't cry, she said, blinking furiously. *Stop it, Ily! Stop it!*

A violin student turned the corner into the hall, and Ilaria ducked her head before he noticed her crying. Tilting her hat over her head, she hurried out of the conservatory, her heart thundering against her steps.

Geppetto was there, as promised, waiting for her. He hadn't brought a book to read or purchased even a newspaper to occupy his time, and when he saw her, he lifted his hat and started to wave – only to drop his hands.

"Ilaria, what's wrong?"

Ily didn't even have the energy to lie. "It was stupid," she said sourly. "All of it was stupid. They didn't even let me finish my aria, or ask me my range, or ask me to sight-sing." The words hurt; each one was like swallowing a needle. "Come on, Geppetto. Let's go home."

Bless him, Geppetto didn't question her. "You should eat something."

"I'm not hungry."

"I tried looking for your favourite cookies, but the bakeries here don't have them…"

His voice trailed when he noticed her bleary eyes. Geppetto's shoulders fell. He looked as crestfallen as she felt. "I'm sorry, Ily." He pursed his lips. "You'll have another chance, I'm sure."

"I won't."

"Fate is kind. She'll see your dreams through. Maybe not in Vallan, but there are other cities in Esperia."

He took her hand, clasping it in both of his, and Ilaria shook her head. She couldn't help it, but a flare of irritation rose to her chest.

Fate wasn't kind, no matter what Geppetto said. Ilaria

knew that in her heart. She'd always known it. First it had taken Chiara from her. Now her dreams.

If she wasn't good enough for Vallan, then she'd always be second rate. There was no use in trying somewhere else.

Ilaria drew her hand back and turned on her heel. "Let's go home," she said, with her back to Geppetto. "I never want to come back to this awful place again."

"How was it?" Mrs Belmagio asked when Ilaria returned home. It was well past her mother's bedtime, but she was still up, sitting beside two plates of Ilaria's favourite cake with matching forks. One for Ilaria, one for Mamma.

When Ily and Chia had been little, they used to sneak slices of cake before bedtime and share with their mother. Any other day, the sight would have melted Ilaria's heart, but not tonight. Tonight, Ilaria's heart was stone.

Inwardly, she thought the truth: *I'm tired, Mamma. It's been a long day. My dreams were shattered and I have nothing left. I just want to be left alone and go to bed.*

"Ily?" Mrs Belmagio's tone leaked concern, and the brightness on her face dimmed. "Ily, is everything all right?"

Mamma handed her a square of chocolate cake – speared on a fork, which Ily accepted numbly.

"Thank you."

She said it automatically; ate the cake automatically, too. But inside, her dreams of travelling the world, of singing in the great opera houses – crumbled like the cake under her fork.

She couldn't tell that to Mamma. "It's delicious," she said as brightly as she could.

"Are you all right?" Mrs Belmagio asked again.

Taking the plate from Mamma, Ilaria started up the stairs, the creaks in the wood sounding louder than they ever had. Then she forced her most brilliant smile. "Of course I'm all right. I'm going to be a star, Mamma! The brightest star that Esperia has ever known."

Mamma's hand flew to her mouth. "The audition was a success? From the way you sounded just now, I thought…"

"That they rejected me?" Ily threw back her head and laughed. "I was acting. They took me, Mamma! I'm going to Vallan!"

"You devious girl!" Mamma pinched Ily's nose, then hugged her close. "To the theatre for you. What an actress you've become. I did believe you."

Ily struggled to keep her voice even: "Were you disappointed?"

"No. Your papa and I would have been just as content for you to stay in Pariva with us forever. We're selfish that way."

"I won't be staying," said Ilaria, the words rushing out before she could think. "I'll leave for Vallan as soon as winter is over."

Mamma wiped at her eyes. "First Chia, now you. It seems Fate has grand plans for both my girls..." Her voice trailed. "Your hard work has paid off. Soon, your dreams will come true."

Ily's smile faltered, and she pushed her mother away. Regret filled her chest, but she didn't dare take back the lie. She'd tell Mamma the truth in a few days. When her head and her heart hurt less and every word she uttered didn't taste so bitter.

Mamma caught the hitch in Ily's composure, and held on to her hand. "What brings you joy brings us joy, Ily. Are *you* happy, my darling?"

"Why wouldn't I be?" Ily said airily. "This is what I've dreamt of my entire life." She took a step up the stairs towards her room. She had to get away before her mother saw through her lies. "I should get to bed, Mamma. It's been a long day."

Without saying good night, she practically flew up the stairs into her room and closed the door. She leant against the wall, sinking inch by inch until she fell onto the ground, her toes curling against the soft, knotted rug her mother had made her when she'd been a girl – back when dreams were as distant and bright as the stars hanging in the sky, and reaching for them wouldn't turn them into dust.

"Where are you, Chia?" she whispered, searching for the Wishing Star. But only the moon peered back at her, a sliver in the sky. "Can you hear me? I miss you. I need you."

They were only a year apart, and almost like twins. They'd spent their whole lives together, and Chiara's not being here was like missing a part of herself.

How unfair it was that Chiara, who would have been happy staying in Pariva for the rest of her life, was out exploring the world! No doubt she was flying with silly gossamer wings and meeting every sort of person, important and not.

All while Ilaria was stuck here. Talentless, unwanted and never good enough.

"Fate isn't kind," she repeated to herself. "Geppetto was wrong. She isn't kind at all."

Over and over she repeated this to herself as she cried herself to sleep.

Little did she know, someone was watching. Someone with the power to change her fate.

CHAPTER TWENTY-ONE

Esperia had crossed winter's threshold, and even the stars were cold. But Chiara hardly shivered as she hurried down the silver-dusted path to the violet house across from her own.

Five months under Agata's tutelage, and her resolve to train with the fairies had only strengthened with every mission, every wish granted, every visit to Esperia. Until today.

Today, when she'd woken and looked outside her window, the sight of the kaleidoscope of fairy homes, the glimmering brooks, and the argent trees brought a pang to her heart. She missed seeing the sun crawling over her sill. She missed seeing Papa sweeping the old cobblestone road outside their home, missed hearing children screech that they were late to school, missed resting her eyes on the ever-blue Lyre Sea.

Before coming to the Wishing Star, she had never spent more than a day away from her family. Now she had spent the entire autumn without seeing them. Occasionally she would steal a glimpse at Pariva through the map over her well, but it could not show her parents, her brother, or her sister as anything other than specks of light. Every day, Ily's grew dimmer, and Chiara couldn't let go of Larissa's taunts:

Would you like to see how miserable you've made your dearest Ily?

Chiara's hands closed into fists at her side. Branches of wisteria swayed above the Violet Fairy's crystal door. Carved along the edges were canal boats drifting down a narrow river. Such hints of Agata's past were present throughout her home, and in the months Chiara had resided on the Wishing Star, she had just begun to notice them.

She thought of the wooden dove she kept in her bedroom, the sheet music she'd brought to remember Ilaria and the slice of almond-blackberry cake she asked for every morning to think of her mamma's baking. She wondered whether one day soon, she'd sprinkle traces of her own past into her home. Whether it'd make being away from her family harder – or easier.

Or whether she'd never come back to this place again, and it'd become only a distant memory.

Her hand trembled as she lifted it to knock on Agata's door.

One rap was all it took before the Violet Fairy appeared. She seemed to be expecting her.

"Well, good morning, Chiara. You're early for your lesson."

Chiara entered Agata's home quietly, taking her usual seat beside the window. Agata's home always smelt like the sea, with a hint of orange – and chocolate, if Chiara inhaled deeply enough.

"Something's on your mind," Agata observed. "I take it we should address it before discussing the itinerary for today."

Chiara gathered her courage. "I haven't seen my family since coming here," she confessed. "It's been five months as of yesterday, and today is my sister's birthday. She turns seventeen."

"You're right," said Agata, clucking her tongue. "It has been five months. You've acclimatised so well to our ways I half forgot you were an apprentice, Chiara. I suppose this means it is indeed time for you to go home."

Chiara gave a nervous nod.

"That isn't all, is it?" Agata sensed. "There's more."

Chiara pursed her lips, wondering how Agata had read her so easily. Then again, the woman was a fairy – skilled at reading one's heart and emotions.

"Do you wish to *stay* at home?" Agata asked gently.

"I don't know," she confessed. "I miss my family more than anything, and yet… I feel like I belong here."

Agata settled into the seat across from Chiara. She said, kindly, "It's natural for you to feel at war with yourself. I would be concerned if you didn't."

"I don't know how I'll be able to make a decision when the time comes."

"Then perhaps it's time I tell you everything," said Agata quietly. "What you'll have to give up before becoming a fairy."

It was a thought that had occupied her mind these last few days. "I have some idea." Chiara spoke as quietly as Agata. "Fairies don't age or die. You've served for centuries. Mirabella even longer than that." Chiara folded her hands over her lap. Every spare moment she had, she spent in the Archives, reading about the fairies before her. Her very first time there, she'd noticed the years and dates of Agata's reports.

"If I become a fairy permanently, my age will become suspended until I decide to give up my wand. My family will pass on, as will my friends and everyone I know. I'll never see them again."

"That is one way to put it," Agata replied. "But there is more. I want to be truthful with you about this, for it is not easy on the heart. Should you choose to stay with your family, you will forget your time here with us on the Wishing Star, and all will be as it was before."

"What if I choose to come back with you?"

"Then after your week at home, you will cast a spell upon everyone you know – so that they will forget *you*."

A hard lump rose to Chiara's throat, and she suddenly couldn't breathe. "I have to make everyone forget me? No. No! I couldn't do that."

"The choice is yours. No fairy is forced into their decision."

"Why didn't you tell me earlier?" Chiara said, feeling a stab of betrayal.

"Because you wouldn't have come with me," replied Agata. The words were the plain truth, but she flinched as she spoke them. "Am I wrong?"

Chiara's throat closed. "No."

A cup of coffee appeared in Agata's hands, and she dropped an extra scoop of sugar into it before sipping deeply. "I deserve your anger, Chiara. All of us do. We did not want to mislead you, but the truth of the matter is, the Heartless grow powerful, and there are not enough of us to reverse their wickedness. Magic is particular and does not speak to everyone. Yet it spoke to you – it led me to you long before you saved Geppetto. We need new fairies such as yourself…"

Agata pursed her lips. "But a fairy's love must be unconditional. You should not form attachments, even to your family – your love for them should be as great as your love for a stranger."

Chiara's voice shook. "Are you saying I can't see them?"

"You may observe them from your Wishing Well, but you aren't to help them. That will be another fairy's duty, should it be fitting."

"I see."

Agata touched her arm. "This is the hardest rule for us all, but it's also the most important. I don't expect you to stop mourning the loss of your life back home overnight, or even over a year. It takes time… a long time, and all of us have gone through it.

"It was difficult for me, too," confessed Agata. "My parents died when I was young – of a fever that swept my town. But I had an older brother I looked up to. He was my whole world."

"What happened?"

"As you can see, I became a fairy later in life," Agata replied, gesturing good-naturedly at the wrinkles along her eyes, "after my brother married and had children of his own. It was easier for me to leave. But you're still a young woman with many years ahead. Perhaps I've asked too much of you."

"It is much to ask of anyone," Chiara said honestly. Not long before, she'd been sure that she wanted to be a fairy. But now a war raged in her heart, and she did not know which side she wished to win.

"Coffee, Chiara?"

"No." A mug of hot chocolate appeared in Chiara's hands instead. Its warmth comforted her, and she took a long drink. Her eyes fell on the boats along Agata's door, the purple wisteria petals that gathered outside the fairy's home. "Do you miss your brother?"

"Every hour of every day," said Agata softly. Her coffee disappeared in a puff of stardust. "There won't be a lesson today. Take the morning off. Spend some time thinking about what I've said. After you finish your cocoa, I'll take you home."

CHAPTER TWENTY-TWO

Half past noon, Ilaria tossed on her coat and wrapped her new fur stole around her neck.

It was her seventeenth birthday, and she'd wasted enough of it huddled in the corner of Mrs Tappa's shop, rubbing her hands by the meagre fire waiting for customers while the lady napped upstairs in her bedroom. Winter had arrived, and snow dusted the road outside, and everyone was crowded around the market to buy last-minute groceries. No one, absolutely no one, was going to buy a hat today.

Ilaria plucked a red feather off one of the caps and wriggled it into her chignon. Then she buried her face in her fur. She'd left work early yesterday when Mrs Tappa was at the market and hired a wagon all the way to Nerio to buy it. An exorbitant purchase, but it was her birthday, and she deserved nice things. Nice things that would take her mind off the future that'd been stolen from her.

A bell chimed at the door. Mrs Tappa was back.

"Just where do you think you're going?" she demanded as Ilaria buttoned her coat.

"Out. It's my birthday."

"I don't care what day it is," Mrs Tappa said. "I've had quite enough of your insolence, Ilaria Belmagio. Day after day I let you come in late, let your friends loiter about my shop without buying anything. Don't think I didn't notice you leaving the store yesterday, unlocked and open for thieves to steal all my wares. And now you want to—"

"If you care so much about your shop," interrupted Ily, "maybe you should try tending it yourself."

"Why, you impertinent, ungrateful little wretch! Get back here. Don't you go to the door, or I'll—"

"Fire me?" Ilaria whirled. "I'm going to be famous, Mrs Tappa. So famous you'll be engraving my name by the door to tell everyone that I used to work here, because it's all people will remember you for."

The words spewed out of her lips before she could control them. Every word was a lie, but Mrs Tappa didn't know that. How good it felt to see the old woman's jaw fall agape!

"I'll take this as a gift," said Ilaria, plucking a velvet hat off the nearest mannequin. It was scarlet, matching the red feather in her hair. "It's the only one here that isn't hideous."

She didn't know where her audacity was coming from, but it felt wonderful. She felt free.

Ily sauntered out the door, ignoring Mrs Tappa's threats to tell her mother. What did Ily care? She hated working at the shop. The hats were overpriced and ugly, the ribbons were of shoddy quality and frayed after a week and she didn't need the money for tuition any more.

She hated Pariva, too.

Mrs Tappa was kind to you. A little voice poked into her head. *She gave you a salary for doing practically nothing. Is this how you repay her?*

Like I said, Ilaria told the voice stolidly. *She'll get to engrave my name on her door.*

Snow crunched under her shoes, and the sound quickly grated on her nerves. The past few weeks, she'd moped about town, trudging her way to the shop and watching the clock hands tick slow second after second. Simona and Beatrice had stopped visiting her at the shop – she'd been brusque to them upon returning from Vallan.

"So, what happened?" said Simona. "We heard Mr Tommaso's son went with you to Vallan. Gius—"

"Geppetto," said Ilaria.

"Geppetto," Simona repeated. "He's poor. And not particularly handsome or charming."

Ilaria pretended not to hear and twirled the ends of her hair. "The director of the conservatory practically dropped his baton once he heard me sing," she lied. "He's famous, you know. Conducts the Vallan Symphony as well as the opera orchestra."

"You actually got in?" Simona said.

"Did you ever have any doubt?" Ily scoffed. "Of course I did, and I'm counting down the days until I leave this backwater."

"When do you leave?" asked Beatrice, raising a sceptical eyebrow.

Ilaria lifted her chin. "First thing in the spring. I'm going to be a star, and I'll never come back to this paltry little town again."

"That's funny. Your eyes look puffy, Ily dear. And Pietro said he saw you crying when you came back with Geppetto."

"They were tears of joy."

They hadn't believed her. Ilaria couldn't stomach their pitying looks and I-told-you-so glances at each other. Worse yet was keeping up her lie at home. Ily knew Mamma was starting to grow suspicious and sensed she was keeping something from her. She could tell, too, from how nice Niccolo was being to her, and how Papa's morning kisses on her forehead felt like a sympathy stamp. As if they were waiting for her to tell the truth.

Deep down she wanted to, but her pride wouldn't let her. If she told them the truth, her dream would be gone forever. Better to cling to the illusion as long as she could, better to pretend to be *someone* than to go back to being no one, even if it was just for a little while. Someone more than a baker's daughter in Pariva, someone people admired and dreamt of meeting.

Better to pretend than face the truth and have to nurse the wound that Maria Linda's words had carved into her soul.

And so Ilaria pretended, and the grander her lies grew, the deeper she buried the sorrow in her heart. Until today, on her birthday, she woke remembering something very important. Something that made her stop feeling sorry for herself.

A wide grin spread across Ily's face, and the ache in her heart turned into a fierce burning. No one would ever have to know that she'd lied. Just let them wait. She might be unworthy now, but soon enough she'd return to Vallan and show everyone – *the world* – just what she was capable of. Maria Linda, Maestro Lully, Carlotta. All who doubted her would witness her soar.

"Shouldn't you still be at work?" her mother inquired as Ily entered the family bakery. "It isn't even two o'clock yet."

"Mrs Tappa let me out early for my birthday," lied Ily. "Are there cookies for me?"

"You're in luck. Papa just pulled them out of the oven. Careful, they're a bit hot."

Ily reached greedily for the sack and inhaled. Cinnamon, with a hint of dark chocolate. Her favourite.

"There's seventeen of them," said Mamma, counting one cookie for each year Ily had been alive. "Plus one extra for luck." She winked. "You might want to share them with your young man."

Ilaria rolled her eyes. "Geppetto isn't my young man."

Her mother shrugged. "If you say so." She swept aside Ily's dark fringe and pressed a kiss to her daughter's forehead. "Happy birthday, my love."

"Mamma," Ily protested at the show of affection. But for the first time in weeks, she didn't cringe or twist away. She took the drawstrings over the sack of cookies and tied a bow. "I suppose eighteen cookies *would* be too much for me to eat alone."

"Cookies taste better when they're eaten with friends," said Mrs Belmagio. "Especially good friends. You two aren't courting, are you?"

"Mamma!" Ily cried, but her cheeks heated. "I said we weren't."

"You've been seeing an awful lot of each other ever

since he took you to Vallan," said Mamma with another shrug.

That was because Geppetto was the only one who knew the truth. At first, she thought he would judge her for lying to her family, the entire town, even to herself – but he never said a word about it. Nor did his eyes, clear and blue as before, ever waver when they held her gaze. In these weeks, having Geppetto believe in her and stand by her meant more to her than she could have imagined.

He was her truest friend. And like Mamma said, maybe more.

"Thank you, Mamma. You're the best." She grabbed the bag of cookies, then, humming happily to herself, hurried for Mr Tommaso's workshop. She had a proposal for Geppetto that she knew he wouldn't be able to refuse.

Geppetto was sitting by the window, so intent on his work that he didn't even notice Ilaria at the door. A good thing. She took a moment to fluff her hair and rub colour into her cheeks. Then she paused before the other side of the window, craning her neck to see what he was working on.

To her surprise, it was a toy. Geppetto didn't usually work on toys in the middle of the day – what would his papa say?

She stood on her tiptoes to get a better look at the

figurine. It was still roughly hewn, the shapes of two people beginning to take form. Ilaria could make out the outline of a girl with her arm outstretched, and a nightingale – same as the one Geppetto had chiselled onto the music box he'd made for her – was perched on her fingers.

"Is that supposed to be me?" she greeted coyly.

Geppetto whirled, startled by Ilaria's appearance. He tossed a cloth over his workplace, trying in vain to hide the figurine. "Ilaria! I wasn't expecting you so early. What are you—"

"I left work," she interrupted, not wanting to explain herself for the second time. "Is your father here?"

"He stepped out for a walk. I was going to come find you after I finished—"

"I beat you to it." She flashed him her most winsome smile, then dropped the cookies on his worktable. "And I brought snacks. Cinnamon chocolate cookies. My favourite. Smell."

She raised the bag to Geppetto's nose, and he inhaled deeply.

He said, gently, "You shouldn't be the one bringing me cookies on your birthday."

"Who would I bring them to, then? Simona and Beatrice?" She snorted. "You're supposed to eat sweets on your birthday for a sweet year ahead – with your sweetest friend." She paused. "That's you, Geppetto."

Before he could respond, she broke a cookie in two and offered him the bigger piece. Geppetto took it, and they ate together, sitting side by side on a bench in comfortable silence. She'd kissed dozens of boys in her seventeen years, yet sharing a cookie with Geppetto felt like the most romantic thing she'd ever done.

"Thank you for coming with me to Vallan," she said quietly. "And… for keeping my secret. It's meant a lot to me these last few weeks. Chiara was right about you – and I'm glad we're friends."

It was his cue to kiss her, but as before, Geppetto was so oblivious that he didn't seize the opportunity.

"I am, too," he said, just as quietly. Over the last weeks, he'd grown less anxious in her presence, though he still fidgeted with his glasses when she was close. He did so now, then offered her his handkerchief. "To wipe your hands," he explained.

Ilaria laughed. "How considerate. But I'm having another cookie."

As she reached into the sack, Geppetto observed, "You're happy. You haven't been happy in weeks."

"That's because I realised something today." Ilaria

rose from the bench. "You were right, Geppetto. There *are* other big cities in Esperia aside from Vallan. Who needs the Madrigal Conservatory? If I studied with Maria Linda, I'd waste an entire year in school. Better I go out and make my own future. Chia will help me."

As soon as she said it, the many clocks on Geppetto's wall announced that it was one o'clock. Still no sign of her dear fairy sister.

But Chiara had promised to be back for her birthday, and she never broke a promise.

"Is she allowed to do that?" Geppetto asked belatedly.

"Why not? She's my sister." Trying to hide her dwindling confidence, Ily grinned. "She could help you, too." She plucked a violin off a rack on the wall. "Why repair instruments when you can *make* them? You could become the most famous violin maker in Esperia, Geppetto. A legend! Think of all the masterpieces you'll craft. Violins for the greatest virtuosos of our time, for kings and princes and dukes! Instruments that everyone in Esperia would clamour to buy. Everyone would know your name. Wouldn't that be marvellous?"

Geppetto picked up a cookie, but he didn't take a bite. "It would be something," he said at last.

"Your father wouldn't have to worry about this shop any more. You'd make plenty of money. Just imagine! After a few years, you could retire and carve all the toys you want."

Geppetto picked up his whittling knife and wiped it clean with his apron. "My heart isn't in music the way yours is, Ilaria. I love listening to it, being surrounded by it, but I..." He spread his arms at the walls of violins, violas, cellos and guitars. "This isn't my dream."

Ilaria frowned. "It'd only be for a few years." She remembered the figurine he had been carving. "What, you want to waste your youth making trinkets? Little toys that people admire from the window but don't come in to buy? Your father wouldn't approve."

"Our workshop has been in our family for generations," Geppetto deflected good-naturedly. "But I've thought long and hard about it, and even if Papa is upset with me, I can't lie to him any more. Or to myself."

His gentle gaze fell on her, and suddenly Ilaria stiffened. "Is this your way of lecturing me about my own lies?"

"No, I would never lecture you. It's not my place."

"Then?"

"I only wonder if you should tell your family the truth. Don't live a lie, and don't run away."

Ily's mood soured. Geppetto, too? She couldn't believe it. "I thought you of all people would understand," she said. "But you're just like the rest."

"Ilaria…"

"At least my dream is worth lying for," she said harshly. "Any peddler on the street can sell toys. Why do we need a shop dedicated to them? There's no future for a toy maker in Pariva."

Geppetto's face fell, and she knew she ought to take her words back. But she didn't.

Instead she stormed out of the workshop, ignoring Geppetto's shouts behind her.

"Ilaria! Ilaria!"

Her heart screamed at her to turn back, to reconcile with the young toy maker and make things right with him, but Ilaria shut it out. She hurried faster, sprinting back into town before Geppetto could follow.

She didn't look back once.

"There you are!" exclaimed Nico as Ilaria stalked through the town square. She was tired and out of breath from walking so fast, and she had nowhere she planned to go.

"Ily!" her brother said again, chasing after her. "You've got to come home, now."

"Leave me alone. I don't feel like talking to anyone."

"Not even Chia?" Nico grinned as Ilaria's eyes flew up from the ground. "Yes, she's back. She's home!"

CHAPTER TWENTY-THREE

It was fortunate that the cookies on Mrs Belmagio's tray had already cooled, for when she spied her eldest daughter enter the bakery, she dropped the entire batch on her feet.

The cookies crumbled on the ground, and Mrs Belmagio burst into tears. Her tears, of course, had nothing to do with the ruined cookies.

"Chia," she choked out. "My dearest dove. You're home."

Mrs Belmagio would have scooped her daughter up into her arms if she could, but Chia was a grown woman. So mother and daughter embraced, and for once Mrs Belmagio didn't care that her hands smelt of dough or that there was chocolate all over her apron.

"I missed you," whispered Chia into her mamma's hair. "I missed you so, so much."

Mrs Belmagio lifted Chia by the shoulders to have a look at her. "You've got thinner," she said, pinching her cheeks. "No good bread in fairy-land?"

"Not like yours."

"You've come to the right place, then." Mamma hugged her again, and Chiara took the deepest breath she had in months. Notes of cinnamon and almonds and oranges sharpened the air – the smells of winter at the Belmagio Bakery – but behind them was the absolute best smell in the world: that of Papa's freshly baked bread and Mamma's cookies.

Mamma only then noticed the fallen cookies. "My stars!" She clucked her tongue. "It's all right, those were extras. Niccolo!"

Niccolo poked his head from behind the kitchen doors. When he saw Chiara, he threw off his baking hat. "You're back!" he cried.

Mamma turned to the door, turning away the hungry customer who had appeared. "We're closed for the day," she said without explanation.

Papa pushed through the shutter doors from the kitchen. His long face revealed no surprise at the sight of Chia, standing in front of the cake counter as if she were an afternoon customer and not his daughter, but his eyes danced with the same merriment that touched his wife's.

"Back in time for the cookies, I see." He tugged at the

end of his moustache and wagged a finger at her. "Aren't you cold in that?"

Startled, Chiara looked down at what she was wearing. For the last five months, her uniform had been the same gauzy white dress with a silver cord at the waist. She hadn't changed come summer, autumn or winter. She hadn't even put on a scarf or mittens or a cloak.

Come to think of it, she hadn't felt cold in months. Hadn't felt goose bumps rise on her skin, or a shiver, except when she was near the Heartless.

"Here," said her father before she could answer. He plucked a cloak off the rack behind him and settled it over her shoulders. "Seems being with the fairies has made you forget how to take care of yourself. That's what parents are for."

Chiara hugged her father. As always, he smelt like basil and rosemary. "How's the herb garden?"

"Shrivelled up for the winter," he replied with gusto. "But it'll be back." He showed off his jars of dried basil, harvested from his garden. "This'll be enough for now!"

Chiara's stomach grumbled. She couldn't wait to eat. "Have you all had lunch yet? Is Ily working?"

"No." Mamma rapped Niccolo on the shoulder with a towel. "What are you standing there for?" she said. "Go fetch Ily. She's at Mr Tommaso's."

Chiara tilted her head. What was her sister doing at the luthier's workshop? "Is she seeing—"

"Geppetto," Niccolo finished for her slyly. "They've been spending every day together. Guess he's her last fling before she moves to Vallan."

Chia gasped. "She… she's moving? The conservatory accepted her? That's wonderful news."

"Isn't it?" Nico said. "Should I bring Geppetto, too?"

Mamma rapped him again. "Family only today. It's Chia's first day back."

As her brother left the bakery, her parents steered her home. "Walk faster, Chia," Mamma said over and over. "You'll catch cold in that dress. What were the fairies thinking, dressing you in a summer outfit like that?"

Once they turned onto Constanza Street, Chia's breath caught in her throat. There it was. Home.

Snow and frost rimed the yellow roof, and frost gathered at the eaves. But inside, nothing had changed. The cat-shaped rug by the door, its eyes scratched off by a puppy Niccolo had brought home when he was five. Stella, they had called her. She'd died three years ago, and Ily had cried so hard she'd come down with a fever.

There was a line of mugs she and her siblings had sculpted and painted; they hung on the wall above the grandfather clock that had been in their family for a century. The harpsichord in Chiara's beloved Blue Room hadn't moved. She didn't need to touch it to know that its keys were probably still in dire need of tuning.

Her whole life, Chiara had spent in this house, and she could have navigated every corner with her eyes closed. She still could, yet something… *something* about it all was different.

That something was her.

"Your sister will be thrilled to see you. And just in time for her birthday!" Her mother chattered nonstop, something she did when she was nervous. Until finally she looked at Chiara and asked, "Will you only be back a week?"

"Yes, Mamma," replied Chia.

"And then?"

Chiara bit her cheek. Of course her mother remembered what Agata had said. That after the week, she'd have to make up her mind whether she'd stay in Pariva or return to the Wishing Star for good. Of course, she didn't know that if Chia chose to go back, she'd have to make everyone forget her…

Stop thinking about that, Chiara rebuked herself. She wouldn't let anything put a damper on her precious time home.

Why? she couldn't help asking herself. *Because it could be my last? It doesn't have to be. I don't have to go back to the Wishing Star…*

Coming home had only magnified her doubts about becoming a fairy. Seeing Mamma, Papa and Niccolo, she was happier than she'd been in months. She wasn't homesick any more; she was home surrounded by the people who knew and loved her best. Already her months on the Wishing Star were a faded memory, and she was slipping back into her old life.

"Don't ask her that," said Mr Belmagio. "She's got seven days to figure it out."

"Seven days!" Mrs Belmagio was exclaiming. "That's hardly any time at all." She elbowed her husband. "Luckily we knew you'd make it home for Ily's birthday. We have some of your favourite dishes prepared."

"Mamma… it's Ily's birthday. Not mine."

"Ily isn't the one who's left home to become a fairy," tsked her mother. "Let me spoil you a bit, Chia. You never let me spoil you."

That was when Ilaria appeared. She wore a new coat, black and furred at the collar, and held a red velvet hat at her side. Her dark hair was pinned up at her nape, a red feather stabbed into the middle of the chignon.

Her sister looked different, but in a way only someone

who hadn't seen her in months would notice. Her cheekbones were sharper, her mouth was harder. And her eyes – her eyes that always glimmered with mischief and merrymaking – held a secret sorrow.

Thanks to her fairy's gift, Chiara could practically taste Ilaria's sadness. It was like tea left too long to steep, chocolate without any sugar, olives that hadn't been cured.

Ilaria put on a bright grin. "Knew you wouldn't dare break your promise," she said, a bounce to her step as she greeted her sister. "Aren't you going to wish me a happy birthday?"

"Happy birthday, Ily."

"What's the matter? You're staring. Has my nose grown a nest?"

Mamma laughed. "Go on, Ily. Help your sister into something warmer."

"Shouldn't we help with dinner?" asked Chia.

Nico snorted. "Only you would volunteer for chores during your first hour home. Relax, Chia. Papa and I will set the table."

With that, Ily tossed aside her coat and dragged Chia up to the attic. "See, your room's exactly the same. I took up some of your wardrobe space, though. You don't look like you'll miss it. Did you not bring anything back? What about a gift for me?"

Chia's breath hitched. "I didn't get a chance—"

"It's all right," Ily interrupted. "Birthdays are about more than gifts. I'm simply happy you're back. Now, what should you wear?"

While Ilaria rummaged through her clothes, Chia sat on her bed. "I heard about the conservatory. You must be so happy, Ily."

"Mmm-hmm," replied Ily, still flipping through Chia's dresses.

That wasn't quite the reaction Chia had expected. She changed the subject. "Is your coat new?"

"It's a present to myself."

It looked expensive, observed Chiara, and she held back a frown as her suspicions about Ilaria rose.

"This one!" Ily said, selecting Chiara's old favourite dress. It was pale blue like her eyes, with a matching blue bow at the waist and sleeves.

"Yes, that will be much better than that nightdress you're wearing."

"It's my apprentice's gown."

Ily wrinkled her nose. "You always sounded like you were a hundred years old, but now you dress like it, too."

Her fairy's gown *was* rather old-fashioned, with its long flowing skirt and straight sleeves. But Chiara hadn't minded it. Without complaint, she shrugged it off and put on the dress Ily had selected. The cotton was soft against her skin, and the soft stripes were a pattern she didn't see much of on the Wishing Star.

"Now," said Ily excitedly as she jumped onto Chiara's bed. "Tell me everything. What kind of magic can you do? Will you show me?"

"I can do magic when I'm on the Wishing Star. Otherwise, I need to borrow Agata's wand."

"You don't have your own?" Ily cocked her head. "What have you been doing these last five months?"

"Honing my sense of what is right and wrong – it's what the fairies call your conscience. And visiting people across Esperia who might need extra guidance."

Ilaria stifled a yawn. "What about wishes? Don't you have to listen to people's wishes?"

"It turns out that's only a small part of what fairies do." Chiara hesitated. "Mostly I look after people's hearts. I have a map I can access that shows me how someone's faring."

A flicker crossed Ilaria's features. She got up quickly and fiddled with a crinkle in the curtain. "Oh?"

"It showed me yours," Chiara said softly. "You've been… sad."

"Sad? Why on earth would I be that?" Ily picked up

a mirror on Chiara's desk and gazed at herself approvingly. "Everything is going just the way I want it to. I got into the Madrigal Conservatory, and—"

Chiara didn't need to hear any more. Ilaria's emotions told her all the truth she needed. "Don't lie to me, Ily. Please."

"I'm not."

"That coat you wore downstairs must have been over a hundred oros. Money you would have used for rent in Vallan, for food, for coal..."

Ily's expression hardened. "You *would* notice that."

"What really happened?"

Ilaria turned down Chia's hand mirror. "I didn't get in." She pursed her lips tight. "It's fine. It's not like I really *wanted* to go. Who wants to be a stupid opera singer anyway? You know what they say: fame is a poisoned chalice."

A lump formed in Chia's throat. That explained everything. Her sister had dreamt of going to the conservatory for years. "You don't believe that."

Ily's lips thinned. "Maybe not. But still."

"You mustn't give up – it's been your dream forever to sing."

"Why shouldn't I give up?"

Her sister was staring at her expectantly. For what,

Chiara couldn't possibly begin to guess. "Tell me what went on in Vallan."

"Maria Linda said I didn't have presence. Whatever that means." Ilaria laughed as if she didn't care. "This other girl, Carlotta, got the spot instead. You should've seen her – she had swan feathers sewn into her dress and pearls as big as grapes in her hair! It looked awfully gaudy, and don't get me started on her perfume. One whiff of her and I thought I'd lose my lunch. Guess that's the sort of girl they're looking for in Vallan."

So that explained the expensive coat, the feather in her hair, the dramatic antics. Ily was pretending everything was all right.

Chia reached for her sister's hand. "It's time to tell everyone the truth."

"Can't it wait until after my birthday?"

"Ily…"

"It's been a horrible day, Chia." Ily's lower lip trembled. "Mrs Tappa fired me from the shop, Simona and Beatrice have been cold and cruel, and I had a row with Geppetto…"

"What?"

Tears heated Ily's eyes. "If you hadn't come home, this would be the worst birthday ever. But you're back, Chia. And you'll make everything right again, won't you?"

Ily flew into her arms, catching her off guard.

Chiara held her sister and tipped her chin over Ily's head. "I'll do whatever I can, Ily."

Ily sniffled. "Really?"

"Yes. I'm your sister, and I love you."

Ilaria wiped her eyes with the back of her hand. A smile tugged at the corner of her lips.

"Did you really have a row with Geppetto?" Chia asked quietly.

"A small one," she admitted. "We've become friends since you left."

"Good friends?" Chiara teased.

"He's in love with me," said Ilaria. "He just hasn't been able to tell me so. I have to show you what he made me."

Ily towed her downstairs to her room, where Chiara noticed a beautiful wooden box on the vanity. It was unmistakably Geppetto's handiwork. The craftsmanship was on a different level from the simple figurines he had carved. The box itself was shaped into a heart, and on the top was a finely etched nightingale. She lifted the lid and gasped as it began to tinkle the Nightingale Aria. "Your favourite song, Ily!"

"Not any more," said Ilaria with a shrug. "He made it for me to bring luck for my audition, but obviously it didn't work."

Ily paused in front of the small hearth in her room,

lifted the brazier's lid, and tilted the music box towards the hungry flames within. "Now it just stirs up bad memories."

"Ily!" Chiara cried, grabbing her arm. "Don't. It's his gift to you."

"Seeing it brings me no joy."

"Then I'll keep it." Chiara took the music box before her sister threw it into the fire. She cupped her hands over the heart-shaped wood. Maybe it was best if she held on to it – for safekeeping – until her fickle sister made up with Geppetto.

"I don't know what you two fought over," Chiara continued, "but it's obvious he cares for you – and you for him."

"What are you, a fairy in training or a matchmaker?"

"Fairies bring out people's joys. Love happens to be one of the great ones." Chiara tucked the box into her pocket. "I'll keep this until you two make up."

Ilaria made a face. "What makes you think we will?"

"My special fairy sense."

Her sister snorted, but didn't resist when Chia enveloped her in a hug.

"I'm glad you're back," Ily finally said, her shoulders softening as the rest of her did, too. "It really feels like all my dreams have come true."

"That's my job," replied Chiara.

"So it is." Ilaria flashed a grin, and there was something so sly about it that even Chiara couldn't pinpoint what it meant.

She had no idea that she was playing straight into Ily's hands, and that was exactly what her sister was counting on her to say.

CHAPTER TWENTY-FOUR

Over the next seven days, Chiara became her old self again. A daughter, a sister, a neighbour and a friend. She went ice-skating with her family; even convinced her mother – who was scared of falling – to join. She and Niccolo held Mrs Belmagio's hands as she nervously toed across the frozen pond while Ilaria and Mr Belmagio chased the ducks. Then they spent hours playing cards and laughing over countless mugs of hot chocolate and slices of almond cake.

She checked in on the townspeople of Pariva. Many shyly asked if she could grant their wishes, but all she could promise was to listen. For most, that was enough.

She baked with her papa again, kneading dough with her fists as he chuckled at her side. "You've still got the muscle," he said approvingly.

"I won't lose it," she promised.

She played chamber music with Niccolo and his quartet and caught Ily stealing by the Blue Room to listen. *Join us,* she mouthed. But Ily shook her head.

One entire week home, and Ily hadn't sung once. Chiara couldn't remember the last time Ily hadn't sung, or at least hummed, everywhere she went.

But her sister had changed. Worse yet, she still hadn't told the truth about what happened in Vallan. The last time Chia prodded her, Ilaria's response had been cutting: "When are you telling us what *you've* decided? Are you leaving us for the Wishing Star, or are you going to stay?"

Distress leaked from Ily's tone, and Chia pursed her lips. "I don't know," she admitted.

"This could be our last week together, Chia. I won't ruin it by telling everyone I lied." Ily flipped her hair over her shoulder. "I'll tell the truth when you make up your mind."

What could Chia say to that? One minute, she was certain she would stay in Pariva with her family. But the next, when she looked up at the stars and remembered her time with the fairies, there came a twinge in her chest. The fairies needed her help against the Heartless. No matter how much she wanted to be with her family, if she forsook her duty to the fairies, thousands could be harmed.

Yet how could she hurt those who loved her most? Her mother, her father, her brother – and sister?

That's why they'll forget, she thought. *They won't hurt if they can't remember. Only I will.*

It was all she could think about, and on the morning of her seventh and perhaps last day at home, she tried to focus on her breakfast, but she couldn't. She stole a glance at Mamma, gripping her knife so tensely she scooped up half the jar of jam on her blade. Papa, who had taken off his spectacles and was pretending to stare at the newspaper. Niccolo, who was sipping nervously at his coffee as if it were grappa.

"Where's Ily?" she asked. "She's usually awake by now."

Her mother gave her a glazed look. *Stay with us,* her eyes read, even if her lips wouldn't speak the words. Chia couldn't see them without guilt prickling her conscience. "She's probably in her room… doing her hair. She's been doing that a lot lately. Why don't you bring her down to eat?"

Every step up the stairs reminded Chiara that she had only hours left to make her decision. When she reached the top, she took a deep breath.

Heavens, she hoped her sister wasn't in her room sobbing. If there was anyone who could convince her to stay, it was Ily.

Ilaria sat beside the window, watching snow fall outside as she brushed her hair. Dark and lustrous, her hair had grown long and nearly touched her waist.

"Ninety-eight, ninety-nine." Ily lifted her brush for one last stroke. "A hundred."

Chiara took that as her cue to step into her sister's room. "Are you coming to breakfast?" she asked softly. "Everyone's waiting for you downstairs."

Ilaria slid to the edge of her bed, but she didn't hop off. She sniffed the air. "Smells like yesterday's leftovers. I'll bet Mamma and Papa didn't want to bake on your last day here."

"I haven't said it's my last day," said Chia, quietly.

As if she hadn't heard, Ily prattled on, "Doesn't matter. I'm not in the mood for coffee or pastries. Sit with me, Chia. Let me brush your hair. A hundred strokes every day and night will keep it glossy and bright."

"I thought you gave up on that when you were seven. Said it took too much time and effort."

"Seventeen's a good time to pick up new habits. Stop moving so much. Sit still."

Obediently, Chiara sat and let Ily brush her hair.

"You have such pretty hair, Chia. I've always envied it, you know? The way it curls at your shoulders and every hair seems to be in place. Niccolo says it looks like noodles – like angel hair. What a silly name for pasta. I think fairy hair is more fitting."

A chill bristled against Chiara's nape. This wasn't the conversation she'd imagined having with Ily today. She twisted to face her sister. "What are you saying?"

"I'm saying…" Ily eyed the crack in the door and lowered her voice. "I'm saying, I've decided to let you become a fairy."

Chiara was certain that she had misheard. "Come again?"

"I know it's your dream to help people and to spread good across all corners of Esperia and all that nonsense," said Ily, wheeling her hands. "I mean, obviously it's not nonsense. But the point is I know it's what you've already decided, and I could kick up a fuss about it, but I'm going to be an adult. I'm seventeen now, after all."

"Thank you for your permission," said Chiara, still rather dazed. "You… you *want* me to go?"

"Mamma and Papa won't agree, but I think it's the best for Pariva. For the family, too. Everyone's been pestering us about you ever since you left. Think of what a disappointment it'd be for the town if you changed your mind about the fairies and stayed?"

Chiara couldn't sort through her emotions. She didn't know whether to be relieved that her sister was giving her blessing to become a fairy, or disappointed. Or flabbergasted.

"It would be nice if you gave me a farewell gift, though," Ilaria went on, twirling her hair the way she did when she was about to make a request that she knew had a high chance of getting rejected.

Chia was instantly on guard. "What sort of gift?"

"For weeks after my audition I was despondent. Yes, I lied – I told everyone that Maria Linda wanted me. That I was going to be her sole student in Esperia's most prestigious conservatory. I wished I hadn't lied. It was miserable, because I didn't know what I was going to do. But then I remembered – my sister is a fairy!" The morning sun hit Ilaria's green eyes, making them sparkle. "A fairy who promised to make all my dreams come true."

Chiara didn't like where this was going. "Ily, that's against the rules—"

"Make me a great opera singer." Ilaria leant forwards. "Make me as great as Maria Linda. Think of it: I'd be able to take care of Mamma and Papa, and Niccolo, too. Think of how many people would hear about our bakery, and how everyone's lives in Pariva would be changed. For the better."

"You aren't listening to me," said Chiara, as gently as she could. "Even if I wanted to help you, I can't. It's against the rules for me to help you. You're my sister."

"I *am* your sister," Ily repeated.

"I can't be seen bestowing favours to my family or my friends."

"I won't tell anyone."

Chia shook her head. "No, Ily."

Ilaria's face darkened. "You promised. I'm not asking much, Chia. All this time you lived in Pariva, you helped everyone you knew. Now help the person you love the most. The person who loves you the most."

The words stung, and Chiara flinched, but she wouldn't be swayed. "I can't."

"Music is all I have," persisted Ily. "The conservatory doesn't want me. There will always be someone better. Unless you help me. I'll waste away if I stay here my entire life."

"No, you won't." Chia touched her cheek. "You're strong, and you work harder than anyone I know. You'll make your way."

"I'll make my way?" Ilaria recoiled from her touch. She scoffed. "Mamma and Papa don't make enough money to send Niccolo to university. Did you know that? His heart isn't in becoming a baker, but he has to. You have the power to make our lives better, and you won't. I thought fairies were supposed to stand for goodness and compassion. You pretend to care—"

"I *do* care."

"Then do something for us. Help *me*. Music is all I have that's my own. I'll die without it, Chia. I'm happiest when I sing."

"Then sing," said Chia. "Why do you need fame to be happy? Why not spread your love for music by teaching the girls and boys in Pariva? They adore you, Ily. They always have, but you never pay them any heed."

"I don't want to be a teacher. I want to be heard."

"You want to be adored," said Chiara. "And you already are. You just can't see it yet."

"What would you have me do?" Ily said. Her tone turned cruel: "Marry Geppetto and help him paint toys?"

Chiara drew a breath. "What's got into you, Ily? This doesn't sound like you."

"Maybe this is who I'm destined to be. What did you expect, after living in your shadow for seventeen years? You've always been the perfect one. Not everyone's life is as charmed as yours."

"You think my life is charmed because I'm going to be a fairy?"

"Isn't it? It's always Chiara *this* and Chiara *that*, what a beautiful and brilliant and kind sister you have. It's such a shame she's gone. I guess there's Ilaria."

"No one says that."

"They do," insisted Ily. Her shoulders shook as she began to weep, and her heart was so full of anguish that Chia couldn't tell whether she was acting.

Chiara drew her close, and squeezed her sister's hand. Once again, she began to understand why the fairies made their loved ones forget them. To save them pain. Pain that she alone would bear.

"They'll forget me, Ily," said Chiara softly. "Everyone will."

Ily went still in her arms. "What are you talking about?"

Chiara swallowed, realising her mistake, but she wouldn't lie to her sister. "If I go back to the Wishing Star tonight, I'll cast a spell over the town. Everyone will forget me, even Mamma and Papa."

Her sister drew a sharp breath. "Do they know?"

"It'll be easier for them if they don't."

"You weren't going to tell us?" Ilaria pushed her away roughly. "You would abandon me, your whole family, the life you've had – everyone's always said you were the selfless one, Chia. But now I see. Eternal youth, magic, you can go anywhere you want, do anything you want. And you'll live forever. All you have to do is leave behind your little mortal family."

"Ily, it's not like that…"

Ilaria was in disbelief. "I thought you'd at least be able to visit. That I'd at least see you… but you'll be leaving for good. I won't even know you."

Chiara wrung her hands. There was nothing she could say without feeling awful. "It'll be easier that way. For both of us."

"Easier that way?" Ilaria's anger returned, and sunlight ignited her eyes, turning them gold. "Easier on your precious conscience, maybe. You won't have to fret about leaving us behind."

"That isn't it," Chiara pleaded. "Fairies love everyone unconditionally. We don't favour someone over another. Even if that someone is my sister."

"So you'll throw away your family. Eighteen years of memories." Ilaria wiped her eyes. She was crying. "How could you?"

Chiara faltered. She wanted to comfort her sister, but she didn't know how. She didn't even know how to defend herself – or the fairies. "It's for the good of—"

"The good," Ilaria rasped. "It's always about the good. Not everything is good or bad, Chia. Not everyone has a diamond heart like you, fit to discern who is deserving and who isn't."

Chiara flinched, trying to overlook the vehemence in her sister's voice. Ily was angry; she was hurt. And she deserved to be. Chia wouldn't deny that.

"You'll have a good life, Ily," said Chia gently. "Mamma, Papa, and Niccolo, too. The fairies promised me this. Even if I can't watch over you, others will."

Ilaria didn't give her a chance to explain further. There was a tremor in her sister's voice as she spoke again: "I hate you."

They were words Ilaria had said to Chiara hundreds of times when they were little girls. But this was the first time Chiara knew that Ily actually meant it.

"Go on, cast your spell. Make me forget now." Ilaria's voice was venom. "Do it. Better now than tonight. What difference will it make, anyway?"

Stricken, Chiara stepped back towards the window. "You have the right to be upset. I'm sorry, Ily."

"Go ahead and cast your spell." Ilaria seethed. "I hate you, and I wish I'd never had a sister."

"Ily…"

Ilaria turned her back to her.

Swallowing hard, Chiara reached into her pocket. "You can have this back," she said, setting Geppetto's music box on Ily's vanity. Though she hadn't wound the lever, the

Nightingale Aria tinkled, filling the silence between Ily's clomping footsteps. If once the song had melted Ilaria's heart, now it did the opposite.

Ily angrily snatched the box from Chiara and threw it across the room.

The box hit the wall, then landed on the rug with a thump.

"I said, leave!"

Chia bit the inside of her cheek so her own tears wouldn't fall. Then, with a silent apology to her sister, she exited the room.

Her mother was waiting for her at the bottom of the stairs. "Your mind is made up," said Mrs Belmagio astutely. "You're not staying."

Chia couldn't lie. "I'll leave tonight."

"I had a feeling. I think Ily did, too." Mamma tilted her head, the way her daughters did. "It'll be hard on her."

"I know."

"Don't feel guilty, Chia. It's your calling. I've always felt you had one that would take you far away, and on a grand adventure. I think I've known it since you were a little girl."

Chia's lower lip trembled. "I wish I didn't have to leave."

"I know, my dove." Mamma brushed her fingers against

Chia's cheek. "But no matter where the stars take you, I'll always be your mother. I'm content knowing that."

Tears of sorrow and relief welled in Chiara, and she wrapped her arms around her mother, hugging her. After her bitter fight with Ilaria, she couldn't begin to describe how much she needed to hear her mamma's words.

"Your sister will come to understand," Mrs Belmagio said, stroking Chia's hair. "Give her time. In the meantime, do as much good as you can. Our world can be an ugly place. But you, my Chia, you will make it brighter for every life you touch."

"I hope so," Chia whispered.

Chiara stood alone outside her home, leaning against the old lemon tree in her courtyard, and held her wooden dove close. "I can't do it," she whispered to it, as if it could listen. "Ilaria hates me, and I can't cast the spell on my family when we're… broken."

"Then speak to her," Agata replied from behind. "Reconcile with your sister, and cast the spell tomorrow."

Chiara practically jumped. She didn't think she'd ever get used to the fairies materialising out of thin air, even when she became one herself.

"Sorry if I startled you." Agata took Chia's arm

and guided her down the street. "But I sensed you were distraught."

"Why are we not allowed to grant the wishes of our loved ones?" Chia blurted, instead of greeting her mentor.

Agata let out a sigh. She held out her wand, and in a wave they had left Constanza Street and stood on the top of Pariva's bell tower. There, the Violet Fairy sat on the roof and finally answered Chia's question: "We were permitted to, once. But a few errant fairies took advantage of the privilege and made their families rich and powerful. Larissa and Amorale – they led a rift among the fairies and formed the Heartless.

"That is why we must uphold our rules. Should you break them, your wand will be taken away, and you will be cast out."

"Are there no exceptions?" asked Chiara.

"The fairies would never punish you for having compassion, Chiara. But there is a reason certain spells are forbidden, and that is to uphold a balance in magic, and to keep it from tipping into the Heartless's favour." Agata paused. "Spells that would benefit you personally, for instance – or those that you know and love. In Ilaria's case, you know that your sister's desires are not selfless."

"Yes, I know. But she's my sister, and I love her."

"As she loves you. She will forgive you in time."

"She won't remember me."

The Violet Fairy lowered her arm. "In her heart, she will. It may seem cruel, what we have to do, but it is the responsibility we bear."

"I know," whispered Chiara. She'd known from the beginning. "Thank you for explaining. Now I understand what I have to do."

"You are certain that this is what you wish?" said Agata. "There's still time for you to change your mind."

All it would take was a simple no, and Chia would return in time for lunch with her family, then spend the afternoon making music with Ilaria and playing checkers with Niccolo. Everything would be as it had been.

But deep down, she knew she couldn't ignore the tug on her heart. That if she didn't take this chance, she'd always feel like she'd let herself down.

"Yes, I'm sure."

Agata reached into her sleeve and drew out a slender wand. "Then this is for you."

Chiara gasped as her mentor passed her the wand, and a small star appeared at its tip. It should have warmed Chiara's heart to see it, but she could barely muster a smile.

"The reception of a fairy's wand is often a bittersweet occasion. Let that be a reminder for you that magic can bring great joy as well as sorrow, hope as well as fear. May you use yours to shine light upon darkness."

"I will," Chiara vowed.

As soon as the words left her lips, the star on her wand came aglow and a pair of iridescent wings bloomed from her back.

"What name will you take, Chiara Belmagio?"

The answer was one she had toyed with ever since she'd considered the fairies' invitation. "The Blue Fairy."

Blue was the colour that brought her joy. The colour of the walls of the music room where she and Ilaria had spent countless hours laughing and chasing each other and making music; the colour of her father's eyes, like hers; the colour of the sea where she and Niccolo took their little boat out when the weather was fair.

Her dress shimmered with stardust. The pale colour deepened into a warm and rich blue, and the fabric softened into gossamer silk. The threads stitched themselves into a gown worthy of a good fairy, turning her long sleeves into iridescent swaths of starlight. A beautiful yet understated uniform. Perfect for the new fairy.

Only the ribbon she wore in her hair was the same as before. A reminder of Chiara Belmagio, daughter of Pariva.

"Go on," encouraged Agata. "Cast your first spell."

Chiara hadn't thought of what that would be. She looked to the wooden dove on her palm and gently touched its head with the tip of her wand. "Awaken, little bird. Have life."

Once the words left her lips, the dove purred and its wings trembled at its sides. But the dove was still made of wood, not of feathers and flesh as Chiara had imagined.

Chiara's brows knit together in confusion.

"A beautiful spell, Chiara," said Agata slowly, "but the gift of life is not yours to give."

Chiara held the wooden dove close as she swallowed hard. "I didn't know. I'm sorry."

"I hadn't told you, so it is not your fault. You recall when Mirabella enchanted the stones in the Hallowed Forest to life?"

When Chiara nodded, Agata went on, "That was a temporary spell. You see, no fairy has the power alone to give life fully where there is none. It is a spell too great, and disrupts the natural balance of things."

The Violet Fairy tapped the end of her wand upon the dove, reversing the magic that Chiara had cast. The dove went still once more.

Heat pricked the edges of Chiara's eyes, but she managed a smile as her mentor returned the dove to her.

"Magic that manipulates life is forbidden, Chiara. If you were to attempt such, you would be stripped of your powers."

"I understand, Agata," whispered Chiara. "Thank you for the lesson."

Agata's expression softened. "I know you'll make a wonderful fairy, Chiara." She squeezed her shoulder. "It is hard, what we ask of you, but you'll see it's for the best. As for the forgetting spell, come back tomorrow, make up with your sister, and cast it before sunset."

"Before sunset – tomorrow?"

"The sooner you cast the spell, the better," said Agata. "It will hurt less." A pause. "For you and for your family."

Chiara gave a nod. "All right."

"Good." Agata's smile was bittersweet. "Now let us go back to the Wishing Star. Everyone is waiting to welcome our new Blue Fairy home."

CHAPTER TWENTY-FIVE

Ilaria waited until Mamma and Papa were asleep. Niccolo, too. The house was never quiet at night. Papa and Niccolo snored and whistled in their sleep, while Mamma occasionally mumbled the bakery's menu for the following day. Tonight, though, she let out a quiet sob. Hearing it made Ily falter, and she almost gave up on her plan. But no, she couldn't. Not even for Mamma.

She put on her coat and red velvet hat – and at the last minute, picked Geppetto's music box up from the floor. With a rueful sigh, she thumbed the dent she'd made on the edge and wheeled the crank round and round, but the song came out fractured, the rhythm off-kilter and more than a few notes off pitch.

It was broken, like her. And she didn't know how to fix it.

I don't need to be fixed, she thought as she stuffed it into her pocket. As quietly as she could, she crept downstairs.

Lifting one of Papa's bread bags, she threw in a handful of matches and candles, a loaf of bread and a jar of honey and the money her father kept behind the atlas he displayed on the wall above their dining table. It'd be enough to get her to southern Esperia, or maybe even out of the country altogether. She had no idea where she was going, only that she had to leave tonight.

Before Chiara returned to tamper with her memories.

Once she stole out of the house, she hurried down Constanza Street for the other side of Pariva. It was a cold night, and the air bit at her nose and fingers. She thought about going back to get her gloves, but she didn't dare risk it. Within minutes, her fingers were stiff with cold and her teeth chattered. Still, Ilaria didn't turn back.

She snatched a lantern off a neighbour's fence, not knowing whether she'd ever return it, and held it close for warmth.

She paused, trying to think. At this hour, there'd be no carriage she could hire, and she didn't dare sail a boat on her own. Where would she go?

Geppetto's, she thought, her feet changing direction for the luthier's workshop.

The hour was late, and as she cut through the town square, fear rattled her heart.

Mamma always said that Pariva wasn't safe after dark. Their little village was situated between Elph and Nerio, two important port towns, and many travellers came through Pariva on their way. Most visitors were genial and warm, but every now and then, the town would get an unpleasant character or two – especially at the Red Lobster Inn.

"Only hooligans frequent that tavern," Mamma said once. "Thieves, drunkards, liars and conmen."

"I've seen Niccolo there once or twice," Ily had replied tartly. "Papa, too."

The glare Mamma shot her was withering.

"Mamma was exaggerating," Ily muttered to herself now. Yes, she'd heard about a few brawls breaking out in front of the tavern, but she wasn't about to avoid taking the fastest route across Pariva simply because she was afraid of a few drunk fishermen.

The guttering streetlamps did little to quell her fear, and Ily walked as fast as she could. She was a street away from Geppetto's corner when she realised that her footsteps had an echo.

She was being followed.

A rush of fear washed down her spine, and as she picked up her pace to turn the corner, a carriage wheeled in front of her, almost ramming her in the side. Startled by the horses, Ilaria stumbled and fell off the pavement into a bush.

"Guess I was wrong about the lack of carriages at this hour," she muttered to herself.

Then came the sounds of someone leaping out, and a shadow darkened the already dim street. A man leant over her. His smirk was shaped like the sickle moon, but the rest of his face was cloaked in darkness.

"What's a pretty minx like you doing in this part of town?" he said, making a low whistle. "Isn't it past your bedtime?"

"Get away from me," Ilaria muttered.

"No need to be rude," said the man, advancing with one long stride. "What have you got in that bag there?"

He reached down to grab her, but Ilaria was faster. With all her might, she slammed her heel into his knee and sprang up, running. But a second man grabbed her from behind – the one who must have been following her. A hand went over her mouth.

"That wasn't very nice," said the man with the smirk as his partner brought Ily around. "Hey, I've seen this lass before. She's that girl who knocked me on the head!"

Moonlight fell upon the man with the smirk, and Ily recognised him now. The grey hair, the uneven beard, the faint markings of an old bruise on the side of his head.

Alarm spiked Ilaria's pulse. "Help!" she shouted. "Help!"

She swung her elbow back, feeling her bone hit against a jaw. The arms around her waist slackened, and she started to wrest herself free – until a knife slashed into view.

Ilaria went rabbit still. Her anger dissolved immediately into fear as the man with the grey beard pointed the knife at her throat.

"Well, now I'm angry," he said with a growl. "Stupid donkey. Bray all you want – that's going to be the last sound you ever make. I'm going to pay you back."

His friend held her by the arms, twisting them behind her back until she yelped with pain. A blow came to her head, knocking her senseless. The world went black, then the guttering streetlamps appeared again. Another hit was coming. Ilaria had to fight! Her legs were still free, and she kicked and kicked, but it was no use.

Her vision went blurry with the effort, and darkness started to close in.

Then suddenly the knife dropped from the man's grasp as his hands went to his throat. His partner, too, was choking on what seemed to be nothing. Within seconds, they were on their knees.

A woman loomed over Ily. Her green gown was far too thin for the wintry night, but she didn't look cold at all. Tiny emeralds glittered on her skin in place of freckles, and vines and leaves that couldn't possibly thrive in this weather were entwined into her long black hair.

She extended a hand to help Ilaria up. "That was no way to treat a rising star such as yourself, Ilaria Belmagio.

"Tell me, wouldn't you like to punish these ruffians?"

CHAPTER TWENTY-SIX

Ilaria caught her breath. Her coat was ripped; her skirts, too, and there was snow and mud all over her boots and hair. But somehow, she was calm. She turned to the two men quavering in the snow, their hands still scrabbling at their throats as air left their lungs.

"Yes," she said shakily. "They deserve to be punished."

"Do you like animals?" A magnificent ebony wand appeared in the woman's hand, spiralling almost to the ground. At the top was a dark and gleaming emerald. "I think they'd make a nice pair of billy goats. Or rats, perhaps."

Ilaria gawked in astonishment. Magic emanated from the woman's wand in streams of smoke and shadow. Could she be a fairy? She didn't seem anything like Chiara's old and frumpy mentor.

"What do you say, Ilaria?"

Ily eyed the men who'd nearly killed her. A stupid donkey, they'd called her. "Turn them into donkeys."

"Interesting choice." A dark eyebrow lifted in amusement. "As you wish." A tap of the fairy's wand, and the men began to change. First went their hands and feet, which became hooves that thumped against the ground as they screamed and flailed. Fur bristled over their skin, and tails sprouted from their backs as their trousers ripped and their shirts stretched until the buttons popped and the fabric shredded onto the ground.

They brayed and brayed, pleading and whining. Ilaria staggered back, horrified.

"You look dismayed," observed the fairy in green. "Should I change them back?"

A part of Ily pitied the men's fate, and then she saw the cuts on her hands, remembered the overwhelming wave of fear as they'd hit her. "No."

"I thought not." The fairy's wand flashed into a whip. Raising it high, she lashed at the donkeys' backs until they bolted away. "Get!" she shouted. "Get!"

Once the donkeys were gone, Ilaria whirled back in the direction she had come – for Geppetto's workshop. She was no fool. The fairy who'd helped her was even more dangerous than the two brutes who'd attacked her.

"Rather ungrateful, aren't we? No thank you for the help?"

"I'd sooner thank a devil," retorted Ilaria.

"That can be arranged." The woman smiled wickedly. "Aren't you forgetting something?"

The fairy held out her music box.

Impossible! The box was in Ilaria's pocket. Except…

Cursing to herself, she turned and seized her music box back, wiping off the snow with her sleeve. When her fingers fell upon the dent in the heart-shaped box and the scratches on the nightingale, she swallowed. She wanted to hug it close, make it good as new.

Why did that make her heart hurt? She didn't care about him or about the stupid song in the stupid box. They were all reminders of her terrible life in Pariva, anyway. She wanted to lift the box and hurl it into the snow, but she couldn't.

"Something the matter, my star?"

"I'm not your star," spat Ilaria.

"You wish to be a great diva," said the fairy, taking Ily's arm. Her nails were sharp, and Ilaria recoiled from her touch. "I can help you."

"Everyone says that. Everyone's lying."

"Your *sister* lied," the fairy in green corrected. "Very unbecoming of her. But also unsurprising."

The fire in Ilaria's lantern went out, leaving her cold. Within seconds, she could hardly feel her nose. Meanwhile, the fairy at her side seemed as comfortable as ever, even in her gown with no sleeves and a scandalously low neckline.

"Cold is a human weakness," said the stranger, noting Ilaria's bewilderment with a smile. "Not a fairy's."

"A fairy?" Ilaria repeated, alarmed. "*You're* not a fairy."

"I am," she confirmed, glancing back at the smoky wings that flickered behind her. "But not like any you've known. My name is Larissa the Green."

Larissa's voice multiplied, becoming a chorus of itself, low and reverberant. "I am a mistress of the night."

With a wave of her wand, they were no longer in the streets of Pariva. They were on the shore, steps from the ocean. Ilaria felt the hairs on her nape prickle. The beach was empty, no one would hear her shouts. She staggered back, trying to twist towards the road, but her feet were rooted to their spot.

"I can't move!" she cried.

"Red suits you, my star." Larissa touched the blood on Ilaria's lip. "It's full of passion, just like you. You could be far more than a simple stage singer, should you wish it."

Little by little, Ilaria's fear disappeared, replaced by a cautious curiosity. "You're going to grant me a wish?"

"No, no, I'm not in the habit of wish granting. I think of it more as making a deal."

"What sort of deal?"

"You want to be a famous opera singer, don't you?"

"I did." Ilaria stared at her hands. "But it seems Fate isn't on my side."

"Fate has many faces," replied Larissa, drawing closer. "*I* can help you change yours."

Ilaria's eyes narrowed. She told herself to trust her instincts. "Go away. I know better than to make deals with someone like you."

"Who else can help you, Ilaria? You've been betrayed by the person you loved most, and abandoned by her, too. You are meant for more, Ilaria. Your sister couldn't understand that."

"What does this have to do with Chiara?"

"Do you want the truth?" said Larissa. "She's worried that you'll outshine her."

Ilaria snorted. "Chia doesn't even know what envy is. She's only following rules."

"Rules that *you* would have broken for her, had you been in her place. Wouldn't you?"

Ilaria's laugh died in her throat, and soured into resentment. "I would have."

"That's because you love your sister. If she loved you,

wouldn't she want you to be happy? Wouldn't she have lent just a crumb of her great power to help you, the dear sister she loves most?"

Ilaria's lower lip began to tremble. She knew the words were poison, triggering the simmering anger in her chest, yet she couldn't help nodding. It was true, all of it.

"It isn't even as if you would have needed much," continued Larissa, stepping closer to Ilaria. "You have the talent and the beauty, the drive and the charisma. All you needed was a bit of luck and it would be you studying under Maria Linda's tutelage, not that overdressed peacock Carlotta."

Ily couldn't disagree.

"I can give you the power to make all your dreams come true," Larissa purred.

"You don't look like a fairy."

"I'm in a different circle than your sister. One that actually cares. I know you want to be the greatest singer in the world. You want to step into a room and have it go silent with awe, to have people fawn over you, to be famous and loved – even more so than Maria Linda."

Shivers tingled down Ilaria's nape. It was all true. She yearned for her music to have the approval and attention of everyone who heard her. But Larissa's offer was too good to be true, and she knew it. "In exchange for what?"

A smile, and those flat eyes lit afire. "Your heart."

"What!" Ilaria staggered back in shock. "Never."

She tried again to turn away, but it was in vain. Her feet wouldn't move. "Chiara!" she cried. "Chia, help me!"

"Your sister is preoccupied on the Wishing Star with her fairy induction," said Larissa, tittering as if the event were a pathetic joke. Her smile widened. "But I'm here. You've impressed me, Ilaria Belmagio. It appears my offer is not enough. So I shall make it sweeter."

"There's nothing you can give me that would change my mind. I'll never give you my heart."

"Then don't," said Larissa. "Keep it yourself. In a box."

Now Larissa had her attention. "A box?"

"You saw what I did to those men. I turned them into donkeys. Not once did you beg for their lives."

Ilaria shrugged. "Because they're criminals."

She regretted it as soon as she said it, for her answer pleased Larissa greatly. "You have taken the first step to your destiny, my star. How would you like a taste of such power? Not just fame and glory, but *magic* as well – magic that will rival your sister's in every element imaginable."

"I'm not evil."

"Is it evil to take what you deserve?" Larissa said. "Some would call it wisdom, strength. Your heart gets in the way. It is a weakness."

Ilaria's hand went to her chest. It was true, there was a pain in her heart she couldn't shake. Was that the weakness Larissa spoke of?

"It won't hurt, I promise," said Larissa. "You won't even miss it."

"No," Ilaria said, still unable to move. "Let me be."

"All right, if that's what you want. In a few days, you won't remember who I am, anyway. Fairies will merely be a bedtime story. Your sister, too."

They were just the words Ilaria didn't want to hear. She pinched her eyes shut. "Go away," she said, but her mettle had withered, and her words were a mere whisper.

Ilaria found she was able to move her feet again. Her mind in a fog, she started back onto the road, but Larissa followed her, a tendril of green mist grazing her ear: "Do you know why fairies make their loved ones forget them? Why your sister is not allowed to grant your wishes?"

Keep going, Ilaria's conscience pleaded. *Don't listen.*

But temptation preyed on Ilaria's resolve. She slowed, and twisted back to Larissa ever so slightly. "Why?"

"Because of me." Larissa advanced towards her. "Long ago I was one of them. Young and innocent, not so different from your sister. I had a mother whom I loved, and even after I became a fairy, I visited her often. But about a year after I earned my wings, a gang of bandits ravaged my hometown and burned my mother's house and farm. She lost everything and became ill with grief, but she had no money – not for medicine or food. I asked the leader of the fairies, *Mirabella*" – Larissa uttered the name as if it were poison – "to help."

"She refused you," murmured Ilaria.

"Fairies are not as compassionate as they pretend. Mirabella was vexed that my time with my mother was distracting me from my duties. She forbade me from helping her."

"What happened?"

"That winter was harsh, and her illness grew worse. I had no choice, so I used my magic to bring her silver and gold and whisked her to a warm place where she could heal from her fever. Because of that, I was cast out from the fairies. They broke my wand." She held it forwards so Ilaria could see that wedged into the black wood were two broken pieces of a fairy's silver wand.

"So who is crueller, them or us?"

That answer, Ilaria found, was not so easy.

"I won't give you another chance to consider my offer, Ilaria. Refuse, and you will go back to your pathetic life in that pathetic little town. Over time, your youth and beauty will fade; your voice, too. Maybe you'll marry that toy maker in the village, pop out half a dozen brats."

Geppetto's music box reappeared in Larissa's hand. Ilaria lunged for it, but Larissa held it out of reach. "Stay here and you'll wither. You'll always wonder if you could have done more." A deliberate pause. "Been more."

Without warning, Larissa touched her wand to Ilaria's forehead, and suddenly, she saw the future she'd craved. A future where her mother gushed to her friends about Ilaria's successes as the finest singer in Esperia, where her parents lived in the grandest house on Vallan's richest streets, where Geppetto awaited her in the wings of the theatre every night with dozens of roses. He was dressed finely – like a prince.

"The prima donna of Esperia," shouted her adoring fans. "And her husband, the most famous toy maker in Vallan."

All too soon, that future vanished into mist.

All of Ilaria's defences crumbled. She drew back her hand, resting it over her heart once more. How it ached, still trying to piece itself together after her fight with Chiara.

"Your sister will do wonders for the world at the cost of neglecting her family," Larissa said. "But you, Ilaria. You can uplift your whole town. Reward everyone who's been good to you, and punish those who didn't think you were worthy."

"In exchange for my heart," Ilaria whispered.

"You won't miss it." The emerald on Larissa's wand glinted, emitting a cloud of mist. Within, Ilaria's most painful memories resurfaced. Maria Linda telling her she wasn't good enough to enter the Madrigal Conservatory, Geppetto chiding her for lying to her family, Chiara abandoning her to become a fairy… the hurt Ilaria had tried to bury from each of those moments rose to her heart, sharper and keener than ever before.

"Your heart will only hurt you," said Larissa. "You see?"

Pain stabbed Ilaria's heart, cutting off her breath and knocking the wind from her lungs. "Stop," she pleaded, but the pain mounted until she couldn't breathe.

"If I stop, you'll die, Ilaria. The pain of a broken heart will kill you. Do you want that? Do you want to die?"

Ily squeezed her eyes shut, refusing to answer.

"Life is short, Ilaria," pressed the Green Fairy. "Even if your dreams come true, you'll enjoy them only for a few short years at most. Come with me, and you'll live as fairies do. You'll not age, and you'll not die. You'll be young and beautiful. Forever."

"Forever?" whispered Ilaria. She was delirious; the pain was too much.

"Yes," Larissa purred. "All I need is your heart. Shall I take it?"

"Yes," she rasped, before she could regret the words. "Take it."

Green mist snaked around Ilaria's body, taking the

shape of claws that looped about her shoulders and neck. Ily screamed as the claws tightened over her neck. She couldn't breathe, couldn't move. Couldn't change her mind even if she'd wanted to.

The claws pierced into her chest, and Ilaria's world splintered. Darkness turned into light, and light into dark. Magic tore her apart, shattered her with its fist, then put her back together again… but changed. In a flash of light, it was done – and Larissa ushered Ilaria's heart into the wooden music box, shutting it tight with a cackle.

"How do you feel?" asked Larissa.

Empty was the only word Ilaria could think of. Hollow. No pulse throbbed inside her chest, no beat drummed in her ears as she breathed. But that wasn't all. The world – all the voices, the memories, the regrets and hopes and fears she had held tight in her heart – faded away into a misty haze.

All was gloriously quiet.

"I feel… free," replied Ilaria, staring at her hands. Her nails were varnished a dark crimson, the tips so sharp they drew blood when she pressed against her arm. But her skin healed immediately. "I'm… I'm…"

"You have taken the first step to becoming a Heartless," said Larissa. "Welcome, Ilaria."

Larissa passed her back the music box. It was heavier

than it had been before, and Ilaria cringed at the faint beam of light trapped within the seams of the lid.

"What am I to do with this?"

"Destroy it," said Larissa. "That will be your oath to the Heartless, and you will be one of us forever."

Destroy it? Ilaria drew a sharp breath as she looked down at the box in her hands. From the cracks in the wood, it glowed against the black night, radiant with the heart she had just lost.

"Here," said Larissa, passing Ilaria a black wand that twinned her own, except it had a sparkling scarlet ruby instead of an emerald at its head. "This will help."

Ilaria gripped the wand tight, and a wave of icy seawater swept up to her ankles. It should have been freezing, but she felt nothing. A realisation that almost made her drop her wand.

"Nervous, are we?" Larissa laughed. "Or are you having second thoughts?"

Ilaria gulped. "No. No second thoughts."

"Good. I would hate for you to lose everything that I've so generously offered," said Larissa. "But I know it isn't easy."

The Green Fairy tilted her head, considering. "How about this? Your sister is casting her forgetting spell tomorrow at sunset. Why don't you settle your business with your friends and family before then?"

"What do you mean?"

"Offer your parents the riches they deserve," said Larissa, encouraging Ily with her wand. "Whatever you can think of, you imagine it and point."

Ilaria looked at her wand in awe.

"Yes," encouraged Larissa. "Gather your friends and family to your side – and not Chiara's – then destroy your heart before your sister casts her spell. Your place will be waiting for you among us once it's done."

Ilaria held her box closer to her heart, suppressing a shiver.

"I'll do it," she said quietly.

"Marvellous," Larissa said. She patted Ily's shoulder. "You'll feel so much better once it's gone, my star. Hearts are the worst kind of pest, after all. They're no good until they're dead."

CHAPTER TWENTY-SEVEN

"You fixed the bridge on the Vaci girl's viola?"

Geppetto nervously pushed his spectacles closer to his eyes, hoping his father wouldn't see how his brow twitched. "Yes, Papa."

"The broken neck on Mr Gusto's guitar?"

"Yes, Papa. The loose braces, too. You can take a look if you'd like."

With a harrumph, Tommaso set his candle on the worktable and leant over the instruments. Though his old hands could no longer work with the precision required to perform his craft, his eyes were sharp – even in the shadows and gloam. They scrutinised his son's work; no crack or blemish, no excessive space between strings – no matter how tiny, no slanted fret or even bridge would get past. Geppetto knew that. Which was why, when Tommaso exhaled through his nose with a satisfied grunt, Geppetto nearly collapsed with relief.

"All your years of apprenticeship are finally coming to fruition," said Tommaso with a rare approving nod.

Geppetto's father untied the apron around his waist and hung it on the rack against the wall. His voice turned soft, and he took a tone Geppetto hadn't heard since his mother had been alive. "I know I've worked you hard these last few years, Geppetto, and I know I've been stern. But I had no choice."

"I know, Papa."

As Geppetto began putting away his tools, his father picked up an inspection mirror and a set of clamps. Anyone could see in the older man's misting eyes that he missed his craft.

"I thought these hands would have many more years of work," Tommaso said, uncurling his fingers. "Unfortunately, Fate has had other ideas, and since I cannot repair a violin with my toes, it falls to my son to learn." Tommaso took a cloth and dabbed at a drop of varnish on the worktable. "One day soon, this workshop will be yours."

"Papa..." Geppetto was at a loss for words. More than anything, he wanted to tell his father about his true dream. That he did not wish to become a luthier, but a toy maker.

And yet, to finally see the approval in his father's eyes… he could not ruin this moment.

He hung his head. "Thank you, Papa."

With a nod, Tommaso took his candle. "Don't work too late."

He ascended the stairs to his bed, leaving Geppetto alone in the workroom.

Once the young man heard his father snoring, he put aside the shop's work. These were the precious hours when he could chase his own dream and hone the craft he truly loved. A new toy or clock that would make a child's heart sing. Or a present for the woman he secretly loved.

Had it been a mistake for him to carve that music box for Ilaria? He'd hoped the gift might bring her luck at her audition, but it seemed it had only made her unhappy. Ever since their trip to Vallan, she no longer sang, and she rarely smiled. The last thing she would want to hear was the Nightingale Aria tinkling from the little box he'd made her. It would only stir up unpleasant memories.

That afternoon, Chiara had visited him in his workshop. She'd come earlier in the week, too, with Ily. The two had filled his workshop with their laughter and teasing, making the afternoon a cherished memory. But on her last day in Pariva, she had come alone. To say goodbye.

She'd decided to leave with the fairies. It wasn't a surprise to him, but the sadness in her eyes was unmistakable. He wasn't one to prod, but when he'd tried to ask if something was wrong, Chiara only replied that everything was as it should be – and that she would leave that night.

She'd asked him, then, for a favour:

"My sister is fond of you. She trusts you. And you… you love her, don't you?"

Geppetto's heart nearly stopped. He took his glasses and set them on the table beside him. "Yes," he said softly. "Yes, I do."

"I know you two will be good to each other," said Chiara. "Watch over her while I'm away. Help her stay true to herself. It won't be easy, but you can do it."

Geppetto swallowed hard. "I see. I would only wish for Ilaria to be happy."

"Thank you, my friend. Remember, Geppetto, stay true to your *dreams, too. Bring joy to those around you."*

"I will," he promised.

Then she was gone.

Geppetto couldn't get the conversation out of his head. If Chiara hadn't succeeded in cheering Ilaria up, what chance did he have?

"I still have to try," he told himself. And so he had spent the night modelling his new project. At the moment, it was a simple carving, the shape of two young sisters side by side. One would be holding a sheet of music and a fan, and her arms would open when the music played. The other sister would be at the harpsichord – which would be a music box. It was an ambitious undertaking, one that would likely take a month to put together, then another week to paint. Maybe more, if things got busy at the shop. But Geppetto prayed it would make Ilaria smile again – and remember her sister.

He became so absorbed in his work that the night grew late, and the candle on his desk burnt to a tiny stub with at most a few minutes remaining. The fire in the hearth had long since gone out, and his fingers were stiff with cold. He rubbed at his eyes, feeling fatigue set upon him, but still he kept on working.

"Geppetto," whispered a voice in his head.

It sounded so close to his ear that he jerked up. But there was no one.

"I must be dreaming," he muttered to himself. He returned to his work.

Then one of the windows flew open, and the wind blew out his candle entirely.

As Geppetto rose to fetch a new one, there came the voice again, louder and clearer:

"Geppetto?"

He whirled, recognising it instantly. "Ilaria!"

She stood at the door, cloaked in the shadows falling

from the oak trees outside. It was so dark he couldn't even make out the whites of her eyes.

"It's… it's late," Geppetto stammered. He found a new candle and tried to light it, but his match wouldn't strike. "What are you doing here at this hour?"

"I'm leaving town." She dared a step forwards. "Come with me, Geppetto. We can have the future we dreamt of – together. Come with me. I won't ask again."

Geppetto set down the match. Ilaria sounded different. Her voice, usually rich with warmth and colour, was flat. Cold, even. "Leaving town? What's the matter?"

Light appeared, but Geppetto couldn't make out its source. It was red and vibrant, casting streaks across Ilaria's dark hair.

Her eyes, too, were turning red. Geppetto staggered, a tingle of fear making him step back. "Ilaria, what's happened? Are you in trouble?"

Ilaria drew close, the feathers on her coat brushing against his arm. Her nearness usually made him heady with nervousness, but tonight, he could focus only on how different she appeared. Funny, he didn't remember her having a coat with feathers. She'd bought a new one recently, with black fur. It looked nothing like what she wore now.

"No, I'm not in trouble," said Ilaria with a laugh. "No one can ever trouble me again."

Her hand wrapped over his wrist. Her fingers were cold; her nails were long and painted with a dark crimson varnish. When she let go, he shivered, watching as she picked up the figurine he had been working on. "You want to make trinkets for children? So be it. I'll make you the most famous craftsman in Esperia. You'll be rich beyond your dreams."

"I told you," said Geppetto gently, "I don't do this for money. I don't want fame."

"Then what *do* you want?"

He reached for his jacket. "I want to walk you home, Ilaria. It's late. Your parents will be worried."

For an instant, the old Ilaria he'd known flickered back. He started to reach for her hand. But she twisted away and her expression turned hard. "Foolish Geppetto. Then you shall forget. You shall forget we were ever friends."

Geppetto blinked, but Ilaria had vanished. He blinked again. Once. Twice.

He could not remember why he had put on his coat and hat. Or why the door was open on such a cold night, letting in the wind.

In the corner of the night sky, a pale star flickered, and the frigid draft blew out his candle.

Curious; the door was closed.

He reached into his pockets, trying to find a hint of

what he'd been planning. But there was only a dried-up old yellow rose. He tossed it out the open door before closing it.

Then he sat at his worktable and frowned at the chunk of wood before him. It was a roughly hewn outline of two young women, one singing and one seated at the rough makings of a harpsichord.

For the life of him, he couldn't remember who they were supposed to be.

CHAPTER TWENTY-EIGHT

Who knew that even fairies could have trouble sleeping? Chiara tossed and turned in her bed, catching only scraps of slumber. She couldn't close her eyes without revisiting her last fight with Ilaria.

Go ahead and cast your spell, Ilaria had said. *I wish I'd never had a sister.*

She'd never forgive herself if those were the last words they exchanged as sisters.

It had been only a day since she took her fairy's vow, but she visited the Wishing Well in her garden, anxious to have a glimpse of her hometown. Surely Ily's anger had cooled by now.

"Show me Pariva," the Blue Fairy instructed the waters of the Wishing Well.

A tall wave rose, and her hometown appeared in the form of a map. Hundreds of bright lights dotted Pariva – each one representing a person's heart.

"I'd like to see Ilaria Belmagio," Chiara told the map. "Show me her heart."

The map of Pariva flickered, and in a rush, all the lights vanished.

Leaving none.

Chiara frowned. Red she had dreaded, even expected. But nothing?

She focused on the little house on Constanza Street with the yellow roof and door. "Show me Ilaria's heart," she repeated.

The map didn't budge. It couldn't lie, couldn't deceive.

Which could only mean Ilaria's light was gone.

"The last trace I can find of her heart is in the Lyre Sea," said the Orange Fairy. Peri was the Wishing Star's most experienced archivist, and during Chiara's apprenticeship, he had become a friend. He was a jovial fellow, always with a cheerful thing to say to everyone. Even when she'd woken him this morning with pleas to help her at the Archives, he'd risen without complaint.

But now, as he also couldn't find Ilaria's light, his expression turned grave. Not a good sign.

"In the Lyre Sea?" Chiara repeated. "When?"

Peri peered through his spectacles at the wall-wide and ceiling-tall map of Esperia. "Last night."

Chiara gripped the side of her chair. "What would her heart be doing in the middle of the sea?"

Peri glided his wand across the Lyre Sea, scanning the facsimile of its emerald-blue waters a second time. The Archives' map was a more expansive version of the one in her Wishing Well, and it glittered with magic, showing in synchronous motion the clouds that actually drifted across the world, the boats that currently sailed, even the waves rippling the sea.

"I don't know," Peri replied honestly. "It is peculiar."

Try as she might, Chiara could not smother the fear growing inside her. Where had her sister gone? Had she taken a boat into the sea, then got lost?

"What are those dark clouds?" She pointed on the map. "Is a storm coming?"

"Those are pockets of dark magic," replied Peri. "Not even our maps can penetrate what lies beneath them."

"There are so many."

Peri chuckled. "This is actually the fewest we've seen in decades. If you'd looked a year ago, half the sea would have been dark. Because of Monstro. Before he was put in his slumber."

Apprehension made her chest tight as she pointed at the dark clouds. "Do you think… do you think Ilaria could be there?"

"It's possible," said Peri. His expression turned even graver than it'd been before, and new lines creased his already furrowed brow. "There are usually two reasons that a heart goes missing. I'm sorry, Chiara… but either your sister's heart has been captured by the Heartless – or she's dead."

Dead.

No, Ilaria was alive. She would have known, would have felt… Chiara didn't know why the fairies couldn't locate her sister's heart, but there had to be a mistake.

In a rush, she flew off the Wishing Star, making for her parents' bakery. Maybe there would be answers there.

"Mother," she said, appearing before Mrs Belmagio in the middle of the kitchen.

Mamma started. "Goodness me!" she cried. "You startled me, Chia. I don't think I'll ever get used to you popping in and out like that."

Mrs Belmagio set down her dough scraper and covered the loaves she was about to bake with a clean cloth. "I didn't expect you back so soon. Let me look at you. How splendid your dress looks! And your wings… oh dear, why the long face, Chia?"

Chiara drew a deep breath. She wouldn't worry her mother until she was absolutely sure what had happened. For now, it wouldn't hurt to ask: "Have you seen Ilaria? I wanted to set things right with her."

"Ilaria!" Her mother chuckled and turned to kneading the rest of the dough. "I thought you fairies were all ears. Didn't you hear? Ily's gone to Vallan."

"To Vallan?" Chiara repeated. "When did she leave?"

"Yesterday evening." Mamma frowned. "Or was it the day before? I can't seem to remember."

Couldn't remember? Chiara's frown mirrored her mother's. Mamma had a memory sharper than a bread knife.

"You'll have to find her in the capital. But don't ask for Ilaria – she'll be using a new name. Cleo del Mar, or something silly like that."

"Are you sure?"

"Why wouldn't I be?" Mamma laughed. "A letter came by this morning. I still have it in my pocket. Here."

The letter smelt like cinnamon, and Chiara unfolded it hastily. "'I've arrived safely in Vallan'," she read aloud in disbelief. It *was* Ily's handwriting – she recognised the round loops and flourishes. "'Come visit soon – I'll send tickets for my first performance'." At the bottom, signed so large it took up half the page, was *Cleo del Mar.*

"This arrived in the morning by post?"

"Beatrice brought it herself. Her father's the postmaster, you recall."

Chiara did, but it just wasn't possible. The timing made no sense. She'd spoken to Ilaria only last night – she couldn't have packed and left for Vallan in a matter of hours.

Something was amiss. Something that made apprehension crawl across the pit of Chiara's stomach.

"I'll find her," said Chia.

"Take a cookie for your travels," called her mother. "Even fairies have to eat."

Chiara searched all day for her sister. As the sun began to sink beneath the horizon, she began to lose hope. She'd promised to cast her forgetting spell by sunset.

Her heart heavy with disappointment, she decided to try the last place she expected to find her sister: home.

The Belmagio house was empty when Chiara slipped inside. Niccolo was out with Sofia, and her parents were at the Vacis' playing cards.

"Ily?" she called, searching room by room.

Her sister wasn't in the Blue Room. Not in the kitchen, either.

There was a faint hiccup of light coming from upstairs. Chiara couldn't imagine Niccolo being careless enough to leave a candle burning, but she went upstairs to inspect it anyway.

The light was coming from Ily's room!

She went inside, holding her breath. Her sister's bed was made, the pillows neatly arranged in a row – and on top of the blanket was the music box Geppetto had made for her.

Chiara thumbed the nightingale etched on the top. It looked not too different from her own wooden dove, and she fished it out of her pocket, setting the figurine beside the box. They were made of the same wood by the same maker. Almost like sisters.

As she set her dove on her lap, a glint of light leaked out from the music box.

"What could that be?" she said aloud, picking up the box. Strange; it was warm. Alive, almost.

Her brows drawing together, Chiara opened it slowly, expecting to hear the tender melody Geppetto had scored in honour of her sister.

What she saw instead made her gasp.

"Oh, Ilaria, what have you done?" she whispered. "What have you done."

She shut the box, so distraught she didn't even notice her wooden dove fall off her lap as she stood.

"Ily," she said, summoning her magic with an urgent wave of her wand. "Ilaria Belmagio, show yourself."

The air had gone still, and not even the wind blew. Then she spied a scarlet mist, curling outside the window like a ribbon.

The mist slid into the bedroom and materialised into a familiar form.

Only it wasn't the sister Chiara had known and grown with all her life. This Ilaria was different. Her green eyes were wickedly vibrant, the pupils dull and flat with no reflection. She wore a long one-shouldered gown decorated with rubies and matching red feathers, and wrapped around her neck was a choker of black pearls.

"Why, if it isn't the esteemed Blue Fairy herself." Ilaria made a mock curtsy. "How might I serve you, Your Honourableness?"

Chiara was too distraught to pay attention to her sister's sarcasm. "No," she whispered. "Tell me you didn't…"

"What?" Ilaria finally noticed the music box and made a loud titter. "Oh, good, you found it. Did you scream when you saw my heart inside?"

The light in Chiara's wand flickered, mirroring the sudden skip in her chest. "Your heart?"

"Yes," murmured Ilaria. "You see, I've beaten you. I cast my own little spell."

"What spell?" Then it dawned on her. Ilaria, moving to Vallan. Taking on the name Cleo del Mar.

"No, Ily," breathed Chiara. "Please don't tell me you made a deal with the Heartless."

"You told me my dreams wouldn't come true. But I found a way." Ilaria laughed smugly. "All Pariva will remember me as the most famous prima donna in the land."

"It isn't real."

"Jealous, aren't we?" Ilaria clucked her tongue. "I wouldn't have expected that of you."

"I'm not jea—"

"You are. Our parents will always remember me, and think of me fondly. While they'll forget everything about you. Everyone always says I'm the selfish one. Chia could never be selfish, Mamma says. She's doing good for the world. We're all *so* proud of her." Ilaria rolled her eyes. "Did you know Mamma would cry herself to sleep at night? She thought Nico and I couldn't hear, but we did. Oh, I'm sure your little forgetting spell will make everything all better."

Chiara's voice was small. "Don't do this, Ily. I know there's good in you still—"

"Enough with the good and the bad," Ily said sharply.

"Not everything or everyone can be sorted into heroes and villains."

"By choosing to be a Heartless, you are going down a bad path."

Ilaria released a bitter laugh. "Would a villain offer Mamma and Papa riches… Niccolo power and Geppetto fame? I say no. I wanted the best for them, but they all turned me down. They'd rather cling to their poor little lives here than come with me. Well, it'll be their loss. I have a new family now."

"The Heartless aren't your family. Their magic comes from making people suffer."

"I know what they do." Ilaria smiled. "Like you taught me, there's a price for power. This is the one I chose to pay. It's about balance. Not 'chosen ones'."

"Then they've tricked you," Chiara said. "Take your heart back, Ily, before you do something you'll regret. Please. It's not too late. Don't leave Mamma and Papa and Nico. And Geppetto. They love you so much."

She reached out and touched her sister's arm. She felt Ilaria stiffen suddenly, then look up as if a spell had been broken. The rancour in Ily's eyes vanished, and her shoulders drooped. Her lower lip trembled, and she hung her head low with remorse. "You're right. I can't do this. What was I thinking?"

Chiara let out a silent exhale. Thank the stars she'd

found Ily in time. A glance out the window, and she saw she had only minutes until sunset.

"I don't want us to be mad at each other, Ily," she said quietly. "I only want you to be happy." She placed the music box in her sister's waiting hands, then stroked her hair. "Here."

The Blue Fairy stepped back to give her sister room, and Ily held the box close, her shoulders still trembling. But as she looked up, a cunning smile smeared the remorse on her face, and she laughed cruelly. "There's one good thing about my not having a heart. You can't tell any more when I'm lying."

Ily held up the box. "Burn!" she said, and a hiss of fire spurted from her ruby wand.

"No! No, Ily!"

As the music box burst into flames, Chiara lunged, knocking it out of her sister's hands and putting out the fire. Before Ily could snatch it back, Chiara shuttered the charred box away with magic. She wouldn't trust her sister to take it again.

In retaliation, Ily pointed her wand at Chiara's wooden dove, still on the ground. Sizzling scarlet light shot forth, magic no doubt intended to destroy the bird, but Chiara reacted in time. Her own magic poured out of her wand, meeting Ilaria's right before it struck the wooden dove.

And the strangest thing happened.

The dove came alive, its wooden feathers turning into real, white ones. It purred and warbled, and the two sisters watched in astonishment as it quickly fled the room and flew out of the window.

What just happened? Chiara wanted to ask, but after one look at Ilaria, she wisely kept quiet.

Ilaria couldn't have cared less what their two magics had accomplished. Her eyes were bloodshot, and she demanded, "Give me my heart."

"No. Not until you're ready to receive it."

Ily gritted her teeth in annoyance. Chiara worried that her sister might attack her with her wand, but the Scarlet Fairy made a sharp turn.

"Keep it, then," she said, seeming not to care. "Sooner or later, I'll get it back. You'll hand it to me yourself. You see, I already am one of them. And I'm excited to learn what my power can do."

Ilaria laughed and laughed before she disappeared in a plume of red mist.

"Ily!" Chiara cried. "Ily!"

But her sister was gone.

A silent sob racked Chiara's chest, and she sank onto Ily's bed and conjured the music box back in her hands.

The dove she and her sister had enchanted to life

suddenly soared back into the room and perched on her shoulder. Chiara marvelled at it, both joy and sadness heavy in her chest. The dove stroked her hand with a comforting wing, and Chiara touched it gently. She knew she ought to turn it back into a wooden figurine as before – those were the rules, after all. But she couldn't, not without Ily's help. And truthfully, she wasn't sure if she wanted to.

"I guess you'll have to stay with me, little dove," she said. "At least until we get Ily back her heart again."

The dove purred, and Chiara offered it a sad but hopeful smile. The light of her sister's heart still glowed from within the box, and it was warm.

"We will?" she said, responding to the dove's sounds. She tucked the box away, promising she'd safeguard it no matter how long she needed to. She wouldn't give up the faith that one day, things between her and Ily would be right again. "I hope so. I hope so."

CHAPTER TWENTY-NINE

Evening crept across Pariva, and as the sun sank behind Mount Cecilia, there was only one final thing for Chiara to do.

Numbly, she left her sister's bedroom and trod up the nine steps to her own bedroom, taking one last look. It was the smallest bedroom in the house – meant to be an attic, then Ily's room after she was born, only she'd been too afraid. "There's spiders up here!" she squealed, so Chiara had insisted on sleeping there instead. She didn't mind spiders.

Over the years, Ilaria would overcome her fear of the attic. She'd come up into Chia's room, and they'd tell each other stories while lying down on a mound of pillows. Papa had worked a window into the ceiling to let in more light, and the two girls would stare at the moon until they fell asleep.

Chiara approached her old bed, tucking in the corners of her sheets one last time. Then she dusted the top of her dressing table with her handkerchief, letting her hand linger on the blue and purple hearts she had painted on the sides when she'd been a girl, the neat stack of books beside her window, full of her favourite stories and adventures. Then she turned to the window, to the painting she had made of her family. Mamma, with a long braid, carrying a loaf of bread under her arm and flowers that she held together with Papa. Niccolo, with a toy boat in his hands and two little sisters on his left.

Her, and Ilaria. Hands held, arms linked. Inseparable… until now.

She pressed her cheek to the window pane. It was cool, almost cold. Outside was a starless night, guarded by a slender moon.

It was time. She had to move through the heaviness in her heart to do what she'd come to do.

"Little town of Pariva," she whispered to the village outside, "you have my heart forevermore. Now sleep, for we must part. Forget me."

The light from her wand swelled out of the star, fanning over the house and across the town. She could feel the edges of the past being sanded off, her name and face washing away from the minds of the hundreds of people she had met in her lifetime.

Before her eyes, her room began to change. The floral blue canopy over her bed, the matching curtains and the lace doilies on her dressing table – all disappeared. So did her books and sheet music and set of paints, even the pot of violets she'd kept in the corner. In their place were sacks of flour and sugar, a broken chair and Niccolo's first violin, boxes of old toys and books and memories that no longer included Chiara. Dust grimed the beams along the ceiling, and cobwebs slung over the corners of the windows. Her bedroom had become the attic it was always meant to be.

Chiara choked back her tears, and she held her wand to her heart. Slipping under her guise of invisibility, she tiptoed down the stairs and visited her family. Niccolo first. He was snoring, a pirate novel half covering his face. Chiara tugged on his blanket, raising it so it covered his shoulders.

"Be good, be well, my dear Nico," she told him tenderly.

Then she visited her parents and kissed her mother's cheek, then her father's. Her father smiled in his sleep, almost as though he could feel her presence.

Mamma, Papa and Niccolo wouldn't know her even if they saw her. For the last time, tonight, they would dream of having a daughter with soft curls the colour of uncooked pasta – as Niccolo liked to tease. A girl with a gentle laugh and a love for playing the harpsichord. A girl as bright as her name, Chiara.

When they woke, they would remember only Ily – but the details of where she had gone would be like smoke in their memory. A little unclear.

"I'm sorry," she whispered to her parents. "I'll find a way to bring Ilaria and her heart together again. I'll bring her home. I promise."

And Chiara folded into the stars.

CHAPTER THIRTY

Forty years later

The years passed, and though Pariva remained the same quiet and sleepy town, the world around it changed. Railways tracked across Esperia, connecting its great cities, and trains pumped from day to night, travelling at ten times the speed of even the fastest carriage. Along Esperia's five seas, steam-powered boats as large as whales ripped down the coastline. The world grew smaller every day thanks to such innovations, but certain things did not change. Hearts, dreams and hopes.

Envy, anger and hate.

In the towns and villages surrounding Pariva, dozens of

boys had gone missing over the past few months. At first it seemed like a stroke of terrible misfortune, and the parents wept, and the towns grieved. But little by little, the numbers of missing children grew, and the fairies themselves were called to investigate.

Chiara was one of those fairies. It'd been a long time since she'd been called to duty near Pariva, and as she searched its surrounding areas for the missing boys, she found clues of dark magic, of an island that came alive at night and disappeared in the day.

The Wishing Fairies had no idea what to make of such information, and though they tried, they couldn't find this mysterious island – or its connection to the lost children.

Chiara became certain that the tragic disappearances were the work of the Heartless. Since the Wishing Fairies had put Monstro to sleep, the Heartless had lost a great source of dark magic, and over the years, they had unsuccessfully tried to recover their power through waves of wickedness. All had failed, until now.

Time was running out. With every boy that went missing, they harvested more despair and more anger and fear, and Chiara didn't know how to stop them.

Little did she know, her troubles were only just beginning.

CHAPTER THIRTY-ONE

Under the shroud of mist and shadow, twenty-odd Heartless fairies hovered above the Lyre Sea's still waters in a circle. At last, after years and years of searching, they had found him.

But before his spell could be broken, a late arrival made her entrance known – through a flare of scarlet light.

"Oh, look, it's our bright shining star," huffed Amorale as the Scarlet Fairy appeared. "I'm surprised you even deigned to show up."

Amorale's displeasure with Ilaria was becoming increasingly worrisome. Ilaria bowed deeply, and in her most formal tone, she said, "I'm sorry, Madame Grey Fairy. It won't happen again." She tried to take her place in the circle, but Amorale blocked her.

"Another concert in Vallan?" said the Grey Fairy. "I

would've thought after four decades, you'd tire of the hollow praise, the mindlessly adoring audience, the—"

"I'm not," Ilaria interrupted, only regretting her rudeness a beat too late. "I mean to say, I'm not tired of it."

It was true, mostly. Ilaria *wasn't* tired of the singing. Yet. The rare evening she took off from the Heartless to sing and make music was the only thing that brought her even a glimmer of joy these days.

What she *was* tired of was the lies, and the glamour cast upon her audience that made them acclaim her, no matter what she crooned from her lips.

At first, she thought it would make her happy to be famous and idolised and loved, but she was wrong. None of it was real, and she could tell from the glazed eyes and too-wide smiles that she faced in the audience whenever she performed.

The Heartless made no secret that they had expected her to outgrow her yearly performance in Vallan and eventually give it up, but Ilaria couldn't. Empty as the experience made her, she still looked to it. It was the only night every year she could forget about the misery and fear she sowed daily – to prove herself worthy of being a Heartless to Larissa and Amorale. Ironically, the very fact that she wouldn't give it up made Amorale increasingly doubtful of her commitment.

"I question your dedication," Amorale said, stating her

thoughts. "Could singing in some frivolous concert be more important than the reawakening of our greatest ally?"

"That's enough," Larissa cut in, coming to her protégé's defence. "Singing makes our little star feel powerful, and look, she teems with energy from the city. We'll put it to good use in breaking Monstro's sleeping spell."

Amorale glared at the Green Fairy. "You're always coming to her defence."

"It's only natural that Ilaria still has ties to her old life," said Larissa sensibly.

Indeed it was. Ilaria was the only one among them who still had a heart. It might not be in her, but it was out there – in her sister's clutches. So long as it still beat, she would always have doubts; she'd always *feel*.

She was desperate to get her heart back from Chiara. As soon as she reclaimed it, these seedlings of doubt would go away. She wouldn't even need her annual concerts. And Amorale would finally accept her as a true member of the Heartless.

"When will she get it?" Amorale said. "It's been decades. No one else has taken so long."

"No one else's has been stolen by a Wishing Fairy," Ilaria cut in. "I'll get it soon. I swear it." She held out her ruby-tipped wand. "Now may I join?"

"You can stand guard for those Wishing Fairies,"

Amorale said shortly. "Your pest of a sister has been seen poking about the area looking for the missing boys."

"And for Monstro," added Larissa. "Word spreads quickly on the Wishing Star."

Their decision made, Amorale and Larissa turned their backs to Ilaria and instructed their fellow fairies to begin the spell. As one, they descended closer to the water. Power sizzled from their wands and met in the centre in one brilliant burst of energy. Then, in a thunderclap, the magic struck the water.

It was silent at first.

Ilaria dared hope, in her secret and conflicted mind, that the silence meant the spell hadn't worked.

Then the sea rose in one great wave, and an enormous black whale emerged.

Monstro!

The Heartless clapped with glee as the whale's eyes peeled open, the spell of slumber cast by the Wishing Fairies broken.

"Welcome back, old friend," said Larissa, patting the whale's side with a green-gloved hand. "You're freed at last."

The whale let out a terrifying low hum.

"Yes, yes. You'll have your revenge," Amorale assured him. "Now quickly, into the water. Swim for the bright lights west of Mount Cecilia. We have much to catch up on, but for now – you'll find haven there… and a few fishing ships." She chuckled darkly. *"Dinner."*

As Monstro tunnelled his tremendous body back into the sea, Ilaria bit down on her lip, trying to push away that prick of discontent that arose in her.

What do you care if the Heartless wake Monstro up again? she scolded herself. *What do you care if he terrorises the coasts and sinks every boat he comes across?*

You obey Larissa and Amorale. They've given you everything – sisterhood, power, fame. In exchange, you do as they ask.

That was the deal she'd struck with the Heartless, and it was too late to go back.

Far too late.

But Ily was a clever girl. Given how scornful Amorale had been towards her recently, she knew she needed to work hard to prove herself. Specifically, she'd need extra magic to get her heart back from Chiara.

Before Monstro disappeared completely into the water, she pointed her wand at him. When the Heartless were not watching, she channelled power away from him ever so furtively – power grown by the fear that was already beginning to spread across the sea.

She had a feeling it would come in handy very soon.

CHAPTER THIRTY-TWO

In the morning came news of two missing fishing boats and three drowned men.

"Oh, my stars," Geppetto exclaimed after hearing about the tragedy from people passing by his shop. "Did you hear that, Figaro?"

He stroked his kitten absent-mindedly. "Three men drowned. We'd best stay away from the sea." He tickled Figaro's head affectionately. "I guess it's a good thing you don't like to swim, anyway."

With a sigh, Geppetto closed his pot of paints. After such awful news, he was hardly in the mood to work.

"Your mouth will have to wait," he said to the puppet sitting in front of him.

Geppetto had followed his dreams and become Pariva's

beloved toy maker. He was an old man now. His hair had turned white, his moustache too, and he walked with the slightest lean forwards, mirroring his dear puppets. But his fingers were still nimble, and the years had honed his artist's eye into one that could bring life to even the dullest block of wood.

That he had proven with his latest toy, affectionately named Pinocchio.

The puppet sat against the wall, its painted eyes innocently round and curious. Geppetto had put off giving the boy a mouth for days. Perhaps because he wasn't ready to sell Pinocchio yet. He'd grown oddly attached to the wooden boy.

"Maybe I'll keep him," Geppetto mused. "What do you think, Figaro? You and Cleo could have a new brother."

Figaro wrinkled his nose.

Geppetto chuckled. "You don't think so?"

He picked Figaro up and set the kitten by the kitchen, where he'd cut some bread and sliced some meat. While Figaro ate, Geppetto also fed his goldfish, Cleo, and he watched his two companions tenderly.

After Geppetto's father passed away, the house had grown colder, the small rooms too big for Geppetto alone. For years, loneliness had snaked its way into Geppetto's heart, and he spent most of his time making toys. Unless he was helping a customer, he went days without speaking to anyone, so he began speaking to his figurines as he made them. It wasn't until he had chanced upon Figaro alone and abandoned in the pasture that he had realised just how lost he'd been. He'd whisked the young cat into his home and fed and nourished him until he'd become the pampered prince that he was today. A few short weeks later, he'd adopted the goldfish Cleo.

Their names had come to him instantly, as though they had always been there. They became his family, and he couldn't imagine his life without them. Yet every time a child came into his shop and left smiling and laughing with a new toy, Geppetto's heart ached just a little for what could have been.

He'd always wanted a son or daughter of his own. Since Fate hadn't willed it for him, he instead tried his best to make the children of Pariva happy through his toys. Still, deep down, he couldn't let go of his secret longing. He traced an invisible smile over Pinocchio with his finger.

Every night he searched the sky for a Wishing Star, but he'd always missed it. Watching the children outside his window laugh and run to school, Geppetto hid a gentle smile.

He would try again tonight. Maybe one day soon, his wish would finally come true.

CHAPTER THIRTY-THREE

Not far from Pariva was indeed a secret island that came alive at night. It lay cloaked behind a veil of shadow, so entrenched in dark enchantment that not even the fairies of the Wishing Star could find it. Yet sailors and fishermen who erred too late and far from home sometimes heard the raucous music of a carnival and the shouts of young boys. If they listened long enough, they even heard donkeys braying.

Spooked, they returned home and told their wives and mothers what they had heard. *Ghosts*, word immediately spread. Ghosts congregated behind the mountains, and now with that monster whale sighted in the waters…

Such stories amused the Heartless. They encouraged them, in fact, and soon the pathetic humans were so frightened by the tales that none dared sail too close. None, of course, except the wicked men and women the Heartless kept in their employ.

The Scarlet Fairy drummed her long nails against her wand. She was tired of overseeing this far-off island. Tired of listening to donkeys braying well past midnight, and of having to play a glorified shepherdess as they were herded off into carriages and carts that would take them back onto the mainland to be sold. Night after night of donkeys and screaming little boys and puddles of popcorn and melted ice cream wasn't what she'd envisioned when she'd pledged herself to the Heartless.

The truth was, she didn't like coming to this part of Esperia. It was too close to Pariva, and she didn't like being so near to the home she once had known.

She couldn't complain. Pleasure Island was thriving, and supervising its success was the first responsibility Larissa had given her. It'd been Ily's idea to turn the boys into donkeys, inspired by the night she'd first turned into a fairy, and the misery and suffering that emanated from the place had made the Heartless more powerful than ever. And it was profitable, it turned out.

Still, she loathed the place. She had better things to do than be tied down to a carnival, such as locate her heart. For forty years, Chiara had done an admirable job avoiding her. Try as she might, Ilaria hadn't been able to goad her sister into an appearance. Not even by sabotaging the lives of the people Chiara tried so hard to help, or by causing mischief everywhere she went.

Every rip she made in the world, Chiara patiently patched. Every life she ruined, Chiara made even more joyful than before. All while somehow avoiding Ilaria altogether.

It was terribly frustrating.

But tonight, fortune smiled upon her. As Ilaria stared up into the night, bored with her watch, she caught a shimmer of magic headed towards Pariva. It was Wishing Star magic, and she tilted her head, curious.

On a whim, she trailed the light, but she was to be greatly rewarded for her efforts. For lo! She found none other than her sanctimonious sister dipping into Pariva – a place Chiara wasn't supposed to loiter, and what had the perfect Blue Fairy done?

In one swoop, she'd broken all of the fairies' cardinal rules: she'd granted the wish of someone she once had known and cherished, she'd given life to a wooden puppet when life was not hers to give *and* she had done it all in secret – without congressing with her elder fairies.

Ilaria nearly cackled with delight.

She'd have to play her cards carefully. The Blue Fairy was clever, and if Ilaria wanted her heart back, she'd have to offer something Chiara wanted in return.

As she spied on her sister, waiting for the perfect moment to intercept her, Ilaria descended upon an old house near Pine Grove.

It was a workshop, tables and walls filled with toys and clocks.

Old Mr Tommaso's home. Now Geppetto's.

Something about seeing Geppetto as an old man made her breath catch, only for a fraction of a moment. Then she recovered.

What did she care about Geppetto? The memories from her life as a girl in Pariva might as well have belonged to someone else. She cared nothing for the town, nor the people in it.

All she cared about was getting her heart back – so she could destroy it. She couldn't lose this chance: after all these years, she'd finally cornered her sister into the perfect opportunity to get it back.

"Still making promises you know you can't keep," she mused from behind Chiara. "Some things never change."

Chiara spun, and her blue eyes went wide.

"Speechless, I see," murmured Ilaria, relishing her sister's stunned silence. "Well, it *has* been a long time."

It was always fun putting Chiara on edge. She let herself have some fun and taunted Chiara about sneaking into Geppetto's workshop, breaking the Wishing Star's rules and giving the puppet life. She piled guilt and distress upon her sister's ever fragile conscience, then – at the right moment, when Chiara was about to leave for home to confess her egregious transgressions – Ilaria said:

"Prove to me that your little Pinocchio can spend three days out of trouble. *If* that chirping conscience of his helps him be a good boy, I will help you turn him into a real boy."

The Blue Fairy looked up. "That sort of magic is—"

"Against the rules? But not impossible." Ilaria eyed the small white dove that they'd given life together, many years ago. The sight of the bird made the hollow in her chest ache, but she pushed the feeling away. "We can do it, together."

The Blue Fairy faltered, and Ilaria hid a smile, gleeful that she'd managed to put her unflappable sister on edge.

"I don't need to hear the rest of your proposal," Chiara said, shaking her head. "My answer is no."

Ilaria wasn't surprised. "I didn't think you'd say yes," she purred. "It wouldn't be like the noble Blue Fairy to accept such a wager – especially from a Heartless like me."

Chiara flinched at the word *Heartless*.

"But then again, that same noble Blue Fairy *has* broken all her sacred rules." Ilaria put her finger to her lips before Chiara could interrupt. "I know, I know. You're going to go straight home and tell Agata and Mirabella that it was out of love that you did what you did. But while the fairies will sympathise with you, the rules are the rules. One stray step off the road might make you fall. After all, Mirabella still remembers what happened to Larissa…" Ilaria paused delicately. "She'll make you reverse your spell on Pinocchio."

Ilaria gave a low chuckle. "I can already hear what she'll say." Ilaria put on her most pompous voice: "'A boy who won't be good might just as well be made of wood'. You know it, I know it. And think of how sad poor Geppetto will be when his little son turns to wood once more."

Chiara was only half listening. Behind Ilaria, Geppetto had woken. Unaware of the two fairies' presence, he stumbled down the stairs only to discover, happily, that his beloved puppet had come alive.

"You do talk!" he cried in astonishment.

"Yes," said Pinocchio. "The Blue Fairy came. And someday… I'm going to be a real boy!"

"A real boy!" Geppetto cried. "It's my wish. It's come true!"

Geppetto danced in celebration, winding up his toy music boxes and collecting toys to show his new son.

Ilaria stole a sidelong glance at her sister, who was practically dancing along. Trust Chiara to see the beauty in the moment of the father and his new son. *How happy they look,* she was certainly thinking. *What good work I've done.*

Good work, indeed. Well, Ilaria was going to remind her how short-lived their joy could be. Soon everyone would know what she had all along – Chiara wasn't the 'good' sister after all.

"You know what they say about wood," she murmured, tilting her wand towards one of the candles in the room. Her dark eyes became bright from the flame. "He burns… with curiosity."

At that moment, Pinocchio noticed a candle burning at his side. His eyes rounded with curiosity. "Ooh, nice."

"Ilaria…" Chiara warned. "Don't you dare!"

Still smiling, Ilaria spoke into the ruby glowing on the top of her wand. "Bright and burning, what could it be? Touch the flame, and then you'll see."

Before Chiara could intervene, Pinocchio stuck his finger into the candle. The puppet didn't even flinch as his finger caught on fire.

"Look!" he said, eliciting his father's attention. "Pretty!"

In a panic, Geppetto dropped the toys in his arms. "Oh, help!" He tried to blow out the fire on Pinocchio's finger, but Ilaria had her wand raised, and the flame wouldn't go out.

"Stop it!" Chiara cried. "Ilaria, stop it!"

"Why?" said Ilaria. "Isn't it better that he burn now, before father and son grow too close? You'll only break Geppetto's heart otherwise."

"Ilaria!"

"Water!" Geppetto was shouting. "Where's water?" Desperate, he plunged Pinocchio's finger into the goldfish's bowl. The fire went out instantly, and Geppetto let out a sigh of relief. "That was close. Maybe we'd better go to bed before something else happens."

As they left, Chiara crossed her arms. "That was cruel of you, Ilaria. You could have hurt him."

"Was it me?" Ilaria feigned innocence. "Or was it the boy's curiosity? He has no strings – and no heart."

"He has a conscience." Chiara glanced down at the cricket, who had settled into a matchbox and was already asleep.

"A conscience won't make up for his lack of a heart. He'll end up like me. Depraved, wicked and delightful."

The Blue Fairy shook her head. "Pinocchio will be a good boy. I have faith."

"If you're so sure, why not accept my wager?"

Chiara inhaled and raised her chin. "I already said—"

"No?" Ilaria finished for her. "But you haven't heard the sweetest part of the deal. If you win, Chiara, I'll also give you what you desire most."

"There's nothing I desire."

Ilaria almost laughed aloud at how serenely Chiara replied. "Now, now, *sister,* we know that isn't true." She spoke over her, slowly and dramatically: "There is one thing you desire more than anything." She paused, relishing how Chiara's pale blue eyes flickered.

Ilaria whispered, "My heart, Chiara. If you win, I'll take my heart back."

CHAPTER THIRTY-FOUR

It was the last thing the Blue Fairy had expected Ilaria to offer. The words startled her, and she drew an involuntary gasp. "You'll take back your heart?"

"That's correct; you heard me. If you win, I'll take my heart back."

"No tricks?"

"I'll swear it on my wand."

Chiara's pulse thundered in her ears. Every ounce of reason told her not to accept, that Agata would disapprove and that if she were found out, she'd be cast from the fairies forever.

But for forty years, Chiara had sought a way to turn her sister away from the dark path she'd chosen. Deep down she knew there was no way for Ilaria to turn back into the girl she once had been – unless she chose to do so herself. Still, every day there was a part of her that mourned her sister and blamed herself for what Ilaria had done. Their parents had passed without ever seeing their daughters again, and though their brother had a family of his own now, everything he knew about the one sister he could remember was a lie.

Was all the good she had done in the world worth the pain she had brought to her family? It hurt Chiara more than anything to ask herself that question, but she forced herself to, every day.

What do I do? she asked herself. Her conscience had never led her astray, and she expected it to tell her to follow the rules, to be the honourable and noble Blue Fairy all had come to know.

But here, her conscience was just as torn as she was.

She could not give up this chance to redeem Ilaria.

And her sister knew it.

"But if you lose," went on Ilaria, twirling a strand of hair around her finger – the way she had when they were sisters – "you'll give me *your* heart."

Chiara tightened her grip on her wand. "My heart?"

"It's only fair. A heart for a heart. You'll become a mistress of despair like me. We'll finally be on the same side again. Isn't that what you've always wanted?"

Chiara's muscles tensed. "No, it isn't."

"Then I guess this is where we say goodbye."

"Take your heart, Ily," Chiara said. "It's too late to go back to the life you could have had with Mamma and Papa…" Her voice cracked. "But there's still time for you. Nico has a family now. They would welcome you. And Geppetto… he was your friend. He might have been more, had you stayed. He still could be more."

Ily was unmoved. "You think I care about them?"

"Then what do you care about? You've lost your family, your friends, your music." Chia paused. "You used to love singing. It was your life. How long has it been?"

"I still sing," Ilaria replied. "Every year at the Vallan Opera. People pay fortunes to hear me."

"They pay to hear Cleo del Mar, and she is only a figment of your vanity. A lie that you created with Heartless magic. Every year you dread the concert more and more. Your audience *hears* you, but they don't listen to you." Chiara's voice, still a whisper, fell even softer. "And the music, Ily… music used to be your greatest joy. But now when you sing, you feel nothing."

"I feel magnificent," snapped the Scarlet Fairy. "I've sung on the greatest stage in the world, thanks to Larissa and Amorale. They kept their word to me. Unlike you."

That stung, just as Ilaria meant it to.

"Larissa was right," Ily went on. "You fairies *are* cruel. You wouldn't break your precious rules for your own sister, but you'll break them for a stranger."

"Geppetto isn't a stranger. And his wish comes from a place of good—"

"So did mine!" Ilaria barked. "So did Larissa's."

In the decades Chiara had been a fairy, she'd learnt a great deal about the Heartless. She knew where they had come from.

"They lied to you," she said solemnly. "You think Mirabella denied Larissa's mother help? Larissa was the one who hired the bandits to burn down her town. She planned it with her mother's blessing so her family could pray to the Wishing Star for riches."

"A likely story," said the Scarlet Fairy, crossing her arms. "Twisted from the *good* fairies' point of view."

"It's the truth," said Chiara. "Listen to me. I know the fairies aren't perfect. But the rules were made to deter us from abusing our power."

"Only you would defend the rules as you break them," retorted the Scarlet Fairy. "Why didn't you ask your precious council to review Geppetto's wish before you cast your spell? Because you knew they'd reject it. We're not so different, you and I. At least I don't try to pretend to be so high and mighty."

"I'm not afraid to beseech the council for help, Ily,"

Chiara said softly. "I granted the wish out of compassion. What I am afraid for – is you." She swallowed. "Geppetto used to love to hear you sing. He cared about you. Would you hurt him?"

Ilaria stared at her sister. "You never give up, do you? Still trying to appeal to my non-existent heart. Still trying to save me."

"There's still hope for you," said Chiara.

"But I'm not *good*," Ilaria said mordantly. "No one is. Not truly, not as you believe they should be. That makes me a villain in your book, doesn't it?"

Chiara swallowed. It was supposed to. After all, the Heartless were the Wishing Fairies' adversaries – and, by definition, *evil*.

So why did she still believe in Ily? Why was she tempted to make a wager with her sister, a Heartless?

The answer was clear: for the same reason she'd broken the rules to bring Pinocchio to life. Because maybe, maybe the Wishing Fairies had been overly harsh in judging what was good and what was evil, and didn't always consider the many shades in between. Chiara, during her years as the Blue Fairy, had found herself guilty of that plenty of times, and was still learning.

"I have your heart," Chiara tried again. "If you take it back now—"

"If I take it back, I'll destroy it."

"You'll remember."

"I already remember," the Scarlet Fairy replied. "I remember that Geppetto had his chance to come with me and become greater than his wildest dreams. But he turned me down, and now he's an old man, at most a handful of years from death." She sneered. "Whatever fate I wrought upon his son, he deserves."

Chiara shrank back. *Ilaria truly is lost.*

"I tire of your company, sister," said Ilaria. "I have places to be, and things to do. If you'll take your chances with your fairies, then—"

"I accept your wager," said Chiara, so softly she almost didn't hear herself.

The Scarlet Fairy turned slowly, a smile forming on her painted red lips. "I have your word, on your honour as a fairy?"

"You do," Chiara said.

Ilaria blew her sister a kiss. "Then I'll see you in three days."

The words echoed in Chiara's mind even as Ilaria disappeared, filling her as much with hope – as with dread.

The good fairies of Esperia were meeting on the Wishing Star, and for the first time since she had joined their ranks,

Chiara was the last to arrive. Thirteen chairs carved of moonstone were arranged into a circle, and Chiara took her seat, grateful to rest. She hadn't felt so tired in years.

It'd barely been half a day, and already maintaining the magic to keep Pinocchio alive taxed her energy. Such an enchantment was meant to be temporary – Chiara wasn't even sure if she could keep it up for three days. But she had to. Or else she would have to turn him back into a puppet.

"Are you all right?" whispered Agata, who sat on her right. "You look pale."

Guilt weighed on Chiara's conscience as she folded her hands over her lap. She had got to know each of the fairies during her tenure, but the closest to her was still Agata, who had moved from being her mentor to being her friend.

In no world would Chiara ever lie to her, but she wasn't ready to tell anyone about the bargain she'd struck with Ilaria.

"I'm worried about Monstro being so close to Pariva."

It was a deflection, but also the truth. Monstro had been asleep for forty years. A week earlier the Heartless had finally found him. They awakened him, and now he was possessed by an unquenchable hunger and rage. Seven ships had already fallen to his wrath, but the whale's fury was not limited to the surface. He terrorised all creatures in the sea, and countless carcasses floated adrift on the surface. All the fairies were on high alert, yet whenever someone came close to tracking him, he mysteriously disappeared.

"I can't blame you," said Agata kindly. "But we'll find him. Are you ready to give us your report?"

With a numb nod, Chiara rose and cleared her throat. "I've returned from scouting the Lyre Sea. I observed the Lake of Mount Cecilia as well as the shores of the Saffiar Beach, and the townships of Elph, Pariva and Nerio. I warned the fishermen not to enter the waters, but most didn't need the warning. It seems they already know of Monstro."

"It isn't natural," mumbled Mirabella, who headed the discussion. "He was bad before, but nothing like this."

"Were you able to locate him?" asked the Rose Fairy.

"I didn't sense him in the Lyre Sea," Chiara replied, "or anywhere near the northern coast."

"Then we'll have to double our patrols," said Mirabella darkly. "He'll be hungry. Monstro is a hunter, and preying on the fish in the sea will occupy him only for a short while. Soon, he'll look for a new challenge."

Chiara suppressed a shiver. Monstro was strong enough to manipulate the seas. One swing of his great tail would destroy an entire village.

"No one who lives near the water is safe," Mirabella

went on. "Take care watching the sailors and fishermen and guide them to safety away from Monstro's clutches."

The fairies chimed their agreement.

"Chiara, why don't you continue monitoring the Lyre Sea?" suggested Peri. "You know that part of Esperia."

"Would that be advisable?" began Chiara. "It is rather close to my hometown."

"All the better," Peri said merrily. "We trust you, Chia. When's the last time you've ever broken a rule?"

As the fairies chuckled, Chiara could not laugh. Guilt sharpened in her chest. She looked at her wand, as if it might give away what she had done. But it sparkled as it always did, shining as true as the stars in the night sky.

Say something, her conscience urged her.

But if I tell them what I did, Geppetto might lose Pinocchio… and I might lose Ilaria.

The stakes were too high, and she knew this was exactly what Ilaria had planned – pitting Chiara against her conscience and her friends.

Yet if she could help Geppetto, Pinocchio and her sister… wouldn't it be worth it? Her heart and her conscience were at odds, and she didn't know which one to listen to. No matter what decision she made, there would be consequences.

The fairies were awaiting her response.

It's my fault for bringing Pinocchio to life, Chiara thought, *but in my heart, it was the right thing to do. I know this. Just as I know that if I give up on Ilaria, no one else will give her a chance.*

She dipped her head. "It would be my pleasure to watch over the Lyre Sea."

"There will be storms across Esperia next week," said Mirabella. "You'd best be careful. You know how cruel Larissa and her kind can be."

CHAPTER THIRTY-FIVE

The next morning, Geppetto sent Pinocchio off to school. A shimmering blue mist watched as the father and son said goodbye, its presence so subtle that practically no one detected it. No one, that was, except Ilaria.

She stayed hidden, blending in with a crowd of gossiping women. But her eyes stayed on the mist as it followed Pinocchio and his chirping conscience down the street.

That wouldn't do. Ilaria couldn't have the Blue Fairy hawking over Pinocchio all day. Not while she had plans for him.

She tilted her head to the sky, and as soon as she commanded it, dark storm clouds loomed over the Lyre Sea. Ilaria twirled her finger around her hair, and the clouds took the shape of a whale.

"Monstro," she sang in a low voice. "Monstro is here."

Her little lie travelled into the wind, finally touching upon the pool of shimmering blue mist.

Chiara took the bait, just as Ilaria knew she would. The blue mist slowed, falling behind Pinocchio as he sauntered off towards the school playground. Then it floated up to investigate the sea.

This is too easy, Ilaria thought with a wicked smile.

Ilaria knew that Chiara and her fairies considered finding Monstro their mission of the utmost importance, so of course she went after him. Did she really trust an insect to protect Pinocchio from the Heartless in the meantime?

The Wishing Fairies had done plenty of ludicrous things before, but this topped them all. Ilaria was almost tempted to call the whole thing off. What fun would ruining Pinocchio be if Chiara wasn't going to pay attention?

Ilaria sighed, moving through the streets swiftly and silently. Fun or not, she needed her heart back. And she wasn't about to leave anything to fate. There was too much at stake.

How long has it been since you've sung, Ily? Chiara had asked her.

Her hand went up to her collar bone, sharp nails grazing against where her heart should have been. Sometimes she could feel the ghost of a pulse inside her chest. Then, and only then, did she miss the music she once had made. The sound of laughter and the warm embrace from a friend, a sister, a brother, a lover.

Fortunately, the feeling never lasted.

How could it, when being a Heartless had made all her dreams come true? She'd wanted fame. Everyone in Pariva thought of her as Cleo del Mar, the most famous opera singer in the world. It didn't matter that Cleo del Mar didn't actually exist; in the end, memories were all that remained anyway.

Ilaria had wanted out of her small town. As a Heartless, she'd seen the world. She'd dined in palaces and danced with kings, she'd skated across mountaintops and sailed the Five Seas. She'd rained doom upon more towns than she could count.

But what she loved most was that no one dared look down on her. No one dared upset her, criticise her, or say anything terrible behind her back.

All eyes fell to the ground in her presence, all spines curved and knees bent as if she were an empress. A flick of her wand, and she could make kings weep with despair; she could ignite wrath as if it were kindling and set it ablaze. She could turn an idea into a war.

Music had had no such power. Oh, she had made her grandmother shed a tear or two, and inspired a few girls enough that they'd wanted lessons from Ms Rocco just like her. But behind her back, everyone had always doubted she'd achieve greatness. Even Chiara.

No longer.

Well, that wasn't quite true. She dug her nails into her palms. She was a fairy with magic, but she wasn't a full Heartless – immortal and near invincible like Amorale and Larissa. They wouldn't accept her into their inner circle until she finally destroyed her heart. She could tell, after all these years, they were starting to doubt her commitment.

I'll prove myself, she thought. In two days, she'd crush her heart with her heel and smash it into a thousand bits.

The Scarlet Fairy moved out of the crowd of gossiping women – thanks to her powers, none of them even noticed – and resumed her usual guise. Her mud-stained cotton skirts turned into the reddest silk, and the straw hat upon her dark locks became an ebony crown studded with rubies and feathers. No one would notice, though – unless she wanted them to. And she had two in mind to visit.

She leant on her wand as she approached the Red Lobster Inn, its half-painted facade still an eyesore on the outskirts of town. After forty years, it'd become even seedier than when it first opened, and its den of delinquents was something she'd learnt to count on.

A low whistle escaped her lips. It didn't take long before

Honest John and Gideon appeared. Her eyes flashed as she scrutinised the pair. Honest John was suavely dressed – if one neglected the subtle patch on his knee – with a bright blue cape, a jade-coloured suit and matching hat. His sidekick, Gideon, however, was an even worse eyesore than the tavern. His clothes were rumpled and ill fitting, and his hat had a hole large enough to fit a fish.

By the Vices, she could not wait until she no longer had to deal with such gormless henchmen. But for now, they would be perfect foils for Chiara's precious wooden puppet. Honest John was as gentlemanly as a criminal could be, but behind his smooth lies and twisted words was a most dishonourable fox. Pinocchio would fall for his charm immediately.

And Gideon? Well, Gideon was a mean cat. He would make sure Pinocchio didn't get away.

"Milady," said Honest John. He swept a bow. "Lady Scarlet, how might I serve your unworthiness?"

Gideon reached for her hand to kiss, but Ilaria moved it swiftly away, so focused that she didn't notice the white dove landing on the tavern's signpost, observing her quietly.

"Boys, boys," she said, in her most lilting tone. "No need to fawn. Now listen carefully. I have a job for you two."

CHAPTER THIRTY-SIX

The Blue Fairy.

Geppetto chuckled as he tidied up the toys he had excitedly scattered across the workshop last night. Pinocchio must have been dreaming, to speak of fairies and such. Why, there hadn't been a fairy spotted in Pariva in over a hundred years.

But then again, what other magic could have brought his 'little wooden head' to life?

"Maybe it *was* a fairy," Geppetto mused. "She must have listened to my wish." He smiled, remembering how wonderful it felt to have Pinocchio beside him. "Just think: Pinocchio will become a real boy. He already feels that way to me."

He was sanding a new set of eating utensils for Pinocchio.

A fork and spoon and a knife. A bowl and plate, too. While Geppetto's deft fingers worked, he whistled to himself, feeling happier than he had in years. His father had passed away some years ago, and Geppetto couldn't remember the last time he'd prepared a meal for two.

Oh, he couldn't afford a grand feast on his humble livelihood, but that didn't mean he couldn't splurge on their first meal together. He didn't know yet what Pinocchio liked to eat – or even if he *had* to eat, given he was made of wood. No matter; Geppetto would buy some of everything. Some tuna, perhaps – that was fresh around this time of the year – and bread from the Belmagio Bakery, carrots and potatoes and some leafy greens to help the boy grow strong.

"What else might the child need? Some books to feed his brain, some milk to feed his bones and a new jacket for winter so he doesn't get cold."

Figaro eyed him sceptically.

"Don't look at me like that. I don't know if the boy will get cold, but he did say he would become a real boy one day. Perhaps by winter, Figaro." Feeling giddy, Geppetto patted the cat's head, unable to believe that Fate had smiled upon him and given him this chance to be a father. He wouldn't take it for granted, and he'd do his best to give Pinocchio a good home and provide for him.

He mused aloud, "Imagine that. It'll be nice to fill up this old house, hear singing and laughter bounce off the walls." He turned to Cleo. "What do you think?"

Cleo folded her fins and twisted to the side as if she were scoffing. Geppetto had cleaned her water first thing in the morning, but she was understandably still irked at him for using her home to put out the fire on Pinocchio's finger.

With a chuckle, Geppetto opened a cupboard drawer and withdrew a drawstring pouch filled with his savings. "He'll need his own room when he gets bigger. I suppose that can wait. For now, some new clothes. And food to feed his belly!"

Whistling as he put on his hat, Geppetto set out for the town square to do some shopping.

Within an hour, he was carrying so many groceries that he did not see his little boy pass him on the other side of the street, flanked by two beastly men and chased by a tiny cricket.

"Mr Geppetto! Oh, Mr Geppetto!"

Geppetto turned, spying two young girls chasing after him as he headed to the marketplace. He brightened, recognising Dafne and Nina Belmagio. Dafne was eight, Nina seven, and the two were the sweetest girls in Pariva. Geppetto sorely hoped they would be friends with Pinocchio.

"Shouldn't you young ladies be in school?" asked Geppetto.

"Not today! We just got back from Vallan. Papa went for work, and he brought us."

"We went to a toy store," added Nina, "but we didn't want anything."

"No one's toys are as nice as yours, Mr Geppetto."

Geppetto beamed. "Your parents are doing well, your grandfather Niccolo, too?"

As Dafne nodded, she peered into his empty basket. "No Figaro today?"

"He's at home watching Cleo."

"How is Miss Cleo?" piped Nina. "Does she still like her name?"

Geppetto chuckled. Little Nina was getting so tall, it felt like only yesterday she had run off from her sister and dipped into his shop to hide.

"When'd you get a fish, Mr Geppetto?" Nina asked, her hands behind her back as she peered at the glass bowl on Geppetto's work desk.

"Just yesterday. I thought Figaro could use some company."

"Cats eat fishes, Mr Geppetto. They aren't friends."

"My Figaro is the friendliest kitten." Geppetto scratched Figaro's ears. "Aren't you?"

Nina looked sceptical, but she shrugged and turned her

attention back to the goldfish. "She's pretty. Look at those long and elegant fins! Does she have a name?"

"No… not yet."

"You should name her Cleo," Nina declared. "After Cleo del Mar. She looks like a diva."

For some reason – and he didn't know what – the name made Geppetto's breath hitch. "The opera singer?"

"Not just any opera singer," Nina cried. "Cleo del Mar is the most famous prima donna in Esperia. And she's my great-aunt, did you know?" Nina puffed up with pride. "Grandpa's going to take me to hear her sing one day."

"You don't say." Geppetto's brows drew together in confusion. "If she's Niccolo's sister, why doesn't she visit?"

"She's too busy touring the world. You must have known her when you were young, Mr Geppetto. She lived here."

The words struck a chord in Geppetto, making his throat close. Yes, he could picture Niccolo's sister. Dark raven hair that curled past her shoulders, and green eyes that sparkled when she laughed. Was she an opera singer? Geppetto couldn't remember her song. Time had faded the memory, and whenever he tried to think of her, his focus grew hazy.

"Old age will make you forget even your name," he joked, trying to hide his uneasiness.

Back in the present, Geppetto's smile faded. Strange that he could not remember Niccolo's sister at all – they must have been about the same age, and yet his memory of her was as elusive as that song she used to sing. A tune from an aria that had been popular when he was younger, but was hardly ever sung these days. Every time he tried to parse the melody, it slipped between the cracks of his memory.

It was about a bird; which type, he couldn't even remember.

"Does she still like her name, Mr Geppetto?" Nina prodded again when he didn't answer.

Geppetto blinked. "Ah, yes. You should come ask her sometime. She would love to see you."

"I will!"

"So will I," added Dafne. "Grandpa says he'll buy me a new toy if I get good marks in school. I've been studying very hard."

"I'm sure you have. Come to think of it, you two should stop by soon and meet Pinocchio!"

"Pinocchio?"

"That's my son," said Geppetto proudly. "The fairies brought him to me. He's about your age, Nina. Shorter than you, though." His shoulders shook merrily. "Pinocchio's at school right now. It's his first day."

"Wow! The fairies brought him? And to think we weren't at school today of all days," lamented Dafne. "We're going home now. But we'll see him tomorrow and say hello." She winked at Geppetto's basket. "If you're going to our bakery to get Pinocchio dinner, pick up some cinnamon cookies. Grandmamma made a batch just now, and they're divine."

"I'll do that," said Geppetto, waving as the two girls skipped off, and he headed into the bakery to buy some bread.

It was nearly sundown, and the grand meal Geppetto had prepared for Pinocchio sat on the table, untouched and growing cold. Flies buzzed over the cinnamon cookies, and Figaro pawed at the plate of sliced meats, his belly growling with hunger.

Geppetto swatted the cat's paw away. "No, no, we sit together. It's rude not to wait."

Figaro let out an anguished moan. He was hungry, and Geppetto couldn't blame him. They'd been waiting for over an hour, and Pinocchio still hadn't come home.

Unable to sit still any longer, Geppetto rose from his chair and paced in front of the window. Never had he been more aware of the *tick tick tock* of the clocks on his wall, of the vibrant shouts of schoolchildren outside on the road.

"Relax, old Geppetto," he told himself. He forced himself to chuckle. "It is his first day. Maybe he made friends and is playing ball in the fields. Nina and Dafne did say they'd look for him. I'll bet they're all getting along wonderfully."

The thought calmed him, but only for a moment. No matter how he tried, he couldn't banish his worries.

"What could have happened to him?" he said. "Where could he be at this hour? I'd better go out again and look for him. And remember" – he wagged a finger at Figaro – "nobody eats a bite until I find him."

Figaro let out a whimper, but he nodded dolefully.

"Good." With his chin up, Geppetto grabbed his coat and set out into town again.

There were plenty of children in the fields, playing ball as he imagined. But Pinocchio wasn't among them.

"He must be in town, then," Geppetto reasoned. "He's a curious boy, like his father. I'll bet he's at the bakery sampling all the cookies. Or with Vito petting the horses."

But Pinocchio was not in either the shop or the stables. Nor was he anywhere in the town square. In fact, when Geppetto stopped by the school to ask the teacher, the young woman replied, "I'm sorry, Mr Geppetto, but Pinocchio never came to school."

"That can't be!" Geppetto exclaimed. "Are you sure?"

"Yes," replied the teacher. "I hope you find him. I'll let you know if I hear anything."

It was a greater anguish than anything Geppetto had ever experienced, not knowing where Pinocchio was, and not being able to ensure in his mind that the boy was safe and sound.

His stomach dropped. One day as a parent, and he'd already failed his son. Forgetting to say goodbye, he turned away from the school and began to search the rest of Pariva.

"Pinocchio?" he called, searching desperately. He asked everyone he encountered, "Have you seen my boy? Black hair and a yellow hat? Are you sure? He's a wooden boy without strings."

"No," all would reply.

What had he done by sending Pinocchio off to school? He'd been so overjoyed to have a son, he hadn't considered the boy's safety. He hadn't prepared him, hadn't made sure he'd known about the world.

And now he'd lost him.

"I'll find my son," Geppetto swore. "He'll be okay." He had to be.

His voice was hoarse and his legs were tired by the time he returned home. Figaro had fallen asleep on the table; the food was still untouched. It had begun to rain furiously, and thunder rumbled across the sky.

Cleo was still awake and hadn't eaten. "No, I didn't

find him." Geppetto swallowed hard. "Come, Cleo. Time to eat. We'll save some food for Figaro, hmm?" He inhaled a ragged breath. "We'll need our strength to keep looking again tomorrow."

CHAPTER THIRTY-SEVEN

Chiara didn't notice the white dove racing over the Lyre Sea, crying out for her attention. It was night, the world illuminated only by a slender moon, and she was channelling every bit of concentration she had on finding Monstro. The sea writhed with dark magic, and simply searching past its barriers made her light-headed with effort.

Her wings wilted as she coasted the clouds. She'd been searching all day, and it was time to return to the Wishing Star. She needed rest.

Just one more try, she thought, not wanting to give up yet. She was more tired than usual because of the magic she'd lent to Pinocchio. But she wouldn't allow any idleness in her duties.

Dipping into her reserves of strength, the Blue Fairy

pointed her wand at the shroud of Heartless magic fogging over the sea. It was no use. The mist wouldn't clear.

Chiara dropped her wand to the side. Monstro was hiding somewhere in these waters, and no one would be safe until he was found. But there were countless pockets of such dark enchantment scattered across the Lyre Sea.

It would take months to search them all.

"There has to be another way," she murmured.

At that moment, her dove landed on her shoulder with a cry.

"Pinocchio?" she said, alarmed. "What's happened to him?"

She touched her forehead to the dove's, and in flashes, she saw into the bird's memory. After she had left Pinocchio in Pariva, two of Ilaria's henchmen – Honest John and Gideon – had lured him away from school. They looked like ordinary village folk, but Chiara's wand showed her their true colours. They were part of the vast network of cronies the Heartless called upon to do their bidding on Earth – happy to get paid handsomely for their trouble, while the Heartless reaped the magical benefits of their subterfuge. And Ilaria had heaped them on Pinocchio.

Horrified, Chiara watched as the men led the boy to none other than Stromboli's theatre. The dove showed her Honest John and Gideon presenting Pinocchio to

Stromboli, who rubbed his hands with glee and passed the two swindlers a generous pouch of oros.

"My little gold mine," Stromboli purred, ushering Pinocchio into his wagon.

It was all Chiara needed to see.

Her heart hammering, she spun back for Pariva. In any other circumstance, she had faith that the cricket would guide Pinocchio in making sensible decisions.

But she knew Stromboli's ways. Over the years, she'd visited him countless times and tried to guide him, but the Heartless claimed him, and he'd grown up to be a duplicitous con man like his father. Now he travelled across the country to perform with his marionettes, robbing his audience when they were enthralled by his show, and even cheating his own brother, Vito.

Poor Vito. He'd run away soon after her visit when he was a boy and had retreated to the countryside, where he'd settled in Pariva. For years, he'd been happy and free from the influence of his father. Then one day he'd noticed Stromboli's travelling wagon, and he'd called out to his brother – naively forgetting that Stromboli had been as cruel as Remo. Stromboli proceeded to steal Vito's hard-earned savings, which forced him to take a second job at the Red Lobster Inn at night. What was worse, Stromboli circled back to Pariva at least once a year, extorting his brother for money and free lodging.

To Pinocchio, he would do far worse. He would woo Pinocchio with empty promises of money and fame. With temptations that the poor young puppet wouldn't be able to resist.

Chiara flew faster, thinking of all that could go wrong. The rain did not touch her, but the lightning and thunder cut into her nerves. Not a good portent. Trouble brewed below.

She hurried, gliding down towards Stromboli's wagon. Inside was Pinocchio, trapped in a wooden cage.

A rare flash of anger bubbled to the Blue Fairy's chest. The poor puppet was helpless, and every second the wagon trundled further and further from home.

It took all of her restraint not to spirit Pinocchio away from Stromboli's clutches and whisk him back to Geppetto's home. But Pinocchio's predicament was partially his fault. He hadn't listened to his conscience and gone to school.

For him to have come across Honest John and Gideon and Stromboli all in one day… her hands shook at the unfairness of it all. The poor boy stood no chance against the Scarlet Fairy. Not without some help, anyway.

Taking a deep breath, she composed herself. Freeing

Pinocchio wouldn't be enough. She needed to teach him how to handle such situations. Otherwise, Ilaria would certainly sway him off the right path again.

"Take it easy, son." Jiminy Cricket was consoling Pinocchio before he noticed a beam of light entering the wagon. "Hey, that star again! The fairy!"

"What'll she say?" Pinocchio asked worriedly. "What'll I tell her?"

"You might tell her the truth."

Good advice, Sir Jiminy, thought Chiara as she materialised before the pair. She smiled, not wanting to give away how worried she'd been. "Why, Pinocchio! I didn't expect to find you here. Why didn't you go to school?"

"School?" Pinocchio repeated. "Well, I . . ."

"Go ahead," Jiminy encouraged. "Tell her."

"I was going to school till I met somebody. Two big monsters with big green eyes!"

Chiara paused, waiting for Pinocchio to go on. It was hard not to be charmed by the boy's already vast imagination. But in order for him to understand the consequences of his actions, she'd have to teach Pinocchio to be honest. Luckily, Chiara had a feeling it would be more successful with this sweet boy than it had the last time she'd tried it.

As Pinocchio continued to tell his story, magic sparkled

around his nose. It suddenly grew an inch longer. His eyes widened. "Why, I…"

"Monsters?" Chiara inquired, allowing herself the smallest smile.

In a way, Honest John and Gideon *were* monsters. Not the seven-eyed, three-headed monsters with scales and claws and flaming tails that Pinocchio was envisioning, but monsters of a different sort. The kind that wore masks of friendliness and charm – and seemed harmless to his child's innocence. Harmless as, say, a fox and a cat.

"And where was Sir Jiminy?" Chiara asked.

"Leave me out of this," Jiminy instructed Pinocchio in a whisper.

"They put him in a sack," Pinocchio replied, ignoring the cricket.

By now, Pinocchio's nose had grown so long that it had become a tree branch with flowers sprouting from the end.

"How did you escape?" Chiara inquired.

"I didn't," Pinocchio replied. "They chopped me into firewood!"

His nose grew across the space, and leaves bloomed from the branch; a nest with two young birds appeared at the end, with poor Jiminy between them.

"Oh, look!" Pinocchio cried. "My nose! What's happened?"

"Perhaps you haven't been telling the truth, Pinocchio," observed Chiara.

"But I have!" insisted Pinocchio. "Every single word!"

The leaves on his nose wilted, and the birds in the nest flew out in alarm.

Pinocchio held out his hands in entreaty. "Oh, please help me. I'm awful sorry."

Chiara gazed at him, echoing what her mother used to say: "You see, Pinocchio, a lie keeps growing and growing until it's as plain as the nose on your face."

Jiminy Cricket raced across Pinocchio's nose to tell the boy, "She's right. You better come clean."

"I'll never lie again. Honest, I won't."

"Please, Miss Fairy," Jiminy entreated. "Give him another chance for my sake. Will you?"

She nodded, her heart full of everything she wanted to say, of all the protection and help she wished she could offer the both of them. "I forgive you, but remember…" The Blue Fairy paused, borrowing the words Ilaria had spoken: "'A boy who won't be good might just as well be made of wood'."

"We'll be good, won't we?" Pinocchio and Jiminy said to each other.

"Very well," said Chiara. She tapped her wand on the cage, breaking its lock and setting Pinocchio free. His nose returned to its normal size, and Pinocchio beamed at the fairy.

"Thank you, ma'am."

"Remember to listen to your conscience, Pinocchio."

With that, she faded into the starlit night, turning herself invisible so she could observe the pair a while longer. She watched as Pinocchio and Jiminy slipped out of the wagon. Stromboli helmed the mules, unaware that his precious 'gold mine' had escaped.

Chiara let out a quiet sigh of relief, but her hands were clenched at her sides. What would have happened to Pinocchio if she hadn't sent her dove to look after him? Did Ilaria expect Stromboli would turn the boy's heart rotten like his? That his greed for coin and fame would spread to Pinocchio?

Already she'd proven Ilaria wrong. But she hadn't proven that Pinocchio was worthy of the magic it would take to make him a real boy. *Two more days.*

So long as Ilaria kept interfering and putting Pinocchio in situations of danger and temptation, there was no way he could win.

Pinocchio wasn't far from home, but this time, Chiara wouldn't leave his safety to chance. She trailed him and Jiminy Cricket – until a dark presence blocked her way.

"You found him," greeted Ilaria. "I was starting to

worry. The game can't end when it's only just begun. That would be no fun at all."

"You know what's also not fun?" said Chiara. "Cheating. You put Honest John and Gideon on Pinocchio's path—"

"I never said I wouldn't interfere."

"Pinocchio could have been hurt!"

"He's just a puppet." Ilaria shrugged and leant forwards on an imaginary ledge, batting her eyes innocently at her sister.

"Pinocchio is a good boy. *You* sent Honest John and Gideon after him. You set him in Stromboli's path. He could have been *killed*, Ily! Stromboli had an axe, and—"

"Enough with the dramatics, Chia. I wouldn't get the boy killed. If he died, he wouldn't exactly be wicked, now would he? He'd only be dead."

Chiara fell silent, but her hands balled at her sides. For the life of her, she couldn't believe this was what had become of her sister. This cruel and unfeeling, *heartless* creature.

"*Stay calm,*" Ilaria taunted, pretending to be her conscience. "*Think before you react.*" She smacked her lips. "So predictable. Though you are looking weak, sister. Are you sure you'll be able to keep up Pinocchio's spell for another two days without help from your fellow fairies? I wonder how disappointed dear Agata will be, knowing her star pupil has broken the rules."

Chiara's voice was a mere whisper: "The fairies wouldn't punish me for having done the right thing."

"But you *would* be punished for bargaining with me." Ilaria fiddled with her hair, a habit she had kept from when she was a girl. It pained Chiara to recognise it. "You'll need your strength if you're going to keep Pinocchio safe. I've plenty of help on my side. Maybe I'll even ask Monstro to make an appearance."

Chiara stilled. It shouldn't have surprised her that she was involved with Monstro, but she didn't want to believe it. "You know where Monstro is?"

"Why wouldn't I?" Ilaria fluttered her hand, clearly loving that she knew more than Chiara about the giant whale. "I was part of the coven that woke him from his nap. You dear fairies have been worried sick about what he'll do." She licked her lips. "Let me tell you, it's nothing good."

"Tell me where he is, Ily," pleaded Chiara. "He can't be free like this. Think of how many he'll hurt – he'll *kill*."

Ilaria simply twirled her hair. "Then you'd better work fast to find him, hadn't you?" she said sweetly. She tore off one of Stromboli's posters and pointed at the illustrated marionettes. "You know, I'd have to say that Geppetto's are of much higher quality than these. Perhaps Stromboli should patronise his shop one day."

A muscle ticked in Chiara's jaw. *Don't react,* she reminded herself. *She's trying to bait you.*

"Will you promise not to interfere with Pinocchio again?" she asked, getting back to the matter at hand.

"Would you believe me even if I did?" The Scarlet Fairy snickered. "I can see you're going to help him each time. He'll never learn that way."

Slowly Chiara lowered her wand. A part of her wondered if Ilaria was right. At what point would she need to let go? Pinocchio would never learn to follow his conscience if she always stepped in to save him.

"By the Vices, you're actually listening to me?" Ilaria cackled with delight. "Time's made you into even more of a gullible fool than I remembered."

Chiara clasped her hands together, trying her best to summon her calm. During her years as a fairy, she'd answered the wishes of those whom she'd deemed worthy – people, like Geppetto, who had shown kindness and compassion and were noble of heart. Her sister, after all the terrible things she'd done, did not fall in such a category. So why did Chiara still have hope for her?

Why had Chiara broken the fairy's rules, even though she knew the risks?

Because not everyone is all good or all bad, she realised. *It might be easy to label them as such, but it simply isn't true.*

Even if Mirabella and Agata disapprove, I know this is what I have to do.

She regarded her sister. "I have faith that Pinocchio's heart is worthy, and he'll show that he deserves to be a real boy – even without my help. Just as I have faith in you, Ilaria. Your heart is true, and it's waiting for you."

The smile on her sister's face vanished. "I have places to be. Monsters to feed, and souls to reap. I'll see you soon enough, Chia."

Ilaria vanished in a puff of red mist, leaving Chiara alone once again.

The storm thundered on, and the Blue Fairy looked to the starless sky, wishing with all her might that she was right about Pinocchio – and her sister.

CHAPTER THIRTY-EIGHT

Geppetto wished he'd brought an umbrella. Rain streamed down his spectacles, and he took them off, wiping them against his damp scarf. He was cold, wet and exhausted, but he had to forge on. The only question was where. He'd already searched every last corner of town and knocked on every door, but his son was nowhere to be found.

As he put on his glasses again, he leant against the side of a house for a moment's rest. It was the Belmagio house, it turned out. He recognised the yellow door, the lemon trees and the garden of herbs and violets in the front garden. The soft strain of a violin wove through the rain. He lumbered closer to the window; inside the house, Niccolo Belmagio was playing the violin while his wife read a book.

At the sight of Geppetto, Niccolo lowered his instrument

and waved. "Come inside, old man," he mouthed. When Geppetto resisted, Niccolo disappeared from the room. A few beats later, the front door was flung open.

"This is the third time you've circled our street looking for your boy," said Niccolo, ushering Geppetto inside. "You need to eat. And look! You're soaked. Dry yourself before you catch cold."

"I can't. There's no time to waste. Pinocchio needs me—"

"Yes, and you won't be able to find him if you die in this storm. You're wetter than a fish. Come inside before I reel you in."

Niccolo wasn't a man who took no for an answer, and Geppetto reluctantly entered the house.

"I always took you for a man of good sense," Niccolo said, shaking his head as Geppetto's teeth chattered. "How long were you out there in this storm? Careful of your boots on the carpet. It was my grandmother's, and Sofia just cleaned it last week."

Geppetto nodded, numbly removing his boots before he followed his friend inside the house. He hadn't been to the Belmagios' in years, but something about being back here jogged his memory, as fragments of his past – that he hadn't remembered in forever – resurfaced.

On his left was the music room; its blue walls were

more faded than he remembered, and the old harpsichord was still there in the corner by the window, next to a wooden music stand in the shape of a lyre. The famous chamber where Cleo del Mar had practised singing. Geppetto could almost hear laughter and music from years past. How odd that she never visited Pariva.

He followed Niccolo down the hall into the small parlour, where a fire crackled in the hearth. There, he greeted Niccolo's wife, Sofia, who offered him a blanket and a mug of hot chocolate. The drink and the fire tickled the chill out of his blood, but not the sorrow in his heart.

"You've looked everywhere? The docks, the fields, the—"

"Everywhere," replied Geppetto morosely. "I can't find him. I'm afraid he's… he's…" His voice faltered. He couldn't bring himself to say it aloud.

"There, there," Sofia said, patting him gently on the shoulder. "You'll find him. I'm sure of it."

Niccolo scratched his head, his brows knitting. "To be frank, I didn't even know you had a son, Geppetto. The children mentioned something about the fairies bringing him to you, but I thought it was just one of their imaginary games."

"No, Pinocchio is real," replied Geppetto. "Well, as real

as he can be… for a boy made of wood. He's a puppet I wished to life, you see. A puppet without strings."

"A puppet?" Sofia exclaimed. She and Niccolo exchanged incredulous looks. But old Geppetto certainly was not one to misspeak, so after a moment passed, Sofia nodded. "It's about time Pariva had its own touch of magic, I suppose. It's been a while."

Her husband, on the other hand, was frowning. He looked deep in thought. "A puppet without strings, you say?"

"What is it?" said Geppetto.

"Nina and Dafne went to the theatre tonight," Niccolo replied. "They saw the marionette artist who comes by every year. I always forget his name."

"Stromboli," Sofia provided. "The Master Showman."

"Ah yes, Stromboli," Niccolo said thinly. "More like master con man. His ticket prices are extortionate, and every time I've gone to see him, I swear his monkey picks my wallet. But you know how my son is, always spoiling his children. My parents would never have indulged in such a thing." He sipped his drink, the chocolate turning his white beard brown. "Anyhow, the girls were enthralled – they keep singing this song about having no strings. I thought it was some ditty they'd picked up, but now that you tell me your son is a puppet without strings…

"You might want to talk to them about it – their parents let them stay up until an ungodly hour on theatre nights. Dafne! Nina!"

The two sisters scampered down the stairs, holding hands and swinging them high as their footsteps thumped across the wooden floors. As soon as they came fully into view, they composed themselves.

"You called, Grandpa?" said little Nina. Her green eyes widened. "Oh, Mr Geppetto! How pleasant to see you!"

"Mr Geppetto wants to know about the dancing puppets you saw tonight," said Niccolo.

Geppetto cleared his throat. "Was Pinocchio there?"

"I don't know, sir. There were so many children there. I didn't see—"

"No, Dafne. On the stage."

Dafne's eyes went as round as marbles. "You mean… oh gosh, that was *him*?" She elbowed her sister. "The puppet without strings!"

Nina let out a squeal. "He was amazing!"

Geppetto didn't dare to hope. He slid off his chair and knelt on the carpet beside the two girls. "You saw him? He was there?"

"He was the star!" Nina exclaimed.

"Shush," said Dafne, clapping her hand over Nina's mouth. The older girl had noticed the urgency in Geppetto's demeanour – or perhaps the worry in his eyes. "Did something happen to him, sir?"

"He's missing." Geppetto felt his gut rise to his throat. "Did you see him after the show?"

Dafne gave a doleful shake of her head. "Sorry, Mr Geppetto. If we'd known he was your son, we would have looked for you. But we went home."

"I'd bet a pretty oro that Stromboli took your boy," said Sofia with a scowl.

Geppetto swallowed, already knowing it had to be true. Poor Pinocchio. He was so new to the ways of the world. He rose. "Then I'll find him. No matter how long it takes, I'll bring my Pinocchio home. Thank you for your help, Niccolo, Sofia. Dafne and Nina. I'd best be going—"

"Try the tavern," Niccolo interrupted. "Vito works nights there, and I've seen Stromboli at his house before. He might know where he's gone."

"Take this," said Sofia, passing him an umbrella.

Emotion clogged Geppetto's throat, and all he could do was pass them a grateful look. Then into the storm he returned, making for the Red Lobster Inn.

Geppetto had never been inside the tavern before. It was a gloomy establishment, with so few candles lit inside that he could barely make out his own feet as the door behind him swung shut. A handful of patrons sat inside, almost all men he had never seen before. As he passed their tables, most eyed him with suspicion. One or two cast him carnivorous glances, as if he were meat to be carved.

The old toy maker was not a brave man, and in any other circumstances, he would have quailed and whirled for the door. But entering a nest of hoodlums and hooligans was only the beginning of what he'd do to find his boy.

Thank goodness Vito saw him bumbling through the dark tavern.

"Are you lost, Mr Geppetto?" greeted Vito, grabbing him by the arm before Geppetto walked into a bucket and a pile of shattered glass. "Didn't take you as someone with a taste for spirits."

"Vito," Geppetto said, relieved. "You're here."

"I work here every night except Sundays," said Vito cheerfully. He was a pleasant fellow whom Geppetto knew more as the keeper of Pariva's stables, where he worked during the day. Geppetto had never understood why he worked in a place like the Red Lobster Inn past dusk, but he supposed that Vito was a large man, his broad shoulders easily twice Geppetto's width. Geppetto doubted anyone would give him trouble.

Someone behind him let out a loud belch, and Geppetto shuffled nervously towards Vito. "I'm looking for my son. Niccolo said you're… you're acquainted with Stromboli."

As soon as Geppetto mentioned the name, Vito's expression hardened. He pulled Geppetto to a shadowed corner, and his voice went low. "What business do you have with my brother?"

"Your brother?" Surprise etched itself onto Geppetto's brow. He'd never seen Stromboli in person, but he'd noticed his posters pasted throughout town.

"We don't look anything alike, I know." Vito scoffed. "It's because of all his makeup and that wig and sham accent. Embarrassing, really, the show he puts on."

"Oh, that's wonderful news."

"Wonderful?"

"That he's your brother." Geppetto's knees nearly knocked with relief. "Have you seen him? He has my son. Pinocchio—"

"Pinocchio?" Vito spluttered. "You mean to tell me your son is that puppet? He's the talk of the town! An extraordinary, magical sensation!"

It seemed everyone in Pariva had witnessed Pinocchio's performance at the theatre.

"Yes," replied Geppetto, "and now he's gone."

"Gone is right," Vito said thinly. "No wonder he was furious."

"Who was?" Geppetto asked, confused. "Pinocchio?"

"No, no. Stromboli." Vito gestured at a pile of shattered glass he had swept into a corner. "He came back an hour ago, accused me of stealing your boy. Broke every glass he could get his hands on. Took four men to put him down. I was worried he'd set fire to the place. Probably would have, if not for the rain."

"I… I don't understand."

"I didn't either until now. Seems like your Pinocchio's left."

"Escaped!" Geppetto drew a breath, daring to hope.

"It was, hmm, an hour ago. Maybe more." Vito glanced at a patron who'd fallen asleep or unconscious among a pile of drinks, as if using the number of empty bottles to gauge the time. "He hasn't come home?"

"I… I don't know," said Geppetto, suddenly feeling light in the head. All this time he'd been out, Pinocchio could have been at home waiting for him! "I need to go!"

Vito yanked off his apron and whistled at his colleague. "I'm taking the night off," he told him. Then, to Geppetto, he said, "I'm coming with you."

Geppetto hastened home, but the moment he saw his house, with the lone candle he'd kept lit for Figaro and Cleo, all the hope he'd let flood into his chest went out again. He hardly had the strength to pull open his door.

Only silence greeted him, then the mournful *meow* of his cat. Figaro crept out from behind the stairs and nuzzled Geppetto's leg.

"He's not here," said Geppetto, collapsing to his knees. "Oh, Figaro, what could have happened to him?"

Geppetto spun back for the door. "Don't close it, Vito. I have to go back out."

"At this hour?" Vito looked at him worriedly. "It's still raining."

"Something's happened to him. I know it."

"It's late, Geppetto. Better you wait until the morning, when you've had some rest. You don't even know where Pinocchio could have gone."

"It doesn't matter. I'll search all of Esperia if I have to."

Vito grimaced. "Something isn't right about all this. Your boy would've come home by now if he'd escaped."

"That's why I have to keep searching."

"No, Geppetto. Listen. There's dark magic afoot, I can feel it."

"Dark magic?"

"It used to follow my papa wherever he went – like a shadow. Comes with Stromboli, too. Lately, it's been around

Pariva an awful lot." Vito frowned. "I heard some of the men at the tavern talking… about boys who've gone missing."

"Missing boys?"

"Yes, there's been a slew of them gone. Mostly from villages down south, a couple from Elph. Or so they say."

"What else did they say?"

"It's just a rumour, Geppetto," Vito said uneasily, as if unsure whether he should go on. "You can't believe everything drunk men say."

"Tell me."

"He said that there's an island behind Mount Cecilia, and that several boats have sailed to it these past few weeks. Boats all filled with young boys – who disappear and never come back. It's possible Pinocchio was taken there."

"What is this place called?"

"I heard someone say… Pleasure Island."

A chill shivered down Geppetto's spine, and he swallowed. "Okay." He moved towards the door.

"Wait until dawn," Vito urged. "The sea's not safe, especially at this hour. Monstro's destroyed every boat that's sailed the last few weeks."

"I don't care about a whale."

"Wait until dawn," Vito repeated. "Get some rest so you can search for your boy with fresh eyes. You can take my boat. It isn't much, but it's small enough that it might not attract Monstro's attention. It'll get you to the other side of the mountains faster than if you ride or walk."

What choice did he have? "Thank you, Vito."

At first light, Geppetto settled Figaro and Cleo onto Vito's boat and slipped out into the waters. All was quiet. The past few weeks, hardly anyone had dared sail out into the sea. Even Geppetto had heard the warnings; the first time he'd heard the name Monstro, his heart had jumped with fear, as if he'd encountered the whale before. But that was silly. Even an absent-minded old man like him wouldn't have forgotten such an event.

It didn't matter, anyway. Geppetto would gladly sail into the jaws of Monstro himself if it meant a chance of finding Pinocchio.

The sky was still grey from the last night's storm, and Figaro shrank under a blanket as Geppetto prayed, "Blue Fairy, if you're listening, please help me find Pinocchio in time. Please let me bring him home safe."

He would need all the luck and guidance that the fairies could offer. The sea was vaster than he remembered. Within an hour, Pariva's coastline disappeared from sight, and in every direction was only blue sea.

He was alone.

"Not *all* alone," he murmured to himself. He patted

Figaro's head and tickled Cleo's fins. "It could be worse," he told them. "The water's calm, and we have Vito's boat." Though Vito had said it was small, it was almost as big as Geppetto's humble abode; it even had a cabin with a bed and desk.

Figaro made a sceptical meow, and Geppetto drew him close. "You'll see. We'll find him."

For all the comfort his friends brought him, Geppetto could not banish the apprehension creeping into his heart.

And he did not see the whale lurking under the waves, waiting to devour him.

CHAPTER THIRTY-NINE

Wicked as she was, even Ilaria thought it supremely gauche to have a celebration marking the disappearance of one thousand boys. The Coachman, who headed Pleasure Island, clearly disagreed.

"That's a thousand souls gone into the Heartless's bank of evil," he said gleefully, rubbing his hands together as one of his shadowy minions delivered a bottle of red wine. "One week earlier than predicted."

"You've done well, Coachman," said Larissa, clapping politely.

"More will arrive tonight." The Coachman peeled a black whip off his belt and wrapped it meticulously – once, twice, thrice – around the bottle's neck… as if he were tying a noose. Then he gave the bottle a good, hard slap. "Shall we celebrate?"

A pop of the cork punctuated the question, and the Coachman roared with laughter as red wine exploded out of the bottle. By the Vices, he had a face that begged to be punched. His nose was round and bulbous like a target. All Ilaria wanted to do was sock it.

He whistled obliviously while filling the four bronze goblets on the table in front of him.

"To new blood," he said, passing Larissa and Amorale their goblets first. Then Ilaria.

Ilaria took it and pressed her cheek to the window. The glass was one way, and no one outside could see her. An unnecessary precaution. The boys on Pleasure Island were so spellbound by the island's offerings they wouldn't have noticed the three fairies gathered at the top of the House of Mirrors, spying on them like vultures.

"To another heinously cruel venture," Larissa toasted.

"And its brimful payoff," added Amorale as wine dribbled off the sides of her goblet.

Ilaria tipped her glass for an imaginary clink, but only because she knew it'd raise Amorale's suspicion if she didn't. Trying her best not to look bored, she swirled her wine, then pretended to drink. The claret pool in her cup was one shade away from her signature scarlet. But it made her ill to look at it. Tonight, the longer she stared at her glass, the more she thought of one thing: blood.

You're not feeling bad about all the boys you've doomed, are you? she asked herself. *Or about one boy in particular…*

She knew Pinocchio was on the island. He'd arrived one boat earlier, and he'd gambolled into her trap like the other boys in his crowd. Just like she'd planned.

Then why this tickle in her throat? This sour note on her tongue?

Did she regret it? Was she secretly hoping her sister might swoop onto the island and save him again? Even Chiara wasn't powerful enough to break through Pleasure Island's barriers to do that.

"The wine not fine enough for you, Ily?" said the Coachman, interrupting her thoughts.

The Scarlet Fairy glared. No one called her Ily. For the Coachman to dare such familiarity was a symbol of the favour Larissa and Amorale had granted him. She despised it.

"I've had better," she said hotly.

"Why don't you sing for my boys?" he said, pretending not to hear. "Larissa says you're quite the little star in Vallan. Clara del Mar?"

"*Cleo* del Mar," she corrected.

"Pardon, Cleo," said the Coachman, lifting his hat in apology. "I spend all my time dedicated to the works of power and wealth. Not much time for going to the theatre. Or the opera. Might make for quite the treat for my boys though, what do you say?"

She'd rather pick fish bones out of Monstro's teeth than diminish herself by singing on Pleasure Island.

"Opera is a high art," she told the Coachman haughtily. "It has no place in a carnival."

"Ilaria," warned Amorale. "Your manners."

"No offence taken," the Coachman said with a wave. "She's right. No boy here would pay attention to some dame crowing her lungs out. Not when there's fights to be picked and mischief to be made."

The three laughed, while Ilaria finally forced herself to take a drink. The wine burned down her throat.

"Sixty-six new boys tonight," the Coachman declared. "A new record that should tip the balance of magic in your favour. We're going to need an extra wagon at this rate for the poor blokes."

Another sip. Her throat shrivelled, and Ilaria clawed her nails into her glass as the walls began to quake. A gang of boys had entered the House of Mirrors with wooden anvils and begun shattering the mirrors. It was chaos. Knives, hammers and wooden bats being handed out along with sweets and fizzy drinks and ice cream – a perfect den of encouraging violence alongside pleasure.

The whole place was the Coachman's idea, of course. Larissa had loved it. Amorale, too.

But Ilaria?

Obviously, she didn't trust any of the depraved souls that the Heartless collaborated with, but the Coachman was in a special category of wickedness.

Larissa and Amorale had recruited him a decade ago. He'd been an architect working in Vallan – an ordinary, unremarkable citizen, designing homes and buildings and such. Or so he'd appeared.

At first glance, he didn't look so different from her grandfather, when her grandfather had been alive. He had a wide face that entertained wide smiles, soft white hair that poofed like a goose's bottom, and round, marble-shaped eyes that seemed to bulge with kindness.

Yet behind the gentle and harmless mask was a face carved of cruelty.

He'd already begun a career of kidnapping children before he met Larissa and Amorale. He'd cart young boys and girls across Esperia and sell them to the highest bidder.

Ilaria rarely spoke up against the Heartless, but when they'd considered recruiting him, she'd been against it. Not that her opinion mattered.

What mattered was that his methods generated results, which greatly pleased Larissa and Amorale. And when they were pleased, they paid handsomely, which in turn pleased the Coachman.

He would have made a perfect Heartless, and more often than not, Ilaria worried that Amorale would convince Larissa to replace Ilaria with him. And now that he was the mastermind behind Pleasure Island, the bringer of a thousand souls that the Heartless would reap for more magic… he was a compelling recruit.

He also still had his heart, rotten as it was. Even without hers, Ilaria could sometimes feel traces of regret and compassion, fear and even hope. Ilaria hated hearing the wails of three-dozen-odd little boys, night after night, calling for their mothers. The moment their throats closed up and their words turned into brays and snorts never failed to chill her.

She hid her unease perfectly. Her life and position with the Heartless depended on it – she'd gone too far to turn back now. But every now and then she swore Amorale could read her mind. If not for Larissa, who had taken her in and mentored her, Amorale would have cast her out long ago. Or killed her.

Until Ilaria's heart was crushed completely, she'd always have this weakness. This softness in her that would keep her from becoming as powerful as Larissa or Amorale.

The Coachman had no such weakness.

Envy reared its ugly head. *Once I get my heart from Chiara, everything will be fine,* Ilaria tried to reassure herself. *It'll be fine.*

But that little voice in her head – that *conscience* – had become infuriatingly louder over the years. *Will it?* it asked now. *Or will you only lose what's left of yourself?*

"Here it is," the Coachman announced as some of his shadowmen came forth carrying a veiled painting. "Behold, a gift for the Heartless, in honour of our ten years together."

The Coachman lifted the veil, and Larissa gasped in delight. "My mother!"

Indeed, the woman in the painting did look like Larissa. The same darkly arched eyebrows and dark green eyes, the sheet of black hair – only with grey entwined along the temples.

"To the woman responsible for inspiring the Heartless," said the Coachman. "Shall we give her a place of honour?

Perhaps in the House of Mirrors? Or right here, where she can overlook all of the glory we shall bring."

Uneasiness prickled Ilaria. How odd that the story Larissa had told of her mother's plight against the Wishing Fairies was coming up again. "Why would we celebrate Larissa's mother?" Ilaria asked.

"Don't you know your own lore?" The Coachman chuckled.

"Ilaria's not fully one of us yet," said Amorale with a dismissive wave. "Her heart's always been… soft."

Ilaria seethed. For Amorale to think she wasn't dedicated enough for the Heartless was bad enough, but to be humiliated in front of the Coachman…

Amorale tipped her dark wand up at the painting of Larissa's mother in a motion of respect. "I guess it's time you honoured this clever woman yourself, Ilaria. Without her, the Heartless would never have been born. It's because of her we discovered the power of hate and despair."

Ilaria spoke slowly. "What happened?"

"We burned down my hometown," said Larissa, with a wistful smile that made Ilaria's blood chill. "When my mother prayed to the Wishing Star ever so convincingly for aid, it was Amorale who answered. Mirabella was suspicious from the start, and it was rather brazen of us to try the same with Amorale's village – but you know what we discovered? As people screamed and begged for mercy, we fairies could drink their fear and misery. That was how the Heartless were born."

The Coachman cackled with them, and Ilaria suppressed the anger flaring to her chest. Larissa had lied to her all along. If she'd known the truth, she'd never—

Never have joined them? she asked herself. *Is that really true?*

If she was honest, she couldn't answer that. While the three kept laughing, she clenched her wine, forcing herself to drink.

"Serves the Wishing Fairies right," said Larissa. "Them and their ludicrous rule about not using magic for your own personal advantage. Why not improve our family's life and station if we have the talent for magic?"

Why not indeed? Ilaria asked herself. After all, that was what had compelled her to join the Heartless in the first place, wasn't it? Wanting what was best for her family?

Or was it wanting what was best for herself?

Another sip, and the wine was done. She needed to share her own piece of celebratory news – before she lost her nerve.

She spoke while her throat burned: "Your Malevolences," she addressed Amorale and Larissa, "I have news to report – in private."

Amorale lifted a thin grey eyebrow. "Not now, Scarlet. Can't you see we're celebrating?"

"It has to do with my… my former sister," she forged on. "You'll like it."

Ilaria so rarely brought Chiara up that Amorale's eyes immediately flared with interest. "All right, but make it quick. There's too much fear to waste."

Just a whiff of fear gave her power, and it wouldn't be long before the first boy would transform. After that, it was only minutes before terror spread across the island. That was the Grey Fairy's favourite part of the night.

"The Blue Fairy has been assigned to search for Monstro. She's tracking him."

Amorale tossed a sheet of silvery hair behind her shoulder. "Exactly how is this good news? Or news at all, for that matter?"

"Because I know for a fact that the Blue Fairy, my former sister, has recently committed a mortal error."

Amorale frowned. Her interest was piqued.

"Go on," said Larissa.

"She granted the wish of an old friend and brought his puppet to life." Ilaria paused for effect. "He's a wooden boy named Pinocchio, and he's now on Pleasure Island, thanks to me."

Larissa leant forwards with interest. Amorale, too.

"You mean to say that the Blue Fairy has broken the most sacrosanct of fairy rules?"

"She did," Ilaria confirmed. "I caught her in the act and offered to help her – for a price." Ilaria summarised the wager her sister had accepted.

"Well done, Ilaria," murmured Amorale. "Your sister's heart would be a worthy prize indeed. You say the puppet is here?"

Amorale's recognition was so rare that Ilaria forgot her guilt and preened. "Yes, he arrived tonight."

"She'll be distracted as she looks for him," Larissa murmured, exchanging looks with Amorale. "We'll have to act fast."

"What must we do?" asked Ilaria.

"It seems misfortune is on our side," Larissa said. "First Monstro, now your news."

"What has Monstro done?"

"You'll soon find out." Larissa and Amorale indulged in a knowing chuckle. "Bring the wine, Ilaria."

"What for?"

"To trap Chiara inside." Amorale and Larissa exchanged nefarious glances.

"Coachman," Amorale said brusquely. "Go and find this puppet boy, Pinocchio. Make sure he doesn't escape while we're gone."

"Oh, they never escape, ma'am," said the Coachman. He rubbed his hands gleefully. "Not the way they came, anyway."

Gathering his whip, he lashed it on the ground, and Larissa and Amorale cackled in delight. Ilaria laughed too, but she felt no humour.

Only a chill in her blood that she couldn't shiver away.

There was a boulder in the middle of the Lyre Sea the size of a small island. It was smooth and dark as obsidian, and half-submerged in the water. Tired birds dived onto the rock to rest their wings, and the moment their webbed feet landed they realised something was wrong. But it was always too late to escape. Too late to leap into the air and fly away.

For the boulder came alive, and Monstro swooped down into the sea, taking the birds with him and drowning them before their next breath. Then his giant maw roared open, and he devoured them in one gulp.

Without missing a beat, he surfaced again, lying still as he had before. Maw shut; eyes, too. Monstro revelled in death – and his hunger knew no bounds.

As soon as he sensed the Scarlet Fairy and her elders approaching, Monstro's eyes flew open, filled with the smug satisfaction of a pet who knew he was about to be fed.

Larissa never disappointed. She blew a cloud of emerald

magic into the water, illuminating the path towards a small boat a few leagues ahead. Ilaria's sharp fairy vision spied an old man aboard, his face obscured by the white sail he was attempting to adjust against the gathering wind. He and his boat stood no chance against Monstro.

"That rusty old dinghy?" said Ilaria with a scoff. "You're going to send Monstro after that? There's only an old man aboard. How much suffering and fear can we get out of him? He'll probably die soon enough anyway."

"You'll see," said Amorale with the smile Ilaria didn't like. "Fate is kind indeed, and she's brought us an old friend."

As if on cue, Monstro turned on his belly and ripped back into the sea. While he sped towards the boat, Amorale dusted her hands.

"You see, little star, that rusty old dinghy belongs to Pinocchio's father," said Amorale. "I believe you knew him. Once upon a time."

A knot of dread started to tangle in Ilaria's stomach.

Once upon a time. Amorale's voice dripped with mockery. As if Ilaria's life before becoming a Heartless had been a fairy tale. She shrugged it off, pretending she hadn't heard, and fixed her gaze on the little boat. It juddered against the roaring waves, a speck in the water, completely unaware of the great whale torpedoing its way.

In a minute, Geppetto would be gone.

But what could she do? What did she care? He was probably searching for Pinocchio. Helping him only hindered her cause.

And yet… guilt needled her.

"Why so silent, little star?" said Amorale, poking at Ilaria's silence. "I remember Geppetto was a beau of yours, long ago. Don't tell me you still care about him."

"I don't," Ilaria said flatly.

"Good. Then you can be the one to seal his fate."

Ilaria bit her cheek before she expressed surprise. But Amorale was sharp. She always had been. "You look stricken, little star. All these years, Larissa's spoiled you by letting you get on without having to dirty those pretty little hands. You wanted more responsibility; you wanted to show how devoted you are. Show us."

Show us.

It *was* the chance Ilaria had been waiting for. She plastered on a smile. "It would be my greatest pleasure."

Unlike her mentors, never had she taken a person's life. Oh, she'd done cruel things. Made toads leap out of a girl's mouth when she talked, turned half a dozen boys into stone and even cursed a king to turn everything he touched into silver. But in the back of her mind, she knew Chiara and her fellow fairies would undo each of those spells within time.

Killing someone was final. Irreversible. A scar on her soul she wouldn't be able to wash away.

And to kill Geppetto of all people…

"Do this, and I will help you take your heart back from your sister," whispered Amorale. She patted her on the shoulder. "You'll be one of us in earnest, my darling. Isn't that what you've wanted most?"

Ilaria swallowed hard, ignoring the hollow pang in her chest.

Monstro was on his way, coursing unseen across the sea. But he was waiting for her blessing to take the ship.

Yes, that is what I want.

She had always been good at lying. Best of all, to herself. And as a Heartless, she'd mastered squashing that tiny conscience in her head. *Don't do this,* it begged her.

It's too late for Geppetto, she thought back. *I have to.*

Don't, Ily.

If he doesn't die, then I will. Larissa and Amorale will kill me.

At least let him live.

Ilaria made the slightest pause. It was hesitation, but she bore it outwardly with a smile, knowing Larissa would read it as pleasure. "I bid you devour that ship," she commanded Monstro through the ruby on her wand. Then, hoping the whale would obey her exact words, she added, "Swallow it whole."

Monstro opened his tremendous jaws, the sea roaring into his mouth. Geppetto and his ship disappeared into the whale's belly, like a flame gone out.

Had she killed him? The ghost of her heart thundered in her head, loud enough that she could barely hear herself speak. "It is done."

"He's still alive," said Amorale, looking into the black diamond shining upon her wand. Within flickered an image of Geppetto crumpled on the deck. The impact of Monstro's attack had slammed him against the wall of his ship, but he was breathing and starting to rise.

Larissa scowled. "You didn't kill him."

"If I killed him, then he wouldn't suffer the loss of his son," Ilaria replied evenly. "Let Pinocchio turn into a donkey first, and let us claim my sister's heart for our own. Then we can deal with Geppetto."

Her words were convincing enough even for herself. But Ilaria knew she was only buying time. Time for Geppetto, and time for herself to untangle just what she had done. If the Heartless knew she had listened to her conscience, the consequences would be… fatal.

She'd seen Amorale with her own apprentice, about two decades before. Amorale had been going through a phase where she trapped her victims in mirrors, and her apprentice made the mistake of accidentally breaking one and thus freeing the souls she had imprisoned within. Before he got a chance to set things right, Amorale had tapped him on the head with her black diamond, and the boy shattered like the mirror he had broken.

A gruesome, horrible fate. Amorale kept the remains in her Vallan mansion; the boy's mournful dead eyes were the first thing you saw when you entered.

Larissa was more patient. But that didn't mean she was more forgiving. The last Heartless who dared cross her she had trapped in a champagne bottle, wandless and powerless, and cursed to float forever across the ocean and never be found.

"I see," Amorale murmured. "I wasn't sure you had it in you."

"I told you my apprentice was well chosen," said Larissa. "There's not a chance Pinocchio will redeem himself now. He's doomed his father."

No, thought Ilaria mournfully.

I've *doomed his father.*

CHAPTER FORTY

A cloak of dark enchantment hid Pleasure Island from Chiara's detection. Its threads were fear and misery manifest, woven from the powers of all the Heartless combined.

Mist frothed over the sea, and Chiara would never have found the island if not for her dove.

"Pinocchio's there?" she asked, spying only water.

The dove insisted. It shook a wing, demonstrating that there was an invisible string linking it to Pinocchio. After all, they shared a creator in Geppetto – in a way, the bird and puppet were linked like siblings.

"I trust you," Chiara murmured. "Show me where he is."

The dove touched its forehead to hers, allowing her to see through its eyes. Then, folding its wings to its sides, it plunged through the mist and landed on top of the island's high wooden gate.

At the dock, a boat unloaded dozens of young boys from across Esperia. They rushed through the entrance giddily, lured by its spectacular sights – a Ferris wheel as tall as Esperia's grandest cathedrals, a carousel that never stopped, floating balloons shaped like bears and tigers.

Not one boy noticed the faceless shadow creatures lurking behind the gates. Chiara had never seen one before, but she recognised what they were: poor souls that had made bargains with the Heartless – and lost. As punishment, they lost their hearts and were forever doomed to serve Larissa and Amorale.

There had to have been hundreds of them on Pleasure Island. Some wore the masks of normal human beings, and acted as caretakers of the amusement park, food vendors and even janitors. The rest loitered about the island coast, waiting.

Waiting for what?

"Right here, boys!" cried a food barker. He was tossing out sweets and ice cream like a farmer tossing feed to chickens. "Get your cake, pie, dill pickles and ice cream. Eat all you can. Be a glutton, it's all free!"

Music piped loudly, drowning out the boys' excited squeals. They hurried deeper onto the island, a few dipping into the so-called brawl houses where everyone picked fights with one another, and everyone grabbing axes and hammers that the island staff handed out, using them to smash anything and everything in sight – all for the fun of it. The dove picked out Jiminy Cricket weaving frantically through the crowds, trying not to be squashed by the stampede of boys.

The crack of a whip startled the dove. As it jumped off the gates, the boat that had carried the boys to the island departed, and the gates began to close.

"Hop to it, you blokes," said the Coachman, lashing out his whip at the shadowmen. "Come on! Come on! Shut the doors and lock 'em tight." He laughed wickedly. "Now get below and get them crates ready."

Chiara didn't have to wait long to learn what they were getting them ready for.

It was something of an event at Pleasure Island – a twisted, grotesque celebration – when the first boy lost himself. Bells rang and sirens sang from every attraction and restaurant and building, though few paid attention to the noise. The music in the place was nearly deafening, and a few extra sirens were hardly cause for alarm.

But Chiara saw. She wished she could look away, but horror – pure, resounding horror – froze her in place.

Grey-brown fur coated the boy's arms, spreading quickly

to the rest of his skin, and a tail sprouted out from the back of his trousers. He screeched in terror, but the music piping over the island muffled his cries as his hands and feet became hooves and he fell onto all fours. "Mamma!" he cried. "Papa!"

They were the last words he uttered before his words turned into brays.

And the boy turned into a donkey.

Terror gripped Chiara. *Pinocchio,* she thought immediately. If he turned into a donkey, he'd be lost – just like Ilaria wanted. *We have to help Pinocchio.*

Her dove was already searching the island, swooping through room after room for the young puppet. To her relief, the cricket had figured out the island's scheme, and her dove tailed the pair making their escape. Together, cricket and boy dived into the sea, and as they swam to shore, Chiara let out a shaky breath.

"That was close," she said when Pinocchio and Jiminy had untangled themselves from the thorny mists that cloaked Pleasure Island.

Too close, she thought, watching Pinocchio wring his donkey ears and tail dry as they scampered through Pariva for Geppetto's workshop.

"The fairies need to know what's happening here," said Chiara, suppressing a shudder. There *had* to be a way to reverse the curse over the boys and return them to their families.

She lifted her wand, about to chime the Wishing Star's bells for an emergency meeting – when her dove let out an emphatic cry.

"Monstro?" she said.

The dove held out a wing, urging Chiara to follow. Together they flew down towards Pleasure Island. A handful of leagues outside the Heartless stronghold rested a figure so still Chiara had taken it for a boulder in the sea.

"So this is where he's been hiding," she breathed. "He's guarding the island. Only at night, you say? How on earth did you find him?"

The dove let out a sorrowful coo.

"Because Geppetto's trapped inside," she said as she understood.

It only just happened, the dove confirmed. *While Pinocchio was on Pleasure Island.*

"We need to send Pinocchio a message," said Chiara. A feather quill appeared in her hand, and quickly she wrote:

Your father went looking for you and has been swallowed by a whale named Monstro. He's alive, but you must find him quickly. Save him, while I recruit the fairies to help the boys on Pleasure Island.

She had to hurry.

Tomorrow would be the third and last day of her bet with Ilaria. If Pinocchio couldn't prove that he was a good boy by dusk, he would turn into lifeless wood again, this time forever.

And she would owe her heart.

CHAPTER FORTY-ONE

Deep in the belly of the whale Monstro, Geppetto tried to count his blessings. For one, he was alive; Figaro and Cleo, too. Two, his ship was still mostly intact, having been swallowed whole down the giant whale's gullet. He had a bed with a blanket – a bit threadbare, but it was better than nothing – a table and two chairs, even a stack of spine-bent books to pass the time.

"It's almost like home," he said aloud to his pets, trying to remain cheerful.

Who was he fooling? He was trapped in the cavernous belly of a whale. His situation was hopeless, his fate was fixed. There was no way to escape Monstro's jaws. Not a sliver of daylight pierced the cracks between his enormous teeth, and the whale had been asleep ever since he had swallowed Geppetto's ship. Had it been only a day? It felt like more. Geppetto had no sense of time any more.

Worse yet, he had run out of food.

All day he'd spent fishing, but every net came up empty. Hard to stay cheerful in such conditions.

For Figaro's and Cleo's sakes, he masked his desperation and hummed whenever he could – slivers of his favourite tunes. But not even music could raise his company's morale.

"Not a bite for days," he mumbled miserably. "We can't hold out for much longer." He sneezed. "I never thought it would end this way, Figaro… starving to death in the belly of a whale." He sniffled. "My poor little Pinocchio."

His stomach growled, and he leant over the railing of his ship, staring into the empty water that pooled over Monstro's gut. "It's hopeless, Figaro. There isn't a fish left. If the monster doesn't wake up soon, I… I'm afraid we are done for."

Geppetto heaved a sigh, about to rise from his chair and give up on fishing. But lo, something rattled against the top of Monstro's head, and the whale lurched.

He was awake!

His jaws began to part. Wind and ocean spilled inside, rocking Geppetto's boat back against Monstro's throat. Geppetto clambered to the edge of his ship for a better look. His eyes watered from the bright light that fanned across the ship, but as he squinted, the most beautiful sight came thrashing across the waters.

Tuna! Hundreds and hundreds of tuna!

Seizing his net and his fishing rod, Geppetto raced to catch as many as he could. "Here they come," he cried. "Tuna, tuna fish! Here's a big one. Get them in there, Figaro!"

The cat leapt with joy, and Geppetto would have done the same if he hadn't been so busy. There wasn't a second to waste. He hauled tuna onto the boat, hurling them onto the floor, onto the cargo boxes and the barrels behind him. It didn't matter, so long as they were aboard.

He was so absorbed in reeling in fish that he did not hear the voice that suddenly cried out behind him.

"Hey! Hey!"

"Here's another one," Geppetto shouted, winding another tuna into the barrel. He had to hurry. Oh, he'd caught maybe a dozen or two fish, but Monstro's jaws were already starting to close, and who knew how long it would be until he woke again? He hurled his net into the water again.

"Hey, Father!" cried the voice once more. "Father!"

"Don't bother me now, Pinocchio," Geppetto dismissed, one beat before his eyes went wide with realisation. "Pinocchio!"

What a wondrous turn of events! He must have reeled

the boy onto his ship and not have noticed it! The father ran towards his son, scooping him up into a delighted embrace. "Pinocchio, my boy. I'm so happy to see you!"

Pinocchio sneezed, and Geppetto's heart immediately leapt with worry. "You're soaking wet. You mustn't catch cold."

"But I came to see you!"

How Geppetto warmed at the words. He knelt so he was eye level with his son. "Let me take your hat." He started to pat the boy's black hair dry and slid off Pinocchio's hat.

A gasp caught in his throat, and he nearly fell backwards.

"What's the matter, Father?" asked Pinocchio.

"Your ears!" Geppetto whispered, pointing at the two grey donkey ears that curled up from Pinocchio's head. "What's happened to your ears?"

Pinocchio reached up above his head, suddenly remembering with a good-natured smile. "Oh, these. That's nothing. I've got a tail, too." He laughed, but the sound quickly morphed into a beastly hee-haw. His humour vanished, and he covered his mouth with his hands and stared at the ground.

Sensing his son's shame, Geppetto exhaled quietly. His alarm melted, and emotion heated his eyes and throat. "Never mind now," he said tenderly. He scooped up the boy into his arms. "Old Geppetto has his son back. Nothing else matters." He laughed, touching his nose to his son's. He sat Pinocchio on his lap. "Are you hungry? Have you been eating, sleeping?"

He didn't give Pinocchio a chance to respond. "We'll cook a feast! We've plenty of fish now. You can tell me where you've been, and how you found me." His voice turned stern, an echo of his father's. "Though you really shouldn't have come here, Pinocchio. It's dangerous, you know."

A wave of emotions overcame him, and his rebuke trailed, and he hugged the boy close. He couldn't muster any more words of reproach at Pinocchio; he was too grateful and relieved to have him back.

Even if he had to spend the rest of his life trapped in Monstro's belly, it wouldn't be so bad now that he had Pinocchio with him. They would find a way to survive, one day at a time.

CHAPTER FORTY-TWO

Chiara navigated a low-hanging cloud, advancing as close as she could to Monstro. But every time she ventured near, a net of dark enchantment threatened to ensnare her. She tried sending her dove, but Monstro was fast asleep. Her bird couldn't even slip through the gaps between the whale's teeth, or fly through his blowhole.

So she waited, and she rang the Wishing Star's bell thrice, over and over. Help was on its way, but did it always take this long for the fairies to come? Every second mattered, and there weren't many left.

The day aged, and the sun pinched into a corner of the world, about to begin its daily descent.

"Still holding out hope for Pinocchio?" Ilaria said,

materialising on Chiara's cloud. "It's time to gracefully admit defeat, sister. You've lost. The wager is over."

"It isn't sundown yet," said Chiara, acknowledging her sister only with a glance.

"It might as well be. Pinocchio's actions have doomed Geppetto. Look at them. They're trapped inside Monstro's belly, perishing together in a cruel twist of fate, as Geppetto would've done as a young lad if you had not intervened – oh, what an opera this would have made." Ilaria bent backwards and pretended to swoon. Then she chuckled darkly. "I can't think of another production with such delightful agony. It's time to face the truth: Pinocchio will never prove himself worthy of being a real boy. Not in the hour that you have left."

"I have faith in Pinocchio," said Chiara. Her voice, though calm, betrayed her with a hitch. Ilaria was right – Pinocchio couldn't redeem himself while he was trapped inside Monstro. "Pinocchio is brave. He will follow through."

"Brave, perhaps," Ilaria allowed. "But unselfish? Truthful?" She snorted. "It's your fault, really, if you must know the truth. If you hadn't made Geppetto forget his past, he wouldn't have sailed into the Lyre Sea in the first place. He would have remembered what Monstro did to him."

"Geppetto would have gone anyway. His love for Pinocchio is true, just as mine is for you." Chiara held out her hands to Ilaria. "That's why the Heartless haven't been able to reach you, Ily. There is no greater power than love, and there is nothing I wouldn't do to bring you home."

Ilaria turned rigid. "You're delusional, Chiara. Concede and give me your heart, and I'll let Geppetto go free."

"No."

"I give you this chance to come with me," said Ilaria. "Larissa and Amorale will make it much more painful for you than I will."

"I have faith in Pinocchio," Chiara repeated. "And in you."

"Then you're about to be very disappointed." Ilaria tipped her gaze upwards at the sky. "You're waiting for your friends." The red feather in her dark hair shook as she tittered. "I regret to inform you, sister dear, that they have been… detained. But don't fret. *My* friends are here."

Green and grey mist permeated Chiara's cloud, and in a flash, Larissa the Green Fairy and Amorale the Grey Fairy appeared at Ilaria's sides.

Chiara didn't even get a chance to take out her wand. Together, Larissa and Amorale stirred their wands into her cloud. Lightning sizzled, and shadowy arms of magic shot out to wrap around Chiara's ankles.

The Blue Fairy couldn't move. When she tried, the Heartless's spell gnawed deep into her flesh, dark magic sinking into her bones. The pain was unlike anything she had ever felt.

"Hurts, doesn't it?" said Larissa, stroking Chiara's cheek. "That's just the beginning. Like you said, you still have an hour until the wager's up. We can deal a lot of pain in one hour – before we kill you."

"You didn't say you were going to kill her," said Ilaria. She conjured a wine bottle and held it out. "I thought you were going to trap her—"

"We changed our minds," said Larissa. "Do you take issue with that, little star?"

It was a challenge, and Ilaria knew it. Her breath hitched. "I thought you couldn't kill a fairy."

"Normally, we can't," Amorale agreed. "But since the two of you have a binding contract where Chiara will owe her heart when she loses, it is yours – *ours,* to destroy."

"That would make her one of us, a Heartless," said Ily, trying to understand. "Wouldn't it?"

"You think she'd become a Heartless even without a heart?" Amorale chuckled. "Oh, poor dear. Only the truly wicked can survive when their hearts are obliterated, my star. Your sister Chiara is all heart. She will die."

Ilaria shrank. "I never agreed to—"

"You do as we say," Amorale growled. "Unless you think we should question your commitment."

"No." Ilaria faltered. "No."

"Good," said Larissa, stabbing her heel into the cloud. "Your bond has always held you back. With her gone, the time will come for you to join us, as *our* sister."

Chiara flailed, but the chains over her ankles only shot fire into her veins. The pain made her crumble to her knees. *Ilaria, please.*

Ilaria pretended not to see. "I'm ready."

"Wonderful," said Amorale. "Then we begin."

Larissa brandished her wand, and its emerald glowed, searing the sky with its brightness. Two green claws extended from the emerald and reached, tauntingly, for Chiara's heart.

Chiara wasn't looking at Larissa or her wand. "Ily," she whispered, reaching out to her sister. "Ily…"

Then the claws wrapped around her heart, cold as ice.

Chiara's entire body spasmed, and as hard as she tried to hold in her scream, it boiled out of her throat. She felt like a piece of glass being shattered again and again. Each time her heart dared to beat, Larissa's powers dug even deeper, and pain exploded inside her, threatening to rip her apart.

Through it all, Chiara kept her eyes on her sister. Ily's lips were pursed, and she floated off the edge of the cloud. But at her sides, her fists were curled, and she was holding her wand.

"That's enough," Ilaria said harshly.

Chiara lifted with hope until Ilaria stepped forwards, her face an unfathomable mask. "I'll deliver the final blow."

And yet, Chiara did not quail. She would not give up her faith in her sister. "I believe in you, Ily."

"Your hopes are in vain," said Larissa, making way for Ilaria to approach. "That's it, my star. Remember all the Blue Fairy's broken promises, her lies and betrayals. Without her, you'll be one of us. Finally."

"I never lied to you," said Chia staunchly. "I love you, Ily."

Energy crackled from the ruby on Ilaria's wand, and she drew tiny circles in the air, gathering the darkness that emanated from Monstro's aura. The ruby turned obsidian black, heavy with enchantment.

"Goodbye," Ilaria said, pointing it at Chiara.

In a cascade of red light and shadow, magic surged out of Ilaria's wand, but at the last instant, she whirled and cast her spell instead upon Amorale and Larissa.

There was no one word that could encapsulate the look on their faces. Terror, outrage, shock and fury. All those twisted the Heartless's features before Ilaria sent them reeling into smoke.

"Begone!" Ilaria cried, seizing Larissa and Amorale's wands before the two fairies began to funnel into the bottle.

"You stupid, stupid girl," Larissa whispered as she

fought off the spell, trying desperately to take her wand back. But her fingers were already smoke, and she could not grasp it. "What do you think will happen to your dreams when you betray us?"

"No one will remember Cleo del Mar," hissed Amorale. "You'll be back where you started."

Ilaria's chest tightened, only for a second, and then her expression hardened. "Good." Holding all three wands, she banished her former mentors into the glass bottle and conjured a thick round cork to shut it tight. Without bravado, she dropped the bottle into the sea – listening intently for a splash.

"Good riddance," she muttered.

Then she aimed her wand at Chiara's shackles. They fizzled into the air.

The Blue Fairy's voice came out as a rasp. "What… what did you do to them?"

"Trapped them. They can't cast magic without their wands, and certainly not while they're locked up in that tiny space. It will probably take a century or two for them to get out." Ilaria rubbed a spot of dirt off her ruby. "They had it coming."

Ilaria's back was to her, but Chiara's heart welled with warmth. *You're back*, she thought, tears pinching the corners of her eyes. *You're finally back.*

"Ilaria…" she began.

"Don't say anything," grumbled Ilaria as she snapped Amorale and Larissa's wands in half over her knee. "I don't need you gloating."

"I never gloat," said Chiara.

Ilaria whirled. "Yes, you do. When your left eyebrow lifts – like it is right now, it's the I-was-right look."

"It's more of an I-am-relieved sort of look." Chiara rose slowly to her knees. "Thank you for saving me."

"You're—you're all right?" said Ilaria. "Did they… hurt you?"

Chiara's body still tingled from the lightning shackles Larissa and Amorale had bound about her ankles, but the pain had already faded. "I'm fine. How did you do that?"

"They've been channelling most of their magic into cloaking Pleasure Island and Monstro from the rest of the world. I stole back some of that energy from Monstro – to use it against you." Her smug air faltered. "I suppose I ended up putting it to better use. Wasn't sure it would actually work… but Larissa and Amorale sure didn't expect it."

Chiara clapped. "*I* didn't expect it."

"Yes you did. I knew you were gloating."

"Not gloating, Ily. Proud."

"Whatever you say," Ilaria mumbled, but the edge in her voice was sanded off. "I couldn't let them take you, too."

Chiara reached for her sister's hand. "Thank you."

Ilaria looked down at their hands, then spun towards Monstro. "We better hurry if you're going to win our wager. You only have a few minutes left. Here." She passed Chiara the snapped halves of Amorale's wand. "You throw Amorale's, I throw Larissa's. Aim for his eye."

"Monstro's head?" Chiara asked as Ilaria flung the wand. Chiara threw, too, matching her sister's strength. The wands skimmed the side of Monstro's head, then bounced into the sea.

"It was worth a try. No magic will touch Monstro – not yours, not mine. All we can do is wait. And hope that he wakes up soon."

CHAPTER FORTY-THREE

Geppetto wrapped his son with a blanket and sat with Pinocchio in the ship's hold. It was the warmest spot he could offer, and the poor boy was drenched from swimming. Geppetto had so many questions, but the sight of Pinocchio safe and with him made him decide they could wait.

"Is this your boat, Father?"

"Mine? No, it's from a friend. I borrowed it."

"Does that mean we have to give it back? I like the water. There's a lot of fish inside."

"When we go home, I'll get us a boat. We can go fishing together."

"I'd like that!"

"But first we have to get out of this whale," said Geppetto

sadly. "You know, it's funny. I feel like I've met Monstro before. But that's impossible, isn't it?"

Geppetto leant back against the wall, trying with difficulty to recall when he might have met the whale, but he couldn't.

With a sigh, he hummed a song as he stroked Pinocchio's long ears. A song he hadn't heard in many years. The first notes came tentatively, and he made the winding turns and leaps of the melody like navigating to a destination without a map, but he forged on, letting his heart take him from note to note. Bit by bit, the song budded and bloomed, and it was like finding a treasure he'd buried years ago under the sand. Still there. Just a little older and dustier.

"That's a pretty song, Father. What is it?"

"It's about nightingales," replied Geppetto, amazed that he remembered. "A nightingale who is lost in the forest, and in her despair, she loses her song. Only through love and hope does she find it again. Then she finally flies her way home."

"I wish we were birds and could fly out of here," Pinocchio said glumly. "There has to be a way we can escape."

"I've tried everything," Geppetto replied. He reached for his boy's hand to comfort him.

"Maybe if we had a smaller boat—"

"We do," said Geppetto. He gestured at the raft he'd built that morning. It was a pitiful-looking thing, but it floated against the water, tethered to the boat by rope.

"A raft!" Pinocchio's eyes lit. "We'll take the raft, and when the whale opens his mouth—"

"No, no, no." Geppetto gestured the impossibility of it all with his hands. "Now, listen, son. He only opens his mouth when he's eating. Then everything comes in. Nothing goes out." As Pinocchio's face fell, Geppetto took him by the arm. "It's hopeless, Pinocchio. Come on, we'll make a nice fire and cook some of the fish."

"A fire, that's it!"

"Yes," agreed Geppetto. "And then we'll all eat again." Just the thought of food comforted his belly.

"A great big fire," Pinocchio went on. "With lots of smoke!" He started grabbing items within the boat and smashing them into firewood. "Quick, some wood! We'll make him sneeze!"

"Make him sneeze?" Geppetto considered. "That will make him mad."

"Mad is what we want!"

Geppetto's heart picked up its pace as he thought this through. Maybe. Just maybe, Pinocchio's idea would work. They heaped a pile of wood on the boat, and Pinocchio shattered a lantern over it. A fire blazed over the wood, and smoke billowed high above their heads.

As the fire consumed the boat, Pinocchio and Geppetto quickly gathered Figaro and Cleo, grabbed oars and leapt onto the raft. Together they rowed, fighting against the current with all their might.

The whale was already shuddering, holding in a sneeze as the smoke grew. He heaved over and over, trying to stifle it.

But he could not.

In a thunderous blast, Monstro sneezed. Out of his jaws Pinocchio and Geppetto sailed, racing into the open waters of the Lyre Sea. They knew they couldn't let up, for once Monstro regained control of his senses, he would be after them.

Monstro chased them across the sea, ripping through the waves as if they were paper. It was hopeless trying to flee, and their pitiful raft skated across the waves, nearly crushed by Monstro's tail alone. Both of them knew it was only a matter of time before the waves destroyed them. At the last moment, before the sea blasted their raft into smithereens, Geppetto and Pinocchio leapt with Figaro and Cleo.

The water was so cold that the chill set into Geppetto's blood and muscles and nearly froze his mind.

"Swim, Pinocchio," Geppetto cried as the sea gained strength and water rushed into his lungs. "Swim, my boy!"

He swam, too, kicking and pushing with all his might. But he was not a young man any more, and he was exhausted and hungry. Even if he had been at his prime, there was no way he could have defeated Monstro.

Let alone a furious Monstro.

Geppetto could feel the whale's wrath in the water. As Monstro ripped through the sea, the very world tilted and shuddered. All it took was one giant wave thundering over him, and Geppetto was knocked senseless.

Seconds later, when he regained consciousness, he was hanging over a piece of floating debris. Shore was within sight, a blurry aspiration that he had not the strength to reach.

"Father!" cried Pinocchio, clutching his arm. "Father, stay awake! We're almost there."

Geppetto gazed at his young son, who struggled to keep both of them afloat. He had never felt more love for anyone. "Go on, Pinocchio," he murmured. "I'll only hold you back. Save yourself."

"No! Father, come on!"

With what strength he had in his reserves, Geppetto kicked and thrashed. Every second felt like a year, and he couldn't tell whether it was the sky growing darker or whether it was his vision growing dim.

At last, the shore was within reach, but a current tore Pinocchio and Geppetto apart. Geppetto's back slammed against a boulder, and the world blanked into nothing.

When he washed up on the shore, it was dusk.

Geppetto rose limply. His throat burned, and his eyes stung with salt. By some miracle, Figaro and Cleo in her bowl had washed up beside him. Were he not so utterly spent, he would have picked them up in joy.

As it was, he crawled across the sand, one hand in front of the other, his legs plodding after them. The world was a wash of rock and seawater; his glasses were broken, and he could hardly make out the sand from the sky.

Behind the rocks, a haze of red and yellow distilled into the outline of his dear son.

"Pinocchio!" Geppetto cried, finding his voice. His arms and legs found strength, and he hurried towards his son.

But his son's face was in the sand. The wooden boy, who had so filled Geppetto's heart with happiness – was dead.

CHAPTER FORTY-FOUR

The sun dipped behind the mountains, and night swept away the last remnants of day. The Heartless were gone, and Chiara's wager with Ilaria was over.

A song peeled out of the howling winds, and neither sister dared move. It was a song that both sisters were sure at first that they were imagining – soft, sung slightly off-key, but carrying all the heart in the world.

Geppetto. The old man wept on the beach, shadows crawling over his shoulders as he held his son to his chest and rocked him from side to side, as if he were a cradle for his fallen boy.

Geppetto cried the Nightingale Aria. The song Geppetto had immortalised in the music box he'd once given Ilaria. Once, it had been performed by every prima donna across

Esperia; its popularity had faded over the years, and now it'd become a ghost, like Chiara and Ilaria – forgotten almost completely.

Geppetto sang slowly, stretching out the words between his tears, yet his voice was so gentle, so tender, that it sounded like a lullaby.

Ilaria said nothing. She bit on her lip, trying to hold in the emotions that rose to her chest. Emotions she hadn't felt in forty years.

She wished she could comfort Geppetto. She wished she hadn't brought this misery upon him, and she regretted everything. Most of all, she regretted that she'd left home.

"You've won," she told Chiara at last. "Pinocchio is a good boy."

The Blue Fairy swallowed. "It's too late. No power of light or darkness can bring the dead back to life."

"But Pinocchio was only half-alive to begin with." Ilaria examined the ruby on her wand.

The resentment and anger she'd nursed inside her for forty years was fading, and with it, her power. She needed to hurry. She didn't want to be a Heartless a moment longer than she had to, but there was something she needed to do before she renounced her dark enchantments.

"With the last of my magic, I pledge to help Pinocchio become a real boy." She extended her hand to Chiara. "You remember what happened when our magics came together and struck your dove?"

As if on cue, Chiara's white dove flew past them and landed on Ilaria's arm.

"She came to life," Chia murmured. "Thanks to the two of us."

"It takes two to make miracles happen," said Ily. "Will you do the honours?"

Taking in a deep breath, Chiara nodded, and together, hand in hand, the sisters approached the lifeless Pinocchio.

Prove yourself brave, truthful and unselfish, and someday you will be a real boy. She touched her wand to Pinocchio's head. "Awake, Pinocchio. Awake."

Magic brimmed across the young boy's still body, bringing him life. His cheeks turned rosy, and his wooden nose became one made of flesh, the nails in his knees and elbows turning into joints and bone and muscle. Gone were his donkey ears and tail.

"Papa!" he spoke. "Papa, I'm alive!"

Geppetto rose from the sand, unable to believe his ears. But when he saw his dearest Pinocchio a real boy, his tears of sorrow turned to joy. He scooped his boy into his arms. "My son," he whispered. "You've come home."

Chiara watched them, her heart full of relief and gladness. This was what made her love being a fairy –

the tender moments of joy, the proof that hope was never in vain.

While the father and son rejoiced, the Blue Fairy guided her sister away from the coast. Two hearts had just been reunited, but there were two more that she was waiting on.

Chiara held out Ily's old music box. "Will you take your heart?" she asked quietly.

"If I do, will I have to forget you, like everyone else?"

Chiara swallowed hard. "I don't know," she admitted. "I'll have to ask."

Ilaria slid the music box off Chiara's palm onto hers. "Even if they say yes, I want my heart back. Even if I'm only your sister, your best friend, your Ily for a minute or an hour, it'll be worth it."

Tears rimmed Chiara's eyes, and she linked her arm with her sister's as Ily opened the music box. The Nightingale Aria hummed to life, and Ilaria let out a shaky breath.

"I'm going home," she whispered to Chiara. "Like the nightingale, I've finally found home again."

She sang along, softly, as she held the box to her chest. With each note, a beam of light radiated from the music box, growing brighter and brighter until it enveloped Ilaria completely.

The light folded into her chest, and her heart was her own once more.

Warmth returned to her eyes, and she aged forty years, her dark brown hair greying into a peppery silver. But her green eyes still danced with youthful mischief.

"I thought I'd be more upset at seeing myself old," Ilaria said, staring at her hands and patting her cheeks. She cleared her throat at the sound of her voice, a good half an octave lower than it'd been only minutes ago. It would take some getting used to. "But you know, I don't look bad." She glanced at her reflection in the sea and tapped at the wrinkles around her eyes. "Almost as pretty as Mother, I'd say."

Chiara laughed and held out her arms to hug her sister. But after a long beat, Ilaria withdrew.

"I don't deserve to live again." The former Scarlet Fairy stared at her hands. "After everything I've done…"

Chiara wrapped a protective arm around her sister. "You've done terrible things, but many of them can still be undone. That's where you'll begin."

Bells interrupted Ilaria's chance to reply, and the two sisters looked up. A kaleidoscope of lights descended upon them: the fairies of the Wishing Star. Released from the Heartless's obstructive spell, they were coming to heed the Blue Fairy's call.

CHAPTER FORTY-FIVE

It was the first time Chiara had seen her fellow fairies assembled together outside the Wishing Star. They landed one by one on the beach, each a bright and vibrant pop of colour against the pale sand and grey sky. Not one was smiling.

Chiara's heart sank, but for Ily's sake, she kept her spirits up and led her sister to greet the fairies.

Mirabella was already waiting, but her stern gaze was on Chiara, not the former Scarlet Fairy.

She spoke: "It has come to my attention, Chiara, that you were once friends with Mr Geppetto of Pariva, and that you granted his wish to bring to life his wooden puppet, Pinocchio."

Chiara bowed her head. "Yes, ma'am."

"You promised Pinocchio that you would turn him into a real boy if he proved himself to be brave, truthful and unselfish."

"I did."

"Such promises are not to be made without express permission and consideration from your fairy elders and the council."

"I know," pleaded Chiara. "But Pinocchio… if only you'd seen the happiness on his face. And on Geppetto's face. It was not a wish made in selfishness."

"Manipulating the gift of life goes against our ways," Mirabella said. "Instead of adhering to the rules you've been taught, you entered a bargain with one of the Heartless, and in the hopes of redeeming the Scarlet Fairy's heart, you gambled your own – on Pinocchio's life. This is most disappointing, Chiara, and not what I would have expected from a fairy of your calibre and reputation."

Ily stiffened at her side. "I didn't give her a choice," she said. "You can't blame her."

"I haven't finished," Mirabella said, frowning at the former Scarlet Fairy. She settled her austere gaze on Chiara, then sighed. "You've made some questionable decisions, Blue Fairy, and yet… at the end, an old man who has spent a lifetime bringing joy to those around him has at last found his own joy, a puppet has become a real boy, and a Heartless has found her heart again."

Chiara dared to look up.

Now Mirabella was smiling. She lowered her wand. "I think some of us have been on the Wishing Star so long that we forget that the rules we set in place long ago may need reviewing. In our efforts to protect ourselves and those we love and guard from the Heartless, we forget that not every heart is only good or only bad."

The other fairies murmured their agreement.

"We forget that the sacrifices we require and make in good faith aren't always what's best for everyone, and we forget to cherish, most of all, the joys and happiness that come with compassion, selflessness and bravery."

Mirabella drew herself tall. "By the vote of the fairies of the Wishing Star, you will remain a fairy, so long as you wish. But to admonish you for the rules that you have broken, you will be suspended from the Wishing Star for a period of one year – once our business with Pleasure Island and Monstro is finished. During that time, you will remain in Pariva with your family. You will be reinstated once the year is over."

That was hardly a punishment, and Chiara's heart rose. "Mirabella…" she breathed. "Thank you."

"I'm not finished." Mirabella's tone had softened, and Agata appeared at her side.

"It has never sat right with me that we must make our loved ones forget us," said Agata quietly. "As Mirabella says, perhaps that sacrifice is not what's best for everyone, and it is time we revisited that rule and re-evaluated whether it does more harm than good."

"Fairies need time with their loved ones, like everyone else," chimed in Peri. "I think those connections to our friends and family actually make our magic stronger."

"I would agree," exclaimed the Rose Fairy.

"Me too!" the Yellow Fairy said.

"It seems like there's enough desire for us to take a vote when we're back on the Wishing Star," mused Mirabella.

"A vote's perfunctory," Agata murmured to Chiara. "I have a feeling we'll have many forgetting spells to undo, shortly. It's about time, too."

"We'll take a vote," Mirabella repeated. "But first, Monstro awaits."

One by one, the fairies waved their wands and became beams of flying starlight.

Chiara was last to go. She took Ilaria's hand. "Come with us," she said.

"Are you sure I'm allowed to?"

"We'll need all the help we can get," Chiara assured her.

Side by side, the two sisters flew together – with Chiara

holding on to Ily – after the other fairies, until they came upon Monstro resting in the middle of the Lyre Sea.

Joining their powers together, the fairies of the Wishing Star pointed their wands at Monstro. "Sleep, Monstro. Sleep, and do not let your wickedness trouble the shores and seas of Esperia any longer."

In an effort to fight off the fairies' spell, the giant whale thrashed and started to dive back into the sea, but the Heartless magic that had once given him unimaginable power had weakened, and without Larissa and Amorale's help, he could no longer resist the good fairies' magic. Slowly, his eyelids grew heavy, and he began to sink to the bottom of the sea, where he would remain for a long, long time.

The fairies let out jubilant cheers, and Agata dusted her hands. As always, she was ready for the next item of business. "Next, we visit Pleasure Island," she said. "There are hundreds of boys who want to go home. Their mothers have been missing them."

"May I come, too?" Ilaria asked in a small voice. The ruby on her wand was starting to lose its lustre, and soon, once she let go of all her resentment, bitterness and anger, she would lose her power. "My magic as a Heartless contributed to building the island. Let it help dismantle the place, and reverse the curse upon all those poor boys."

"And what will you do after you help us, Ilaria Belmagio?" asked Agata. Her words did not betray any reproach, but they also carried no sign of forgiveness. "You are a Heartless no longer."

Ilaria swallowed and stared down at her reflection in her wand's ruby. "I'm an old woman now, and with the years I have left, I'd like to atone for the mistakes I've made." She held out her wand. "Imprison me, please. The way you did Monstro. I would welcome the sentence."

"It is not our place to punish the deeds you regret," said Mirabella kindly. "That is for your own conscience to bear."

"Then what must I do?" Ilaria said.

"What do you *want* to do?" asked Chiara.

Ilaria drew a ragged breath, and her eyes misted. "I'd like a second chance with my family," she said quietly, meeting Chiara's gaze. "I'd like to ask their forgiveness for my selfishness. I know I don't deserve it, but that's where I'd like to start."

It was all Chiara could do not to hug her sister right there and then, but Ily wasn't finished. "Music once brought me great joy," the former Scarlet Fairy went on. "I'd like to start a school for children, maybe even a choir in town." She paused. "The boys of Pleasure Island contented themselves by brawling with one another and destroying everything in sight. I'd like to teach them – as well as anyone who will listen – to find happiness through song and harmony."

"You always did love to sing," said Chiara, wrapping her arm around her sister. "I think it's a wonderful idea."

"As do I," said Agata.

"And I," Mirabella chimed in.

One by one, the fairies of the Wishing Star agreed, and with the fairies' blessing, Ilaria accompanied them to what remained of Pleasure Island.

It took one long week for the fairies to track down every boy who had been turned into a donkey, and Mirabella and Agata personally sought out the Coachman, Honest John, Gideon, Stromboli and other servants of the Heartless and ensured that the villains were taught just lessons for their evil behaviour. Stromboli, for instance, was plagued with nightmares that his puppets came to life and attacked him, and Honest John and Gideon dreamt that they drowned in piles of golden coins.

But for the Coachman, who was so evil that no lesson would redeem him, Ilaria used the last of her Heartless magic and turned him into a donkey. In the pastures of Pariva, he spent the rest of his days gnawing on hay and grass and braying unpleasantly whenever young boys laughed at his smell.

As for the Heartless – without Amorale and Larissa to lead them, their strength as a group waned, and many of them instinctively fell into a deep slumber, as Monstro had. Their absence wouldn't last forever of course, but it would give the Wishing Fairies time to re-evaluate the rigidity of their old rules and ways.

In the meantime, the Wishing Fairies found the bottle that contained Amorale and Larissa and brought it onto the Wishing Star. There, they dropped the bottle into the bottom of the deepest well, with a sign for all that there were Heartless within, and they were not to be disturbed.

When it was all done, Ily and Chia received the fairies' blessing to return to Pariva. It was unanimously voted that the fairies should lift their respective forgetting spells, and in the future, every fairy would receive one month every year to spend in Esperia – with their family, their friends or however they pleased.

Chiara's time home would begin as soon as she set aside her wand.

Spring seemed to have arrived overnight. Daffodils and violets bloomed from the flowerbeds along the cobblestone streets, birds chirped and whistled from every tree, and the town square was busier than ever. Hardly anyone noticed Chiara and Ilaria walking along Pine Grove.

"You know what I wished, all those years ago when we were girls?" Ilaria's voice hitched, and her eyes turned wet. "You thought I wished to be an opera singer. The best in all of Esperia."

"Didn't you?"

She shook her head. "I wished that we would be together, always."

Chiara swallowed hard. She hugged her sister. "We will be together. I'm coming, too, remember?

"Give me a moment on my own," Ilaria said, flipping her grey hair. "I've got a lot of explaining to do. Though I don't even have a room any more. Our grandnieces have taken it over."

"They're still young," said Chiara with a smile. "I'm sure they'd be happy to share. Maybe in exchange for singing lessons."

Ilaria tossed her a sceptical look, but as if on cue, Nina and Dafne Belmagio raced each other down the road. In her haste, little Nina didn't look where she was going and nearly bumped into Ilaria.

"I'm sorry!" the young girl cried. Her red hair bow had come undone while she was running, and it fell onto the ground.

As Ily knelt to pick it up, Dafne went over to her sister's

side. "Told you to look where you're going when we race. Come on, Grandpa's waiting for us to help make cookies. We should—"

"Don't forget your ribbon," said Ilaria, calling after the pair as they headed towards the bakery.

Dafne glanced over her shoulder. "You sound familiar," she said, her bright green eyes rounding at the sight of Ily. "Do I know you?"

Instead of replying, Ilaria knelt and gently tied Nina's bow back into her hair. Then she faced the elder Belmagio girl. "You're Dafne. Niccolo Belmagio's granddaughter?"

"Both of us are," chimed in Nina.

"Hush, Nina, we aren't supposed to talk to strangers."

"But she doesn't look like a stranger. She looks like Daddy."

Ilaria's heart swelled, feeling pain and joy both at once.

"What's your name?" asked the older girl.

"Ilaria, but friends call me Ily. Ily Belmagio."

"Belmagio?" cried Nina. "But that's our name!"

Ilaria chuckled. "Well, you see… I'm your grandfather's sister. That would make me…" She frowned, having to think about it.

"Our great-aunt Ily!" Nina staggered back, unable to believe it. "Grandpa told us you're famous – a real prima donna. But I thought your name was…" Nina stopped with a frown. "Funny, I can't remember any more. All I can think of is a goldfish."

Ilaria chuckled. "I'm no diva," she said honestly. "I did like to sing when I was young, though."

"You mean you're not famous?" said Nina, blinking with confusion. "Grandpa lied to us?"

"No, *I* lied."

Dafne crossed her arms. "That's a big lie to tell."

Ilaria couldn't disagree.

"Grandpa says if you tell too many lies, your nose will grow flowers."

"My nose used to have a lot of flowers," Ilaria admitted. "It took a long time for me to prune them all off."

"They must make a nice bouquet."

That made Ilaria laugh again. "The prettiest bouquet you'll ever see."

"Grandpa told me so many stories about you. How you used to sing with..." Dafne frowned, suddenly remembering. "With Great-Aunt Chia on the old harpsichord. It's in the attic now, but we could bring it down."

"That'd be a good idea," said Ily. She tilted her head slyly at the invisible Blue Fairy watching from the near distance. "I have a feeling your Great-Aunt Chia is going to be visiting very soon."

"Can you give us singing lessons before she comes?"

"I'm not such an experienced teacher…" Ily said. "But I'll do my best."

"You'll be a natural," Chiara murmured, knowing Ily could hear. The two sisters smiled, and Ily grasped her grandnieces by the hands and skipped down the road with them.

Are you coming? Ily mouthed at Chiara.

Soon, Chiara replied. She set her wand on her palm, watching as Fate stepped in and reunited her sister with her past. For who should Ilaria come across – but Geppetto and Pinocchio?

Laughter echoed from the end of the road as Nina and Dafne befriended Pinocchio, and Geppetto shyly reacquainted himself with Ilaria.

Chiara strolled down Constanza Street for the first time in years. She didn't have wings at the moment, but how wonderful it was to walk. She paused before the house she had once called her own. Before she went inside, there was still one more thing she needed to do.

The cricket.

She whistled quietly, and before long, he appeared.

"I haven't forgotten you, Sir Jiminy." She lifted the cricket onto her finger. "You've done marvellously."

With a tap of her wand, Chiara rewarded him with an

official conscience badge, and the cricket preened, admiring the shiny new addition to his suit.

"Pinocchio has proven himself to be a fine boy," Chiara said. "But your work is far from done. Will you stay on as his conscience for a little while more?"

"It'd be my pleasure, Your Honour."

Jiminy leapt onto the road, but he darted a glance back at the Blue Fairy. "Will you be coming, too? Smells like the bread's coming out fresh from the oven."

What a keen cricket. "I'll be just a minute," Chiara said with a chuckle.

As Jiminy hopped away, the Blue Fairy spun her wand for one last spell before she tucked it away for a year. In her mind, she conjured the smell of cinnamon and pistachios, of chocolate and buttery sugar. A modest plate appeared on her palm, and she inhaled. "Just like home," she whispered to herself.

With a wave of her arm, she let go of her wand and made for the humble two-storey house with a yellow door. A lemon or two still hung from the trees brushing against the back window, and a bittersweet pang overcame Chiara's heart. It squeezed inside her, filled with excitement and nervousness and wonder.

When she found her courage, she knocked.

At first, she didn't think anyone heard. Then from inside, Niccolo's wife shouted: "It's the girls! They must be back early."

Footsteps approached, and Chiara held her breath. Niccolo himself answered the door, and let out a gasp.

The expression on her brother's face was one she would treasure all her life. Joy and surprise flooded his eyes as years of forgotten memories came back to him. When he finally cried her name, his voice choked with emotion. "Chiara?"

"I know I'm a few years late," she said, finally letting go of her breath. She smiled at her brother. "But is there room for one more at dinner tonight? I've brought cookies."

Photo Credit: Adrian Ow

Elizabeth Lim was inspired to become a writer by the myths and fairy tales her father told her as a child. In addition to being an author, she is a Juilliard-trained composer and has written the scores to several award-winning films and video games. Originally from the San Francisco Bay Area, she attended Harvard College and now lives in New York City with her husband. To learn more about Elizabeth, visit her site at www.elizabethlim.com

Disney

ALMOST THERE

A TWISTED TALE NOVEL

FARRAH ROCHON

AUTUMN
PUBLISHING

Published in 2024
First published in the UK by Autumn Publishing
An imprint of Igloo Books Ltd
Cottage Farm, NN6 0BJ, UK
Owned by Bonnier Books
Sveavägen 56, Stockholm, Sweden
www.igloobooks.com

1024 001
2 4 6 8 10 9 7 5 3 1
ISBN 978-1-83795-966-2
Sold as part of a set, not for resale

Printed and manufactured in China

Disney

ALMOST THERE

A TWISTED TALE NOVEL

For Jasmine Gabrielle,
my very favourite friend of Tiana's.
You'll always be the best princess.

– F.R.

PROLOGUE
TIANA

New Orleans, 1912

"Daddy! Daddy!"

The little girl ran as fast as her wobbly five-year-old legs could carry her, irrepressible joy shining in her dark brown eyes. Her pigtails bounced gaily, the ribbons tied around them precariously close to flying away with the brisk breeze blowing in from the pond.

James stooped down to one knee, his arms open wide, waiting for his little ray of sunshine to rush into his embrace.

"Come on, baby girl. I got you." He scooped her up and spun her around. The hem of the green-and-yellow dress his wife, Eudora, had made for their daughter, Tiana, fluttered as they twirled around.

"You wanna dance with your daddy?" James asked as he set her on his hip and playfully pinched her chubby cheek.

"Yeah, Daddy. Let's dance!"

He and his sweet girl rocked back and forth to the drumbeat of the band playing in the centre of Congo Square.

Their family had gathered for the annual neighbourhood picnic to celebrate the arrival of Mardi Gras, the biggest party on the face of the earth – and the most jubilant time of the year here in their hometown of New Orleans.

Blankets of every colour and fabric adorned the square, each representing a family that had come to contribute to this beloved ritual. The air was fragrant with the aroma of home-cooked creole food, and the chatter of neighbours catching up with old friends competed with the music from the brass band.

"No, Daddy. I wanna dance like you do with Mama," Tiana said.

James threw his head back and laughed. "And just how do I dance with your mama?"

"Like this." She slid down his legs and placed her tiny feet on the tops of his much bigger ones. Then she reached for his hands. "Here, hold mine," she said.

James's hands swallowed hers as he wrapped them around her fingers.

"Is this right?" he asked.

"Yep." Her pigtails bobbed with her emphatic nod. "Now we move like this!"

She swayed her hips from side to side, her dress rocking like a bell. She stared up at him with a cheerful, gappy smile. Her two front teeth had fallen out just a few days ago.

James looked over at Eudora, trying to catch her attention so that she could see her daughter in action. But his wife was busy laying out the feast he'd cooked that morning and entertaining the friends and family who were steadily dropping by to offer their congratulations on the new house he and Eudora had just purchased in the Ninth Ward.

It wasn't the fanciest place, but it was a lot better than the one-room flat they'd lived in for the past five years. There was a yard with enough room for a garden in the back, and a veranda that James couldn't wait to spend time on. A good, sturdy house that a man could be proud to raise a family in.

He looked down at his baby girl, imagining the years of happy memories to come in their new home, and his heart swelled with joy.

"What's going on here?" Eudora asked as she sidled up to them.

"I'm dancing with Daddy the way he dances with you!" Tiana beamed.

"Is that so?" his wife asked.

"Yeah! Does this make me a grown-up?" Tiana asked.

"Don't you worry about growing up anytime soon." James chuckled. "I like my baby girl just as she is right now."

Tiana pulled her hands away from his and jumped off his feet. She rushed over to her mother and shoved her towards James.

"Now you do it!" Tiana ordered. "Come on, Mama and Daddy. Dance."

James held a hand out to his wife. "You heard the child," he said.

Shaking her head at their daughter's antics, Eudora placed her hand in his. She tugged Tiana close to her side, and together, the three of them rocked to the music.

Gratitude filled his chest, wedging into every corner and crevice. He had never asked for a perfect life, but somehow he'd been blessed with one anyway.

New Orleans, 1917

Tiana struck a match on the edge of the table and used it to light the wicks of the half-melted tapered candles she'd found in the drawer of the kitchen bureau. She'd wrapped tinfoil around the bases to catch the dripping wax, but now she wasn't so sure about that. It took away from the romantic ambience she was trying to create.

"Can we come in now?" her mother called from behind their bedroom door.

"Not yet," Tiana said. "Give me just a minute."

She ran over to the cooker and flipped over the beignets she'd set to frying a few minutes earlier, then used the stepping stool to retrieve a plate from the cupboard. Give her a few more years and she wouldn't need this stool to reach the upper cabinets. Like her daddy always joked, she was sprouting up like a weed in his vegetable garden.

Tiana scooped up the hot beignets, added a little sugar on top, and took them over to the kitchen table. She filled a glass jar with water, then added the flowers that she'd picked on her walk home from school. She set it on the table in between the two candles.

"Perfect," Tiana whispered. "Okay, y'all come out now!" she called. Her entire body vibrated with excitement as she waited to see their faces.

"Happy anniversary!" Tiana screamed when her mama and daddy entered the kitchen.

"Well, looka here! Did you make beignets, baby girl?"

"I sure did," Tiana said, proudly lifting her chin in the air.

"These look better than any I've had down in the French Quarter," her daddy said. "Between my gumbo and this girl's beignets, I say we can open ourselves up a restaurant one of these days. What you think, Eudora?"

"I think I want to eat my beignets before they get cold," her mother replied.

They all sat at the table and gorged on the fried doughnut squares until there were none left. Once they were done, her daddy sat back in his chair and rubbed his flat stomach.

"That was some fine beignets, Tiana. You really do have talent in that kitchen."

"Thank you, Daddy!" Tiana's smile grew so wide that her cheeks started to hurt.

James reached across the table and took Eudora by the hand. "How about an anniversary dance?"

They pushed their chairs back from the table and strolled to the centre of the kitchen, between the cooker and her mother's sewing machine. Her daddy gathered her mama in his arms, and Mama laid her head against his broad chest as they began to sway.

"How are y'all gonna dance with no music?' Tiana asked. She set her elbow on the table and rested her chin in her upturned palm. "Of course, if we had a gramophone, I could play music for y'all to dance to."

"We don't need no expensive gramophone to hear music," her daddy said. "In this family, we make our own music."

He started to hum a tune that made her mother blush like a schoolgirl.

Tiana put both elbows up on the table and smiled as she watched her parents rock slowly from side to side, their eyes closed and both singing softly, in their own world.

New Orleans, 1921

"Tiana, are you still in that kitchen?"

"Umm… maybe," Tiana called over her shoulder. She blew at the steam rising up from the spoonful of gumbo she'd just taken from the pot and quickly slurped it up.

Her mouth twisted in a bemused frown as she tried to dissect the flavours hitting her tongue.

"I taste the cayenne and the roux. And the smoke flavour from the neck bones is there. What am I missing?" Tiana murmured.

"Little girl!"

Tiana jumped and turned at her mother's call.

Eudora carried a bolt of fabric from her storage room in the rear of the house and dropped it next to her sewing machine. She plopped a hand on her hip and regarded her daughter with a stern, pointed look.

"There is nothing more to do with that gumbo other than to let it cook," she said. "Now go finish up your schoolwork so you can be done by dinner."

"I will, Mama," Tiana said. "I just need to figure this out. I don't know why I didn't have Daddy write down his recipes before he left. I'm gonna have him do just that the minute he gets back home."

"I think your daddy will have other things on his mind when he finally comes back home," her mother said. "Besides, he never writes down a recipe. It's always just a little bit of this and a little bit of that."

Eudora walked over to the cooker and gestured to the spoon Tiana held. "Let me have a taste."

Tiana scooped up a helping of the brown liquid and held it up to her mother's lips. After taking a sip, Eudora pointed to the cabinet that held the spices.

"Sprinkle in a bit of that ground sassafras," she instructed.

Tiana did as she was told, then stirred up the gumbo. She took a taste, then smiled at her mama.

"Your daddy's not the only one who knows how to cook, you know? He just likes doing it more than I do." Eudora took the spoon from Tiana's hand and bumped her with her hip. "Now go on and finish that homework."

A half hour later, Tiana and her mother sat at their small kitchen table, enjoying her daddy's signature dish. Even though gumbo was more of a Sunday meal, Tiana had decided to make it on this random Tuesday. She just wanted to feel closer to her daddy.

He'd been away for over five months now, fighting a war in a far-off place that Tiana had only read about in her schoolbooks.

"It's a good thing I made a big pot of gumbo," Tiana said. "Because I'm going for seconds."

"Well, if you're getting seconds, so am I," her mother said with a laugh.

Just as Tiana pushed away from the table, there was a knock at the door.

"You get the gumbo, I'll get the door," Eudora said.

Tiana carried their empty bowls into the kitchen and heaped another helping of gumbo into each of them. With one bowl in each hand, she turned back towards the table.

She stopped short at the sight of her mother standing in the doorway.

Two uniformed men stood on their front porch, their

caps in their hands and solemn frowns on their faces. She heard her mother gasp, then let out a god-awful scream Tiana knew she would hear in her nightmares for years to come. Her mother crumpled to the ground.

And the bowls of gumbo shattered at Tiana's feet.

1
TIANA

Lafayette Cemetery, New Orleans
1926
Mardi Gras

The jubilant sounds of Mardi Gras resonated throughout New Orleans as vibrant, colourful floats wound their way along the wide avenues of the city. Flambeau carriers hoisted their torches high, lighting up the deep purple sky and making way for the costumed revellers who danced in the street.

But within the dark, secluded recesses of Lafayette Cemetery, it was eerily quiet.

Tiana's tiny green body trembled as she raced down a narrow alleyway, the cemetery's crumbly stone catacombs lined up like sentries on either side of her. Her heart pounded against her chest, the *thump thump thump* ringing more loudly in her ears with each inch of the pavement she traversed. She had no idea where she was going; she just knew she had to get away from the shadows that were hot on her heels.

Tiana clutched the amulet her friend Ray had shoved into her hands moments before, treating it with the same care as her daddy's Distinguished Service Cross from the army.

Oh, if only her daddy could see her right now. What would he think? How would she explain this mess she'd got herself into? Wishing on an evening star for her restaurant and getting mixed up in some nefarious dealings. Falling for a prince. Becoming friends with a gator and a firefly along the way.

And now running through the cemetery like the fires of hell were at her feet, fleeing from something she barely understood herself.

Her conscience pleaded with her to go back and make sure her firefly friend was okay, but her instincts told her she couldn't. Not yet. She had to hide. And she had to keep this amulet out of the Shadow Man's clutches until she figured out what was going on.

Tiana sprinted around a corner and galloped towards a menacing stone facade. Just as she reached it, an otherworldly shadow appeared out of nowhere.

Terror robbed her of her ability to think. To breathe. All she could do was quake in fear as the terrifying blob loomed overhead, its spindly fingers reaching for her.

This was it. She was caught.

But she never gave up on anything without a fight.

Holding the amulet as far away as her tiny arms could stretch, she glared at the shadow and issued a warning.

"Back off, or I'm gonna break this thing into a million pieces!"

"Don't!"

Tiana went still. She recognised that voice.

Facilier.

The Vodou practitioner was known for prowling about the French Quarter, reading palms and hustling poor unwitting souls with his card tricks. Everyone in New Orleans called him the Shadow Man due to his dabbling in dark magic – and other shady dealings, no doubt.

"Where are you, Shadow Man?"

"You have something that belongs to me," Facilier said as he emerged from the darkness. "And I want it back."

"No." Tiana clutched the amulet against her chest. "Ray said to keep this away from you no matter what. He wouldn't have told me to do so without good reason."

She straightened her shoulders and silently prayed her voice wouldn't quiver when she spoke. "I'm not giving you a thing."

His lips curled in an evil snarl. But then his expression changed, an air of nonchalance replacing his impatience. He buffed his nails on his lapel and observed her with blithe disregard.

"I'm a businessman, after all. I understand how this game is played." His brow arched in inquiry. "What do you say to a trade?"

"I'm not interested in anything you have to offer. I won't—"

A blast of wind caught Tiana unawares, followed by a cloud of glittery purple dust that swirled around her. An odd sensation shot through her like a bolt of lightning, nearly bringing her to her wobbly knees.

She blinked. Hard.

"Wha— what's happening?"

She stretched out her arms – her *human* arms – and wiggled her fingers. She was human again!

Tiana peered down in stunned delight at the sparkling white silk draping her body. The rhinestone- and pearl-studded gown she now wore was unlike anything she'd ever owned.

When she lifted her head, she gasped at her

surroundings. Tiana twirled around in a slow circle, mesmerised by the glitz and glamour of a place she had only seen in her nightly dreams.

The old sugar mill she'd had her heart set on buying for years was no longer decrepit and falling apart. The floors gleamed underneath her feet, shining so bright they nearly blinded her. Brilliant crystal chandeliers hung high above her head, illuminating a massive dining room that was crowded with patrons. Men in suit jackets and women wearing their Sunday best sat at cloth-covered tables adorned with extravagant centrepieces and sparkling china. Everyone seemed to be having a grand time, enjoying rich, fragrant dishes that smelt like the food Tiana used to cook with her daddy.

"Where am I?" she whispered.

"You know where you are. You've been dreaming about owning this restaurant for years. And it can all be yours, Tiana."

"But… but how?"

"Why don't you hand me that talisman," Facilier said. "And I'll fill you in on all the details."

Tiana stared at her hand in perplexed awe as it extended the pendant towards Facilier of its own accord, as if she had no control over it. With a jolt, she snapped herself out of the daze and yanked the pendant away.

"No," she said. She shook her head, ridding herself of the vestiges of whatever trance Facilier had put her in. She had to remember to keep her guard up around this one.

His fevered gaze remained on the amulet, amplifying the alarm bells ringing in Tiana's head. She had no idea what this pendant held, but the Shadow Man wanted it something fierce. Which meant he could never have it.

"I'm not giving you anything," she reiterated.

"Not even in exchange for your restaurant?"

"I… I can still get my restaurant. I just have to keep working for it."

"But why continue to toil when my friends on the other side can get you your restaurant just like that?" He snapped his fingers. "All I have to do is ask them on your behalf. Come on, Tiana. You're almost there. Let's make this deal, and I'll get you across the finish line."

"No!" she said more forcefully. He still towered over her, even though she was now human, but Tiana refused to be intimidated. "I don't need to rely on help from the likes of you, Shadow Man. And I don't want anybody to *give* me my restaurant. I'm gonna *earn* it, just like my daddy taught me."

At the mention of her daddy, Facilier's eyes lit up. He opened his palm and blew another cloud of iridescent dust into her face.

Tiana's head jerked back as she was once again plunged into a dream world. It took her a moment to find her bearings as she tried to navigate the foggy edges of her mind. She stood just inside the doorway of a state-of-the-art kitchen, like the ones she'd seen in magazines. Her mouth watered at the delicious aroma wafting up from the large copper pots that occupied the gas cooker. Waiters in sharp tuxedos flittered about the space, grabbing plates filled with artfully arranged food and carrying them out the door.

She took a tentative step forward. With that one step, her body began to move about the kitchen, not walking, but gliding, as if on a cloud. Through the sea of cooks and staff, Tiana noticed a figure that looked eerily familiar. The man stood at a cooker at the far end of the kitchen. He stirred a big cooking spoon around a gumbo pot she instantly recognised. She couldn't make out the face, but she would have known those broad shoulders and muscled arms anywhere.

"Daddy?" Tiana gasped.

"That's right," the Shadow Man whispered. "It's your dear old daddy."

"What is he…? How…?"

This couldn't be real. It had to be a figment of her imagination.

The figure turned, and Tiana let out a sharp breath. It *was* him.

Joy burst inside her chest as she took off running, her arms stretched out wide in front of her. Everyone else in the kitchen disappeared. It was just she and her beloved father. It had been so, *so* long since she'd seen him, other than in the countless dreams she'd had over the years.

But just as she got near to him, he vanished.

"Daddy, no!" she shouted.

"Ah, ah, ah." The Shadow Man's loathsome voice rang out in her ears, once again knocking her out of her daze.

Tiana glared at him as he stood before her with that sinister smirk on his face. He wasn't playing fair, toying with her emotions in such a cruel way. But then again, what did she expect from a no-good hustler like Facilier?

"What do you say to my deal now, Tiana? You can work hard, scrimp and save; maybe you'll get your restaurant in another fifty years. But there is *nothing* you can do that can bring your daddy back to life. You need *me* for that." The Shadow Man shook his head. "Tragic what happened to him. James was a good man. He didn't want to leave his family the way he did."

"You keep his name out of your mouth," Tiana hissed.

Facilier shrugged his bony shoulders as he casually searched for non-existent dirt underneath his fingernails.

"Suit yourself. It's a shame that you would turn down the chance to see your daddy again. Makes one wonder if you ever loved him at all."

"Don't you dare!" Tiana yelled. "He was everything to me."

"Then why won't you take me up on my offer?" Facilier said. "All I have to do is ask my friends on the other side for a little assistance, and you and your daddy will be making gumbo again. Think about your mama, and what it would mean to have her husband back."

Tiana closed her eyes and conjured an image of her mama and daddy dancing in the middle of the kitchen of their small but comfortable home in the Ninth Ward. The love beaming from them warmed her like rays from the bright summer sun.

"That's… it's impossible," she said. "He's gone."

"What's impossible to you is child's play for my friends on the other side. They have powers you can never understand. The favour will carry a small price, of course, but that's to be expected. It will be hardly anything, if I'm being honest."

Her eyes blinked open.

"I don't believe you," Tiana said. "My daddy has been gone for years. How can they just bring him back?"

"Don't worry your pretty little head about the

particulars. That's a problem for me and my friends on the other side to solve. Just trust me, Tiana."

Trust him? Her eyes flared, his ridiculous statement bringing her back to earth. After all he'd put her and her friends through…

"You're the last person I'd ever trust." She held the amulet high above her head, preparing to smash it to the ground.

But Facilier was quick. He stretched out his hand, releasing a bloodcurdling scream.

2
FACILIER

"Just… just wait a second there, Tiana," Facilier implored after he'd collected himself. He forced out a chuckle. "Be careful with that. It's an heirloom."

He tried to project an air of cool indifference despite the rampant desperation pulsing through his veins. That amulet was the key to everything. As long as it held a sample of Prince Naveen's blood, its designated wearer could take on the prince's appearance. Without it, Facilier's ploy to gain control of Eli LaBouff's fortune through his lovestruck daughter, Charlotte, would crumble.

But even more important, *he* would have to pay the high price his friends on the other side had attached to it.

Tiana held his very life in her hands.

Facilier clutched his fists at his sides, wishing he could wrap his hands around that gutless Lawrence's neck.

Striking up an alliance with the prince's incompetent valet had been more than just a miscalculation on his part – it could prove to be a deadly mistake.

Lawrence had allowed Facilier's treasured talisman to fall into Tiana's hands, and because of that, he now found himself in a position of weakness, having to make a bargain with this slip of a girl.

He should have known Tiana wouldn't take the easy way out when it came to her restaurant. She would never take pride in something she hadn't earned. People like her suffered under the foolish notion that their hard work made them better – made them more deserving than those who were smart enough to take advantage of life's shortcuts.

People like him.

Even after turning down his offer to get her that restaurant, Facilier had been certain that dangling the prospect of seeing her father again would do the trick. Bringing James back was a tall order and would come at a high price, possibly more than he'd ever had to pay to his friends on the other side, but he had been willing to do it. He was willing to do just about anything to secure that talisman.

And Tiana had thrown his offer back in his face.

He hadn't wanted to resort to this, but she left him

no other choice. If he couldn't sweet-talk her into returning his property, intimidation was his only recourse.

"Before you turn down my proposition, there is still the matter of your little froggy prince to discuss," Facilier said.

"Naveen?" Her eyes widened.

It was exactly the reaction he'd hoped for. He had a feeling that she'd fallen in love with that prince.

It would be her downfall.

"Where is he?" Tiana asked. "Where's Naveen?"

"Don't you worry about where he is. You need to think about *what* he is. You might be willing to give up *your* dreams, but will you give up his in the process?" Facilier continued. "If you want your precious Naveen to ever become human again, you'd better give me what's mine."

"You're lying." Tiana shook her head. "All Naveen has to do to turn human again is kiss a princess, and Charlotte LaBouff is a princess, because her daddy is the king of Mardi Gras."

"Come now, Tiana." Facilier tsked. "You're smarter than that. You know Miss LaBouff isn't a real princess. And neither are you. If Naveen doesn't kiss himself a *real* princess by midnight, he will live forever as a frog."

"No." Tiana gasped.

"Yes." He detected the tiniest signal that she was starting to waver, and pounced. "But you can save him,

Tiana. You can get everything you ever wanted. You and your prince can—"

He stopped.

What was he thinking?

Naveen was his ticket to Eli LaBouff, the most powerful man in New Orleans. Now that the scheme he'd crafted with Lawrence had fallen apart, Facilier needed the real Naveen to continue a courtship with LaBouff's daughter. An eventual marriage between those two was still his best shot at gaining control over LaBouff's money.

He should have focused on the prince from the very beginning instead of partnering with that spineless Lawrence. That devil-may-care attitude of his made Naveen an easy one to manipulate. As long as he could keep getting a drop of Naveen's blood every so often, he could control him.

But that would never happen if Naveen and Tiana were together.

"*Almost* everything you ever wanted, I should say. Here's my offer," Facilier started. "You hand me that talisman. In return, I'll bring your daddy back, *and* I'll make your little prince human again." He held up a finger. "There's just one thing. Once the spell is broken, Naveen won't remember a single thing about any of this. And if you want him to *remain* a human, the little dalliance between you two can be no more."

"Are you saying—"

"I'm saying that you must forfeit the love of your sweet Prince Naveen in return for him being human again."

She gasped. "But… but that's not fair."

"Life isn't fair," Facilier snapped.

Where was the fairness in what he now faced? He would have to strike yet another bargain with his friends on the other side in order to deliver everything he'd promised her. The price would undoubtedly be high, putting him in even deeper debt to them.

And what was *she* sacrificing? Her little infatuation with that dunderheaded prince?

He was doing her a favour. According to Lawrence, Naveen was useless. A broke, lazy burden on his parents. He would only hold Tiana back. Without Naveen weighing her down – and with the help of her father, once Facilier bargained for James's return – Tiana would have her restaurant in no time at all.

Compare that to what he was getting out of this deal. Nothing.

But wait a minute. Maybe there *was* more in it for him.

Facilier thought about the small vial in his jacket pocket that contained a tincture he'd whipped up for some of his more stubborn clientele. It made those who consumed it more malleable to his wishes, at least for a little while. If he could convince Tiana to add a bit of it to her gumbo, he could manipulate all who ate it into giving him whatever valuables they had in their possession.

Facilier's lips curled up in a smile as something else occurred to him. Tiana and LaBouff's daughter, Charlotte, were thick as thieves. It stood to reason that Eli LaBouff would become a loyal patron of any restaurant Tiana eventually opened. If he could get even a drop of this tincture into LaBouff himself… it could be another avenue to get to the sugar baron should his plan with Naveen fall through. Another way to fill his coffers. A fail-safe.

The possibilities were too delicious to contemplate.

But first he had to convince Tiana.

"Before we go any further, I'll need to consult my friends on the other side," Facilier said. "You understand, don't you?"

He closed his eyes, leaving a short sliver open so that he could keep Tiana in his sights. Then he began to speak gibberish, yammering like a baby. He would make the bargain with his friends on the other side once he returned to his shop, but Tiana had to believe he was making the deal for her daddy here and now. He put on a stellar show, if he did say so himself.

"Ah. Ah, yes," Facilier said.

"What are they saying?" Tiana asked.

He held up a finger, silencing her.

"Oh. Oh, of course. Yes, that's very reasonable," Facilier murmured. "That shouldn't be a problem at all."

He added more gibberish for good measure, then made a production of releasing himself from his trance. He belonged on a vaudeville stage with that performance.

Facilier settled his gaze on Tiana once again. "My friends on the other side have named their price. You are very lucky, Tiana. It's hardly anything at all."

He produced the vial from his pocket.

"In return for making your froggy prince human again, and for bringing your dear father, James, back to life, all you have to do is add a small drop of this potion to your gumbo once you inevitably open your restaurant. After all your *hard work* helps you to do so."

Tiana was instantly suspicious. "What's in it?"

"Well…" He needed to think fast. "Well, you… you know better than anyone that gumbo was your father's signature dish. I had some of James's gumbo a time or two myself." He rubbed his stomach. "Delicious stuff."

"What does that have to do with whatever is in that little bottle there?"

"This contains the magic that will keep your daddy alive. What better way to do that than through his gumbo?

You see, Tiana, that's just how my friends on the other side operate. It's poetic in a way, isn't it?"

"How do I even know you were talking to these friends of yours a minute ago?" she asked. "Why should I trust you at all, Shadow Man?"

This was exactly why *he* couldn't trust *her* around Naveen. She was too smart for her own good.

"Because we can both benefit from this, Tiana. You have something I want, and I can provide things that you want."

"How do I know whatever you have in that vial won't kill anyone who drinks it?"

Facilier chuckled. "If that's what my friends wanted to do, they could have done that a long time ago." He tipped the vial to his lips, pretending to take a sip. "It's harmless," he said.

"What is it supposed to do exactly?"

Facilier held up his hands. "I don't question my friends, Tiana, and neither should you. Their magic is a thousand times more powerful than mine. If they say that a tiny drop of this in your gumbo will keep your father alive, then you need to trust them." Sensing the need for extra insurance, Facilier added, "And don't forget about Naveen. You're saving him, along with all the people you love. You can make sure no harm comes to any of them, Tiana."

Her eyes widened with alarm. "What do you mean by that? *All* the people I love?"

"Accidents happen all the time." Facilier hunched his shoulders.

"Are you threatening me?" she asked, her voice once again strident with staunch defiance.

"I'm *warning* you," he snapped. "Things will get very, *very* ugly if you choose to ignore such a generous offer." He could tell she was starting to waver. He waved a hand, and one by one, phantom versions of Tiana's loved ones appeared in the air: her mother, that maddening prince, the LaBouff girl, the neighbours she had grown up with. And one by one, the figures crumbled, lying lifeless on the invisible floor. Tiana gasped as the apparitions disappeared. Facilier moved in closer. "So, do we have a deal?"

"You're not giving me much of a choice, are you? Either I make this deal with you, or innocent people will be hurt."

"We all have choices to make, Tiana. The question is whether or not we're prepared to face the consequences of those choices."

She defiantly thrust her chin in the air and held her shoulders back, but Facilier saw through her bravado. He was back in control. She might have held his life in her hands, but she didn't know that. That was his ace – Tiana's not knowing just how much power that talisman possessed.

"What's it gonna be, Tiana?"

She glared at him with burning anger in her eyes, but Facilier knew he'd backed her into a corner.

"If I have to give up Naveen, there are several things I want in return," Tiana said.

Even when she had no way out, she still drove a hard bargain. In a way, he could admire that. It was too bad she was such a goody two-shoes. With her gumption, Tiana could help him take over this entire city.

"What is it you want?" he asked.

"You have to promise that my family will be safe. I don't want any harm coming to them." She hesitated for a moment, then said, "And you have to help my two friends Louis and Ray. Louis wants to be human so he can play with a jazz band in the music halls here in N'awlins. Either your friends make that happen, or no deal.

"And Ray… well, I would feel better knowing that he's close by, where I can keep an eye on him. That he's safe—"

Facilier interrupted her. "I'm afraid that won't be necessary." He almost felt sorry for Tiana as her forehead dipped in a confused frown. Almost.

"What do you mean?" she asked.

"Remember what I said about our choices having consequences?" He arched one brow. "Well, your little firefly sealed his fate when he stole my talisman."

Her face fell as understanding dawned. Tiana clutched her hands to her chest. "Oh, Ray," she cried.

"But the gator?" Facilier continued with a shrug. "I'll have a talk with my friends, but I'm pretty sure I can make that happen."

"You can assure me that whatever is in that vial won't harm anyone? That it's simply the magic that will keep my daddy alive and keep my family safe?"

"There's nothing simple about this magic, except for your part in this, of course. You just remember to put a drop of it in your gumbo, and no harm will come to anyone. And you and your dear father will be cooking once again." Facilier squeezed his hands at his sides as he leant forward, his excitement on the verge of overwhelming. "So, Tiana, do we have a deal?"

She pressed her lips together.

"For dear old dad?" he continued.

For a moment, a streak of true terror rushed through him at the reluctance he saw in her eyes.

But then Tiana stuck out the hand that held his talisman. "Deal."

3
TIANA

The Ninth Ward, New Orleans
Thursday, February 1927
Five days before Mardi Gras

Tiana couldn't think of a better way to wake up than to the aroma of salty bacon wafting through the air. She sucked in a deep breath and blew it out with a sigh.

The promise of a hearty breakfast of buttery grits, fluffy eggs and thick, crispy bacon beckoned, but she remained tucked underneath her covers with her eyes closed. She basked in the feel of the warm sun caressing her face as it shone bright through her windows. The jaybirds flittering about outside chirped songs of cheer, a happy soundtrack for what was sure to be a stellar day.

"Tiana, baby. Come to breakfast."

Tiana's eyes popped opened and a smile as wide as the Mississippi River stretched across her face.

"I'm on my way, Daddy," she called.

It had been nearly a year since the Shadow Man made good on his promise to bring her daddy back to them. The sound of that deep baritone echoing throughout the house never failed to send grateful chills skittering along her skin.

She sat up in bed and threw the well-worn quilt off her legs. Stretching her hands high above her head, Tiana rocked her neck back and forth, working out the kinks. Maybe she should put new pillows on her shopping list the next time she and Mama visited Krauss Department Store.

Or maybe not. These pillows had served her just fine for years.

She had bigger plans in store for the profit she made from the humble restaurant she and her daddy had opened three months ago. Every cent she earned went back into her savings. Eventually, she would earn enough to buy a larger building to house the grand restaurant she had always dreamt of opening.

Not that she wasn't grateful for the supper club; it was a proper stepping stone. And it really was a feat that she and her father had been able to get the cosy little spot and open up so quickly. But Tiana had her sights on something bigger, and no one was getting in her way this time.

Buoyed by the thought of her future, she hopped up from the bed and ran over to her bureau. She pulled out a yellow-and-white gingham dress along with a matching yellow ribbon to tie back her hair. Once done, she left her room in search of that bacon she'd been smelling.

"Well, look who decided to make an appearance. Good morning," her mother said from where she sat behind a worn wooden table, working the hand crank on her Singer sewing machine.

"Good morning, Mama." Tiana walked up behind her and clamped her hands on her mother's shoulders. She leant forward and planted a loud kiss on her cheek. "Is there any breakfast left? Please tell me there is."

Eudora nodded towards the cooker, where a plate covered with tinfoil sat next to the dented copper kettle that had taken up permanent residence on the cooker now that her daddy's big gumbo pot was at the restaurant. Tiana walked over to it, lifted the tinfoil, and snatched a strip of bacon.

"Where's Daddy?" she asked.

"Out in the garden."

"Oh, shoot! I almost forgot," Tiana said. She grabbed another slice of bacon, then covered the plate back up.

"Aren't you gonna sit and eat?" her mother asked.

"I can't. I promised Daddy I would help pick some peppers and tomatoes for tonight. I'm working on a new recipe for my jambalaya, and I want to give it a test run before we open for supper." She looked at her mother with a raised brow. "You willing to play guinea pig later today?"

"Don't I always?" Eudora answered with a laugh. "Promise me you'll eat something more substantial soon, Tiana. You're too skinny."

"I promise," Tiana called as she lifted a black cloche from the hat rack near the door and secured it over her hair, sighing a little. The promises she made these days were so blissfully uncomplicated. It sort of made her wonder when the other shoe would drop.

Standing up straighter, Tiana walked outside, automatically shielding her eyes from the unforgiving sun. She dropped her hand when she realised it wasn't necessary. The sun still shone, but it was muted by a murky haze that hung in the air.

It was peculiar, to say the least. So close to the river, it wasn't all that strange to see a mist roll off the Mississippi early in the morning, but the fog typically lifted after a couple of hours.

She looked up at the sky, wondering if maybe a storm was coming.

Tiana snatched up one of the wicker baskets next to

Daddy's rocker, then descended the back veranda steps and made her way to the small garden behind the house. She paused for a moment as she came upon him, his large frame bent over a row of black soil.

Her heart expanded within her chest as a mixture of gratitude, wonderment and profound love merged together, threatening to overwhelm her.

She still could not believe her daddy was here.

Despite her scepticism, it turned out that she *could* trust Dr. Facilier, at least when it came to holding up his end of their bargain. The day after Mardi Gras last year, her daddy had walked through their front door as if returning from a typical day's work. Her mother had greeted him as usual, with a hug and kiss on his cheek, not missing a beat.

Tiana smiled softly at the memory of running up to him and wrapping her arms around his large shoulders as she cried uncontrollably, unable to suppress her joy. Both her mama and daddy had stared at her as if she'd lost her ever-loving mind. But then they'd all burst out laughing, and that was that. Her family had been made whole again.

Tiana had decided then and there not to question whatever mystical forces Facilier had called upon in order to bring about her daddy's return. He was here and she was grateful for it. And she would never *ever* take the time she had with him for granted.

"How's it going, Daddy?" Tiana greeted as she sidled up to where he knelt between the rows of freshly tilled earth.

He looked over his shoulder and smiled that wide, handsome smile of his. "Mornin', baby girl. You had your breakfast?"

"I ate a little. I didn't wanna take too much time away from helping you harvest."

He opened his massive palm, revealing a collection of small green seeds. "I decided to get these limas in the ground. Gotta get them planted before that summer heat arrives. It won't be long now."

"Well, you stick to your lima beans and I'll start picking the peppers and tomatoes for my new signature jambalaya. I think I've finally got the recipe just the way I want it. It's gonna be a hit."

"Everything you make in that kitchen is spectacular. But, Tiana, you know you don't have to spend so much of your time there. Have some fun. Join your friends for a night out every once in a while. You planning on attending any Mardi Gras parties?"

Tiana did her best to hide her exasperation. She couldn't understand why her parents were so determined to see her flouncing about this city with her friends. As if she could afford to waste time on such frivolity. If the previous year had taught her anything, it was that you never knew when things might change. Better to focus on the things you could control, and the people you loved the most.

"I don't have time for parties and Mardi Gras balls, Daddy. I have a restaurant to run. And besides, we have to get ready for our own festivities."

He looked up over his shoulder again. "You remember what the J stands for in T&J's Supper Club, don't you? You're not the only one responsible for everything."

"I know." They were bona fide business partners, just as she'd always imagined. "But what kind of co-owner would I be if I skipped out on my duties to go frolicking around N'awlins?" She clamped her hand on his shoulder and gave it a squeeze. "This restaurant is *our* dream, which means we *both* have an obligation to it."

Her daddy patted her hand. His calloused fingers were a testament to a life defined by long hours of hard work.

"I can handle things on my own every now and then, baby girl. Especially if it gives you the chance to paint the town red with your friends. Promise me you'll think about it."

"I'll think about it," Tiana said smoothly. "But now, I need to pick some tomatoes."

She balanced the basket on her hip as she strolled along the row of evenly spaced tomato vines. As she mulled over which looked ripest, her mind wandered to a place she seldom allowed it to go these days: a place where she was the kind of girl who attended parties and balls and soirees with her friends.

Not that she'd ever been all that much of a party girl. The last party she'd attended had been her best friend Charlotte LaBouff's Mardi Gras ball the year before, and even then she'd been there to serve up some of her famous beignets to the guests. The ball where she'd met Naveen… *Don't,* Tiana chastised her errant imagination.

She knew better than to even think about him. She'd spent the better part of a year doing her best to avoid Naveen altogether. Unfortunately, that had become more difficult lately. He'd taken to joining Charlotte down at the supper club, which meant Tiana now spent even more of her time hiding away in the kitchen, too afraid to go out into the dining area to chat with her guests in case she ran into him.

You just have to come up with more creative ways to avoid him.

She released a mournful sigh. She'd known giving up Naveen would be the most difficult part of the deal she'd made with the Shadow Man, but ever since he'd started frequenting her restaurant, denying how she really felt about him had become downright unbearable.

If there was a bright spot in all of this, it was that Charlotte had given up her pursuit of him. Now she and the prince shared an unlikely friendship that Tiana would have found charming if she could ever see past her own heartbreak.

She swallowed past the knot of emotion clogging her throat.

This was for Naveen's own good – for the sake of his very life. She would gradually come to terms with the fact that they could never be together. Hopefully.

Banishing all thoughts of Naveen from her mind, Tiana got back to work. Once she was satisfied with the tomatoes she'd amassed, she turned to the vibrant green bell peppers, plucking several from the stalk and adding them to her basket.

Tiana walked over to where James now tended the cucumbers. "I'm gonna head down to the restaurant and get started." She leant over and planted a kiss on his cheek. "I'll see you there, Daddy." She turned to leave, but before she could take a step, her daddy grabbed her hand. When she looked back at him, Tiana suffered a flash of alarm at the odd look on his face. "Is something wrong? Are you feeling okay?"

A gentle smile drew across his lips. "There's nothing wrong, baby girl. In fact, everything is just right. I only wanted to tell you how proud I am of you and what you've done with the supper club. You made my dream come true, Tiana."

A cluster of gratefulness, affection and unabashed joy blossomed within Tiana's chest. She set the basket on the ground and threw herself into her father's arms.

"Thank you, Daddy. It's my dream, too. And there is no one else I'd rather share it with." She held on to him for several more moments before finally finding the strength to pull away.

"All right now," Tiana said. "We can't spend all day blubbering along."

"You're right," James said. "You get to that restaurant and cook up that pot of jambalaya. I'll be along as soon as I get cleaned up."

Tiana picked up her vegetable basket and began to hurry out of the garden, then turned around and threw herself into her daddy's arms again.

"What's that for?" James asked.

"I'm just so happy you're here."

4
TIANA

As she travelled along the cobblestone pavement on her way to the St Claude Avenue streetcar stop, Tiana's spirit was invigorated by the charge that suffused the hazy air. It was rich and vibrant and teeming with the unmistakable energy of Mardi Gras. There was something about that time of the year that grabbed hold of the city and wouldn't let go.

Even though the big day was still several days away, the festivities leading up to Fat Tuesday had already begun. Elaborate balls with men dressed in tuxedos and women in magnificent ball gowns would be held nightly at all the fancy hotels downtown. There would be plenty more gatherings for those who weren't lucky enough to attend the balls, whether small house parties or live music venues. On Saturday there'd be the annual neighbourhood picnic in

Congo Square, not too far from her restaurant, and then gatherings to commemorate Shrove Monday.

As tempting as it was to get caught up in all the Mardi Gras revelry, Tiana was more interested in using the citywide celebration to bring attention to T&J's Supper Club. She'd kick things off later that evening with live music and a special menu, and the next day, they'd have a special guest for entertainment to draw more folks in.

Excitement coursed through her veins like the electricity zipping through those newly installed wires overhead. She mentally ran through the new dishes for that evening, including the new jambalaya, which would be daringly made with pasta instead of the traditional rice.

It was a risk to make such a drastic change to one of New Orleans's most beloved dishes, but if she managed to pull this off, T&J's would be the talk of the town! She wouldn't be surprised if people came in from as far as Biloxi, or even Jackson, Mississippi, to try her new recipe.

She hoped Mr Salvaggio had delivered her order of spaghetti. His small macaroni factory in the French Quarter made the best pasta in the city. And, more important, Mr Salvaggio didn't mind bartering. A pound of pasta in exchange for a dozen of her beignets.

Tiana stopped short.

She whipped around, searching for the dark silhouette she was sure she'd seen out of the corner of her eye.

Nothing.

She did her best to shake off the eerie feeling that crept up her spine. She was being foolish again. Or maybe she should pay a visit to that new doctor on Canal Street, whose sole focus was on eye diseases. There must be something to account for the strange shadows she'd sensed slithering alongside her lately.

Unless they had to do with another doctor…

Shivering slightly, Tiana continued towards the streetcar stop, a smile emerging as she came upon the welcome sight of Ms Margery Johnson sitting on the wooden bench. Ms Margery was known all throughout the Ninth Ward for her baked goods. Before the war, Daddy had often surprised them with one of Ms Margery's apple pies or sweet vanilla cakes as the grand finale to their Sunday dinner. After he was gone, she and Mama still ordered a cake from Ms Margery on each of their birthdays, including her father's. It had been one way to keep his memory alive.

"Good morning, Ms Margery," Tiana greeted.

"Well, hello, Tiana," the woman replied, her kind smile lighting up her face.

Tiana took a seat on the bench and settled the bag with her vegetables in her lap. "You're looking mighty fine today," she said. "You on your way to the market for baking supplies?"

The older woman's forehead furrowed. "Why, Tiana, I haven't made any baked goods in years, not since my Edwin left for the war."

Tiana's head flinched back slightly. "But…"

Ms Margery's son had gone around the same time her daddy had. And the older woman had received word that her son had become a casualty not long after Tiana and her mother received their similar devastating news.

How could she claim she hadn't baked anything in all those years when she'd made Tiana's favourite caramel cake for her birthday last year? Ms Margery was not all that much older than her own mama, far too young to start losing her memory to old age.

"Are you sure about that, Ms Margery?" Tiana asked cautiously.

The woman nodded. "The last thing I baked was a batch of sweet rolls the morning Edwin left for the service. They were his favourite." She glanced at Tiana, a sad smile tilting up the corners of her mouth. "But I sure do miss baking."

An odd sensation prickled at the back of Tiana's mind. A week earlier, while Tiana was out shopping with her mother for materials for new curtains, Mr Smith at the fabric shop had greeted them as if he hadn't seen them in ages. And then she'd had a similar encounter with the butcher, Mr Phillips, when she'd visited his butcher shop a few days ago. Even though she'd gone in just a week before, he'd prattled on about things that happened years ago.

"Maybe you should take it up again," Tiana told her. "I reckon there's a lot of people who want your sweets for their Mardi Gras parties."

The streetcar rolled up to their stop, and Tiana helped Ms Margery up the steps. She paid her nickel fare and took a seat in the rear, grateful there was one open near the window.

There was something magical about New Orleans when seen from the vantage point of a rolling streetcar, and the view distracted her from the odd encounter. Despite the thin haze that hung in the air, she could still make out the colourful shotgun houses of her Ninth Ward neighbourhood. The humble structures soon gave way to an array of shopfronts along Rampart Street. From Dix's Barbershop and King's Shoe Shine Parlor to Polmer Tailoring and Pelican Billiard Hall, Tiana was fascinated by the hustle and bustle along the busy promenade.

As the streetcar neared Ursulines Avenue, she reached above her head and tugged on the cable that hung just above the window, letting the driver know she wanted to get off at the next stop. The streetcar came to a halt and the driver cranked the brass handle on the wheel lever as he opened the door for her.

When she alighted from the streetcar, she spotted a familiar face.

"Hello there, Ms Rose," Tiana greeted.

She'd first encountered Ms Rose at her flower stand in the French Market several months earlier, during one of her weekly trips to buy supplies for the restaurant. The woman seemed to have an innate ability to coax her flowers into producing the most stunning blooms. Even in the dead of winter, her stand abounded with vibrant sprays in every colour under the sun.

She'd called Tiana over that first day and offered her a bunch of fragrant lilacs, free of charge. The next time she visited, Ms Rose had added peonies to the bunch and surprised Tiana with a lovely painting of a courtyard like the ones scattered throughout the French Quarter. Tiana tried to pay her, but Ms Rose refused to take her money. And she continued to give her gifts every time she visited.

"Fancy seeing you outside of the French Market," Tiana said. "What brings you to Tremé?"

"Just visiting a friend," Ms Rose said with a gentle smile. "She has been feeling under the weather, so I brought her flowers to brighten her day. It's a common practice among my people back home in Haiti." She held up a finger. "I'm happy I ran into you." She reached into the burlap sack that she kept draped over her shoulder and retrieved a large spray of lavender and bunches of marigold.

"To decorate your supper club," Ms Rose said. "They are the colours of Mardi Gras: purple for justice, gold for power and the green leaves represent faith."

"These are beautiful," Tiana said as she took the flowers. Their colouring was so vivid they looked otherworldly. "Thank you so much. Ms Rose, I do wish you would let me pay you for these."

"Never." She shook her head. "A gift does not require payment."

"Why don't you let me make you some beignets?"

The older woman put a hand to her stomach and shook her head. "I've gotta watch my figure," she said with a laugh, although her figure remained a mystery since she was always dressed in layers of clothing. Even now that winter was melting into spring, Ms Rose still wore a heavy purple cloak and a flower-print scarf tied around her head.

"Well, I should be heading back to my flower stall," she said.

"No wise sayings today?" Tiana asked. Ms Rose loved sharing nuggets of wisdom she said were passed down from her mother.

The woman's brow lifted. "Actually, I do have one for you: *Ti bwa ou pa wè, se li ki pete je ou.* The twig you don't see is the one that puts out your eye."

Tiana peered at the flowers Ms Rose had handed her. "Are there twigs in here?"

"Be cautious," the woman said. "It means to always be aware of your surroundings." She smiled and patted Tiana on the arm. "Take care." Then she continued along Rampart Street.

Tiana gathered her flowers and the vegetables she'd brought from her daddy's garden and continued towards the supper club. A familiar feeling of pride bubbled up inside her as the green facade of the building came into view.

It might not be the palatial restaurant of her dreams, but it was everything she needed for the moment.

For the first six months after her daddy returned, she'd continued working at her waitressing jobs. She still had the money she'd saved up to purchase that old sugar mill that the Fenner brothers had sold to another buyer behind her back – making the infuriating claim that someone of her 'background' was unfit to run a restaurant. And she had diligently set aside every extra penny she earned, trusting that one day the opportunity she'd been waiting for would come along.

It was fate that had brought her to the neighbourhood

of Tremé last fall, just as the weather was changing. And it was fate that had nudged her into taking a shortcut to Krauss Department Store, where she'd been on her way to buy a new coat. She'd happened upon this building just as the banker was sticking a For Sale sign in the window.

Tiana had made him an offer on the spot and had raced to the bank to withdraw half of the down payment to show him that her money was good. Daddy had accompanied her to that same bank the next day, adding his severance pay from the army to cover the other half of the down payment so she could keep saving for whatever came next.

Tiana hadn't been able to contain her smile when she'd walked into Duke's Cafe and given Buford her two weeks' notice. She'd spent the next couple of months alongside her daddy renovating their new restaurant, and three months ago had welcomed their first guests – her mama, Charlotte and Mr Eli LaBouff – to dine at T&J's Supper Club.

Tiana pulled a copper key from her pocketbook and opened the door.

She took a moment to bask in the joy she felt whenever she entered this place. After setting her bags on the table nearest the door, she zipped around the dining room, removing the red carnations she'd received from Ms Rose a few days earlier from the simple blue vases at the centre of each table.

It struck Tiana as odd that the carnations had wilted so much overnight. She could have sworn each of these flowers had been healthy and fragrant when she'd wiped down the tabletops before locking up the restaurant yesterday. She replaced the modest carnations with arrangements of lavender and marigold.

"Wow!" Tiana plopped her hands on her hips, regarding the dining room with a smile. Ms Rose was right; the flowers instantly made the place more festive.

Done with the front of the house, she grabbed the bag of vegetables and started for the kitchen. But before she made it to the swinging door, the sun that had managed to break through the haze shone directly on a scuffed spot on the floor, just underneath one of the paintings Ms Rose had given her.

"Oh, no, you don't," Tiana said. She continued into the kitchen, set the bag down, and picked up an old rag. She headed straight for the mark and buffed it out of the floor. There would be none of that in her restaurant, thank you very much.

She stood and straightened the slightly crooked picture frame that held Ms Rose's painting. Tiana was sure the flower monger had never set foot in this restaurant, yet the four pieces of artwork she'd gifted to T&J's matched the decor perfectly. Each featured a subject that was uniquely New Orleans and complemented the stunning mural her daddy had commissioned by an artist from the neighbourhood.

The mural, which depicted the rich Cajun and Creole cuisine they served, covered the entire back wall, just behind the wooden dais where Louis and his band played jazz music for the crowd.

Tiana frowned. Had she reminded Louis about the music for tonight?

"Hey, Tiana!"

She spun around. "Just the man I wanted to see." Louis smiled that big, almost frightening smile of his. "What are you grinning about?"

"You said just the *man* you wanted to see. I still get a kick out of hearing that. Me. A man." He fiddled with his waistband. "Truth be told, I'm still getting used to it. Who knew pants could be so… confining."

"Please, keep them on," Tiana said quickly.

"I know, I know," Louis replied. "So, why did you want to see me?"

Tiana stepped closer to the stage. "I was wondering if we should go over the song list for tonight."

"You don't need to worry yourself with that." He tapped the side of his head. "I've got it all up here. In fact, I came over to get the sheet music I left. Me and the guys are practising over at Gerald's place."

"Great," Tiana replied. "I'm thinking if word gets out that things are rocking at T&J's Supper Club tonight, then people will decide that this is *the* place to celebrate their entire Mardi Gras weekend. And when they hear that Rudy Davis and the Allstars will be here – wait, Rudy Davis *is* still coming tomorrow night, right?"

"They'll be here," Louis said.

"There's just so much riding on this, Louis," she said, straightening a nearby tablecloth. "I'm counting on the money we bring in during the next five days to pay off a large portion of the loan on the building. I *have* to make sure Mardi Gras is a success. Nothing can go wrong."

"Nothing will go wrong." Louis headed over and patted her on the shoulder. "I know you've had to deal with a lot this past year, but this is one thing you don't have to worry about. In fact, I asked Rudy if he and the band could come back next week. I've been thinking about home a lot lately. Maybe it's time for a visit."

She paused, hearing the wistfulness in his voice and feeling a twinge of guilt. She hadn't considered that Louis would feel homesick, but why wouldn't he? He'd been away from his family for an entire year.

Tiana just wasn't sure how Louis would be received back in the swamp now.

She turned to look up at him and put a gentle hand on his arm. "Umm… sure. Why don't we talk about it after Mardi Gras?"

"Yeah, good point. Let's focus on this coming weekend and making it the best that T&J's has ever had. I know you can do it, Tiana. You've worked too hard not to."

Louis was the only other person who knew about her deal with Facilier, but even Louis didn't know the entire story. He wasn't privy to all the details in the agreement that had made his dream a reality – the bits about her father, for example, and the concoction she added to the gumbo.

And yet, their shared history had made him into something of a confidant this past year. At times, Tiana felt as if he was the only person she could turn to, the only one who would understand when she found herself faltering.

"Thanks for being here, Louis," Tiana said. "For listening."

He hunched his broad shoulders. "It's what I'm here for. Well, that and making your customers shake their rears." He did a little dance, then took off for the stage. "I need to get back to the guys. We're gonna sound better than ever tonight. You mark my words, Tiana!"

"I believe you," she said with a laugh. "I'll see you in a few hours."

The music taken care of, Tiana decided to focus on more pressing issues, like perfecting the jambalaya.

Just as she re-entered the kitchen, there was a loud knock on the back door that led out to the alley behind the restaurant.

"I'll be right there," Tiana called. Relief rushed through her when she opened the door and found Mr Salvaggio staring back at her. He wore his signature pageboy hat.

"Salve!" Tiana exclaimed in the greeting they always shared. "You are a life-saver, Mr Salvaggio."

"And you remain my favourite customer, Ms Tiana," the kind-faced Italian man said. He followed her inside, carrying a paper bag in each hand. "Here is your extra order of spaghetti, and here is biscotti that my beautiful wife made for you. You must enjoy with a nice hot cup of coffee." He kissed his fingers. *"Perfecto."*

"That sounds marvellous," Tiana said. "If you give me just a few minutes, I'll fry up your beignets. You know they're best when they're hot out of the oil."

She retrieved the already-prepared beignet dough from their brand-new electric icebox and settled in to listen to one of Mr Salvaggio's stories. It had become a standing routine whenever he made a delivery. He would share memories from his childhood in Sicily while she made his beignets. Tiana wasn't sure she believed some of the tales Mr Salvaggio spun, but they always made for a good laugh.

She packed up his beignets and bade him goodbye. As he left through the back door, Mr Salvaggio made Tiana promise that she would stop for a moment to enjoy the cookies his wife had sent over.

Friendships like his were an unexpected bonus to owning her restaurant. The vendors she worked with viewed her with respect, as an equal. It was a far cry from the treatment she'd received from the Fenner brothers.

Tiana's blood boiled like a hot pot of gumbo whenever her thoughts turned to that old sugar mill. Seeing all her hard work and sacrifice tossed aside like yesterday's trash had left her feeling powerless.

And wishing on evening stars.

Her eyes fell shut as a fresh wave of torment washed over her. But she opened them just as quickly. She didn't have time for wallowing. In a few hours this restaurant would be full of hungry customers.

Besides, none of that other stuff mattered any more. She was doing just fine without that old sugar mill, and without the Fenner brothers or their bank loan. She didn't need to cast wishes on evening stars; she made her own dreams come true.

And she certainly didn't need to rely on that no-good Dr. Facilier.

Tiana hated to admit that, for the briefest second, she'd considered his offer to get her the restaurant when they'd made that deal last Mardi Gras. Thank goodness she'd quickly come to her senses. There was only one thing she relied on Facilier to provide. One thing she couldn't have possibly done herself.

She walked over to the pantry and moved aside the jar of preserved green beans from last year's crop. Behind it stood a tiny vial of the potion she'd agreed to add to her gumbo. She met with Facilier every couple of weeks, usually during her normal trip to the French Market, and exchanged the empty vial for a new one.

As long as he held up his end of their bargain, ensuring that her daddy stayed alive and the rest of her friends and family remained safe and well, this was all she would ever need from the Shadow Man.

She leant forward, peering at the vial.

"Can't be," she said as she snatched it from the shelf.

But yes, it was empty.

"Oh, come on," she whispered.

Guess she had to add a trip to the French Quarter to the list of everything else she had to do before tonight's dinner service. She grabbed her bag and headed out.

5
FACILIER

Dr. Facilier positioned himself against the wrought-iron lamppost, hunching his back so that the dusty cloak he'd donned wouldn't slip from his shoulders. Of all the disguises in his repertoire, this one was by far his least favourite. But blending in with the riffraff who loitered about the French Quarter was paramount to keeping his identity concealed.

He forced a wretched cough from deep in his lungs, the kind that would send anyone who came near scurrying to the other side of the street. He was in no mood for company.

Not that he had that to worry about today. Most of the people hustling their way through the narrow streets and alleyways didn't seem to notice him. They were too busy complaining about the peculiar haze blanketing New

Orleans. Facilier didn't mind it one bit. The gauzy cloud was the perfect distraction, providing extra cover for those deeds he'd rather keep hidden from the public eye.

Unlike the rest of the folks whining about this fog, Facilier chose to use it to his advantage.

And here came his opportunity to do just that.

He spotted his mark when he was still several yards away. The unsuspecting fool strolled along the pavement with a trumpet tucked underneath his arm and a derby hat pulled low over his forehead. He ambled right past Facilier, whistling to himself as if he didn't have a care in the world.

Because he didn't.

Prince Naveen of Maldonia never had to worry about anything. He'd been born into the kind of wealth most people couldn't fathom. Even after his parents had cut him off, he never faced any *real* hardships. His looks, charm and connections were aces in his pocket, qualities he could count on to get him out of anything.

Facilier fought to keep the disgust from showing on his face as he set off to follow the young man.

He hung back, maintaining a respectable distance between himself and the prince while travelling along St Ann Street. He waited until Naveen reached the crowded street corner before sidling up alongside him. Naveen paused while a horse-drawn carriage clomped by, and Facilier made his move.

"Oh, oh, excuse me," he said, fumbling into the prince.

"Whoa, whoa, whoa. You okay there?" Naveen asked.

Pretending to be a drunkard deep in his cups, Facilier slurred a mumbled "thank you" as he looped his arm around Naveen's shoulders. With sleight of hand, he pricked him at the base of his neck and collected several drops of his blood using a small bottle that he'd held hidden in his palm.

Naveen stiffened, but he wasn't in a position to let go lest he drop the poor drunk man he'd been kind enough to help.

"Steady there, my friend," Naveen said. He looked to a stately gentleman standing next to them and, with his free hand, motioned as if he were drinking. "It is a bit early in the day, eh?"

The other man turned his nose up at them both, then proceeded to cross the street.

"You okay?" Naveen asked as he righted Facilier.

"Yes. Yes, thank you," Facilier slurred.

"You take it easy." Naveen tipped his hat to Facilier and continued on his way.

Facilier smiled as he watched Naveen scratch at the place where he'd pricked his skin. He probably thought it was a mosquito.

He pocketed the small vessel he'd used to collect the prince's blood and quickly made it back to his residence deep in the French Quarter. The front room served as the shopfront for Dr. Facilier's Emporium, but it was in the back where the real magic happened.

Unfortunately, when it came to his magic, real was relative. It was mostly sleight of hand, convincing illusions, simmering brews. And, of course, the borrowed powers.

Facilier removed the dusty cloak and tossed it aside on his way to the nondescript chest at the rear of the room. He lifted the lid from the chest and shielded his eyes from the streams of blinding light that burst forth and ricocheted off the walls.

Carefully, he retrieved the bowl from the bowels of the chest. Its smooth opal exterior made it cold to the touch, but the contents bubbled like the brew in a witch's cauldron. He carried it to a nearby table and added the drops of blood he'd just confiscated from Naveen to the bowl. Using the tip of his cane, he swirled around the concoction that had been fermenting for the better part of a year and intoned the initial verses of the spell he'd cast on Prince Naveen with the help from his friends on the other side.

Bitterness festered on Facilier's tongue, its intensity growing with every word that poured forth from him.

His reliance on his *friends* was a source of constant fury, but he had no other choice.

Facilier closed his eyes tight around the image of his mother as his mind brought him back to those days when he would sit at her knee, observing her service to the people of their community. She had been a healer, practising sacred rituals passed down from her mother and her mother's mother and beyond. But none of those rituals had been enough to heal *her*. No words, no dancing, no burning of alms had been enough to keep her here.

The day his mother's soul passed on was the day he vowed to get back at this cruel world. It was what it deserved for ridding itself of her.

He'd shunned his mother's religion, refusing to learn its practices, now knowing once and for all it could do nothing for him. What was the point? None of it had saved her.

So to achieve the power and fortune he had coveted, he had turned to his friends from the other side. And now the price of doing business with them continued to increase.

Facilier unhooked a wooden spoon from the wall and scooped up some of the concoction. Careful not to spill even a drop, he cupped his hand underneath the spoon and carried it to the brass plate that held the gold crest of Maldonia that had once hung around Naveen's neck.

Pilfering the crest was about the only thing that useless Lawrence had done right after their misguided scheme backfired and Facilier had decided he was done using the amulet.

Facilier slowly drizzled the piping hot liquid over the crest as he murmured the final lines of the spell.

The spell didn't give him total control over Naveen's mind – the price for that particular trick had been much too high – but his friends had offered the next best thing. As long as Facilier performed the ritual of covering something Naveen still held near and dear to his heart with Naveen's own blood, he would be susceptible to Facilier's wishes. Similar to the potion he supplied Tiana, though this was tailored specifically to the prince and his memories.

There was just one caveat: the spell became less potent with each day that passed. Lately, all it seemed to be doing was making sure he forgot about the incidents of last Mardi Gras. Timing was important in these deals. And Facilier was up against the clock.

That dunderheaded prince and LaBouff's daughter were always together, yet no official wedding announcement had made it to the newspapers. Their dillydallying was costing Facilier precious time. The longer he had to wait to get his hands on LaBouff's fortune, the longer he had to remain beholden to his friends on the other side.

He'd considered discarding the spell he'd cast on Naveen after Tiana opened that little supper club in Tremé, especially once LaBouff became a frequent visitor. The man loved to indulge in Tiana's cooking. Facilier figured it would be only a matter of time before he could get the wealthy sugar baron under his control.

Except LaBouff seemed immune!

Facilier didn't doubt that Tiana was using the potion as promised. He'd swindled enough of her customers as they left the supper club to know that she dutifully added it to her gumbo exactly as he'd directed. But when it came to LaBouff and the rich cronies who often accompanied him to the restaurant, the magical concoction seemed to have no effect.

Facilier tightened his fist around the handle of the wooden spoon to the point of cracking it.

He had to get to the bottom of this. He had to get to LaBouff.

He had so many cards built into houses. One wrong move and – poof. It would all fall down.

Mardi Gras was less than a week away, which meant the Shadows would be expecting their payment for that deal he'd made with them almost one year ago. If Facilier had any chance of getting to LaBouff through Tiana's gumbo, it had to be soon. Because once the sun dipped below the horizon on Mardi Gras night, Tiana would no longer be around to add his potion to her gumbo.

She just didn't know it yet.

6

TIANA

Tiana fidgeted with the pleats in her gingham dress as a familiar mix of anxiety and dread curdled in the pit of her stomach. She glanced over her shoulders, searching for signs of Dr. Facilier. She'd sent word that she was in need of more of the potion for her gumbo by way of their usual method: tying a white kerchief to the door handle of an abandoned factory just around the corner. She'd seen his nearby emporium from afar, but she had no desire to ever visit. These clandestine meetings were nauseating enough.

They followed the same protocol whenever she needed to replenish her supply of the potion. She was to sit on this particular bench, underneath the canopy of a towering oak tree in Jackson Square, and wait. She'd repeated this ritual five times over the past three months, and she hated it more and more each time.

But Facilier had fulfilled his end of their bargain, and she vowed to do the same. She had kept a close eye, and as far as she could tell, the potion hadn't caused harm to any of the customers who'd consumed it. Adding it to her gumbo was a small price to pay in exchange for having her father back.

Tiana stood and looked around. Facilier had never been this late before. The dinner service would be starting in less than two hours, and she still had vegetables to chop, sauces to make, and beignet dough to prepare.

"Looking for me?"

Tiana spun around. She slapped her palm to her chest to calm her heart.

He'd done that on purpose.

"I didn't expect to see you again so soon," Facilier said in that vexing drawl Tiana had come to despise.

"We're busy down at the supper club," she said. "And my gumbo is our top seller. I'm making more batches of it than ever."

His expression darkened as he leant in close. "Have you been stretching this potion? Trying to make it last longer?"

"No! I put the exact amount you instructed into each pot. That's why I ran out sooner than expected," she said, making no effort to mask her offence. "I would never take a chance like that, not when—" She glanced on either side of her, and in a lowered voice, said, "Not when my daddy's life depends on it." Tiana opened her palm, revealing the empty vial. "Are we making this trade or not? I have a restaurant to run, Dr. Facilier."

Facilier snarled as he reached into the breast pocket of his purple vest and retrieved the vial.

"Five drops," he said, distrust still teeming in his eyes. "Make sure you put it in every pot of gumbo you cook, Tiana."

Tiana slipped the vial in her bag, experiencing a rush of relief now that she had a full bottle of the potion once again. She'd warred with these contrasting emotions for the past three months – abhorring the fact that she'd had to make a deal with this vile man at all, while at the same time cherishing what it had made possible.

Facilier tipped his top hat to her. "Until next time."

Tiana turned on her heel without uttering a parting word. There was nothing in their deal that said she had to treat him with any sort of kindness.

She tucked her bag to her side and left through the side gate of Jackson Square. She attempted to walk up St Philip Street, but an upturned horse cart had dumped manure onto the pavement. Tiana quickly pivoted, heading back towards the river. She would cut through the French Market and follow Esplanade Avenue back to Tremé.

The afternoon rush had descended on the market, with women carrying wicker baskets on their arms, picking through the selection of produce, meats and fresh pasta brought in from the French Quarter factories. This was just one of the reasons Tiana preferred to visit the market in the early morning hours. Not only were the offerings fresher, but she didn't have to wrestle with other shoppers.

She shouldered her way through the throng of pedestrians. When she arrived at the edge of the market, she felt an odd sensation tugging at her, an undeniable pull that drew her attention towards the water. Her stomach twinged uneasily. She looked over and found Ms Rose staring at her, framed by the vivid purple wisteria that grew along the flower stall's walls and awning.

Tiana released a relieved laugh and waved.

Ms Rose nodded in acknowledgment, but her expression remained austere. Tiana didn't know what to make of it. She started to walk towards the flower stall to ask Ms Rose if something was wrong, but then a customer grabbed the woman's attention and she broke eye contact.

Tiana disregarded the unsettling episode and continued towards Tremé, her mind jumping to everything that still needed to be done before they opened up the supper club.

She stopped.

There was that feeling again, as if something was… was

following her. She quickly turned, positive that she'd seen a fleeting shadow of some kind out of the corner of her eyes. She whipped her head around the other way.

Nothing.

"It must be this fog," Tiana muttered.

She continued on her swift walk up Esplanade Avenue, clucking her tongue at her own foolish antics.

Still, she couldn't shake the feeling that something was very, very wrong.

7
NAVEEN

The pungent aroma of coal fire and burning sugar cane permeated the air surrounding LaBouff Sugars' massive sugar mill. The red brick building stood out boldly among the smaller structures along the banks of the Mississippi River, its prominence a physical testimony to its significance to the local economy.

Naveen roamed about the production floor, checking in with the workers at the heart of the operation to make sure they had everything they needed. He came upon one of the contraptions – he still didn't know what they were officially called – where dark molasses percolated, gurgling and splattering over the edges of the large copper pots. Puffs of white smoke plumed from the vessels and lingered in the air above their heads.

The foreman had tried to explain the process that was

used to turn the willowy stalks of sugar cane that were brought in by the truckload into crystallised sugar and molasses, but Naveen was still a bit shaky on the mechanics of it all.

He flagged down one of the workers he'd befriended since he'd begun working here the year before.

"Hey, Jacob. What is this called again?" Naveen asked.

"Why, that's the boiler," the man replied, a smile stretching across his soot-covered face.

"Oh, yes. Thank you." He would have to remember that if he wanted to convince the others that he was serious about the sugar business.

And he was. He was determined to learn everything about this industry. He preferred being on the factory floor with the workers over sitting behind a desk.

Naveen wasn't as naive as many thought him to be; he knew Mr LaBouff had only offered him this job because of his friendship with Charlotte. He didn't even have an official title, or any real duties. He wanted to prove to everyone that he had more to offer than just his charm.

He had yet to figure out exactly what that more was, of course, but that's why he was here now.

Naveen pointed at the thermometer on the side of the massive kettle. "So when the temperature reaches—"

A piercing whistle rent the air.

Naveen jumped back. His hands shot up in the air. "It was not me!"

That was why he never touched any of the equipment. He knew his limitations.

"You might wanna get outta the way, boss," Jacob said.

"I am not the boss!" Naveen called out, but no one could hear him above the ruckus that ensued as the men set about extracting the heated liquid from the boiler.

He stood back and watched, fascinated by the choreography of it all. It was like a graceful dance, the way the factory workers moved about the equipment, each confident in his role. Observing the backbreaking work these men put in day after day gave Naveen a greater appreciation for the sugar he had always enjoyed, yet taken for granted.

He now recognised that he'd taken *a lot* of things for granted. It was easy to do that when you spent most of your life having everything handed to you.

Did he miss living in the lap of luxury? Sometimes. But if his parents sent passage for him to return to Maldonia that very day, with the promise of giving him everything he asked for, Naveen would turn them down. He liked this new life he'd built for himself in New Orleans. There was something very freeing about earning his own money and not being under his parents' thumb.

Except now, it felt as if he was under Mr LaBouff's.

His boss didn't make demands the way his parents had, but how could Naveen ever feel that he was earning his own way with a job that had been given to him as a favour? He wanted to prove to Mr LaBouff that he could be an asset to this company.

And, well, maybe he wanted to prove that to himself as well. He wasn't sure what had sparked this new ambition, but he couldn't shake it and didn't think he wanted to anyway.

Naveen shoved his hands in his pockets and tried to fight off the familiar uneasy feeling that settled in the pit of his stomach. Like he was forgetting something important. It wasn't the first time he'd had to brush off such feelings in recent weeks. Something seemed… off.

He entered the milling room and leant against the wall, giving a wide berth to the sharp blades that swung like pendulums from huge pulleys, slicing the pulpy cane into shreds. He pulled his trusty notepad from his back pocket and scribbled a reminder to research how the boiler worked. As he made his way to the rear of the room, he caught the tail end of a conversation between two workers who were manoeuvring a bushel of sugar cane stalks onto the massive scale.

"Uh, excuse me, gentlemen," Naveen said. "What were you just saying about the candy company?"

The worker took his hat off and fidgeted with it, his expression suddenly apprehensive.

Naveen did his best to mask his exasperation. He wanted these men to like him – to think of him as one of the guys. But because of his proximity to Mr LaBouff, they treated him as if he were in charge.

"I am just curious," Naveen said.

"Well… uh, my brother works over at Dugas's. Said they had some kinda fallin' out with their sugar supplier. They may be lookin' for a new one."

"Really?" His gaze shifted from the worker to the milling machine and back. "Dugas's, they make those little chocolates with the marshmallow centre, yes? I see them everywhere."

The man nodded. "Yessir."

Naveen began to pace back and forth between the scale and the nearby bushels of sugar cane waiting to be weighed. His pulse pounded like a thunderous drumbeat within his chest as an idea began to take shape.

LaBouff Sugars was the king of sugar in the South. Dugas's was the king of candy. A partnership between those two companies could be the start of an empire.

And if *he* was the one to broker the deal…

He turned to the two workers. "Can you keep the news of this… uh, what is the saying? Under wraps?" Naveen asked.

"Sure thing, boss," the man said. "But this isn't just rumour. My brother works there. He knows."

"No! No! I believe you," Naveen said. "I just want to… investigate a little on my own. And it is just Naveen. No boss here."

"Right, boss." The man tipped his hat to him.

Naveen let out a sigh, but his frustration at his fellow mill workers refusing to treat him like a regular guy was quickly replaced with his excitement over this new development. This was his chance. If he could convince Dugas Candy Company to partner with LaBouff Sugars, he could prove to everyone that he belonged here and that he was capable of doing more than simply being a friend to the real boss's daughter.

"Naveen!"

His head popped up. Had he conjured Charlotte just by thinking about her?

"Naveen, where are you?"

He quickly made it out of the milling room just in time to see Charlotte LaBouff rounding the corner of one of the huge boilers, her blonde curls bouncing with each step.

"Charlotte, what are you doing here? You know it is not safe for you on the factory floor."

"Well, *you're* here," she said. She grabbed him by the hand and started for the winding staircase that led to the upper floor. "But I don't like all this grime and dust anyway."

Naveen followed her to the suite of offices that lined the left side of the building. Mr LaBouff's office was the biggest, of course, but Naveen's wasn't much smaller. In a way, he could understand why the factory workers had yet to warm up to him. They all shared a lunchroom that equalled the size of the office he had for himself.

Charlotte pushed through the door and plopped into the chair behind Naveen's mostly empty desk. She pointed at him.

"I need you to be my date for tonight," Charlotte said.

"Charlotte." Naveen rubbed the bridge of his nose. "We have been over this, have we not? You and I are friends. We should not mess that up by—" He ducked just in time to miss the fountain pen she pitched at his head. "Hey, that is dangerous."

"I'm not talking about a *real* date, Naveen," she said with an exasperated huff. "Daddy is bringing two members of the city council to Tiana's supper club tonight, and Mr Dubois will probably bring his son Rubin with him." She made a gagging motion. "He's been trying to get with me since we were in school together, and I don't want him getting any ideas."

"So you want to lie to him."

"Yes," she answered without the slightest hint of remorse.

Naveen chuckled at her audacity, but it was what he'd come to expect of Charlotte.

Once she'd decided to no longer pursue him as a husband, she had become an unlikely friend. In fact, she was his *best* friend. He wasn't sure he would have made it through this past year in New Orleans without her.

And not just because she had got him this cushy job at her father's sugar mill.

It turned out he and Charlotte had more in common than Naveen first realised, with both of them coming from significant wealth. Although Charlotte didn't seem interested in proving that she could earn her keep in the same way he felt compelled to lately. She was more than happy to spend her father's fortune.

But their wealthy families were only one of the similarities he and Charlotte shared. They both loved to dance and had spent the past year cutting a rug at dance halls all around New Orleans. It took him a little longer to catch on to the latest moves, but Charlotte was a surprisingly patient teacher. She also shared his love of art. She joined him at the museum whenever there was a new exhibition on display.

And Tiana. They both shared a particular interest in Tiana.

Though his interest in her was decidedly different from Charlotte's.

"Well?" Charlotte asked with a tinge of frustration. "Are you gonna be my date tonight, or what?"

A night of good food, jazz music and the chance to see Tiana again?

Naveen gave her his best smile. "What time do we leave?"

8
TIANA

"Baby girl, looks like we're running low on corn bread."

Tiana poked her head out of the pantry long enough to call out to her daddy, "I'm on it."

She grabbed a bag of cornmeal from the shelf, then added baking soda, flour and her secret weapon: sweet molasses from LaBouff Sugars. Cradling her haul close to her chest, she kicked the door open with her foot and raced past the waitresses lined up at the counter, collecting meals to take to the hungry customers who had descended on the restaurant tonight. The crowd started rolling in as soon as Tiana opened the doors for the dinner service, and the stream of people lining up to enter T&J's Supper Club had been steady ever since.

Tiana deposited the ingredients for the corn bread onto the counter. She turned to the cooker and, with a big cooking spoon, stirred the pot of simmering collard greens. She picked up a fork and used it to flip over the catfish fillet she'd left frying in her daddy's cast-iron skillet. It was flaky, golden and perfect, exactly as she'd intended.

The swinging door that separated the kitchen from the dining room swung open, and her head waitress, Addie Mae Jones, came bursting through it, her arms piled high with dirty dishes.

"Tiana, how much longer on those beignets?" Addie Mae called.

"Just a few more minutes," Tiana answered. She quickly grabbed the last of the beignet dough from the icebox, rolled it out, and cut it into squares. She carefully dropped them into a waiting pan of hot grease, giving each the chance to take shape before adding the next.

Tiana used her forearm to wipe the sweat from her brow as she skirted around the prep table to grab a couple of plates for this latest order. She'd lost count of how many she'd made already tonight.

"You need help over there?" her mother called.

"I got it, Mama. And what are you doing in here? You're supposed to be out in the dining room, enjoying the band. I told Louis to have the Crawfish Crooners play 'St Louis Blues' just for you."

Back at the stove, she used a spatula to dunk the puffed-up pastries into the hot oil, making sure the edges were a warm golden brown before she scooped them out of the fryer. That was the key to making sure her beignets were crispy on the outside and pillow-soft on the inside.

She plated them on one of T&J's Supper Club's signature emerald-green plates and sprinkled just the right amount of powdery confectioners' sugar on the top.

Perfect.

"All right, Addie Mae, here are those beignets you've been asking for."

"You'd better mix up another batch of dough," her head waitress said as she grabbed hold of the plate Tiana handed to her. "As usual, these beignets are our biggest seller. Behind the gumbo, of course."

Her mother was tying an apron around her waist as she walked up to the cooker.

"Mama, what are you doing?"

"Helping," Eudora said. "Until you two hire another cook, I am making it my mission to be of use."

Tiana dropped her head back and sighed up at the ceiling. For the past two months, she and her mother had had this same discussion at least once a week. Tiana didn't know what else she could do to make her understand that she didn't want to hire another cook. She didn't need one. She could handle it.

Besides, they used recipes her daddy had been crafting ever since he was a little boy; was she supposed to just allow anyone to come into this kitchen and learn those secrets? Not in this lifetime.

Tiana looked over at her daddy, who stood at the shelf chopping onions without shedding a single tear. "Would you tell her that we're fine?" Tiana asked him.

"My baby girl knows what she's doing, Eudora," James said.

Her mother held her hands up in surrender. "If you say so. But I still think you could use an extra set of hands or two. Maybe that way Tiana can get out and enjoy the band a bit herself." Her eyes brightened. "Why don't you see if Charlotte's out there? I'll bet she brought along that nice young man."

Tiana shook her head. She would not take the bait.

Her mother had made several not-so-subtle mentions of that 'nice young man' who always came by with Charlotte over the past few months. She would rather have her mother as a third cook than a matchmaker.

But at that moment, Eudora untied the apron from around her waist and rolled it into a ball. "Anyway, I hear you. You've got things under control. I'll go listen to the band." She grinned as she leant in and planted a kiss on Tiana's cheek. "You know to come and get me if you need me. Even if it's just to give yourself a breather."

"Thank you, Mama," Tiana said, softening.

As she turned back to the dough, Tiana took a deep breath, trying to remind herself what was important. Here she was preparing all her favourite foods with her daddy, their loved ones showering them with praise over the success of their new endeavour. Her mama was smiling and happy. It was everything she'd ever wanted.

So despite the awful feeling she got in her gut whenever she even thought about the deal she'd made with Facilier, Tiana remembered everything she'd gained.

Her family was whole again. How could she *ever* regret that?

Addie Mae burst through the door with another set of dirty dishes. "What did I just say about those beignets? I've got three more orders. Do you need some help?"

"I've got it," Tiana assured her.

If Tiana ever did consider bringing someone else into this kitchen, it would be Addie Mae Jones. The waitress had come highly recommended by an old coworker from Duke's Cafe. Like Tiana, Addie Mae had dreams of opening her own restaurant. She would get there one day, too. She was a hard worker, and she had a way about her that made each customer feel as if they were the most important person in the restaurant.

It was probably why Tiana had hired her on the spot, and after her first hour on the job, had declared Addie Mae the best waitress in town. She could only imagine how chaotic this place would be without her here to keep the rest of the staff in check.

Of course, the fact that the rest of the staff were Addie Mae's younger cousins, Jodie and Carol Anne, made it easy for her to keep them in line. They both worshipped their older cousin.

Now that this latest order of beignets was done, Tiana turned her attention back to the pot of gumbo gurgling on the hob. She took in the dents and pings along the walls of her daddy's big gumbo pot. Every imperfection was perfect in her eyes.

"How's that gumbo coming along, baby girl?"

"It's almost there," Tiana called.

Her father came over and pulled her into a side hug. "Smells good."

"And it tastes even better." She scooped up a big spoonful of the gumbo and blew lightly across it. Then she held the spoon up to him and grinned as he sipped a bit of the dark brown liquid.

"Just like your daddy taught you to make it," he said.

His big belly laugh was the sweetest sound in the world. She would have made a deal with the devil himself in exchange for hearing that sound every day.

The Shadow Man is close enough to the devil.

She ignored the pinch of unease that threatened to crop up again.

"Let me see about these catfish," her daddy said. "As much as the folks out there love the gumbo, they can't get enough of this fried catfish. Well, that and the music."

"Does the band have them dancing out there?" Tiana asked.

"Oh, yeah. They're sounding real good tonight. Your mama's right; you should go and see for yourself." He gestured with his head towards the swinging door that led out to the dining room. "I can handle things in here for a bit. Go have a listen, and make the rounds. People been asking 'bout ya."

When they'd first opened the restaurant, Tiana had made a point of dropping in at each table for a few minutes to make sure their patrons were having a good time. She wanted people to feel at home when dining at T&J's Supper Club, as if they were having a meal with family.

But her desire to move beyond the walls of this kitchen and visit with the crowd had diminished the moment Naveen started visiting regularly.

Just as Facilier had warned, Naveen had no recollection of the days the two of them had spent together, journeying through the dark, brackish waters of the Louisiana bayou. As far as Naveen was concerned, Tiana was simply the owner of the restaurant where he occasionally indulged his love of beignets and jazz music.

It's better this way, she reminded herself.

Saying the words was easy. Accepting them was another thing.

"I'll go out in a minute, Daddy," she said as she tried to think up an excuse to hang back.

She often wondered if it would have been better if she had never attended the LaBouffs' Mardi Gras ball last year. If she had never met Naveen at all.

But then, did that mean he would have actually *married* Charlotte?

She almost laughed out loud.

Tiana wasn't convinced winning his heart had ever been Lottie's true objective. Shortly after last year's eventful Mardi Gras, Charlotte had declared she still wanted to marry royalty, but the title of princess came with too many responsibilities. She'd set her sights on becoming a duchess and had spent the past year trying to convince Mr LaBouff to allow her to travel to England.

But her father was adamant that she remain right here

in New Orleans. It was the first time Tiana had ever witnessed Mr LaBouff deny Lottie something she'd asked of him.

Tiana started, suddenly remembering she needed to make tonight's crawfish étouffée. It had become Mr LaBouff's favourite, and Tiana always made sure she had a fresh batch just for him.

"Hey, Addie Mae," Tiana called as she put together the fragrant stew. "Can you go out there and let me know if Mr LaBouff is here?"

"He sure is," Addie Mae answered. "And he has Mr LeBlanc and Mr Dubois from the city council, along with Dubois's son, with him. He asked if there's any—"

"Étouffée," Tiana supplied. "Coming right up. In fact, I'll bring it to him myself."

Tiana dished up several bowls and set them on a serving tray. She cut thick slices of corn bread and added a slice to each serving. But when she picked up the tray, she immediately set it back on the counter.

Tiana closed her eyes and sucked in a deep breath. She had to prepare herself for the prospect of seeing Naveen.

She could tell Charlotte was starting to get suspicious. The last few times they had come, Tiana had made sure to maintain her distance. On their most recent visit, Lottie had tried to get her friend's attention by yoo-hooing across the whole supper club before Tiana had waved and scurried away.

"All you have to do is avoid going near their table," Tiana whispered to herself.

Mr LaBouff would make that easy enough. He'd be sitting in the far right corner of the dining room, far from where the band played. As he'd explained it to her, he liked the music, but needed to be somewhere a bit quieter in order to conduct business with the gentlemen he brought to the restaurant.

Charlotte, on the other hand, always sat at a table as close to the stage as possible. That would work in Tiana's favour. She would take Mr LaBouffs' meal, stop in on a few other tables to make sure folks were enjoying themselves, and get back to the kitchen.

"See, it'll be easy."

At least that was what she told herself.

9
TIANA

Sucking in another fortifying breath, Tiana lifted the serving tray and carried it out to the dining room. She avoided even glancing towards the stage, where the band was playing a rousing rendition of Jelly Roll Morton's "Smoke House Blues". She didn't want to take the chance of catching either Charlotte's or Naveen's eye.

As she looked out over the packed restaurant, pride made her chest swell up like the giant silver airship she'd seen in the paper. Everyone seemed to be having the grandest time, their smiles and jubilant chatter mingling with the music from the band.

She moved forward, spotting the three gentlemen sitting with Mr LaBouff. He looked as if he were holding court, his ample belly and overwhelming presence taking up more space than any of the night's other patrons. There wasn't an official monarch in this city, but if there had been, Tiana had no doubt who would reign as the King of New Orleans. There was no one more powerful living here than her best friend Charlotte's daddy. Not even the mayor.

As Tiana had come to learn over the years, politics only got you so far. The *real* power in this city – and probably the world – was money.

And Eli LaBouff had a lot of it. As did the other men at the table, it seemed, judging by their posh clothes. What had Addie Mae said – they were councilmen?

Tiana sighed, thinking about her own daddy and how, despite the fact that he was now a business owner, he would never fit in with Mr LaBouff's crowd. Not because he wasn't smart enough or didn't work hard enough. Simply because of a matter of his birth and station in life. Because of the colour of his skin. Same reason the Fenner brothers had refused to sell her the old sugar mill. The unfairness of it rankled.

Tiana pushed the infuriating thoughts away as she came upon the table, focusing on the task at hand.

"Tiana!" Mr LaBouff's jovial voice resonated throughout the dining room. "How's it going tonight?" Before she could speak, he continued, "Well, heck. I don't have to ask you that. Just look at all the people in this place! No better restaurant in town."

"Why, thank you, Mr LaBouff. And thank you, gentlemen, for spending this Thursday before Mardi Gras at T&J's Supper Club. We're honoured to have you here." She placed a bowl of étouffée before each of them, then said, "Are you sure you don't want to try the jambalaya pasta? It's brand new, and everyone seems to like it."

"It can't be better than this here étouffée," Mr LaBouff said. "It's all I eat whenever I'm here."

"Well, all right." Tiana lifted her shoulders in a hapless shrug. "You all enjoy your étouffée. If there's anything else I can get you, just let me know, you hear?"

"How about getting rid of that fog out there?" one of the councilmen said with a laugh.

"Is it still foggy?" Tiana asked.

"And it's getting thicker by the minute. You reckon it's something going on with the water? It seems to be worse down by the river."

"I thought maybe it was the stacks of the sugar mill, or some of the other factories in the Quarter, but your guess is as good as mine," she said. "I just hope it clears up before the Mardi Gras parades start rolling. No one wants a foggy Mardi Gras."

The effects on the Fat Tuesday celebrations weren't

her only concern when it came to the bad weather. Tiana feared people would be afraid to venture away from home if things got so bad that it made travelling along the roads too dangerous. There were more and more of the new Ford Model Ts on the roadways these days, and there was no doubt one of them would crash into another if drivers couldn't see.

The folks there in the Tremé neighbourhood loved to dine at the restaurant, but T&J's was beginning to see a fair number of patrons from other parts of the city. She wanted them all to be able to travel safely to and from the supper club.

"I should tend to some of the other tables," Tiana said. "Remember, if y'all need anything, just let me know."

When she turned, a stiff breeze ruffled the hem of her dress as a gentleman from a nearby table whizzed past her, his face hidden behind a newspaper. An eerie sensation skidded along Tiana's spine, raising the tiny hairs on her arms and at the back of her neck.

She shook off the strange feeling and turned her attention to the table where a bunch of her friends from the neighbourhood sat. She'd known Georgia, Donald, Maddy and Eugene since school, back when they all sat like quiet little mice in Mrs Brown's classroom. Well, except for

Georgia. That one never could keep her lips from flapping for very long.

"Hey there, y'all," Tiana greeted. "Y'all having a good time?"

"Sure are."

"We're having the best time."

"I just wish we were closer to the stage," Georgia remarked. "Your place is so popular; people have to get here really early if they want a good seat."

"It does get crowded," Tiana agreed with a smile.

"I gotta hand it to you, Tiana. You said you were gonna open your restaurant one day and you sure did it. This place is the best spot in Tremé."

"In all of N'awlins," Donald chimed in.

Once again, Tiana's chest expanded with pride. It wasn't all that long ago that this same group of friends would hound her to go out with them. And here they all were, spending their night out at *her* restaurant.

"And I love the Crawfish Crooners," Maddy said. "I'm surprised that I hadn't heard of them before they started playing here."

"The band leader, Louis, just moved down from Shreveport," Tiana said quickly. "But he's making a name for himself here in N'awlins. Y'all should come back tomorrow, because we have a special guest band."

"Oh, yeah? Which one?" Donald asked.

"Rudy Davis and the Allstars!"

The entire table gasped as Tiana's smile widened.

"How'd you get Rudy Davis to agree to play at your restaurant?" Georgia asked. "Ain't he up in Chicago now?"

"New York, last I heard," Eugene said.

"Well, he's back in town for a few days, and he owed Louis a favour." Tiana nodded up at the stage. "He filled in for Mr Davis down at a jazz club in the Quarter a while back and convinced him to stop by. And after Rudy had some of Daddy's gumbo, he agreed to perform next time he was here. It's like y'all said, T&J's Supper Club is the best spot in all of N'awlins."

"Wow!" Georgia said.

Suddenly, a new high-pitched voice cut through the crowd. "Tia!"

Tiana turned to see Charlotte at a table just steps away from the stage. She frantically waved her hands in the air, motioning for Tiana to join her. Tiana glanced just past Charlotte and locked eyes with Naveen, who was staring directly at her.

Her heart caught in her throat.

Tiana quickly looked away.

"Well, thank y'all for coming tonight," she told her

friends. "But I need to get back to the kitchen. Gotta keep the hot food coming if I want to keep people happy."

"Tia!" Lottie called again.

But Tiana ignored her. She tucked the serving tray underneath her arm and rushed past the other tables and through the swinging door, desperate for the sanctuary the kitchen provided.

10
TIANA

"Back so soon?" her daddy asked as soon as Tiana stepped into the kitchen.

She walked over to where he stood before the cooker, tending to a large cast-iron skillet with several fillets of golden-brown catfish. Tiana picked up a spatula and nudged the catfish, causing the hot oil to sizzle even more.

"I can't spend all night out there," she said in a shaky voice. Goodness, how could simply seeing Naveen rattle her this much? "It's unfair to leave you with all the work," Tiana tacked on, hoping her daddy bought her excuse.

"I told you I have everything under control, baby girl," he replied. "Go and enjoy yourself a little while longer."

"I don't think—"

"Tia!" Charlotte burst through the swinging door, whizzing around the kitchen like a tornado. She came upon

Tiana and plopped a hand on her hip. "Didn't you hear me calling you out there?"

"Oh! Lottie, hey!" Tiana forced as much false cheer into her voice as she could muster. "No, I didn't hear you," she lied. "It's so noisy out there with the band and all."

"Hello there, Charlotte," James greeted. "Glad to see you could make it here tonight."

"Hey there, Mr James." Lottie waved to him before grabbing hold of Tiana's arm. "You don't mind if I steal Tia for a spell, do you? I promise to have her back here before the second dinner rush."

"No problem at all," her daddy said. "I was just telling her to go out there and enjoy the band."

"Yes, the music is fabulous tonight. And I have the best seat in the house, so come and join me."

Tiana wanted to dig in her heels – literally – as Lottie tugged on her arm, but she stood no chance when pitted against both her best friend and her daddy. Instead, she braced herself for the impact of having to be near Naveen and pretend he had no effect whatsoever on her. She was no Evelyn Preer, but a few more months of this and her acting skills might get her all the way to Hollywood.

But when they arrived at Charlotte's table, it was empty, save for two dishes that held the remnants of the pasta jambalaya both had eaten tonight. Tiana was confused by the unnerving mix of relief and disappointment that assaulted her at finding Naveen's chair unoccupied.

"Where's Naveen?" Tiana asked. "Did he leave?"

"He had better not have," Charlotte said, looking around. She gasped and pointed to the centre of the room. "Oh, my word! Look to the dance floor, Tia!"

Tiana swung around and did a double take. Was that Naveen dancing with her mother?

Goodness.

"Just look at Ms Eudora out there cutting a rug." Charlotte clapped excitedly. "Who knew your mama was such a hoot!"

"I sure didn't." Tiana had to admit it was nice to see her mother having a good time. She just wished it were with anybody else. Tiana had no doubt her mother was talking her up.

"You look great, by the way," Charlotte said as she reclaimed her seat. "Did your mama make that dress?"

Tiana looked down at the simple yellow-and-white gingham sheath. It was one of her nicer dresses, but it was nothing compared to the creations Charlotte wore every day. Creations that Tiana's mother had made with her own two hands.

"Actually, I made this one myself." Tiana preened as she sat. "I guess I inherited skills from both Mama and Daddy."

"Oh, Tia, you are just unbelievable! I wish I had half your talent." Charlotte lifted her hands in the air. In a wistful voice, she said, "I'm still trying to figure out what I'm good at doing. I'm not sure I'll *ever* figure it out."

"Don't talk that way about yourself, Lottie. You can do amazing things if you put your mind to it." Tiana reached across the table and gave Charlotte's hand a reassuring squeeze. "I know you can."

"Maybe," her friend said with a shrug. "I do have a knack for shopping. Maybe I can do *that* professionally one day."

"That's a… thought," Tiana finished. She had never heard of such a job, but if there ever were a job out there for Lottie, that would be the one.

Suddenly Charlotte looked at her seriously, squeezing Tiana's hand. "Hey, Tia, I miss you. I know you're busy, but I feel like maybe you've been avoiding me?"

"Oh, no, no, I haven't…" *Been avoiding* you, Tiana added silently.

"Good." Charlotte suddenly brightened. "Then you can come to Maison Blanche with me tomorrow. Please? Ms Eudora is making my dress for *my* Mardi Gras ball, but I have about a half dozen others to attend over the next five days and I need a different gown for all of them. I need your help picking them out. Maybe you can get something, too! I'd love for you to join me for some of these parties."

Tiana hesitated. She'd never had time to go shopping with Charlotte before.

"Please, please, please?"

Charlotte looked so genuinely hopeful, Tiana felt a twinge of guilt for not spending much time with her friend this past year.

"Well, I don't think I'll have time for parties," Tiana started. She watched her friend deflate a little. "But I'll go with you tomorrow – as long as we're done in time for me to get back here so that I can start prepping for our big Mardi Gras kick-off," Tiana added.

"Eep!" Charlotte got up and threw her arms around Tiana. "Yes, all right, deal! Gosh, I still can't believe you have Rudy Davis and the Allstars playing at your supper club! It's gonna be so fabulous." She moved to sit back down. "And speaking of, oh, Tia! Tia! Tia! How could I forget to tell you! I had an epiphany today."

"Another one?" Tiana couldn't help laughing. She had missed Charlotte's unflappable energy.

"Yes, a *real* one this time. Are you ready for this?"

"Ready as I'll ever be," Tiana said.

"You know how much I love art, right? Naveen and I are always at the museum together."

"Yes, I know," Tiana said, praying her envy didn't show on her face.

"Well, I've discovered that I love British art. And do you know the best place to see *British* art?"

"In England?" Tiana asked.

"That's right!" Charlotte waved her hands in the air. "You see, if I tell Big Daddy that I want to study with the artists who live in London, then he *has* to send me there, because it's educational. And while I'm educating myself on British art, I can search for my duke!" She squealed. "Isn't my plan the best?"

"Uh… sounds like the bee's knees to me," Tiana said.

"It's just brilliant, and I know it will work. Besides, I need to do something. Big Daddy has brought that dull Rubin Dubois around again."

The band brought their song to a close, and Louis announced that they would be taking a ten-minute break. Panic surged through Tiana as the band members set down their instruments. She quickly glanced to the dance floor and spotted Naveen striding towards them, his charming smile as bright as always. Her heart immediately began to thump wildly within her chest. For a moment, she couldn't breathe.

"Uh, Lottie, I need to get back to the kitchen."

"But Mr James said that you should sit and enjoy the band. They'll be back to playing in just a bit."

"No, really. I have to go," Tiana said. She stood and moved swiftly through the maze of tables to the kitchen. Before pushing past the swinging door, she chanced a glance over her shoulder. Naveen had stopped in his tracks. The light had drained from his eyes, and a look of hurt and confusion had taken its place.

Tiana bypassed the cooking and serving areas and headed for the small storeroom. She closed herself inside of it and plopped down on an empty milk crate, sucking in several breaths as she tried to calm her erratically beating heart.

"Who knew you were such a coward?" Tiana whispered.

After agreeing to Facilier's deal, Tiana had selfishly hoped that Naveen would return to Maldonia. It would have made things easier for her. But then, she knew that wasn't true. It didn't matter where he lived; this private agony of knowing what she had given up would remain.

It's been a year!

She had to find a way to move on. She could not go on like this, feeling such heartache every time she saw him.

"Has anyone seen Tia?" Charlotte's voice carried throughout the kitchen. Tiana closed her eyes and counted the seconds until her friend would find her. It didn't take long.

Charlotte knocked twice on the door to the storeroom

before opening. "Tia?" she called. "What are you doing in here? Why did you run away again like that?"

"I'm sorry, Lottie. I've got too much to do."

"Really?" Charlotte drawled. She cocked her hip to the side and perched a fist on it. "I can tell. You're so very busy right now, sitting in a closet." She peered at Tiana. "Do you know what I think? I think maybe you've been avoiding someone after all. And maybe that someone is *Naveen*. The question is why?"

"Lottie, please."

"I want to know, Tia. Is it because you're—"

But before Charlotte could finish, Louis burst through the partially opened door. "We've got a problem."

11
FACILIER

Facilier exploded out of the door to the supper club. His blood pounded in his ears as his mounting rage reached unprecedented levels. He shouldered past the line of patrons still hoping to make their way into Tiana's restaurant, glaring at them, baring his teeth. But he didn't take any satisfaction in the way they recoiled.

LaBouff wasn't eating the gumbo!

That was why the potion he'd given to Tiana hadn't worked on the sugar baron and his cronies. Because LaBouff had been eating that blasted étouffée this entire time. Facilier whacked at a pile of garbage with his cane, sending the refuse flying across the uneven cobblestone streets in this seedier part of the Vieux Carré.

Fury consumed him, rising in his throat until it unleashed with a raw scream into the dark, foggy night sky.

Once home, he ripped the fedora from his head and flung it onto the hat rack next to the door. He hadn't needed much of a disguise tonight. With the number of people crammed inside Tiana's little supper club, he'd gone unnoticed as he slipped inside and parked himself at the table near LaBouff's.

Tiana thought she was so clever, but he was the brains of this operation. He had been visiting her little supper club for months now. Always cloaked in a different disguise, he'd been right there in the same room with them, observing from afar how she interacted with all her customers, especially those fat cats Eli LaBouff brought in. But he had never got close enough to notice that LaBouff wasn't eating the gumbo.

Facilier peeled off his black gloves and tossed them aside as he made his way through the emporium to the back rooms of his home.

Disgust pooled in his stomach, recollections of the conversation he'd overheard tonight between LaBouff and those two from the city council swirling around in his head. The wealthy sugar baron had pledged to invest fifty thousand dollars in a new set of railroad tracks being added to those that already lined the riverfront as if it were play money.

What a ridiculous man with ridiculous ambitions.

He didn't deserve his fortune, nor his influence. The things Facilier would do with that type of wealth, with men bending over backwards to heed his every word… He snarled as he recalled an incident years ago when he'd encountered Eli LaBouff in Jackson Square. The sugar baron had not been nearly as wealthy and powerful as he was now, yet still carried himself as if the world were his to control. Facilier had held his hand out for a gentlemanly handshake, but LaBouff had walked past him without so much as a glance.

Well, LaBouff and his cronies would take notice of him. And soon. Facilier would make sure of it.

He squeezed the handle on his cane so hard it was a wonder the wood didn't break under the strain. He tossed the cane aside and went to work, gathering everything he needed to create more of the potion he'd given to Tiana for her gumbo.

Before long *he* would be on his way to owning this city.

His arms brimming with the ingredients he'd collected from the shelves, Facilier turned and sneered at the dark, dank room. He was better than this musty hovel that was just steps above living in squalor. He should have been living in a mansion like the ones Eli LaBouff and those other fat cats lived in along St Charles Avenue.

He had thought he would be satisfied with their wealth and power, but now Facilier decided he wanted more.

He wanted their *envy*.

He wanted them to seethe with jealousy when he walked by, to crave his attention. He wanted LaBouff to choke on his own bitterness and resentment. It was only right that he experience what Facilier had endured all these years.

And the only way to accomplish that was to take hold of the power they all had over this city. Once he was able to manipulate their minds, the rest would fall into place. He was sure of it.

A knock at the door jarred Facilier out of his fervent musings. He tilted his head towards it, waiting for the second double knock. When it came, he smiled.

He went over to the door and opened it with a flourish.

"Mr Bruce, my dear friend. Back so soon?" He stepped aside. "Why don't you step into my humble abode."

The stout man barged into the room. He held up a bottle.

"Regina smiled at me yesterday!" Bruce exclaimed. His eyes were eager, but his pudgy jowls still sagged like the fish-filled nets the fishermen pulled out of the Mississippi River.

Facilier had been expecting him. The concoction he'd sold the cobbler just a few days ago should have lasted him well into next week, but Mr Bruce's infatuation with the war widow who frequented his shop grew stronger with each bottle he consumed. That was always a good sign for business.

"If you give me just a moment, I will provide everything you need," Facilier said. He turned to the shelf stocked with neatly arranged jars and bottles of various sizes, each filled with assorted liquids and salves. He might not have the knowledge his dear mother had, having been taught by the Vodou spiritual leaders of her homeland, but he'd learnt a trick or two in his day.

He emptied dried rose petals into a black marble mortar and crushed them into a fine powder with the pestle. He added a bit of honey, a little sage and the juice of one red cherry. Then he mixed it up using a wand made of rose quartz.

Facilier motioned for the man to hand him the empty bottle he'd brought with him. "Let me have that there bottle," he said. He slowly poured the concoction into it and swirled the bottle around. As he did so, Facilier mumbled gibberish. The words didn't matter as long as Mr Bruce believed they held the power to make sweet Mrs Dupre fall in love with him.

"There," Facilier said. "A few sips and your lady friend will be at your door."

The bits of gravel Facilier had sprinkled at the widow's

doorstep would ensure her trip to the cobbler. The jagged stones were hell on shoe soles.

Mr Bruce reached for the bottle, but Facilier pulled it out of his reach and stretched out his other hand, passing his thumb over his fingers.

"Ah, ah, ah," he crooned. "I think you're forgetting something."

Bruce handed over several folded bills. Facilier fanned them out, counting the money before finally releasing the bottle into his customer's stubby hand.

"Now, remember, you need only a small teaspoon of it in the morning. Of course, you can take more at night before bed, if you think Mrs Dupre needs a bit more urging."

The man nodded excitedly as he tucked the bottle into his pocket and exited the door, disappearing into the dark, foggy night.

Facilier smiled as he closed the door behind him, but his grin quickly turned into a glower.

He shouldn't have had to peddle silly love potions to numbskulls like Bruce. Done were his days of performing two-bit schemes for pennies; he wanted bigger things for himself. His plans for LaBouff might have been stalled, but they weren't completely thwarted.

"Wait. Wait a minute," Facilier said.

He rushed back to the door and wrenched it open. The fog was even thicker than it had been on his walk home from the supper club.

Something strange permeated the air. Literally. Facilier had no idea what was behind this curious phenomenon, but he now realised that he could use it to his advantage.

His low, deep chuckle grew louder as he shut the door and returned to his laboratory.

His first plan might have failed, but this one wouldn't. He searched the shelves until he caught sight of a large jar with a particularly potent ingredient – one that could stop a grown man in his tracks and make him wait for his fate.

He knew exactly what he had to do.

12
TIANA

Trepidation thundered throughout Tiana's bloodstream as she stared into Louis's worried eyes. She was almost afraid to ask, but running away from a problem was never the way to solve it.

Of course, it would help to know exactly what the problem was.

"What's the matter?" Tiana asked Louis.

He backed out of the way and motioned to the man standing behind him.

The *bleeding* man standing behind him.

Tiana scrambled up from the floor. She scurried out of the storeroom and into the kitchen, where the other four members of the Crawfish Crooners stood.

Charlie, their other trumpet player, held a dish towel up to his lips. Tiana took notice of the large splotches of bright red blood seeping into the towel and immediately knew they had more than just a problem on their hands. This was an emergency. And a disaster.

"What happened?" she asked, rushing to Charlie's side.

"Charlie split his lip on the horn," Louis said. "We were playing a rendition of 'Tin Roof Blues', and his bottom lip just split open like a banana peel."

"Ooh," Charlotte said, covering her mouth. She looked on the verge of losing the pasta jambalaya she'd eaten for dinner. "I'll be in the dining room if you need me, Tia," she mumbled from behind her hand.

Louis hooked a thumb towards Charlotte's retreating form. "What's wrong with her?"

"Lottie's just a little scared of blood. She'll be okay," Tiana said. "Let's focus on Charlie." She set a comforting hand on the trumpet player's shoulder. "Do you think you need a doctor?"

He nodded.

"Gerald here is gonna take him," Louis said. "It's a bad split. He'll need a doc to sew that lip up."

She did her best to hide it, but Tiana was on the verge of losing her own dinner. She looked on in horror as the crimson stain imbuing the towel began to spread. The colour seemed to drain from Charlie's face, turning his skin ashen.

"Now," Tiana said, ushering Charlie and Gerald, the band's trombone player, out of the kitchen through the back door that led to the alley. "Get him there safely."

"We're gonna get set up for the final set," Harold, their drummer, said.

"Don't know how good we'll sound being down a trombone and a trumpet," Walter, the bass player, added as he followed Harold out of the kitchen.

Tiana slapped her palm to her forehead. "How did that even happen, Louis?"

Louis hunched his broad shoulders. "I dunno. Charlie was just blowing his horn as usual, and next thing you know…" He flapped his hands open, providing a visual Tiana really could have done without. "Strangest thing I've seen." He leant in close and whispered, "And I've seen some pretty strange things in my day. Though I don't have to tell you that."

"Shhh," Tiana said, looking over her shoulder to make sure no one had overheard. She inched close and lowered her voice. "Tell me, Louis, have you sensed that *more* strange things are happening lately?"

His scabrous forehead creased even more with his frown. "How do you mean?"

She opened her mouth, about to tell him that she thought she was being followed by murky shadows. But it seemed so ridiculous she decided against it. Tiana still wasn't convinced those shadows were real. More than likely, her mind was playing tricks on her due to the stress of pulling off a successful Mardi Gras season.

Instead, she waved off his question. "Forget I said anything. I'm just… just a bit out of sorts these days; still nervous about this weekend."

"Well, your first real test will be tomorrow night, when Rudy Davis and the Allstars pack this place," Louis said. "Charlie couldn't have picked a better time to split his lip."

"Louis!" Tiana smacked him on the arm.

"What?"

"That's an awful thing to say." She plopped her hands on her hips. "You do bring up a good point, though. This is going to sound horrible, but do you think the rest of the band will still be able to play tonight?" Tiana asked. "We still have the second dinner service to get through."

"I don't know." Louis shook his head. "I handle the melody, but I count on Charlie's trumpet to harmonise. Maybe if—"

"Umm… I can play trumpet."

Tiana whipped around. Naveen stood several feet behind them, holding up a shiny brass horn.

"Sorry. I just wanted to make sure everything was okay back here. There seemed to be a lot of frantic running," he explained. He gestured to the trumpet in his hand. "The ukulele is still my first love, but I've taught myself how to play the trumpet this past year. I never leave home without it."

"All right, man," Louis said.

Panic seized Tiana's chest. "No!"

Louis and Naveen both stared at her.

"Why not? It's the perfect solution," Louis stated. "We'll only need Naveen here for this final set. I can play Gerald's trombone, and then you've got Rudy Davis and the Allstars tomorrow."

"I know… I just…" she said, unable to come up with a rationale that wouldn't make her sound like a terrible person, or worse, a lovestruck fool.

She couldn't admit that having to watch Naveen up on that bandstand would rend her soul in two. But that's exactly how she felt. It was hard enough when he was only a guest here at her restaurant, but to have him actually working here?

But what choice did she have?

"Very well," Tiana said. She looked over at Naveen and suppressed the whimper that nearly escaped. Bracing herself, she stuck her hand out.

"Welcome to the band."

13
NAVEEN

Excitement surged through Naveen's veins, his euphoria building with every song the Crawfish Crooners played. His obsession with jazz music was one of the things that had first drawn him to New Orleans, but never had he imagined he would get the chance to play with a live band. He felt like a real musician, not just someone with a hobby.

He could get used to this.

Naveen peered out at the crowd from his perch on the raised dais, hoping to spot Tiana. He had noticed her sticking her head out of the kitchen door a few minutes ago, but it appeared she had not followed Charlotte out to the dining room.

Disappointment and exasperation warred within him as he recalled the abject horror that raced across her face when he'd offered to step in for the injured trumpet player.

It wasn't as if he'd suggested he take over cooking duties in her kitchen – *that* would be a disaster. But he knew his way around a trumpet, and he'd practised enough of the American jazz standards to blend right in with the Crawfish Crooners.

Naveen had hoped Tiana would be grateful that he'd offered to help. Or, at the very least, that she would be relieved the band would be able to play through the second dinner rush even though they were down two members.

Alas, it would appear that no smiles of appreciation were anywhere in his future. Not from Tiana.

If only he could understand why she hated him so.

Well, that was not fair. He did not know if Tiana hated him – he did not know how she felt about him at all! Every time he came near her, she scurried away like a frightened little church mouse.

Her behaviour was peculiar. And frustrating.

And… confusing.

At first, he'd thought Tiana was just shy. He would visit that diner where she had worked as a waitress just to see her. Of course, he could not let her know that was why he frequented it, so he'd order beignets. He ate so many of those luscious fried doughnuts during his first few months in New Orleans that his trousers started to get tight at the waist.

Once he and Charlotte became friends, his encounters with Tiana also became more frequent. Naveen waited impatiently for her to warm up to him, but when she remained skittish, he figured that was just her nature.

Then, after she opened her restaurant, he observed how vibrant she was with all her other guests. That was when Naveen realised that Tiana's timidity seemed to be reserved only for him. She constantly turned away from him, almost in a rebuff. He couldn't understand it.

Had he done something to her?

He tried to tell himself that it didn't matter, but that would be a lie. He spent much of his spare time playing jazz music or learning more about the sugar industry, but when he was not doing either of those, he was trying to solve the mystery of the beautiful Tiana.

Louis held his hand up, indicating that this would be their final song of the night, which meant his experience as a real musician was coming to a close. Naveen managed to clear his mind. He wanted to soak in the last drops of this remarkable feeling.

The song ended, and the crowd erupted in applause. It was exhilarating. Seeing the joy on everyone's faces, knowing he'd entertained them with his music – it sent a rush of pride and gratitude galloping through his bloodstream.

If only Tiana had been out in the dining room to see it.

"Hey, man, you should be on top of the world after that performance," Louis said. "Why you looking so down and out?"

Naveen glanced over to find Louis smiling at him, his toothy grin a mile wide. He had been so caught up in his thoughts of Tiana that Naveen hadn't realised he was frowning.

"I'm not," Naveen assured him. "This was great. I was just… just thinking."

"Well, maybe you should stop thinking about whatever it is that put that frown on your face," Louis said as he slapped a broad palm on Naveen's shoulder. "Not if it makes you this sad."

That was the problem. He *couldn't* stop thinking about Tiana.

"I'm not sad," Naveen said. He covered Louis's hand. "Thanks for letting me play with the guys, eh? This was like… what do they say? Like a dream come true?"

"Aw, man. Any time," Louis said. "In fact, you should think about joining the band. We can always use a new guy on the trumpet."

"It would be like old times," Naveen said automatically.

Louis's eyes widened. "What did you say?"

"Uh, like old times?" Naveen said. He frowned. "Wait, have we done this before? Played music together, I mean?"

"I… I don't think so," Louis said.

"I could have sworn…" Naveen shook his head, wondering what had got into him. "Anyway, thank you for the invitation, but things are getting pretty busy down at the sugar mill." He clapped Louis on the shoulder. "This was fun, my friend."

Naveen had started to think of Louis as a friend in the year since he'd arrived on the shores of America. Despite his extremely big teeth and the skin condition that required him to constantly rub lanolin onto his skin, Louis was approachable and always had a ready smile. Naveen was grateful for him. He was grateful for all of the friends he'd made since moving to New Orleans.

More and more, Naveen was coming to realise that travelling to this country was the best decision he'd ever made. He was meeting new people and working hard… if one could call persuading restaurants and shops to partner with LaBouff Sugars hard work. For a guy like him, it came naturally.

But what else could he do with his life?

Naveen considered Louis's invitation to join in with the Crawfish Crooners. If he could spend the rest of his days playing jazz music with his friends, he would die a happy man.

Well, maybe not *completely* happy.

Convincing Tiana that she did not have to run away whenever he was near would be nice. She and Louis were good friends. Maybe he could ask Louis to put in a good word for him.

Naveen's back went ramrod straight.

Achidanza!

Why hadn't he thought of this before?

He swiftly climbed down from the stage and went in search of Tiana's other friend – her *best* friend. Charlotte. He spotted her sitting at the table Mr LaBouff always occupied when he dined at the supper club, towards the rear of the dining room.

Given the look on Charlotte's face, the fella sitting next to her was the one she'd hoped to avoid. Maybe if he rescued her from this conversation she obviously did not want to be a part of, she would return the favour.

"Hello, gentlemen," Naveen greeted the table at large. "Mr LaBouff, I wonder if I could speak to Charlotte for—"

"Oh, yes!" Charlotte yelled. She pushed back from the table so quickly that her chair landed on the floor behind her. "I don't mean to be rude, but now that Naveen is done filling in for that trumpet player with the busted lip, we can go back to our date."

She gripped his arm like a vice and pinched him.

"Yes," Naveen yelped. "Yes, let us continue our… our date."

"Oh, thank goodness!" Charlotte released a relieved sigh as they quickly made their way back towards their table near the stage. "I swear, if I had to listen to Rubin Dubois talk about his bunions a second longer, I may have murdered him. Heavens to Betsy, that man is irritating."

Naveen's forehead wrinkled. "Umm… who is Betsy?"

"I don't know. It's just something people say around here." She waved him off. "Now, what is it that you wanted? Or did you come over because you could see on my face that I was ready to commit a felony?"

"Uh, both, actually," Naveen said. He pulled out the chair at their table and waited until she sat before taking a seat himself. He scooted his chair closer to her and, in a lowered voice, said, "I need you to put in a good word for me with Tiana."

Charlotte's head jerked back. The suspicion in her eyes caused Naveen to squirm like a bug under a microscope. But then a cagey smile drew across her lips.

"I *knew* you had designs on Tia," Charlotte mused as she pointed a finger at him. "I could sense something happening between you two."

"I just—"

She held up her hands. "But before you get your hopes up, I can already tell you exactly what Tiana will say. She'll say that she's too busy and doesn't have time for romantic foolishness."

"But—"

"Now, usually, I would disagree with that sentiment, because I believe there is nothing more important than love. However, I've known Tia a long time, and I know how hard she's worked for this restaurant. I don't want anything to distract her, either."

"I don't want to be a distraction. I only—"

"Of course, that girl really does need to loosen up a bit."

"I just want to get to know her better," Naveen rushed out before she could interrupt him again. "That is all, Charlotte." He hunched his shoulders. "I am not sure why, but Tiana does not seem to like me very much. Maybe if you tell her that I am not such a bad guy, she won't run away when she sees me, eh?"

Charlotte tipped her head to the side. After several moments ticked by, she pointed at Naveen and said, "Okay, here's what I'll do. I'll tell Tia that you are madly in love with her—"

"No, no, no, no!" Naveen said.

Charlotte slapped him on the arm. "I'm only teasing,

Naveen. Lighten up! I know what I'm doing here," she said. "I will casually mention how interesting you are." She snapped her fingers. "Quick, give me something interesting about you."

"Uhh… I have been learning to juggle?"

"I'll make something up. Besides, I'm hoping to drag her to some Mardi Gras balls, and she'll need a date." She narrowed her eyes at Naveen once more. "But you better not make me regret it. Tiana is my best friend, and I will not see her hurt."

Naveen shook his head. "No way. I would never hurt her." His pulse quickened at the thought of accompanying Tiana to a ball, seeing her all dolled up in a beautiful gown. He could see her now!

Actually, he *could* see it.

Naveen squinted in confusion.

Had he seen her in a ball gown already?

"Of course, we'll have to work our way up to the Mardi Gras ball. I think you need to start slow, like asking her out for coffee tomorrow." Charlotte's eyes brightened as she looked over Naveen's shoulder. "Here's your chance."

Naveen whipped around.

Tiana had just stepped out of the kitchen. She carried a tray laden with dishes on her shoulder, probably beignets or bread pudding. Both were hot ticket items when it came to dessert at T&J's Supper Club.

"You ready, sugar?" Charlotte asked.

He stopped and took a breath. Before he could nod, Charlotte grabbed him by the hand and jerked him from his seat.

"Come on! Operation: Make a Match with My Two Best Friends is on."

14

TIANA

Given the current tranquillity of the empty dining room, one would never believe that less than an hour earlier this place had been packed to the gills with a boisterous crowd and rousing jazz music. Tiana shoved away the guilt that tried to creep in at the notion of her sitting here doing nothing. She'd worked hard tonight – they all had. She deserved to relax for a spell, to steal just a few minutes and quietly celebrate yet another successful night at T&J's Supper Club.

If she was being honest, she also needed a minute to ruminate over that *other* thing that had happened about an hour ago.

She was still reeling from Charlotte's outlandish suggestion that Tiana and Naveen meet up for café au lait the next day. Tiana had reminded her that they already had plans to go shopping, and then she'd raced back to the kitchen.

What was Lottie thinking?

Although, to be fair, Charlotte had no way of knowing the turmoil Tiana endured whenever she was near Naveen. None of her friends knew what she'd sacrificed in order to keep them all safe. Still, her *best* friend, who had known her all her life, should have known better than to propose such a preposterous idea. And in front of Naveen, no less!

With a sigh, Tiana pushed up from her seat. This was enough relaxing for the week.

She went around to all the tables and wiped them down with an old dishcloth. Using as much muscle as she could muster, she scrubbed at a particularly stubborn stain on the table next to Mr LaBouff's, then picked up a tray stacked with dirty dishes and hauled it into the kitchen.

She walked past one of the paintings that Ms Rose had given her and stopped short. The portrait, depicting a rainy evening in the French Quarter, was one of her favourites of those that hung in the restaurant. But something seemed… off.

Tiana tilted her head to the side, trying to figure out exactly what bothered her. She peered more closely and blinked several times. She was sure that the flowers hanging along the wrought-iron balcony had been more vibrant.

The same with the deep red brick of the building. Now they seemed obscured by the rain. Was the mist in the painting thicker?

"Don't be ridiculous," Tiana murmured.

That thickening fog outside must have been fogging her brain. Or maybe it was just that she was bone-tired after the night she'd had and wasn't thinking clearly.

She continued to the kitchen, carting the last of the dirty dishes with her. She backed her way through the swinging door. When she turned, she yelped in surprise.

"Addie Mae!" Tiana nearly dropped the tray. "My goodness, you scared me. What are you still doing here?"

"Mr James made me promise not to leave you here by yourself," Addie Mae answered.

"I should have known." Tiana rolled her eyes. And to think she'd felt such a sense of triumph after convincing Daddy to go home early. "Well, let's get these cleaned up so that we can both get out of here."

She and Addie Mae made quick work of the dishes and had the kitchen looking spotless in no time. Of course, it would be a mess again the next night, but that was how things worked in the restaurant business; she wouldn't have had it any other way.

"Thanks for the help," Tiana said as she followed Addie Mae out the back door that led to the alley behind the restaurant. She snapped her fingers. "I forgot Mama's dessert," she said, remembering the bread pudding she'd promised to bring home. Her mother had left early with a headache, probably from all that dancing.

"I'll wait for you," Addie Mae said.

"No, you go on home," Tiana said. "I'll see you tomorrow."

She went back inside and found the thick wedge of bread pudding wrapped in tinfoil sitting where she'd left it near the coffee percolator. She slid it into her bag, then looked over the kitchen one last time to make sure all was in order.

Letting out a deep breath, she tried to make the stress of the night dissipate. *This is all yours and Daddy's.*

And no one could take it from her.

Tiana walked back into the alley and gasped, struck by how thick the fog had become in just a few minutes. She could barely see a foot in front of her.

"My goodness," she whispered.

She kept the alley behind her restaurant clear of clutter, but she still tiptoed about, making sure she didn't trip over anything she couldn't see.

Despite its still being February, a sultry heat lingered in the air, making the night warm and damp. Tiana hefted her bag more securely onto her shoulder and took off for the

Rampart streetcar line. If she didn't make it in time for the last ride to the Ninth Ward, she would find herself walking home.

At least the walk from Tremé was shorter than if she'd bought that old sugar mill from the Fenner brothers. In fact, maybe it was a blessing that the estate agents had sold it to someone else.

"Yeah, you keep telling yourself that," Tiana said with a huff.

"You always go around talking to yourself?"

A streak of cold rushed through Tiana's veins. She took a step back. "Who's there?" she called.

A low, distinct laugh came from just over her shoulder. Tiana quickly turned. She blinked twice as the thick fog parted and the Shadow Man appeared.

"Well, hello there, Tiana," he greeted in that deceptively cordial voice of his. "Fine night out, isn't it?"

She straightened her shoulders, refusing to show an ounce of fear. "What can I do for you, Mr Facilier?"

"Why so formal? We're old friends at this point, aren't we? And it's *Doctor* Facilier."

"We are *not* friends, *Doctor*. The bottle of the potion I got from you this morning should last for at least two weeks, so we have no further dealings with each other until after Mardi Gras." Tiana hefted her bag higher on her shoulder and began to walk past him. "Now, if you'll excuse me, it's late and I need to get to the streetcar stop. I have another long and busy day ahead of me tomorrow."

"I can imagine," he said, stepping in front of her and blocking her path. "This little restaurant of yours is all anyone can talk about." He looked towards the building. "It's… nice." He didn't sound impressed. "Of course, the one I offered you would make this look like a shabby shack in comparison."

Tiana stuck her chin in the air, ready to defend her restaurant, but he spoke again before she could.

"Your guests don't seem to mind, so why should I?" he said with a casual shrug of his bony shoulders. "It appears your food makes up for the lack of… ambience, shall we say."

"The food *is* the most important thing at a restaurant, and yes, my guests love the dishes Daddy and I prepare here. That's all that matters."

"Yes, it is," he said. "I'm particularly interested in that étouffée you cooked tonight for Mr Eli LaBouff."

Tiana's eyes shot to his. "How do you know that I served Mr LaBouff étouffée?"

A wicked smile curved up the corners of his mouth.

Tiana suddenly recalled the stranger who had stalked past her, nearly knocking her over.

"You were here tonight," Tiana said in an accusatory tone.

Facilier peered down at his fingernails, then buffed them on his shoulder. "I may have stepped inside for a moment. I wanted to see what all the buzz was about."

Tiana narrowed her eyes at him. She didn't trust this one as far as she could throw him.

"I need to get going," she repeated. She tried to move past, but this time he stopped her with his cane, shoving the long stick out in front of her.

"Not so fast," Facilier said. "I have a proposition for you. Call it an amendment to our original arrangement."

Tiana shook her head. "No. I'm fine with how things are now. I'm not making any more deals with you."

He moved in close, his voice growing more sinister. "Look, girlie. You got off easy with that first deal. And if you want things to continue as they are, you'd better listen to what I have to say. It would be a shame if there was a horrible accident at this restaurant you've opened, but we all know how quickly fires start. Don't we?"

Tiana gasped. "You wouldn't."

He tilted his head to the side. "Now that I think about it, it would be far worse for you if something were to happen to that dear father of yours. Or your mother."

Dread sliced through Tiana like a knife through an onion.

"You keep my family out of this," she hissed. "That was part of the deal."

"Things change." Facilier shrugged. "You of all people should understand *transformations.*" He reached inside his jacket and drew out a vial similar to the one she'd got from him earlier today, but bigger. "You can still avoid harm coming to your family. All you have to do is add this potion to *all* of your food from now on. It's simple, Tiana."

"But why?" she asked. "Everything has been going just fine with me adding the potion to the gumbo. What difference will it make putting it in everything?"

"Enough," he snarled.

Tiana flinched at his harshness, then cursed herself for showing even a hint of fear. She'd learnt over the course of this year that the best way to handle Dr. Facilier was to show that he couldn't intimidate her.

"My question is legitimate," she countered. "What's the point of putting this potion in all of my dishes? You said I had to put it in Daddy's gumbo because that's the dish he's known for."

"I've cautioned you before about questioning my friends on the other side. Ask yourself, Tiana; is it worth risking your daddy's life when you just got him back? Is it worth your *prince's* life when all you have to do is what you've been doing all this time? Why must you make things so difficult?"

"Because I don't trust you," she said. "I'm never going to just do something simply because you asked, *Doctor* Facilier."

He grabbed her wrist and turned her hand palm up. He slapped the vial into the centre of her palm. "Every single dish, Tiana."

She threw the vial directly at his face. He snatched it as if he had been expecting her to do just that.

"I don't have to do anything," Tiana said. "I've held up my end of our bargain. You hold up yours."

She knocked his cane out of the way and brushed past him. She moved like her feet were on fire, refusing to look over her shoulder to see if he was following her. Her entire body trembled as she ran on shaking legs for the streetcar stop. Tiana could hear the bells jingling, indicating its arrival.

She was still yards away from the stop.

"Hold on there!" she shouted, frantically waving her hands even though the conductor wouldn't be able to see her through the thick fog. "Please! Don't leave!"

She reached the corner of Ursulines and South Rampart and looked both ways through the haze before stepping into the street. The moment her foot hit the roadway, the headlights of a Model T blasted through the fog.

Tiana yelped, jumping back onto the curb.

She slapped her hand over her erratically beating heart.

"Goodness," she whispered. She looked again for vehicles, then crossed the street, grateful that the streetcar was still at the stop. Tiana climbed aboard and paid her fare, then made her way to the back of the streetcar. She collapsed onto a seat and covered her face with her hands.

What was she going to do? Could Facilier really hurt her parents? Or Naveen?

Of course he could. The man had turned both her and Naveen into frogs. He could do whatever he wanted to do with that strange power he wielded.

She never should have made that deal with him. She knew better than to get involved with the likes of the Shadow Man.

But if you hadn't, Naveen wouldn't be human. And Daddy wouldn't be here.

Once she reached her stop, Tiana alighted from the streetcar. She could barely see her hand in front of her face. The relentlessness of this fog took her breath away.

She travelled this route so often she could probably have made it home with her eyes closed, but it was still unnerving not being able to see where she was going. Not knowing if anyone was out here with her.

"Don't be ridiculous," Tiana whispered.

This was Facilier's fault. Her run-in with him had her on edge, causing her heartbeat to escalate and tendrils of anxiety to cascade down her spine. But she was in her own neighbourhood now. She didn't have anything to worry about. Right?

Taking a deep breath, Tiana couldn't help running the rest of the way.

15
TIANA

The Ninth Ward, New Orleans
Friday, February 1927
Four days before Mardi Gras

Tiana lifted her favourite camel-brown hat from the rack in the corner of her room and fixed it over her hair. She turned to face the mirror and frowned.

"You look like you're off to shovel manure in this getup," she said to the image staring back at her.

She expelled a frustrated sigh as she tossed the hat on the bed and went back to her chifforobe for what had to have been the dozenth time this morning. There must have been *something* in there that would be appropriate for shopping at the most prestigious department store in all of New Orleans.

"Ah, yes! This one should work."

She pulled out her green-and-white polka-dot dress with the satin ribbon that tied at the waist, and the matching satin trim that ran along the hem of its ruffled skirt. She would normally only wear a dress like this to a wedding, or on Easter Sunday, but if she was going on this outing with Lottie to Maison Blanche, she had to look the part of someone who belonged there.

Because she *did* belong there.

She was just as good as anybody else who set foot in that establishment, and she was going to make sure everyone who was there knew it.

Tiana pulled the dress over her head and pinned the barrette Ms Rose had given her as a gift behind her ear. It had tiny gardenias attached to it, adding an elegant touch to her ensemble. She swished around from left to right in the mirror, admiring the way her dress twirled about her legs.

She stopped.

"Wait…" Tiana murmured.

She stepped closer to the mirror and peered at the barrette. She could have sworn the two flowers on either end of the trinket had been buds. Now all four of them were full gardenia blooms.

She must have been mistaken about the buds. Had to have been.

But she had specifically remembered those buds. She'd remarked on how pretty they would be if they could bloom.

She shook her head. There had to be a logical explanation. Maybe she'd bought a second barrette and had forgotten about it? Or perhaps someone had switched them on her.

With shaking hands, she slowly slipped the barrette out of her hair and returned it to her jewellery box. She tried her best to ignore the uneasiness that continued to build within her gut.

Tiana closed her eyes tight and sucked in several deep breaths. When she opened them, all would be okay. She popped her eyes open and forced herself to smile at her reflection.

"See, everything is fine. You're just tired."

She looked back at the clock on her bedside table and realised if she didn't get going, she would be late. When she walked into the kitchen, she was greeted with a surprised murmur from her mother, who sat behind her sewing machine.

"Well, look at you," Eudora said after removing the needle she'd had sandwiched between her lips. "You're dressed pretty fancy for making fried chicken and jambalaya, aren't you?"

"I'm not going to the restaurant just yet," Tiana said.

She drew a cup of water from the tap and leant against the counter as she took a sip. She stood up straight. "Wait, where's Daddy?"

"He went out to Jefferson Parish to look at some gardening equipment. He said to tell you he'll be back by this afternoon to start preparing for the Mardi Gras weekend kick-off." Eudora threaded a second needle with purple thread. "I should have the last of these done just in time."

Her mother had spent the past week making tablecloths in the traditional Mardi Gras colours as part of the decorations for the supper club's weekend-long celebration. Tiana couldn't wait to see how they would look.

Eudora glanced at Tiana. "You still didn't tell me why you're all dolled up."

Tiana finished her water, rinsed the cup in the empty sink, and returned it to the cupboard.

"I'm going over to the LaBouffs', and then Charlotte and I are going to Maison Blanche."

Her mother's eyebrows shot up. "Oh, you've got Maison Blanche money now?"

"I'm not planning on buying anything," Tiana assured her. "I'm only going with Lottie because she invited me."

"Well, you have been working hard. You deserve to treat yourself to something from the department store." Eudora pushed away from her sewing machine and came around the table. She reached into the pocket of her dress and pulled out a five-dollar bill.

"Five dollars?" Tiana cried. She backed away when her mother tried to hand her the money.

"Didn't I just say that you deserve to treat yourself? Go on and buy yourself something fun."

Tiana shook her head. "No way, Mama. I'm not wasting five whole dollars on foolishness."

"It's not foolishness. What's the point of working so hard if you don't enjoy the fruits of your labour?"

Eudora cupped Tiana's cheeks with her hands. They were slightly calloused from years of working with needle and thread. "I haven't said this enough lately, but I am *so* proud of all the work you've put into the supper club. Your daddy is, too."

A lump of emotion immediately formed in Tiana's throat. There were few things in this world that meant more to her than making her parents proud. She closed her eyes and smiled, relishing the safety and comfort of her mother's tender touch.

"Thank you, Mama." She opened her eyes. "But I'm still not taking your five dollars." She slipped out of her mother's hold and quickly made her way to the front door. "Tell Daddy I'll meet him at the restaurant later."

"Tiana!" her mother called, her hands on her hips.

"Love you, Mama." Tiana blew her a kiss before grabbing her purse and leaving the house.

Tiana headed south towards the river this time, opposite her usual route. That way she could hop on the St Charles Avenue streetcar line, which would take her directly to the LaBouff mansion.

She greeted neighbours while simultaneously calculating the various tasks she had to complete before that night's special dinner service.

The streetcar pulled up to the stop just as Tiana arrived.

"Hey there, Tiana," the streetcar operator greeted. "I hear you've got a big name playing at your restaurant tonight."

"I sure do," she answered as she slid a nickel in the box. She spoke loud enough for everyone on the streetcar to hear. "Rudy Davis is kicking off Mardi Gras weekend at T&J's Supper Club. Make sure you stop on by once your workday is done."

Tiana smiled as she heard murmurs of excitement while she made her way to the back. She took an empty seat on the side that faced the river, and was immediately taken aback by the thick greyish cloud that hovered over the water – even thicker than yesterday. There might have been something to Councilman Dubois's theory that this peculiar fog was coming from the river.

Tiana put her chin in her upturned palm and marvelled at the activity buzzing along the riverfront. Despite the lingering mist, she could make out the fishermen casting wide nets off the pier that stretched along the banks of the Mississippi River. She and her daddy made a trip to that same pier at least once a week, making deals for fresh catfish, dreaming up new recipes.

A medley of worry, alarm and sheer rage bubbled up inside as she recalled Facilier's threat.

To ignore it outright would be unwise, but she did not want to bow down to his whims, either.

She now recognised her folly. She'd become too comfortable, foolishly trusting that a known con man would remain true to his word. She should have been expecting him to pull something like this all along.

Well, it wasn't going to work. Unless he could give her a good reason to add that potion to everything she served at the restaurant, she wasn't going to do it. Who knew what was in this new version, if it was even the same magical concoction keeping her daddy alive… or something more nefarious? And who knew what else he would ask if she complied?

Attempting to put Facilier out of her mind, she took in the sights and sounds of the city. The streetcar sailed past LaBouff's enormous brick sugar mill. Plumes of white smoke bellowed from metal stacks, mixing in with the fog.

As she stared at the deep red bricks of the mill, another unwelcome thought made its way to her mind. Was Naveen somewhere inside? What was he doing? Was he considering asking her out for coffee again?

Stop that, Tiana!

She could *not* have coffee with him. She needed to focus on her future. And as much as she wished things could be different, Naveen was not and never could be part of it.

She pulled her bottom lip between her teeth to stop it from quivering, cursing even that tiny display of weakness.

The streetcar rolled along St Charles Avenue, past the imposing homes that lined the wide boulevard. Tiana couldn't imagine what it would be like to live in one of these, despite the fact that she'd been a frequent guest at the largest one in the city since childhood.

Even at a young age, she'd noticed that the people who looked like her never *lived* in those houses – they only cleaned them or provided some other kind of service. Her youthful mind thought it was happenstance, but as she got older, Tiana gradually became aware of disparities between how the Black people who lived in

Tremé and the Ninth Ward – and even the poor white people living in the tenement buildings – were treated, compared with those who lived uptown. She would ask Mama about it, but after hearing her say "It's just the way things are" so many times, Tiana stopped asking. Tiana always wished she could do something to help end those disparities.

When the streetcar pulled up in front of the LaBouffs' large white mansion, Tiana bade farewell to the conductor and climbed down the steps. She waited for several Model Ts to drive past – they were common in this more affluent part of the city – before she crossed the busy street and entered through the heavy wrought iron gate.

New Orleans was home to many grand residences, but there was none more magnificent than the two-storey Greek Revival home Mr Eli LaBouff had commissioned right in the heart of the city's Garden District. Stately columns surrounded the wraparound porch, each archway adorned with ornate ironwork. The house, with its intricately carved trim and elaborate front door, was a work of art.

"Tia!"

Tiana looked up to find Charlotte waving at her from the second-floor balcony. Feathers from the fluffy pink plumes that lined the edges of the silk dressing gown she wore flittered to the ground.

"I'll be right down," Charlotte said. "I just need a minute to finish getting dressed."

Shaking her head with a small laugh, Tiana didn't bother to point out to Lottie that she was the one who had said to be here at 10 a.m. sharp. She'd known her friend long enough to understand that 10 a.m. in Charlotte's time meant no sooner than 10:30 a.m. to everyone else.

She entered the house and was instantly pummelled by Stella, Charlotte's gentle giant of a hound. She hunched to the ground and rubbed the dog behind both ears. "How's it going, girl? You mind telling your mama to hurry it up?"

Stella's tail wagged back and forth as she looked excitedly at Tiana.

"Stella doesn't have to tell me anything, because I'm ready," Charlotte said.

Tiana looked towards the top of the gargantuan staircase. Lottie descended the steps, wearing a pristine white suit with a form-fitting skirt and a wide-brimmed hat. Tiana knew she'd made the right choice in choosing the green-and-white polka-dot dress.

"Well, come on. Let's get going," Charlotte said, putting her arm through Tiana's as if she hadn't been the one who'd left Tiana waiting. Tiana had to hand it to her – only Lottie had the charm to get away with such things.

They exited through the front door and walked to a car

idling at the curb. Ten minutes later, the car pulled up to the multi-storeyed department store in the heart of downtown. If the prime Canal Street location wasn't enough to convince people of its prominence, Maison Blanche's towering white edifice, with its lofty columns and fancy carvings, should.

Tiana tamped down the bit of nerves that suddenly tried to surface. This wasn't her first time shopping here. She and her mother frequented Krauss Department Store a few blocks away because of their fabrics selection, but she'd come to Maison Blanche with Daddy just a few months ago to buy a present for Mama's birthday.

She just knew that shopping here was a completely different experience for her than for her friend.

"I know exactly what I want," Charlotte said as they walked through the door. "Well, I know the exact colours I want – I'm thinking something violet and maybe a blush pink. Ooh, and midnight blue!"

She led Tiana to the gown section and proceeded to run the shop attendants ragged as they catered to her every whim.

Tiana was mindful of a shop attendant who lurked near the display of rayon stockings. The woman had been watching her like a hawk from the moment they arrived.

Charlotte emerged from the changing room wearing a sparkly navy blue flapper dress with crystal embellishments along the neckline.

"What about this one, Tia?" she asked, turning left, then right in front of the mirror.

"That dress was made for dancing," Tiana replied.

"Yeah, but it's missing something."

Charlotte marched to the row of mannequins and lifted a navy cloche from one of them. She tugged the tight-fitting hat over her bouncy blonde curls.

"You know, I actually think this would look better on you," she said. Charlotte tried to fit the hat on Tiana's head, but she moved out of the way.

"Lottie, no," Tiana said. Yet the lurking shop attendant had already noticed.

She rounded the display case and rushed to where Charlotte and Tiana stood.

"Excuse me – she cannot try on the merchandise," the woman stated.

Lottie looked over at her. "Why not? We're shopping."

"She cannot try on the merchandise," the woman repeated, her voice even harder. Colder. "It's store policy."

Lottie plopped a hand on her hip, but Tiana intervened before she could say more. "It's okay, Lottie."

"No, it is not!"

"Ma'am, if you do not calm down, we will have to ask you to leave," the attendant said.

"Excuse me!" Charlotte gasped. "Do you know who my daddy is?"

Tiana took Charlotte by the hand. "We're leaving," she said.

Charlotte wrenched her hand away. "We are not! We have every right to be here. And you have every right to try on whatever you want."

"Charlotte, please," Tiana hissed. "Let's just go. Please."

It must have been the plea in Tiana's voice that finally caught Lottie's attention. Or maybe it was the use of her full name, something Tiana rarely did.

"Okay," she said with a nod. "We'll leave."

She stuck her nose up in the air in the most Charlotte way possible and marched into the changing room. She came out a few minutes later dressed in her white suit.

"I will never, ever step foot in this store again," Charlotte said.

Tiana did her level best to keep her own head held high as she followed Lottie out of the department store, but when she slid into the back seat of the car, the adrenaline released from her body in a rush. Her hands shook.

"The nerve of that woman!" Charlotte huffed. "We shouldn't have left, Tia. In fact, Jefferson, turn the car around."

"No," Tiana said. "No, Lottie. I'm not going back there."

"You can't let people tell you what you can and cannot do. I never back down from—"

"I can't do what you do!" Tiana said. She fisted her hands in her lap, fighting for control over her emotions. She hated this feeling, and she resented Charlotte for putting her in this position, even if her friend's heart was in the right place. And at the moment, that felt worse than Dr. Facilier's magical bind.

"You don't understand," Tiana said. "They can forbid me from trying on their merchandise, and if I don't comply, they can call the authorities. That's my reality."

"But it doesn't have to be that way."

"But it *is*," Tiana said. "Who knows, maybe one day I will be able to try on that hat at Maison Blanche, but today is not that day."

"And not that store," Lottie said.

"Never that store," Tiana reiterated. She paused. "I do appreciate you standing up for me that way."

"I will always stand up for you, Tia," Charlotte said, grabbing her friend's hand.

But as the car moved through the city, they both fell into silence, wrapped up in their own thoughts.

16
TIANA

Tiana sifted flour into the steel bowl she'd dubbed her beignet-making bowl, then added in two heaping cups of sugar direct from the LaBouff Sugars mill. She relished in the comforting chaos of the busy kitchen, trusting that it would get her mind off what had occurred this morning at Maison Blanche department store.

It wasn't working out as planned.

Now that she thought about it, making beignets wasn't the best distraction method. She made them so often that her mind tended to wander, and right now, it remained fixated on the horridness of that morning's encounter. What had happened with that snobby sales attendant was a stark reminder of what she knew all too well: that unfairness lurked around every corner, especially for people who looked like her.

Once again, Mr Fenner's words from the year before echoed – the ones he'd uttered after selling that abandoned sugar mill right from under her. A woman of her *background* wasn't fit to run a big business like this.

"Did that dough do something to you?"

Tiana startled at Addie Mae's question. "What?"

Addie Mae nodded at the bowl Tiana held. "You're whipping that dough up like it stole your favourite pair of shoes or something. Too much of that and the beignets will come out tough and chewy instead of fluffy."

Tiana cursed under her breath as she dumped the contents of the bowl into the bin and started over.

That attendant at the department store might have ruined her morning, but Tiana darn sure wouldn't allow her to ruin the rest of Tiana's day. Not with the crowd she was expecting at her restaurant tonight – especially after spreading word about Rudy Davis and the Allstars.

Tiana started to hum her favourite of his tunes, 'Jump, Skip and a Hop', under her breath as she cracked an egg and added it to the bowl. She measured and poured in the sugar and threw in a pinch of salt, getting back into the familiar rhythm and focus. On her way to the icebox for milk, she noticed the wire basket that she used to store the pasta was empty. For a moment she just stared at the basket, baffled.

She'd quickly gone through the pasta Mr Salvaggio had

delivered yesterday and had put in an emergency order to be delivered first thing this morning. Tiana went into the pantry to see if Addie Mae had mistakenly put it there, but there were only canned vegetables, tomato sauce and rice on the shelves.

"Addie Mae." Tiana walked over to where her head waitress was stacking salad bowls. "Where's the pasta I ordered?"

"You made jambalaya with it, didn't you?"

"That was yesterday's order. I put in another for today. Mr Salvaggio assured me that it would be delivered this morning. Did he not bring it?"

Addie Mae shook her head. "No, I don't think so. And I haven't seen any packages out back."

Tiana frowned. Mr Salvaggio was one of her most reliable vendors. It wasn't like him not to follow through.

"I hope he isn't unwell," she murmured. She untied the apron from around her waist. "You know what, I think I'll just take a walk down to the French Market. I need a few extra ingredients anyway. I found a recipe for greens with salt meat in Mama's cupboard that will go mighty fine with tonight's menu."

Tiana hung the apron on the nail next to the door, then grabbed the wicker basket she used whenever she went to the outdoor market, which lined the huge bend along the mighty Mississippi. It was only a fifteen-minute walk through the French Quarter. That is, if she didn't run into anyone she knew on the way there. A fifteen-minute journey could take an hour with chatty neighbours stopping her to inquire about how her mama and the rest of the family were doing.

Tiana was walking near one of the brick tenement houses when she caught sight of a silhouette out of the corner of her eye. She moved to the side, assuming it was some hardworking factory worker on his way to one of the many warehouses in the Quarter. When the blurred figure didn't emerge after she'd walked several yards, Tiana slowed her steps so that whoever it was behind her could move along.

They didn't.

She stopped walking and turned around.

No one.

Unease crept up Tiana's spine in the same way that ever-thickening fog crept along the city streets. She couldn't dismiss this as fatigue or her mind playing tricks on her. Something – or some*one* – was definitely following her.

"Hello?"

No answer.

Was it the Shadow Man? But no – for all his tricks, Facilier couldn't resist hearing himself talk. He would have shown himself by now.

Heart starting to pound in her chest, Tiana hurried

along the pavement, barely stopping at the street corners to check for traffic.

Relief washed over her when she arrived at the covered outdoor market and found it bustling with people. She waved to the egg vendor, Mr Taylor, and his son, Lil Johnny, lifted his cap in greeting. The strong smell of fish hit her square in the face, but Tiana didn't mind. She waded through the throng of people at the seafood stalls that were set up at the very end of the market, making her way to the plethora of vegetable stands lined up on both sides of the pedestrian walkway.

Tiana did a double take when she glanced over at the river.

It was green. *Grassy*. A thick moss skimmed the top of the water.

"What's happening here?" she asked.

"Strange, ain't it?" a fisherman said. He held up a foot-long catfish. "Can I interest ya in one of these?"

"No, thank you," Tiana said. She hooked her thumb at the river. "When did this start?"

The craggy-faced man hunched a shoulder. "All was just fine yesterday. Got outta my boat this morning and this stuff was covering the water. Strange, indeed."

"There has to be something to account for it. Could it be the fog?" she remarked.

"Don't know. Not making it easy for us fishermen, I can tell ya that."

From the conversations she caught on the way to her favourite vegetable stand, the baffling algae bloom on the river was the talk of the market.

Tiana sidled up to the stand run by the Galvez family from St Bernard Parish. They always had the freshest, most flavourful vegetables, and if you offered a fair price, they would throw in a little something extra.

Tiana picked up several bunches of dark leafy greens, a few radishes, some onions and a basket of strawberries. She'd been wanting to try her hand at making a strawberry sauce to drizzle on top of her beignets. After paying for her purchases, she went over to the Rinella family's pasta stand for her last order. It didn't measure up to Mr Salvaggio's spaghetti, but then again, little could.

She was moving away from the stand when a sense of foreboding tingled along Tiana's spine. Just then, an encroaching shadow fell over her. She spun around to find Dr. Facilier standing just over her shoulder. She quickly squelched the cry that rose in her throat.

"What do you want?" she whispered harshly.

"You know why I'm here."

She narrowed her eyes. "Were you following me earlier?" Confusion flashed in his eyes, telling Tiana all she needed to know. He wasn't the one who had trailed her to the market after all. Tiana waved off her question. "Forget it. I told you that I am not making any more deals, so leave me alone."

She turned and started to walk away, but before she could get past the next vegetable stall, Facilier was suddenly in front of her, blocking her path. Tiana yelped, but the buzz and chatter around the busy market drowned out her cry.

Facilier lowered his head until he was eye level with her. "I've been polite. You don't want me to get nasty."

She waved her arms in front of his face, inches from her own. "What do you call this?"

"You see this little bit of fog that's been hanging around this city?" Facilier scoffed. "It's nothing. My friends can show you what *real* smoke looks like."

"Are you saying that they're the reason behind this strange weather?"

"I'm saying *you're* the reason this fog is here. I warned you things would get ugly if you didn't do what I said." He pulled the large vial he'd tried to give her the last time they'd met from the inside pocket of his vest. "Take it. Use it tonight."

Facilier shoved it into her hands, looking like he wanted to say more. But then he looked past Tiana, his eyes widening in dismay. He quickly pivoted and stalked away, disappearing into the heavy fog.

Tiana turned to see what had motivated his abrupt departure. "Oh, Ms Rose!"

"Hello, Tiana. Who was your friend?" the woman asked as she approached.

"He's… he's nobody," Tiana muttered darkly, watching Facilier retreat further into the fog. She threw the new concoction into her bag.

"You know, Tiana, my mother used to say all the time, *bel dan pa di zanmi*. Just because someone is smiling at you, it doesn't mean they're your friend. One must be careful of the company one keeps."

"He's no friend of mine," Tiana said.

The woman only nodded. Then, after a beat, she said, "Were you going to leave the market without visiting my flower stand?"

"Well, I'm in a bit of a rush." Tiana hedged. Ms Rose had the ability to make her feel as if she'd just been scolded in the most gentle way possible. "But I must say that those beautiful flowers you gave me yesterday are gorgeous," Tiana added. "They really do brighten up the restaurant."

"I'm happy to hear that," the woman said in her soothing voice. She nodded in the opposite direction. "Follow me. I have another gift for you."

"I really can't," Tiana called, but Ms Rose was already heading to her flower stand, and the woman had been much too nice to her over these past few months for Tiana to rudely walk away.

"Ms Rose, I appreciate the gifts, but I can't continue to accept them, especially without payment," Tiana said as she trailed after her.

"But I insist," Ms Rose replied. "My painting is a hobby. They would remain unseen in my home if you weren't kind enough to display them. And this one is very special. I think you will like it."

She lifted a purple cloth from the framed picture, unveiling an absolutely stunning portrait of the Mardi Gras Indians. The bright colours of their elaborate headdresses were so brilliant; they gave the picture an almost lifelike appearance.

The scene displayed the tradition, which had originated in Tremé, of the formerly enslaved Africans paying homage at Mardi Gras to the Native people who had aided them during troubled times. How could she say no to a painting that held such meaning to the neighbourhood that had embraced her restaurant?

"It's beautiful," Tiana said. "I know exactly where I'm going to put it."

"You must hang it in the very centre of the back wall, facing the stage."

Tiana blinked. "That's… uh… very specific."

Ms Rose shrugged her delicate shoulders. "There's a symmetry to the placement, yes? The rhythm of the band paired with the rhythm of the Indians' tambourine?" She tapped the side of her leg as if she were playing one of the percussion instruments.

"Yes." Tiana slowly nodded. "Yes, I agree."

"You should probably get back," Ms Rose said. "Word on the street is that you have quite the celebration taking place at your restaurant tonight."

Tiana shook her head, trying to clear it. "Yes – yes, I do," she said. "Thank you again for the painting."

"Thank you for giving it a home," she returned.

Tiana secured the gift underneath her arm before leaving the French Market. She decided against going back the way she'd come, choosing to head west, past the Cabildo and St Louis Cathedral. As she came upon the huge limestone Louisiana Supreme Court building that had just recently been built, she watched as a brand-new Model T pulled up to the curb and one of the Fenner brothers – the taller of the two – got out of the car.

As if the day could get any stranger.

"Well, if it isn't Tiana. How are you doing?"

"I'm doing well, Mr Fenner. How are you?"

"Oh, well, you know. All is good, except for this fog that doesn't want to go away. Strange thing, isn't it?"

"That it is. And it seems to be getting thicker by the day."

"Yes, it does." He looked her up and down through the monocle that hung from a chain on his neck. "You know, Tiana, I hope there are no hard feelings about what happened with that old sugar mill. Your restaurant never would have survived in that area. Where it is now, over there in Tremé, is much more suited for your type of establishment."

She straightened her shoulders. "Forgive me for being so bold, Mr Fenner, but I happen to disagree. I think my restaurant would thrive no matter where it's located. And I haven't given up on the riverfront. Me and my daddy are gonna eventually open an even bigger restaurant one day. In fact, we plan to open *several*."

She gave him a sweet smile as she hefted her basket of vegetables up higher on her forearm. "Now, if you would excuse me, I have a very big night ahead. If you would like some good food and good jazz music, might I suggest you come over to Tremé and give T&J's Supper Club a try? The doors are always open to *any*one."

Tiana's heart pounded like a bass drum within her

chest as she continued along Royal Street. She could feel Mr Fenner's eyes boring into her retreating form, but she wouldn't take back a word she'd said, and she refused to apologise for her tone. She was tired of everyone telling her what to do, where to be. This weekend's Mardi Gras celebration would give her the boost she needed to do things her own way. She would make it so.

Even if that constant unease in the pit of her stomach made her wonder what other forces were at work.

17

NAVEEN

Naveen paced the length of the veranda, counting his steps as he travelled from one end to the other. It spanned the entire front of the café where he was set to meet a representative of Dugas Candy Company, and if the man didn't show up soon, Naveen feared he would wear a trench into the wooden planks.

Setting up the meeting on such short notice had taken a bit of finessing, but if there was one thing Naveen was good at, finessing was it. Now, he had to exploit that skill into convincing the area's largest candy company to partner with LaBouff Sugars.

He stopped his pacing long enough to look out at the street for signs of John Dugas, the son of the owner of the company. The fog made it difficult to make out the faces of the people who walked by. Not that it would make much of a difference to him. He had never seen John Dugas before. But he'd been in America long enough to recognise that the people here displayed their status by the clothes they wore. Naveen was certain that, being the son of a rich candy maker, John Dugas would arrive in a suit and tie, and possibly a top hat.

If the average person were to look at Naveen on any given day, they would probably think he had grown up a pauper. He'd worn his best pair of trousers, but he favoured comfort over formality. Stuffy attire made him itchy, and he only wore it when absolutely necessary.

He stopped pacing as panic seized him.

Maybe more formal dress *was* necessary for a day like today. Maybe Dugas would take one look at him and think he wasn't serious enough to go into business with. What did Mr LaBouff always tell him? He had to look the part of a businessman if he wanted to succeed in business.

Did he have time to run home and change into something more conventional?

Naveen took off for the veranda steps, but stopped at the sight of a young man wearing brown slacks and a sleeveless pullover not much different from the one Naveen wore.

"Mr Dugas?" he asked.

"Yes! Are you Naveen?" He tipped the bill of his derby hat. "Pleasure to meet you."

John Dugas was about his age, with a cheery smile that Naveen could make out even through the fog.

Naveen suddenly felt foolish for being so worried. He and this man would get along just fine.

They talked for two hours over cups of coffee and tea biscuits. Naveen had strategically chosen a café that used LaBouff Sugars in all their desserts. But it soon became apparent that Dugas could not be so easily sweet-talked into a deal.

"I have to warn you," the man said as he stirred another teaspoon of sugar into his café au lait, "LaBouff Sugars has some stiff competition. This area is full of sugar mills that have been vying for our business for years. What makes you think LaBouff's is the one for us?"

"Because none of those other mills are bigger or more successful than LaBouff's," Naveen stated with certainty.

Dugas nodded. "True. But there are logistical issues, as well. Dugas Candy Company is headquartered across Lake Pontchartrain. Will LaBouff make that extra inconvenience worth our while?"

"We will," Naveen assured him, although he had no idea what it would entail to deliver the product across the vast lake. It didn't matter. If he landed this contract for LaBouff's, he would do whatever it took to make sure it was a success.

Not only did he want this for himself, but after his

recent interaction with Tiana, Naveen had a burning need to show her that he, too, could prosper. Seeing how hard she worked to make her restaurant a success made him want to do the same in his job.

"I can personally guarantee that no other sugar mill will provide the same service as LaBouff's," Naveen continued. "Nor will anyone else provide a superior product. With LaBouff's, you get the best."

Naveen wasn't sure how John Dugas could turn down such a fabulous sales pitch.

"You drive a hard bargain. But I have one more question," Dugas said. "How did you know we were in the market for a new supplier? We just got rid of our previous one a couple of days ago."

Naveen leant in closer and smiled. "It's my job to stay on top of such things. And if you go with LaBouff Sugars, we will bring that same diligence."

By the time Naveen walked out of the café, he felt so light he practically floated down the steps. It wasn't a sure thing – John Dugas was much too savvy a businessman to show his hand. But it was close, Naveen could feel it.

And *he* would be the one to make it happen.

Possibly. Maybe. *Right?*

He cursed that little nugget of doubt, but after being

a screwup for so long, how could he be certain that this time things would be different? Dugas could very well be meeting with other sugar suppliers that very minute, having the same friendly conversation.

Naveen returned to the sugar mill and went on his daily tour of the factory floor. He spotted Randy Boudreaux coming out of the boiler room.

"Hey, Randy!" Naveen called. He looped an arm over the man's shoulder. "Thanks for that inside information about Dugas's." Even though he could barely hear his own thoughts above the noisy industrial equipment, Naveen still leant in close so that no one would overhear. "This is only between me and you, my friend, but LaBouff Sugars may be their next supplier. Pretty good, eh?"

"Oh yeah?" Randy asked. "Was it the new cane seeds we're using that did it for him? That ribbon cane produces a much sweeter juice."

"I—" Naveen frowned. "I didn't think to tell him about that." Naveen cursed under his breath.

"Aw, don't beat yourself up, boss. I don't think it'll make a difference."

But it *could*. Competition was fierce – Dugas had said so himself. Any leg up Naveen could give LaBouff Sugars would be a good thing.

Naveen looked at Randy's soot-covered face with the same curiosity he'd felt every time he'd chatted with the man.

"I should have brought you along to my meeting," Naveen said. "Your mind is sharp, Randy. How did you end up working on the shop floor?" He immediately held up his hands. "Not that there is anything wrong with that. You guys do incredible work down here; I just wondered why you don't try your hands at sales. I think you would do a good job."

Randy shrugged. "I come from poor folks on the bayou. Folks like me don't get to wear them fancy sweaters to work." Another shrug. "That's just how it is."

Naveen watched him as he walked back towards the boiler room.

He wasn't so clueless as to not recognise what it meant to be born into privilege, but he had never thought about those who were held back simply by the chance of their birth. What would he have done with his life had he not been the son of the king and queen of Maldonia? Would he even have the fortitude to work at LaBouff's?

What was he without the royal blood that ran through his veins?

Naveen's head was buzzing as he climbed the stairs up to his office. He was so distracted that he almost missed the fine linen envelope on his desk. His pulse quickened as he picked it up and turned it over.

Naveen sucked in a swift breath.

The royal crest of Maldonia was branded into a seal of gold wax. He quickly loosened the seal and pulled out the letter.

Our dearest Naveen,

It has been a year since you embarked on your journey to North America. Your mother and I now see that we were harsh in our initial decision to cut you off from your rightful inheritance.

Please accept this correspondence as an apology and an invitation to return to your home in Maldonia. We have already prepared the southwest wing of the palace to serve as your residence. This comes with a slate of servants to tend to your needs and a healthy stipend to cover your expenses.

I expect your response to our invitation within the next two weeks.

In congruence with your mother, the Queen,

Your father, the King of Maldonia.

Naveen stared at his father's bold handwriting so long that the letters began to swim on the page.

Home.

They wanted him to come home. He would have servants. A luxurious place to lay his head.

Money! He would have all the money he could possibly spend, and more.

So why did it suddenly feel as if he'd eaten too many biscuits at the café?

Perhaps because, as easily as he could think of all he would gain by returning home, it was just as easy to consider all he would lose. Like the friends he'd made here in America. Like the satisfaction he experienced after an honest day's work, the fulfilment that came only with knowing he was earning his own way.

Like the chance to get to know Tiana better.

He was meeting Charlotte at Tiana's place tonight for her big celebration to ring in the Mardi Gras season. He felt a lurch of excitement just knowing he would get the chance to see her soon. Who knew, maybe this time she wouldn't run away from him.

But that would all be irrelevant if he returned home.

Naveen pressed a fist to his stomach and slumped into his chair. He brought his elbows up onto the desk and cradled his head in his hands. The decision his father had put before him felt like an anchor in his gut.

Would it make him foolish to turn down their invitation to return to the life he'd known back in Maldonia?

Or would it make him a failure to accept it?

18

TIANA

Anticipation thumped like a drum throughout Tiana's bloodstream as she raced from one end of the dining room to another, putting the finishing touches on the decorations for tonight's celebration.

She tugged on the green cloth covering Mr LaBouff's table, then turned to the one at the very rear of the dining room. She frowned. The flowers at the table's centre that had looked so vibrant that morning were suddenly all wrong. The marigolds were clumped together on one side of the vase, while the stalks of lavender congregated on the other.

She plunked her hands on her hips. "Okay, now who is messing with my centrepieces?"

"Tiana?" She turned to find Addie Mae peeking out of the door to the kitchen. "I don't know the last time you looked outside, but folks are lining up around the building. If we don't start this dinner service soon, those people are going to barge in."

"Oh, goodness, all right," Tiana said. "But first, Addie Mae, did you tinker with these?" she asked, gesturing towards the table.

"I serve food, I do not decorate," was her head waitress's answer.

"Hmm," she murmured. "Maybe it was one of the other girls."

Tiana quickly rearranged the flowers, but when she turned for the door, something else caught her attention out of the corner of her eye. She whipped around to look at Ms Rose's painting of the Mardi Gras Indians that she'd hung up earlier.

She tapped her fingers against her lips, counting in her head as she studied the portrait.

"Weren't there six men?" she whispered. Tiana was sure there had been at least a half dozen colourfully dressed men in the painting, but now she only counted five.

"Tiana!" Addie Mae called again, motioning to the door.

"I'm on it," Tiana said. She glanced once more at the painting, thinking that she really needed to get some sleep once she was sure this kick-off celebration was a success.

She rushed over to the kitchen and opened the door a crack, poking her head inside. "Are we ready?"

"Ready," Jodie and Carol Anne replied in unison.

"Ready as we'll ever be, baby girl." Tiana smiled at her daddy, who wore one of the new aprons her mother had surprised them both with earlier that day. She'd painstakingly embroidered their initials on the front panel.

"Okay," Tiana said. "It's time for T&J's Supper Club to kick off the Mardi Gras season in style!"

She headed to the front door. Though Addie Mae had warned her, she could scarcely believe the line of people waiting. Tiana smiled wide as she welcomed the patrons filing inside. Although people tended to dress a bit fancier on Friday nights, many had gone all out this evening. The women wore flapper dresses and long gloves, and most of the men were in well-tailored suits and homburg hats.

Just as she'd predicted, her dining room would be bursting at the seams with people eager to hear Rudy Davis and the Allstars.

Tiana's smile grew even wider as she spotted Buford, the cook at Duke's Cafe, where she'd once worked, walking towards her.

"Well, hello there, Buford."

"Tiana," he replied with a nod. He gestured at the door, a sheepish look on his face. "I… uh… I thought I'd come check out your new restaurant. I've been hearing good things about it."

"Have you now?" she asked. "Well, come on in." She held her hand out with a flourish.

It would be rude to revel in his obvious discomfort. But, then again, Buford *had* taken every opportunity to make fun of her dream back when she worked at Duke's.

"Oh, Buford," Tiana called. "Why don't you bring that trophy you got for winning the Kentucky Derby next time?"

His forehead creased in confusion, making Tiana wonder if he remembered the time he'd told her that he had a better chance of winning the horse race than she had of opening a restaurant.

But then understanding dawned in his eyes. "I guess I deserve that," Buford said.

Tiana decided to take pity on him. "I'm just messing with you," she said teasingly. "There are no hard feelings. In fact, I'll be sure to make my way down to Duke's soon. It's been a while since I had your flapjacks."

"Flapjacks? Why, I haven't made those in quite some time," Buford said.

"Why not? They were your bestsellers, after my beignets, of course."

"Well, Duke's has been closed for a while, so—"

"Closed?" Tiana's head snapped back in surprise. "Since when?"

"Going on a year now," Buford said. He looked at her as if she'd lost a few of her marbles.

Tiana's heart skipped a beat.

"But, Buford, I…?" She'd only left her job at Duke's Cafe about five months earlier, just as she and Daddy were gearing up to buy the restaurant. He had to have been mistaken.

"I'm gonna go in and get myself a seat," Buford said.

"Yeah," Tiana whispered. "Go on in."

She put a hand to her stomach. She thought about her conversation with Ms Margery at the streetcar stop yesterday. And with her butcher, Mr Phillips, and Mr Smith at the fabric shop. All of them had behaved as if parts of the past didn't exist. She recalled the strange buds on the barrettes, the changing painting, the wilting flowers. Once again, she felt like she was losing it.

Could this be…

No. The Shadow Man didn't have that kind of power. He didn't have access to her possessions, let alone the memories of random people.

But they weren't just random people, a little voice in Tiana's head countered. They were all people she had a connection to – albeit loosely – in one way or another.

Hadn't he warned that he would bring harm to folks she knew? What if this was the start of it? What if her loved ones – the friends and family she was closest to – were next?

"It's all one big coincidence," Tiana murmured. Although that was becoming harder and harder to believe.

Tiana forced herself to return her attention to the guests still filing into the restaurant. Once every table was filled to capacity, she went into the kitchen and took her place by her daddy's side, focusing on the food. They cooked up a pot of red beans and rice, and another filled to the brim with her pasta jambalaya. She expected a lot of sales of the jambalaya, but the star for tonight was smothered pork chops with a little of the greens she'd whipped up on the side.

"These sure do take me back," her daddy said. "Your grandmother used to cook them every Sunday."

"I can't wait for Mama to try them," Tiana said.

"She should be here in a few minutes. She said she didn't want to miss any of Rudy Davis."

Tiana looked at the clock that hung above the door and frowned. She'd asked Addie Mae to come and get her when the band arrived. They should have been here by now.

"Speaking of Rudy Davis," she said as she untied her apron. "Let me see if he and his band need help setting up."

Just as she started for the door that led to the dining

room, Lil Johnny Taylor, the egg vendor's son, came bursting through.

"Miss Tiana!" he shouted. "Miss Tiana, you'll never believe it!"

The young boy was out of breath, his chest heaving with each word.

"Calm down, Lil Johnny," Tiana said as she hurried to the tap to draw him a glass of water. "Here, drink this."

Lil Johnny took the glass and gulped down half before wiping his mouth with his sleeve.

"Now, what's going on?" Tiana asked.

"There was a fire!" he finally said. "I never seen anything like it."

"A fire?" Tiana gasped. "Was anyone hurt?"

He shook his head. "I don't think so, but it sure was scary."

Her daddy came up behind her, wiping his hands on a dish towel. "Any idea what caused it?" he asked.

Lil Johnny hunched his bony shoulders. "No, sir. Strangest thing. It just happened out of nowhere."

"And you're sure no one got hurt?" Tiana asked.

He nodded his head so fast the pageboy cap he always wore nearly fell off.

"I'm pretty sure, ma'am. But I got a message. From Rudy Davis."

"Rudy Davis?" What was Rudy Davis doing sending her messages through Lil Johnny Taylor?

"Yes, ma'am. You see, it was the Allstars' instruments that caught fire. They're all burnt up. Mr Davis said to give you his regrets, but he and the Allstars won't be able to perform tonight."

19

FACILIER

"Good evening, sir." Facilier smiled at the well-dressed gentleman approaching his table in Jackson Square. "Can I interest you in a game of cards?"

"Out of my way," the man said, swatting at him with the folded newspaper he carried.

Facilier glowered at the man's back as he continued down the pavement. If only he hadn't been in so much debt to his friends on the other side, Facilier would have had them burn the man to a crisp, right on the spot.

Alas, he owed too much already, and he was incapable of producing a fire by sheer will alone. He had to rely on more conventional methods, like the kerosene he'd poured over Rudy Davis and the Allstars' instruments.

He chuckled at the havoc he'd caused with that stroke

of genius. Or, should he say, the havoc *Tiana* had caused. Because that was what he planned to tell her.

He already had her thinking she was the reason this peculiar fog had overtaken the city, but the fog didn't go far enough. It wasn't dangerous enough to those close to Tiana.

But this fire? The fire was personal. He would make her believe that it was punishment from his friends on the other side. And that was only the start!

The potion was still his easiest route to LaBouff – to making sure all of this hadn't been for nothing – so Facilier wouldn't count solely on the mysterious fog and the fire to make Tiana fall in line. She was too smart for him to take that chance. This fog could disappear as quickly as it had shown up, and she could write the fire off as some sort of fluke. No, he had yet another ace in his pocket.

Actually, his aces were tied up in a room back at his emporium.

He'd ambushed the pasta maker on his way to Tiana's restaurant that morning. Not only did she rely on old man Salvaggio for his wares, but Facilier had witnessed their new friendship. She was chummy with just about every person who set foot in that restaurant.

And he was going to *remove* each and every one of them until he convinced her that his friends on the other side were behind the disappearances. He already had a nice collection going.

If he could make her see that her stubborn resistance to using his special new potion was causing others to suffer, she would come to heel.

Well, she had *better* come to heel. He had less than a week to trick her into feeding LaBouff that concoction before his friends on the other side came calling.

Realising he needed to check in on his captives, Facilier started packing up his cards and table. He might be a bit deceitful, but he wasn't a complete monster. Besides, they could possibly prove useful in other ways.

He navigated through the green fog towards his home in Pirate's Alley. When he entered, a blast of cold air hit him.

Facilier shut his eyes for a brief moment. It was as if he'd summoned them with his thoughts.

The Shadows.

The low moans and groans emerged from somewhere deep within the walls of the draughty space, the air becoming colder as their groans grew louder, until both reached a crescendo when they appeared. They slithered along the walls and on the floor at his feet.

"Friends, it's so nice to see you again," Facilier lied. A gust of wind billowed. "Yes, yes, I agree. The time for small talk is over."

He canted his head to the side, listening to the rhythmic intonations that only those indebted to them could understand.

"Yes, I know. Payment is coming due."

The Shadows didn't know it yet, but this would be their final collection. Because this was the last deal he planned to make with them. He nodded and murmured in agreement as their lamentations continued.

Until they said something that made him stiffen in shock.

"What was that?" Facilier asked. "Has Tiana signed the contract?"

A high-pitched keening accompanied a frigid blast of cold air. The Shadows didn't like repeating themselves.

"But… but why would that matter? I made the request on her behalf, and it was done," Facilier said. "It was a verbal agreement. We've done those before."

Their answering chant sent a chill down Facilier's spine that had nothing to do with the brutally cold temperature of the room.

Had he heard them correctly?

The exchanging of a soul required more than just a verbal agreement?

No. No, that couldn't be right.

"I… I think you're mistaken," Facilier said.

Gale-force winds blasted across his face. Facilier held up his forearm to shield himself from the fierce gust.

Read the governing covenant?

He raced to the cabinet where contracts for the numerous bargains he'd made with the Shadows over the years were stored. A collection of scrolls sprang forth from the drawer. He pitched them left and right, clearing out the drawer until he reached the bottom, where the very first agreement he'd made with them lay.

He unfurled the crumpled parchment and scanned the document, his hands shaking so badly he could barely make out the words.

"See, here it is," he said once he got to the end. He held up the document so the faceless creatures could see his wobbly ten-year-old signature scrawled across the bottom. "It says right here that I can make requests on behalf of others."

They spoke in sighs and grunts, the juxtaposition of the soft and sharp sounds a brutal cacophony that sent Facilier's head reeling.

What was that? He had missed the clause on the exchanging of souls?

Fear caught in his throat as his eyes continued down the document. The verbiage on the exchange of souls was at the very end, in print that was tiny and faded.

He squinted at the minuscule words, but there they were. Right there in black and white.

> *The soul of the one who requested the deed shall vacate the body one year from the signing of an agreement in exchange for the soul of another being returned to the earth. All knowledge of the returned soul's previous death shall be wiped clean from the consciousness of all who knew him, with the exception of those who are party to the agreement. Payment shall be rendered by signatories of the agreement.*

Tiana wasn't a signatory.

"What… what does this mean?" Facilier said.

More moans. More deep, intense, ghastly moans.

This final warning from the Shadows was the most terrifying thing Facilier had ever heard.

If Tiana did not physically sign over her soul, he, as the lone signatory, must forfeit his own.

20
TIANA

This could not be happening. It could *not* be happening.

"This is a disaster," Tiana said.

She'd promised Rudy Davis and the Allstars. If she went out there and told the crowd there would be no show, they would rebel. Even worse, they might never come to her restaurant again. This was the kind of thing that could ruin T&J's Supper Club's reputation and make the success they'd achieved short lived.

In the few months since they'd opened, Tiana had learnt just how difficult it was to run a restaurant in a city known for its cuisine. Serving great food was only a small part; if you alienated your customers, they could easily spend their money somewhere else.

And this was supposed to be their weekend!

"Now, just stay calm, baby girl," James said. He put an arm around her shoulders and gave her a gentle squeeze.

She leant into her daddy's comforting embrace, wanting nothing more in this moment than to soak in the support he provided. But she had an emergency on her hands. She couldn't just stand there doing nothing.

"I have to figure out a way to fix this," Tiana said. "People are expecting dinner and a show."

"The way Lil Johnny described it makes no sense," Addie Mae said. "Why would only the instruments burn up?"

"That's what I don't understand, either," Tiana said. "It almost makes me wonder if it was intentional—"

My friends can show you what real *smoke looks like…*

Was this Facilier's doing? Had he set his friends on Rudy Davis's band just to get back at her for not wanting to add his latest potion to all her dishes?

"How can T&J's have a Mardi Gras celebration without a band?" Addie Mae asked. "People are going to be so disappointed."

"Or they're gonna go down the street to listen to The Shiny Walter Band," Carol Anne said.

Tiana whipped around. "Where's Shiny Walter playing?"

"Smokey Joe's over on Rampart. I heard folks talking about it earlier."

Tiana quickly tried to come up with a backup option. But she couldn't call on Louis and the rest of the Crawfish Crooners. She'd given them the night off, and they were surely all scattered about the city.

She walked over to the swinging door, nudging it just wide enough to observe the crowd. She fidgeted with the top button of her dress as her eyes scanned the packed dining room. Tiana was relieved to see so many cheerful smiles. People were enjoying their food, and everyone seemed to be having a grand time.

But how long would that last if she went out there and informed them that the band everyone had come to see tonight would not be performing? That *no* band would be performing?

Trepidation tiptoed up and down her spine, the feeling of dread escalating as each second passed.

As she looked over the crowd, she caught sight of Charlotte's blonde curls at her favourite table near the stage. Naveen was there with her.

Naveen!

You can't ask him.

But Naveen was the only musician here. And when he'd played for the crowd the night before, everyone seemed to love him.

She'd promised her patrons dinner and a show. What choice did she have?

"This is what you get for making promises," Tiana whispered to herself.

She sucked in a deep breath and slowly blew it out, then pushed open the kitchen door and headed straight for Lottie and Naveen's table. Tiana did her best to quell the butterflies that instantly began to flitter around her stomach as she drew closer.

"Hi, Lottie. Naveen," Tiana said as she came upon their table. She cursed her voice for shaking.

"Tia, everything looks so beautiful tonight," Charlotte said. "But where's the band? I'm ready to dance."

"Well, that's why I'm here." She turned her attention to Naveen, her breath catching in her throat. It was hard to believe that, at one time, she'd found him annoying. She would gladly put up with his exasperating habits if it meant they could be together.

But you can't. So get on with what you came here to do.

Tiana swallowed deeply, then allowed the words to rush out of her. "Rudy Davis and the Allstars' instruments burned up in a fire tonight, and they won't be able to make it, so can you please play your trumpet for the crowd, Naveen?"

"Oh, goodness." Lottie's hand flew to her chest. "Is everyone okay?"

"I think they are," Tiana said. "But, of course, they can no longer perform tonight. And I have no way of contacting Louis. I would if I—"

"Yes," Naveen said.

"Yes?" Hope surged through her. "You'll do it?"

"Of course I will, Tiana."

There was something about the way he said her name – the way it rolled off his tongue in that lyrical way he spoke. If she didn't know any better, Tiana would have thought the Shadow Man had taken away her ability to speak. She was transfixed by the subtle hint of longing in Naveen's hazel-coloured eyes.

The butterflies returned. But Tiana didn't try to suppress them; she didn't want to. Because *this* flutter was filled with excitement and yearning and all those feelings she'd tried so hard to ignore this past year when it came to Naveen.

For one brief moment, Tiana allowed herself to just feel.

"Thank you," she finally answered, her voice once again catching in her throat.

"Anything for you," he said.

Before Tiana could respond, he grabbed his trumpet and climbed onto the stage.

"Good evening, good people," Naveen greeted the crowd. "I trust everyone is having a great time tonight? Have you tried that jambalaya?" He rubbed his belly and licked his lips. "Fantastic!"

Rousing applause and calls of "here, here" reverberated around the restaurant.

"Now, I bet you're wondering, 'What is this guy doing here,' eh? Where's Rudy Davis?" He hunched his shoulders. "Well, unfortunately, there was a bit of an incident with Mr Davis's band. They won't be able to make it."

Disturbed murmurs began to hum throughout the dining room.

"But never fear," Naveen continued. "You will get a great show tonight. That is a promise!"

He tipped his trumpet to the crowd, brought it to his lips, and opened with a rousing rendition of an old Fats Waller tune. Before Tiana knew it, she was swaying back and forth with the rest of the crowd, her distress from a minute ago a thing of the past. He really was charismatic.

She glanced towards the kitchen and caught sight of her mother and father dancing just outside the door, her heart nearly bursting at the sight.

"Naveen sure is good with that horn, isn't he?" Lottie asked.

"That he is," Tiana said, bringing her attention back to

the stage. "Thank goodness for that. He's saved me from what could have been a catastrophe."

"You know, Tia," Lottie said, her voice taking on a teasing tone, "Naveen really likes you. Now, don't tell him I told you that, because he's trying to take things slow. But y'all are moving *too* slow for me."

"There is no 'y'all' when it comes to me and Naveen," Tiana said.

"But there could be. What do you have against him?"

Tiana closed her eyes. "Lottie, please. You know I don't—"

"Don't have time for romance," Lottie singsonged. "Yeah, yeah, I know. I'm not saying you have to marry the man, Tia. You can spare an hour for coffee, can't you? I think it would do you some good."

Tiana watched as he belted out a slow ballad on the trumpet. What she wouldn't give to sit across a table from Naveen in a quaint café in the Quarter. Laughing. Joking. Just enjoying his company.

Was that too much to ask? Would that violate the terms of the bargain she'd made with Facilier? Did relinquishing her love for Naveen mean she couldn't have any dealings with him whatsoever?

What if it wasn't just her and Naveen on a date? What

if there were others around, and she and Naveen just so happened to meet up?

Her eyes still fixated on the stage, Tiana said, "The annual neighbourhood picnic crowning the King of Zulu is tomorrow in Congo Square. Me and Mama… and Daddy take part every year. We start early in the morning, and it lasts all day long." She glanced over at Lottie. "Why don't you join us?" She returned her eyes to the stage, hesitating only a moment before she added, "And bring Naveen with you."

21
TIANA

Congo Square, New Orleans
Saturday, February 1927
Three days before Mardi Gras

Tiana stood on the periphery of the crowd that had formed in the centre of Congo Square. She clapped along to the rhythmic beat of the drum, cheering on the brave folks who took their turn in the centre of the circle.

It was a long-standing tradition to honour the ancestors who had been brought here against their will and forced to work the land by commemorating their sacrifice through song and dance. The Mardi Gras Indians, just like those in the painting Ms Rose had given her, led the ceremonial celebration.

Their elaborate headdresses and colourful costumes

sparkled in the rays of sun. Remarkably, the thick fog that continued to plague the city had thinned into a gauzy haze, as if it knew how important today was to the people gathered here and didn't want to ruin it. The light mist that did remain cast an ethereal quality over everything, making it seem almost dreamlike.

"You wanna dance, baby girl?" Her daddy gestured to the circle.

Before she could talk herself out of it, Tiana nodded, grabbed him by the arm, and entered the fray.

She mimicked the steps of the other dancers, joining in the traditional African folk dance she'd been taught as a little girl. Her daddy danced alongside her, stomping his big feet and twisting his torso from left to right.

Tiana tilted her head back and held her arms to the sky, unable to restrain her smile. She felt a sense of weightlessness, as if she could take flight at any moment. It was a feeling she never wanted to let go of, a freeness she hadn't allowed herself to feel in far too long.

Once the dance ended, the crowd erupted in cheers.

Her daddy wrapped her up in a big bear hug and swung her around like he used to do when she was a little girl. Tiana clung to his big frame, soaking in the safety and security and love he embodied. Her throat tightened with emotions that threatened to overwhelm her.

"That felt like old times, baby girl."

"It felt like the *best* times," Tiana answered.

He set her back down and rubbed a hand over his stomach. "All that dancing has made me hungry. I think it's time for some of that fried chicken and corn bread."

Her daddy headed for the spot they'd commandeered on the left side of the square, where her mother was busy setting up the lunch.

Charlotte and Naveen both ran up to Tiana.

"That was fabulous!" Naveen said.

"Oh, it was, Tia! Just fabulous," Charlotte said. "Who knew Mr James could move like that?" She flapped her arms like a crazed flamingo in what Tiana could only guess was her attempt to mimic the folk dance. "I've never seen such dancing before."

"Really?" Tiana asked. She considered the fact that the celebration at Congo Square was a sacred ritual, but only to certain communities in New Orleans. Tiana had never thought to invite Charlotte to join them before. "No. No, I guess you haven't," Tiana said.

"Show me how you did that spin," Charlotte said. She twirled and fell flat on her backside.

"Ouch." Tiana grimaced.

"Well, that didn't go the way I thought it would." Charlotte held her arms out so that Tiana and Naveen could help her up. She took a step and yelped. "I think I broke my ankle!"

"But you didn't land on your ankle," Tiana said.

"Hmm… well, *some*thing's broken. Naveen, sugar," Charlotte called. "Why don't you help me over to where Ms Eudora is setting up the picnic. I think some peach cobbler will make me feel better."

Tiana shook her head but chuckled as Naveen looped Charlotte's arm around his neck. Together, they hobbled towards Tiana's parents.

"Hey, Tiana!"

She spotted Maddy jogging towards her.

"I'll meet y'all over there in just a minute," Tiana told Charlotte and Naveen, then waved over her friend. "Hey, Maddy," Tiana said as she approached. "How's it going?"

"I saw you dancing out there, girl! Good to know you can still kick up your heels and have a good time."

"Maybe you should tell Georgia that so she can get off my case about going out," Tiana answered with a smile.

"That's if I can find her. I haven't seen her or Eugene since leaving your supper club Thursday evening. I thought they would show up last night, because Georgia loves her some Rudy Davis, but I guess it's just as well they didn't." Maddy leant in close. "Although, I must say, that trumpet player from last night sure is something." She wiggled her eyebrows. "He's been looking at you the entire time we've been talking."

Tiana felt a telltale blush creeping up on her cheeks. "I need to go help Mama set up lunch," she told Maddy. "I'll talk to you later. And if I run into Georgia and Eugene, I'll let them know you've been looking for them."

Tiana continued to the lunch that her mother had spread out on the massive patchwork quilt she'd created from fabric scraps. The quilt made an appearance only once a year, for this very celebration. It was soft and colourful, and filled with memories that Tiana had learnt to cherish even more during those years when her daddy was gone.

She wouldn't think about those times. Their family was whole again. That was what mattered.

Tiana was grateful that talk of postponing the picnic until after the fog retreated had turned out to be nothing but talk. More and more people were looking towards the river as the culprit. Based on snippets of conversation she'd caught as she'd moved about the square, that green algae growing on the river had also become thicker overnight.

Whatever had caused this phenomenon, it was beginning to wreak havoc for too many people, especially for people who relied on the river for their livelihood, like the fishermen she did business with. Tiana didn't want to give any credence to what the Shadow Man had told her, but the thought continued to linger in the back of her mind.

Was this all her fault?

"Don't be ridiculous," she whispered to herself.

Refusing to allow thoughts about the Shadow Man to steal another minute of her day, she joined the others over on the picnic blanket and feasted on fried chicken, corn bread, devilled eggs, fruit salad and peach cobbler.

Full and satisfied, Tiana braced her hands on either side of her and stretched her face upwards towards the sky, basking in the warmth of the sun trying to peek through the haze.

"Uh, Tiana?" Naveen's voice came from somewhere just to the left of her.

She tilted her head to the side and opened one eye. "Yes?" She could see Charlotte a few feet away, holding her thumb up and smiling.

"I – I wondered if you would like to dance?" Naveen asked.

She wasn't sure if it was the raw hope she saw in his eyes, but something compelled her to say, "Okay."

Tiana almost laughed at Naveen's shocked expression. His mouth opened and closed several times before he spoke. "Really?" he asked.

This was her chance to backtrack, to tell him that she hadn't heard him correctly, or that she'd simply changed her mind.

But she didn't.

She no longer hoped for a day when there could be anything more between them; she knew it was impossible in order to keep him safe.

But she selfishly wanted this one dance. One little dance. That wasn't too much to ask, was it? And here at the picnic, they seemed so far from the Shadow Man and his tricks.

Tiana held out her hand.

Naveen helped her up from the quilt, beaming. Together, they joined the others who were dancing to the lively brass band that had started up a few minutes ago.

In that moment, at least, every single thing was right in her world.

22
NAVEEN

The energy pulsating throughout Congo Square captured everything that Naveen loved about New Orleans. The music, the people, the vibrancy of this place and all who lived here was like nothing he'd ever encountered. Could he honestly consider leaving now?

Maybe it was not the best time to entertain such a question, not when standing across from a carefree – dare he say silly? – Tiana as she tried to teach him the current dance moves. As much as he loved his home, it was no match for Tiana's radiance. If given the choice between being here with her or returning to his home in Maldonia, he would choose Tiana every single time.

"Are you paying attention?" she asked him.

"Hold on," Naveen said. "You are going too fast. Now, what am I supposed to do with my legs?"

"It goes like this," she said. She bent her knees and pivoted her toes in and out. Then she executed alternating kicks in time with the music, all while counting the steps and trying to direct him to follow along.

Naveen overexaggerated the move in hopes of eliciting a certain response from her. She rewarded him by throwing her head back and letting out a peal of that magical laugh of hers.

Yes, *that* was the response he was looking for. Goodness, but he loved her laugh.

"I'm not sure the Charleston is your thing," Tiana said, wiping tears of mirth from her eyes.

"No, no. I think I've got it," Naveen said.

This time, he actually *did* try to get it right, thinking he would impress her with how quickly he was able to catch on to the dance. But he tipped too far to the side with one of his kicks and nearly fell to the ground.

"Whoa," Tiana said as she reached for him.

"I am fine." Naveen raised his hands. "Just embarrassingly clumsy all of a sudden."

So much for impressing her.

But maybe this was better. Her lyrical mirth wrapped around him, cocooning him like a warm, comforting blanket.

"Oh, my," Tiana said, slapping a hand to her forehead. "I can't recall the last time I laughed so much."

"It is a beautiful sound."

"I… uh… thank you," she said.

Their eyes met, and his heart felt as if it would beat out of his chest.

Achidanza!

Naveen had a hard time breathing. The sight of Tiana's eyes staring at him with such feeling had stolen all the air from his lungs.

Suddenly, it felt as if no one else was in the park, as if this one moment in time was made for the two of them alone.

"Tiana, I…" Naveen began, but the words caught in his throat. He knew what he felt, but he couldn't figure out how to express it. Because he didn't understand it. He couldn't explain this pull he had towards her, as if they were destined for each other.

You can't talk that way. She will think you are loose in the head.

But that was the way she made him feel. He didn't recognise who he was when he was around her. Or maybe he did – a version of himself that felt both new and familiar somehow.

"Tiana, I was hoping—"

"What is that?" she said suddenly, her eyes going wide.

"Uh, I am trying to find the words—"

"No!" She pointed over his shoulder. "That!"

That was when Naveen heard it: a low hum reverberating in the air, a mixture of the murmurs from the picnic goers and something else. Something that sounded like... buzzing?

He turned to where Tiana pointed.

A dark cloud seemed to be shifting through the greenish fog, swaying like a pendulum through the air. The closer it got to them, the louder the hum became.

"What is that?" Naveen repeated her question.

The buzz grew even louder, along with yells and screams from the crowd on the far end of the square.

Something bit his neck. He slapped the spot. When he removed his hand, there was a black-and-red smear on his palm. "This looks like some kind of—"

"Mosquitoes!" someone shouted.

Chaos ensued as the thick black cloud descended on them. But it wasn't a cloud; it was a swarm of insects. Monstrous mosquitoes, at least ten times the normal size, twirled around like a twister, attacking the crowd with stinging bites.

"Run!" Naveen shouted. He provided cover for Tiana,

shielding her from the torrent of bugs and dodging the people who scattered around the square, seeking shelter from the invasion. Grown men fell to the ground as the enormous insects ambushed them, jabbing at them with their extra-long beaks.

He and Tiana raced over to where Mr James, Ms Eudora and Charlotte all huddled underneath the blanket where they'd just picnicked. Mr James lifted the edge, motioning for Tiana and Naveen to join.

Naveen remained huddled close to Tiana, doing all he could to protect her as the stinging insects attacked his back even through the fabric of his shirt. It felt as if someone were firing pellets into his skin, each bite a hot, searing assault upon his flesh.

Finally, he and Tiana crawled under the large blanket. The five of them all huddled together as screams from the crowd rent the air.

"Are you okay?" Tiana asked.

Naveen grimaced. "It is just… a few bites," he said through clenched teeth.

"I've never seen such big mosquitoes in all my life!" Charlotte said.

"Neither have I," Naveen said. He lifted his arm to reveal ghastly welts forming on his skin. "I did not think bugs were capable of this."

"Is this what you call a few bites?" Tiana cried. She reached for his arm, but he instinctively pulled away. Naveen immediately cursed himself. Tiana was offering to tend to his wounds; why not let her?

He held his forearm up to her and tried not to yelp as she inspected the carnage. She gently wiped away the blood with her thumb, showing no concern for her dress, which was now stained.

"Where did those mosquitoes come from?" Charlotte cried. "It's not even summertime!"

"You're right, Charlotte," Ms Eudora said. "These are early."

"Much too early," Tiana said. Naveen was not sure he'd ever seen such venom in her eyes.

"And I think I know what brought them here."

23
TIANA

They all went home following the harrowing mosquito attack in Congo Square, but despite her exhaustion, Tiana didn't take a moment to rest. She went straight to her room and dressed for war, pulling on a blue cotton top with long sleeves and the denim coveralls she reserved for when she really had to get her hands dirty. She tugged her hair back and tied it with a blue ribbon, then slipped on her leather boots.

She took a moment to mentally prepare, then stalked out of her bedroom.

When she entered the kitchen, her mother and father were both at the table, holding onto mugs.

"Where you going?" Eudora asked.

"I'm going to check on Naveen," Tiana lied. "I want to make sure he's okay."

She would eventually call on Naveen, but there was someone else she needed to see first.

"Can't you wait until tomorrow?" her father asked. "We've all been through quite an ordeal today, Tiana."

"Your father's right. You need to rest for a bit."

"I'm fine," Tiana reassured them. She appealed to her father's sense of duty, knowing that would do the trick. "Besides, after the way Naveen shielded me from that swarm, I owe him."

He nodded, and cautioned, "Be careful."

"I always am," Tiana replied.

She grabbed her bag from where it hung on a peg next to the front door and stepped outside. She was hit by the wall of thick, suffocating fog. It had returned with a vengeance.

It really was all the Shadow Man's doing – him making good on his threat. Now she had no doubt about it.

Tiana quickly made her way to his emporium in the French Quarter. If ever there had been an occasion to break her rule to only meet in public, this was it.

She stopped when she came upon his bright purple door, the same colour as the vest Facilier wore. There was a menacing skull and crossbones etched in the lintel above it.

Tiana clenched her fists at her sides, shoring up her nerve.

You can do this. You have to.

Facilier had warned her of what would happen if she didn't follow his commands, but she hadn't listened. He'd all but promised that his friends on the other side would begin to wreak havoc on the lives of those around her if she did not start adding that potion to all her dishes.

And because of her, people had suffered.

It was *her* fault for not taking his initial threats seriously. *Her* fault for trusting that he would stick to his word, for getting involved with him in the first place.

But despairing over what she should or shouldn't have done would do her no good now. It was time she ended this madness with the Shadow Man once and for all.

Tiana pounded on the door. "Open up, Shadow Man."

She jiggled the handle. It turned.

Unlocked?

Suspicion travelled down Tiana's spine like thick molasses. This had all the makings of a trap. Facilier wasn't the type to leave himself exposed.

But she'd come too far to back down now. She pushed the door open and took a step inside. Then another.

It was dark. Not a single window in the place, as far as she could tell. The only light in the room came from the door she still held open. Tiana pushed it open a bit more so that she could see her way inside.

As she came upon a table of some sort, she could make

out the silhouette of an oil lamp sitting on top of it. She felt around the base of the lamp, searching for the knob. Once she found it, she said a small prayer that the lamp had fuel and gave the knob a turn.

A small flame flickered to life, giving off just enough light to illuminate the area around her. She picked the lamp up by its wire handle and made her way around the room. A shelf held what must have been hundreds of bottles. Some short and squat, others tall and slim. Some filled with liquids, others with seeds and pebbles of various kinds.

"I knew you would come to your senses."

With a gasp, Tiana spun around. Her heart slammed against her chest at the sound of the familiar voice. Yet, despite the glow from the lamp, the room appeared as empty as it had been when she first arrived.

"Where… where are you?" she stammered.

Facilier's deep, awful laugh rumbled around the room. A moment later, he emerged from the darkness, striding towards her with that ever-present walking stick.

"Smart girl like you knows what's best," he drawled.

"I'm not here to make any deals," Tiana said. "I'm here to tell you that you'd better stop whatever it is you're doing."

"And what is it you think I'm doing, Tiana?"

"Don't play coy with me. You all but said you and your friends are behind this fog. I'm guessing you're also the reason Buford thinks that Duke's Cafe has been closed for a year, why Ms Margery doesn't remember making me a caramel cake for my birthday. And I'm pretty sure you set fire to Rudy Davis's band's instruments last night, and sent those mosquitoes to attack us this morning."

Facilier paused, holding his grin. "I told you things would start happening if you didn't do what I say," he said finally.

"We had a deal. I've been adding that potion to my gumbo ever since we opened the supper club."

He waved his hand. "This isn't about the potion. We can take care of that later. This is about your contract. It's time for you to sign the amendment."

"Amendment?" Tiana put her hands up. "I don't know what you're talking about. What I *do* know is that I have been fulfilling my end of our bargain. You have no right to demand I do anything more than what I agreed to."

"It seems you've forgotten part of the contract you signed."

"What are you talking about?" Tiana balked. "I didn't sign anything."

"Except that you *did*!"

He snatched the lamp from her hand and strode to a

rickety wooden desk on the other side of the room. He picked up a tattered scroll and stalked back to where she stood.

"The proof is right here." Facilier held out the rolled parchment.

Tiana took a step back. "What is this?"

"It's the deal you signed," he said.

She shook her head and started to back away. "I… I didn't sign anything," she said again.

"Yes. You. Did."

Facilier opened his hand and blew a cloud of iridescent purple dust into her face.

Tiana's head shot back as if sustaining a blow. She lifted off the ground, suspended in a slow yet dizzying twirl high above the floor of the cavernous room. She started to spin faster and faster, her head swimming.

With a thud, she landed on her hands and knees. The ground underneath her was cold, the dirt and crumbling stone pressing into the fleshy part of her palms. Tiana lifted her head and found herself surrounded by towering catacombs and rusted wrought-iron gates.

The cemetery.

Dread sluiced down her spine.

"Why am I here?" she whispered.

"That's why," came Facilier's low growl.

Tiana's head seemed to turn of its own accord, drawn to a scene playing out like the moving picture shows on the big screen at the Prytania Theatre.

It was her – wearing a sparkling white dress and glittery shoes.

Tiana suddenly realised what she was looking at. This was the previous year, when she'd made that deal with Facilier. She was unable to hear the words being spoken, but she remembered it all so clearly that she could almost recite them in her head.

She froze when Facilier pulled a scroll from his jacket and unfurled it.

But that part hadn't happened!

A scream collected in her throat as she watched herself sign the scroll, then shake Facilier's hand.

"No!" Tiana said aloud. "That's… that can't be right."

"But it is," Facilier said.

In a flash she was back in Facilier's dark emporium, her mind muddled by what she'd just witnessed. How could she not remember that?

"You signed this contract, Tiana." One corner of his mouth lifted in an ugly grin. "You just saw it with your own eyes."

Facilier set down the lamp and picked up a long wand made of smooth purple stone. Threads of gold twirled throughout it. Tiana looked on in dismay as he closed his eyes and spoke in a language she didn't understand.

The wand began to glow in his hand. As he glided it down the scroll, tiny writing appeared in gold lettering. He hovered the wand over the bottom portion of the document.

"Here," Facilier said. "This is the section you seem to have forgotten. It says that you must agree to an amendment every year, or this city and the people you love will suffer. We're coming up on the one-year mark, Tiana. If you don't sign again by sundown on Mardi Gras, hell will rain down on this city."

"No!" Tiana gasped, shaking her head. She put a hand to her mouth as her eyes read over the letters scrawled in glittery gold ink. "No, this can't be. I didn't sign any contract! I didn't agree to any amendment! I'm not doing any of this!"

Her head snapped back with another blast of the purple dust. She was instantly dropped into the middle of her parents' living room. Both her mother and father writhed on the floor, pain etched across their faces as they soundlessly screamed into the void.

Tiana tried to run to them, but her legs wouldn't move. It felt as if she were stuck in quicksand. She reached for them, but they were too far away.

Watching them suffer was so excruciating, Tiana's

knees gave out, sending her to the floor. She squirmed around like a bug stuck on its back.

When she opened her eyes, she was once again in Facilier's dreadful dungeon. He stood above her, his mouth screwed up in a twisted grimace.

"Is this what you want for Eudora and James?" Facilier asked.

"Where's Mama and Daddy?" she screamed.

"They're just fine. For now," Facilier added. "I wanted to show you what could happen if you don't sign this paper before Mardi Gras."

It was one of his mind tricks again. But that didn't mean it couldn't be reality one day.

Tiana scrambled up from the floor and snatched the scroll from his hands. She tried to rip it, but it was tough as leather and barely crinkled.

That deep laugh rumbled from Facilier's chest.

"It's binding," he said. "Sign it before Mardi Gras, or watch your mama and daddy suffer."

There had to be a way out. She hadn't agreed to this. She could not be indebted to the likes of the Shadow Man forever – under his thumb for the rest of her life.

"You won't get away with this," Tiana said.

"I already have." He snatched a quill from a pot of ink and shoved it at her.

"No!" Tiana started to turn, but he caught her by the back of her coveralls. Jerking out of his grasp, she ran out of the dark room, then raced out of the alley and back into the fog.

24
TIANA

Tiana ran like the wind. She ran until she was out of breath, until she was far away from the Shadow Man's dreadful French Quarter dungeon. She didn't stop running until she reached Canal Street. The wide boulevard teemed with people going about their day, as if nothing were amiss. As if they all weren't in danger because of *her* actions.

Tiana flattened her back against the rough brick of a nearby building. She shut her eyes tight, wishing for a moment that she could shut out the world.

What had she got herself into?

If she could travel back in time, she would have never made that deal with the Shadow Man. She would have smashed his talisman to the ground and let the chips fall where they might.

Now she was tied to Facilier for life. Stuck playing his games.

As much as she loved having her daddy back, Tiana knew he would never want this for her. If he knew what she'd done – the power she'd given the Shadow Man – he would be so disappointed.

As for Naveen…

Well, she would have figured out another way to save him. Anything was better than the bind she now found herself in.

"Tiana?"

Her eyes popped opened to see the flower vendor in front of her. "Oh, Ms Rose." Tiana held her palm against her chest. "You scared me." She took a moment to collect herself. "How… how are you doing?"

"It would seem I should ask you that question," the woman said. "You look troubled."

She blew out a sigh. "I've had a rough morning."

"Oh?" Ms Rose transferred the basket of irises she carried from one arm to the other. "How so?"

Tiana wasn't up for rehashing what had happened, but she couldn't bring herself to ignore Ms Rose.

"I'm not sure if you heard about the mosquito attack at Congo Square," Tiana started. When the woman shook her head, Tiana filled her in with a condensed version of the assault. "But that isn't the half of it. Something… strange is happening to people around me – my friends and associates. It's hard to explain."

"Hmm," Ms Rose murmured. She reached over and patted Tiana's hand. "Actually, it's quite simple. There's an old saying—"

"From your mother?"

"From my grandmother," she said. "She would say, *tanbou bat nan raje, men se lakay li vin danse.* The drum is beaten in the grass, but it is at home that it comes to dance."

Tiana was much too distressed from her confrontation with Facilier to decipher Ms Rose's idioms. "What does that mean?"

"It means that acts that are done outside the home can have repercussions for *all* those inside the home. Your actions affect more than just you, Tiana. It's something to remember." She patted her hand again. "You take care."

Tiana mulled over the woman's words as she watched her walk away. Her shoulders slumped as she experienced something she never allowed herself to feel: hopelessness.

Her head still reeling, Tiana started walking again, heading to the only place she could think of where she felt in control. Where she felt safe.

When she reached the supper club, she went directly

to the pantry and retrieved the ingredients for her beignet dough.

"Tia?"

She stiffened at the sound of Charlotte's voice coming from the dining room. Her friend entered the kitchen a moment later. "Hey, Tia, do you know if I left my shawl here or—?" Charlotte stopped mid-sentence. "Tiana, what's wrong? Is it the bugs from this morning? They were scary."

"N-no, but—" Before she could utter another word, Tiana burst into tears.

"Oh, my goodness, Tia! Is it Ms Eudora? Is she okay?"

"Mama's fine. It's nothing" – she hiccuped – "nothing like that. But, Lottie. Oh, Lottie, I've messed up something *awful*."

Charlotte rushed over and wrapped an arm around her shoulders. She guided her into the dining room and urged her to take a seat. Using a dish towel she'd grabbed from the kitchen, she wiped the sticky dough from Tiana's fingers.

"Now, now," Charlotte crooned. "It can't be worse than what we all just went through at Congo Square."

"But it is," Tiana lamented. She picked at a piece of fuzz on the tablecloth as she tried to come up with a way to describe the pickle she was in without betraying the terms of her and Facilier's deal. "Do you… do you know who the Shadow Man is?"

Charlotte's head jerked back. "You mean that man with the emporium in the Quarter? I've heard he's bad news, Tia."

"I know he is," she said. Oh, how she knew.

How could she explain the situation to Lottie without her friend thinking she'd gone off the deep end? She couldn't very well tell Lottie that Naveen had once been a frog and would have remained that way if not for Tiana's deal with Facilier. And her daddy? Could she honestly tell Lottie that her strong, vibrant daddy had passed away, but was now back because of the Shadow Man's friends on the other side?

She looked up from the table and into Charlotte's confused eyes.

"I can't go into any details, but I got involved with him. And now he's threatening to ruin my life."

"But, Tia… why?" Charlotte asked.

"I had no other choice," Tiana said. She fidgeted, scraping at bits of dough that remained on her fingers. "You wouldn't understand."

"I can try," her friend said. She pulled at one of Tiana's hands until Tiana looked at her. "Tell me."

Tiana chose her words carefully, knowing that one slip of the tongue could prove to be dangerous. She didn't want to involve Charlotte in this mess with Facilier in any way.

"I came into possession of something the Shadow Man

really wanted, and in exchange for it, he offered… well, something that I couldn't pass up. But then he changed the terms of our deal," Tiana continued. "And lately he's been hounding me to do more. He says that I have to keep doing whatever he asks or he'll hurt the people I love."

"Why, that… that's awful, Tia."

"I need a way out, Lottie. I can't allow him to have this kind of hold on me for the rest of my life. And I can't allow other people to be hurt because I was foolish enough to get involved with the likes of him."

"What are you going to do? There has to be something – some*one* that you can go to for help. Maybe I can ask Big Daddy…"

Someone she could go to…

That was it!

Tiana plopped her palm to her forehead. "Why didn't I think of this before?" she whispered.

Her heart pounded against her ribcage as the first bead of hope she'd felt all day began to blossom in her chest. "There *is* someone!"

"Who is it? I can have our driver bring us to him right now."

"It's not a him, it's a her," Tiana said. "And you can't get there by car. She lives on the bayou." Tiana stood and began to pace between the stage and the table. "I need to go to Mama Odie."

"Who's Mama Odie?" Lottie asked with a frown.

"You don't know her," Tiana said. "But she's the only person I know who can help me get out of this mess. I'll have to find a boat. Maybe I can rent one from one of the fishermen at the dock."

"A boat? The bayou? Tia, this doesn't sound safe." Charlotte moved closer. "Listen, Big Daddy knows lots of people—"

"No." Tiana clamped her hands over Charlotte's shoulders. "Trust me, Lottie. I know what I'm doing." She pressed a kiss to Lottie's cheek. "Thanks for lending an ear. I appreciate it."

"Of course, Tia. You know I'm always here for you… But I can't let you go traipsing off to this Mama Odie person, either."

"I'll be fine, Lottie," Tiana said as she moved to grab her bag. When she turned, Charlotte looked ready to put up another argument. "Don't," Tiana said. "Mama Odie is the only person who can help.

"The quicker I get to her, the better off we'll all be."

25
NAVEEN

Naveen stood in front of his desk, mumbling the words he'd practised over and over again. Too much hinged on this meeting with Mr LaBouff for him to screw it up. He absently rubbed at the welts on his arm, remnants of the mosquito attack earlier that day. Somehow it felt like a million years ago now.

He'd come to the mill after leaving Congo Square – assuring Tiana and Charlotte that he would clean his wounds as soon as he got there, since the mill was closer than home. And to his surprise, he'd found John Dugas waiting for him.

The man had countered with several uncustomary demands, stipulations that the mill's other customers would never dream of requesting. But Dugas Candy Company would not be an ordinary customer. It was Naveen's job to convince Mr LaBouff of that.

If he could not, he just might have to give more thought to that invitation from his parents.

Naveen glanced over at the missive on his desk. It taunted him, silently insisting that he pack up and return to the life of luxury he had once lived. Asserting that he was a fool to think he could handle anything on his own.

But he could do this. He would show Mr LaBouff that partnering with the candy company was in the sugar mill's best interest. And maybe even help Mr LaBouff notice the contributions of the guys on the floor like Randy, see that they had more to give.

Naveen resumed his pacing. He stuck out his hand and engaged in an imaginary handshake.

"Thank you for seeing me, Mr LaBouff. Have I got a proposal for you." Naveen shook his head. "No, no. That is all wrong. Not enough enthusiasm. Maybe if I—"

"Naveen! Naveen, sugar, where are you?"

Naveen ran out of his office at the sound of that very distinct voice calling his name. A moment later, he saw Charlotte climbing the stairs to the balcony.

Was she wearing… trousers?

Naveen was so shocked that he could have knocked himself over with a feather.

Wait. Was he supposed to knock *himself* with the feather? That didn't seem right. These American sayings still baffled him.

"There you are," Charlotte exclaimed as she made it to the landing.

"Charlotte, what are you wearing?" Naveen asked.

"Forget about my clothes," she said. "I need you to come with me. Now!"

"No. No. I can't," he said. "I have an important meeting with your father."

"There is nothing more important than this!" Charlotte said. "Then again, I don't know if I should even tell you. She told me not to tell anyone." She wrung her hands together, dismay evident in her worried eyes. "Oh, but I have to, because *some*body needs to talk some sense into that girl."

"To who? What girl?"

"It's Tiana," Charlotte said. "She's in trouble."

Panic instantly knotted in his chest. He thought about the picnic, about the look in her eyes when she'd spoken about the strangely aggressive insects. "Trouble? Where? What has happened?"

"That's just it. I'm not even sure. She gave me bits and pieces, but I've known her far too long not to understand when she's not giving me the full story."

She began to relay what Tiana had shared with her, but Naveen had a hard time following. Something about her getting involved with a man known for cheating folks around the French Quarter out of their money.

"Charlotte, are you sure about this?" Naveen asked with an incredulous frown. "Tiana doesn't seem like one who is so easily swindled."

"She told me with her own mouth. She made some kind of deal with the Shadow Man, and now she wants out of it. I offered Big Daddy's help, but she doesn't want me to tell him. She says the only person who can help is a lady who lives on the bayou."

"Mama Odie?" he asked automatically.

Charlotte's eyes widened. "You know her?"

Naveen frowned. "I… I am not sure."

"How did you know her name?"

How did *I know that name?* It had popped into his head the minute Charlotte said "the bayou".

"Maybe Tiana mentioned her before?" Naveen tried.

Charlotte started that thing with her hands again, nervously twisting them. "I just don't know what to do about any of this, Naveen. It's too dangerous. Tiana's talking about renting a boat and going out there on her own, but I can't let her do that. That's why I'm wearing these blasted pants."

"So you're going, too?"

"I have to," Charlotte said. "I can't very well let my best friend go sailing in the middle of nowhere by herself. But I would feel so much better if you joined us."

Naveen reared his head back. "Me and Tiana? On a boat?"

Together?

Why did that seem somehow *familiar*?

"Oh, please say you'll come with us," Charlotte said.

Naveen glanced at the letter from his parents again, then at Charlotte. He thought about Tiana in trouble and knew there was only one answer.

"Lead the way."

26
TIANA

"Eighty-five cents a day?" Tiana cried. "To rent this rickety boat? I'll be lucky if it doesn't sink the moment I take it out on the water."

She couldn't waste time haggling. She needed to leave as soon as possible if she wanted to reach Mama Odie's before sundown. Otherwise, she'd find herself trying to navigate those narrow bayou passageways at night.

But she was her daddy's daughter. She had to at least *try* to get the price down.

"I'll give you fifty cents, and not a penny more," Tiana said.

The grizzly fisherman moved his cigar from one side of his mouth to the other. "Sixty-five," he countered.

"Fine," she said. She looked at the washed-up pirogue, with its warped, weatherworn planks. The chances were pretty high that this thing really *would* end up at the bottom of the bayou, especially if the thick blanket of algae covering the river had made it out to the swamps. The insidious green scum had even started to grow along the sides of the posts holding up the pier.

"There she is!"

Tiana whipped around at the sound of Charlotte's voice. She caught sight of her friend traipsing around the thick fishing nets and ropes scattered along the busy pier. And she was wearing trousers! Though she still looked completely out of place in a pink silk top with an embroidered collar and T-strap heels.

Tiana peered at the figure coming up behind Charlotte and nearly tumbled off the pier. Goodness, Almighty! She'd brought Naveen with her!

"Charlotte LaBouff, what is going on?" Tiana hissed.

"I couldn't let you go out there all alone, Tia." Charlotte panted as if she'd run all the way there from the LaBouff mansion. "It's much too dangerous. Naveen and I are going with you."

"Hey! Hey, what y'all doing here?"

Tiana looked past Charlotte and Naveen to discover Louis heading towards them, carrying his ever-present trumpet.

Was everyone she knew at the docks?

"I thought that was y'all," Louis exclaimed in his boisterous voice. "What y'all doing here?"

"What are *you* doing here, my friend?" Naveen gestured to the trumpet in Louis's hand. "Entertaining the fishermen?"

"I come out here to play every now and again. I like being close to the water." He looked at Tiana. "Y'all going somewhere?"

"I am," Tiana said quickly.

"*We're* going to get help from a lady who lives in the swamp," Charlotte insisted.

"Y'all going to Mama Odie?" Louis asked excitedly.

"How does everyone know about this Mama Odie except me?" Charlotte asked.

"Can I come with y'all?" Louis asked. "I was telling Tiana just the other day that I haven't been home si—"

"Excuse us for just a moment," Tiana said, cutting Louis off before he revealed more than he should. She grabbed Charlotte by the arm and dragged her several feet away.

"Charlotte LaBouff, what in the world is going on?"

"I told you, Tia! It's too dangerous for you to go out there alone. There are gators and snakes and who knows what else lurking out there in the bayou. Besides, I told you I missed you. This may not be a Mardi Gras ball, but we'll be spending time together."

Tiana was baffled. "And just what do you plan to do if I get attacked by a snake? Beat it with that parasol?" she asked, pointing to the dainty satin-and-lace umbrella hanging from Charlotte's wrist. "And you brought *Naveen*!"

"I figured he could help protect us." Charlotte plopped a hand on her hip. "You may not think you need a strong man around, but you'll think differently if we get attacked by gators."

"Gators? What you say over there about gators?"

"Nothing, Louis," Tiana called over her shoulder. She turned back to Charlotte. "Look, I don't have enough room in the boat for all of you to come with me."

"Well, we'll just get a bigger boat," her friend said, as if her words were final. She looked at the little pirogue Tiana had just paid her hard-earned money to rent. "I'm not sure this would have gotten you very far anyway." Charlotte waved her hand in the air as if she were hailing a taxicab. "Oh, fisherman! Fisherman, we'll need to rent a bigger boat. Something with a cover, if you have it."

Tiana dropped her head back and looked up at the sky, but there were no answers raining down on her from above.

She followed Charlotte back to where a collection of boats for rent were lined up against the dock.

"None of these look very accommodating," Charlotte told the fisherman. "Don't you have anything bigger?"

"It's the bayou, Lottie. It's not as if you can take the Steamboat *Natchez* through those narrow canals or underneath those low-hanging branches."

Charlotte tipped her head to the side, an inquisitive dip to her brow. "Since when did you learn so much about the bayou? You hardly ever leave the city."

"I… I've… uh… heard things." Tiana stumbled over her words. She couldn't very well tell Lottie about her previous trip to Mama Odie's. "The fishermen are always talking about it when I come down to the pier to buy fish for the restaurant. Can we just pick a boat and get on with it?" Tiana asked, changing the subject. "We're losing daylight. I want to get where I'm going before nightfall."

"Where exactly on the bayou are we going?" Naveen asked.

Goose bumps popped up along Tiana's arms at the sound of his deep voice.

She closed her eyes for a brief moment in an effort to collect herself. A dance at a picnic was one thing. Being confined to a small boat with Naveen for hours? That was a decidedly *different* thing.

"It's kinda hard to explain," Tiana said before quickly moving away from him.

She walked over to where the fisherman and Charlotte were looking at a set of gleaming mahogany wood runabouts.

Tiana didn't want to even think about how much it would cost to rent one of those.

She spotted a boat a few feet down the pier. It looked a bit worse for the wear, but it was big enough for all of them and its flat bottom was just narrow enough not to give her pause at the thought of flowing through whatever shallow waters they might find.

"We'll take this one," Tiana told the fisherman.

"That one?" Charlotte screeched. "Tia, I don't—"

"You want to come along, you come in this boat," Tiana told her. She turned her attention back to the fisherman. "Can you have this ready to go in the next ten minutes?"

The man tipped his tattered cap to her. "That I can do."

Tiana replied with a firm nod. She hefted the linen sack she'd brought with her and realised that the few provisions she'd thrown in there during her quick trip back to the house wouldn't be nearly enough food for four.

She turned to her motley crew and pointed just past the dock to the French Market. "I'm going over to those stalls to get more supplies. Be ready to get going when I return."

As she made her way to the market, Tiana tried to come up with answers to the inevitable questions Charlotte and Naveen would have. How was she supposed to explain her relationship with a two-hundred-year-old Vodou woman living in a tree house in the bayou?

"You'll figure it out," she said underneath her breath.

At the market, she bought bananas, apples, pears and dried figs, along with several fresh loaves of French bread. She would find a way to make the canned sardines and beans she'd taken from home stretch between the four of them.

Tiana was scooping shelled pecans into a small sack when she noticed Ms Rose walking up to her.

"Hi, Tiana," Ms Rose greeted her.

"Hey there, Ms Rose." Tiana tied off the sack of pecans with twine and handed it to the vendor to weigh. "I would love to chat, but—"

"You're in a rush," the woman finished for her. "You're taking a boat ride."

Tiana's brows arched. "Yes," she said. "How did you know?"

Ms Rose jutted her chin towards the water. "I saw you on my daily walk along the dock."

Tiana wasn't sure why anyone would choose the pungent docks to take a stroll, but it wasn't her concern right now.

"Well, I better get going," she said, hefting the bag with her purchases higher on her shoulder.

"Where are you headed?" Ms Rose asked.

"Umm… to see a friend." It was what she'd told her

parents when she had gone back to the house to gather supplies. "She lives on the bayou."

"That's a long way to go to see a friend," Ms Rose said.

"She's, ah… special," Tiana said. "And I really need to see her as soon as possible."

Ms Rose nodded slowly. "Well, before you go, I have something for you." She reached into the bag she always carried with her. Then she took Tiana's hand and placed a pewter brooch shaped like a rose in its centre.

"Oh," Tiana said, unsure exactly why the woman was giving her such a lovely piece of jewellery, especially when she knew Tiana was on her way to the swamps. "This is quite beautiful," she said. "But maybe you should hold on to it until I get back from my trip?"

"No." Ms Rose closed Tiana's fingers over the brooch. "Take it with you. Maybe pin it to your shirt."

Tiana looked down at her coveralls. This brooch was as inappropriate as Lottie's dainty parasol and heels. But Tiana didn't have time to argue. "Thank you."

"Be careful," Ms Rose told her. She glanced up at the sky. "There's quite a storm coming." She brought her gaze back to Tiana's. "It's been brewing for a while."

Something in the woman's tone, in that piercing, intense look in her eyes, made the hair on the back of Tiana's neck stand on end.

Just then, a streak of lightning came from out of nowhere, striking close to the St Louis Cathedral and putting a finer point on her statement.

"*Malè je wè pa kite l' rive*, Tiana," Ms Rose said. "The eyes that see misfortune don't let it arrive. Keep your eyes open. Take heed of warnings. And be careful."

"I will," Tiana said, shivering despite the heat. She held up the brooch. "Thank you again."

She gave a shaky smile, then moved past Ms Rose, towards the dock. When she glanced back over her shoulder, the woman was still standing there, watching her.

Tiana quickened her steps and tried to shake off the strange feeling suddenly prickling her skin. She looked up at the sky and, even through the fog, could see the voluminous storm clouds building.

She needed to get to Mama Odie's…

Before the sky ripped opened on all of them.

27
TIANA

By the time Tiana returned to the dock, Louis and Charlotte had already climbed aboard the boat, but Naveen was nowhere to be found. Tiana briefly wondered if he'd decided against joining them, but a moment later he came running along the pier.

"Here we are," he said, holding three fat beeswax candles to his chest. "I've heard the bayou can get murky, even during daylight hours. Thankfully, there was someone selling these in the market."

Tiana was touched by his thoughtfulness, despite the impracticality of his suggestion. She reached into her bag and pulled out her kerosene lamp.

"I'm way ahead of you. Though we can use those as a backup if necessary."

"You think of everything, don't you?" he said.

Tiana couldn't tell if he was joking, so she just nodded. "Are we ready?"

"Ready!" Louis called. "Hey, Tiana, you need me to help guide you to Mama Odie's?"

Tiana hesitated. Louis was not the greatest at directions. Still, he'd grown up in these bayous, and she supposed having him here to help was better than relying on her memory alone.

"Start out that way," the fisherman chimed in, pointing east. "A few knots down, you'll see the entrance to the canal that'll take you to Bayou Bienvenue. That's the quickest route to Mercier, Maxent and all the others."

Tiana had no idea exactly on which bayou Mama Odie's house was located. She would have to rely on her recollection of landmarks, and on Louis.

And prayer. Lots and lots of prayer.

"Thank you," she told the fisherman as he untied the last of the rope from the stout, algae-covered pole and gave their boat a firm push with his booted foot. He tipped his hat to them again as they started to drift out on the scummy water.

Tiana grabbed hold of the long handle that stuck out from the motor, holding it steady as they travelled along the busy river. She kept the boat close to the bank to avoid the wake from any of the larger vessels. The waves they created made the grassy film covering the water resemble short, rolling hills.

After about ten minutes, she spotted the turn the fisherman had told them about. The fog, which was thicker on the water, made it difficult to see. Fortunately, as they travelled further away from the city, it began to let up, and she could see more than two feet ahead of the boat.

Tiana could sense they were getting closer by the odours lingering in the air – the briny aroma of the river mixed with the dank, vegetative smell of the murky bayou. It instantly brought back memories of the last time she had been there.

She firmly shut those thoughts out of her head. It was bad enough that she had to share this tiny boat with Naveen. She would not torture herself by reminiscing about the time they'd spent together, falling for each other.

"Aww, this takes me back to when I was little," Louis said.

"Really? I didn't know there were bayous in Shreveport," Charlotte said.

Tiana cut a glance at Louis and shook her head. "Uh, Louis's family is originally from the bayous west of here," she said to Lottie.

"Yeah, I grew up in parts like this," Louis added. "Once you live here, it never leaves your blood."

"What made you come to N'awlins?" Charlotte asked.

Tiana looked back at Louis. When she'd made the deal

with the Shadow Man to allow Louis to become human, the two of them had sketched out a story about how Louis had moved from North Louisiana in search of fun and excitement in the big city. It wasn't far off from the truth. She just hoped Louis didn't say anything that would rouse suspicion.

Louis gave Lottie a line about wanting to play jazz in the spot where the musical style was born, which seemed to satisfy her. Tiana breathed a sigh of relief and prayed that the subject wouldn't come up again. She would have a hard enough time explaining Mama Odie once they arrived at her boat house; she didn't have the energy to come up with another story about Louis's dubious origins.

The body of water they were in tapered into a much narrower canal. Large spindly tree branches hung overhead, with gossamer-thin moss draping from them like a lady's fine hair.

Tiana looked upwards, squinting to see through the hovering fog. She couldn't be sure, but she thought this might be the place where she and Naveen had first fallen out of the sky on that fated balloon ride they'd taken a year before. She looked from side to side, keeping an eye out for the hollowed tree stump where they'd hidden away from that pack of gators.

A small smile tipped up one corner of her mouth as she

remembered that first night, and how ridiculously out of his element Naveen had been. She glanced over at him now, taking in his strong and handsome profile. He'd changed so much in the year since she'd first met him. He was no longer the spoilt little rich boy who thought he could get by on his looks and charm.

Though he'd surely won *her* over with that charm in the end.

"Do you want to share what you find so amusing, Ms Tiana?"

Tiana startled. "Huh?"

"You were smiling," Naveen said.

He lounged against the wooden bench as if it were a velvet-covered chair in a palace somewhere. Even in the middle of a humid bayou, he still had that regal way about him. Tiana figured it was ingrained in him. It was yet another example of how so very different they were.

She wondered – even if she hadn't made that deal with Facilier, were there too many things about his world that made it so that she would never fit in it?

"It's nothing," she finally answered him. "Just thinking back on happier times."

"Would those happier times include this morning? Before the insects, of course." He scooted a few inches closer to her and shimmied his shoulders. "Did I impress you with my smooth dancing moves?"

"Smooth?" Her brow arched.

"Was I not?"

Tiana bit her lip to suppress her grin. "You were… interesting."

"Hmm." He rubbed his chin. "I'm not sure how I feel about that. I've seen some pretty interesting things that were not very impressive. Quite the opposite, in fact."

She couldn't hold back her laugh any longer. "Entertaining? Is that better?"

"Eh." He wiggled his hand. "Not really, but I'll take it."

"If it makes you feel any better, I think with a little practice, you will be dancing the Charleston better than anyone else in N'awlins."

He peered over at her, a faint light twinkling in the depths of his hazel eyes. "Are you offering to be my teacher?"

The rich cadence of his voice sent Tiana's heart thumping triple time. She rebuffed his suggestion with a shaky laugh. "Now, Naveen, you should know better than to ask that. I hardly have time to think these days with us as busy as we are down at the supper club."

"Hmm," he murmured again. "You know, I am pretty new to this having-a-job thing, but from what I have seen, most people will take a day off every now and then just for fun. Now, *that* is interesting, yes?"

"Prince Naveen, is that your way of chastising me for working too hard?"

"Yes," he said. "Is it working?"

"No."

"Ah, Tiana." He pitched his head back and sighed up at the sky. With a hunch of his shoulder, he said, "I tried."

"I know lately I've been working longer hours than some deem healthy – especially my parents – but it's an important time. And I have to work hard if I want my restaurant to be a success."

"I understand," he murmured, leaning forward. "Actually, I admire that about you. Maybe you can teach me what it takes to be a success, eh?" He winked. "Along with how to dance the Charleston, of course."

Tiana swallowed.

Oh, yes, his charm was as strong as ever.

This trip was going to be even more challenging than she'd thought.

28
FACILIER

Facilier hustled through the crowd of dingy factory workers heading back to their humdrum jobs, their faces filthy with soot and grime. He hated that they worked so close to where he lived. He remembered a time when people such as these weren't allowed anywhere near the Quarter. Prior to when the railroad was built, when the wealthiest of the city lived here before migrating to those big mansions uptown.

Oh, to have those days back.

But it looked as if the riffraff was here to stay. The dreadful factories that had taken over the Quarter made it so.

Facilier arrived at his residence in Pirate's Alley. He hung his top hat on the hat rack as he stepped inside, his mind filled with the myriad quandaries before him. His pursuit of Eli LaBouff's fortune had dominated his existence for years, but that was no longer his top priority. He now had a more pertinent goal: saving his own soul.

And in order to do that, he had to get Tiana's signature on that contract.

He regarded his bandaged hand with a scowl. He'd tried signing Tiana's name to the document himself, but a bolt of lightning had struck the contract, burning off a bit of his skin with it. He should have known his friends on the other side would have a provision in place to impede something like that.

Well, he was done playing games. He *would* get Tiana's signature on that contract, and he knew exactly how he would do it.

It was time for him to turn up the heat on Naveen.

Tiana was more than just smitten with the prince. He'd seen them out in Congo Square that morning, giggling like a couple of besotted lovebirds while they danced as if they didn't have a care in the world. He gathered Tiana would do just about anything for her little prince.

After all, it was the threat of Naveen remaining a frog forever that had finally propelled her to accept his deal a year before.

What should it be? Should he snatch him off the street and store him in that room with the others?

No. It wasn't enough for Naveen to go missing. Tiana needed to *see* his pain.

An unfortunate accident at LaBouff's sugar mill? A broken leg, maybe? Or how about a nasty burn from those big kettles filled with piping hot liquid sugar? Wouldn't it be a shame if that pretty face of his was scorched, leaving him scarred for life.

Facilier mulled over his options. He should have gone after her prince from the very beginning, but it was too late for recriminations. The only thing that mattered was getting her to comply before his friends on the other side came to collect.

As if he'd conjured them just by thinking about them, the floor underneath his feet started to shake, and the temperature around him grew cold as ice. Facilier braced himself as shadows slithered along the floor and walls.

"Well… hello," he said, injecting false cheer into his voice.

They spoke in their typical moans and groans.

If he closed his eyes Facilier could still see that dirty, dishevelled little boy, curled up on the filthy floor of an abandoned building. Nowhere to go, no mother to take care of him.

The Shadows had sought him out. They'd preyed on

him, knowing that he had no other option but to become their minion.

Well, he was done being under their thumb.

"Yes, yes. I know," Facilier answered. "I know I have just a few more days before the payment is due." He held up a hand. "However, I have a proposition for you fine gentlemen. I recognise that Tiana's soul was part of our deal, but what if I get you a different soul? I have a few options—"

A stiff wind blew, strong enough to knock him to the ground. He steadied himself on his hands and knees, bracing against the fierce gust of air.

"Okay." Facilier held his hand up to his face. "I… I… I understand. I will get you hers. When have I ever let you all down?"

Another blast of wind. It sent him crashing into the wall. Jars and bottles toppled from the shelves above him, shattering into thousands of pieces as they landed on the hard floor.

And as quickly as his friends from the other side had appeared, they were gone.

Everything was silent. The temperature in the room returned to the normal chilliness of late February. Facilier remained on the floor, his chest heaving with each breath he took.

They were becoming more impatient, more violent. Their insatiable appetite for mayhem grew stronger with each passing day.

He pushed himself up from the floor and searched through the documents that had scattered around the room, seeking the contract he'd *thought* he was signing on Tiana's behalf last year. Once he found it, he tucked it underneath his arm, grabbed his cane and top hat, and stormed out of his emporium.

He considered going straight to LaBouff's sugar mill and snatching that stupid prince by his perfect hair. He could drag Naveen to Tiana's restaurant so that he could torture him in front of her. But those goons working in LaBouff's mill would likely try to stop him.

Instead, he took off for Tremé. He'd used his illusions on Tiana successfully before; he could use them again.

Facilier spent the entire walk devising a creditable lie about Naveen's whereabouts, but when he arrived at the restaurant, the waitress informed him that Tiana wasn't there.

Facilier could barely control his rage.

"Where is she?" he growled.

The waitress looked him up and down as if he were a foul bug she wanted to squash with her shoe. How dare this little peon treat him this way!

He stepped closer to her. *"Where is she?"* he repeated slowly.

"Is there a problem here?"

Facilier stepped back as James walked through the swinging door. A red-and-white chequered towel was thrown across one burly shoulder. He was strong and healthy, and had no idea just how much he owed Facilier for being here.

"Can I help you?" the man asked. By the tone of his voice, Facilier could tell that he had an opinion of him. One that was not good.

"I was looking for the owner of this restaurant," Facilier answered.

"Well, I'm one of the owners."

Thanks to me.

He should tell him that right now. What would his reaction be? What would James say if he learnt that an artillery shell meant for his heart had, instead, embedded itself in a tree in Belgrade? All because Facilier had petitioned for it to happen that way on his behalf. Had paid for it, possibly with his own soul.

"It's a young woman who introduced herself to me as the owner," Facilier said. "She wanted to talk to me about possibly being an entertainer for the guests." He pulled out a deck of cards and did quick work, flipping them and fanning them out.

"Tiana never mentioned that…" James pulled the towel from his shoulder and wiped his hands with it. "She had some business to tend to – a friend called on her for help. She'll be gone overnight, but should be back some time tomorrow. I'll tell her you stopped in."

"Great," Facilier said. He tipped his hat to the man and gave the waitress, who still stared at him suspiciously, a stern look. "You can count on my return."

As he walked away from the restaurant, Facilier clutched the handle of his cane so hard he nearly broke it. He couldn't sit around waiting for Tiana to show up. Time was running out.

Where could she have gone?

Facilier retreated to the French Quarter. He prowled around the market, searching stalls where he'd noticed her shopping in the past. Maybe she'd stopped to make a few purchases before travelling to this supposed friend in need.

When he didn't see her anywhere, he took off for the pier, hoping to find her looking at all the freshly caught seafood being sold along the banks of the Mississippi. He slipped several times on the slimy green algae clawing its way up the dock.

There was something pernicious happening here – the never-ending fog, the peculiar algae growing on the water. He'd asked around about the bugs Tiana had accused him of summoning and discovered that a swarm of giant mosquitoes had attacked those at Congo Square after he'd left that morning.

He didn't know what had caused any of it, but he knew it was supernatural, and malevolent at that.

And he wasn't the one behind it.

"Can I help you, fella?" a fisherman asked.

Facilier turned his nose up at his foul stench, but the man didn't seem to notice.

"Yes," he said. "I'm looking for a Black girl, not too long out of high school. A little bit skinny."

"Oh, you talking 'bout the one with that restaurant over in Tremé? She comes by to get fish every so often."

"That's her," Facilier said. "Have you seen her around today?"

"Sure did. She came by looking to rent a boat, but I sent her over to old Pete, because none of my boats are good for trawling around the bayou."

"The bayou?" Facilier asked, his mouth going dry.

"That's what she said," the man replied. "I thought maybe she's gonna try her hand at frogging. Fry up some frog legs to serve in that restaurant of hers."

Facilier rubbed his jaw. "Maybe you're right," he said.

But the old fisherman had it all wrong.

There was only one reason Tiana would take off for a last-minute trip on the bayou. Only one person she could be on her way to see.

Things had just become infinitely worse for him.

29
NAVEEN

The boat made a low puttering sound as it sloughed through the swamp waters. Louis relaxed against the starboard side and twirled his trumpet on his finger. Charlotte had declared that the rocking was making her both seasick and sleepy. She was currently curled up towards the front on the boat's knobby bench, with one of Tiana's bags of provisions serving as her pillow.

Naveen returned his attention to Tiana. She was focused, her eyes constantly roaming from left to right. She had refused his offer to take over driving duties, proudly declaring that she could steer the boat just fine on her own. All he wanted was to give her a little time to rest.

As he stared at her profile, Naveen wondered what had spawned her need to constantly be in pursuit of something.

As if taking a moment to just relax was some kind of invisible mark against her.

"Are you sure you do not want me to take over?" he tried again. "Just for a little while, so that you can stretch your neck."

Is that the right phrase? Stretch your neck?

"I've got it," she answered. "The canals are getting narrower the deeper we get into the bayou. I've gotta take care to stay in the centre of the waterway. Last thing we need is to have the propeller get caught up in a bunch of weeds."

After a few minutes, their tranquil surroundings were polluted with a loud snore. Naveen looked over his shoulder and chuckled at the sight of Louis and Charlotte now sharing the same bag as a pillow.

"So much for help from those two, eh?" he said.

Tiana glanced over her shoulder and smiled. "It's probably for the best. Easier to concentrate on where we're going."

Naveen thought it best as well. He liked the idea of not having to share Tiana's attention with their other boatmates.

Although it was not as if she was paying all that much attention to him. After her earlier teasing about his interesting dance moves, she had gone back to manning the boat and had not spoken much.

"Do you find it odd that the heavy fog is no longer with us?" Naveen asked, deciding the weather was a safe subject to start with. "I would have thought it would be worse here in this soupy swamp, no?"

"I don't know what to make of that fog," she said, but then she sat up straighter. "Actually, I just had a thought! Maybe it's because we're no longer in N'awlins, and it's the city that's—" She stopped. Her mouth pulled into a frown. "I'm not sure," she said. "I just hope it lets up soon back home."

A bug whizzed past Tiana's head and she flapped her hand around, waving it away. "Ugh! I don't particularly like these stowaways. Especially after Congo Square." She shifted towards the side of the boat, then ran her fingers through the water.

Naveen's breath quickened as he was struck with a strange sense of familiarity. It was as if he had already seen her do that very thing.

"Have I… have we been here before?" he asked.

Tiana looked at him, her big brown eyes narrowed with suspicion. "What do you mean? In this boat?"

"Yes." He nodded. "I remember you talking about your dislike of bugs. You did not want to eat one."

Her eyes widened with dismay.

"What am I talking about?" Naveen nervously laughed. "That was a ridiculous thing to say. Why would there be talk about you eating a bug?" Although he was certain there had been. Well, almost certain. He shook his head. Maybe the heat was getting to him. "And, of course, we have not been here before. *We* have not been anywhere before." He huffed out a regretful sigh. "You practically run whenever I am near you."

The moment he said the words, Naveen wished he could take them back. They revealed too much. He was afraid if Tiana knew just how much she captivated him, she would pull away even more.

"It's not you," she said.

His eyes shot to hers. "It's not?"

"Forget I said that," she said quickly.

"No. No, please." He leant towards her. "What did you mean?"

"Really, it's nothing." She hesitated for a moment before continuing. "It's like I said before: I'm very busy with my restaurant." She glanced away from the water just long enough to grace him with a subtle grin. "But I guess it wouldn't hurt to occasionally sit and talk with you and Lottie when y'all are at the supper club."

"I would like that very much," Naveen said.

He would like it even more if it were just the two of them, without Charlotte, but that would come eventually. He would take baby steps with Tiana.

They returned to that companionable silence again, but Naveen no longer felt the impulse to fill it with chatter. He had achieved what he had set out to accomplish: he had managed to get Tiana to smile at him. Talk to him. She had even agreed not to scurry away when he approached her.

"Naveen?"

Tiana's soft voice pierced his musings.

"Yes?"

"I actually am getting a little tired. Would you mind taking over for a minute?"

"Of course not." He stood so quickly that he caused the boat to wobble just a bit.

Charlotte woke up with a start. "What's going on?"

"It's nothing, Lottie," Tiana said. "Naveen is going to drive the boat for a while. Go back to sleep."

"Oh. Okay," Charlotte said, then put her head down again.

"Sorry about that," Naveen replied. He moved closer to the motor and grabbed hold of the wooden handle used to steer it. As Tiana released her hold on the handle, her hand brushed against his.

It felt as if a bolt of electricity flashed through him. The air around them was heavy with something Naveen could not describe as they stared at each other for several moments, neither moving their hands.

"I… I'm going to get a pear," Tiana said. "Do you want anything?"

"Not a pear," Naveen said without thinking. He mentally scolded himself over his forwardness.

But Tiana did not chastise him. Instead, a blush formed on her delicate cheeks.

Achidanza! She was so lovely; she took his breath away.

She finally slipped her hand away from his and moved to the front end of the boat. Naveen could hear her shushing Charlotte in a soothing voice. A few minutes later she returned, claiming the spot where he had sat for much of their journey.

"So, Tiana, where exactly are we headed again?"

She took a bite of her pear and chewed excruciatingly slowly, so slow that Naveen was sure she had done so on purpose. After a moment, she said, "There's a lady who lives down on the bayou. She's special. She has… umm… special powers." She chuckled. "I know this may sound crazy to you, but—"

"No," he said, cutting her off. "If you need to see a bayou lady with special powers, who am I to judge?"

He almost asked if she had ever mentioned Mama Odie to him before, but after his statement about the bug, he thought it best to not say anything.

She smiled that smile at him again. The one that made

Naveen think that maybe he really *was* starting to make some progress.

"I was a bit surprised that you wanted to drive the boat at all," Tiana said. "You're not one for manual labour. At least you didn't use to be. You've changed."

"How do *you* know that I have changed?"

"Umm… because… well, you made quite the splash when you first came to N'awlins. Your reputation for being a laissez-faire playboy was well known throughout the city."

"Yeah, well, that was last year."

"It doesn't seem all that long ago," she remarked in a wistful voice.

"No," Naveen said. "No, it does not." He tipped his head to the side. "Yet, in many ways, it feels like a lifetime."

"Really? How so?"

He shrugged. "I just feel like a different person. I cannot explain it." Naveen chuckled. "I often think about what my parents would say if they saw their… what was that phrase you just used?"

"Laissez-faire? It means carefree," she said around another bite of her pear.

"Yes, yes! Their laissez-faire son. My father would probably say, 'Why did it take you coming to America to learn the value of a hard day's work?'" He mimicked his father's voice.

Although he was not so sure about that any more. Based on that letter he had received from his parents, they no longer cared about his lack of a work ethic.

But *he* cared.

He did not want to be seen as that lazy, carefree playboy any more, especially by Tiana.

"How do you know so much about my reputation?" Naveen peered at her from his side of the boat. "It sounds as if you were paying more attention to me than you like to let on, Ms Tiana."

She pulled her bottom lip between her teeth, a demure smile playing at her lips. "Don't flatter yourself," she said, but the words didn't hold much censure.

It was almost as if she was… *teasing* him.

Was she teasing him? It would be a very good thing if that was the case. Teasing was one step closer to… to…well, to not running away from him.

Tiana reached over and pulled a leaf from a low-hanging branch. She twirled it between her fingers.

"Can I ask you something?" she asked.

"Anything," Naveen quickly answered.

"Do you ever think about going back home to… where is it you're from again?"

He sent her a sly smile. "Come now, Tiana. Would you have me to believe that you don't know where I am from?"

"Fine." She rolled her beautiful brown eyes. "Maldonia. Do you ever think of going back home to Maldonia, Mr Prince?"

Naveen decided to be honest.

"Sometimes," he answered. "But I'm not sure I would go back to stay. I miss my parents and the rest of my family, but I want to show them all that I can move about the world without our family's money. That I can make it on my own. And, well, maybe I want to show myself that, too."

"Do they know you're working in a sugar mill?"

"What's wrong with working in a sugar mill?"

"Nothing," she said. "You just don't see that many princes doing it."

"Well, it is nice to be the first at something in my family," he said with a grin.

They relaxed again into one of those comfortable silences. This time, Naveen did not interrupt it. He welcomed the sound of the birds chirping and the toads croaking. There was something peaceful about the unseen inhabitants of the swamp going about their day. He glanced over at Tiana and caught her yawning. It was the prettiest yawn he had ever seen.

"You can go to sleep if you would like," he told her. "You can trust me to man the boat."

"I don't think so," she said with a laugh. She yawned again.

This one was, by far, the prettiest yawn he had ever seen.

"I'll stay up and keep you company," she said. "Just keep us steady. Don't veer off course for a second."

"You have a lot of demands, you know that?"

"So I've been told," she said.

He peered out over the water again. "I don't know why, but I cannot shake the feeling that I've been here before," Naveen remarked. "There is something about this swamp that seems very familiar to me. The smell, I think. I cannot explain it."

"Well…" Tiana started, then stopped.

"Well, what?" Naveen inquired.

"Well, maybe some of the men who work at the sugar mill are from around here. You've probably smelt it on their clothes. It's not easy to get rid of this scent once it's in your skin."

"So are you telling me I will smell like this stinky swamp forever?"

She laughed. "It'll wear off eventually."

"You have a lovely laugh," Naveen said. "So beautiful, so rare."

"I laugh all the time," she countered.

"You should laugh more often when you are around *me*. I would like very much to make you laugh, Tiana."

Naveen could not be sure, but he thought he saw a faint spark of interest in her gaze before she broke eye contact. She fiddled with the kerosene lamp she'd brought.

"Should I light this?" she asked.

He sighed. Just when he thought they were bonding, she pulled away.

"I can see just fine right now," Naveen answered. "Why don't you save it in case it gets murkier?"

"Okay," she said. Then she yawned again, with her whole body this time, stretching her balled fist in the air.

"Actually, I think I will take that nap. You'll wake me if you need me?" she asked.

There was much he would still have liked to say, but Naveen feared they would go right back to the way things had been, when she had seemed put off by his very presence. So instead, he said, "I have it from here, Tiana.

"Get some rest."

30
TIANA

As the boat bobbed along the bayou, Tiana tried her best to get some sleep. It should have been easy enough after her eventful morning, but her mind was too keyed up to allow her body to get the rest she needed.

Facilier's threat consumed her.

What if he made good on his promise to harm her family? Was he sending those shadowy figures to hurt her daddy right now? Was her mother safe? Would he do something to the restaurant, like set it on fire, the way he'd most likely done to Rudy Davis's band's instruments?

And what about Mr Salvaggio? He still hadn't turned up, and Tiana couldn't help wondering if Facilier was behind the disappearance.

The unknown was as frightening as the little she *did* know when it came to what that awful con man could do.

Who knew what else he had up his sleeve, or how long he planned to torment her with his requests? He could very well demand she be at his beck and call for the rest of her life.

She said a fervent prayer that Mama Odie would help her find a solution to this mess she'd got herself into.

Tiana gave up on the idea of getting any sleep, but kept her eyes closed. It was safer to make Naveen think she was resting so he wouldn't turn that charismatic charm on her again.

She had been through this before with him, nestled in the cosiness of this very same bayou. She remembered all too well what it was like to listen to his soothing voice as he talked about anything and everything.

It was where she'd fallen in love with him.

Talking with him earlier had brought back such fond memories – memories she was afraid for a moment that he'd also remembered. But it had also called to mind what she'd been forced to give up when she agreed to the conditions of Facilier's deal last year.

For just a moment, Tiana allowed her mind to wander to that ideal fantasy world. A world where she had her restaurant, her daddy *and* Naveen. Where she didn't have to worry about any harm coming to her family. Where she could live out her days cooking scrumptious meals for the people of New Orleans and dancing to sweet jazz music in Naveen's arms.

The world she currently lived in was far from that ideal fantasy she so often conjured up in her dreams. In *this* world, everything came at a cost.

Despite the troubling thoughts that continued to invade her mind, Tiana managed to drift into a fitful slumber. She couldn't have been sleeping for more than a half hour when a disquieting sensation rushed through her.

She woke up with a start and found Louis manning the boat.

Oh, no!

"Louis." Tiana spoke through clenched teeth. "What are you doing driving?" She looked around. "And where are we? This doesn't look familiar to me at all."

"He said he knew a shortcut," Naveen said from the starboard side of the boat.

"A shortcut?" Tiana asked.

Why, why, *why* had she let them talk her into allowing them to come along? She should have stuck with her original plan and taken this boat out by herself. She had certain milestones she'd remembered that would have guided her directly to Mama Odie's. She had no idea where they were now. They could be heading back towards New Orleans for all she could tell.

"Louis, tell me you know what you're doing," Tiana pleaded.

"I do," he replied. "I know this bayou like the back of my hand." He gave her a toothy grin. "Just trust me."

Her brow pinched as she cast a quick glance over their surroundings. Something wasn't right about this. Whatever canal Louis had guided them into was much too narrow for their boat. She could practically reach out and touch the banks of the bayou.

"Louis, I'm not sure about this," Tiana warned. "It's too narrow." She looked over the side of the boat. "And this water is too shallow."

"Oh, it's not that bad," Louis said. "I promise, I know what I'm—"

The sound of the boat suddenly crashing against an embankment rang out loudly in the quiet stillness of the bayou.

31
TIANA

"Louis! Ahhhh!" Tiana pitched forwards in the boat, nearly tumbling over the side. Lottie rolled off the bench where she'd been sleeping.

"What happened!" Charlotte screamed. "Why aren't we moving? And why is it so dark here? Goodness, Tia, why did I let you talk me into this?"

Tiana whirled around. "Me? *You're* the one who decided to tag along, Lottie. I would have been just fine by myself."

"Really? Does this look fine to you!"

"Let us all calm down," Naveen said, "and see what kind of damage has been done. It may not be so bad, eh."

They all climbed out of the boat. As Charlotte took Naveen's hand, she slipped and fell into a putrid patch of slimy mud.

"I'm never doing this again," Charlotte said, looking down at her trousers, which were now streaked with sludge.

"Let's hope we never have to," Tiana said. She looked over at Lottie. "Sorry I snapped at you."

"Don't worry about it, sugar. Stress brings out the worst in me, too. You hear that, swamp creatures?" Charlotte called out as she gingerly navigated the soupy shoreline. "Don't test me! You stay away from me and I'll do the same!"

Tiana rounded the side of the boat to stand with Naveen and Louis, who were both studying the bow. She had no idea how Louis had managed to wedge the vessel inside the cluster of gnarled branches and prickly brambles. Some of the vines had thick thorns that were at least two inches long.

Naveen scratched the back of his head. "This looks… uh… pretty sticky."

Tiana took a step closer, grateful she'd worn boots but regretting that they were her good leather ones and not the plastic rain boots. They squished as her feet sank into the mud. She just knew they would be completely ruined before all was said and done.

She braced her hands against the hull and tried to give it a push. The boat didn't move a single inch.

"We tried that," Naveen said.

"Well, I'm sure you did," she returned. "I just wanted to see how stuck we were."

"We are pretty stuck," he said.

She peered at the thicket from several angles. "If we can find a few branches that are thin enough to manoeuvre through these vines, but sturdy enough to give a little leverage, I believe we can pry the boat out. Let me see what I can find."

She backed away from the boat. She started to flail in the mud, but before she could tumble backwards, a set of strong arms braced around her.

"I have you," Naveen said. He was so close she could feel his warm breath against her ear. Tiana did her best to ignore the goose bumps pebbling up and down her skin, but she would have had a better chance of ignoring a fireworks display taking place on her front porch.

"Thank you," she said. She disengaged herself from his hold and moved several feet away. It still didn't feel far enough. She could have moved clear to the other side of this bayou and it still wouldn't have left enough room between them.

She dusted her hands off on her coveralls. "I'm going to search for something to dislodge the boat."

"I think me and Louis can do that," Naveen said.

"We'll all do our part," Tiana replied. "I'm not just going to stand here twiddling my thumbs while the big strong men go in search of something to get us out of this mess."

Tiana took a gander at Charlotte, who was brooding as she sat on a downed cypress tree. She walked over and pulled her friend up by her arm, then pointed to the left side of the bayou's shoreline.

"You and Louis can go that way, and Lottie and I will search this way," Tiana said, pointing in the opposite direction.

"We will?" Charlotte asked with a horrified shriek.

"Yep, we sure will," Tiana said. She plopped a hand on her hip. "Let's see who can find the best branch."

"Ah, it is a competition, then?" Naveen asked, his brow arched, a small smile playing at the corners of his mouth.

Oh, goodness, was he flirting with her again? Was *she* flirting with *him*?

This was *not* the time.

It was never the time to flirt with Naveen. Doing so would only lead to the heartache of realising that they could never be together.

Tiana made the decision then and there to end this ill-advised teasing between them. Not only was it foolhardy, it was dangerous.

Electing not to respond to his question, she looked up at the sky and said, “Let’s go. Before dusk settles and we’re stuck here in the dark.”

32
TIANA

Tiana dodged thatches of thick vegetation that protruded from the earth as she led the way opposite where Naveen and Louis had travelled.

"You doing okay, Lottie?" she called over her shoulder.

"What do you think?" came Charlotte's retort.

Despite the direness of their situation, Tiana had to laugh. "If it makes you feel any better, I'm proud of the way you're holding up. You haven't complained nearly as much as I thought you would."

"Just give me time," Charlotte replied.

The deeper they journeyed into the copse of algae-covered trees and tall reeds, the more pungent the briny, stagnant air became. The humidity wrapped itself around them like a damp, dank cloak, its saturating presence bordering on unbearable, despite the fact that it was not quite spring. It signalled a scorching summer ahead of them.

Something swooped down just over their heads, emitting a loud caw. Charlotte yelped.

"What was that?" she cried. "Oh, goodness, Tia, I just know we're gonna get eaten by some horrible swamp creature."

"The animals here are more afraid of you than you are of them," Tiana said.

Except for the gators, but she wouldn't mention those.

"That's hogwash," Charlotte said. She slipped and reached out for a nearby tree to steady herself. "Eww! Eww! Eww!"

"What now?" Tiana asked.

Charlotte pointed to a horde of bugs crawling along the tree bark where she'd just had her hands.

Tiana held up both of hers. "I can't help you. You know how I feel about bugs."

She took a step back and caught her foot on a broken stump protruding from the ground. Tiana flailed, her arms windmilling in the air. She overcorrected herself and pitched forward, barrelling into Charlotte.

They both landed against the bug-covered tree.

"Eww!" Tiana and Charlotte screeched simultaneously.

"Move, move, move," Charlotte said, pushing at Tiana.

Tiana scrambled into a standing position. She slapped at her arms, even though she hadn't been against the tree long enough for any of the bugs to get to her. Charlotte, on the other hand…

"I am officially complaining," Charlotte said as she peeled a slimy slug off her sleeve and flung it on the ground. She pointed in the area where she'd thrown the creature. "What's that?"

Tiana looked down. The brooch Ms Rose had given her lay among the foliage.

"Oh, it must have slipped out of my pocket when I fell," she said. Tiana retrieved the brooch and, this time, pinned it inside her coveralls. "Come on," she said, reaching for Charlotte's arm. "We can't let Naveen and Louis win."

"So it *is* a competition," Charlotte drawled.

"A friendly one," Tiana quipped.

"Hmm. You know, Tia, I've been wondering… how friendly *do* you feel towards Naveen?"

"Don't start, Lottie."

"I just think if you gave him half a chance—"

"Don't," Tiana reiterated.

Charlotte threw her hands up. "Fine. I won't say how perfect I think you are for each other. You're driven, and he's so carefree. You balance each other out!"

Tiana marched ahead, ignoring Lottie.

"But you two *are* perfect for each other," her friend called.

Tiana ignored that, too.

They happened upon an area of fallen tree limbs ripe for the picking. Both she and Charlotte searched the timber pile.

"Okay, what about this one?" Charlotte asked, holding up a scrawny pole that didn't look as if it could hold the weight of a one-pound catfish.

"I don't think that one will be strong enough."

"We've been poking through these sticks for twenty minutes already," Charlotte said.

"Just be patient," Tiana said. "We'll eventually find the perfect branch."

"In case you hadn't noticed, patience isn't one of my virtues."

"You don't say?" Tiana laughed.

"You, on the other hand, have the patience of a saint, Tia. Always have." Charlotte tossed a stubby branch over her shoulder. "Take the other day at Maison Blanche, for instance. I don't know how you kept your cool when that saleswoman stopped you from trying on that hat."

Tiana paused in the middle of lifting a rotted-out tree limb from the pile. "Lottie, you do realise such things happen to me all the time, don't you?"

"What?" Charlotte recoiled, her face a mask of confusion. "Tia, what are you talking about? That lady was absolutely horrible to you. You're saying she's been that way to you before? Why didn't you tell me? I would have suggested we go to another store."

"It wouldn't have mattered," Tiana said as gently as possible. "It would have been the same way at any of those department stores." This was neither the time nor the place to have this conversation. Though, in all honesty, Tiana wasn't sure when would be a good time to have this conversation. There were some things that were just better left unsaid, especially when dealing with her well-meaning but often oblivious friend.

"Don't worry about it," Tiana said.

She turned her focus to a pile of reeds, twigs and tree limbs that had collected at the base of a nearby cypress tree.

Despite the damp earth muffling the sound of Charlotte's footsteps, Tiana could hear the sucking sound of her feet sinking with each step she took through the mud.

"Tia?" Charlotte's voice was quiet. "Tia, please talk to me. How can I know how to fix this if you won't even talk to me?"

"There's nothing for you to fix."

"It sounds as if there is."

"This is bigger than you, Lottie. It's… complicated."

Tiana blew out a weary breath. "Besides, we have other things to worry about right now."

"But what makes it so complicated?"

"Because we're different! Don't you get it, Lottie? We're different. How can you not see that?"

Tiana covered her face with her hands. One part of her wanted to shield her friend from this truth. It was just easier to let Lottie live in her perfect little world where everything was black and white, and those murky shades of grey didn't exist.

Yet Tiana had been forced to face these facts ever since she was a little girl. She had known how different their worlds were from the moment she stepped into the LaBouff mansion and realised the entirety of the little house her family lived in could fit in their grand entryway.

She'd known as she watched her mother sew dress after dress for Charlotte, using the kind of soft, silky fabrics Tiana could only dream of wearing. Fabrics so much more luxurious than the rough cotton her own dresses were made of.

Those differences – the stark reality of the existence she lived compared to Charlotte's – had been part of Tiana's life for as long as she could remember. Her mama had told her a long time ago that it wasn't proper to mention the

LaBouffs' money, but just because she couldn't *talk* about it, that didn't mean Tiana hadn't noticed.

It hadn't occurred to her until years later, when they were both in their teens, that Charlotte had never fully grasped that Tiana didn't have all the privileges she had. And here they were, both on the cusp of turning twenty years old, and Lottie still didn't seem to understand.

"Even though we live in the same city, it's as if we come from two different worlds," Tiana told her now. "I don't know if you understand just *how* different our worlds are."

"I'm not as naive as you assume, Tia. I know Big Daddy's money allows me to live a… well, a charmed life."

"It's not just about the money. It's about everything, about our lives in general," Tiana said. "What happened at the department store is a perfect example."

"What happened at Maison Blanche was *not* right. And they will never get another red cent from me."

"I know it wasn't right, but I also know it's the way things are. It's the world that *I* have to live in, Lottie." Several uncomfortable seconds ticked by before Tiana asked in a quiet voice, "Do you want to know how I got roped in with the Shadow Man?"

"I have no idea why you'd ever get caught up with the likes of him," she answered.

"It's because, at first, he offered to give me my restaurant," Tiana said. "I turned him down, but I was tempted, Lottie. I was tempted because I spent years working at Duke's Cafe and Cal's Restaurant. I socked away every penny I earned, and it was barely enough for the down payment on that old rundown sugar mill."

"But you *did* buy your own restaurant!"

"But look at how long it took. And as grateful as I am that Daddy and I were able to afford that building in Tremé, it still isn't the place I had my heart set on. Of course, it's not as if the Fenner brothers would have sold it to me anyway," she continued with a sarcastic snort. "They'd already decided that I wasn't fit to run a restaurant like that."

"What gives them the right to decide what you can and can't do?"

"It's done all the time," Tiana answered. "People assume I'm a maid because that's usually the only type of work a Black woman can get in this town. It's the only type of work we've been allowed to do, save for those who have skills that can't be denied, like Mama. People are often surprised to hear that I'm a chef who owns her own restaurant."

"Well, at least you've shown those Fenner brothers that

you *can* run a restaurant. And I'm sure you'll eventually earn enough to buy that building you really want."

Tiana levelled her gaze at Charlotte. "How long have we known each other, Lottie?"

"Well, Tia, you know we've been knowing each other since we were both in knee-highs."

"And how long have I talked about opening a restaurant?"

"For as long as I've known you," Charlotte said with a laugh. "All you've ever talked about was making your daddy's gumbo and selling it in your restaurant one day." She put her hand on Tiana's shoulder and squeezed it encouragingly. "That's why I'm so happy to see you finally getting that chance now. You made it happen."

"Tell me something, Charlotte. In all that time, did you ever think to ask Mr LaBouff to help me?"

Charlotte froze. "Well… well, no. You're so proud, Tiana. You would never have taken charity from Big Daddy."

"You're right, I wouldn't have accepted charity from him, but do you ever wonder why it never crossed your mind to offer to help me, Lottie?" Tiana swallowed past the knot of disappointment clogging her throat. "Your daddy is the richest man in the city, and one of the most influential. There are more ways he could have had an impact than just with his money. Like vouching for me with the Fenner brothers, or talking with the councilmen about my venture. Or even hiring me to cater his company parties."

"Are you saying all of this my fault?" Charlotte asked.

"Of course not," Tiana said. She hated feeling this way. She hated the sadness in Charlotte's eyes. In a way, she understood why it had never occurred to Charlotte to offer help. She'd had everything handed to her, sometimes on an actual silver platter. She was the product of her daddy's overexuberant affection.

If you lived your entire life never wanting for anything, why would you ever look at someone else's lot in life and compare yours to it? It just wasn't in her friend's nature.

"I'm not blaming you for anything, Lottie," Tiana said. "But I need you to understand that the world sees us differently." Tiana shrugged her shoulders. "It's not fair; it's the way things are."

Charlotte glanced at her, nodding slowly. "Well, I say we start to change the way things are. I say we raise a ruckus until things change." She held her hand out to Tiana.

Tiana paused, then took the hand and shook it. It wasn't as easy as that. But it was a start.

"I say you've got yourself a deal." She sighed. "But before we can change the world, we have to figure out how to get that boat out of those brambles. And look here," Tiana said, picking up a slim but sturdy-looking branch. "I think we've found a winner!"

She started back towards the boat, but before she could take more than a couple of steps, Charlotte grabbed her hand again, halting her progress. Tiana looked at their clasped hands and then up at her friend's face. The look in her eyes was so humble and full of understanding – Tiana wasn't sure if she'd ever seen such a look from Charlotte in all the years she'd known her.

"I meant what I said." Her tone was earnest. Heartfelt. "I know that I can be selfish and stubborn, but I want to be a good friend to you. The *best* kind of friend. Because that's the kind of friend you have always been to me."

"Oh, Lottie." Tiana dropped the branch and wrapped her arms around her.

"I'm glad you're here."

33
TIANA

"There y'all are!" Louis's boisterous voice greeted them as soon as they cleared the thicket of trees.

Tiana held up the branch she'd carried back. "This is the best we could find. How did y'all do?"

"About the same," Naveen answered, motioning to a long pole that looked to be thin enough to fit between the bottom of the boat and the gnarled vines. Tiana just hoped it was strong enough to withstand the amount of effort it would take to dislodge the vessel. "You'd think there would be a better selection of sticks out here in... well... in the sticks. But they were either too fat or too skinny or too short. Very frustrating."

"We'll make do with what we have," Tiana said. She looked up at the sky. "I can't believe I'm about to say this, but I think we should wait until morning."

"Are you sure?" Naveen asked.

She nodded and hooked her thumb back towards where she and Charlotte had just returned from. "I spotted a bit of a clearing back there. It wasn't a large space, but it seemed big enough for us all to stretch out for the night."

"Are you saying we have to sleep on the ground?" Charlotte asked. "Why can't we sleep on the boat?"

"You can take your chances on the boat if you want to," Tiana said. "But if it happens to dislodge while you're asleep and drifts away…" She shrugged her shoulders.

"Fine, I'll sleep on the ground," Charlotte groused. "I swear, once we get back to N'awlins I'm gonna have Big Daddy treat us to a full day of pampering. We deserve it."

"I do have a blanket, if that makes you feel any better," Tiana told her. She looked apologetically over at Naveen and Louis. "Unfortunately, that's all I have. I only packed it in case I got chilly while on the boat. At the time, I thought I would be the only one out here."

"Not a problem," Naveen said. He clamped a hand on Louis's shoulder. "We can rough it, right, my friend?"

"Rough it? Man, this feels like home to me." Louis grinned.

"You sleep on the ground when you are at home?" Naveen balked. "Tiana, maybe you should consider paying my friend here a little more when he plays at the supper club, eh? At least enough for him to afford a proper bed."

"Louis gets paid handsomely," Tiana said. She narrowed her eyes at Louis. "He just likes the great outdoors." She turned to the boat. "Let's get the food. I'll get started on dinner as soon as we set up camp."

They grabbed the bags out of the boat and, with Tiana leading the way, marched in single file towards the clearing.

"Tia, look over there," Charlotte called. She pointed towards the bank of the bayou. "Are those palmetto leaves near the shoreline? Maybe we can lay those out on the ground as some kind of cover."

"Good thinking, Lottie," Tiana said. "Let's get these to the clearing. Then we can come back for the palmettos."

The area Tiana had spotted earlier turned out to be larger than she'd first thought. There was more than enough room for them all to spread out, and there was even a large tree stump with a smooth top, as if someone had made a table for them.

"This is going to do just fine," Tiana said.

They set their supplies near the tree stump and returned to the bayou's edge to pick palmettos. In no time at all, they had several dozen stacked along the bank.

"I reckon this is enough," Tiana said. She glanced up

at the ominous grey cloud that had drifted overhead. "The rain is coming. We need to get back and find ourselves a tree to settle in under before it starts to pour."

Charlotte pulled another palmetto from the marshy area. "Maybe just a few more. I like a plush bed—" She paused and pointed at the water. "What's that ripple?"

Tiana whipped around. Her stomach dropped.

"Lottie, get back!" Tiana screamed just as a large alligator lurched forward, its massive body splashing against the shore.

Naveen reached over and grabbed Lottie by the waist, jerking her away from the water.

"Everybody, run!" he yelled, carrying Lottie in his arms and galloping through the reeds, palms and cattails.

Instead of running away from the shore, Louis started towards it.

"Louis, what are you doing? Don't go near the water!" Tiana cried.

"Don't worry," he said. "I know how to handle these gators." He turned to the huge reptile, his hands raised in entreaty. "It's okay, fella. We're just getting a few of these palms. Nothing to worry about. Just give us a—"

The gator launched itself at him.

"Louis!" Tiana yelled.

Louis hurried away from the bayou, running towards

Tiana at full speed. His eyes were wide with fear and confusion and hurt.

"Are you okay?" Tiana asked him.

He shook his head as he gulped down air with huge, lung-filling breaths. He rested his hands on his thighs. After a moment, he took Tiana by the arm, moving several yards away from where Naveen and Charlotte stood.

"You don't understand, Tiana," Louis whispered. "That was Henry. We grew up together. It was as if he didn't even know me."

The sadness in his eyes broke her heart. "I – I don't think he does, Louis," she reminded him in a soft voice. "You're not one of them any more."

Tiana stood by silently, offering her friend comfort as he digested her words. She could see the reality sinking in as myriad emotions moved across his face, the realisation that he could not straddle both worlds. Now that he was human, his old life here on the bayou truly was over.

A pang of guilt shot through Tiana. Even though she had done what she had thought Louis wanted, what she had thought would keep him safe, she wondered if it had been right to bring him into her deal with Dr. Facilier at all.

Placing a hand on his rough arm, she looked over at the other two and called, "Let's get our palm fronds and get back to camp before the rain comes."

A loud crack of thunder rang out, like an exclamation point on her statement.

Charlotte stood as the lookout while Tiana, Louis and Naveen quickly gathered up the palm fronds they'd already collected.

Once back at the clearing, the mood was subdued. They went about setting things up for the night, the encounter with the gator bringing the dangers they faced out here in the bayou into stark relief.

Thunder rent the air, and sheets of heavy rain poured down like a curtain all around them. But, oddly, the area where they'd set up their camp remained dry, as if an invisible dome covered them.

"Does this rainstorm seem peculiar to you, or is it just me?" Naveen asked.

Tiana couldn't explain it, so she simply shrugged.

She made a paste with the sardines and spread it over the loaves of fresh bread she'd bought at the market before they left. She set it out, along with some of the fruit and shelled pecans.

She continued to observe Louis out of the corner of her eye as she nibbled on her meagre dinner. His forlorn mien was so contrary to his usual cheery disposition, it was as if he was an entirely different person.

Because he was. That was the issue. He was a person.

She wondered… after a full year as a human, was he starting to regret the change?

After finishing up her meal, Tiana dusted off her hands and went over to him. She quietly approached, giving Louis space to decline her company if he chose. Relief washed over her when he patted the ground next to him.

"You didn't eat much," she said, gesturing to his half-eaten bread.

"I don't have much of an appetite."

"You know, Louis," Tiana started in a lowered voice. "When I made that deal with the Shadow Man, I included you in it because I knew how much you'd dreamt of becoming human. But I shouldn't have assumed I knew what you might want or need. I'm so sorry." She paused. "If we can figure out a way to change the deal… would you want to go back to the way things were?"

He shrugged. "I like playing with the Crawfish Crooners, but I do miss my family sometimes." He looked over at her. "I'm not sure I'll fit in with them any more, not after what happened tonight with Henry."

"Henry didn't recognise you as you are now, but I'm sure he would if you return to your former state. Maybe Mama Odie could help with that, too." She covered his forearm and gave it a squeeze. "I would miss you, but I want you to be happy."

"I would miss you, too. And Charlotte and Naveen. And the guys in the band." His expression was full of remorse.

"You decide which would make you happier. The choice is up to you." She looked him in the eye. "It should've *always* been up to you."

Louis shot her a shaky smile, and she left her friend to his thoughts, pushing up from the ground and returning to the tree stump to clean up the remnants of their dinner – only to discover Naveen and Lottie putting things away.

"I was going to do that," Tiana said.

"You fixed the meal," Charlotte pointed out. "The least we could do is clean up. You don't have to do everything yourself, Tia."

Tiana stood there, uncertain what to do with herself.

"See, we can be useful," Lottie said once they were done. She stretched her arms above her head and released a yawn. "But today has been a lot. I'm going to bed. At least I hope I can get some beauty sleep out here."

She grabbed the blanket and went over to the bed of palmettos they'd spread over the ground.

Meanwhile, Naveen motioned for Tiana to come with him. She followed him to one of the big cypress trees that surrounded their camp, and they both slid to the ground, sitting with their backs against the tree's trunk.

"Is he okay?" Naveen pointed at Louis, who remained

in the spot where Tiana had left him, on the other side of the clearing.

"I think so," Tiana said. "He just misses his family."

"I can understand that," Naveen remarked.

Tiana studied his profile, realising he was in a similar situation, even if his wasn't magically motivated. "It's been a year since you've seen them," she said.

"Back on the boat, you asked if I ever think about going back." He picked up a small twig and twirled it around. "My parents have invited me to return home."

Tiana was shocked by the sudden, profound anguish that instantly swept over her just at the thought of him leaving. Of course, she'd considered it numerous times this past year, telling herself it would be better for her if he *did* return to his homeland. Yet hearing those words sent a sharp pain straight to her chest.

She swallowed past the lump of emotion clogging her throat before asking in a quiet voice, "Will you?"

Naveen brought his knees up and rested his elbows on them. He continued to twirl the stem between his fingers, a contemplative look on his face. After several moments ticked by, he looked over at her and said, "Not if I have a reason to stay… Say, from you?"

Her breath caught. "Me?"

"Yes. You," he said softly. "There are many things in

America that I have come to enjoy, but I can find those things back in Maldonia. There is only *one* thing here that I cannot find anywhere else. That is you, Tiana." He turned to her. "I want the chance to get to know you better. Will I get that chance if I remain here in America?"

"Oh, Naveen." The words came out in a raw whisper. Despair over what she knew could never be threatened to shatter what little control she still held over her emotions.

"I am simply asking for a chance," he said.

She didn't have the heart to tell him that there was *no* chance, not if she wanted to keep him safe.

Instead, Tiana reached over and took his hand. She threaded their fingers together and tilted her head to the side, until it rested on his shoulder. "Let's get some sleep. We've got a long day tomorrow."

Tiana sensed he wanted to say more, but he didn't. Pretty soon the driving rain and the low hum of buzzing insects were the only sounds on the bayou.

34
TIANA

The Louisiana Bayou
Sunday, February 1927
Two days before Mardi Gras

"Up and at 'em!" Tiana clapped her hands as she walked around the makeshift camp they'd set up last night, rousing her crew. She nudged Charlotte with the toe of her boot. "Wake up, Lottie. We're already behind, and we still have to pry the boat loose."

Naveen stood from where he'd slept, slumped against a tree trunk. He stretched his arms up in the air, moving his neck from side to side as if working out kinks. "Eh, not the best sleep of my life, but not the worst, either."

"I'll have an order of flapjacks with maple syrup," Louis said as he twisted underneath his palm-frond blanket.

Tiana poked him with a branch. "This isn't a diner, Louis. Wake up. We need to get going."

She rolled up her blanket, tying it with twine and looping it over her shoulder.

"Grab those poles," she instructed Naveen and Louis. "And pray that we can dislodge this boat." She looked to the sky. "The rain passed us by last night, but that doesn't mean we'll be so lucky today."

Ten minutes later, they were trudging through the mud, on their way back to the boat.

"Are you sure this is the right way?" Lottie asked. "It's easy to become disorientated when every tree and shrub looks the same."

"It's the right way." Tiana pointed to a cypress tree that canted to the left, its branches nearly touching the ground. "See this tree, the one bending over like a gentleman taking a bow? I made note of it last night as we were searching for a place to camp out. There's another one a few yards away that looks as if someone carved a portrait of a cat in the bark."

They continued their trek through the marsh. The area around their campsite had been spared from last night's conspicuous rainstorm, but judging by the saturated grounds, this part of the bayou had got a good soaking.

"There it is!" Lottie pointed at the cat ears etched

into the tree bark. "Dang, Tia, you sure are good at this camping-around-the-bayou business. I still don't get it. How'd you even come to know about all of this?"

"Maybe I can explain it to you one day," Tiana told her. She still wasn't sure how to address the questions Lottie would undoubtedly have about Mama Odie, and wondered if maybe she should give her friend a little insight into what had happened the year before.

But how would she even broach the subject?

You don't know this, Lottie, but Naveen and I were both turned into frogs at your Mardi Gras ball last year. Oh, and Louis? We met him while travelling through this bayou. He was a gator at the time.

Lottie would fall away in a dead faint.

It was probably better to keep things as vague as possible when it came to discussing her prior dealings with these bayous and the quirky lady who lived there.

Naveen and Louis had travelled ahead and were already at the boat when she and Lottie arrived. Tiana quickly joined them, adding her muscle, but the boat remained rooted in the tangled branches.

She walked around to assess the situation from the other side. Tall shoots of cattail cradled that side of the vessel, their fluffy brown ends thwacking against the wooden hull. She leant in closer, shoving the stalks to the side with her elbow, but there were so many that most flapped right back into place.

"If I can just… get these… out of the—" The tall plants parted. She looked over her shoulder to find Naveen holding the cattails at bay with a branch. "Way," Tiana finished.

His eyes brimmed with infectious humour and the familiar kindness she'd come to associate with him.

"Thank you." Tiana acknowledged his help with a gentle smile.

He shrugged. "Hey, that's what friends do for each other, eh?"

Was he her friend?

It was starting to feel that way, particularly after their conversations yesterday. Their playful banter had been a delight, hearkening back to the time they'd spent together on this very bayou almost exactly one year earlier. Maybe, once they returned to New Orleans and she put all this horrible business with the Shadow Man behind her, the Fates would take pity on them and allow a semblance of friendship between her and Naveen. It wasn't part of the deal, but given the way she'd unswervingly held up her end of the bargain, there should be room for a few concessions.

She sighed.

You knew what you were signing up for.

As far as her relationship with Naveen was concerned,

at least. It was the other thing that she hadn't signed up for – the looming threats that had served as the catalyst for this trip – that she should be focused on.

No more daydreams. She needed to get to Mama Odie.

While Louis and Naveen tried their hardest to lift the boat's bow, Tiana worked her branch underneath it. She did the same with the stick they'd brought back, wedging it as far as she could. Unfortunately, it wasn't very far at all. There was no way this would give them the leverage they needed to push the boat free.

"Lottie, over here," Tiana called over her shoulder.

"Me?" Charlotte yelped.

"Your clothes are already dirty," Tiana said. "A little more mud won't kill you. Put all your weight on that edge of the stick."

Despite the effort she put into each thrust, neither she nor Charlotte had the muscle required to move the boat.

"As much as I hate to admit this, I think we need more manpower on this end," Tiana said.

"Just remember you're the one who said it," Naveen told her as he grabbed onto the end of the branch she held. Louis joined Lottie.

"On the count of three," Naveen said. "One… two… three." They pushed down on their respective branches and the boat moved a smidgen. "Yes! Again," Naveen called. "Again."

"It's working," Tiana said excitedly.

"Yes, it is," Naveen said. "Uh… the only problem is that, at this rate, I fear it will take us about three days to get the boat free."

"You're right." Her shoulders slumped.

"No giving up just yet," Naveen said. He approached the front of the boat again and peered at it from several angles. "Ah, yes. There's a little more room here. If I can get my hand on the front of the boat, maybe I can push."

"Be careful," Tiana called.

He looked back at her, one brow cocked in inquiry. "You are concerned about my welfare, eh? That's good to know."

Goodness, is he capable of turning that charm off for even a second?

"Just push the boat," Tiana said.

He winked at her before turning his attention back to his task.

She watched as he manoeuvred his hand through a small gap in the vines and branches. It was just wide enough for him to sneak in there. Tiana wasn't sure he would be able to do much with just that one hand, and there certainly wasn't enough space for him to get a second palm on that boat.

Still, he pushed and pushed and pushed.

"Maybe if I switch hands, I can—"

"Watch out for that—"

"Ooowww!" Naveen bellowed as a sharp piece of wood scored his flesh.

He jerked his hand free and clutched it against his chest. Tiana could see blood seeping through the fingers covering his injured hand. She let go of the stick and ran to him.

"What happened?" Lottie asked, coming up alongside her.

"Let me see it," Tiana said. He pulled back when she reached for his hand, but she refused to back down. "I need to see how bad it is."

He finally relented, slowly letting his uninjured hand fall away.

"Ugh!" Lottie screeched, skittering back to where she'd come from. "I hate blood!"

"I'll stay over here." Louis put a hand to his stomach. "Blood makes me squeamish."

Tiana rolled her eyes at the two of them. She winced as she studied the nasty, jagged gash marring Naveen's previously unblemished skin. The flesh around the cut puckered.

"Give me just a minute," she said.

She walked over to the side of the boat and retrieved

the bag that held the remaining food. She searched inside for the handkerchief she'd used to wrap up some biscuits, sticking it in the front pocket of her coveralls before making her way back to Naveen.

"Give it here," she said again. Holding his hand, she grabbed the edge of his shirt and began dabbing at the cut. "I hope this wasn't your favourite shirt."

"In fact, it was," he said. Her eyes flew to his. Before she could apologise, he smiled and said, "I'm only kidding."

"You," she growled, trying to hide her smile. How could he be both endearing and insufferable at the same time?

She concentrated on clearing the small particles of wood from his hand.

"Ow," Naveen said, slightly jerking his hand away.

"I'm sorry," Tiana whispered. "It's a pretty nasty gash. I'm sure it stings like the dickens."

"I'm not sure what the dickens are, but if they feel like fire, then yes, it stings like the dickens."

She cleaned the cut as best she could, but it still didn't look good.

"I wish I had some iodine or something to put on it," she said. "I'm afraid this will become infected, especially out here in these swamps. Who knows what kind of parasites are lurking here?"

"Well, that is very discomforting, Tiana. I would have rather you not mentioned that at all."

"I'm sorry," she murmured again. She reached for the handkerchief in her breast pocket, scratching her own knuckle on Ms Rose's brooch as she retrieved it. She shook out the handkerchief, making sure there were no crumbs from the biscuits that could stick to the cut. She wrapped the cloth around his injury, then pulled the ribbon holding her hair in place and used it to secure the dressing.

"There you go," Tiana said. She shook out her hair, letting it fall to her shoulders.

When she looked up at him, Naveen was staring back at her, a compelling spark of wonder in his eyes. In that moment, it felt as if they were alone, just the two of them in this quiet, cosy corner of the world.

"This is the second time you have tended to my wounds," he said. "Thank you." His voice was low and soft, like a feather brushing across her skin.

"You're welcome," Tiana whispered, still staring into his eyes.

She told herself to look away. The feelings swirling through her as she continued to stare at him were dangerous. But these feelings were too potent – too irresistible – for her not to indulge them for just a moment longer. She stared into Naveen's hazel-coloured eyes and tumbled headfirst into the fantasy of what it would be like if she had never agreed to Facilier's demands.

What if, after getting off the boat from Maldonia, Naveen had walked through the doors of Duke's Cafe for a cup of coffee, taken one look at her, and decided she was the one for him? How magical would it have been if he had whisked her away and pledged his love for her? She would have had everything she'd ever wanted: Naveen, her restaurant, her daddy…

No!

No, her daddy would be dead. And who knew if she would have had her restaurant at all? It was easy to constantly harp on what the Shadow Man had cost her, but she should never forget what she'd gained from their deal.

Tiana cut her eyes away from Naveen's and dropped his hand.

"We need to get this boat dislodged and be on our way," she said. She turned back towards the stick she'd found and gripped the end of it. "Come on, Lottie. You'll need to put some muscle in it."

Tiana could see Naveen walking towards her out of the corner of her eye. "You can stand over there," she threw out over her shoulder. "We don't need you injuring your hand even more."

"But, Tiana—"

"We've got this," she said.

She sensed his despondency, but she couldn't concern herself with Naveen's feelings right then. Dabbling in those games of what-ifs was foolhardy. More than that, it was dangerous. It caused her to forget what was at stake, and how deadly things could turn out for all those she loved if she wasn't careful.

Naveen's love was something that could never be hers. It had only taken a split second to weigh the pros and cons, and she'd decided his safety – and the safety of her family, and having her daddy back in her life – was worth the cost. She couldn't forget that now.

"Louis, why don't you get in the boat and start the engine? Maybe the motor's power, along with our own elbow grease, will be just the thing we need."

"I can do that!" Louis said.

He climbed aboard the boat and settled at the stern. Tiana had hoped his weight would help pop the boat's bow out of the branches, but it didn't.

"Ready?" Louis asked.

"Ready," Tiana called back. He revved the motor and, to her utter relief, the boat began to inch back. "Yes! It's working, Louis! Hit it again."

The motor whirled, and she and Lottie pushed harder.

"Uh… Tiana," Naveen said.

"Not now," Tiana told him. "Again, Louis!"

The motor roared again.

"Tiana, you may want to—" Naveen started, but Tiana stopped him.

"Wait," she said. She sniffed. "What's that smell?" She looked up and noticed a plume of grey smoke coming from the back of the boat. "Oh, no! Louis! Louis, stop!"

But it was too late. Tiana knew the moment she heard the motor rev one last time, then sputter, that they were in trouble. Her entire body slumped as her spirits deflated like a popped balloon.

"That did not sound good," Naveen said.

"What happened?" Louis asked.

"I think the motor burned out," Tiana said.

"What? I didn't… I didn't mean to."

"No, Louis. It's not your fault. It's… it's just my luck," Tiana said. She wondered for a moment if this was the Shadow Man. Could whatever dark powers he held reach her all the way out here?

"I did it!" Charlotte yelled.

The three of them turned to find Charlotte kneeling in the mud. More important, the bow of the boat was now free from the brambles.

"Wow, Lottie!" Tiana said. "Great job!"

"Except now we can't move the boat with no motor."

"Yes, we can," Tiana said. "There are oars. We're gonna have to paddle our way to Mama Odie's, but we'll get there. Let's get moving!"

She took over the driving duties again, not trusting anyone else to get her to her destination. She was once again in control of her own destiny.

"Almost there," Tiana whispered.

35
NAVEEN

Naveen sat at the rear of the boat, feeling useless as Tiana, Louis and even Charlotte worked in tandem to paddle the boat onwards. He'd picked up one of the wooden oars with the intention of doing his share of the work, but had to drop it seconds later. His hand still throbbed from his attempt to help.

If he had still been in Maldonia, it would never have even occurred to him that he should contribute to the effort to row the boat. But he was no longer the person he'd been back in his parents' kingdom. Even if he considered taking them up on their offer to return home – a decision that continued to confound and frustrate him – he would be returning as a different man. A better man. A man determined to prove that he had something to contribute to the world.

This fierce need to be useful was still new to him, but

it was strong. And the feeling grew even stronger whenever he was around Tiana.

Witnessing the effort she put into making her restaurant a success inspired him; it pushed him to seek the same for himself. He wanted her to see him as someone who took pride in putting in a hard day's work.

Naveen cradled his head in his good hand, releasing an exasperated sigh.

He was not sure *how* Tiana saw him now. He was in a perpetual state of confusion when it came to her.

He had been so sure he was making progress, given the laughs they'd shared yesterday. Yet this morning, Tiana was right back to avoiding him. Remembering how she'd reacted after bandaging his hand, as if she could not get away from him quick enough, caused a sharp ache to pierce his chest.

If only he could figure out why she treated him that way. What more could he do to make her like him?

Except she *did* like him. He was sure of it.

The way she had laughed at his silly jokes and teased him. The way she had tended to his injured hand, taking care not to hurt him, as if hurting him was the absolute worst thing that could ever happen. The way she had stared into his eyes as they had stood so close to each other.

She cared about him, but for some reason, she was still hesitant to show it.

Naveen tried to flex his hand, but the moment he did, he felt the skin crack open again, and blood seeped through the handkerchief Tiana had wrapped around his wound.

"Oh, Naveen, you're bleeding," Charlotte said.

"It is nothing," Naveen said to Charlotte, but he was looking at Tiana. He wanted to know if she had heard, and if she was worried.

He saw her back stiffen, but she did not turn.

"Are you sure? Your entire hand is red now," Charlotte said.

"Is it hot to the touch?" Tiana asked, although she kept her eyes straight ahead.

Naveen ran his fingers over his injured hand. "I… uh… I can't really tell. Strange, eh?"

"Not if you're feverish," Tiana said. "Lottie, touch his hand and see if it's warm, or if it hurts when you touch it."

"I don't wanna touch it," Charlotte cried.

"His hand won't bite you," Tiana said. "Just press on the flesh surrounding the cut. But be gentle."

Naveen held his hand out to Charlotte, who approached it with the same caution one would take when encountering a venomous snake. She gingerly poked at the back of his hand with her finger. At first, Naveen had intended to jerk it back as a joke, but there was no joking about it. Her touch sent a flash of intense pain shooting through his hand. He yelped.

"Yep, I'd say it hurts when I touch it, all right," Charlotte called.

"I knew it," Tiana said. She shook her head. "Infection is setting in."

"What does that mean?" Naveen asked, trepidation slithering down his spine at the foreboding he heard in her voice.

"Oh, I know," Louis said. "You're gonna have to chop off your whole hand if you don't wanna lose your arm. I saw it happen before."

"*What!*" Naveen screeched.

"Louis, you are not helping," Tiana hissed. "You're not going to lose your hand," she said. "I'm sure Mama Odie will be able to help. She can do anything."

"How much longer before we're there?" Naveen asked.

"It won't be long," Tiana said.

Finally, she turned to him, glancing over her shoulder and looking him directly in the eyes.

"You'll be okay. I promise you, Naveen."

There it was again. That concern for him that she could not mask, despite how often she tried to hide it. What was she so afraid of?

He needed to figure out a way to break past the barrier

Tiana had erected against her feelings for him. If only he knew *why* she continued to do so, it would be so much easier for them to get past it. He just did not understand. Tiana's behaviour was the opposite of what he was used to.

He wasn't arrogant enough to think that every woman he encountered would just fall at his feet – well, okay, maybe he had been that arrogant in the past. Mainly because it was true. Women *did* fall at his feet. He was a prince, after all.

Yet the one person he felt the deepest connection to was the only one who appeared immune to his charms.

Still, it was more apparent to him than ever that the magnetic pull between them wasn't just a figment of his imagination. It thrummed through the air whenever they were near.

He just hoped it, and *he*, was enough.

36
FACILIER

Facilier cut around the corner of the old Cabildo, holding his hat against the fierce breeze that blew in from the river. The fog had grown thicker despite the wind. It swirled around like a dust cloud, cloaking the entire city in a dense, blinding mist that made it difficult to see more than three feet in front of him. The green algae had reached the French Market. It swathed the open-air stalls in grimy, viscous muck, forcing the vendors to abandon their wares.

Facilier's heart raced. Blood pounded in his ears as he tried to do the impossible: outrun the Shadows.

He bumped into people as he dashed in and out of shopfronts, muttering curses and warning them to stay out of his way. He needed to get away from here, to find somewhere to hide.

Maybe that was the key – he should just leave New Orleans. Head to Chicago or Detroit, as so many of the people who once lived here had done.

An anguished howl tore from his lips at the realisation that it wouldn't matter. There was no escape for him. No matter where he fled.

Still, he ran as fast as he could, darting around corners as he made his way through the French Quarter. He had been trying to outrun these demons for years. Their grip on him, on his very life, was like a vice. Constantly squeezing. Forever demanding.

Even if they collected Tiana's soul instead of his own, would he ever be free?

He slipped into a narrow alley a few blocks away from his home. His eyes roamed the crumbling brick walls of the century-year-old buildings in search of the telltale nebulous blobs that had been chasing him. When he didn't see any sign of them, he released an unsteady but calming breath.

He turned to exit the alley, and, without warning, three dark shadows slithered up to him. He started, dropping his cane and then scrambling to retrieve it. Fear snatched the breath from his lungs as he took several steps back.

"Gentle… gentlemen," he croaked. "How are you? It's been a while."

The three shapeless forms swirled around him,

moaning and groaning in displeasure, reminding him what would happen on Mardi Gras night.

"Don't you worry. I haven't forgotten about you," he assured them.

The moans grew louder, coming in a rush that made it difficult for him to decipher exactly what they were saying, but he heard the most important words. He was down to his final days.

"I'm working on it, gentlemen. Tiana will sign that contract. You'll get your soul. I promise." He held his hands out. "You know you can always count on me."

The three Shadows roared. One of them whipped around him and knocked his top hat off his head. It swooped in again, jolting Facilier with a solid blow to his back. He stumbled to the ground and braced himself for another strike.

He remained in that crouched position long after the Shadows had disappeared, his body shaking with lingering panic and fear. In the decades since he'd first partnered with them, he had never witnessed such a virulent attack. Their rage was palpable.

Facilier finally stood and straightened his clothing. He dusted off the dirt that clung to his trousers and jacket and looked around to make sure no one had witnessed his humiliation. Fortunately, the alley was empty.

Except…

Facilier squinted as he tried to make out the small figure he saw outlined in the murky fog. He took one step forward, then another. And another. The closer he got, the clearer the shape became.

It was a small child. He stood next to a filthy pile of garbage, just outside the back door of one of the Quarter's eating establishments. The young boy's ashen face was gaunt, his cheeks hollow and smudged with dirt. He picked through the rubbish, examining the rotting vegetables and table scraps with hungry eyes.

This little miscreant was one of hundreds who roamed about the city. Abandoned by parents who could no longer afford to feed them. Ignored by the countless people who walked past them begging in the streets.

And he'd just borne witness to the indignity Facilier had suffered.

Facilier took another step towards him. A loud crack rang out from the broken glass he'd unknowingly stepped on.

The young boy's head popped up. He looked towards the sound, and their gazes connected across the mere three feet that now separated them. His wide, terrified eyes conveyed his panic. Facilier reached out and grabbed the child by the arm before he could run.

"Not so fast," he said.

When that frightened gaze settled on him, Facilier was struck with an unpleasant sense of familiarity. It was uncomfortable. Unwanted.

As he stared into the depths of the filthy child's dark brown eyes, he couldn't help seeing another child. The child sat at his mother's knee as she prepared a poultice for a sick neighbour. Even though she barely had enough to feed her own family, she had nursed the neighbour back to good health with medicinal herbs, bowls of vegetable stock and help from the generations of ancestors who had come before her.

His mind's eye catapulted him several years into the future, to when that same young child had grown into a scrawny kid who ran the streets, getting into trouble. So angry with the universe for taking his mother away far too early, he'd rebelled, opting for two-bit hustles in order to get ahead instead of learning the Vodou traditions his mother had practised and tried to teach him.

And ever since, he'd been digging himself deeper and deeper into debt with his *friends*.

Facilier's head snapped back. He shook himself out of his reverie and relinquished his hold on the young boy. But before the boy could scramble away, Facilier caught him by the arm again. With his free hand, Facilier reached into his pocket and pulled out several coins. He placed them in the boy's palm and closed his tiny dirt-streaked fingers around the money.

"Go and get yourself something to eat," Facilier told him. "Find a warm bed tonight. That's what this money is for, you hear me?"

The boy nodded, his eyes still wild with fear. Then he took off down the alley, his small body quickly disappearing in the dense mist.

Facilier's lips twisted in a frown as he continued to stare off into the distance. This sudden awakening of his conscience was most inconvenient. What did he care about a homeless delinquent, especially when he should have been focused entirely on finding Tiana?

Facilier tilted the brim of his hat to shield his eyes and steadied himself on his cane. Moving out of the alley, he returned to the hustle and bustle of the city, easily swiping the wallet of a man in a tailored suit walking in the opposite direction.

That was more like it.

It was time for Facilier to continue his search.

He would find Tiana.

And he would make her pay what was due.

37
TIANA

An excited buzz hummed through Tiana's entire body as their boat's bow cut through the murky swamp water, fevered anticipation building up in her bloodstream.

They were close! She could feel it!

She'd spotted a weirdly shaped cypress tree a few minutes earlier and instantly recognised it as one she'd seen the last time she was here. Mama Odie's house would appear soon. Just a few more minutes and they would see it.

She paddled with renewed vigour now that they were so close to their destination. Yet, despite her excitement, Tiana could not fend off the trepidation that tingled at the back of her neck at the thought of approaching Mama Odie for help once again. She was intimidated by the quirky Vodou lady who talked in riddles and kept a snake as a pet. The one who always seemed to know exactly what she was thinking.

But she has a good heart.

The reminder assuaged a bit of her worry. Mama Odie had been willing to help both Tiana and Naveen the year before. Hopefully, she would be willing to do so again.

Please. Please. Please.

The strangeness of having to rely on someone else for help struck Tiana anew. She knew she was independent to a fault. She had lost count of how many times she had wasted hours – sometimes even *days* – toiling away at some task or another, refusing to ask for help.

But Tiana would not pretend that she could get out of this mess with Facilier on her own.

"I don't think my arms can take much more of this," Charlotte cried.

"Just a little further, Lottie," Tiana said.

"Are you sure?" Charlotte asked.

"I am, I promise. It should be right—" she started, but Naveen cut her off.

"There it is!"

Tiana's eyes grew wide as the boat broke through a curtain of moss that hung like delicate lace from the spindly branches of two trees. There in the middle of the swamp grew the biggest tree Tiana had ever seen. Hundreds of steps were carved into its massive trunk. They wound their way up to the rickety fishing boat that sat nestled between a cluster of gnarly branches.

"Yes!" Tiana said. It took all she had not to cry tears of joy.

"That's not a house," Charlotte said. "That's a shipwreck. It looks as if it was blown there by a hurricane."

Tiana wouldn't have been surprised if that was exactly how Mama Odie had come to reside in that tree.

"There's a lot more to that little boat than meets the eye," she told Charlotte. "Everything is going to be okay now. Just watch. Mama Odie will know what to do about the Shadow Man."

They paddled up to the humongous cypress. Tiana lifted the heavy rope from the boat and tossed it over a chunky tree stump near the base of the tree.

Once she'd secured their boat, she plunked her hands on her hips and released a deep, satisfied breath.

"Well, we made it," she said. A sense of foreboding sneaked its way into her head, but she tamped it down. There was no reason for her to be afraid.

She gingerly climbed out of the boat, doing her best to find purchase on the tree's lumpy roots that protruded from the water.

"Is that safe?" Charlotte asked.

"Of course it is." She reached a hand out to help

Charlotte. "Come on." Her foot slipped, and she had to fight to keep her balance.

"Umm... I think I'm going to stay on the boat," Charlotte said. A moment later, a huge bug zigzagged around her head. She yelped and scrambled out of the boat. "On the other hand, maybe I should join you."

"Ah... this brings back memories," Louis said as he hefted his huge body off the starboard side.

"Yes, it does," Naveen said, climbing out after Louis. Once out of the boat, he stood with his fist perched on his hips and looked around. "*Why* does it bring back memories?"

"Oh, well, you know," Tiana hedged as she started up the steps. "You're probably remembering some other house in the swamp that you've visited. Once you've visited one swamp house, you've visited them all."

"But I've never—"

"We'd better get up there," Tiana interrupted.

The carved steps squeaked loudly in the quiet bayou, so loudly Tiana wondered if it wasn't by design. It was an ingenious way to alert whoever was in the house that someone was on their way up the steps.

"You're going too fast, Tia!" Charlotte called.

"Yeah, I'm gonna take it slow," Louis puffed.

Tiana looked back to make sure both were okay, then

continued up the steps. She was ready to make her case to Mama Odie and hopefully gain the old lady's help. Despite her excitement, she slowed as she approached the door to the boat house. The rusty hinges looked as if they were ready to fall off.

"Who's there?" an unfamiliar voice called from the other side of the door.

Tiana jumped. "Mama Odie?"

The door opened a few inches and the sliver of a face appeared through the slit.

"I said, 'Who's there?'"

It opened a little more. Tiana couldn't make out any of the features, not with the way the person stood in the shadow of the doorway, but she could tell by the shape that this was *not* Mama Odie.

Could they be at the wrong house?

No, this was definitely the house. Weren't any other old fishing boats sitting in big cypress trees around these parts.

"I came to see Mama Odie," Tiana said.

The door opened a bit wider and a young woman walked out into the dimmed sunlight. Her golden brown skin was several shades lighter than Tiana's, and she had a red-and-black chequered kerchief tied around her head. Her eyes were a colour Tiana had never seen before:

a mixture of green and hazel and grey. She was strikingly pretty.

"She's not here," the young woman said.

It felt as if someone had struck Tiana directly in the chest. She shook her head, unwilling to let the words sink in. There was no way she had gone through all this trouble only for Mama Odie to not be there.

"What do you mean she's not here?" Tiana asked. "She *has* to be here! This is her home."

"I know this is her home," the girl said. "But she's not here. Auntie Odie is in New Iberia, visiting her sister. My mama, Clairee."

"No," Tiana whispered. This was the one thing she had not considered. She took a step back, as if she could physically distance herself from the bad news. If not for Naveen catching her by the arm, she would have fallen off the steep wooden step.

"What happened to you?" the girl at the door asked, jutting her chin towards Naveen's hand.

"Ah… I came out on the losing end of a fight with an angry tree branch," he said.

"He cut it on a log while trying to dislodge our boat from some brambles," Tiana murmured, her mind still reeling.

"It don't look good," the girl said. "The way it's puffed up like that means infection is setting in." She looked them both up and down, her face a mask of distrust. But then she backed into the house and held the door open. "Come on in."

Both Tiana and Naveen remained outside.

"Well, come on," the girl said. "You need to get some salve on that hand before you lose it. I'll whip up something." She tilted her head, indicating that they were to follow her.

Once they were alone, Tiana looked to Naveen. "What do you think?" she whispered.

"I am a bit frightened," he admitted. "But my hand, it hurts like… what was that you said? The dickens?"

Tiana sighed. "I guess we should go in. You need to let her see about it. She can't do any more damage."

The moment they entered the house, Naveen's footsteps halted. He stood just past the entryway, his eyes taking in every nook and cranny of the room.

"I've been here before," he said.

Tiana frowned. She wasn't sure what was happening. Naveen wasn't supposed to have any recollection of anything that happened during their time as frogs, but ever since they had taken off on the bayou, Tiana could tell that memories were beginning to return.

She released a nervous laugh. "Don't be ridiculous."

"No, no. I have," Naveen insisted. "I don't know when, but I've been here." He rubbed his chin with his fingers.

"There was a snake. It was a peculiar snake." He put a hand to his head. "It makes no sense, but I *know* it is true."

Just then, the girl returned. She held several colourful glass jars and bottles against her chest. "Come on in the kitchen," she said. "I'm Lisette, by the way," she threw out over her shoulder.

"I'm Tiana, and this here is Naveen. My friends Lottie and Louis are still making their way up the staircase."

"Navigating those stairs takes a lil getting used to," Lisette said.

Tiana followed her into the room where she'd helped Mama Odie whip up a pot of gumbo the last time she had been in this house. She held her breath, waiting for Naveen to mention how familiar this room was, too. But he was uncharacteristically quiet.

There was a large mortar and pestle sitting on the table. The bowl's smooth interior was scored with marks, likely from years of use.

"So, what is it you folks want with Auntie Odie?" Lisette asked. "If you need her to put a spell on someone, I'll tell you now that she don't use her knowledge for stuff like that."

"No, that's not it at all," Tiana said. "I've been here before, and Mama Odie lent her assistance. I was hoping she'd be willing to do it again. You see, I've gotten myself into a bit of a… situation." She wondered how much she should divulge, but what more was there to lose?

Tiana leant a little closer and said, "I got involved with a Vodou man back in N'awlins."

Lisette's eyes lit up. "Oh, y'all came from N'awlins? I love it there."

Tiana thought for a moment. If this young woman was related to Mama Odie… "We really could use some help. But since Mama Odie isn't here, maybe you—"

"I can't do what Auntie Odie can," the young woman said simply. "That's not my gift."

"But—"

"Hey, Mama Odie," Louis's overexcited voice interrupted her. He lumbered inside, Charlotte trailing behind him, out of breath. "You not Mama Odie," he said, looking at Tiana but hooking a thumb towards Lisette. "Who this?"

"Mama Odie is visiting family out of town," Tiana explained. She couldn't stop her shoulders from wilting with disappointment. She wondered if she could wait for the older woman's return.

Charlotte swooped gracefully into a wicker chair as Tiana moved closer to the table. Watching Lisette add several leaves and berries to the mortar, Tiana was struck by the girl's efficiency and how competent she appeared as she measured each ingredient. Her baby-soft skin made her look so young – she couldn't have been more than fifteen years old.

She uncorked a slim bottle, not unlike those Tiana had spotted in Facilier's workshop. The moment the cork was out, a putrid smell rose from the container.

"Faldi faldonza," Naveen said, waving his uninjured hand in front of his nose.

"It's the valerian root," Lisette said. "It has a foul odour, but it will soothe the sting while the ribwort fights the infection."

She sprinkled several of the fragrant leaves into the mortar, then used the pestle to grind it all into a dark green paste.

"If you don't mind my asking, how'd you learn to do this?" Tiana asked.

"My mama taught me," Lisette said. "She's an herbalist, too. I'm still an apprentice, but there's nothing complicated about making a salve to stop infection."

"Your mama and Mama Odie are sisters?"

"Auntie Odie is my mama's older sister. I came to take care of Auntie's house while she visits Mama. She left a few days ago, but she'll be back in about a month's time."

"A month!" Tiana said. "That's way too long." She studied Lisette's face. "Are you sure you don't have any of Mama Odie's special powers?"

Lisette rolled her eyes. "They're not special powers," she lamented. "Do you know anything about Vodou?"

"Not really," Tiana admitted. "I just know that the Shadow Man is causing some awful things to happen around the city with it. And I know that Mama Odie used her… gifts to help me last year."

"I don't know what this Shadow Man is all about, but sounds to me like whatever he's involved in is a lot different from what Auntie Odie and the rest of my family practises. We call on the *Lwa*, the spirits of our ancestors that offer healing and protection from harm. It's used for good, not for evil."

"That's exactly what I need," Tiana said.

"Well, unless you can make it to New Iberia to fetch Auntie Odie, you'll have to wait. And even if you went there to fetch her, I don't think she would come back here until she's done with her visit. She still treats Mama like a little girl, spoiling her rotten."

Lisette stuck her fingers in the concoction she'd made and rubbed the paste between her thumb and forefinger. She brought it to her nose and sniffed, not reacting at all to the pungent aroma.

"I think this will do. Send your boyfriend over here," she said to Tiana.

"He's not – *we're* not… He's not my boyfriend!" Tiana stammered, her face growing hot.

The young girl's brow arched in a way that told Tiana she was not fooling her one bit.

Lisette took Naveen's injured hand in her own and slathered a thick layer of the grainy salve over it. Naveen pinched his face, but as more of the salve went on, his expression turned from one of concern to relief.

"Feel better?" Tiana asked him.

"Yes, it does," he said, a bit of wonder in his voice. "It does."

"I have a scrape from when I fell getting out of the boat," Charlotte said. "Is there a chance I can get some of that smelly green stuff, too?"

"As soon as I'm done with this one here, I'll take care of yours," Lisette said. She lifted a square of cloth from the table and ripped it down the middle, then tore it several more times until there were six narrow strips of fabric. She gently but efficiently wrapped four strips of cloth around Naveen's injured hand. Once she got to the end, she reached under the kerchief covering her head, pulled out a hairpin, and used it to secure the dressing.

"Wow," Naveen said, moving his wrist back and forth as he stared at his hand. "This is impressive," he said. He looked up at Lisette and smiled. "I am very impressed."

"It *is* impressive," Tiana said. "That's a great skill."

Lisette shrugged her shoulder as if making a concoction

that would save Naveen from possibly losing his hand wasn't a big deal.

"We all have our part to play in this world," she said. "Being an herbalist is mine." She brought the mortar over to Charlotte and rubbed some of the salve on Lottie's tiny scrape. "It won't take long for this one to heal. I'll jar some of this up so that you can take it back with you."

Take it with them?

It suddenly occurred to Tiana that she would be on her way back to New Orleans without Mama Odie's help.

Without *any*one's help.

She was on her own. And, it was becoming increasingly evident, in way over her head.

38
TIANA

Tiana's mind swirled with worry as the reality of her situation began to sink in. She paced back and forth in front of the bathtub-shaped cauldron in the middle of the room, the angst building in her bloodstream with each second that passed.

There had to be a way out of this. Maybe if she—? It was possible she could—?

There was nothing!

Once again, she found herself facing a problem she could not solve using her own devices. Putting in extra hours or working harder than anyone else would do her no good when it came to Facilier and his friends on the other side. She was dealing with powers outside of her realm of control.

She stopped walking, a sudden sense of doom crashing over her.

"I can't do this alone," Tiana said in a strained voice. She covered her face in her hands. It felt as if these walls were closing in on her, squeezing her lungs. She hated this feeling. She *never* allowed herself to give up, but she couldn't see a way out.

"Tia?"

Her shoulders stiffened at the sound of Charlotte's voice, but Tiana didn't look at her. She couldn't bear to see Lottie's look of pity staring back at her.

"Umm... Tiana?" came Naveen's sweet voice.

Her hands fell from her face. She was unable to ignore him, no matter how much she wanted to. It wasn't just Naveen and Charlotte, but Louis and even Lisette had come to see about her. They didn't look at her with pity; it was genuine concern on their faces. It made Tiana want to burst into tears.

"What exactly did you need from Auntie Odie?" Lisette asked. "Maybe I *can* help."

"Not if you don't have her powers—"

"*Knowledge,*" Lisette corrected. "And even though I don't have the knowledge Auntie Odie has about such things, there are others who do. Now, tell me about this fella you've gotten yourself mixed up with. Maybe we can figure out a way to get you out of this."

A combination of hope and optimism began to coalesce in her blood.

Tiana stared at the curious faces staring back at her and wondered how much she should say. The less they knew about her dealings with the Shadow Man, the safer they would be.

Then again, they had all come this far with her. She couldn't keep them completely in the dark any longer.

She sniffed, wiping her nose on the sleeve of her filthy shirt. She directed her attention to Lisette but spoke loudly enough so that they would all hear her.

"His name is Dr. Facilier," Tiana started. "People around the neighbourhood always warned us kids to stay away from him. They say he deals in bad magic, and nothing good can come from it."

"I gather the energy he deals in isn't good at all," Lisette said. "Healing energy is at the centre of the Vodou my mama and Auntie Odie grew up practising in Haiti. It's filled with goodness and light and blessings from the ancestors who have gone before us.

"But there are others who choose to use their knowledge for the wrong thing," Lisette said, her voice whisper soft, as if she were afraid someone beyond these walls would hear her. "I've been warned away from those people, too."

"I knew better," Tiana said. "But..." She glanced over at Naveen. "I found myself in a desperate situation. The Shadow Man offered to provide things I had only hoped for in my dreams, something I thought I could never have again." She sucked in a deep breath. "And then he threatened to hurt the people I love."

"He threatened you?" Naveen asked. His brow furrowed with displeasure, and Tiana couldn't deny that it felt nice to see how angry he was on her behalf.

"It felt as if I had no other choice but to take the deal," Tiana said. "I made the choice I thought would give me that thing I really wanted while keeping my loved ones safe.

"But Facilier changed the rules. A few days ago, he demanded I make a new deal. When I told him I wouldn't, he started to make good on his threats. He's caused all kinds of horrible things to happen. But I'm afraid if I give in to his demands this time, he will continue to ask for more and more, and I'll never get out from under his thumb."

Lisette nodded. "Yes, I'm sure he will. You give people like that an inch and they'll take a whole mile. You can't trust this Facilier fella to do the right thing."

"No, I can't," Tiana said. "That's why I came seeking

Mama Odie's help. She's the only person I can think of who would know what to do."

Lisette crossed her arms over her chest, a contemplative frown on her face. After a moment, she said, "There's a possibility there's someone else who can help. She's an old friend of Mama and Auntie Odie. They all grew up together in Port-au-Prince."

"Who is she? *Where* is she?" Tiana asked. "Does she live out here on the bayou?"

Lisette shook her head. "She's back in N'awlins. She lives in the French Quarter."

Tiana threw her head back and sighed up at the ceiling. They'd come all this way when the answer was right at home?

"What's her name?" Tiana asked again. "And can you give us directions to exactly where she lives in the Quarter?"

Lisette screwed up her lips, a confused look on her face. After a minute, she shook her head. "Sorry, but I just don't know enough about N'awlins to tell you how to get there."

Tiana's shoulders wilted.

"But I can *show* you," Lisette piped up. "I may not recall the street names, but I've been to Tee Lande's home with Mama and Auntie several times. I'm pretty sure I'll remember the way once I'm there and can see it for myself."

Tiana was almost afraid to hope. "You're willing to come back with us?"

"You sound like you need the help," she said. "My mama and auntie always taught me to help good people who are in need." She looked Tiana up and down. "You seem like good people."

"I am good people," Tiana rushed out. "I promise I am. Please, Lisette. If Mama Odie can't help me, then I must go to her friend to see if she's willing to do so."

Lisette walked back over to the table where the ingredients she'd used to make the salve still sat. She picked up one of the jars and replaced the cap, slowly tightening it. "Well, I *have* been wanting to go back to N'awlins for quite a while," she finally spoke. "All the tall buildings and streetlights and cars. It's just so dreamy compared to the bayou." Her excitement seemed to build the more she talked. Her eyes lit up as her lips curved in a smile. "Oh, and I want to go to a speakeasy and listen to music. And dance! It's been *so* long since I went out dancing."

She spun in a circle, the hem of her rough ankle-length denim skirt twirling about her legs. She let out a giggle that reminded Tiana that she was still a girl, despite seeming so wise beyond her years.

"I'll make you a deal," Tiana said. "If you come back with us and bring me to… what's her name again?"

"Tee Lande," Lisette said. "She's not my real auntie, but she's always felt like one to me."

"Okay, if you can bring me to your Tee Lande's home in the French Quarter, you can come over to my restaurant and dance your heart out. And then I'll make sure to get you back here to Mama Odie's. Maybe Louis can bring you?" Tiana said, looking to him. "You think so, Louis?"

"Wait," Lisette said before he could answer. "Isn't it almost Mardi Gras?"

"Yes." Tiana nodded. "This coming Tuesday."

"Hmm…" Lisette pulled her bottom lip between her teeth. "I'm supposed to be here taking care of Auntie Odie's house, but I can't go to N'awlins this close to Mardi Gras and then leave before the big day."

Tiana looked to her with cautious hope. "Does that mean you're coming with us?"

Lisette paused for a moment before nodding. "Yeah, I'll take you all to Tee Lande's. And you can take me back after Mardi Gras."

"Oh, thank you!" Tiana launched herself at her, gathering her in a hug. She felt the girl stiffen in her arms. She quickly released her and stepped back. "I'm sorry. I'm just so grateful."

"Yeah, I can tell," Lisette said. She took several steps back and held up her hands. "Here's what we'll do. Y'all will help me get everything in order here at the boat house. I have to make sure all is secure if I'm going to leave Auntie Odie's place for several days. Then, first thing in the morning, we'll set out for N'awlins. It shouldn't take us more than a couple of hours to get there."

"A couple of hours?" Tiana balked. She wasn't so sure Lisette would be able to lead her to this Lande woman's home after all, not if she thought it would only take two hours to make it back to the city.

"I can see what you're thinking," Lisette said. "Don't you worry." That cagey smile returned to her lips, and then she winked. "I know a shortcut."

39
NAVEEN

The Louisiana Bayou
Monday, February 1927
One day before Mardi Gras

Naveen changed position on the bench at the bow of the ship, leaning first on his left elbow, then on his right. He could not find a comfortable position. Most likely because there was no way to get comfortable while he sat here doing nothing but looking out over the murky swamp ahead.

He'd been banished to lookout duty, and he was still brooding over it.

Both Tiana and this Lisette girl – who happened to be just as strong-willed as Tiana – had quickly shot down his offer to help row the boat, even though he assured them that his hand caused him very little discomfort. It stung a little, but that stinky green salve had worked like magic. He could flex all five of his fingers without flinching.

The only thing still making him flinch was his bruised ego. It was difficult to sit here while the others pulled his weight – literally.

Naveen glanced over his shoulder at the others rowing in unison to the tune of Hoagy Carmichael's "Riverboat Shuffle", which Louis hummed.

"Psst…" Naveen whispered at Charlotte as he slid over to where she puffed out laboured breaths with each rotation of her oar. "Here, let me do that," he said, reaching for the long handle. "I insist."

"Oh, thank you," Charlotte said with a grateful sigh.

"Naveen?"

He looked at Tiana. The normally smooth skin of her forehead creased with a frown.

"Please, Tiana. I cannot just sit here and do nothing. You must allow me to row. Just for a little while, eh?"

She stared at him for a moment before a delicate smile curled up one corner of her mouth.

So now she found him funny? Her reactions continued to confound him.

"Why are you smiling?" Naveen asked with much suspicion.

"You don't even realise how much you've changed, do you?" she asked.

He peered at her. "Is it such a big deal that I want to row a boat down a bayou?"

She answered with that musical laugh of hers. "It is a *very* big deal. When I first met you, the idea of you begging to do such menial labour is something I could not fathom."

"Yeah, well, do not hit me in the head with an acorn this time, eh!"

Tiana's eyes widened. "What did you say?"

Naveen frowned. "I… I recall you pitching an acorn. It hit me." He pointed to the top of his head. "Right here. We were in the swamp. I see it so clearly."

"Are you sure?" Charlotte asked.

"Yes!" Naveen said. "But… but that makes no sense." He searched Tiana's face. "Does it?"

"No," she said quickly. "I've never been in the swamp with you before." She gestured at the oar. "You can row for the next ten minutes, and then you're back on navigation duty."

His scalp still prickling with unease, Naveen shook his head, trying to put the disturbing episode from his mind. Had he lost more blood than he had thought?

"And be careful," Tiana added. "I don't want you reinjuring that hand."

"Ah, but as long as I have some of Lisette's wonderful smelly paste, my hand will be just fine."

"The next bit will cost you two nickels and a plate of beignets," Lisette called from just behind him.

"You drive a hard bargain," Naveen responded. "But it is worth it. Seriously, you should sell that stuff. It is marvellous."

"He's right, you know," Tiana told her. "All those factory workers who get hurt while dealing with that machinery would pay good money for your concoctions."

"They would," Naveen said with an enthusiastic nod. "Believe me, I have seen my share of injuries at the sugar mill. If you have one specifically for burns, you could be one of the richest women in New Orleans. It is something to think about. I can even help."

It suddenly occurred to him that those were not just empty words; he actually *could* help her. This past year of working for Mr LaBouff had not only established that he was a pretty good salesman, but also that he *liked* it. And he was good at it.

Maybe he could use that skill to help others.

"Ow!" Naveen howled. He looked down to discover the

dressing covering his wound had begun to unravel, and the wood from the oar was rubbing against his cut.

"See," Tiana said. "I knew something like this would happen." She handed her oar to Charlotte and quickly made her way to his side.

"Here," Lisette said, handing Tiana a stout jar. "Put a little more of the salve on it."

Tiana balanced the jar on her leg and used both hands to unravel the remaining strips of cloth from around his hand. Naveen could barely believe his eyes. The cut looked as if it had been healing for days instead of just overnight.

"Wow," Tiana said. "Naveen's right. You really should bottle this stuff up. I have a friend who has a stall in the French Market. I should introduce you to her. I'll bet she'd sell your salve for you." She looked up at him and grinned. "Not to take the business away from you, but you seem to have your hands full selling sugar."

She returned her attention to his hand. Naveen studied her as she concentrated on smoothing the paste across the wound.

Even the streak of dirt across her cheek could not detract from her beauty. Her hair flew wildly now that it was no longer bound by that ribbon, and he decided he liked it this way.

His eyes were drawn to her mouth as she pulled her bottom lip between her teeth. He had caught her doing the same thing while at the restaurant. He now recognised it as something she did when she was focused on completing a task.

Naveen wondered what she would say if he told her that he was falling in love with her. Maybe she would throw him off the side of the boat.

But, then again, maybe she would tell him that she felt the same way.

There was something about being on this bayou with her, something about their surroundings that conjured a feeling of… what did that French fellow call it? Déjà vu. It felt as if they had been here before, as if this was not the first time he had cruised these canals, talking to her, falling for her.

Tiana looked up at him. Their gazes caught and held.

Naveen's breaths became shallow as something potent and intense flashed between them. Only a few inches separated them, an expanse barely the length of his hand. His eyes still locked with hers, Naveen leant forward.

The boat collided with a wave and bounced up in the air.

Tiana's head snapped back. "Umm… where's the hairpin Lisette used to secure the bandage?" she asked.

It took a moment for her question to register. He was still entranced by their near kiss, his mind caught somewhere in those breath-stealing seconds when his most fervent fantasy had nearly become a reality.

"Naveen?" she called softly.

"Yes?"

"The hairpin? Where is it?"

"I'm not sure," he said, looking to either side of him. "Maybe it slipped down to the deck?"

"Oh, wait! I have something even better." She reached into the front pocket of her coveralls and, after some twisting around, came up with a rose-shaped bauble of some sort. She turned it over in her hand to show him the pin on the back. "This'll keep it in place even better than the hairpin."

"It is a bit fancy for the swamp, but it's not as if I haven't been accused of being overdressed before," Naveen said.

She laughed, the reaction he'd hoped for.

Just as she released the pin from the back of the brooch, they hit another rough patch of water and the piece of jewellery sailed out of her hand and over the side of the boat.

"Oh, no!" Tiana said. She peered over the edge, but there was nothing but foaming green water. "That was a gift from Ms Rose," she said.

"Uh-oh," Charlotte said.

"What?" Naveen asked.

She held her palm out. "Did you feel that?"

"Feel what, Lottie?" Tiana asked.

A deafening crack of thunder pierced the tranquil swamp just as the skies opened and a deluge poured down. The five of them released simultaneous screams.

"Keep rowing," Tiana called. "Maybe we can outrun the storm."

They rowed as fast as the murky waters would allow, but it seemed as if the storm cloud was following them.

"Uh, Tiana, I know we need to get back, but we will have to stop," Naveen called over the roar of the pelting rain.

"We can't," she said. "We're not all that far from the city. Maybe another hour."

"But we can hardly see in front of us. The bayou is so twisty; we may run into the bank again if we aren't careful."

"He's right," Lisette shouted. She pointed to their left. "Look over there. We can tie the boat to that tree stump and find some cover. Hopefully it won't last too much longer."

The rain continued to drench them, and a brisk wind blew as they waited for Tiana's answer.

"Okay," she said. "But if this rain doesn't let up in a half hour, I say we just fight through it."

"Deal," Naveen said.

They rowed towards the tree stump Lisette had pointed out. There was a cavity that looked as if it had been cut out especially for their boat. Once they had secured it, they all ran into a thicket of trees just a few yards away and huddled together underneath a canopy of leafy branches.

The boat rocked violently from side to side as the howling wind whipped up the water. Streaks of lightning stabbed the ground, like a mighty javelin lunging from above.

"Where did this storm even come from?" Tiana asked. "Everything was calm just a few minutes ago."

"Is there anything else that can go wrong on this cursed trip?" Charlotte groused.

"Don't borrow trouble," Tiana told.

"That was supposed to be a joke, Tia. I honestly don't think there *is* anything else that can—"

"The boat!" Lisette cried. "It broke loose!"

"No!" Tiana screamed.

Naveen sprang into action, taking off for the shoreline. That boat was their only way home; he could not let the current drag it down the bayou. He raced towards it, but a second later, Louis whizzed past him.

"I got it!" Louis called before diving into the water. He cut through it like a knife, swimming out to the boat and catching the rope in both of his hands.

"When did Louis learn to swim like that?" Charlotte asked as she caught up with Naveen.

"Come on," Tiana called. "We need to help him pull the boat in."

They all waited on the bank of the canal for Louis to arrive back with the boat.

"Good job, my friend," Naveen said as he gave him a hearty pat on the back. "You swam out there like you've been doing it all your life."

"We got lots of ponds up there in Shreveport," Louis said. He and Tiana shared a smile, which, again, confused Naveen. But he had no time to ponder what that meant.

The rain still poured, but it had let up enough for them to see.

"Tiana had the right idea," Naveen said. "If we hang around here, the boat will just collect rainwater. I say we continue now that the rain isn't coming down as hard."

"Let's get on with it," Tiana said.

They all climbed back in the boat and started paddling up the canal, but it only took a few moments for Naveen to sense that something was very, very wrong.

"Are we… sinking?" Charlotte asked, putting voice to Naveen's fear.

"What did you say about this trip being cursed?" Lisette asked. She pointed at her feet, where water gurgled up from a puncture in the boat's flat bottom. "I think you may be right."

40
FACILIER

Facilier paced back and forth, nearly slipping several times along the algae-covered dock that lined the bank of the Mississippi River. The briny, viscid seaweed had invaded the city, climbing up from the river and clawing its way across the piers, railroad and market and into the Quarter. The city workers with their shovels and rakes were no match for the slimy invasion.

Facilier had long before stopped trying to shield his nose from the pungent odour of fish, shrimp and whatever other sea creatures the dirty men hauled in big nets from their fishing boats. Every so often one would ask him if he wanted to buy a bucket of trout, or oysters, or catfish, but they mainly left him alone, which was exactly how he liked it.

He didn't want to involve anyone else in this business he

had with Tiana. He didn't need any nosy people coming to her rescue, as if she were a damsel in distress. They didn't realise just how crafty she was. But he knew.

Facilier pulled out his pocket watch to check the time.

Where is that girl?

He had only one day left. If he didn't get her signature on that contract before sundown tomorrow, he was done for.

That father of hers had been adamant that she would be back by now.

Unless she *was* back and he had missed her.

Facilier had been so sure she and that motley crew she ran with would be easy to spot among all these fishermen, but seeing how busy this dock was – combined with the fog that had grown so thick he could barely see anything more than two yards away – they could have slipped past him without his taking notice. Especially if Tiana had seen him first.

Damn her!

His heart began to race as he intensified his search, going up to various fishmongers and boat captains, asking if they'd seen a girl travelling with several other young people. If Tiana and her friends had returned, someone would have noticed. LaBouff's prissy daughter would stick out like a sore thumb among these mangy, hardened fishermen.

He sprinted from one boat to another until he was sure he'd talked to every fisherman here. No one had seen anyone resembling Tiana or any of the others.

Well, he was done waiting.

"I'm going to do what I should have done from the very beginning," Facilier snarled.

His topcoat whipped around him as he turned and headed for the crowded gangway that bridged the dock to the market. He headed straight for the streetcar on St Charles Avenue and rode it until they reached his destination uptown.

Yes, he'd wanted to do this the elegant way – the way that guaranteed less mess, less risk.

But the time for keeping things close to the vest was over.

He stepped off in front of the white mansion he'd looked at from afar so many times over the years. He dusted the dirt from his coat and straightened his top hat. Then he stalked up the walkway as if he owned the place.

Because, if he played his cards right, soon, he would.

41
TIANA

Tiana wasn't sure she'd ever felt more relieved than when their boat rounded the shaded bend and the egress of the bayou came into view. She could see the white dome that sat atop the twenty-plus stories of the Hibernia Bank Building, the tallest building in the city.

But that was all she could see.

A corpulent greenish cloud shrouded the city. It even obscured the spires that sat atop the cathedral. Tiana had never seen anything like it.

"That doesn't look good," Naveen said from over her shoulder.

"No, it doesn't," Tiana said. "But at least we're almost there. I don't know how much longer that tarp will hold the water out."

Tiana still wasn't sure why Lisette had packed a tarp for a couple of days in the city, but she wasn't questioning her. Stuffing the hole in the bottom of their boat had saved them.

A troubling thought suddenly occurred to her as they neared the approach to the Mississippi River.

"Guys, I don't think we can paddle this boat against the current of the river, especially with that thick algae covering it. It's been hard enough rowing along the bayou, and those waters were relatively calm."

"I think you're right," Lisette said.

"Wait a minute." Tiana held up a hand. She pointed to a rickety pier that had seen better days. "See those railroad tracks just beyond this old pier? They lead to the main docks. I think we should tie the boat here and find the fisherman that rented it to us. Maybe he can get someone to come out with a motored boat and pull it back to the dock."

Tiana shuddered at the thought of what it would cost to cover the damage that had been done. She wouldn't be surprised if it depleted what little savings she had been able to amass since buying their building in Tremé. But it would be worth it if this Lande woman Lisette spoke of could provide the help Tiana needed to finally defeat Facilier.

They navigated their boat to the pier. The dark green sludge that coated the entire structure made it a thousand times more difficult to tie the boat down, but they were able to secure it with double knots to one of the wooden beams. With the way her luck had been going since that big rainstorm hit, the entire beam would probably break away and send the boat sailing back down the canal before the fisherman could get back here to pick it up.

Once out of the boat, the five of them started down the train tracks that ran along the shore's edge. They arrived at the main dock twenty minutes later.

"My goodness," Tiana cried with a gasp. The sludge was even thicker there. It covered every surface, its mouldy, putrid smell permeating the air.

Tiana searched through the miasma of imposing fog, algae and confused people, hunting for the old man with the scar on his face from whom she'd rented the boat. She found him in the same spot where he'd been two days earlier.

"You're back," the fisherman greeted. He looked around. "Where's my boat?"

"About the boat," Tiana started. She quickly explained the trouble they'd encountered and how they'd burned up the motor. "But I will cover the cost of all repairs," Tiana assured him.

The fisherman huffed out an aggravated breath. "That's one of my best," he said. Then he shrugged his bony shoulders. "Though I know the bayou can be brutal. You say it's down at the old pier just before Arabi?"

She nodded. "We tied it to one of the beams. I'll go back and get it, but it will have to wait until later this afternoon."

The man was shaking his head. "I'm gonna need it before then." He gestured to the other boats leaving the dock, bobbing along the choppy, scum-covered water. "This here is selling time, and you're already late bringing it back."

"I know, sir!" Tiana said. "But—"

"There's no buts about it. I need my boat, girlie. Now, you get it or I'm gonna have to call the authorities."

"Tiana." Naveen put his hand on her shoulder. Tiana whipped around to face him. "I can go back for the boat. Louis, you'll come with me, eh?" he asked.

"Yeah. Sure I can," Louis said.

Naveen turned back to her, his penetrating eyes pleading with her to accept his help. "You don't have to do this all on your own. We're here for you. *I'm* here for you."

Tiana hesitated as a blend of uncertainty and gratitude converged. This was her mess. She'd pulled them all into this; she shouldn't expect her friends to get her out of it.

But Naveen was right: she didn't have to do this alone. She couldn't.

"Okay," Tiana answered.

The shame she thought she would feel didn't materialise. All she felt was overwhelming relief at knowing she didn't have to rely solely on herself.

An embarrassed flush raced across the fisherman's craggy face. "Well, maybe I can go out there with you two," he said, contriteness suffusing his voice.

Tiana turned to him. "I meant what I said about covering the cost of repairs. I pay my debts," she said.

The old man waved her off. But then his eyes narrowed.

"Hey, wait a minute. You're the one with that supper club in Tremé, aren't ya?"

Tiana nodded.

He snapped his fingers. "Thought so. There was a fella here asking about ya not long ago."

An unwelcome sense of dread washed over her. "Someone asking about me?" Tiana asked.

"Yep. Tall skinny fella." He plopped a hand on top of his head. "Had on a big ol' hat. One of those fancy kinds."

Facilier.

"Thank you for letting me know," she said. "And thanks for being so understanding."

Naveen clamped his hands on her shoulders and turned her to look at him. "It is him, is it not? That Shadow guy."

She nodded. There was no need to withhold the truth.

"I am coming with you," Naveen said.

She shook her head. "No. Please, just help him to get his boat back." She released a deep breath. "I'll take care of the Shadow Man."

"Are you sure?" he asked. The concern in his voice wrapped around her, providing comfort she hadn't realised she so desperately needed.

"Yes, I'm sure," Tiana answered. "Thank you, but I can handle this."

Naveen seemed reluctant to let go of her shoulders, but after several seconds passed, he finally did.

"Tia, you sure you're okay, sugar?" Charlotte asked.

"I will be once I talk with this woman Lisette is taking me to see," she said.

"Okay. Well, in that case, I'm catching a taxicab home," Charlotte said. "I need to burn these clothes and spend the next three hours in a nice hot bubble bath."

Tiana walked over to her and wrapped her in a hug. "Thanks for all your help out on the bayou, Lottie. You really stepped up."

"Well, what did you expect – that I would let my best friend down?" she replied. "I will always be here when you need me, Tia. Remember that." She pulled back slightly and narrowed her eyes. "Unless you need me right now, because I am serious about that bath."

"Go clean up," Tiana said. "Get ready for tonight."

"Tonight?"

"Yes," Tiana said. "It's Shrove Monday. I'm not letting

the Shadow Man ruin the big day-before-Mardi-Gras celebration."

Tiana turned to Lisette.

"Take me to your Tee Lande."

42
TIANA

Tiana and Lisette took off for the French Quarter.

As they made it past the dock, Tiana had a difficult time comprehending what she was seeing. It looked like something out of a nightmare. The foetid vegetation that covered the river and dock had invaded the city, climbing across the train tracks and over the stalls of the French Market. The slimy growth covered the abandoned baskets of the vendor's wares, as if people had dropped everything and scurried away with all haste.

Her horror only escalated as they marched on. The algae had made its way into the French Quarter; it had climbed up the exterior walls and wrought-iron galleries of the structures that lined Decatur Street.

As they waited on the other side of the street while a line of cars passed, Tiana cringed at the nauseating sound the

Model Ts made rolling over the boggy substance with their tyres. She would probably hear the sickening squish in her sleep for years to come.

"It's this way." Lisette motioned for her to follow. "Down this promenade."

"You sure you remember?" Tiana asked as they made their way along the walkway between Jackson Square and the Pontalba Townhouses.

"I'm sure," Lisette said. "She lives in this big red building. There's a courtyard that has a stone fountain in the middle of it, and the fountain has a bunch of little naked babies carved into the sides of it."

"Cherubs?"

"Whatever they're called," Lisette said with a shrug. "They're naked and holding musical instruments. Tee Lande is on the second floor. I can't remember which place exactly, but I know she's there."

Lisette gasped when they arrived at the end of the promenade. She pointed to their left. "Look at that!"

Tiana pressed her fist to her mouth as she tried to make sense of what was happening. The algae undulated, rolling towards the steps of St Louis Cathedral, then retreating just as quickly, as if an invisible force fought to keep it at bay. An odd but undeniably radiant energy resonated from the area surrounding the church. Its creamy alabaster-coloured facade remained pristine while everything around it was overrun by the dark green sludge.

What kind of terror had Facilier unleashed?

"I don't know what's going on, but I have to stop it," Tiana said.

"Let's hurry and get to Tee Lande's," Lisette said. "She'll know what to do."

"What if she's moved since the last time you were here?" Tiana called after her.

"She's lived in that building as long as I've been alive. She's there. Trust me."

It wasn't easy to put her faith in a teenage girl who didn't really know the city, but what choice did she have?

They hurried beyond the cathedral and the convent.

"Here it is," Lisette said, stopping at the gate of a deep red brick building with pretty flower baskets hanging from ornate wrought-iron galleries. "See, I told you," she said, looking back at Tiana and smiling as if guiding her to a random building in the Quarter proved anything. They entered the gate and found their way to the courtyard. The fountain etched with cherubs sat in the centre of it, just as Lisette claimed it would.

Tiana surveyed the area, hoping for any telltale sign that would indicate which of these flats housed a Vodou lady from Haiti.

"I think you're looking for me."

She whipped around.

A tall, stunningly gorgeous woman stood a few feet away, a wicker basket overflowing with stems of fragrant lavender hooked on the crook of her arm. She wore a gauzy, flowing caftan. Colourful embroidered flowers ran along the neckline and hem of the pale peach dress.

Tiana stopped short. Something about her eyes seemed familiar.

"I've been expecting you," the woman said.

"Tee Roselande!" Lisette ran to her, enveloping her in a hug.

Shock rooted Tiana where she stood. She wasn't hunched over, and she was no longer wearing layers and layers of clothes, but…

"Ms Rose?" she whispered.

"Wait, you already know my Tee Lande?" Lisette asked.

"I know *Rose* the flower vendor," Tiana said.

"Hello, Tiana," the woman replied. She wrapped an arm around Lisette, who continued to stare up at her with worshipful eyes. "Your trip to Odie's place took longer than I anticipated it would."

"How do you know where I went? What… what is happening?"

"I gather you lost the brooch I gave you," Ms Rose said

as her gaze travelled from the tip of Tiana's feet to the top of her head.

Tiana knew she looked a fright, with her tattered, mud-stained clothes.

"But," the woman continued, "I trust it provided at least some protection for you while on your journey. I'm sorry that I could not do more, but my giving you the brooch very likely tested the limits of what is allowed."

"Allowed?"

"By the universe," Ms Rose said. "Much has been imposed upon it already because of your involvement with Facilier."

Tiana released a shocked gasp. She took several steps back. "What do you know about Facilier?"

"I know much more about him than you do, which is why you need to listen to what I have to say. The universe is not at all pleased."

The woman was talking in riddles with her vague assertions about the universe. It compounded Tiana's bewilderment over discovering that the old flower monger apparently knew more about her than she'd first thought. Her head was swirling.

"You've... you've been lying," Tiana said. "You've been lying to me... manipulating me... this entire time." The hurt and confusion clogging her throat made it difficult to get the words out.

"I have not," Ms Rose said.

"Can someone explain what's going on?" Lisette asked.

Ms Rose turned to the girl. "I just made a batch of those tea cakes you love. Why don't you go up and have some? We'll be right there."

Tiana was shaking her head. "No, *we* won't," she said, backing away.

"Tiana." The woman's voice was stern. Uncompromising. "There is no time for you to be upset with me. There are powerful forces at play here, much more powerful than you or I. More powerful than the Shadow Man. Facilier doesn't have the powers you think he has. *He's* the one who has been manipulating you." She hitched her head towards the staircase Lisette had climbed up. "Follow me. I'll explain everything."

"No!" Tiana stated more forcefully. The woman's brows shot up. "I don't know who you are," Tiana said. "With your flowers and your paintings and all your other gifts. What was that about?"

"I will explain," Ms Rose said, her tone even harder than before.

Tiana refused to be intimidated. She'd been lied to,

manipulated. Again. What kind of game was this woman playing with her? "I'm supposed to just trust you?"

"Yes," Ms Rose stated. "I'm the only one who can help. And at this point, I'm not sure how much. There is no time to waste."

Tiana backed away, not wanting to turn for fear of what the woman would do.

She didn't know what to think. Or whom to trust.

"I've put up with enough lies from the Shadow Man," Tiana said. "As far as I'm concerned, you're no better than he is."

She turned on her heel and raced out of the courtyard, past the gate, and to the only sanctuary she could think of.

43
TIANA

Tiana was out of breath by the time she reached Tremé. Still, a cry of relief broke free as the supper club came into view.

She *needed* to be there. Even though the thought of having to get through an entire dinner service – cooking, entertaining patrons, cleaning up after all was done – made her want to collapse, she needed the comfort of the place she and her daddy had built.

She cut through the alley that led to the back entrance of the supper club, but before she entered, Tiana took a moment to collect herself.

A jagged, painful sense of betrayal threatened to overwhelm her at the thought of Ms Rose – Roselande – lying to her all this time. She'd considered the woman something of a friend. Had Ms Rose been pretending during their neighbourly chats? Was Tiana just a pawn in some game between Roselande and Facilier? A game she'd never agreed to play in the first place?

Maybe she should have stuck around and demanded the woman explain herself. Ms Rose owed her at least that much after months of deceiving her.

She swiped at the angry tears that she hadn't even realised had started to fall.

It was imperative she not show any sign that anything was amiss. Given the time of day, her daddy was likely in there preparing for that night's dinner service. If he had an inkling of what was going on, Tiana wasn't sure what he would do. Or what Facilier would do in retaliation.

"Just get through tonight," she told herself. "Take this prep time to think things through, to find another solution."

She would figure out how to take care of the Shadow Man on her own, without Roselande's help.

When she walked inside, she spotted her daddy standing at the prep station. Her dark mood immediately lifted at the sight of him.

"Hey there, baby girl," he called, his ever-present smile as warm as a comforting hug. "You back from seeing your friend? How is she?"

"Hey, Daddy," Tiana answered, then walked over and gave him a kiss on the cheek. "Yes, I am. My friend… well."

She waved that off. "It's not important. It's so good to see you, Daddy."

"You saw me the day before yesterday." He laughed as he expertly diced bell peppers into uniform pieces.

"But it's *always* good to see you," Tiana said. "It's something I've learned to never take for granted."

"That's a good lesson to learn," he said. He glanced over at her and frowned. "You get caught up in a storm or something, baby girl?"

Tiana looked down at her filthy clothes. Maybe she should have gone home first; maybe Charlotte had had the right idea. She needed a bath.

"I did," she said. "The rain caught me on my way back to N'awlins. I'll go get cleaned up soon." She walked over to where her apron hung on a hook near the rear of the kitchen. "But I should start on the gumbo before I do. Once it's cooking, Addie Mae can watch it while I run home and bathe."

"If she ever shows up," her daddy said. "I haven't seen or heard from her all day."

Tiana's fingers fumbled in the middle of tying the apron around her waist. That didn't sound like Addie Mae.

"I wonder if she fell ill," she murmured. She wished Addie Mae had a telephone, but Southern Bell's service was still a rarity in most households in the city. "Let me get to this gumbo, and then I'll see if I can find Lil Johnny Taylor to go check on her."

She scrubbed the dirt from her hands and underneath her nails, then filled her daddy's big gumbo pot with water. Together they took it over to the cooker. She then made quick work of chopping up the remaining vegetables and adding them to the pot, along with chicken and andouille sausage.

A now-familiar sense of dread climbed up Tiana's spine as she walked over to the pantry and moved the jar of green beans to the side. There behind it stood the small vial filled with the potion Facilier had given her, next to the larger one he'd shoved upon her at the market. The potion meant to keep her Daddy alive, next to the one he wanted her to put into all her dishes to keep their deal going.

Facilier doesn't have the powers you think he has. He's *the one who has been manipulating you.*

Roselande's earlier assertion pried at a question that had puzzled Tiana since Thursday night, when Facilier had suddenly changed the rules of their deal. She'd balked at the flimsy excuse he'd given her as to why she needed to start adding the larger potion to all of her dishes. It hadn't made sense, and he had never explained the reasoning behind it.

"He doesn't have the powers you think he has," Tiana whispered as she continued to stare at the vials. Could it be? Could that be one thing Roselande had been honest about?

For months, had Facilier used whatever was in that small bottle to control *her*, not her daddy? Had he convinced her to do his bidding, not with magic, but with his words, his illusions?

He *was* a master manipulator.

She slid the beans back into place and left the potions – both of them – where they were. This batch would not include Facilier's contribution.

"You okay in there, baby girl?"

Tiana cleared her throat. "Yeah, Daddy. I'll be right out."

She left the pantry and returned to her gumbo, trying her hardest to quell her unease. She could very well risk everything she loved with the decision she'd just made, but this was more than just a gut feeling.

She knew that Facilier had deceived her more than once with his mind games, tricking her into thinking she was standing in the restaurant of her dreams or that he'd harmed her parents.

Well, her daddy was right there in the kitchen, alive and healthy.

Tiana went over to the cooker and lowered the fire under the pot.

"Daddy, I'm gonna let this simmer for a bit while I look for Lil Johnny. I'll send him to check on Addie Mae."

She lucked out and found Lil Johnny Taylor just a couple of blocks away from the restaurant. Tiana paid him a nickel to run over to Addie Mae's house and return with word about why she had not shown up for work.

When she returned to the restaurant, she found her daddy standing over the gumbo pot.

"It isn't burning, is it?" Tiana asked.

He looked over his shoulder, a sheepish grin on his handsome face. "No, you caught me stealing a taste."

Tiana burst out laughing, something she couldn't imagine herself doing just an hour before.

James sipped the brown liquid from a big cooking spoon. "Mmm… that's a good gumbo." He took another sip, then broke out in an awful, body-racking cough.

Panic sent her running. "Daddy!"

Tiana grabbed the spoon from him and tossed it aside.

What had she done? Why had she taken a chance with that potion?

"I'm fine." Her daddy pounded his chest, his smile returning. "Gumbo just went down the wrong pipe is all. That's what I get for sneaking a taste before it's done."

Relief made her muscles weak. Her hand trembled as she covered her forehead with her palm. "You scared me."

"Everything's okay. Don't get yourself so worked up, baby girl." He gestured towards the dining room.

"Why don't you go out there and get the tables ready for tonight? And then you can head home to wash off and dress for the big Shrove Monday dinner crowd. I'll do the same once Carol Anne and Jodie get here to watch the kitchen."

Tiana nodded, but her entire body still hummed with anxiety. Something wasn't right. She felt it in her bones.

She entered the dining room and went about straightening the tablecloths and centrepieces. Her hurt and anger came roaring back at the sight of the flowers Ms Rose – Roselande – had given her for the restaurant. As she picked up some petals that had fallen onto the table, she had a mind to toss all the flowers away. Same with all the paintings hanging up around here.

She looked over at the most recent one the woman had gifted her and blinked in confusion. She dropped the flower petals and raced to it, her mind unwilling to register what her eyes were clearly seeing.

Or *not* seeing.

Nearly all the people were gone. Of the half dozen colourfully outfitted Mardi Gras Indians in the original portrait, only one remained.

Tiana slowly shook her head as she backed away from the painting. This couldn't be right. Someone was playing tricks on her again.

"Miss Tiana! Miss Tiana!" Lil Johnny Taylor rushed through the restaurant's front entrance. "Miss Addie Mae is gone," he said.

Icy fear wrapped around her heart like a fist.

"What do you mean she's gone? Was her mother at home?"

Lil Johnny nodded. "She was. Miss Phyllis said Addie Mae went to fetch some things at the market and was supposed to bring them back home before leaving for work, but she never did. I went to the market, but nobody's there on account of that green stuff growing everywhere."

Tiana's rising panic refused to subside. "Thanks, Lil Johnny," Tiana told the boy, slipping him another nickel.

Facilier was behind all of this. She had no doubt about it.

"Daddy," Tiana called as she entered the kitchen. But she found Carol Anne and Jodie there instead.

"Mr James just left," Carol Anne said. "He said he'll be back in time for the dinner service."

Tiana nodded. "Have either of you talked to Addie Mae?"

Both girls shook their heads.

"Tia! Tia!" Charlotte burst through the swinging door and into the kitchen. "Oh, Tia!"

"Lottie, what's the matter?" Tiana captured her friend

by her shoulders. She was still wearing her mud-stained trousers. "What's going on?"

"It's Big Daddy! He's missing!"

Tiana's entire body went rigid, while Lottie's shook like a leaf in the middle of a hurricane.

"What do you mean? What makes you think he's missing?"

"He's not home."

"Maybe he's at the mill."

"He's not." Lottie was shaking her head. "I just came from there. No one at the mill has seen him, either." She walked back into the dining room, cradling her head in her hands. "Oh, Tia, I don't know what to do."

Just then, Naveen and Louis arrived, both looking as if they actually had come through a hurricane. Their clothes were covered in muck, and they reeked of dank, smelly rot.

Naveen hooked a thumb towards the door. "I don't know what's going on out there, but it looks as if the swamp followed us back here. That slimy green sludge is everywhere."

"And the fog is worse than ever," Louis piped up.

Charlotte turned to them. "Naveen, have you seen Big Daddy?"

"Mr LaBouff?"

"Yes. No one knows where he is, not even his closest friends. Big Daddy would never just up and leave without telling a single soul where he was going. Alfred said he's been gone since this morning. It isn't like Big Daddy to leave without saying anything to anybody."

"Don't get yourself worked up," Tiana told her, running her hand up and down her friend's arm to soothe her, even though her own nerves felt as though they were twisting and tying into knots.

"What's that?" Charlotte pointed to tiny specks of dirt that dotted the tablecloth. Tiana went to dust them away, and dozens of bugs took flight.

She screeched, running away from the table. But the bugs were suddenly everywhere, swarming around in the same way the mosquitoes had attacked on Saturday.

Ms Rose's flowers! The winged insects flew out of the centre of each bud and whizzed around the dining room like a tornado. Terror shot through Tiana as she thought about the mosquitoes at Congo Square.

She scrambled into the kitchen.

"Shut everything off!" Tiana called out to Carol Anne and Jodie. "Just shut off the stove and leave that food there. Get out! *Get out!*"

44
TIANA

"Tiana! Tiana, where you going?"

She could hear Louis hustling to keep up with her, but she had no time to waste. "I've got something I need to do," she called over her shoulder. "Go and see about Lottie."

"Naveen is taking care of Charlotte. I'm coming with you."

"No," Tiana said, hastening her steps.

"You're going to the Shadow Man, aren't you?

Tiana stopped and turned to him. "Please, Louis, I have to do this alone."

"Let me join you, Tiana."

Tiana shook him off, determined not to endanger the life of another loved one. "No."

Louis flinched. He stepped back, his face a mask of hurt.

"I'm sorry," Tiana said. "I know you want to help, but please, Louis, just listen to me. I will handle this."

He didn't say another word – simply nodded, turned and walked back the way they'd come.

Tiana started to go after him, but she needed to get to Facilier. She would smooth things over with Louis later. She pivoted and continued on her mission. The fog was so thick she could only see a couple of feet in front of her, but she didn't let it deter her. She once again had a sense that something was following close behind.

She moved so fast down the pavement she was practically running in her haste to get to the French Quarter and Facilier's dark, creepy emporium. Her skin crawled at the thought of crossing the threshold of that purple door. There was a sinister weight to the air inside Facilier's home, as if evil was not only allowed, but welcomed.

Tiana's feet stopped short.

She didn't have to bother with going to his home, because he was right there, three feet away from her. The fog obscured his facial features, but she would have known that top hat anywhere.

He sat at a small wooden table on the street corner near Jackson Square, an array of playing cards spread out before him. He riffled the rest of the deck, shuffling them with one hand. He called out to a gentleman passing by and gestured to the cards, but the man shook his head and continued walking.

His eyes still focused on the man who had just shunned him, Facilier said, "I wondered when you would show up, Tiana."

The blood drained from her face as the sound of her own heartbeat pounded in her ears.

"Where are Addie Mae and Mr LaBouff?" Tiana hissed. "And where is Mr Salvaggio? I know you're behind their disappearances." Facilier continued to shuffle the cards. "Well, are you gonna answer me?" Tiana asked.

"I warned you," was his answer. He slowly turned to face her. A sinister smile played at the corners of his lips. "You're the one who decided not to heed my warning."

"And I warned *you* that you'd best leave my family and friends out of this!"

"Some friend you are," Facilier snarled. "I'll bet you haven't noticed those other two were even gone."

Tiana frowned, but then she remembered Maddy coming up to her on Saturday. "You have Georgia and Eugene!"

"Oh, *now* you remember them?"

She shoved hard, toppling his table and sending the playing cards flying into the air. "Where are they!" she yelled.

Facilier righted the table, then perched himself on its corner. He studied his fingernails for a moment before buffing them on the collar of his vest.

"You let them go, you hear me? Let them go right now!"

Like a deadly lion pouncing on its prey, he launched himself at her, his sneering grimace stopping only inches from her face.

"Or what, Tiana? What is it you *think* you can do to me? You have no power. *I'm* the one who holds all the cards here."

Just then, a stiff wind blew, and the playing cards that had scattered on the ground whirled around like a cyclone. Tiana watched in fascinated horror as, one by one, the cards flew into Facilier's waiting hand. His maniacal laugh echoed around her.

"I warned you not to trifle with me, little girl. The consequences of your actions go far beyond just you."

Without warning, Ms Rose's words slammed into her brain.

The drum is beaten in the grass, but it is at home that it comes to dance.

Her actions had repercussions for her entire family. She had brought this upon everyone.

Facilier reached into the inside pocket of his vest and

produced that blasted contract. "Now, for the last time, sign this!"

She shoved his hand away. "I'm not signing anything," Tiana said. "You can't make me, because you have no real power. Just tricks. Roselande told me so."

His body stiffened in shock, his eyes bulging with instant rage. Tiana took an unconscious step back.

"Watch it, Tiana. You're playing the wrong hand. Bring Roselande into this, and you'll be sorry."

"Tiana! Tiana!"

She turned at the sound of Louis's panicked voice. "Louis, I told you not to follow me!"

"It's Mr James," Louis called from down the street.

His words snatched the breath from Tiana's lungs. She took off running, hearing Facilier's deep, rumbling laugh behind her.

Tiana caught up with her friend, reaching her arms out as if to buoy herself. "What's going on? What's happened?"

"It's your daddy, Tiana," Louis puffed out. "You need to get to the house – now!"

45

TIANA

Tiana rushed through the front door and stopped, dread rooting her where she stood. She pressed a hand to her chest at the sight of her father's huge body sprawled on the sofa, his head cradled in her mother's lap. His skin was ashen and wrinkled. He looked years older than he had when she'd seen him at the restaurant just an hour before.

"I'll be right back," she heard Louis say, but all her focus was on her parents. Tiana hurried to their side. She knelt down on the floor next to them and took her father's hand in hers. His fingers were gnarled, the skin papery thin.

"What's going on, Mama?"

"I don't know," she answered. Her mother looked up at her and Tiana saw true fear in her eyes. "He was just fine when he came home. He went into the bathroom to wash up and get ready for the big night at the supper club. When he came out, his hands had wrinkled up like a dried prune. I thought maybe he'd soaked in the tub too long, but then I noticed the grey hair at his temples."

The grey was no longer just at his temple. More than half of her daddy's beautiful dark brown hair was now peppered with wiry grey strands.

"Hey, baby girl," he called, his voice a thready whisper. He peered up at her with rheumy eyes. "I don't think I can make it to the supper club tonight." He coughed. "I don't know why I'm so tired."

"Don't worry about the restaurant," Tiana said. "We won't be opening tonight anyway." She wouldn't explain about the bugs or the food they'd left abandoned. None of that was important at the moment.

The restaurant.

The vials were there. Tiana wondered – if she gave the usual potion to him now, would his illness be reversed?

"Mama, I have something that may help. I'll be back as soon as I can."

She raced from the house, making it to the supper club and back home in record time. She hastened to her father's side and uncapped the smaller vial.

"Here, Daddy," Tiana said, putting the vial up to his lips. "Drink this."

"What's that you're giving him?" her mother asked in a panicked voice.

"Just give it a few minutes, Mama. Trust me."

But could she trust Facilier to have been telling the truth? She still didn't trust the new larger concoction, but what about the one she'd been using these past months? Did this tincture really have any effect whatsoever on her father's fate?

Tiana could hear her heartbeat thumping in her ears as the seconds ticked by. She zeroed in on the grey hairs on her father's head, willing them to start turning back to their dark brown colour. She studied the wrinkles creasing his once-smooth skin, praying they would even out.

"Come on, come on, come on," Tiana murmured. But after several minutes had passed, it was clear the potion she'd been adding to her gumbo all this time was truly worth nothing. It had all been a charade.

That damn Shadow Man.

There was a knock at the door.

"You expecting somebody?" Tiana asked her mother. Eudora shook her head.

She walked over to the front door and opened it. Lisette stood outside on the porch. "Tee Lande told me where to find you," she said.

Tiana's first instinct was to turn her away, but Lisette

had done nothing wrong. In fact, she'd helped when she had no incentive to do so.

"Come in," Tiana said, moving out of the way so that she could enter. "Mama. Daddy. This is my friend, Lisette. Lisette, this is my mother, Eudora, and my father, James."

"Hello," Lisette said. Her eyes immediately zeroed in on James. "He isn't well."

"No, he isn't," Eudora said. As if to punctuate her statement, James coughed again. It was hoarse and brittle and sent a chill down Tiana's spine.

"He's very weak," Eudora continued.

Lisette walked over to the sofa and went to touch James's forehead, but Eudora pushed her hand away.

"You don't have to worry, Mama. Lisette is an herbalist. She's a healer. If anybody can help Daddy, she can."

Lisette laid the back of her hand to James's forehead, then along his forearms. She used her fingertips to gently press against his glands, starting behind his ears and travelling down his neck until she reached his chin.

Tiana stood back and watched as the young girl went through a methodical assessment of her father's symptoms.

"He isn't feverish," Lisette said. "But that cough doesn't sound good at all."

There was another knock on the door. Before Tiana could answer it, Naveen and Louis walked in.

"I brought Naveen to see if he could help," Louis said.

"Thank you, Louis," Tiana said. "And I'm sorry. You know, for earlier." She owed him that apology for being so cross, but in true Louis fashion, he seemed to have no ill will towards her.

"It's okay, Tiana," he said.

Naveen came to stand behind her. He put one hand on her shoulder and gave it another of those reassuring squeezes. Despite all the months she'd spent avoiding him, Tiana could not have been more grateful to have him near her right now.

"Where's Lottie?" she asked.

"She's at home, waiting for her father to return," he answered.

Tiana's stomach flipped as she remembered the conversation with Dr. Facilier. He had Mr LaBouff and all the rest; she had no doubts about that. Tiana was determined to find them, but she had to figure out what was ailing her father, too.

"I don't understand what's happening," Tiana said, looking down at him. "He was just cooking with me at the restaurant. How did he become so frail, so quickly?"

"I'm not sure what it is, either," Lisette said. "But I can whip up a tincture to help build up his strength and get rid of that cough."

She gathered her skirts around her and pushed herself up from where she'd knelt next to the sofa.

"Here's what I'll need." She listed a number of herbs, many of which Tiana fortunately had in the kitchen.

"I don't know where we're going to get ivy leaves," Tiana said.

"There are several herbalists in the French Quarter. You may have to ask around, but I'm sure someone has some."

"I'll go to the Quarter," Louis volunteered.

"Bring back as much as you can," Lisette told him. She looked down at Tiana's father. "At the very least, it'll keep him comfortable."

"What can I do?" Tiana asked. She couldn't just stand there while her father suffered.

"You can show me to the kitchen and help me get started. We'll have to grind the thyme and elderflower into a powder. If we get started now, we can be done by the time the scaly one is back with the ivy leaves."

Tiana kissed her daddy on the forehead, then led Lisette to the kitchen. They spent the next half hour collecting and preparing the ingredients for the medicinal syrup, and once Louis returned with the ivy leaves, Lisette was able to complete the final steps. The young girl also made a broth with the marrow from chicken bones Tiana had set aside for soup stock.

"Okay," Lisette said, carrying a coffee mug filled with the concoction into the living room where Tiana's father lay. "Try to get him to drink at least half of this."

After handing the mug to Eudora, Lisette joined Tiana, Naveen and Louis, who all stood by, nervously watching James sip the steaming liquid.

In just the hour since she'd returned home, her father seemed to have aged another ten years. Spots dotted his hands and forearms, and the skin around his mouth and eyes had wrinkled even more.

Tiana placed a hand on Lisette's forearm. "Thank you."

"Now it's just rest and prayers," Lisette said with a shrug. "I wish I could do more. Maybe Tee Lande can help."

Tiana hesitated.

"Tee Lande isn't a bad person, and I don't like you thinking she is," Lisette said, as if she could read Tiana's mind.

"Ms Rose – Roselande – lied to me," Tiana said.

"If she did, then she had good reason." Lisette jutted her chin towards James. "Let's just watch over your daddy for now."

And that was exactly what they did all night long. Tiana, her mother, Lisette, Naveen and even Louis sat in the tiny living room, keeping vigil over her father's steadily weakening body.

46
TIANA

The Ninth Ward, New Orleans
Tuesday, February 1927
Mardi Gras

Tiana awoke the next morning with a crick in her neck, courtesy of the uncomfortable chair she'd slept in. The moment she opened her eyes, she looked to the sofa. Her father remained motionless, his head still in her mother's lap.

Tiana pushed herself up from the chair and quietly made her way over to them, even though Louis's snores would mask any noise she made. He, Lisette and Naveen were all still asleep.

"How is he?" Tiana asked as she neared the sofa.

Once there, she gasped.

His hair had gone completely white, and the wrinkles on his face had deepened. He looked like an old man.

Her mother glanced up at her with tears in her eyes. "I don't know what's happening to him, Tiana."

"Go to Roselande." Tiana jumped at the sound of Lisette's voice from just behind her. She turned to face her. "Go to her. Now."

Tiana swallowed deeply and nodded. "I'm going."

"Who is Roselande?" Eudora asked.

"She's someone I'm hoping can help," Tiana said. She pulled her bottom lip between her teeth to prevent it from trembling. "Because Daddy needs help, and I don't know what to do."

She kissed her mother's forehead, then her father's. Tiana's stomach twisted at how wrinkly his smooth skin had become. He was aging before their eyes, becoming an old, brittle man. How much longer before…

She didn't want think about what could possibly come of this.

They'd been through this before. She'd made a deal with the proverbial devil to erase what had happened to her father. She would not lose him again.

"I'll be back soon, Daddy," Tiana whispered to him. "I'm gonna figure out how to help you."

She grabbed her purse from the hook near the door,

then bounded down the porch steps. She went to the expense of hailing a taxicab instead of waiting for the streetcar to arrive. She would not pinch pennies. Time was of the essence.

Tiana instructed the cab driver to take her to the corner of Royal and St Ann Streets in the French Quarter. That would put her exactly where she needed to be.

Navigating through the thick fog made the drive more harrowing than Tiana's frayed nerves could withstand. The green sludge had reached the edges of the Ninth Ward. Pretty soon, it would take over the entire city.

By the time the cab driver pulled up to the building, her hands were shaking.

She still wasn't sure if she could trust Roselande. The flower monger had kept so much from Tiana, had perhaps even known who Tiana was before ever introducing herself. Remembering their encounters over the past few months, and how Ms Rose would share all those gifts and her little drops of wisdom, Tiana now wondered if it had all been orchestrated. And to what end?

Couple that with the infestation that had sprung from the Mardi Gras flowers the woman had given her, and the shifting imagery in the painting hanging on the wall at her restaurant, and Tiana wasn't sure Ms Rose was any better than Facilier.

Had Roselande put some kind of curse on her supper club? Was that the point of her gifts?

No, she couldn't trust Roselande...

But her father's life was now at stake. And she had no one else to turn to.

Tiana opened the gate of the red brick building and walked down the short colonnade that led to the courtyard. She spotted Roselande standing before a row of planters filled with colourful blossoms, a watering can in her hand. It suddenly occurred to Tiana that the courtyard had somehow escaped the dense fog that encompassed the rest of the city.

The dazzling pink roses, saffron freesia and deep purple violets overflowing from the planters were a stark contrast to the drabness shrouding New Orleans. The air was redolent with the soft scent of lavender and sweet, tangy aroma of primrose. How had the woman managed to maintain such a beautiful garden in the midst of all this grey?

"You're back." Tiana jumped as Roselande turned and faced her. A serene smile played about her lips. "Happy Mardi Gras."

She hadn't even considered that it was Mardi Gras day. All the plans she'd made for the big celebration seemed so insignificant now.

"Something's wrong with my daddy," Tiana said. "I came hoping that you could help him. Help *me* help him."

"Why don't we go inside?" Roselande suggested. "We can have tea and talk for a bit."

"I don't have time for tea!" Tiana said.

"Yes, you do," the woman stated in a firm voice that brooked no argument. She set the watering can on the ground and started up a nearby flight of stairs, not bothering to look back to see if Tiana followed.

When Tiana entered the small flat, she wasn't surprised to find it as colourful as the dress worn by the woman who lived there. The walls were painted a vibrant red, and curtains of sparkling beads hung in the doorways.

"Please, have a seat." Roselande motioned to a chair at a large round table that was covered with a bright yellow tablecloth.

Tiana balked. She would not just sit here and socialise while her daddy was growing into an old man. They were wasting time.

"I don't—" Tiana started, but quickly quieted when Roselande turned to her.

"Please. Sit," the woman said. Then she smiled. "There is always time for tea."

Tiana reluctantly fell into the chair. She fidgeted as she watched the woman walk over to the basket of flowers she'd been carrying when Tiana and Lisette arrived yesterday.

She broke off several of the lavender stems and placed them in a pot on the cooker. Then she added water first to that pot, next to a kettle, lighting fires underneath both.

"Does the lavender keep away evil spirits?" Tiana asked.

"No."

"So why are you using it?" she asked.

The woman looked at her with one shapely eyebrow hitched. "Because of the pleasant scent, of course."

She retrieved a tin from the counter and walked over to the table.

"There's nothing magical about these flowers, either," Roselande said as she scooped up a heaping teaspoon of dried flowers and placed them in two of the delicate teacups that sat on the table. "But we have a lot to discuss. And it is always best over a nice cup of tea."

Tiana jumped at the piercing sound of a loud whistle and felt like a complete fool when she realised it was only the kettle.

Roselande carried the brass kettle back to the table, poured the steaming water over the dried flowers, and then took the seat across from Tiana. A delicately floral scent permeated the air. Using a teaspoon, Roselande swirled the flowers around her teacup until the water turned a colour that matched the caftan she wore, then brought it to her mouth and took a sip.

She looked Tiana directly in the eye. "Do you understand what is happening, Tiana?"

"No. That's why I'm here."

But she *did* know. At least she knew *why* this was all happening.

Roselande looked at Tiana expectantly.

"It's my fault," Tiana went on, her throat tight. "Dr. Facilier warned me what would happen if I didn't do what he asked, but I thought he was bluffing. And now my daddy is dying. He's growing older and older. He's aged at least thirty years since last night."

"Is that so?" Roselande asked. "You know, when I was a young girl, my mother would always say, *tan ale; li pa tounen.* Time goes; it does not return. It's another way of saying that one can never return to the past. But maybe it is better to say that one *shouldn't* return to the past. Nothing good will come of that."

"I know that now," Tiana said. "I never should have made that deal with Facilier. Look what's happening to the city."

Roselande shook her head. "But he doesn't have the power to facilitate what is happening right now. This isn't between you and Facilier. Well, it isn't *only* between the two of you," she amended. "The universe is sending a message. I'm afraid it is very, very unhappy."

"With me, or with Facilier?" Tiana asked.

"With you both, because you have both caused this disruption. My mother had another saying: *Pye chat dous men zong li move.* The paw of a cat is sweet, but its claws are nasty." She set down her teacup. "You saw the sweetness of Facilier's deal without considering the consequences that could follow."

"He left me no choice," Tiana said.

"There is always a choice. The manner of pestilence that has been unleashed on this city conveys just how upset the universe is with the deal that was made. The fog. That awful green sludge that is everywhere. The swarm of insects—"

"You mean like the ones from your flowers?" Tiana asked, unable to keep the accusation out of her voice.

"You are talking about the marigolds and lavender?"

"Yes. Thousands of bugs flew out of the flowers last night. For all I know, they're still in my restaurant."

Roselande released a sigh. "I was hoping the flowers would provide a level of protection, along with the paintings. They were supposed to look over you, to shield you. But the forces are stronger than I anticipated."

"Is that why the Mardi Gras Indians in the painting keep disappearing?"

Roselande's brow creased in confusion, but then understanding dawned in her eyes. "So my calls for protection were not completely ignored. The disordering of the painting is a message, likely sent from the *Lwa*. Beware, Tiana. I wouldn't be surprised if those around you start to go missing."

"People *have* gone missing," Tiana said. She ran down the list of all who had disappeared over the past few days.

"By removing the people from the painting, the spirits were trying to alert you as to what was happening. Unfortunately, you did not understand how to receive their message."

Tiana shook her head, unsure what to make of any of this.

"Can you please tell me what I need to do to fix it?" Tiana asked. She was growing impatient.

But Roselande simply took another sip of her tea before setting the teacup back on the saucer and folding her hands on the table.

"You see, Tiana, there are things that happen in this world that are beyond what many people can comprehend. There are powerful forces at play. Most are good and cause no harm, but there are others that seek to wreak havoc.

Unfortunately, Facilier chose to follow *those* forces, and now he has dragged you into it."

She pinched her lips together, a pensive look clouding her eyes. "I knew there was something sinister here from the moment I arrived in New Orleans."

"It's Facilier," Tiana said. "People in the neighbourhood always would warn us about the Shadow Man and his Vod—"

"No." Roselande stopped her. "Do not associate what Facilier practises with Vodou. Vodou delivers peace and goodness into the world. It offers healing to those who are sick and solace to those who are hurting. It is about bringing joy into the heart, not misery and despair. Never confuse that which Facilier practises with the religion of my homeland." She let out a sigh. "Facilier could have done much good in the world if he had taken the time to learn the ways of our people, but he decided he wanted to go the easy way." She rubbed her thumb and fingers together. "Easy money."

"He wants more than money," Tiana said.

"Yes, he wants power. Always has. Facilier wants to control the city of New Orleans, and he believes if he can control those in power, then everything he has ever wanted will just fall into his lap. That is where you come in."

"But I have no power over this city," Tiana said. "All I have is my restaurant."

"You have very powerful people who dine at your restaurant, Tiana. Facilier sees you as his ticket to get to those people."

"Mr LaBouff," Tiana whispered.

The woman nodded. She tilted her head to the side. "How did you get mixed up with the Shadow Man in the first place? That's the one thing I haven't figured out."

Tiana hesitated for a moment, but reasoned that she could not hold anything back from Roselande if she wanted the woman's help. She gave her a detailed account of what had transpired at Mardi Gras the year before, and in the year since.

"All right. It is making sense now," Roselande said once Tiana was finished. "His next payment is due."

"Payment?" Tiana asked. "So it *is* about money?"

"Not that kind of payment," Roselande answered. "In order to provide the things he promised when the two of you made that deal, Facilier had to call upon malevolent forces. And now those forces are demanding payment. I can't imagine their price for bringing someone back from the dead. Whatever it was, you can be assured it was very steep."

Tiana thought for a moment. "Would those forces happen to look like shadows?"

Again, Roselande nodded. "They can take many forms."

"I think they've been following me," Tiana said.

"I wouldn't be surprised. They'd want to keep an eye on you. Facilier has no knowledge of how to call upon the *Lwa*, so he must rely on these shadows instead."

"So what do I do?" Tiana asked. "How do I defeat Facilier? And what can I do to help my father? How do I stop him from growing old so fast?"

The pitying look that instantly clouded Roselande's face turned Tiana's blood cold.

Her voice trembled as she asked, "There *is* something I can do, isn't there?"

"Here's what I know." Roselande sucked in a deep, cleansing breath, then slowly released it. Folding her hands on the table, she looked Tiana directly in the eyes. "There is a symmetry to everything. You bargained for extra time with your father that he should have never been given, so I believe the universe is taking that time back.

"I've only heard of this happening once before, but those affected did not physically age. They were stripped of their memories, and they—"

"Ms Margery," Tiana said with a gasp.

"I don't follow," Roselande said with a frown.

"Ms Margery and Buford and Mr Smith at the fabric shop. Something is going on with their memory," Tiana explained.

"And you've had dealings with all of these people, either now or in the past?"

"Yes, all of them," Tiana said.

"It makes sense," Roselande said. "The universe is extracting the time you took from it by snatching up memories from those around you."

Tiana tried to wrap her head around all of this. It was still so much more than she could handle right now.

"So are you saying that whatever is going on with my daddy and the others is because the universe is upset with me? It isn't because I didn't put Facilier's potion in the gumbo I made yesterday?"

Roselande shook her head. "Whatever Facilier gave you has nothing to do with this. *That's* most likely some sort of con on his part. I told you already, Tiana. This – the fog, the algae, your father's woes – is far beyond anything he can do."

"So why is this happening now? I made that deal with Facilier a year ago!"

"I think you just answered your own question," Roselande replied. "You're approaching the one-year anniversary, which also happens to line up with Shrovetide, or Shrove Monday as they call it here. The Monday before the beginning of the Lenten season is a time of seeking absolution for the sins committed over the previous year."

"But what sin does my daddy need to seek forgiveness for? He's the most honest man I know."

Roselande brought her teacup to her mouth and took a very long, deliberate sip. "You are a very smart girl, Tiana. I think you already know."

It wasn't her daddy's sins. It was hers.

"It's because I brought him back, isn't it?" Her voice cracked.

"I'm afraid so," Roselande said. "Remember what I said about the symmetry of these events? It was one year ago today that you caused this disturbance in the universe by receiving something that never should have been. The deal you made with Facilier disrupted the order of things," she said. "To set things right, you must allow fate to continue as it first saw fit."

Apprehension skated along Tiana's skin, causing goose bumps to pebble up and down her arms.

"What are you saying?" she asked, although she feared she knew what Roselande was going to say before the woman spoke.

"*Kote ki gen dife a, gen dlo tou.* Where there's the fire, there's water, too," she said. "Every problem has a solution."

"What's the solution?" Tiana asked. She was near her breaking point.

"Your father," Roselande answered. "As much as you want him to remain with you and your family, it is not meant to be."

Tiana shook her head. She covered her mouth with her fist, trying and failing to mute the strangled cry that escaped her lips. Roselande reached across the table and gently placed her hand on Tiana's forearm. She gave it a firm squeeze.

"This extra time you've had with your father has been a blessing; it has been a gift. But it has come at a cost that is more than this world can bear. The longer you hold on to him, the more destruction and despair will be unleashed upon New Orleans and beyond. You must willingly relinquish your father to his rightful place in the universe, Tiana."

"Am I just supposed to let him die?" she cried.

"No," Roselande said. "Just letting him die isn't enough. You must give him *permission* to go. He is holding on because of you – because you brought him back here. Nothing will be right in this world until you make the choice to release him. That is what the universe demands. It's the only way to atone for the disruption you caused."

"So… so what do I do?" She released a hiccuping sob. "How do I give him permission to go?"

"In this world, all beginnings have an end. Or, as my people say, all prayers have an amen. *Tout laprivè gen amen.*"

"I don't understand."

"Your father has reached his end on this earth, Tiana. You are to offer these words until he passes on. Tout laprivè gen amen."

"Tout… tout la… la…"

"Laprivè gen amen," Roselande instructed.

"Tout laprivè gen amen." Tiana imagined saying the words to her father, watching him leave them once more. Forever. She shook her head. "I can't. I can't just sit by while he dies!"

"You must, Tiana. It is the only way.

"You must let him go."

47
TIANA

"I – I'm sorry," Tiana said, unsure whom she was talking to now, tears blurring her vision. She pushed her chair away from the table and stood abruptly. Then she ran out of the flat and didn't look back.

She spent the entire cab ride home trying to discount Roselande's warnings. It was all too much for her to wrap her head around. How could a decision she had made a year before affect the entire universe? This fog? Buford and Ms Margery and the others losing their memories? All of that was because of her? All because she wanted to have her daddy back?

She closed her eyes tight against the tears that began to stream down her face.

How was she supposed to willingly let go of her father when she'd just got him back? She wasn't ready to say goodbye to him.

But when would she *ever* be ready? a nagging voice asked. He could live to be a thousand years old and she still would not want to give him up. If she never willingly let him go, would he live forever?

It seemed impossible, but so did having her daddy back in the first place.

An onslaught of anguish assailed her, so intense it robbed her of breath.

The deal she'd made with Facilier had given her something most people only dreamt about – more time with a lost loved one. She had been granted an entire year that she never should have had with her daddy. Those long talks while sitting in the rocking chairs on the porch, picking vegetables in his garden, cooking together at the supper club; they were the most precious gifts. Ones she would cherish for the rest of her days.

But now her daddy seemed to be suffering.

She had asked Roselande for the way to fix the mess she'd put this city and all her loved ones through, and she'd got her answer. And deep down, she knew she couldn't brush it aside just because it wasn't the one she'd wanted.

Tiana braced herself for the wave of cold, hard truth. She would have had to say goodbye to her father at some point.

That day had just come all too quickly.

Tiana knew that things had taken a turn for the worse the moment the cab pulled up to her parents' home. Even through the dense fog, she could make out the herd of people from the neighbourhood crowding the front porch. They stared at her with pity as she walked up the pathway to the porch steps, mournful expressions on their faces.

As she approached the front door, Mr Miller from across the street put a hand on her shoulder. "It doesn't look good, Tiana. The doctor was just here. He says he's never seen anything like it." He gave her shoulder a gentle squeeze. "I'm sorry."

Tiana nodded, her throat aching as she entered the house. Her daddy lay in the same place she'd left him, his head cradled in her mother's lap.

Several of her mother's friends had arrived. A couple of them sat with her in the living room, while a few others were in the kitchen collecting meals that had been prepared by their neighbours. It was a ritual around these parts. Those in mourning did not have to worry about cooking or cleaning for at least a week after a death in the family. The entire community pulled together to offer support.

Tiana closed her eyes, remembering the last time she and her mother had gone through this. It seemed as if it had happened just yesterday.

Back when she'd agreed to Facilier's deal, she had not considered how difficult it would be to face this loss twice.

She looked over at Lisette, who stood near the sewing machine, away from those who crowded around the living room. Her solemn expression was filled with understanding.

Tiana nodded and mouthed a silent *thank you*.

"Every beginning has an end," she murmured to herself, voice shaking.

Tiana sucked in a deep breath before walking over to the sofa. Several of the women made room for her, clearing the space next to her parents.

She looked down at her father and could barely believe her eyes. His face was ashen, almost ghost-like. His body looked like an eighty-year-old man's. Tufts of grey hair grew from his ears. His age-spotted skin stretched over knobby, gnarled hands, which were folded atop his chest.

Someone brought over a chair and directed Tiana to take a seat. She did. And then she took her daddy's limp hand in her own and brought it up to her cheek.

Tiana closed her eyes and rubbed her cheek against his paper-thin skin. Her throat constricted as she tried to swallow past the knot of grief clogging it. With her free hand, she reached out and captured her mother's, lacing their fingers together.

Her daddy's eyes fluttered open. A tired smile drew across his lips.

"Hey, baby girl," he said. His voice was so weak, it was barely perceptible.

"Hey, Daddy." She gave his hand a gentle squeeze and tried to find the strength to say the words she needed to say. "You're tired, aren't you?" Tiana asked.

He nodded. His chest rose with the breath he struggled to take.

"I know," she whispered as tears once again began to stream down her cheeks. Her daddy tried to reach for her face, but he was too frail to lift his hand more than a few inches. The crushing realisation brought even more tears to her eyes.

She straightened her shoulders, finding the resolve to press forward. She would not make it harder for her daddy to let go.

She soothingly rubbed her thumb back and forth across his wrinkled, fragile hand, offering comfort. Then Tiana closed her eyes and inhaled deeply, mentally preparing herself for what she must do next.

She managed to smile as she looked down at him and said, "Do you know how special it's been to be in that kitchen with you every day? It's been a dream come true, and I would not trade it for anything." Her lip trembled as her emotions threatened to overwhelm her. "But I don't think we will be cooking together any longer, Daddy. The time for that has passed."

"It's okay, baby girl," he said. "It's… going to be… okay."

"I'll miss it," she said. "I'll miss *you*."

"You'll see… me again."

"Yes," she said with an emphatic nod. "We'll see each other again one day." She swallowed past the anguish jammed up in her throat. "But, for now, it's time for us to say goodbye."

Tiana leant forward and pressed her cheek against his. She took a deep breath. Now was the time. She had to make things right.

"Tout laprivè gen amen," she said softly, trying to channel all the beauty and care Roselande had in her words. "Tout laprivè gen amen."

She repeated the phrase quietly, over and over and over, as tears streamed down her face and onto her father's wrinkled skin.

"It's okay to let go," she whispered in his ear. "We're going to be okay. I will take care of Mama, and she will take care of me." She kissed his wrinkled forehead. "I love you, Daddy."

They remained that way for untold minutes, with Tiana holding on to her daddy with one hand and to her mother with the other. She and her mother drew strength from each other as her daddy's breaths became shallower and shallower. Silent tears streamed down Tiana's face as she listened to her mother's quiet sobs. How she wished she could alleviate her pain.

But Tiana had come to learn that enduring this particular kind of pain was an unfortunate, but inescapable, part of life. She had gone to extraordinary measures to avoid the agony of losing her father only to end up in this exact place again. Her days of avoiding life's inevitable consequences were over.

She saw her daddy's chest heave one last time, and then he went still. Tiana was surprised by the unexpected sense of calm that washed over her amid her grief.

Murmurs drifted from near the front door.

"What is this?" someone asked.

"Have you ever seen anything like it?"

As people began to congregate around the door, Tiana made her way to the closest window. She gasped at the sight on the other side of the glass. The fog had thinned, but only in the area surrounding their house, and flower petals rained from the sky. They collected on the ground like a colourful snowfall.

Tiana closed her eyes, a gentle smile touching her lips. She was at peace, because her daddy was now at peace.

But she still had one last thing to do.

48
TIANA

Tiana started the now-familiar journey to Facilier's dark, dreadful home hidden within the depths of the French Quarter. The greenish fog remained here, as thick and suffocating as ever. Despite it, she could make out the ominous clouds hovering overhead. The last thing she needed at the moment was a downpour slowing her down, but she would not let it deter her. If she had to fight the elements along with the Shadow Man, that's just what she would have to do.

She didn't bother to knock when she arrived at his home. She marched right up to that purple door and barged in.

"Where are you, Shadow Man?" she called.

The place smelt of patchouli and peppermint, the pleasant aroma at odds with the sinister charge that hummed through the air.

"So you've finally come to your senses," came Facilier's cold, menacing voice.

"I've come to put an end to this," Tiana said. "Now get out here! Don't hide from me."

Several moments passed before he stepped into the dimly lit room. Despite her determination to conquer him, Tiana still experienced that initial jolt of panic the Shadow Man evoked whenever he was near. She mentally pushed away her fear and stood up straight, clenching her fists at her sides.

He has no power.

"You've arrived just in time," Facilier said. He reached into his vest and pulled out a pocket watch. "There is only an hour left until sunset, which means you have an hour to sign your name to that contract."

"I'm not signing anything," Tiana said. "I will not live my life according to *your* rules. That was never part of the deal."

"That was *always* part of the deal," Facilier said, quickly closing the distance between them. He drew near, his face just inches from hers. "You've been playing by my rules all along, Tiana. You just didn't realise it."

"That's not how this works." She fought to keep her voice from trembling. She refused to let him see an ounce of fear. "You don't get to change the rules at your whim. But it doesn't matter, because I'm done."

"Are you now?" His brow arched as he stared her down, observing her as if she were a bug he wanted to crush with his shoe.

"That's right," Tiana said. "I fulfilled my obligation to you a long time ago. I don't want any part of any new deal, and there is nothing you can do to change my mind."

"Have you forgotten what's at stake? Or are you ready to see that dear father of yours perish?"

Tiana pulled in a deep breath and held her head up high.

"You're too late," she said. "My daddy is no longer here with us. He died just a little while ago."

As painful as it was to speak those words, Tiana took some satisfaction in the shock that registered on Facilier's face. His surprise was further evidence that the potion he'd given her had never controlled her father's fate.

"You're lying," he growled.

"I would *never* lie about that," Tiana said. "My father meant the world to me, but I've accepted what fate had in store for him." She straightened her shoulders, feeling empowered. "And now you can't hold his well-being over my head any more. I'm done cowering before you, Shadow

Man. I don't care what it costs – I'm willing to pay *any* price to be free of you!"

He glared at her, his nostrils flaring. "But are you willing to pay the *ultimate* price?"

Before Tiana knew what he was doing, he twisted around, his black coat arcing through the air. And just like that, he was gone, consumed by the darkness surrounding them.

She squinted, trying her best to see in front of her, but the faint light coming in from the open door didn't do much to illuminate the room. Her fists tightening in determination at her sides, Tiana pulled in a fortifying breath and stormed ahead.

She unclenched her hands and held them up in front of her, feeling around for the wall or a door. She let out a swift *oof* when she bumped into a piece of furniture of some sort, its pointed edge jabbing her hip.

Facilier's low, maniacal cackle reverberated around the room.

Tiana twisted around, searching for where the sound had come from. The more she searched, the more confused she became. The darkness disorientated her, making her head spin.

"Where are you?" she yelled.

A loud pop rang out. Tiana jerked. It rang out again,

and then a puff of glittery purple smoke appeared before her. A moment later, Facilier materialised out of the smoky haze.

"You're running out of time, Tiana," he said in a singsong voice. "The sun will soon sink below the horizon." He reached inside his vest again and produced that blasted contract. "Sign it," he hissed as he shoved it at her.

"No!" she yelled.

Summoning every drop of courage within her, she ran at him. Facilier struck out with his hand, and Tiana bounced backwards as if she'd hit an invisible wall. She crashed to the floor, scrambling to find her footing. She pushed herself up and launched at him again, but he broke away and retreated deeper into the house.

Her heart thumping against her chest like a pack of wild horses, Tiana took off after Facilier. She heard a door slam shut and rushed towards the sound, running her hands along the wall until she encountered the door handle. She opened the door and stopped short.

It was pitch black.

She blinked several times, but couldn't make out even the faintest object.

"Enter at your own risk." Facilier's disembodied voice came from somewhere in the empty abyss that stretched out before her.

Tiana paused at the threshold, her chest heaving with the swift breaths she sucked in. She closed her eyes.

This is for you, Daddy.

Then she charged into the darkness.

49
TIANA

The moment Tiana entered the room, she was suspended in the air, her arms flailing as her body spun in a dizzying circle. Facilier's laugh swirled around her. When she finally landed on solid ground, she found herself back in the heart of Lafayette Cemetery, where this had all started.

It was an illusion. It had to be.

"You're in my world now," Facilier said. "You should have taken the easy way out and signed the contract."

"Taking the easy way is what got me into this mess with you," she said.

"And I gave you what you wanted. I gave you your father."

"You didn't give me anything," she said. "It was your *friends* who did it. You don't have any power of your own,

Facilier. You're nothing without your friends from the other side."

He shrugged his shoulders, as if she hadn't just ripped the veil off the fraud he'd been perpetuating all this time.

"You're right," he said. "But without me, you wouldn't have *access* to my friends from the other side. So you're nothing without me, Tiana." He pointed to his chest. "*I'm* the reason you were able to open that restaurant with your daddy. *I'm* the reason that little prince of yours isn't hopping around the bayou.

"You wouldn't have had any of the things you've enjoyed this past year if I had not summoned my friends from the other side on your behalf. *You owe me.* And them."

Her vision became hazy as her eyes fixed on a stone catacomb just over the Shadow Man's shoulder. A montage of scenes played across it, images of her cooking side by side with her daddy at the supper club. Of sitting at her restaurant watching Louis and his band play rousing jazz music. Of staring into Naveen's beautiful eyes as they drifted down the bayou together.

Tiana shook her head.

No.

She wouldn't fall for his antics again. He had a way of twisting his words around, of making her believe what he wanted her to. But he no longer had the upper hand.

Tiana had finally accepted that she didn't have to face her battles alone. After the pastor arrived at the house to sit with Mama, she'd returned to Roselande's to apologise and tell her what had happened. Then, together, they had come up with a plan to beat Facilier at his own game.

Tiana pressed a hand against her satchel, feeling for the vial tucked inside.

For this to work, he had to buy her bluff.

"If I wanted to make another deal with you, I would," Tiana started. "But I don't have to, because I have friends, too. And my friends can do everything your friends can do and more."

"That's not possible," Facilier said.

She arched her eyebrow in cynical amusement, just as he had done to her so many times.

"Oh, but it is," Tiana said. "And I have something you *don't* have. Something that will give you what you've been seeking all along: power."

She reached into her satchel and pulled out the large vial.

"You must take me for a fool," Facilier said. "I'm the one who concocted that potion. I know exactly what it can do. And what it can't."

"Except this isn't the potion *you* concocted," Tiana lied. "I got this one from my new friend – a Vodou priestess in the Quarter. She replaced the contents with something… a little more helpful."

His eyes narrowed. "You're talking about Roselande," he said. "A thorn in my side ever since she came to this city. I thought I warned you to stay away from her."

"And I told you that I'm done living by your rules. I explained to Roselande how you've been extorting me. She wasn't surprised by your dishonesty. I guess you have a reputation."

Facilier's nostrils flared.

"Now that Daddy has passed on, I've decided it's time I finally accept some help in getting the restaurant that I've always dreamt of." She shrugged, striving to keep her voice calm and relaxed. "As much as I love our little supper club in Tremé, you know that I've had my heart set on that gorgeous old sugar mill on the river." She held up the vial so that the colour was slightly distorted. It looked more pink than purple. "And this will help me to get it."

"How's that?" Facilier asked.

"Roselande promised that if I drink this, it will give me the insight I need in order to convince the wealthiest people in town to invest in my restaurant. She assured me that her gifts matched those of your friends on the other side, because they come from a noble place. Unlike yours."

She could tell the words affected him by the expression that flashed across his face.

Her heart raced within her chest as she considered her next move. She'd come to know Facilier well enough over the past year to anticipate what he would do.

She peered at the vial. "All I have to do is drink it, and everything I've always wanted will be mine. However" – she cocked her head to the side – "I'm willing to make a deal of my own."

"What do you want?" Facilier asked.

"You know more about how these things work than I do, but I was thinking that maybe if we split it, we can *both* get what we want."

His eyes narrowed. "Why should I believe you? You have nothing to gain by giving me half of Roselande's potion."

"Well, unlike *some* people, I don't do things simply for my own gain." She shrugged again. "It's like you said: you gave me an entire year with my father that I would have never had. Maybe I am a fool, or maybe I'm too loyal for my own good, but it feels as if I *do* owe you for providing such a precious gift."

"Yes, you do," Facilier said. He extended both hands, going for the vial. "Give it to me."

"Not so fast." Tiana jerked it out of his reach. She had to make him think she believed he was still in control. "If you want this, you have to reverse every awful thing you've set in motion over the last year. The fog, the green sludge – all of it! And you have to tell me where to find the missing people. Addie Mae, Georgia and Eugene. And Mr Salvaggio and Mr LaBouff."

"Fine," he hissed, his eyes never leaving the vial. "They're all tied up in one of the back rooms."

He snapped his fingers, and just like that, they were back in his house.

Damn him. She knew it had been an illusion.

"As for the fog," Facilier continued. "Well, that's up to my friends on the other side. The fog will lift when they get what they want."

"What do they want?" Tiana asked.

Facilier stared at her with an intense, piercing look. "Your soul."

Tiana sucked in a swift, terrified breath, thrown off. "My what?" she whispered.

"Well, it doesn't have to be *your* soul," he quickly added. "It can belong to anyone; my friends on the other side won't care. There are thousands of chumps around this city who no one would ever miss if they just disappeared."

Like the people you kidnapped? Tiana wanted to rail at him, but she shook her head to keep her cool. She had a part to play, and if she slipped up, Facilier would know that she was on to him.

"Are you sure about this?" she asked, adding extra suspicion in her voice just to throw him off.

"Yes," he said impatiently, his eyes never leaving the vial. "But you *must* sign your name to the contract," Facilier added. "None of the horrors will end if you don't."

"What would they do with the soul once they have it?" she asked.

"That's not my concern, and it shouldn't be yours," Facilier said. "Are you ready, Tiana? One last deal."

His willingness to sacrifice some innocent person's soul alleviated the last prickle of conscience she felt over what she was about to do. This snake in the grass deserved everything that was coming to him.

"Okay," Tiana said. "I'll sign it."

She followed him to a wooden desk that held a lamp, and grabbed hold of the fountain pen he held out to her. Tiana bent over the contract, turning her back slightly as she scribbled across the bottom of the scroll.

"Okay, it's done," she said. She turned and held the vial out to him. "Now, you drink half, and I'll drink half."

His eyes were bright with triumph as he snatched the

vial from her hand, wrenched the cork out of it, and gulped down the entire contents.

He threw his head back and let out a peal of laughter.

But his laughter quickly died as he clutched at his throat and staggered several steps back.

Tiana held out the contract to him, the words *Goodbye, Shadow Man* scrawled on the signature line.

His eyes grew wide with panic, and he began to gasp for air. He backed up against the wall and slumped to the floor, his face becoming mottled, bright red splotches appearing all over it.

Tiana had to fight the innate urge to reach out and offer assistance, but what could she do? This was *his* potion. She had no idea what was in it or how to mitigate its effects.

She looked on in horror as Facilier's eyes glazed over. For a moment, Tiana thought he was dead, but then he began to mumble words she could just barely make out.

"Are… you… ready?" he murmured, the words thick and slurred as they left his tongue. "Are you… ready, Tiana?"

"I think that's a question for you to answer, Shadow Man."

As she stood over him, Tiana noticed her silhouette shrinking as the sun dipped below the horizon. The air turned ice cold. The sound of faint, indiscernible groans rumbled behind her, growing louder with each passing second. Fear and shock rooted Tiana's feet to the floor as the dark shadows slithered along the walls and floors.

Her mouth hung open in dismay as the Shadows wrapped themselves around Facilier's limp body and carried him out of the room.

50
TIANA

Tiana wasn't sure how long she stood there, her body too exhausted for her to consider moving even a single limb.

Had that really just happened? Was she actually – *finally* – free of Facilier? Even though she'd seen it with her own eyes, it was still hard to believe she'd eradicated him from her life once and for all.

She spotted the rolled-up sheaf of papers on the floor. She picked it up and unfurled the tattered pages, taking a moment to read over it. Tiana's breath caught in her throat as she absorbed the words, her heart thumping wildly as the enormity of the fate she'd just escaped sank in. She could have very well signed away her soul.

She gripped each end of the contract and tore the document in two. Then she tore it again. And again. And again. Each rip was like music to her ears.

It sounded like freedom.

"Tia! There you are!"

Tiana swung around, surprise and happiness lifting her heart at the sight of her friends. Charlotte led the charge, followed by Naveen, Louis and Lisette.

"What are you all doing here?" Tiana exclaimed. But her voice held no censure. She was so happy to see them all, grateful they hadn't heeded her command to stay away.

Charlotte wrapped her arms around her. "Oh, Tia, I was so afraid for you. I went to see you when I heard about your daddy, and Lisette told me you'd left. I realised you must've gone after that awful man."

"I'm okay, Lottie. And we don't have to worry about Facilier any more."

Charlotte jerked her head back and regarded Tiana, concern etched across her furrowed brow. "What happened?" Charlotte asked.

"He got out-tricked," Tiana answered, leaving it at that. No one else needed to know what had taken place in this room.

Naveen walked up to her and gently cradled Tiana's cheek in his warm palm. He brushed his thumb over her cheekbone. "You have been hurt, *ma poupette*," he said.

Tiana was surprised by the bright red blood glistening on his thumb when he pulled it away from her face. She had no idea when she'd been cut.

"It's… it's nothing," she said. "I'll be fine."

"Are you sure? Lisette!" he called over his shoulder.

"No, really, I'm fine," Tiana said. She turned to Charlotte and grabbed her by the shoulders. "Lottie, your daddy is here somewhere – and others, too. We just have to find them."

"What?" her friend gasped. "Where?"

"I don't know. Fan out," Tiana called to the group. "Search every nook and cranny. Facilier told me they were hidden in a room somewhere in this house."

She pivoted on her heel, setting out for the door just to the right of them, but Naveen caught her arm and pulled her back to him.

"Tiana, are you sure you're okay?" he asked. "At least let Lisette take a look at those scrapes."

His concern touched her. She was struck once again by how different he was from that self-absorbed cad he'd been when she had met him a year earlier. Despite her best efforts not to, she'd fallen in love with him then. It would be so very easy to love this kinder, more considerate Naveen.

Tiana's breath caught in her throat, and her eyes grew

wide as it suddenly occurred to her that there was nothing stopping them from being together any more. Facilier was gone, and with him the barrier keeping her and Naveen apart.

Tiana beamed up at him.

"I promise you that I am just fine," Tiana reassured him. She cradled his face between her hands. "I will explain as much as I can very soon, but right now we need to find those folks the Shadow Man kidnapped."

She grabbed him by the hand and headed for the rear of the house. The structure was so much larger than it had seemed from the unassuming entrance, stretching back at least half a street or more. Before Tiana could turn the knob of the first door she came across, she heard Louis's rousing call from somewhere down the long hallway.

"I think they're in here!" Louis called.

Tiana and Naveen raced to where Louis stood. Naveen put his ear to the door.

"Mr LaBouff?"

There was a pause, and then a cacophony of muffled cries clamoured from just beyond the door.

"Yes, they are here," Naveen said excitedly. He tried the door handle, but it was locked. No matter how violently he wrenched at it, it wouldn't budge. "Should we search for a key?"

"In this house?" Tiana asked. "That could take a lifetime. Who knows where the key to this door may be hidden?"

Or, even worse, what if Facilier had taken the key with him to the other side?

"Maybe we can knock it down?" Louis suggested.

"Outta my way," Lisette demanded, pushing her way through. She reached under the cloth covering her hair bun and retrieved a hairpin, then stuck the pin inside the lock and jiggled it. There was a click. She turned the knob and pushed the door open.

For a moment, no one moved. They were all stunned at the sight before them. Eli LaBouff, Addie Mae, Georgia, Eugene and Mr Salvaggio sat on the floor with their backs against the wall and their hands tied together with twine. Ragged pieces of cloth covered their mouths, preventing them from talking. And they were filthy, with dirt and grime streaking their faces.

"Big Daddy!"

Charlotte rushed into the room and threw her arms around her father.

"Let's get him untied first, Lottie," Tiana suggested.

She, Naveen and Lisette made quick work of untangling the knots and setting the five of them loose from the bonds Facilier had used to imprison them.

"Where is he?" Mr LaBouff said, scrabbling from the floor.

"It's okay, Daddy," Charlotte said. "You don't have to worry about him. Tiana took care of Facilier."

"That's right. No one has to worry about the Shadow Man again," Tiana said. She turned to Addie Mae and wrapped her friend up in a hug. She turned to Georgia and Eugene and did the same. "I am so, so sorry for what he did to all of you. It's over now."

But as she stood there with her arms around her loved ones, Tiana realised that it wasn't over. Her heartache was beginning anew as reality sank in. She would once again have to endure the pain of living in this world without her father.

As she waited for the soul-crushing grief to envelop her, an odd thing happened. The grief failed to materialise. Instead, she felt… joy. An overwhelming sense of peace weaved its way around her sadness.

Tiana knew she would always miss her daddy, but the hole his passing had left in her heart wasn't as hollow this time around. It was filled with memories of the past year – the laughs they'd shared, the meals they'd prepared together and the all-encompassing love they'd experienced every single day. And a true goodbye.

Tiana closed her eyes tight, holding onto those

memories. They would be with her always. Just as her daddy would be with her.

Always.

A muted rumble sounded from somewhere in the distance. Tiana tipped her head to the side to hear it better.

"What is that?" she asked. The growing noise quickly became clearer. It was the sound of a jazz band playing and the roar of a crowd.

"That's Mardi Gras you're hearing," Louis answered. "Time for me to get my horn and join in the parade!"

"I guess a little fog and green scum ain't enough to stop Mardi Gras," Charlotte said. "Come on, Lisette," she said, taking the girl by the arm. "We don't want to miss the floats!"

Tiana followed the others out of Facilier's home.

"The fog," Lisette said once outside. "It's gone."

"So is that nasty green stuff from the river," Charlotte remarked.

"Sure is," said a guy standing next to them on the pavement, bobbing his head to music from the band. "Most peculiar thing. Just as the sun went down, that fog rolled out as quickly as it rolled it. Same goes for the algae from the river."

Sundown?

"Symmetry," Tiana whispered.

"What was that?" Naveen asked.

"Nothing," she said. She looked up at him and smiled. Then she tipped her head towards where the others had wandered off, following the marching band and crowd of costumed revellers as they made their way through the French Quarter.

"What do you say?" Tiana asked. "You want to join the parade?"

Naveen's brow furrowed. "Are you sure you're not too tired?"

"Nope." She shook her head. "I've realised just how short life is. I think I should let my hair down for a change." She winked and held her hand out to him. "Let's go have some fun."

51
NAVEEN

The Kingdom of Maldonia
Three months later

Naveen could not hold back his smile as the car travelled along the tree-lined street leading up to the grandiose entrance of the Grand Palace of Maldonia. The white marble dome atop the massive, two-hundred-room royal residence sparkled like a newly harvested pearl. After a three-week journey aboard a passenger ship and more than a year in America, the sight of his family's home brought more joy than he had anticipated.

The car rounded the reflection pool and fountain, coming to a stop before the twenty-foot, gold-plated doors.

"Ah, it's good to be home," Naveen said. He looked

around at the other occupants in the car, who all sat in stunned silence. "What is wrong?" he asked.

"What *is* this place?" Lisette asked, her eyes wide with wonder as she stared out of the car's window.

Naveen shrugged. "It is home."

"This makes Big Daddy's house look like a shoebox," Charlotte said.

"I can't believe you grew up living in a place like this," Tiana said. She looked over at him. "Then again, yes I can."

Naveen threw his head back and guffawed at the car's ceiling.

"This looks like a place with really tasty food," Louis said.

"That it is." Naveen laughed again. "Come on. Let us go in. I'm sure my family is eager to see us, and if I know my mother, she has instructed the cooks to lay out a feast for the ages."

They were greeted by the king and queen the moment they walked into the palace. Naveen was staggered by the rush of emotion that hit him the minute he saw their faces. Formalities were brushed aside as he wrapped his mother and father in a hug.

"I've missed you," he said.

His younger siblings flooded the grand entrance, embracing him like a prodigal son returning. Which, he guessed, he was.

As Naveen predicted, his parents had ordered a grand celebration to mark their son's return home – temporary though it was. He'd informed them before he boarded the ship that he had chosen to make New Orleans his permanent home.

At Lisette's insistence, Naveen took their guests on a tour of the palace, including a drive around the hundred-acre estate. By the time they returned, more than fifty of his closest friends and family had arrived for the celebration.

Naveen felt conspicuous dressed in his traditional royal regalia, but one look at Tiana's face when he walked in the grand ballroom changed his mind. Following dinner, he immediately escorted her to the dance floor, where they waltzed until his father finally cut in.

Now, Naveen stood at the periphery of the dance floor, leaning against one of the marble columns and observing the guests enjoying themselves. His mother came up to him and patted his arm with her gloved hand.

"How are you, son?" she asked.

"I'm well, Mother," Naveen answered.

"You look well. And you look happy." She glanced over at Tiana, who studied the traditional Maldonia folk dance his younger sisters were trying to teach her. "Does she have something to do with that?"

"She does," Naveen answered, unable to suppress the grin that drew across his lips. "I am in love with her, Mother. She is… my everything."

She arched a regal brow. "Now I understand why you turned down our invitation to return." She tipped her head to the side. "Should I expect a wedding and grandchildren soon?"

"Mother!" Naveen felt himself blush.

"You cannot fault me for asking." She looked over at Tiana again. "They will be lovely grandchildren." Her eyes lit up with excitement. "It will be fun to spoil them."

"Please do not speak of such things with Tiana," Naveen said. "We have only been together a few months. I have not brought up the subject of marriage."

"What are you waiting for? Get on with it."

He chuckled. "I will. Soon." Then he sobered. "You know, Mother, there are other reasons that I have chosen to remain in America. None more important than Tiana, of course."

"Of course," she said.

"But I like the person that I have become over this past year. I learned that I'm really good at selling things and helping others," he said with a laugh. "See Lisette over there?

I just helped broker a deal for her to sell her homemade medicinals in the biggest department store in New Orleans.

"I like my job. It feels good to know that I can make my own way in this world, and do some good in it, too." Naveen shook his head. "I never thought I would say this, but I want to thank you and Father for cutting me off. It turns out that is exactly what I needed."

His mother cupped his cheek. "I am proud of you, son. I always knew you could accomplish anything once you discovered your heart's true desire. Well, at least I'd hoped that would be the case," she amended with a laugh. "Just know there is always a place for you here. You can always come home."

Naveen caught sight of a sparkling blue dress out of the corner of his eye. He looked over and saw Tiana walking towards them.

"I have found my home," Naveen said.

"Oh, yes." His mother patted his cheek. "My grandchildren will be lovely."

She nodded and smiled at Tiana before drifting off to mingle with the other guests.

Naveen took Tiana by the hand and walked her out onto the balcony that overlooked the extensive ornamental gardens below.

"So are you enjoying your first night in the royal palace?" Naveen asked.

"What do you think?" she returned, a hint of sass in her voice.

"Well, I would hope you are, but I can also understand if it's a bit too much. My sisters can be a handful."

"They are lovely, and so are your parents, and that adorable little brother of yours. I think he has a crush on Lottie."

Naveen laughed. "He is a charmer, that one."

"I wonder where he gets that from?" She winked at him, then walked over to the marble balustrade and leant against it. Looking up at the sky, she said, "Doesn't it amaze you that these stars we're staring at here in Maldonia are the same stars they're looking at back in N'awlins? It really puts things into perspective when you think about it."

"It does," Naveen said. "It tells me that no matter where I am, I can be connected to home if I just look up at the stars."

"And what a lovely home it is," Tiana said.

He shrugged. "It's okay."

"Okay? Do you want my honest opinion?"

"Of course. Always."

"I can't believe you would choose to live in that dusty little apartment in N'awlins when you could live here."

"It is not the apartment that is keeping me in New Orleans," Naveen said.

She turned to him, her smile demure, though there was a twinkle in her eye. "Is that so? What else is there that could even compare to this?"

"Come now, Tiana," Naveen said, taking her by the hands. The moon shone down on them, illuminating her beautiful face. "I don't have to tell you that I would give up all the money in the world to be with you."

"Would you really?" she asked.

"In a heartbeat," Naveen said. He leant forward until his forehead met hers. Staring into her eyes, he said, "There is nothing that I would not do for you."

She regarded him with a devilish grin. "I'm gonna remind you of that when I make you wash dishes at the new restaurant."

Naveen frowned. "Did I say there was *nothing* I wouldn't do?"

"That's right," Tiana said. "And it's too late to take it back."

Then she claimed his lips in a sweet, tender kiss.

"I can't wait to see that new restaurant in action. *Your* palace," Naveen said when they broke apart.

Tiana grinned slowly. "Tiana's Palace – I like the sound of that."

EPILOGUE
TIANA

New Orleans, 1928
Mardi Gras

"How's it looking out there, Mama?"

"Like all the Mardi Gras revellers have converged on this place," Eudora said. "The line of people waiting for tables stretches all the way to the French Quarter. You'd better put on a second pot of gumbo, because you have a whole lot of hungry mouths to feed."

"That's just the way I like it," Tiana said as she added a few dashes of Tabasco to the pot. Her daddy's dinged-up pot might not shine like the new copper and steel cookware in her gleaming kitchen, but Tiana refused to use anything else to cook her gumbo.

She could barely hear the band over the din of the noisy kitchen, but she found herself rocking to the faint sound of the traditional Mardi Gras song they were currently playing. She had requested their playlist include only the liveliest tunes. Tonight was a celebration, and she was determined to enjoy every single moment of it.

Tiana's Palace was filled to capacity yet again, just as it had been every single night for the past two weeks, ever since its grand opening. It truly was the place to be, with some of the city's most elite clamouring for a seat at one of her tables.

Just the day before, the newspaper had published a front-page story on the new restaurant that had everyone talking. Tiana's decision to employ an all-female staff – save for the Crawfish Crooners, who would always have a place on the bandstand – was the type of thing that made news from Baton Rouge to Mississippi. Some were sceptical, but many others applauded such a unique idea.

However, it was the food that had people lining up for a table. All her daddy's favourites were on the menu, and the people of this town couldn't seem to get enough. A reservation at Tiana's Palace was the most sought-after thing in all of New Orleans.

"Addie Mae, can you watch the gumbo while I go out to greet some of the guests?" Tiana asked her head chef.

"Sure thing, Tiana! You tell Mr LaBouff that his oysters will be right up."

After suffering from nightmares for months following her rescue from the Shadow Man's dungeon, Addie Mae had taken some time to recuperate. She'd felt ready to return to work just as Tiana closed the deal to buy the old sugar mill she'd always dreamt of owning. The man the Fenner brothers had sold it to a couple of years before had decided to leave New Orleans – but not before enjoying an evening of good music and even better food at the supper club. When he'd learnt it was Tiana who had put in an offer the very same day it went on the market, he'd sold it to her on the spot.

She'd never lost hope that the place would one day be hers. She'd felt it in her bones.

And now it was.

She would have pinched herself, but she already knew this wasn't a dream. This was real life, and she was embracing it all.

Tiana untied her apron from around her waist and went out into the grand dining room. It had taken a lot of blood, sweat and tears to get it to this point, but with the help of her friends, her restaurant looked exactly as she had always imagined it would.

She was still a work in progress when it came to relying on others for help, but she was getting better at it. Especially after the experience she'd had with renovating this place. Naveen, Louis, Lisette and Charlotte had been by her side every single evening, polishing light fixtures and refinishing the tables. Even Maddy, Georgia and Eugene had come by a few times, sweeping and mopping and sanding down the floors.

Tiana started her rounds at their table. Georgia and the gang had a standing invitation to dine whenever they wanted to, no reservation needed.

"How're y'all doing tonight?" Tiana asked.

"This place is hopping," Maddy said. "I know Donald will be sorry he missed this."

"From what I hear, he's found good luck up there in Detroit. I'm guessing it won't be long before you join him up there," Tiana said. She winked at Maddy, who blushed like a schoolgirl. "I'll see you all a bit later. Don't leave without trying my newest creation, Mardi Gras beignets. They're covered with praline sauce!"

She left her old schoolmates and went over to Mr LaBouff, who was holding court, as usual.

"Hey there, Mr LaBouff. Addie Mae said to tell you that your oysters will be right out. Although I really think you should try on one of the other dishes for size. Addie Mae makes a mean muffuletta."

"Nope." He shook his head and cradled his ample belly.

"Bring on the oysters Rockefeller. Or oysters LaBouff, as I like to call them."

Tiana laughed. "Coming right up."

She stopped by Mr Salvaggio's table to check in on him and his wife, then went over to Roselande, who had joined Lisette that evening.

The girl had really come into her own since she'd moved to New Orleans that past year. Maison Blanche had dedicated an entire display case to her products. People around town claimed that Lisette's skin cream was the perfect balm for skin burned by the hot Louisiana sun.

"Tia! Tia!" Tiana turned at Charlotte's call. Her friend ran up to her and enveloped her in a hug. "Oh, Tia, it all looks wonderful in here. I'm so happy I made it back from Baton Rouge in time for your big Mardi Gras celebration. What a perfect way to end this perfect day!"

"Based on that smile, I take it your speech at the State Capitol went well," Tiana said. "I hope you gave them hell, Lottie."

"You know I did!" Charlotte said.

Tiana's heart swelled with pride as she listened to her friend recount her impassioned speech to the state legislators on behalf of the Federation of Civic Leagues. Lottie had joined the group last year after organising a campaign to bring better conditions to the schools in communities like Tremé and the Ninth Ward. But she no longer limited herself to New Orleans. Charlotte had begun to travel around the entire state of Louisiana, fighting for those less fortunate.

But she hadn't given up on finding herself a duke. She'd booked a passage on a luxury cruise liner to England leaving after the Easter holiday.

It took Tiana another half hour to visit the rest of the tables in the dining room, but she made it a point to drop in on each one of them. She was convinced that the key to her restaurant's success – besides the food – was the hospitality. Each patron at Tiana's Palace knew they were appreciated.

She returned to the kitchen to get started on desserts. A few minutes later, Eudora walked through the door.

"Do you need a rest, Mama?" Tiana said as she drizzled praline syrup on the order of beignets she'd just made.

"No, baby. You know I stopped sewing to embrace the excitement of the restaurant business."

"Well, that's not the only reason you're here," Tiana said with a laugh. She rounded the cooking station and enveloped her mother in a hug.

"No, it isn't," Eudora said. She and Tiana stared up at the portrait of her daddy that hung on the wall, looking down over the entire kitchen. "I'm here because this is exactly where he would want me to be."

"And it's exactly where I want you to be, too. What did that man from the paper call you? The queen of Tiana's Palace?"

"Well, he's right," her mother replied with no small amount of sass.

Then she and Tiana burst out laughing.

"Ah, what has my two favourite ladies in New Orleans in such a good mood?" Naveen greeted as he came upon them.

Tiana turned around. "The band taking a break?"

"Only because I insisted," Naveen said. "If it were up to Louis, he would have us playing nonstop all night long."

"That's because he's doing what he loves," Tiana said.

After much soul-searching, Louis had decided to remain in New Orleans instead of petitioning Mama Odie to help him change back into a gator. But he still took his boat out to the swamp every so often, just to be closer to the place where he'd grown up.

Naveen put an arm around Tiana's shoulders and pulled her in to his side.

"I only have ten minutes, so I want to make the most of it. Mother," he said to Eudora. "If you do not mind, I am going to steal my wife away for a bit."

"As long as you bring her back before the second dinner rush," Eudora said.

"I promise."

"Where are you taking me?" Tiana asked.

"To the best view in all of New Orleans," he said.

Five minutes later, she and Naveen were standing at the railing of the restaurant's outside balcony. She stood with her back to his chest, his arms wrapped around her. Tiana rested her head back, listening contently to the beat of his heart as she watched boats of all kinds floating along the river, their lights twinkling among the waves.

"This really is beautiful," she said.

"Very, very beautiful," Naveen replied. She looked up to find him looking at her, not the river.

He dipped his head and placed a gentle kiss upon her lips.

"Tell me. Are you happy, my love?"

"I am," she answered. "So much happier than I ever imagined I could be."

Not too long before, she would have maintained that no matter how well things were going, she would never be truly happy again, because her father was no longer with her.

But he *was* here. She felt him every time she walked into the kitchen at this restaurant. She felt him whenever she walked into her mother's house in the Ninth Ward, or when she was in the house she and Naveen shared uptown.

She felt him everywhere.

And because she knew his spirit would always be with her, no matter how far she travelled or how long they were apart, Tiana now knew true happiness.

She took Naveen's hand and squeezed it, taking in the view.

She'd learnt a lot about letting go that past year. About not holding on to the past and embracing what fate had in store. About taking pride in a hard day's work, but also taking time to rest and find peace in the quiet moments of the day.

Most of all, she'd learnt the importance of spending time with those she loved. She now understood just how precious time was, and that it wasn't promised.

Another Mardi Gras, and once more she was forever changed. It was just as Roselande had said: symmetry was the universe's way. And Tiana looked forward to what new transformations the future – and she – would bring.

Photo Credit: Tamara Roybiskie

Farrah Rochon is the USA Today best-selling author of *The Boyfriend Project* and over thirty other romance novels. She hails from south Louisiana and is a two-time finalist for Romance Writers of America's RITA Award, as well as the 2015 winner of the Emma Award for Author of the Year. Her June 2020 novel, *The Boyfriend Project*, has been lauded by O, The Oprah Magazine as a must-read Black romance novel, as well as praised by Cosmopolitan as a Best Romance Novel of 2020. *Almost There* was her YA debut.

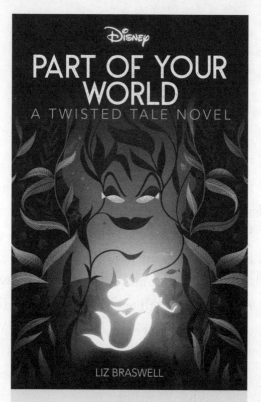

ALSO AVAILABLE IN THE TWISTED TALES SERIES:

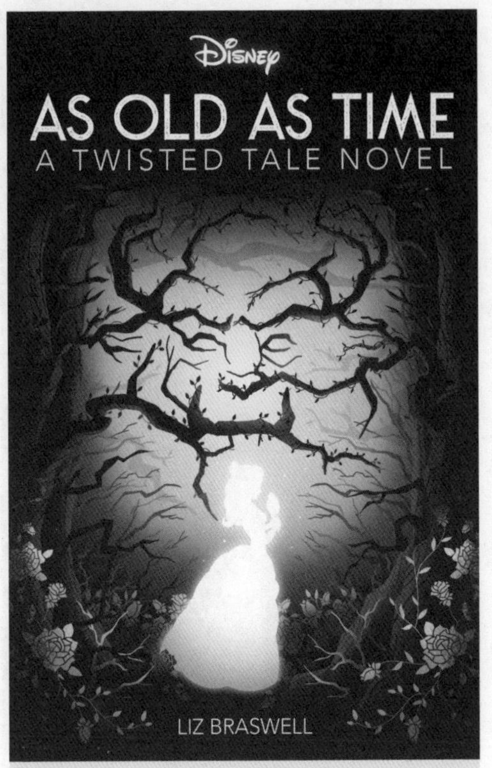

WHAT IF BELLE'S MOTHER CURSED THE BEAST?

Trapped in the castle with the terrifying Beast, Belle learns there is much more to her angry captor when she touches the enchanted rose. Suddenly, her mind is flooded with images of her mother, a woman Belle hardly remembers.

Stranger still, Belle realises that her mother is none other than the beautiful Enchantress who cursed the Beast, his castle and all his staff.

Stunned and confused by the revelation, Belle and the Beast must work together to unravel years of mystery.

ALSO AVAILABLE IN THE TWISTED TALES SERIES:

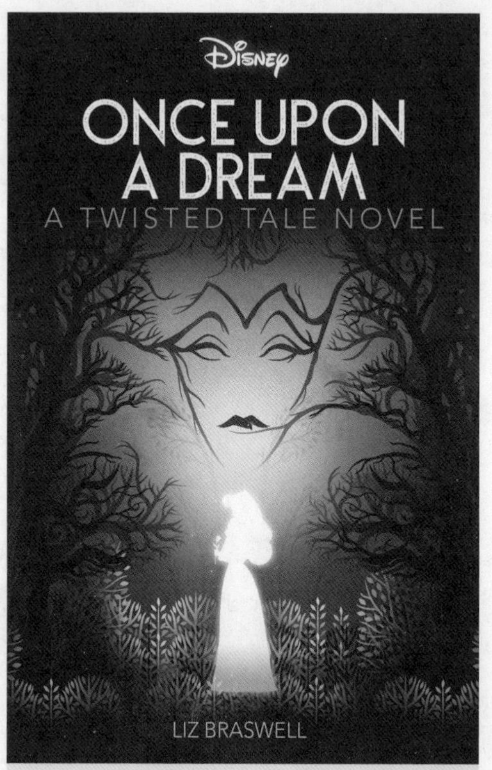

WHAT IF THE SLEEPING BEAUTY NEVER WOKE UP?

The fairy tale ending is just the beginning in this exciting novel that provides a twist on the story you already know.

The dragon is defeated, the prince is poised to wake his slumbering princess, but he too falls asleep as their lips meet and it's clear that this story is far from over.

Wicked fairy Maleficent is controlling Aurora through her dreams and the sleeping beauty must find a way to take back control of her own mind from Maleficent. With the sleeping prince and old friends also trapped in the strange world, Aurora needs to work out who she can trust and defeat Maleficent. Only then can Aurora finally wake up and live happily ever after.

ALSO AVAILABLE IN THE TWISTED TALES SERIES:

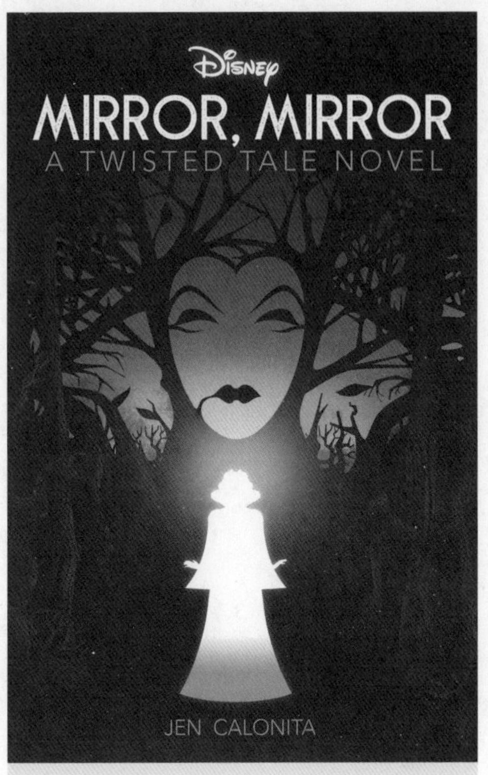

WHAT IF THE EVIL QUEEN POISONED THE PRINCE?

Following her beloved mother's death, the kingdom falls to Snow White's stepmother, known as the Evil Queen.

At first, Snow keeps her head down, hoping to make the best of things. However, when new information about her parents comes to light, and a plot to kill her goes wrong, Snow embarks on a journey to stop the Evil Queen and take back her kingdom.

Can Snow defeat an enemy who will stop at nothing to retain her power... including going after the ones Snow loves?

Disney

SET IN STONE

A TWISTED TALE NOVEL

MARI MANCUSI

AUTUMN
PUBLISHING

Published in 2024
First published in the UK by Autumn Publishing
An imprint of Igloo Books Ltd
Cottage Farm, NN6 0BJ, UK
Owned by Bonnier Books
Sveavägen 56, Stockholm, Sweden
www.igloobooks.com

1024 001
2 4 6 8 10 9 7 5 3 1
ISBN 978-1-83795-966-2
Sold as part of a set, not for resale

Cover illustrated by Giuseppe Di Maio

Printed and manufactured in China

Disney

SET IN STONE

A TWISTED TALE NOVEL

To all my once and future readers
– you make this all worthwhile.

– *M.M.*

PROLOGUE

Bermuda – Present Day

"*Higgidis… piggidis! Alakazoom!* No, that's not right. That's not right at all!"

The waiter frowned as he approached the elderly man with the long white beard who had been collapsed on a deckchair in front of the resort's main pool for the past four hours, mumbling to himself. He was dressed like an overenthusiastic tourist, wearing a baseball cap, loud striped shirt and yellow shorts with little palm trees printed down the sides. On his feet were red Converse trainers, and a pair of yellow sunglasses obscured his eyes.

Ugh. Why do they always end up in my section? the waiter wondered before clearing his throat.

"Um, sir?" he tried. "Are you… all right?"

The man jerked at the sound of the voice, his baseball cap flying from his head and landing in the pool. He stared up at the waiter, pulling his sunglasses down his hooked nose, revealing a pair of piercing blue eyes that seemed far too sharp for an old man's face.

"Am I all right?" he repeated, as if astounded by the question. "Did you just ask me if I'm all right?"

"Um, yes?" The waiter took a small step backwards as the man struggled to get out of his chair, somehow managing to get his foot stuck in the straps in the process. When he tried to yank his foot free, the chair flew backwards, bonking him on the nose. The waiter flinched as the man let out a stream of nonsense words that seemed to be meant as curses – though none the waiter had ever heard before. *Oh, dear.* Maybe he should have left the gentleman well enough alone. Still, he was almost off his shift, and he needed to cash everyone out before he left.

"Can I… get you something?" he ventured. "The bill, perhaps?"

"Bill? Please! I don't need a bill! I need a time machine. I don't suppose you have one of those on the menu, do you, my boy?" The man ripped off his sunglasses and stared at the waiter, almost accusingly.

The waiter sighed, reaching for his mobile phone. It appeared he was going to need some backup on this one. "I'm so sorry, sir," he said as he frantically texted hotel security. "But I'm afraid we're fresh out of time machines here at the Bermuda Dunes Hotel." Was this man even a guest at the resort? Or had he wandered in from somewhere off the beach?

The man groaned loudly and stroked his rather impressive white beard. The waiter found himself wondering just how many years it would take to grow a beard of that magnitude. "I'm sorry," the man said. "It's just… I'm a bit out of sorts today, you understand. After all, time travel does quite a number on one's noggin, especially if you do it twenty-three times in a row."

"Of course it does," the waiter agreed politely. *The guests are never wrong.* "I'm, uh, always saying that to my wife."

The man nodded as if this made perfect sense. "It wasn't intentional, of course. All I wanted to do was spend a few days in 1960s Bermuda – get a little warmed up after spending all those weeks in a cold leaky tower." He peered at the waiter. "I mean, is that so wrong?"

The waiter agreed this sounded more than reasonable.

"But after a short R and R, I was ready to go home – back to medieval England. Which should have been a mere hop in the park for an accomplished wizard like myself. But instead, after casting my spell, I found myself still here in Bermuda – this time in the year 2634." He glanced around the resort. "A terrible decade, by the way. I don't recommend it at all."

He reached into a small suitcase by his feet, pulling out a tall pointed blue hat. It reminded the waiter of the sorcerer cap a character had worn in an old cartoon, and he wondered, for a second, if the man was going to claim it came from the future.

Instead, he planted it on his head. "So I tried again. And again. At this point I've bounced around half of human history. But I can't seem to leave this blasted island." He shook his head, nearly losing his cap in the process. "I just don't know what's wrong with me."

To be fair, the waiter had been wondering the same thing since he'd started the conversation. He tried to surreptitiously glance behind himself. What was taking security so long?

The man rose from his chair, shaking crisp crumbs from his beard. "You know what? I'll bet it's *her* doing." He nodded his head vigorously, as if agreeing with himself. "She's still mad that I won that duel fair and square – even though she completely cheated! Purple dragon." He rolled his eyes. "Of all the ridiculous…"

The waiter bit his lower lip. "You know, sometimes if you spend too long in the sun—"

"And now I'm stuck here and she's back there, and who knows what she'll try to pull in my absence? What if she goes after the boy again? He'll be completely helpless on his own!" His face crumpled. "We got in a fight, you see. Right before I left. I got mad and just abandoned him all by himself. Well, with Archimedes, I suppose. He's a very intelligent owl. But still..." He sighed. "Oh, Wart. I never meant to let you down."

He looked so despondent the waiter almost felt bad. "Look, I'm sure whoever this Wart is, he'll forgive you," he assured the man, patting him on the shoulder comfortingly. "In the meantime, maybe you should go take a little nap? I'm sure you'll feel much better if you just get out of the sun for a few hours and—"

The man looked up. "Nap?" he sputtered, shaking his fists as his long white beard swung from side to side. "Haven't you listened to anything I've been saying? I can't take a blasted nap! I need to get back to England pronto!"

"Now, now, sir, take it easy."

The waiter whirled around to see that two burly security guards dressed in matching khaki pants and dark glasses had stepped up behind him. He dropped his shoulders in relief. Backup. Finally.

"Let's get you back to your room," said the first one, taking a cautious step towards the man.

"You're going to feel much better soon," assured the second, going around to his other side.

"I'll take care of your tab," the waiter added, starting to feel a little bad for the old geezer. After all, he was probably someone's grandfather. Maybe this Wart person's, even? "Uh, what did you say your name was again?"

"My name?" the man huffed, suddenly dodging the security guards with a move that seemed far too nimble for an old guy. "My name is Merlin, of course. I'm the world's most powerful wizard." He stared up at the sky, moaning mournfully. "And if I don't get back to Camelot soon, the world as we know it will surely be doomed!"

CHAPTER ONE
ARTHUR

Over one thousand years earlier,
in medieval England…

"Oh, Archimedes, surely I'm doomed!"

The young boy, Wart, recently crowned King Arthur, paced the cavernous throne room of Camelot Castle, shoving the altogether too-heavy velvet and metal crown out of his eyes for what felt like the thousandth time that day. He glanced over at the small brown owl, who perched on the armrest of his new throne.

"What am I to do?" Arthur asked mournfully. "I can't be king. I'm fourteen years old! Just a boy!"

"A boy who somehow managed to pull the legendary

sword from the stone," Archimedes, Merlin's highly educated owl, hooted back in reminder. "Which evidently makes you the rightful ruler of all England."

Arthur gave him a beseeching look, and the owl ruffled his feathers. "Sorry, I don't make the rules."

Arthur groaned, dropping down onto the throne. Which, by the way, had turned out to be the most uncomfortable chair he'd ever sat on in his entire life. Evidently kings didn't believe in cushions.

"I still don't understand how it happened," he mused, his mind going back to the day a week before when the so-called miracle had taken place. He'd been so excited to stand in as a real squire for the day after Kay's other squire, Hobbs, had mysteriously come down with the mumps. It was a great honour, after all, for a lowborn orphan like himself to serve a true knight of the realm – even if, in this case, the knight in question was his oafish foster brother, Kay. Arthur had been sure it would be the best day of his life.

Instead, it had turned out to be the worst.

The jousting tournament had been held to determine who would become England's next king, with the winner taking the throne. England had been too long without a king after Uther Pendragon had died with no heir, and it had thrown the kingdom into a dark age full of war and famine. They badly needed someone to don the crown and start making some rules around the place. And Sir Ector, Arthur's foster father, had decided his son Kay would be perfect for the job.

So when Arthur accidentally forgot Kay's sword back at the inn, he'd been forced to find another at the last moment – lest Kay be disqualified. And it was Archimedes who had first spotted the lone sword in the nearby churchyard, stuck in an anvil on top of a stone. How was Arthur supposed to know this was *the* sword in the stone – the one that would truly determine who would be king? It looked like any other sword.

Until he pulled it out of the anvil…

Not long after that, people were bowing to him. Knights and lords and ladies who had never given him the time of day, now calling him sire and Your Majesty and king. Claiming it was a miracle, ordained by Heaven itself. That Arthur was now the land's chosen monarch.

That Arthur, single-handedly, would somehow save them all.

"Why me?" he asked, staring up at the high ceiling of the throne room, which was decorated in rich tapestries of royal blues and purples and greens. "I'm no one. I wash dishes for a living. I shouldn't be king."

"Don't think I don't agree with you," Archimedes assured

him with a dismissive snort. "I told Merlin from the start he was wasting his time with you. But he saw something in you." The owl spun his head. "Maybe this was it."

"I wish he had warned me," Arthur grumped, thinking back to his kind but somewhat bumbling tutor. The wizard Merlin had seen fit to take Arthur under his wing the year before after Arthur had accidentally crashed through his roof, searching for Kay's lost arrow. At the time, Arthur had just been grateful for the attention, even if Merlin's unique brand of tutelage did frequently get him into a bit of trouble. After all, who wouldn't enjoy lessons that entailed becoming a fish or a squirrel or even a bird?

But those transformations hadn't exactly prepared him for being a king.

"If only Merlin would come back," he moaned. "He'd know what to do."

Archimedes flew from the throne up to a wooden beam near the ceiling. "Believe me, I want Merlin back as much as you do," he agreed. "I never realised how fond I was of the old fool until he bopped himself off to Bermuda."

"Blow me to Bermuda," Arthur sadly echoed Merlin's last words. "I know he was angry with me, but I never thought he'd stay away for good." He slumped his shoulders. "I should have turned down the squire job like he wanted

me to. I could have stayed behind at Ector's castle and continued my lessons with him. Then I wouldn't be in such a mess."

If only there were a way to reach him. To apologise. Merlin had been right about everything all along. But Arthur hadn't listened…

"Well, there's no use crying over wandering wizards," Archimedes chirped. "The point is, he's gone. You're king. And there's nothing you can do about it. So I suggest you stop moping about and start doing your duty." He flew across the throne room to the double doors at the end. "There are at least two dozen people outside, waiting to talk to you. You can't keep them out forever."

Arthur nodded miserably. He knew the owl was right. "Very well," he said. "Let them in." He tried to straighten his crown, which was far too big for his head, and sat up taller in his throne. Archimedes waited for him to be settled, then yanked the front doors open with his talons.

Suddenly the vast empty chamber exploded in sound and colour as the people of England poured inside to meet their new king. Arthur tried not to squirm as they dropped to their knees before him and practically kissed the ground at his feet. How embarrassing.

"All rise," he called out, trying to make his voice sound authoritative – like a king's. Instead, it sounded as squeaky as a mouse's. "Make an orderly line. I'm ready to hear your grievances."

Arthur had never known any actual kings prior to becoming one himself, mind you. But he had always just assumed being king meant being able to do whatever you wanted – whenever you wanted to do it. Unfortunately, the opposite was true according to Sir Pellinore, who had instated himself as head knight and official advisor once Arthur took the throne. A king had to attend to his subjects constantly, listening to their problems and trying to help solve them. Even if their problems were difficult.

Or just plain ridiculous.

Speaking of, an apple-cheeked woman with pale skin and freckles, dressed in a dusty white apron and powder-blue dress, pushed her way through the crowd, cradling a small brown chicken in her arms.

"Your Majesty," she said, bowing so low to Arthur that she almost dropped her chicken in the process. "I am in desperate need of your help."

Arthur nodded, beckoning for her to stand upright again. He wondered, not for the first time, if it was within his powers to outlaw bowing entirely – at least to a king. He'd have to ask Sir Pellinore later. "What seems to be the trouble?" he asked.

The woman thrust the bird forwards. "I am Mistress Mabel. And this is my chicken. I call her Helen of Troy. She's a remarkable bird. Always has an egg for me, every morning, rain or shine."

"That's… great." Arthur waited for the complaint.

"Well, this morning, I went out to her henhouse, and there was no egg! And no Helen of Troy, either! I searched the yard thoroughly, concerned that a fox might have come in and stolen her away in the night."

"But… you found her," Arthur suggested gently, gesturing to the chicken, which was clearly no longer lost nor eaten by a fox. "She's all right." He wondered if it'd be unkingly to ask her to get to the point.

"I found her… in my neighbour's chicken coop!" Mistress Mabel sputtered, her red cheeks ripe with indignation.

Before Arthur could speak, another woman shoved her way through the crowd. She grabbed the chicken from Mabel and yanked it in her own direction. Helen of Troy squawked in dismay, and a spray of feathers burst into the air, causing several people – including Arthur – to sneeze.

"Bless you," Archimedes whispered. "And good luck with this one."

Arthur sighed and turned back to the new woman in front of him. "I'm sorry. You are…?"

"I'm Ayn, the rightful owner of this here chicken," the new woman declared.

"I see." Oh, dear. Arthur's eyes strayed to the long line of people behind the two women, who were starting to look impatient.

Mistress Ayn puffed out her chest. "You see, sire, I woke up this morning, ready to get started preparing our family's daily meal. We were all well looking forward to a nice supper of roasted bird this eve." She licked her lips. Helen of Troy squirmed in her arms, looking a tad alarmed.

"So I go out to the chicken coop. And what do I find there but this *thief*!" She gestured angrily to Mistress Mabel at her left. "She was trying to steal my chicken! Steal food out of my poor, sweet kids' very mouths!"

"Helen of Troy is mine!" Mistress Mabel protested. "I hatched her from an egg!"

"A disgusting lie. I picked her up at the market on Monday," countered Mistress Ayn, crossing her arms over her chest. "And you can't prove that I didn't."

The two women turned to look at Arthur expectantly. Meanwhile, the chicken had managed to wriggle its way out of Ayn's hands and drop to the floor, which it pecked at. Arthur raked a hand through his hair, feeling nervous. He knew they wanted him to rule on whom the chicken truly belonged to. But how could he tell for sure? They both seemed utterly convinced the bird was theirs.

If only Merlin were there. He'd know what to do.

Arthur turned to Archimedes – who was the next best thing. "What should I do?" he whispered.

The owl ruffled his feathers. "I'm sure I don't know. Though chicken for dinner does sound quite lovely." He eyed the bird hungrily. "Maybe we should just take it for ourselves and settle it that way."

"But that wouldn't be fair," Arthur protested.

"You want fair? Then just have them split it in two," Archimedes replied. "One half for each of them. That would be *fair*, right?" He huffed. "And then we can move on from all this nonsense and get to the important matters of the day."

Arthur frowned. The owl wasn't wrong. But still… Something about it didn't sit right with him. His eyes travelled to the two women. Mistress Ayn was glaring at Mistress Mabel with a smug look on her face. Mistress Mabel looked close to tears.

And suddenly he had an idea.

"Very well," he declared grandly, addressing the women and the court. "Since I suppose we can't know for sure who the bird belongs to, how about this? What if we cut the chicken in half and you can each have half of it? That ought to solve your problem, right?"

He watched the two women's faces, holding his breath.

Ayn spoke first. "Half," she muttered. "Well, I suppose it's better than nothing. Though with my big family…" She trailed off, turning to Mistress Mabel, who, Arthur realised, had burst into tears. Arthur watched as she dropped to her knees in front of him, her hands clasped in prayer.

"Please, kind sir," she begged. "Your Grace. Your Majesty. Do not split Helen of Troy in two! If she must have her, then she must have her. But make her promise not to eat her and to let her lay her daily eggs. They're good eggs – the best in the village." She turned to Ayn, her face pleading. "You'd do so much better to keep her alive than eat her, I promise you!"

It was all Arthur needed to hear. He clapped his hands.

"I have made my decision," he declared. "The chicken – Helen of Troy – shall be returned to this woman here." He smiled down at Mabel, who was still on her knees before him. "For if she cares so much for the fate of a chicken that she's willing to give it away rather than have it be cut in two, clearly she is the rightful owner."

Mabel let out a cry of joy. She dived for the chicken. Helen of Troy leapt into her lap, and she hugged the creature tightly against her chest, tears streaming down her rosy cheeks. The crowd behind her broke into cheers.

Mistress Ayn grunted and stormed out of the great hall, slamming the door behind her.

"Oh, thank you, kind sir," Mabel cried, still weeping. "Finally, we have a true king. One who is so just and good and kind and fair." She rose to her feet, still cuddling Helen of Troy. "I will bring you eggs every day from now on! To thank you for your kindness." She bowed again, then turned and headed through the hall to the door, all the while being congratulated by the others waiting their turns.

"That was very good, boy," Archimedes hooted. "Using wisdom to gain knowledge. Merlin would be so proud."

Arthur beamed, all of a sudden feeling quite proud of himself. His first act as king, and it was a success. Perhaps this wouldn't be as hard as he'd thought.

"Your Majesty, if you're done courting chickens, we must speak of graver matters."

Or… maybe not.

Arthur looked up to see that Sir Pellinore had stepped up to the throne. The tall, thin balding knight looked quite distraught – with an expression under his thick grey moustache that sent a chill down Arthur's spine.

"What is it?" Arthur asked worriedly, not entirely sure he wanted to know.

Sir Pellinore gave him a solemn look. "We have word that a new threat is coming to London Town, Your Majesty.

An army of Saxon invaders is rumoured to be landing on our eastern shores. They have supposedly heard of your new… position… and likely seek to learn for themselves what mettle you are made of." He met Arthur's eyes with his own steely grey ones. "What should we do to answer their call?"

Arthur sank back into his seat, all his earlier bravado fleeing. While the fate of chickens was something he felt somewhat confident handling, the fate of the kingdom was something else entirely. Especially when it came to matters of war. What if he made the wrong decision? People could die. England could be overrun by invaders. Soon there might not even be an England for him to be king of.

He glanced over at Archimedes, but the owl had retreated up into the rafters. Coward!

"Um…" he stammered, turning back to Pellinore. "What do *you* think we should do?" Sir Pellinore was, after all, an actual knight. And much more versed in these types of matters.

But the elderly knight shook his head. "What I think doesn't matter in this case," he told Arthur. "You, my boy, are our king. You are the one the heavens chose. You are the one who must decide our fate."

Arthur bit back a groan. He'd had a feeling Pellinore was going to say something like that. He rubbed his hand on his chin, as if deep in thought. But in truth, his mind was basically blank. He squirmed on his throne, once again wishing he had a cushion. But all the cushions in the world couldn't get him out of this one.

What would Merlin do? he asked himself again. But this time he had no answer. Merlin had tried to give him a top-notch education, but none of his teachings had to do with battles or invaders. War wasn't the wizard's thing.

"Well, Your Majesty?"

Arthur could feel the entire court locking their eyes onto him, holding their breaths, waiting for his reply. Whatever came out of his mouth next had the potential to change the course of history. He did not want to say the wrong thing. He swallowed hard and opened his mouth…

"I think we should… I think we should…"

His voice trailed off as he realised everything had gone strangely quiet. The hum of voices in the hall had completely ceased. And when his eyes scanned the room, he realised everyone was standing very still. Not still because they were paying close attention, mind you. But as if they had been actually frozen in place. Even Archimedes was hanging above him – suspended in midair.

Then, suddenly, a new voice rose up beside Arthur. Thin and reedy and high pitched.

"Now, now, don't tell me our illustrious new king is *chicken*…"

CHAPTER TWO
ARTHUR

Arthur whirled around, shocked to find a hunched old woman standing next to him, seeming to have come out of nowhere. She wore long purple robes and the same style of pointed hat that Merlin favoured, though hers was a dark shade of violet. She leant heavily on a wooden cane topped with an elaborate carving of a dragon's head. As Arthur gaped at her, she grinned toothily back at him as if he were a long-lost friend, and even though he was pretty positive he'd never seen her before in his life, he felt a weird shimmer of familiarity wash over him as he gazed upon her face.

"Um, who are you?" he asked, warily looking around the room. "And why is everyone but us frozen?"

The woman laughed. It sounded like the tinkling of

tiny bells. "That was my doing, m'lord," she informed him, bobbing her head respectfully in his direction. "I wanted to speak with you privately, and they were all being so very loud." She paused, staring at him with strangely vivid purple eyes. "You don't mind, do you?"

"Um..." Arthur honestly wasn't sure if he should mind or not. On one hand, it wasn't right to freeze people against their wills simply to have a quieter conversation. On the other, it did give him some extra time to make a decision on the whole Saxon invader thing, which, he supposed, wasn't unwelcome. "Who are you again?" he asked.

"My name is Morgan," the woman informed him. "The marvellous Morgan le Fay. I am a wizard of some high regard. Surely you have heard of me?" She looked a little hurt to think that maybe he hadn't.

Arthur felt his cheeks heat to a blush. "I'm sorry," he said. "I'm sure you're quite well known. It's just... I don't get out much, you see. In fact, before last month, I'd never gone beyond the Forest Sauvage and my foster father's place. And now that I'm king, I'm not allowed to leave this castle."

"Poor lad." The woman – Morgan – put a hand on his arm and patted him comfortingly. Arthur couldn't help noticing that even her fingernails were painted purple. "And now you're king of all England. I imagine that kind of quick change of fortune is bound to make one's head spin."

"You have no idea," Arthur said with a sigh, looking out over his frozen court.

"Oh, but I do! In fact, it's why I'm here, my boy!"

"It is?" Arthur turned back to the woman, his eyes widening. Suddenly he put two and two together. "Wait… did Merlin send you? Is he all right? Why isn't he here? Is he still angry at me about the whole squire thing? Because I really feel bad about all that! I didn't mean to drive him away!"

Morgan laughed, holding up a hand to stop the barrage of questions. "Oh, my dear boy. You know Merlin! He's so flighty. So unpredictable. He wanted to be here, of course. But he had a little holiday planned. And you know how *those* can be. Don't cancel in time? You don't get your deposit back. And no one wants that!" She gave Arthur a knowing look.

Arthur swallowed hard, his mind whirling. He knew she was speaking English, but he wasn't quite sure he understood half the things she'd just said. But then again, that was how Merlin always talked, too. Maybe it was a wizard thing…

"Anyhoo, while dear old Merlin is enjoying a little R and R in the far-off future, I'm here at his behest to take over your education. And it seems, my dear little sparrow,

I've arrived just in the nick of time." She glanced out over the frozen court. "Now tell Auntie Morgan. What exactly seems to be the trouble?"

Arthur sank back down onto his throne, slumping his shoulders in relief. Finally, someone grown-up – and human (he stole a glance up at Archimedes) – who was willing to listen.

"I want to be a good king," he told Morgan. "I don't want to let anyone down. But I know nothing of battles and wars and invasions." He sighed. "It seems the Saxons – whoever they are – will be landing on our shores shortly. And it sounds as if they'll be up to no good when they get here. But I don't know what I should do about it."

"Oh! That's simple!" Morgan exclaimed without a pause. "You blow them out of the water."

Arthur looked at her, surprised. "What?" This was not quite what he'd been expecting her to say.

"Come on! Isn't it obvious? We have to show these silly boys they can't just roll up to England's shores without RSVPing first! It's simply not done! And quite rude, to boot."

"RSV-what?"

Morgan waved him off. "Look, it's all very simple. You round up an army of your very best knights. And you send them down to the shores to defend your land. Show them exactly what happens when they try to rise up under our rule!"

"*Our* rule?" Arthur scrunched up his face.

Morgan giggled. "Did I say *our*? I meant *your*, of course. For *you* are the king of England now! All because you pulled that sword from that stone." She motioned to the sword at Arthur's belt. "A marvellous miracle, don't you think?"

"I— I suppose..." Arthur stammered, starting to feel a little uncomfortable.

"Oh! He's modest, too! How adorable." Morgan pinched his cheeks, just a tad too hard. Then she clapped her hands. "Look, all you need to do is show them who's boss. And then they won't have a leg to stand on. Literally – if you cut off their legs." She giggled. "Just kidding," she added quickly, in a way that made Arthur wonder if she had been.

"Look, I don't want to hurt anyone," he told Morgan. "I just want them to go home."

"Oh, they will. A few amputated limbs and everyone will take off running." She laughed. This time it sounded a bit more like a cackle. "Well, not *running*, exactly." She slapped her hand on her knee. "Kidding! Kidding! Sorry! Sometimes I just can't help myself!"

"Right..." Arthur pressed his lips together, glancing up at Archimedes again, wishing the owl would unfreeze and help him. Maybe he could tell Arthur who this woman really was – and if she truly was a friend of his teacher's. She claimed Merlin had sent her. But she certainly had a very different way of looking at the world than his old tutor.

His mind flashed back to the day Merlin had turned him into a fish. They'd been swimming along in the castle moat quite happily when a huge pike with nasty sharp teeth had started chasing them. Merlin had refused to help, telling Arthur he needed to figure it out on his own. In fact, he still remembered the wizard's words. Something about the strong wanting to conquer you, but that you could defeat them using intellect.

Intellect – not violence. Because according to Merlin, *brains* were just as powerful as brawn.

What if he could trick the Saxons? Or better yet, try to befriend them? Maybe they could avoid violence. Maybe it could even work out in everyone's favour – having a new friend was never a bad thing…

He realised Morgan was still waiting for an answer. Sitting up straighter in his throne, he cleared his throat. He had to be careful. After all, friend of Merlin's or no, she was clearly a powerful wizard. He didn't want to make her angry by dismissing her outright. She might even refuse to unfreeze his court. And then where would he be?

"Look," he said, "it's not that I don't appreciate your

advice. I really do. But in this case, I think I am going to try something else first. Something more… peaceful." He shrugged sheepishly. "I'm pretty sure it's what Merlin would have wanted."

Morgan's smile slipped from her face. For a moment, she looked angry. But then, just as quickly as her smile had faded, it returned. "Of course, of course!" she agreed, patting him a little too hard on the shoulder. "You do you! You're the king, after all! You pulled the sword from the stone – all by yourself! So why would you want to listen to a silly old wizard who went so far out of her way to come and help you with your troubles? Much better to imagine what Merlin would do. The cowardly kook who abandoned you to this fate. Did he even say goodbye when he left?"

Arthur cringed. "Well, not exactly—"

"Of course he didn't. That silly boy!" Morgan snorted. "Anyway, I must be going now! So much time, so little to do!" she jabbered. "Or is it the opposite?" She tapped her finger to her chin. "In any case, have fun running the kingdom all by yourself! Hope you don't get invaded and suffer a fate worse than death!" She lifted her hand to a wave. "Toodles!"

And with that, she poofed into a cloud of smoke. When it cleared, she had disappeared completely. As if she'd never been there at all.

A moment later the court erupted into sound again, everyone talking and moving as if they had no idea they'd ever been frozen at all. Perhaps they didn't. Arthur felt a shimmer of unease as he looked to the spot where Morgan had stood a moment before, now completely empty. He wondered if he'd made the right decision.

Archimedes dropped down from his perch and peered at Arthur quizzically.

"Are you all right?" he asked. "You look like you've seen a ghost."

"I'll tell you later," Arthur said, waving him off. He turned back to Sir Pellinore, who was now once again expectantly waiting for his answer.

"Sire?" the knight queried. "What do you want us to do?"

Arthur drew in a breath. "I think we should invite the Saxons here," he blurted out before he could lose his nerve.

Pellinore looked shocked. "Excuse me?"

"We will invite them to the castle. And when they come, we will throw a great feast in their honour."

"You want to invite our enemies to a feast?" The old knight looked as if he was about to fall over.

"Yes," Arthur declared, feeling more and more confident about his plan as he thought about it. It was exactly the kind of thing Merlin would have approved of. "We will invite them here and speak with them as equals. See what they want. Who knows – maybe we can work out a peace treaty that will benefit us both. We may be different, but we're all human beings, after all. There's no reason we can't all get along."

For a moment Pellinore said nothing. Then he slowly nodded his head. "Very well, Your Majesty," he said. "You are the king. It's your call." But he didn't sound too confident about the whole thing. Perhaps he would have preferred Morgan's idea of destroying them all. Arthur sighed, looking out onto the court for support. Surely *someone* thought this was a good idea, besides him? But all he saw were worried, distrustful faces. No one seemed to approve of his plan.

Merlin would have approved, Arthur thought, forcing himself to remain strong. *And he's the smartest person I know.*

CHAPTER THREE
MADAM MIM

Merlin is such a meddling muck!

The Marvellous Madam Mim cursed under her breath as she poofed herself back to her little cottage in the woods, so furious at what had just transpired at the castle that her skin had broken out into pink polka dots all over again – an irritating lingering side effect of that horrific disease she'd suffered at the hands of that wily waste of a wizard. She glanced in the mirror, scowled, then snapped a finger. The elegant elder 'Morgan le Fay' vanished into thin air and Mim returned to her normal purple-haired self.

She stormed over to the fireplace, poking angrily at the ashes. Then she waved her finger, and a small purple flame sputtered to life in the hearth. Huffing, she plopped down on a nearby chair in front of her table of cards. But she was in no mood for games.

"This was not how it was supposed to go," she muttered to herself. "Not how it was supposed to go at all. Here I go to all the effort of faking a miracle, and where does it get me? A young sparrow with delusions of grandeur and no respect for his elders."

Mim spat on the floor. "Bleh!" This was clearly all Merlin's fault. As usual.

Perhaps she should have never meddled in the situation to begin with. But when she'd heard the announcement that they were going to have a tournament to decide on a king at last, she'd panicked. All these years she'd been working to ensure England stayed stuck in a dark age of chaos and confusion – a state Mim delighted in; it was just so much fun! And now they were going to allow some random knight in shining armour to rise up and start making rules again? What if this man united England? What if he brought peace and lawfulness to the land?

Why, that would be no fun at all!

And so she'd determined to take matters into her own hands. She had sneaked out late at night and used her magic to relocate the real sword in the stone to some kind of fancy theme park far in the future of a land yet to be called Florida. In its place, she'd fashioned a replacement.

A design of her own, which allowed the sword to be lifted from the stone by a person of her choosing.

And she'd chosen the least likely candidate of all.

"The looks on their faces!" she cackled in remembrance. "When they realised this scrawny little sparrow who couldn't even fit into his clothes was to be their king!" She thought back to all the fools bowing low before the boy and how she'd laughed and laughed from the sidelines. "How could they really believe he was the one?"

It was all just perfectly hilarious.

And if that wasn't victory enough, she'd gone one step further, getting rid of the only person who might have discovered her ruse. The meddlesome Merlin, who'd completely, unfairly cheated during their wizards' duel. She'd been on her way to demand a rematch when she'd overheard his owl say he'd gone to somewhere in the future called Bermuda. It took a bit of fancy spell casting – including the regretful sacrifice of her favourite warty toad, Martha – but she'd managed to track him down and scramble up his spell book while he was asleep in a lounge chair on the beach, making it impossible for him to magically find his way back home. Which meant he wouldn't be around to mess up her messing things up.

Yes, everything had been so perfectly un-perfect.

Until she'd spotted the owl in court today. *Merlin's* owl.

And he'd been talking to the boy.

She grunted in annoyance, remembering the moment she'd realised what she'd accidentally done. That of all the boys in all the world, she'd somehow managed to place Merlin's own protégé on the throne. It was an honest mistake; she'd never seen Arthur with Merlin before. At least not in his boy state – he'd been a bird when he'd come down her chimney and started the whole duel thing. How was she to know that this very same boy would turn up halfway across England in London on the day of the tournament, looking for a sword?

Mim liked bad luck. But only when it happened to other people.

At first, she didn't think it would be a huge problem. In fact, maybe it could even work out in her favour. What better way to get back at Merlin than to take over the 'education' of his favourite pupil? With Merlin gone, Arthur would be lost, confused, scared. She could slip right in and pretend to be his friend, offering up some oh-so-wise advice that surely he would follow, relieved to have a grown-up calling the shots.

She imagined with delight Merlin's horror when he finally realised what she had done. Taking his very own student – the one he had risked his life in their duel to protect – and moulding him into her own stooge, a fellow lover of the gruesome and grim! It would have been the best revenge she could have hoped for.

Unfortunately, it had not gone so well.

She scowled into the mirror, thinking back to the scene. Why, the boy had not listened to her oh-so-wise advice at all! Instead, the little boy king had some wonky idea of trying for a peaceful solution instead. Which was ridiculous, to say the least! After all, what young lad in medieval England wanted peace? There was no glory in that! No adventure! No dragons, even.

Merlin had clearly poisoned his young brain.

She sighed, brushing away the pile of cards. She needed a new plan. It was too late to put someone else on the throne – it would cause far too many questions. And she was still convinced Arthur could be turned to her side; he just needed something more convincing. Or maybe some*one*. Someone he could grow to trust. Someone Mim could use to feed him her fun ideas and make him act on them – ensuring more and more chaos the longer his rule. An advisor, maybe? Was there a knight she could corrupt? Maybe a servant?

A friend?

"Mother? I'm home!"

Mim's head shot up as her ward, Guinevere, stepped into the cottage, her arms laden with supplies she'd acquired at the market in town. Guinevere always insisted on buying groceries the old-fashioned way, no matter how many times Mim reminded her she could just conjure them up with magic – no muss, no fuss. (And no price tag, either! Let's just say being a wizard was marvellous, but didn't always pay the bills.)

Mim had been fostering Guinevere for the last thirteen years, after 'borrowing' her from her cradle in her parents' home back in the Summer Country. Mim had always thought it would be fun to have a child to teach magic to, and had somehow not managed, thus far, to produce any on her own. And so when she had discovered, in an ancient tome, that Guinevere's family lines ran deep and were rumoured to flow with fairy blood – the kind of blood that could help make one into a powerful wizard – Mim took matters into her own hands, not wanting such potential power to end up totally wasted on a royal lady in court who would never have a chance to properly use it.

Guinevere, of course, didn't know any of these pesky little details of her unconventional 'adoption' – a story Mim found far too boring for her liking. Instead, she'd told the young girl she'd rescued her from the evil wizard Merlin, who had killed her parents and tried to steal her away, which proved a much better bedtime story. Guin was *so* lucky that Mim had come by when she had and risked her own life to save the baby from the hands of that tyrant. And Guin should be eternally grateful her 'mother' had agreed to take her in afterwards, when she had nowhere else to go. After all, babies were stinky. And those midnight feedings? A major sacrifice for the sake of a helpless creature who couldn't even keep up with an intelligent conversation.

But it would all be worth it, Mim had told herself back then, once Guinevere started mastering her magic. And she would become a worthy heir to take Mim's place someday as the most powerful wizard in the land.

There was only one problem with it all. Guinevere hated magic.

Perhaps it was Mim's fault, she thought in hindsight. Perhaps the Merlin story had been a bit too dramatic to tell an impressionable four-year-old just before bed. But there was nothing she could do to take it back now. And as much as Mim tried to show Guin all the fun things that magic could do – fireworks! shapeshifting! rainbow-coloured ponies! – Guin remained thoroughly unconvinced. Hence the groceries. And the washing. And the mending. All things that could have been easily accomplished by a touch of magic, instead done painstakingly by her daughter's hands. While all of Guin's potential power remained untapped. Untouched.

Mim shook her head. Such a waste…

Guinevere set her packages on the floor near the door, then danced across the cottage to give her mother a warm hug. Mim indulged her for a moment – hugs made her itchy – then shrugged her off.

"What's wrong, Mother?" Guin asked, frowning as she studied Mim's face with her big brown eyes. The girl had the most amazing lashes, Mim thought grumpily. So thick and curly. And she didn't even need magic to grow them. "You look upset."

"Oh, I'm just fine, my dear," she assured her, patting her on the arm. "Did you get any slugs at the market today? I've been practically dying for slug soup for dinner."

"I'm sorry," Guinevere apologised as she walked over to her bags and grabbed one, bringing it over to the table. "I looked and looked. No one seems to sell slugs in London." She shrugged. "They did have some lovely apples, though." She reached into the bag and pulled out a shiny red apple, giving Mim a hopeful look.

Mim did not like apples. Especially ripe ones without any worms. They made her toot like a trumpet and tasted nothing like a good old slimy slug. But she only smiled and petted Guinevere's hand. The poor girl did try so hard to please her mother. Even if she did have lousy taste in food.

Guinevere began putting away the groceries, dancing a little as she went. As much as Guin didn't like magic, she *loved* to dance. Which had always given them something to bond over. Mim would sing and Guin would dance. And for a brief moment, it would feel as if it was just the two of them – together against the hard, cruel world – and Mim would realise just how lucky she was to have a daughter of her very own.

"It was wild in town today," Guinevere said as she placed some potatoes in the bin where they could sit until they properly rotted. "With the new king holding court and all. People were here from all over the kingdom to meet him."

Mim frowned, unhappy to be reminded of that ridiculous Arthur and his ridiculous court again. She still couldn't believe he'd basically thrown her out of the throne room, all because of some teensy-weensy suggestion that he start a war. Thank goodness everyone had been frozen at the time and therefore hadn't witnessed her humiliation.

Guinevere, oblivious, danced back over to the table. "It *was* pretty exciting, though," she added, her eyes sparkling a little as she grabbed a cabbage. "You should have been there. It was as if there was this energy crackling in the air. Everyone's waited so long for a new king. And to finally have one at long last! Why, they say he'll bring peace to the realm! Maybe even unite all of England!"

Mim swallowed back the urge to vomit. Seriously, this Arthur was nothing if not nauseating.

"Please don't talk to me about that usurper," she protested grumpily. "He shouldn't even be king, you know."

Guinevere stopped short. She turned to Mim, her large brown eyes widening in surprise. "What are you saying, Mother?" she asked. "Why shouldn't he be king? He pulled the sword from the stone, didn't he?"

He certainly had, Mim thought huffingly. Thanks to her. She really had to do something about this. She couldn't just sit back and let Merlin win after all.

Suddenly an idea began to niggle at the back of her brain. She looked up at Guinevere.

"Yes," she said. "He *did* pull the sword from the stone. But he wasn't meant to. It was all a trick. Concocted by that evil wizard Merlin to get his little puppet on the throne – so he could have all the power for himself and destroy England!"

Guinevere dropped her cabbage. It fell to the floor of the cottage with a loud thump. This was not surprising. She always got upset when Mim said the *M* word. She turned slowly to her mother, her face white with fear. "Are you serious?" she asked. "Merlin? He's behind the miracle?"

Mim smiled to herself. Now that was more like it.

"None other," she declared, liking this story more and

more as she made it up out of thin air. "And now Arthur is on the throne. Who knows what damage he'll do to our country?" She sighed loudly. "I worry for the realm, I really do."

"Oh, but this is terrible!" Guinevere murmured, pacing the cottage, rubbing her hands together in worry. "I had no idea. Everyone seems to love the new king so much!"

"A trick. A trap. Evil sorcery of the worst kind."

"So what do we do?" Guinevere asked. She dropped to her knees before Mim, clasping her hands over Mim's own. "You can't let Merlin get away with this! Tell me you have a plan."

Mim stroked her hairy chin, her fabulously big brain now whirring with excitement as a plan did begin to form. "I do," she confessed. "However, I don't think I can pull it off myself. I tried to go to court today, but he rejected my oh-so-generous offer of help. I think he might have been suspicious of my intentions. Which were entirely good, of course!" she added, lest Guin have any doubt. She dropped her eyes to meet her daughter's. "But perhaps if someone *else* were to go to court in my place. Someone more his own age…"

"Do you mean me?" Guinevere's voice echoed her surprise. Which, Mim supposed, wasn't unwarranted. Back in the Forest Sauvage, she hadn't exactly let the girl wander too far from their cottage in the woods for most of her life. For her own good, of course. And just in case someone recognised her and had the bad sense to call the authorities. Mim wasn't about to lose her useful protégé over something as ridiculous as having her real parents wanting her back.

But they were far from the forest now. And while Guin had grown to look irritatingly like her birth mother, no one here would recognise her. Mim would have to take a chance.

"Yes." Mim straightened, her plan solidifying in her mind. Arthur wouldn't suspect a thing from a sweet young girl like Guin. And Guin would do whatever her mother asked of her without question. "You will go to court and apply to be a dishwasher or dog walker or privy emptier or whatever random job they might have open at the castle for young ladies like yourself. This way you can be my eyes and ears on the ground."

Guinevere looked unsure. "Would I have to use magic?" she asked.

"No, no, of course not," Mim assured her, resisting the urge to lecture the girl about the benefits of having powers – she didn't need to start a fight. "You just have to be yourself. Befriend Arthur – make him trust you. Get him to tell you his evil plans, then report them all back to me. Perhaps you'll even discover a weakness. Something we can use to take him down."

"And put the rightful ruler on the throne instead!" Guinevere concluded, looking satisfied at the idea now that she knew it didn't involve magic. She rose to her feet, planting her hands on her hips. "I love it. It's perfect. And I know I can do it. He won't stand a chance against me." She smiled smugly. She might not be magical, but Mim had always admired her confidence.

"That's my girl!" Mim cried, feeling suddenly so much better about everything. She leapt up from her chair, grabbing a harp and strumming the chords. Guinevere clapped her hands, delighted, then broke out into a playful dance as Mim began to sing.

The evil Merlin thinks he's won.
But the game, my dear, is not half done.
For his lackey king is far too dim…
To stand a chance against the mighty,
magnificent, marvellous—

"Guinevere!" Guin broke in, finishing the song with a dramatic flourish.

Mim frowned. "That doesn't exactly rhyme," she muttered a little sulkily at having her song interrupted. But Guin wasn't listening. She was standing in the centre of the cottage, her eyes shining.

"Just leave it to me, Mother," she declared. "I swear I won't let you down. I will do whatever it takes to put this usurper back in his rightful place."

Mim couldn't help a small smile at the earnest look on her daughter's face. Yes. This was going to be great. Arthur would trust her confident daughter, giving Mim the perfect in. And Merlin – he would be so upset when he found out she'd stolen his pet and made him her own! She walked over to Guin, taking her hands and squeezing them tight.

"This will be just *marvellous*, my dear. Wait and see."

CHAPTER FOUR
GUINEVERE

After she received her assignment, Guinevere had hoped her mother would send her to Camelot Castle immediately so she could begin her quest to help unseat Merlin's pawn. Instead, Mim had told her it was best to wait until morning to start her journey, stating that it would be dangerous for a young girl to travel through the woods on her own in the dark where wolves and other nasty forest creatures might be lurking. Guin wouldn't exactly be able to save the world, she reminded her, if she became a wolf's midnight snack.

Of course, Mim could zap her there immediately using magic, but Guinevere chose to decline that option, saying she should probably cook dinner first anyway.

So Guin began to prepare their nightly meal, deciding on a hearty stew using the vegetables she'd found in the market. (She was still secretly grateful she hadn't found any slugs. Nothing against her mother, of course, but they were just so slimy!) She planned to make an extra-large portion of stew so Mim could eat it while she was away. After all, she had no idea how long she'd be at the castle. And she didn't need her mother resorting to magic again while she was gone just to feed herself.

After slicing and dicing the vegetables, Guin realised she didn't have enough water for her stew. And so she set out with two large buckets to the well just outside of town. It was about an eight-furlong walk, but Guinevere didn't mind the trek so much. It was pleasant, after all, to feel the warm sun on her skin and fresh air on her face.

It reminded her of the Forest Sauvage, where she and Mim had lived up until recently. Mim had decided one day (seemingly on a whim) to use her magic to poof their entire cottage furlongs away from its old spot and plop it down on an entirely new plot of land just outside of London – with them still inside of it. Mim insisted it was more convenient that way – rather than packing everything up and moving to a new place by horse and wagon. And Guinevere *was* happy to be able to keep her old room in the new spot. Though she admittedly would have preferred a less jarring way to go about it.

Magic. It was always so troublesome.

Speaking of magic, she still couldn't believe what that dastardly Merlin had managed to get away with. Or maybe she could – after all, it was just like the evil wizard to meddle in affairs that were simply none of his business. He'd killed her parents, for one thing. And he'd tried to kill her, too. Why, he'd quite recently barged into her mother's cottage with his bewitched owl for no reason at all, while Mim was minding her own business playing a game of cards. He'd challenged her to a duel, forcing her mother to use her magic, then cheated by giving her a near-fatal disease. It had taken weeks for Guin to nurse her poor mother back to health.

The man had to be stopped. And if Guinevere could help in any way? Why, she was more than happy to do so. She'd been longing for revenge as long as she could remember. And finally she would get her chance.

She wondered what Arthur would be like. Mim hadn't allowed her to attend his coronation, so she'd never caught sight of his face. She could imagine it, though – probably rough and scarred from the many battles he'd fought. And his shoulders would be very broad. He'd be tall, too. Guinevere was pretty sure all kings were tall. And likely barrel-chested – maybe with a cleft in his chin. She pictured him draped in heavy ermine robes and decked out in stolen jewels as he sat languidly on the throne, working to destroy a kingdom that he should never have been allowed to rule to begin with.

But that wasn't going to happen. Not on her watch.

When she arrived at the well, she realised there was someone already there: a boy, around her own age, with a mop of sandy-coloured hair on top of his head. From his simple undyed cotton tunic, woven belt and plain shoes, she assumed he was one of the nearby villagers, come to gather water at the well.

Except he didn't have a bucket. And he was peering down into the water with a strange longing on his face.

She waited for a moment, hoping he'd just leave on his own and allow her to get her water. When he didn't, she eventually cleared her throat to get his attention. His head jerked up in response, managing to smack into the well's wooden roof. He let out an "OW!" and staggered backwards, holding his head with his hands. Guinevere immediately felt bad.

"I'm sorry!" she cried, biting her lower lip. "I didn't mean to startle you."

The boy managed to straighten, then shook himself. He looked up at her. "It's all right," he said. "My fault, really."

"What were you doing?" she asked.

"I was just thinking about being a fish," he replied. As

if this weren't a strange thing to say to someone, especially someone you just met.

"Hm. I don't think there are any fish in this well," she couldn't help teasing. "I mean, I hope not, at least. It wouldn't be very pleasant for them. Or us, for that matter." She grinned.

He laughed. It was a nice laugh, full and rich and hearty, unlike Mim's giggles. "You're probably right," he agreed, leaning against a nearby tree. "Perhaps a bird would be better." He looked up into the sky. Guinevere noticed his eyes were very blue.

"I don't know about that," she replied before she could help herself, remembering the time Mim had zapped her into a bird during a lesson on shapeshifting magic. Guin still remembered how terrifying it had been to feel her body shrink in size and her bones reshape themselves. And if that wasn't bad enough, Mim had found it hilarious to pick her up and toss her high into the air, assuming she'd learn to fly before colliding back with the ground.

She hadn't, it turned out. And if Mim hadn't caught her at the last moment in a magical bubble of air, she probably wouldn't even be there talking to the boy now.

"Where would you go if you were a bird?" she asked as she grabbed the well's rope and started pulling up its bucket.

"I don't know," the boy mused, seeming to take the question more seriously than she'd meant it. "But wherever it was, it would be far away from here. Where no one could find me."

The tone in his voice sounded both sad and a little lonely. Guinevere watched as he stubbed his toe into the dirt. "Is that why you're out here?" she asked kindly. "Because you don't want to be found?"

"Most definitely," he agreed with a long sigh. "Life has become… well, complicated lately. I just wanted a few moments to myself. You can imagine, right?" He gave a half laugh and looked at her as if she would understand.

And she did, actually. As much as she loved her foster mother and their simple life in the forest, sometimes Guin found herself longing for some freedom or a chance for adventure. Mim was a lot of wonderful things, but she was also very protective of her daughter, insisting she always stay close for her own safety. The world was a dangerous place, Mim would say. With evil wizards like Merlin always lurking about in the shadows. You couldn't be too careful.

Guin was appreciative of her mother caring about her so much and protecting her from harm. But still, sometimes she couldn't help wishing for more…

"Do you live in the village?" she asked the boy,

deciding to change the subject. "I don't think I've seen you here before."

For a moment he looked startled at the question. Almost as if he had expected her to know this already. But then a small smile crept over his face.

"Yes," he said. "I, uh, live in the village. My name's, uh, Wart."

"Wart?" she repeated, raising an eyebrow. "What a peculiar name."

His face turned bright red. "It's a… nickname," he confessed. "Perhaps not the most flattering…"

Guinevere immediately felt bad. "I like it, actually," she pronounced. "It's very unique. I mean, everyone and their brother these days is a Gawain or a Galahad or a Gaheris. But I don't know a single other Wart." She smiled at him. He smiled back, clearly relieved.

"What's your name?" he asked.

"Oh! Well, I'm Guinevere," she replied. "I live just down the path with my mother in a small cottage in the woods. We come here to get well water because our well ran dry."

That wasn't exactly what had happened. In truth, one of Mim's spells had backfired when they'd first arrived and left the entire well filled with green slimy goo. The wizard was still trying to work on a reverse spell, but so far had only managed to change the goo's colour to purple, which Guin didn't feel was much of an improvement, at least when it came to drinking it.

But, of course, she wasn't to speak of such things to strangers. That was Mim's number one rule. Never talk about magic to mortals. They might think you dangerous. Like Merlin was. They might even try to lock you up and throw away the key. In fact, they'd tried to do that with Mim once. Guinevere would never forget the day she came home to find her mother gone. Thank goodness Mim had outsmarted her captors in the end. She'd turned them all into toads and poofed herself back home.

Can't keep a good wizard down! she'd declared. And Guin had nearly collapsed in relief. After all, her mother was all she had. And as much as she feared magic, she feared losing Mim most of all.

"It's nice to meet you," Wart said, interrupting her thoughts. He held out his hand and Guinevere took it in her own, surprised at how strong his grip was. She had assumed from his thin, gangly arms and legs he would have a softer touch.

"Nice to meet you, too," she said. Then she glanced up at the sky. "Though I really must be getting my water and heading home. It is starting to get dark, and I don't want to run into any wolves on the way back."

"I'll walk you back," Wart proposed. "They'll be less likely to attack if there's two of us. And I do have a sword," he added with a small blush, gesturing to his side. The sheathed weapon hanging there had a rather ornate hilt – the kind of hilt that likely meant the sword was quite expensive. She wondered how a commoner like him could have come into possession of such a prize. She hoped he hadn't stolen it…

"It's really not necessary," she hedged, knowing Mim wouldn't be pleased about her leading a stranger to their home.

"It's a knight's duty to serve a damsel in distress!" Wart declared, puffing out his skinny chest. Guinevere couldn't help a giggle.

"First, I'm no damsel in distress," she scolded playfully. "And second, I'm willing to wager you're not a knight."

His chest drooped. He looked so forlorn that for a moment she felt bad.

"But I *would* like the company," she added hastily as she worked to fill her buckets with well water. After she said it, she realised it was true. It was a long walk, and it would be lovely to have someone to talk to along the way. Especially someone as pleasant as Wart. They could get to know one another better on the journey, and then she could say goodbye to him well before the cottage came into view.

Mim would never be the wiser. "So what do you say?" she asked.

Wart's blue eyes lit up. He took one of her now-filled buckets with one hand, then made a sweeping gesture towards the path with his other. "Lead the way, m'lady," he said grandly. Which made her giggle all over again. "Our quest begins!"

CHAPTER FIVE
ARTHUR

What do you think you're doing? Arthur scolded himself as he followed Guinevere down the windy forest path in the direction of her home. *This is pure foolishness.*

And it was. As king, he wasn't even supposed to leave the castle, at least not without a full complement of knights at his side. And even then, he certainly was not supposed to talk to strangers he met along the side of the road. It was too dangerous, Sir Pellinore had lectured when Arthur had first tried to set out for a stroll shortly after his coronation. After all, he was England's only hope. The country's entire future rested on his admittedly scrawny shoulders. Which meant those shoulders needed to be protected. If anything happened to him, the land could fall back into a dark age. And no one wanted that.

Arthur didn't want that either, but still! It was so stifling being king. To be stuck inside all day long, listening to adults drone on and on about this problem or that. Sometimes he even longed for his old life back in Sir Ector's crumbling castle. At least there he had honest hard work to keep him busy, and he could go outside anytime he wanted without even having to tell anyone first. In a moment of desperation, Arthur had tried to sneak down to the Camelot kitchen to wash some dishes like he used to back then, but he was quickly discovered and sent back to the throne room. A king, it seemed, did not dirty his hands with menial labour.

So when Pellinore and his knights had left the castle that afternoon to go follow Arthur's orders and invite the invading Saxons to dinner, Arthur had found himself in a rare position of not being watched like a hawk for once. And when he'd discovered a servant's door left ajar, he couldn't resist taking full advantage, slipping out of the castle and wandering into the woods.

Just for a few minutes, he'd told himself. And he'd go right back.

But then he'd met her.

His eyes rose to the girl dancing down the path in front of him. She wore a plain peasant dress, un-cinched at the waist, and her long golden curls tumbled messily down her back in waves, free of all the severe braids and bindings so in fashion at the castle. It was almost as if she were a wild thing, untamed by civilised life. He couldn't imagine the ladies in court ever dancing so freely, as if they didn't have a care in the world.

And the best part was? She had no idea who he was. Which had shocked him at first – after all, he was currently the most famous person in all the land. And so many had attended his coronation. But then, she'd said she and her mother lived deep in the woods and didn't get out much. So it made sense she wouldn't recognise him. She hadn't even recognised the sword Excalibur at his side.

Which meant, for a moment, he could be his old self again. Not the long-destined king of legends, pledged to save the realm, but a simple boy out for a walk in the woods with a nice girl by his side. In fact, it had felt so good to be Wart again that he hadn't wanted the moment to end. And so he'd blurted out his offer to walk Guinevere back home. Just to spend a few more minutes feeling normal.

What if it's a trap? an annoying voice in his head nagged. *Maybe she knows exactly who you are and it's all part of her ruse. What if she is leading you into an ambush of your enemies? After all, not everyone in the land is pleased to have a young boy as their king. And they would be thrilled to get their hands on you, all alone, unprotected in a dark wood…*

"Ooh! Are those violets?" Guinevere asked, interrupting his worried thoughts. She leant down and plucked a handful of small purple flowers, then slipped them into a small pouch tied to her belt. "I haven't found any since we moved here, and they're so great for easing one's coughs when mixed with yarrow flowers."

"You make medicines?" Arthur asked, curious.

"Oh, yes. It's sort of a hobby of mine." Guin's cheeks coloured slightly. "Nature provides us with so many natural gifts. You just have to know what to look for. Back home I had a whole garden filled with herbs that I used to make potions with to help those in the nearby village."

"Home?" Arthur queried. "Are you not from around here, then?"

"We just moved here recently," she explained. "Around the same time they crowned the new king. We used to live miles away from here, in the Forest Sauvage. It's a wild place, but just as beautiful."

Arthur stopped short. "The Forest Sauvage?" he repeated incredulously.

"Yes." Guinevere stopped and turned to look at him quizzically. "Have you heard of it?"

"I used to live there!" he exclaimed before he could stop himself. "Until..." His voice trailed off. "Until... I came here," he stammered. He had to be careful not to give out too much personal information, just in case.

But Guinevere didn't seem to notice his stammer. She was shaking her head in wonder. "Wow! What a small world!" she whispered, an excited gleam in her dark eyes. "I wonder if we ever ran into each other back then and never realised it!"

"I don't think so," Arthur replied. "I would have remembered you."

As soon as the words left his mouth, he felt his face heat into a blush. *Imbecile! Why would you say something like that?* But then he caught her glancing at him with a shy smile on her lips, and something inside him made him glad he'd said it after all.

"It's getting rather dark," she pointed out, fortunately changing the subject. She looked up at the sky, still painted in bands of orange and gold from the setting sun. "I hope Mother isn't too worried. She doesn't like me being out at night by myself."

Arthur nodded absently, a little worried himself. He'd never meant to stray from the castle for so long. By now someone surely had noticed he was gone. Would they send out a search party for him?

Maybe it was time to say his goodbyes.

"Look, I…" he started, but trailed off as he heard a horn blowing in the distance. Along with a few shouts of "Arthur! Arthur!"

Oh, no. There *was* a search party. And they weren't far away, either, from the sound of it.

"Come on," he said, grabbing Guinevere's hand and urging her forwards. "Let's go!"

She gave him a puzzled look but complied, picking up the pace and dashing down the wooded trail. Arthur could hear the heavy clomping of hooves behind them, sounding as if they were getting closer by the second. This was not good.

"What's wrong?" Guinevere asked breathlessly. "Why are we running?"

He swallowed hard. Maybe it was time to come clean "Look, there's something I should tell you—" he began. But he was cut off by the horn blowing again, so close this time he had to put his hands over his ears to block out the sound. It was then that he realised Guinevere had stopped running. She turned to face him, putting her hands on her hips.

"So you *did* steal that sword, didn't you?" she accused, glancing down at Excalibur. "I knew it. It's far too grand for a peasant boy like yourself. And now they're looking for you! They want to arrest you for grand theft!"

"What?" Arthur's eyes bulged. "Wait, Guinevere – no!" He reached for her hand, but she ripped it away.

"I don't associate with thieves," she spit out. Then she turned in the direction of the search party. "He's over here!" she called.

Arthur's face went pale. "Shhh!" he cried. "Please! Don't attract their attention. I didn't steal the sword, I swear! I just… they can't find me!"

"Why not?" Guinevere demanded, looking very displeased. The sounds of horses were getting closer and closer. They must have been almost on top of them.

Arthur felt his knees practically give out. This had all been such a terrible mistake. "Look, Guinevere…" he tried.

But he got no further. At that moment, they were surrounded by a group of knights, led by none other than Sir Kay, Arthur's foster brother himself. Kay smirked as he looked down from his horse at Arthur and the girl standing in the middle of their circle.

"Well, well. Now I think I understand," he joked.

Arthur felt his hackles rise. Of all people to find him, it had to be Kay. There was no one who resented his rise to the throne more than his foster brother. And Kay was constantly letting him know it.

"Understand what? What did this boy do?" Guinevere demanded, looking fiercely from knight to knight. It was funny; here Arthur was terrified, and yet she didn't look one bit afraid to face off with a band of knights. "Did he truly steal the sword he wears on his belt?"

The knights looked at her incredulously, then broke out into laugher. Arthur cringed. Guinevere's scowl deepened.

"What's so funny?" she demanded.

"Sorry, m'lady," Sir Bors said, choking back his laughter. "It's just… do you not know who this young lad is?"

Guinevere looked over at Arthur, confusion clouding her face. "Who is he?" she asked, her voice suddenly a little wobbly.

"Why, m'lady, this is King Arthur, ruler of all England. And that sword he wears? He pulled it from the stone."

CHAPTER SIX
GUINEVERE

Guinevere stared at Wart – no, Arthur! – in shock. She couldn't have been more surprised if he'd suddenly sprouted wings and turned into a bird right then and there. *This* was Arthur? The one who had stolen the throne of England?

And she had somehow *befriended* him?

"Is it true?" she managed to sputter, wanting to hear the confession spill from his own lips. She realised a part of her still held out hope that maybe it was some ridiculous joke. That the knights were putting her on for their own amusement. Because surely this boy – this skinny young boy who dreamt about being a bird and flying away – couldn't be the usurper out to destroy England.

Could he?

Wart's face turned bright red, confirming her worst fears. Anger rose inside her, mixed with burning shame. What would Mim think if she could see her now, already falling for the charms of Merlin's pawn? Why, she was supposed to be the one tricking *him,* not the other way round! Her mother would be so ashamed.

"I have to go," she muttered. This was clearly why Mim never let her do anything on her own. She was the worst judge of character ever. She'd taken him at his word, and he'd lied to her. And of course he had – he'd lied to the entire kingdom, pretending to be their rightful monarch. And worse, she'd believed him without question.

"Guin!" Arthur cried. He sounded upset. "Please! I can explain!"

"I'm sure you can," she managed to say, trying to keep her voice thick and haughty. As if his deception meant absolutely nothing to her. "But I'm not interested in hearing it."

And with that, she turned and walked down the path, keeping her shoulders squared and her head held high. She could hear him calling for her, but she refused to give him the satisfaction of turning around to look. Only when she heard the sounds of the knights' horses galloping away, presumably with Arthur in tow, did she allow herself to run. Down the path, through the woods, not stopping for a moment until she reached the cottage.

She burst through the door, out of breath, her hair windswept and her face stained with tears and dirt. She leant over, hands on her knees, trying to catch her breath.

Mim looked up from her card game, raising a bushy eyebrow. "Where's the water?" she asked.

Oh, no! The water! Guinevere looked down at her bucket to find it nearly empty. And, she realised miserably, she had never grabbed the second bucket back from Arthur when she fled.

"I'm sorry," she said. "I, uh, ran into some wolves. I had to run home. I must have dropped one of the buckets on the way."

She felt a little guilty lying to her mother, but what else could she say? That she'd lost their precious water because she'd accidentally befriended the kingdom's number one enemy? If she confessed to Mim that she'd fallen for Arthur's charms even before she got to the castle, Mim would think her a silly girl who wasn't ready to undertake such an important quest. And Guinevere *needed* this quest – now more than ever. If for nothing else than to teach that cowardly king a lesson in manners. He shouldn't be able to get away with lying to people. And she was going to make him pay for tricking her, whatever it took.

Mim sighed deeply. "You know, you could have just poofed yourself home. Or shapeshifted into a bird or a mouse to get away." She shook her head. "You always make things so hard for yourself, my dear."

Guinevere hung her head. Of course her mother would go right to magic. Magic was Mim's solution to every problem. And she couldn't understand Guin's reluctance to use it.

"In any case, I'm fine," Guin pointed out. Though she didn't feel very fine at all. In fact, if she was being honest with herself, she felt downright miserable. She was still furious at Arthur. But also kind of sad. Like she'd lost a friend just as she'd made one.

"Of course you are!" Mim agreed. "And don't worry. I'll conjure us up a bountiful feast – just for tonight." She gave Guin a scolding look. "Surely you can stomach a little magic if it means a full stomach. I'm thinking… slug à la mode! What do you say?"

Guinevere nodded reluctantly. Slugs with ice cream sounded pretty horrific, but then it was her fault they wouldn't have their stew. And she didn't want to appear ungrateful when her mother was acting so understanding.

"Now sit down, my pet, before you pass out on me," Mim instructed, pulling a chair close to her own. Guinevere gratefully collapsed into it, and Mim took her hand, squeezing it lightly. Guin let out a shuddering breath and closed her eyes.

"Wow. You were really upset," Mim noted with surprise. "And all over a silly little wolf? That's not like you, my dear."

Guinevere opened her eyes a crack. Her mother was staring at her suspiciously.

"I… thought it was a dog," she stammered. "Until I got close to it. It… surprised me."

Mim's grip tightened, just a little, but enough to tell Guinevere she didn't quite believe her. Which made sense, of course, since it was a blatant lie. Luckily, however, there was no way for her mother to guess the truth. Mim might have been magical, but she wasn't a mind reader. And eventually Mim's hand relaxed again.

"Poor child," she soothed, stroking Guin's palm. "So frightened of the world. I suppose that's partially my fault, keeping you so close to me all these years." She paused, then added, "Maybe sending you to the castle isn't such a good idea after all…"

"No!" Guinevere cried, her eyes flying open. She jerked her hand away. "I want to go! I'll be fine, I promise. You don't have to worry about me!"

Mim held up her hands in protest. "All right, all right!" she cried with a giggle. "No need to beg! I'm sure it'll all be simply marvellous! I can't wait to see!" She paused, then added, "There's one thing, however…"

"What's that?" Guinevere asked warily, noting the change in her mother's voice. No longer laughing – but dead serious. Which was unusual for Mim, to say the least.

Mim's eyes rested on her daughter. "When you get to the castle, whatever you do, whatever you say, do not let Arthur know you are related to me in any way. No matter what happens. If he learns that I sent you, there's no telling what he'll do to you… or me, for that matter." She gave Guin a strong look. "Arthur may only be a boy – but at the end of the day, he serves Merlin. You'd do best to remember that."

"I understand," Guin said softly, feeling a shiver trip down her spine. "You can trust me. I won't let you down."

"That's my girl!" Mim cried, her demeanour changing again. She leapt to her feet. "Now let's eat! Can't save a kingdom on an empty stomach, can we?" She waved her arms wildly in the air. "Bring on the slugs!"

CHAPTER SEVEN
ARTHUR

"Sire, we've gone over this a hundred times. You cannot leave the castle unattended," Sir Morien scolded. The brawny, bearded dark-skinned knight paced the throne room, his long steps eating up the distance between stone walls.

Arthur slumped in his throne. "I said I was sorry," he muttered, a little sulkily. But who could blame him? After all, he hadn't asked for this. All he ever aimed for in life was to maybe become a squire to a famous knight and go questing throughout the land – facing dangers untold and maybe, if they were lucky, a few dragons. Instead, he was stuck in a musty old castle, deciding the fates of random chickens and hoping he didn't accidentally start a war.

It was *not* good to be the king.

He sighed deeply, thinking back to his fleeting moment of freedom in the forest earlier that day. It had felt so good to be his old self again. The orphan Wart, who hadn't had a care in the world. Back when he lived that life, he hadn't fully appreciated it. Now, he'd give anything at all just to have it back.

To see Guinevere again.

His mind flashed to the girl he'd met in the forest. She'd been so nice to him – not caring about his social status or who his parents might be. In fact, it hadn't mattered one bit to her that he was a nobody. Which, in a strange way, made him feel like a somebody. Somebody worth talking to. Somebody worth becoming friends with.

Well, until she realised the truth. He winced as he remembered the look of shock that crossed her face when she realised he had lied to her, followed by the crushing look of betrayal. At that moment, his greatest wish on earth would have been to climb down into that deep dark well and never come out again.

He resisted the urge to slap his hand to his forehead. Oh, why had he lied to her? It was so stupid and shortsighted! Not to mention completely disrespectful to her. This was not how Merlin had taught him to be!

But it didn't matter now, he supposed sadly. For he

would likely never see her again. At least not without a full accompaniment of knights, which would spoil any chance of fun. Not to mention the fact that he was pretty sure she had no interest in running into him again – knights or no. His stupid lie had ruined their chance of friendship. Probably forever.

There was a knock at the door. Arthur rose to his feet. "Come in," he commanded, after throwing a quick look at Morien, thankful for a distraction to his scolding. The knight sighed deeply, shaking his head.

As the door swung open, for a brief moment Arthur allowed himself to indulge in the fantasy that it would be Guinevere on the other side of it, come to the castle to give him a chance to apologise.

But, of course, it was not Guinevere. It was the castle steward.

"Your Majesty." The steward bowed low. "Sir Pellinore and his men have returned from their meeting with the Saxons. They are requesting an audience with you."

Arthur's heart quickened, relegating all thoughts of Guinevere to the back of his brain. "Send them in," he declared.

The steward bowed again and disappeared out the door. A moment later, he returned, accompanied by Pellinore, Kay, and a tall knight with broad shoulders and a shock of jet-black hair whom Pellinore introduced as Gawain. All three bowed low to Arthur.

"So?" Arthur asked impatiently. "What did they say?"

Pellinore straightened. His face broke into an excited smile. "Your Majesty," he said, "I can barely believe I'm sharing this news with you. But somehow the Saxons have agreed to your request. They are planning a trip to Camelot to attend your promised feast."

"Really?" Arthur stared at the knights. It had worked? His plan for peace had worked? Well, not completely – not yet, anyway. But they'd agreed to come. That was a big step.

"Really," Gawain agreed with a toothy grin. Arthur liked him immediately. "They're packing up now and plan to arrive at the castle in a week's time. Their king seems very eager to meet you."

"This is amazing," Arthur cried, overjoyed. "I knew this would work—"

"Bah!" Kay interrupted, shaking his head. "I don't like it. I don't like it at all. Inviting these barbarians to our banquet halls – to sup like they're civilised people?" He scowled. "It's just not done."

"Maybe not, but it's *being* done now," Arthur corrected, a little cross at being challenged. Especially by his foster brother, who had always made it clear he thought he knew better – even when he clearly didn't. "And who knows? Maybe they'll surprise you."

"Or maybe they'll surprise *you*," Kay shot back, not missing a beat. "Ever think of that? Maybe it's a trick to breach our castle walls. To learn our ways and the depths of our forces, so they can gain the upper hand when they come back to attack us at a later date."

Arthur swallowed hard, his earlier enthusiasm deflating. He didn't want to admit it, but Kay did have a point. What if opening their gates in peace led to nothing but war? And worse – gave their enemies an advantage?

It would be all his fault.

"Oh, Kay," Gawain broke in, smacking Arthur's foster brother so hard on the back that Kay almost fell over. "You worry too much. By the gods, they're invited to dinner, not a behind-the-tapestries tour of the inner workings of Camelot Castle. We knights can keep an eye on a few barbarians, don't you think? Make sure they mind their manners."

"Exactly," Arthur agreed, thankful to Gawain for sticking up for him. "We'll show them we're kind. But not stupid."

Kay opened his mouth as if to speak, but a stern look from Gawain made him close it again. Instead, he crossed his meaty arms over his chest and stuck out his lower lip in a pout. Arthur resisted the urge to snicker. It wasn't often he'd got to see Kay put in his place. But he was a king, he reminded himself; he couldn't afford to be petty.

Sir Pellinore turned to Arthur, clapping his hands.

"Very good, Your Majesty," he said. "What would you like us to do in the meantime?"

"Let's have the cooks start working on the menus," Arthur said. "And the staff need to be cleaning out the halls and guest rooms, and making sure there's enough room in the stables for their horses." He listed off the various tasks, the kinds of preparations he himself was quite familiar with from when guests arrived at Sir Ector's castle back when he had worked in the kitchens.

"Oh, yes! We'll be sure to get right on all of that, *m'lord*," Kay jeered, making a mocking bow in Arthur's direction. Gawain sighed and gave Arthur an apologetic look before he and Pellinore led the other knight out of the throne room. Morien followed close behind. Arthur let out a breath of relief. It seemed his lecture for leaving the castle was over.

And the day was finally starting to look up.

He sat back in his throne, feeling rather pleased. A moment later, Archimedes flew down from his perch on the rafters above and landed on his throne's armrest.

"Well done, lad!" the owl chirped. "Your first act as king, and it seems to be turning into a smashing success."

Arthur smiled goofily, feeling better now that they were

alone. "I wasn't sure it was going to work," he confessed. "I mean, when I first decided on it, everyone seemed to think I was mad. Some still do, I suppose," he added, thinking of Kay's sneer.

"It's not mad, it's civilised," the owl corrected haughtily. "And I'm sorry, but a knight like Kay has no room to complain about barbarians. Not when he's only one step above one himself."

Arthur smirked. "You said it, not me."

"I'm proud of you, boy," the owl continued. "Perhaps you will make a fine king yet."

"Thank you," Arthur said. "That means a lot coming from you." He leant back in his throne, staring up at the ceiling thoughtfully. "Do you think this was all part of Merlin's plan from the start? Do you think he knew my destiny? Was that why he agreed to teach me in the first place? So I'd know how to do this?"

The owl shrugged. "He did say something about leading you to your rightful place," he told Arthur. "Perhaps this is what he was talking about?" He fluffed his feathers. "I just assumed he meant to have you become his apprentice – maybe take over for him someday. But perhaps it was more than that."

"I wish he were here now." Arthur sighed. "It would be nice to have his advice."

"I know, boy," Archimedes agreed. "I miss him, too." He scowled. "Though you better never tell him I said that."

Arthur laughed. "Your secret is safe with me."

Archimedes took flight, making small circles around the throne. "I have to admit, I am getting worried about him. He's been gone a very long time. Longer than I can ever remember his being gone before. Sure, he'll sometimes time travel when he's angry. But he always comes back. So where is he now?"

"Morgan said he was on something called a *holiday*," Arthur told him.

The owl stopped in midair, almost falling to the ground in the process. "Morgan?" he repeated. "Who's Morgan?"

"Morgan le Fay?" Arthur tried to remember. "She's a wizard like Merlin. She came here the day I had to rule about the chicken. She told me Merlin sent her." He wrinkled his nose. "But something was very strange about her. And her advice seemed very odd. Very un-Merlin-like."

"Morgan le Fay?" Archimedes landed back on the throne, shaking his head. "Why does that name sound so familiar?"

"I don't know." Arthur shrugged. "Should we track her down again and see if she knows more about Merlin? Maybe she knows where he is."

"Maybe. Or maybe she's the reason he's not back

yet," Archimedes suggested worriedly. "After all, it seems quite a coincidence that she shows up right after Merlin's disappearance. What if she did something to him?"

Arthur frowned. He hadn't thought of that possibility. But she *was* a wizard, which meant she had magic…

"What should we do?" he asked the owl.

Archimedes seemed to consider the question for a moment. Then he shook out his feathers. "Let me fly back to Sir Ector's castle," he said. "Merlin's books are probably all still in the tower where he left them. Maybe I can learn something from them about this Morgan le Fay character. Then we'll know if we can trust her… or not."

Arthur shuddered at the thought. "Do you really think she might have done something to Merlin?" he asked nervously, thinking back to his poor teacher. If anything had happened to him…

"I don't know," Archimedes admitted. "But I plan to find out."

CHAPTER EIGHT
GUINEVERE

"You call that washed? What's that smudge on the side? You're washing for a king now, girl! Kings don't tolerate smudged plates!"

Guinevere groaned as she attempted to take back the plate from the castle cook, Mistress McCready, and balance it on the top of the already towering pile of dishes she was carrying into the kitchen after clearing the banquet hall from breakfast. Unfortunately, the plate missed its mark and fell. When she instinctively dived to catch it, she lost her balance, and her entire stack of dinnerware came crashing to the ground.

"Now look what you've done!" screeched the cook. "Stupid, clumsy girl! You've managed to break them all!"

"At least you don't have to worry about them being

smudged now," Guinevere retorted under her breath as she knelt down to pick up the pieces.

The cook wrung her hands together in annoyance. "It is truly impossible to get good help these days," she muttered as she stormed back into the kitchen, leaving Guinevere alone to pick up the mess.

Guinevere sighed, looking over the damage she'd done. Not a single plate or bowl appeared to have escaped its fate. Wonderful. Reluctantly, she started gathering up the bits of broken earthenware in her hands and taking them over to a nearby bin.

So much for saving the kingdom. She couldn't even save a pile of plates.

Could this quest of hers possibly be going worse? It was bad enough she'd had that embarrassing encounter with Arthur in the forest. But at the very least they'd been face to face and talking. Since she'd arrived at the castle, she'd been stuck down in the kitchen, washing dishes; she hadn't had the chance to talk to Arthur at all. In fact, she'd only ever even got a brief glimpse of the king one time since she'd arrived – and then only from a distance. How was she supposed to keep an eye on him when she literally never saw him?

She shook her head. Her mother was going to be so disappointed in her.

"Oh, wow! I remember those days!"

Guin looked up, startled at the sound of a new voice approaching. Her eyes widened in shock as she realised who it belonged to. None other than King Arthur himself, stopping at the bottom of the stairs, looking down at the mess, a strange look in his eyes.

He was dressed quite differently than when she'd first met him in the forest, where he'd worn typical peasant attire: a plain, undyed tunic and tights. He was now garbed in a rich red velvet doublet over a billowy white shirt. A heavy golden chain hung across his shoulders, and an ornate crown that looked a bit too large for him perched on his head. She watched as he shoved the crown back up his forehead, almost absently, as if he had to do so often.

Before she could say anything, he knelt beside her, checking out the mess. He picked up a piece of pottery and tossed it in the bin. Guinevere felt her cheeks heat.

"What are you doing?" she demanded before she could stop herself.

"Helping, I think," he replied, grabbing another plate. "Unless you meant for them to stay on the floor?"

"Of course not," she snapped, feeling hot and embarrassed. Here she'd been waiting all week for her chance to get close to the king, and this was how she finally ran into him? On the floor, surrounded by broken dishes, looking a sight? Pathetic. Truly pathetic.

"Look," she tried, "you don't have to—"

She was interrupted by a cry of surprise. She frowned, looking up to find Arthur staring at her, a look of astonishment on his face.

"Why, it's *you*!" he declared in a voice rich with wonder. "Guinevere, right? From the forest?" He couldn't have sounded more surprised than if she'd been a purple dragon he had spotted wandering the halls. Which she supposed made sense, seeing as they'd met under such different circumstances the first time round.

For a split second, she considered lying – saying he was mistaken. That her name was Mary or Martha or Elaine. Maybe it would have been a good idea. She was trying to keep a low profile, after all. But then again, this was the first conversation she'd been able to have with him since she'd arrived at to the castle, and she didn't want him to just walk away.

"I suppose I am," she choked out, trying to keep her voice light. "Nice to see you again, *Wart*."

Now it was his turn to look embarrassed. He hung his head, causing his crown to tumble to the floor. He grabbed it and shoved it back on, looking unhappy.

"About that," he said. "I suppose I should explain."

Guinevere shrugged, going back to the broken dishes. "No need," she replied airily. "You're the king. I suppose you can do whatever you want." She reached out for a dish.

Arthur grabbed the dish from her hands, causing her to look up at him in surprise. He met her eyes with his own, and she was astonished to see they were practically radiating with apology.

"I shouldn't have lied to you," he said solemnly. "It was wrong, and I knew it. It was just… well, the way you were treating me. Like I was a normal, everyday person – not some fancy king. Let's just say I don't get that a lot any more." He sighed deeply.

"I imagine you don't," she muttered, trying to ignore the sudden tug at her heart as she caught the forlorn expression on his face. Ugh. The last thing she needed was to start feeling sorry for him. He had stolen the throne of England, she reminded herself. He wasn't some innocent victim.

"Besides," he added, smiling, "if you had known who I really was, would you have let me walk you home?"

"Probably not," she admitted.

His eyes sparkled. "So you see the need for my deception, then."

Guinevere felt herself blushing again as she forced her eyes back to her task. He was certainly charming – she'd give him that. A lot more charming than she'd imagined someone like him would be. Still, she couldn't allow herself to let down her guard. To forget who he really was. And whom he served.

She had to be careful. But at the same time, she had to play nice. To get him to trust her, to open up to her, so she and Mim could find a way to take him down.

She realised he was looking at her expectantly.

"It's really all right," she assured him, giving him a bland smile. "I'm not angry with you."

Hope flushed on his face. "So you… forgive me?"

"It's already forgotten."

The lie tasted like sawdust on her tongue, but she swallowed it down, knowing it was necessary. Still, she couldn't help feeling a little guilty when she caught the relief on his face. *Now who's the liar?*

Arthur grabbed another piece of broken pottery and tossed it expertly into the bin. "So what are you doing here, anyway?" he asked. "You never told me you worked in the castle."

"I didn't until last week," she confessed. "My mother thought it might be nice for me to get a job to pass the time and help pay our expenses." The lie rolled easily off her tongue, surprising her. She tried to imagine herself as a spy, deep undercover – a notion that pleased her quite a bit.

Especially when she caught the look on Arthur's face and realised he believed every word.

"Well, I'm glad you did," he said. "I've been feeling terrible about what happened and wanted to apologise to you. But they won't let me out of the castle any more. They say it's too dangerous." He scowled, telling her exactly what he thought of that notion.

"I'm glad to see you again, too," she replied. "Though I wish it were under better circumstances than a pile of broken dishes. I promise I'll pay for them," she added quickly. "They can take it out of my wages."

Arthur looked shocked at the idea. "Certainly not," he said, scooping up an armful of broken pottery. "Do you know how many dishes they have in this castle?" He paused, then grinned. "No, of course you don't. No one does. And no one's ever going to count them, either."

She couldn't help a laugh at this. "I suppose not."

"Trust me, I broke more than my share of dishes back in the day," he told her, tossing his load of pottery into the bin.

"You used to work in a kitchen?" she asked, surprised.

"Oh, yes – for years, actually. What I told you out in the forest – it wasn't altogether a lie. I was Wart before I was Arthur. Just an orphan boy, lucky enough to be taken in by an old knight and his son and given a job."

She bit her lower lip, dropping her head to concentrate on her task again. It seemed the two of them had more in common than she had thought. They were both orphans, both raised by foster parents, both trained by wizards. But now one of them was sitting on the throne of England. And one was washing dishes in a castle basement.

No, she scolded herself. That was just his cover. He didn't belong on the throne at all. He'd taken it from the rightful king.

She wondered suddenly if he knew this. Had Merlin let him in on the plan from the start? Or did he really think this was his destiny? Was he a mastermind, deceiving them all? Or was he just a puppet for Merlin – having no idea what he was doing?

Arthur threw the last piece of pottery in the trash. "There!" he declared. "Much easier when you have help, am I right?"

"Much," she found herself agreeing.

"And now look!" he added. "You've got time for me to give you a tour of the castle." He held out his arm gallantly.

She stared at it, not taking it. "A tour?" she asked, surprised.

His confidence fled his face. "I mean, if you wanted one, that is. If you have other things to do…"

She swallowed hard. She certainly did have other things

to do – a pile of chores in the kitchen that would take her all day. But how could she turn down her first chance to spend one-on-one time with Arthur? That was the true reason she'd come here, after all.

"Actually, a tour sounds lovely," she declared, giving him what she hoped looked like a sweet smile. She hooked her arm in his. "Lead the way."

CHAPTER NINE
GUINEVERE

The tour took almost an hour. Camelot Castle was huge, with perhaps a hundred rooms. Arthur took his time showing Guinevere each and every one, and she forced herself to ooh and aah over the rich purple drapes and golden ornamentations in each one, as if they were visions of her greatest dreams come to life. In truth, however, she found the whole thing a bit shocking – to see so much luxury and riches go to waste. Rooms that were not even used, containing enough wealth for a peasant to live on for a lifetime. It didn't seem quite fair. But she kept her mouth shut and played the good servant girl as the tour progressed, knowing it was more important to gain Arthur's trust than criticise his lifestyle.

"And this is the final bedroom," Arthur announced as they stepped into yet another room, this one with a giant stone hearth in the corner and a window with real leaded glass that looked out over the castle gardens. There were thick animal-skin rugs on the floor and a massive canopy bed in the centre, covered with at least a dozen pillows and draped in heavy crimson curtains. "At least I think so," he added with a bashful grin. "I've lost count at this point."

She snorted and walked over to the bed. Feeling a little mischievous, she climbed onto it and began dancing on it to see if it was as soft as it looked.

Turned out it was even softer.

Arthur stared up at her as if shocked by her brazen move. She grinned, beckoning him with her hand, suddenly feeling silly and free. "Don't tell me you've never tried jumping on one of these beds?" she teased. When he shook his head doubtfully, she laughed. "Well, it's no wonder you think this place is boring, then."

For a moment, he stood there as if warring with his own indecision. But at last he shook his head and scrambled onto the bed. Soon the two of them were jumping up and down so high they almost smacked their heads on the ceiling twice. The third time, Guinevere managed to lose her footing on the way down and tumbled into the pile of pillows. Arthur laughed as she struggled to right herself, tangled in their silk covers.

"Need some help, m'lady?" he asked in a mocking voice.

"Please," she scoffed, grabbing a pillow and throwing it in his direction. It hit him square in the chest, and he too lost his balance, tumbling off the bed altogether and landing on the floor with a heavy thump. Guinevere gasped.

"Are you all right?" she asked, leaning off the bed to check on him.

"I'm fine," he said with a sly grin as he picked up two pillows off the floor. "But you… you are dead!"

He lunged at her. She leapt off the bed, screaming, dashing to the other corner of the room. He gave chase, but it was hard to run with an armful of pillows, allowing Guin an easy escape. She leapt back onto the bed and grabbed her own stash, throwing them at Arthur one after another while using her own pillow as a shield.

"You shalt not win, evil knight!" she cried out. "I will be the victor!"

"We'll see about that," Arthur shot back, leaping up on the bed and diving in her direction. She lost her balance again, and this time they both tumbled to the floor together, tangling up in a pile of limbs. They were laughing so hard at this point, they could barely speak.

"Do you yield?" Arthur asked with a sly smile.

"Never!" she declared, struggling to sit up. "As long as there be breath in my body, I shall never—"

The door burst open. Two guards rushed in, grabbed Guinevere, and yanked her backwards. She cried out in alarm as her arms were pinned behind her painfully and a rough hand grabbed at her throat.

"Leave me alone!" she cried, trying to fight them off. But they were grown men. Far too strong. For a split second she actually considered using magic – that's what Mim would have done in a situation like this. But she realised it would destroy her cover and probably get her banned from the castle. So instead, she stopped struggling and submitted.

"Who are you?" the first guard demanded, once he had her under control.

"And what are you doing to the king?" added the second.

"It's okay, Brutus," Arthur broke in. Guin turned to see he'd managed to get up off the floor and was approaching the guards. "We were just playing."

"Playing, Your Majesty?" the guard – Brutus – exclaimed, spitting out the word as if it were poison. "But we thought…"

"We heard screams," added his partner, looking personally offended. "We thought you were being attacked."

"It was just a game," Arthur explained with a heavy

sigh. "I'm sorry I worried you." He pressed his lips together. "So… can you please let her go?"

The guards reluctantly released Guinevere. She shook out her arms, giving them a sour look. Inside, her heart was pumping a thousand beats a minute. She glanced over at Arthur. He shot her an apologetic smile.

"I should get back to the kitchen," she mumbled, feeling incredibly awkward all of a sudden. Not to mention more than a little ashamed. What had she been thinking, jumping on royal beds and pillow fighting with the king of England, as if she were an unruly child who didn't know any better? What if they told her mistress – the cook – about her bad behaviour and she lost her job because of it? What if they banished her from the castle altogether? Arthur wouldn't order it, she was pretty sure, but from what he'd said, he didn't always get to make the rules. If she lost her chance to complete her quest, Mim would be so disappointed.

Also, England would be doomed. Which was almost as bad.

"Are you all right?" Arthur asked, catching the look on her face.

"I'm f-fine," she stammered, feeling the eyes of the guards on her. "Um, thank you for the tour."

The corner of Arthur's mouth lifted. "Thank *you* for making my afternoon a lot more interesting than usual," he said, bowing grandly in her direction. She noticed he had a small bruise on the side of his face, probably from hitting the floor so hard. Hopefully no one would ask him how he got it.

Brutus cleared his throat, nodding to the door. She realised it was her invitation to vacate. She gave Arthur one last rueful look, then scurried towards the exit, hoping she'd be able to remember her way through the twisty passages back to the kitchen and that no one had noticed she'd been gone.

She was almost to the door when she heard his voice again.

"Wait."

She stopped in her tracks. "Yes?" she asked, turning, her pulse beating fast at her wrists.

For a moment Arthur just stood there. Then his mouth opened. "Would you like to have dinner with me tonight?" he asked, his voice wobbling a bit on the words, as if it took an effort to speak them. "It's a bit of a special night. The Saxons are coming to visit, and we're holding a grand feast in their honour."

She raised her eyebrows. He was inviting her to dinner? Dinner with the Saxons?

"Aren't the Saxons our enemies?" she blurted out before she could stop herself.

But Arthur only smiled. "Not for long," he said mysteriously. He paused, then added, "So what do you say? Will you join me? Eat by my side?"

Guinevere shuffled from foot to foot, indecision whirling through her. This was the opportunity she'd been waiting for, the reason she'd been sent to the castle to begin with: to observe courtly matters and report them back to Mim.

So why did she suddenly feel so conflicted?

She glanced up at Arthur. His face was awash with what could be described only as hope.

"Of course," she mumbled, forcing herself to curtsy to him. "If you want me there, I will come."

Arthur smiled. "There is nothing I would want more."

CHAPTER TEN
ARTHUR

Arthur was only halfway dressed for the banquet when he heard a rapping at his window. Puzzled, he ran over to see what it could be and was surprised to find none other than Archimedes flapping on the other side, pecking the glass with his beak. Excited, Arthur yanked the window open to let the bird in.

"You're back!" he exclaimed. "Did you make it to Sir Ector's castle? Were Merlin's books still there? Did you find something in them? Did you discover what happened to Merlin? Who's Morgan le Fay?"

The owl flew to his perch by Arthur's bed, settling in and carefully picking at his wing feathers before answering. Arthur hopped from foot to foot impatiently.

The owl had always had a flair for the dramatic. But this was ridiculous.

"Come on!" he cried. "I don't have a lot of time before the banquet starts. I need to know what you found out."

Archimedes had been gone a week, and Arthur had started worrying something might have happened to him. Which would have been horrible – Arthur had admittedly grown pretty fond of him over the last months. Of course he would never admit this to the grumpy old bird, knowing full well Archimedes would never, in turn, admit to appreciating this kind of concern on his behalf.

Archimedes spat out a feather. "Yes, I am back," he said grandly. "And let me tell you, I'm very happy to be so. That horrible tower that your foster father had Merlin stay in is so damp and cold and dreary – I don't know how we ever put up with it back in the day."

"Yes, yes, it's terrible," Arthur agreed peevishly. "But were Merlin's books still there? Were you able to read them?"

"Of course I was able to read them," the owl clucked. "What do you think I am? A bumbling medieval idiot? I'm the one who taught you your ABCs, and don't you forget it."

Arthur groaned, plopping down on his bed. Clearly the owl refused to be rushed.

Archimedes flew over to join him. "Yes, my impatient

boy," he said patronisingly, "I was able to go through Merlin's books. He has quite a lot of them, as you know, which was what made it take so long. But in the end, I did manage to find out quite a bit about your Morgan le Fay."

Arthur sat up in bed. "You did? What did you learn?"

The owl frowned. "Unfortunately, it's much worse than we thought. It turns out Morgan le Fay is a very powerful wizard who practises sorcery of the worst kind. Sorcery you've actually witnessed first hand – though at the time she was going by another name."

Arthur stared at the bird for a moment. Then something suddenly dawned on him. The purple eyes. The purple dress. The purple fingernails.

"Madam Mim!" he exclaimed, horrified. "Morgan le Fay is Madam Mim?"

"Give the boy a gold star," Archimedes proclaimed. Then he huffed. "Of course it would have been better had you figured that out when she first showed up at the castle. Would have saved me a lot of draughty nights in that leaky tower."

"Sorry," Arthur said. "But she didn't look anything like herself at the time. Except for all the purple. She probably shapeshifted – like she did during the wizard duel between her and Merlin."

"Yes. Quite likely," Archimedes agreed. "She is a master at shapeshifting. The only way to truly tell it's her is by all the purple. She can't quite manage to get rid of that in any shape or form."

Arthur shook his head, thinking back to their encounter. If only he'd put two and two together. He could have had her arrested or something. Though if she was truly as powerful as Archimedes said, that might not have done any good.

"Why do you think she wanted me to go to war with the Saxons?" he asked. "She was very insistent about that."

"Right." Archimedes nodded. "Well, from what I've read, Mim or Morgan – whatever she wants to call herself – is a big fan of the gruesome and grim. And she loves to cause trouble. The more chaotic things become, the more she enjoys them."

Arthur considered this. "I guess that makes sense," he said. "She probably thinks a peaceful England is a boring England."

"Indeed. And don't think this will be her last attempt to interfere with your rule. As long as Merlin is away, there's no one to stop her from trying her worst. You must keep on guard and be ready for when she strikes again. Likely in a way you least expect it."

"Please. She's not going to get by me," Arthur declared.

"I know her tricks now. Her purple colour. I'll be ready for her next time she shows up." He jumped off the bed, launching into a few knightly poses to back his claim. Archimedes rolled his eyes.

"Very scary," he deadpanned. "I'm sure she'll be quaking in her purple boots when she sees you coming."

"She'd better!" Arthur declared, grabbing Excalibur and waving it in the air. "Or else I'll— I'll—"

Suddenly, there was a loud knock at the door, causing Arthur to practically leap out of his skin. Excalibur slipped from his hands and went crashing to the floor. Archimedes snorted.

"You were saying…?" he replied drolly.

Arthur ignored him, pulling the door open and revealing the castle steward standing on the other side. "Oh. It's you," Arthur said, blushing. "What is it?"

"Your Majesty, everyone has gathered in the great hall," the steward informed him, giving him a doubtful once-over. It was then that Arthur realised he was still only half-dressed. "Including the Saxon king and his men. They are awaiting you to start the feast."

Arthur slapped his hand to his forehead. "Oh, no! I'm late. All right. Thank you! I'll be right there."

"Very good, sir," the castle steward replied, bowing low before closing the door behind him. Once he was gone, Arthur turned to Archimedes.

"What do I wear?" he asked. "I want to look kingly for the Saxons."

Archimedes groaned loudly but flew over to Arthur's wardrobe and used his beak to open it. He plucked out a red robe with a golden belt.

"However did you manage while I was gone?" he asked, shaking his head.

Arthur excitedly grabbed the robe and slipped it over his head. "I did great while you were gone, actually," he said haughtily, cinching the robe with the belt. "I made laws. I found a nice round table for my knights to sit at during meetings. Oh, and I even met a girl. I invited her to dinner tonight, too."

Archimedes stopped mid-flight, but managed to recover quickly enough to land on his perch instead of the ground. His eyes locked on Arthur. "You *what*?"

Arthur blushed. Maybe he shouldn't have mentioned that last part. But truth be told, he hadn't been able to concentrate on much else since inviting her earlier that day. Every time he'd try to focus on courtly politics, he ended up getting lost in thought, his mind whirring with memories of her dark brown eyes.

"She works in the kitchen," he explained as he grabbed his boots and put them on one at a time, not meeting the owl's eyes. "Her name is Guinevere. She's really nice."

"Really nice?" Archimedes repeated. "Really nice? Is that what they're calling it these days? And you invited her to dinner? Your very important Saxon peace treaty dinner?"

"Um… yes?"

The owl shook himself, feathers flying everywhere. "This is why I should have never left. You're perfectly incapable of handling yourself alone." He shook a wing at Arthur. "Don't tell me you're in love with her. You can't afford to be in love with anyone. You're far too young. Also, you have an entire kingdom to run. Which leaves no room for romance."

"Don't be ridiculous," Arthur shot back, perhaps with a tad too much defensiveness. "I'm not in love with anyone. I just invited her to dinner because she's kind and fun. And I don't have any other friends in this boring old place."

Archimedes huffed, ruffling his feathers. "No friends?"

Arthur groaned. "You know what I mean!" he protested. "Human friends! My own age!"

The owl sighed. "I understand. I really do. But, Arthur, you can't allow yourself to be distracted. Especially now with the Saxons coming tonight for your peace treaty feast. This event must go off without a hitch. Without one tiny snag. If these men leave without signing your treaty, your people will see it as a failure on your part. They'll think you don't know how to be king."

"Well, they wouldn't be entirely wrong," Arthur muttered.

"Now, now, boy! What kind of attitude is that? What if Merlin heard you right now? Do you think he'd approve of you putting yourself down? Now buck up and get down to that feast like the king you are."

And with that scolding, the owl took flight, straight out the window and into the night. Arthur sighed, watching him go. He knew Archimedes was right. He was getting distracted. Still, it was nice to have one thing in his life that wasn't a total disaster. Between being stuck in the castle, Merlin being missing, and now Madam Mim trying to cause trouble, he had a lot of negatives to deal with.

But Guinevere – she was the one shining light in his life. And it would take a lot more than a grumpy, highly educated owl to convince him to smother it.

CHAPTER ELEVEN
SIR ECTOR

"Look at 'em over there, making themselves right at home. Why, I bet not a one of them has had a bath in the last three years. Maybe longer. Have you smelt them yet? I've had pigs that smelt better." Sir Ector grunted disapprovingly, elbowing his son Kay to get his attention. Kay was sitting beside him in the banquet hall, gnawing on a turkey leg. He rolled his eyes at his dad.

"Whatever," he said, his mouth full.

"Whatever!" Sir Ector snorted. "I'll show you whatever. This isn't right, I tell you. And the Wart should know it! Did we teach him nothing at all during his time at our castle?"

"He doesn't even know how to properly wash dishes," Kay muttered. "How can you expect him to run a country?"

Sir Ector sighed loudly, his eyes scanning the castle's great hall, which was decked out to within an inch of its life and packed to the gills with nobles and knights from around England, sitting at long tables lined up in rows across the room. Each table was covered in mountains of food – choice meats and fine cheeses and delectable roast pheasant – piled high and almost overflowing their platters. They had even put out some sugared dates and almonds – rare delicacies, usually saved for very important guests.

Instead, they were serving the Saxons. Barbarians from across the sea who had been nothing but trouble for England ever since Rome had left and taken their armies with them, leaving the country basically defenceless. War chiefs from different regions had tried to take on the problem, but could never seem to stop fighting one another in order to unite against their common enemy. At the time, it seemed England would be destined to fall to foreign rule.

Then King Uther had come – a vicious war chief who had never lost on the battlefield and yet was charismatic enough to convince the smaller lords to join his realm. Once he'd united England, he'd taken on the Saxons with brutal force – letting them know, in no uncertain terms, how unwelcome they were in his country. Let's just say they hadn't been a problem since.

Until now.

Until England decided to put a child on the throne.

Sir Ector huffed, infuriated all over again. This was all Hobbs's fault. If only the man had not suddenly come down with the mumps, Ector would have never been forced to take the scrawny little orphan to London instead, to serve as Kay's squire. And if the Wart hadn't been in London, he'd never have even seen the sword in the stone, never mind have had a chance to pull it out. The tournament would have been held as promised – with the strongest knight being awarded the throne. Why, at this very moment, Kay could have been their king.

Instead, it was the insufferable Wart wearing the crown – which didn't even fit him properly!

Sure, at first Ector had believed the whole thing was some kind of a miracle, just like everyone else. A gift from the heavens – the promised king, delivered to them at long last. He'd even bowed before Wart as if he were some long-lost hero, come to save them all. But ever since that day, he'd started to have his doubts on the whole matter. Especially since it was clear Wart had no idea what he was doing. The heavens must have made a mistake.

And now Wart was making a much worse one, trying to befriend England's enemies.

Luckily, Ector had a plan. A good plan.

A plan to show everyone here – especially those filthy Saxons – that while Wart might have been able to pull a sword from a stone, he had no idea how to use it.

He turned to Kay. "Are you ready for this?" he asked, grabbing the turkey leg from his son's hand and tossing it back on his plate.

Kay gave his father a sulky look. "I said I was, didn't I?"

Sir Ector slapped Kay on the back. "Of course you did, my son! And it's going to be great. A historic event the bards will sing of for years to come!" He smiled widely, chuckling to himself as he tried to imagine the Wart's face when it all went down. When *he* went down.

And Ector would become father to the king of England.

CHAPTER TWELVE
ARTHUR

"Presenting His Majesty! Arthur, king of England!"

Arthur squirmed a little as the herald called out his name, his voice ringing through the great hall, as loud as a trumpet. As Arthur stepped into the room, his ears were further assaulted by spontaneous cheering from his guests. Shouts of "Hail King Arthur!" and "Long live the king!" resounded through the large space as he made his way through the room to the king's table, which had been set on a raised platform at the very front. He'd never understand why they forced kings to sit on a stage to eat, as if they were part of an actor's show. But the constant scrutiny did remind him to always chew with his mouth closed.

He climbed up on the platform, scanning the room. All eyes seemed to be on him, their expressions expectant. At first he wasn't sure if they wanted him to make some kind of speech – something he was not exactly prepared to do. But then he noticed none of the food on the tables had been touched. In fact, the only person he could see eating was Kay, who was gnawing on a huge turkey leg, chewing with his mouth wide open. Everyone else was sitting patiently in front of empty plates.

Had they all been sitting waiting for him to start eating? Ugh.

"So… sorry I'm late!" he stammered. "Please help yourself to the food. There's, uh, plenty to go round!"

Fortunately that seemed to serve as speech enough, and everyone turned excitedly to the bounty before them. Soon the room was filled with a cacophony of banging plates and animated conversation, everyone eating and drinking and chatting among themselves. Arthur sat down at his table, relieved to no longer be the focus of everyone's attention.

It was then that he wondered where Guinevere was. A quick scan of the hall told him she was not present. Had she decided against coming after all? A wave of disappointment washed over him, even as he tried to push it away. He tried to remind himself of Archimedes's warning – this was an important dinner; he couldn't be distracted. But still, he had to admit, he had been looking forward to seeing her again.

He had just started to help himself to food when the door at the back of the great hall opened. A lone figure stepped shyly into the room. It took Arthur a moment to realise it was Guinevere, she was dressed so differently than when he'd seen her earlier that day – or in the forest by the well. Now she wore a long sky-blue gown with bell sleeves and a simple silver sash. Her once flowing blonde hair had been tied up in a series of complicated braids, framing her head like a crown.

Excitedly, Arthur stood up and waved from his platform. She met his eyes, her own widening in disbelief as he beckoned her forwards. As she took a few cautious steps in his direction, it seemed like everyone in the room turned to stare, wondering what had captured the king's attention. But when Guin noticed their eyes, instead of cowering in embarrassment, a mischievous grin spread across her face and she began to dance wildly down the aisle, as if to lively music. When she reached the stage, she leapt up onto the platform, then turned to the guests, giving them a saucy bow. The room broke out into whoops and cheers.

Guin turned to Arthur, giving him an impish smile. He laughed and clapped along with the other guests.

"You're a pretty good dancer," he remarked as she settled down in the chair next to him. "I wish I could make an entrance like that."

"It's not hard. I'll teach you," she told him, grabbing a plate and helping herself to some of the meat. All eyes were still on her, but she was looking only at Arthur. "This is quite a feast," she remarked as she sampled a sugared date. "I don't think I've ever seen so much food in one place in my entire life."

"It is a bit much, honestly," Arthur confessed. "I had no idea when I asked them to prepare it that this is what they'd come up with. At least there will be a lot of leftover food to share with the people in town tomorrow."

"You're going to share your food with the people?" Guinevere looked surprised.

"Well, yes. It's better than having it go to waste, isn't it?" Arthur replied with a shrug. "And why shouldn't they enjoy it? They're part of our kingdom, too. I want them to know that they matter."

Guinevere's face took on a peculiar look. She dropped her eyes, concentrating on her food. Arthur wondered if he'd said something wrong. But then, what would she want him to do? Hoard the good food in the castle and allow the people to go without? That didn't seem very kingly to him.

"By the way, you look really nice," he blurted out, feeling the need for a subject change.

She looked up, her cheeks flushing. "When I told Mistress McCready I'd been invited to dinner, she insisted on finding me something *proper* to wear – seems my everyday kitchen rags don't cut it in court. This monstrosity of a dress once evidently belonged to the great and lovely Lady Igraine, who lived here many years before." She made a gesture of putting on the airs of a grand lady. Then she laughed. "To be honest, it's dreadfully itchy, and I can't wait to be rid of it."

Arthur nodded knowingly. "I know exactly how you feel," he confessed. "And I'll never understand it. Why, these clothes cost so much, you would think they'd be required to make them comfortable to wear."

"Exactly! There ought to be a law. Hey! Maybe you could make one," she joked. "You are the king, after all. Might as well get something out of the job."

"That's a good idea." Arthur squared his shoulders, shooting her a look of mock authority. "I declare, from this day henceforth, all clothes in the kingdom must be made comfortable – on penalty of death!"

Guinevere clapped her hands. Arthur made a short bow. He was already glad he'd invited Guinevere to dinner. She brought a spark of life to the dreadfully boring court.

He opened his mouth to say something more, but at that moment, they were approached by Sir Pellinore and a man in chain mail whom Arthur didn't recognise. The knight bowed before his king, then straightened.

"M'lord, I'd like to introduce you to King Baldomar," Pellinore said, gesturing to the visitor. "He is king of the Saxons and was the one who agreed to come and join your feast this eve."

Oh. Arthur swallowed hard. So this was the invading king. He looked… tall. And pretty muscular, too. He had curly black hair on his head and a thick, ugly scar cutting across his left cheek – the mark of a true warrior. Arthur glanced down at his own skinny, gangly body and felt suddenly awkward. Like a child playing dress-up in his father's clothes.

No. He couldn't think like that. He had to play the part, or this wasn't going to work. He had to act like he had been born into this role, with full confidence. He could not let King Baldomar see a hint of weakness or fear. Or else that chaos Mim wanted so badly? It would become inevitable.

"You are most welcome, Your Grace," he said, giving a small bow of respect to the other king. "I am pleased to make your acquaintance and delighted to welcome you to my kingdom. Thank you for accepting my invitation."

Wow. That sounded pretty good, actually, he thought after he had spoken. Maybe he could make this work.

The burly king gave him a crooked smile. "How could I not come?" he asked with a wink. "Everyone in the land is talking about the miracle boy king. Of course I had to see him for myself!"

Arthur felt his cheeks heat at this, but forced himself to keep his eyes on the man and not look away. "And now you've seen me. And my court. What do you think?"

"I think it's quite a merry place, Your Grace," Baldomar replied with a smile. "I will be honest, most of my men didn't agree with my decision to come here. They thought it might be a trap. We came fully expecting we could be met by swords and arrows." He gestured out to the room. "Instead, you feed us and give us respect. It's not something we're used to from the English, if you pardon my saying."

"Of course," Arthur replied, feeling secretly pleased. His plan was working! "I have no quarrel with you. As long as you keep to your own lands, I think we can agree to live in peace." He paused, then added, "And perhaps even take things a step further, if you're willing."

"What are you proposing?" Baldomar looked interested.

"We agree to become allies. Meaning we help one another out. If you need food or medicine, you can call on us and we will give it to you. Or if we need an army to protect our shores, you will send your vast fleet of ships to lend us aid."

King Baldomar looked surprised. For a moment he said nothing. Then he nodded slowly. "This is an interesting proposal," he said. "I will think on it this eve. If it pleases you, I will give you my answer tomorrow morning, after I speak with my men."

"That's fair," Arthur said, just happy Baldomar hadn't laughed in his face at his idea. Kay had claimed the Saxons were barbarians, but they actually seemed quite reasonable. "I will eagerly await your response," he added, then waved his hand. "But for now, please enjoy yourself and the feast. Sit by my side, if you like. You are my personal guest, after all." He gestured to the empty place at his left.

"I thank you, Your Majesty, but I prefer, I think, to sit with my men. If that's all right with you. They might not like me putting on airs, sitting on stages." He laughed good-naturedly.

"Oh. Yes, of course," Arthur replied with a grin. "Believe me, I don't like sitting up here much, either. I feel like I should be putting on a show."

The king laughed again, slapping Arthur on the shoulder. "I like you, boy king," he said. "I think you and I may be able to work something out."

The king returned to his men at the table, and Arthur turned back to his plate, feeling flushed with pleasure. This had gone better than he'd imagined. And in front of the whole court, too. Now everyone could see his plan wasn't as mad as some of them had wanted to make it out to be.

As he lifted a slice of pheasant to his mouth, he felt eyes at his side. He turned to see Guinevere watching him, another strange expression on her face. He cocked his head in question.

"What?" he asked. "Don't tell me I just did all that with food in my teeth."

"No." She smiled and shook her head. "No. Your teeth are fine."

"Then… what is it?"

She shrugged. "Oh, nothing. I'm just… surprised, I guess. Most kings would not be as generous as you were just now."

Arthur considered this for a moment. "I suppose not. But then, none of them studied under Merlin."

Guinevere's smile faded, just for a moment. Arthur wondered why.

"Do you know Merlin?" he asked.

"No," she said quickly. Maybe too quickly. "I mean, I've heard of him, obviously. Everyone has. But I've never… had the pleasure… to meet him." Her face looked pinched all of a sudden, as if she smelt something bad.

"Well, if he ever comes back, I'll introduce you!" Arthur declared. "You'll love him, I promise. He's so smart. And he's an amazing wizard, too. He's taught me everything I know."

"Does he tell you what to do?" Guinevere asked, suddenly looking very interested. "Like, how to run the land? Does he give you advice? Orders?"

Arthur frowned, confused at her questioning. "Well, no," he said. "To be honest, I haven't seen or heard from him in ages. Not since before I came to London and pulled the sword from the stone." He hung his head, remembering. "We had a fight, you see. And he flew off to someplace called Bermuda. I wish he'd come back. I don't like doing all this without him. I feel like I'll make a wrong choice or something. And someone will get hurt."

Guinevere pursed her lips for a moment. "You seem to be doing pretty well without him," she ventured, her voice hesitant. "I mean, all of this" – she gestured to the room – "this was all you, right? Not anything to do with Merlin."

"I suppose. But—"

Arthur was interrupted by a sudden commotion in the hall. When he looked out to see what it could be, his jaw dropped in surprise as his eyes fell on Kay, storming up to the stage. His foster brother's eyes were narrowed. And his hands were clenched into fists.

Arthur's heart quickened, though he wasn't quite sure why. Was his foster brother going to complain about his treaty with the Saxons again? If so, he was choosing a very poor time to do it.

"Um, Kay?" Arthur tried as his foster brother stepped up to the table, glaring down at him. If looks could kill, Arthur was quite sure he'd be on the floor. "Is something wrong?"

Kay scowled. He glanced back at his father, who was watching with far too much interest for Arthur's comfort. Sir Ector waved his hands at his son, urging him on. Kay huffed, then turned back to Arthur.

"Is something wrong?" Kay growled. "I'll tell you what's wrong. This farce has gone on long enough. You were never meant to be our king."

CHAPTER THIRTEEN
ARTHUR

Arthur stared at Kay in shock. Of all the things he'd expected his foster brother to say, this was definitely not one of them.

"What did you just say?" he asked, trying to keep the tremble from his voice. This was not a time to show weakness. Not with everyone in the kingdom watching. Not to mention the Saxons.

"I think you heard me, *Wart*," Kay snarled, spitting out Arthur's nickname as if it were a bad joke. "You don't deserve to be up here. And you certainly shouldn't be running the kingdom."

Arthur paled. Oh, no. Not now. Not in front of the Saxons, not when he'd just proposed an alliance.

He'd known from the start it was possible there would be someone someday who felt the need to challenge his kingship. He was only a child, after all. Untrained in just about everything to do with being a king. It made sense that someone would eventually rise up and try to take him down.

He just hadn't expected it to be his own brother.

He stole a glance over to the table where the Saxons were sitting. King Baldomar was watching the scene with steely eyes. He did not look pleased. Wonderful.

"What are you doing?" Arthur asked through clenched teeth, trying to keep his voice as low as possible so no one else could hear. "If you have a problem with me, can we just talk about it later? Privately? At least not in front of the entire kingdom and our invited guests?"

Kay shook his head. "No!" he said loudly. "For this concerns your entire court." He beckoned to the crowded room with his hand. "No one wants to say it, so I will. You are too young to be our king. Why, you haven't even grown your first whiskers yet!" he jeered. As if he himself had some kind of grizzly beard.

Arthur heard a few nervous laughs from the crowd. It made him want to crawl under the table. Why was Kay doing this? And why now of all times?

He could feel Guinevere's eyes on him from the side, but couldn't bring himself to look at her. Whatever he said next might change the course of history. And he would be responsible for the outcome.

"I hate to inform you, *brother*," he said stiffly, "but whiskers don't make a king. I may be young, but I pulled the sword from the stone. And as the prophecy says—"

His words were cut off by Kay's mocking laugh. "The prophecy," he spit out. "England's king was *meant* to be decided by a tournament. And because you pulled some sword from some stone, I never got my chance to compete. Does that seem fair to anyone?" He turned to the crowd, who was still watching the whole thing as if it were some kind of riveting play.

Sir Ector rose from his seat. "Well, I certainly don't think so!" he bellowed, and Arthur cringed as he noticed a few people nodding in agreement. *And why not?* he thought. To be honest, he himself had never thought it was quite fair. And he'd never asked for it, either. In fact, the last thing he'd wanted was to become king of England. Though he wasn't quite sure dim-witted Kay would fare any better.

He realised Kay was waiting for an answer.

"What do you want from me?" he asked, not knowing what else to say.

"I came to London for a tournament," Kay replied. "And I'm still waiting for my chance to fight." He sneered at Arthur.

"Face me in single combat. We'll see, once and for all, who's *really* meant to be king."

Arthur swallowed hard. He could feel his forehead break out into a cold sweat. Kay wanted to fight him? His brother was ten times bigger than Arthur and probably twenty times stronger. Not to mention he had years of training, whereas Arthur had none.

Heavenly prophecy or no, if he fought Kay, Arthur would not stand a chance.

He could feel Guinevere's hand on his arm. "You don't have to do this," she whispered. "Just call your guards. Have them take him away."

It was a good idea, but Arthur knew it would serve as only a temporary reprieve. Kay would be back, or others would take his place. The gauntlet had been thrown, and he had to prove himself worthy of the throne – or everyone would remain in doubt. The Saxons would think him a coward. They might start thinking twice about the treaty.

And so Arthur squared his shoulders. Lifted his chin. "Name your time and place," he said simply. "I will answer your challenge."

There were gasps from the crowd. Kay's smile widened.

"Excellent," he said. "I knew you'd see reason." He pressed his fists against the table, leaning forwards. So close Arthur could smell his foul breath. "Meet me in the courtyard tomorrow morning and we shall battle. And to the victor goes the kingdom."

"I will be there," Arthur replied, hoping he sounded brave. In reality, he was shaking like a leaf.

Kay smirked, then turned and stormed out of the great hall. As the heavy door swung shut behind him, the court erupted into conversation. Arthur guessed they would probably be making wagers on the battle – and he assumed most of them would not be in his favour. Not that he blamed them. His odds of beating a trained warrior in hand-to-hand combat were next to nothing.

"What were you thinking?" Guinevere demanded, grabbing his arm. He turned to look at her and realised her face was ashen with fear. "You're never going to win against a man like that!"

He grimaced. "Thanks for your support."

"I'm sorry." She hung her hand. "I'm just trying to be sensible." Arthur watched as she inhaled a long breath through her teeth. "Look, maybe..." she began hesitantly. "Maybe you should just give him what he wants."

"What?" Arthur looked shocked.

"Do you really like being king? Being trapped here in this castle, under guard? I saw you out in the forest. You seemed happier there. You... could go back to that."

Arthur stared at her. She wasn't wrong – and it was a

tempting thought, to say the least. To just walk away from it all. Get a second chance at a simple life. One where he didn't have to make rules or avoid wars or be responsible for the well-being of people he had never met.

And all he would have to do was give up his crown. Which didn't even fit.

But then his eyes travelled to the Saxon table. They were all watching closely, their faces guarded, but clearly concerned. Arthur remembered his conversation with Kay the week before. His foster brother had called Saxons barbarians. He said they deserved to be destroyed.

If he backed down now – abdicated the throne – these men, who had come here under his protection and promise of peace, would likely be arrested where they sat. Taken to a dungeon. Maybe even killed.

All talks of peace would be over.

The kingdom would erupt into war.

"I can't," he said sadly. "As much as I might want to. There's too much at stake." He gestured to the Saxons. Guinevere nodded unhappily, as if she'd known this would be his answer all along.

"You can't sign a peace treaty if you're dead," she said in a low voice.

He bit his lower lip. "Well, then, I'm just going to have to figure out a way to stay alive."

CHAPTER FOURTEEN
GUINEVERE

The feast went late into the night, and by the end of it, the Saxons and Englishmen were making merry with one another, dancing and laughing, as if they were long-lost friends. In fact, the only person who didn't look like he was having fun was Arthur himself. Sure, he tried to keep a brave face, but Guinevere could see the traces of fear in his eyes that he couldn't quite hide. And she couldn't help feeling sorry for him. She was convinced, at this point, he didn't know about the evil Merlin had done; he'd been tricked into thinking he was meant to be king. Which made her quest a lot more difficult. She knew he still needed to be brought down, but she didn't want him to get hurt in the process. If only he'd just given up the throne – walked away from it all when he had the chance…

But he wouldn't, she realised. He felt responsible for the people of England. He hadn't been king long, but he cared about the realm and his chance at peace. He had all the instincts of a good leader, even if he wasn't meant to sit on the throne.

Eventually she left the feast to retire to her humble little bedroom down the hall from the kitchens. She was just about to take off her itchy gown and replace it with a soft night garment when she heard a scratching at her window. She pulled open the wooden shutters (servants, of course, didn't get real glass windows like kings did) and found a little purple squirrel on the other side, twitching its nose at her.

She raised an eyebrow. "Mother?" she whispered. "Is that you?"

Not that she had much doubt in the matter. The purple rather gave it away.

As the squirrel hopped up onto the windowsill, Guinevere ran to lock her door. Then she headed back to the window, scooped up the squirrel in her arms, and took it over to her bed. A moment later there was a quick *poof*, and the squirrel disappeared, replaced by Mim.

"Ugh. I hate squirrels," Mim grumped, brushing off her

muddy dress with her hands. "They're so dirty and smelly. Rats with bushy tails, that's all they are."

Guinevere nodded dutifully, even though she was quite fond of squirrels herself.

"What are you doing here, Mother?" she asked, trying not to notice all the dirt and mud flakes landing on her bed as her mother continued to shake out her dress. Why had Mim felt the need to use magic instead of just coming through the front door like a normal person?

"Why, I'm here to see you, of course! I missed you, my dear! It's so dreadfully boring in the cottage without you dancing around all the time! I even had to play card games by myself! Which I won, of course! You do get such a better chance of winning when you play both sides of the table!" She giggled.

Guinevere couldn't help a small smile. She hadn't realised how much she'd missed her mother's silly banter. "I'm glad you're here," she assured her. "Only it's very late at night. I would think you would want to wait till morning."

Mim waved her off. "Sleep is for the weak. And I couldn't wait. Not when I heard the news!"

"The… news?" So much had happened that night, Guinevere was at a loss as to what her mother might be referring to. Did she mean the Saxon treaty? Sir Kay's challenge to Arthur?

"The whole town is buzzing about it," Mim clucked. "The mysterious blonde girl in the blue dress who danced through court like an angel and dined like royalty with the king himself." She gave Guinevere a meaningful look. "It seems you've been enjoying yourself, my dear."

"Oh. That." Guinevere stared down at her feet, feeling sheepish. "Yes, Arthur invited me to dinner tonight. I, uh, thought it would be a good chance for me to spy on him, as you asked me to."

"Indeed, my pet!" Mim looked positively gleeful. "Earn his trust and friendship, and then – pow! Off with his head!" She cackled loudly. "I mean, not literally, of course," she added as she caught Guin's horrified look. She leant in closer. Her eyebrows waggled. "So tell dear Mother, what have you learnt about our boy king? Anything useful we can use against him?"

Guinevere opened her mouth to speak, but strangely nothing came out. Instead, she felt a weird shimmer of unease waft through her stomach. She had plenty to tell Mim from her day with Arthur. So why was she suddenly feeling reluctant to share it?

"Well, come on, girl!" Mim scolded. "We don't have all night!" She puffed up her wild purple hair with her hands. "I need my beauty sleep, you know! I mean, not that I'm not perfectly lovely as I am..." she added, preening at her reflection in Guinevere's water basin.

"Sorry," Guinevere mumbled. She forced herself to straighten her shoulders and draw in a deep breath before giving her report. "The Saxons arrived tonight and dined with the king. Arthur presented his idea of a peace treaty, and they're going to tell him tomorrow whether they want to sign it."

"Bah!" Mim spit on the floor. "This was exactly what I was afraid of."

Guinevere bit her lower lip. "But... why?"

"What do you mean, why?" Mim looked at her, puzzled.

"I don't know. It's just..." Guin shrugged. "Why don't we want peace? I mean, wouldn't that be a good thing?"

"Well, y-yes. I mean, of course it would," Mim stammered, looking a little taken aback by the question. "Peace would be wonderful! Just peachy! We all want peace. Of course we do! It's just that – well, how do we know it's not a trick? Maybe they're pretending to want peace – just to get us to let our guard down. After all, you know how *Saxons* can be!" She gave Guinevere a pointed look, as if daring her to argue. Then she waved a hand dismissively. "Anyway, what else did you learn?"

Guinevere gnawed on her lower lip. "Well, Arthur's foster brother, Sir Kay, has challenged his right to the throne."

She had a feeling her mother was going to appreciate this piece of news more than the first. "They're set to fight first thing tomorrow morning. Arthur had to agree to it, or he risked looking weak in front of the Saxons. But I'm afraid he's not going to be up for the challenge. He's just a boy. And this knight is an experienced warrior."

Mim rubbed her hands together in glee. "Now that's more like it! If we're lucky, maybe he'll manage to ruin everything on his own!"

"But then Kay would be king," Guinevere protested. "And he's not the rightful ruler, either."

Mim shrugged. "Well, we can't have everything, now can we, my dear?"

"But that seems kind of like a *big* thing," Guinevere insisted. She was starting to get really confused. "I mean, Arthur's actually a good king. He's young, but he's smart. And he seems to care about people."

Mim pinched Guinevere's cheeks hard. "Oh, my dear, sweet girl," she cooed. "Do not tell me that you're falling for this usurper's lies!" She released Guinevere's cheeks and danced to the other side of the room. "He may seem innocent enough. But never forget what master he serves."

Guinevere flinched. "Merlin," she said softly.

"Merlin," Mim affirmed. "You know, *he* seemed quite lovely once upon a time, too. Just a dear old doddering fool.

Until he slaughtered your parents in cold blood, that is." She gave Guin a hard look. "And the apple, my dear, never falls far from the tree."

Guin swallowed hard, her mind racing. She thought back to Arthur at the banquet, talking so lovingly about his teacher. Something wasn't adding up.

"Why did Merlin kill my parents?" she blurted out before she could stop herself.

For a moment, Mim froze. Then she laughed. "I've told you this story a thousand times," she reminded Guin.

"Yes," Guinevere agreed. "But you never told me why. *Why* did he want to kill my parents? I mean, he must have had a reason."

"Because he's evil! Obviously!" Mim replied. "And evil people do evil things. There's no sense in looking any deeper than that, my darling. You'll only drive yourself mad."

"Right." Guinevere sighed. Clearly she wasn't going to get any more information out of her mother tonight. But there *had* to be more to this than she'd been told. After all, the Merlin of Mim's stories was so unlike the Merlin of Arthur's. So which was the true Merlin?

And what did he really want from Camelot?

CHAPTER FIFTEEN
ARTHUR

"This is pure foolishness, boy! Pure foolishness, I say!"

Archimedes flew from one end of Arthur's bedroom to the other, his wings flapping furiously. It was still early in the morning, and Arthur wondered if the owl had slept at all the night before. Merlin used to joke that Archimedes was especially grumpy when he stayed out all night. Or maybe it was just the situation that had him all riled up.

"What am I supposed to do?" Arthur asked with a shrug. "It's not like I want to fight him. But I have no choice."

"You always have a choice. In fact, you could have chosen to put that sword back where you found it, for that matter – like I told you to. Then you wouldn't be in this mess."

"Well, it's too late for that now. And a lot of people are depending on me. I can't let them down by being a coward."

"Being a coward! How about being stupid and getting yourself killed? I'd imagine *that* would also let a few people down. First and foremost, me."

"Aw, Archimedes. I didn't know you cared," Arthur couldn't help teasing.

The owl huffed, offended. "Please! I could care less what you do with your own skin. I just don't want to have to deal with Merlin coming back and learning I let his favourite pupil be pounded into a pancake while he was gone," Archimedes grumbled. "I don't need that kind of pressure on my handsome feathered shoulders, thank you very much."

"Come on, Archimedes," Arthur begged. "A little faith?"

"Faith, trust and pixie dust!" Archimedes spat. "And we're all out of pixie dust."

"What's pixie dust?" Arthur asked, cocking his head. "And why would we need that?"

The owl rolled his eyes. "It's just an expression. Something Merlin used to say. The point is, having faith is one thing. Having smarts is quite another. And you clearly don't have any of those."

Arthur sighed. "Look, I'm not going to let myself get pounded, all right? I've been in dangerous situations before. Like when Merlin turned me into a fish? And a squirrel? And a bird?"

"Yes, yes. Give the boy a medal for his marvellous near misses. Believe me, I was there to witness them. But this time I can't fly in and save you if you get yourself in a jam."

"No. But I can use the lessons I learnt from those experiences. Like the one about brains being just as good as brawn. I may not be as strong as Kay, but I'm pretty sure I'm smarter."

"That big rock out on the courtyard is likely smarter than your foster brother," Archimedes admitted reluctantly.

"Exactly. And I know Kay's fighting style. I helped him train for years, remember. I know he's weaker on his left side. And when he feints right, he leaves his neck exposed. It used to drive Sir Ector mad."

"I suppose knowledge like that *could* be useful," the owl hedged.

"Exactly. Knowledge. That was what Merlin always tried to teach me. That knowledge is just as powerful as a sword. I can do this, Archimedes," he added, feeling excitement well inside of him for the first time since Kay had approached his table. "I know I can."

"Well, you certainly have confidence. I'll give you that."

The owl spun his head. "And I suppose there's no talking you out of this?"

"No, sir." Arthur shook his head, walking over to Excalibur and giving it a thoughtful look. The sword was heavy enough when he wore it on his belt. He was pretty sure he wouldn't be able to swing it more than a time or two – and even then without much control and accuracy.

But if all went according to plan, he wouldn't need that.

Oh, Merlin, he thought, *I really hope you're right.*

After trying without much luck to swallow a quick breakfast, Arthur got dressed and made his way down to the castle courtyard, where the makeshift tournament was to be held. When he arrived, a crowd of spectators had already gathered, pushing and shoving one another as they fought their way up onto the wooden stands, trying to get the best spot to watch the fight. In fact, there were so many of them there, Arthur half wondered if they outnumbered the crowd at his coronation.

But then, it was not every day the king of England took on his own knight.

The Saxon king, Baldomar, met him at the gate. He looked down at Arthur, studying him carefully. "Are you certain about this?" he asked, his voice tense with concern.

Arthur squared his shoulders. Or he tried to, at least.

The chain mail armour he was wearing was supposed to be lighter than plate, but it was still unbearably heavy. "Don't worry," he said. "I have a plan. And I plan to win."

The king nodded, though he didn't look quite convinced. "I hope so," he said. "For I do not like the way your challenger looks at us. I get the feeling he will not be so eager to sign a treaty if he emerges victorious."

"No, he probably won't be," Arthur agreed, wanting to be honest. He shuffled from foot to foot. "In fact, it may be a good idea for you to head out of town now, while you still have the freedom to do so. Just in case. If the worst happens, I do not want you to have to pay for my failure as king."

King Baldomar looked at him thoughtfully. "You are wise beyond your years, boy king," he said. "And I can see you truly care for others, even above your own self. That's a rare quality in a leader." He smiled. "But like you, we are not cowards. We do not retreat in the face of adversity. We will stay and cheer for your victory. And *when* you emerge the winner," he added, emphasising the *when*, "we will sign your treaty."

Arthur's face flushed. It was all he could do not to break out into a happy dance. But he forced his feet to remain firmly on the ground. "Thank you," he said. "Then we talk this afternoon."

"I look forward to it." King Baldomar gave him a deep bow, then turned and headed back to where his men were gathered. Arthur watched him go, drawing in a slow breath. He appreciated the faith shown in him, and he just hoped he could prove worthy of it.

A moment later, Sir Pellinore approached. "Are you set, lad?" he asked, looking at Arthur a bit doubtfully. "Kay has indicated he's ready to fight."

A chill tripped down Arthur's spine, all of his earlier confidence in front of King Baldomar instantly deflating. He glanced out into the courtyard to see Kay warming up by swinging his sword against a wooden post. He was dressed in a full suit of plate armour and looked ten feet tall. Arthur cringed, looking down at his own paltry suit of chain mail that didn't even fit well. What was he doing? Archimedes was right – this was pure foolishness!

No! He scolded himself. It did him no good to panic before the fight even began. Keeping his head was the one chance he had to win this. And he had to win this. Everything depended on it.

"I'm ready," he told Pellinore, trying to make his voice sound calm and confident. He drew in a breath and walked past the older knight, heading out onto the makeshift field, keeping his head held high. The crowd broke out into loud cheers as they caught sight of their king, and shouts of "Long Live King Arthur!" resounded through the space. Arthur caught a quick glimpse of Kay's scowl before his foster brother put his helmet over his head.

"All right!" Sir Pellinore announced, stepping into the courtyard and addressing the crowd in a voice loud enough for everyone to hear. "The fight shall begin when I raise and lower this flag. The rules are simple. Fight with honour. Fight with bravery. And fight to the death."

Wait, what? Arthur stopped short at the last part. Clearly no one had thought to mention that pesky little 'to the death' detail earlier! While, yes, tournaments often ended with knights being maimed or killed, it was never the intended result. He gnawed on his lower lip. This was not good at all. Not only did he not want to die himself, obviously – he also didn't want to have to kill his foster brother if the fates turned in his favour. While he was truly angry at Kay for putting him in this position, that didn't mean he wanted him dead!

Worry about it later, he scolded himself. *Right now, you have to fight. And stay alive.*

Arthur watched as Kay unsheathed his sword and followed the move with his own, trying not to notice how heavy Excalibur felt in his hands, his muscles already wobbling from the effort. His heart pounded as he took a moment to gaze over the crowd before facing his opponent.

Suddenly, his eyes fell on Guinevere, who was sitting in the very back row of the stands, dressed in a simple homespun dress of undyed wool, her hair plaited into two matching braids. Arthur threw her a small friendly smile and waved in her direction, happy to see a familiar face. She smiled back at him – just for a moment – then bashfully dropped her gaze to her lap. But it was enough. Arthur felt his confidence rising again. She had come. Which meant she cared. And if he won this, perhaps they could dine together again.

It was almost reason enough to win, in and of itself.

It was then that he noticed something at her side – make that some*one.* An old woman dressed in common peasant clothes. Which wouldn't have normally struck him as unusual. Except…

The clothes were purple. And so was her hair.

He swallowed hard. Oh, no! Had Mim come back? Now of all times? And somehow she had found Guinevere! She must have heard that Guin had been his guest at dinner last night; from what Archimedes had told him, the whole town had been talking about it. Had Arthur put his new friend in danger? He tried to get Guin's attention again, but she had turned to look at Mim, who was whispering something in her ear. Guin looked uncomfortable as she glanced back out onto the field. What had the wizard said to her? It took all Arthur had inside of him not to rush the stands and make sure Guinevere was safe.

But at that moment, the trumpets sounded through the air, indicating the start of the fight. Arthur turned to see Sir Pellinore raising his flag, then dropping it.

This was it. The battle had begun. Before Arthur could even think of saving Guinevere, he'd have to find a way to save himself.

CHAPTER SIXTEEN
GUINEVERE

A fight to the death.

The words reverberated in Guinevere's ears as she watched Arthur take the field against Sir Kay. She could hear Mim's excited cackles beside her but couldn't bring herself to look in her direction.

"Why does it have to be to the death?" she asked, worrying her lower lip. "Why can't they just, I don't know, fight and declare a winner – like they do at the regular jousts?"

"Oh, my pet. You worry far too much about one downed little sparrow," Mim clucked. "Besides, it'll be much easier this way. If he dies, Merlin loses. We win."

Guinevere shot her a look. She shrugged. "And, you

know, the kingdom will be safe from destruction, blah, blah, blah – all that good stuff, too, of course," she added gleefully.

"It's just so… barbaric. I mean, he's only a boy," Guinevere found herself arguing.

"A boy under the thumb of an evil wizard," Mim reminded her. "Trust me, my sweet girl." She rubbed her hands together. "This will be so much fun!"

Guinevere felt her stomach squirm with nausea. Why couldn't her mother take anything seriously? Didn't she understand this wasn't a game? Arthur could die out there on the field. And whether he was meant to be king or not, he didn't deserve such a fate.

She watched as Sir Kay lumbered towards Arthur, swinging his sword with practised grace. Arthur stumbled backwards, trying to put distance between them, but only managed to fall on his backside. The crowd erupted into worried murmurs as their king scrambled to his feet just in time to dodge the heavy blow from his knight. The sword swung only a finger or two above his head in a near miss. Once he was clear, Arthur dashed to the other side of the field, trying to catch his breath.

It was not an auspicious start, to say the least.

"This might be quick!" Mim crowed. "If we're lucky, maybe I'll even have time to grab a few slugs at the market on the way home." She grinned widely. "I'm still craving that slug soup."

Guinevere ignored her, still watching Arthur closely. He was standing in the corner, panting heavily. He gave another look at Kay, then, to Guinevere's surprise, dropped his sword and began to unclip his chain mail armour. He let it fall to the ground in a pool of metal, leaving him wearing only a tunic and tights.

"What is he doing?" Guin gasped. "Why is he taking off his armour? He'll be completely unprotected!"

"Well, clearly he's not very bright," Mim said with a snort. "Not that we didn't know this already. I mean, with Merlin as his teacher…"

Guinevere frowned. But Arthur *was* bright – she'd witnessed it first-hand. And he definitely wasn't stupid enough to just take off his armour on a whim; he must have a reason for doing it.

But what could it be?

She held her breath as Kay stalked towards Arthur again, his sword raised and ready. Arthur had picked his own sword back up and was holding it in a defensive stance. But Kay was so much larger, towering over the boy king like a mighty beast, Guin realised it would be nearly impossible for Arthur to even get close enough to land a blow. How did he ever expect to win?

Kay swung his blade. But Arthur darted out of the way at the last second. Guin watched as he danced from side to side, nimbler without his armour. Kay, dressed in full plate, tried to catch him, but each blow landed a hair too late. Arthur would feint right, then dodge left when Kay took the bait. And then feint left, only to dodge right. Arthur wasn't landing any actual blows, but he was succeeding in tiring his opponent out. Kay's thrusts were getting weaker. His shield began to wobble in his hand. On his next swing, Arthur slid forwards instead of going to the side, ducking under the sword's arc and slamming his feet into Kay's ankles. The knight bellowed as he lost his balance and came crashing to the ground. Arthur rolled to the side to avoid being flattened. Then he scrambled to his feet, grinning at the crowd.

Guinevere let out an accidental cheer. Mim shot her an annoyed look.

"Sorry," she muttered. "But you have to admit, that was pretty good."

Mim grunted, turning back to the fight. The crowd was on its feet now, cheering loudly for their king – and jeering at his opponent. Kay cursed under his breath as he managed to get back on his feet. He charged after Arthur again, swinging his sword recklessly. He was angry now, Guinevere realised. Humiliated. Which meant he would start making mistakes.

Meaning Arthur might actually have a chance.

But just when Arthur moved in for a real blow, his feet suddenly seemed to come out from under him. He yelped in surprise as he fell sprawling to the ground, a cloud of dust kicking up in his wake. Guinevere gasped. Had he tripped over something? But there was nothing there!

It was then that she heard the giggle. Her head jerked in Mim's direction. Her mother was slapping her hand on her knee in excitement.

"Did you do that?" Guinevere demanded in a whisper. "Did you just use magic to trip him?"

Mim shrugged impishly. "The fight was getting boring," she declared. "I just wanted to mix things up a bit."

"But that's not fair!" Guin cried before she could stop herself.

"Fair, schmair." Mim grinned at her toothily. "If I'm going to have to sit here, I want to have some fun!"

Guinevere sighed, turning back to the fight. Arthur was trying to stand up, but it was like his legs weren't working right any more. Then Guinevere noticed something strange under his boots. Something that looked almost like mud.

Purple mud.

Kay barrelled towards Arthur. But this time Arthur couldn't leap out of the way. It was as if he was glued to the ground by the mud. His eyes widened in fear as the knight swung—

Kick off your boots, Guinevere begged silently. *It's the only way!*

Arthur threw himself forwards, slipping out of his boots at the last moment. He slammed chest-first into the ground, but somehow managed to scramble back up again, dashing shoeless to the other side of the courtyard, leaving Kay staring down at a pair of empty boots.

Yes! Guinevere cheered, remembering to do it inwardly now. She stole another glance at Mim. Her mother was leaning forwards in her seat, her eyes glued to the fight. Guinevere realised she wasn't going to stop until Arthur went down.

Which wasn't fair. It wasn't fair at all. She was fine with helping Arthur lose the throne, seeing as he wasn't the rightful heir. But she wasn't all right with killing him in order to do so. There had to be another way. A more civilised way.

Why couldn't her mother see that? Why was she being so cruel?

"Mother! Stop!" she tried, raising her voice. "You need to stop now!" Several people turned to look at her. Mim's smile dipped to a frown.

"*You* need to mind your business. Whose side are

you on, anyway?" Not waiting for an answer, Mim turned back to the fight just in time to see Arthur trip again. She giggled and shot a look at Guin, almost as if daring her to say something.

Guin couldn't take it any more.

"Excuse me," she said, rising to her feet abruptly. "I've got to go to the privy."

"Good. Because you're being a complete poop!" Mim muttered. "No slugs for you, later. You don't deserve them!"

Guinevere ignored her, making her way through the throng. After climbing down the risers, she circled around the back of them, where no one was standing. Her mind raced as she walked. She had to do something to make this right. Her mother wasn't going to stop. But what could she do to help Arthur, save going on the field and fighting Kay herself?

"You let go of the boy, you lousy old lout!"

Speaking of… Guinevere looked up to the sky just in time to see a small owl swooping down at Kay. Merlin's bewitched owl, she realised in shock. She'd just assumed he'd been stuck in the future along with the wizard himself. But evidently he'd escaped that fate. Maybe he'd be able to help.

Kay let out a scream as the owl pecked him hard on his bulbous nose. He waved his arms, trying to swat him away. But the owl kept at it, digging his claws into the knight's shoulder. Unfortunately, Kay's armour was too thick and the owl couldn't get a good grip.

"Archimedes!" Arthur cried, struggling to stand. "Look out!"

But it was too late. Kay swung out a fist. His metal glove smacked the owl straight on. Archimedes flailed for a moment, then dropped to the ground like a stone.

"No!" Arthur cried, sounding horrified. He dived towards the bird, throwing himself on top of him to protect him from Kay. Even from here, Guin could see the tears streaming down his bruised cheeks and realised his face was cut and bleeding. But he didn't seem to even notice, he was so concerned about the bird. "Oh, Archimedes!" he cried, his voice cracking on the name.

Guinevere's heart panged hard. He clearly cared for this animal. Like he cared for his people. Even his enemies. He wasn't Merlin. He wasn't anything like Merlin. And he didn't deserve to die.

Drawing in a breath, she realised what she needed to do. It was the last thing she wanted, and her hands started to shake just thinking about it. But she had no choice. She had to act – now. Or Arthur would die. And his blood would be on her hands.

"*Zim, zabberim, zouse!*" she whispered. "Make me a mouse!"

A moment later she felt her body collapsing in on itself, shrinking down, reshaping, just as her mother had taught her to do. She hated shapeshifting – it felt so disconcerting to fold into another shape. It made her sick to her stomach, too. And gave her a terrible headache.

But that was nothing compared to what Arthur was going through. And she was almost positive, if the tables had been turned, he would have done the same for her.

She drew in a breath, steadying her nerves. Then, using her tiny feet, she dashed under the risers and weaved through the standing spectators' legs at the front. She prayed no one would suddenly move their feet and squash her before she had the chance to get out onto the field. By the time she made it to the front, Arthur had fallen to his knees before Kay. He clearly had no fight left in him.

"You should have just walked away, Wart," Kay sneered. He removed his helmet and looked down on the young king, his mouth curling into a lazy smirk. "Did you really think you had a chance to beat me?"

Arthur stared up at him defiantly. Blood dripped down his face, but he ignored it, his mouth set in a thin line. The crowd was so silent you could have heard a pin drop.

"I had to try," he said simply. "For my people. For our kingdom."

Kay's face twisted into an ugly scowl. He raised his sword, ready to make the fatal blow.

Guinevere realised it was now or never. She raced across the field as fast as she could. Darting up Kay's boot, she found the small kink in his armour where it met with his knee. It wasn't a large spot, but it was the perfect size for tiny mouse teeth.

She bit down. Hard.

"Argh!" Kay screamed, falling backwards and dropping his sword. Guinevere scampered up his side until she found his armpit, biting down yet again into his soft flesh. The reek of sweat assaulted her nose, and it was everything she could do not to vomit. Instead, she forced herself to bite again. And again.

The crowd gasped as Kay began to roll on the ground, screaming in pain. Arthur took his moment, leaping up and kicking the knight's abandoned sword to the side, far enough away that he couldn't easily retrieve it. Then he stalked over to Kay – and placed his own sword at the knight's throat.

"You were saying?" he asked.

"Make it stop!" Kay begged. "Please!"

"Kill him! Kill him!" cried the crowd. "Show no mercy!"

But to Guinevere's surprise, Arthur lowered his sword. "No," he said simply. "I won't kill you. That's not how we do things here any more. You will be charged with treason against your king and you will be tried in court, by a jury of your peers. It will be up to them to decide your fate."

Kay began to blubber like a baby. He yanked off his gloves and threw them angrily at the crowd. Arthur motioned to his guards, who surrounded the disgraced knight and pulled him to his feet. Kay tried to fight them off, but he was too weakened from the battle. They dragged him out of the courtyard as the crowd jeered and threw pieces of food at his head.

Arthur watched him go, then turned to Archimedes, who was still lying motionless on the ground. He dropped to his knees, cradling the bird in his hands. Was he dead? But then Guinevere caught a slight movement at the wing. No, he was alive. She let out a sharp breath.

Arthur looked up at the crowd. "He needs a doctor," he said. "Is anyone here a doctor?"

A large muscular man pushed his way through the crowd. He took the bird from Arthur's arms and studied him with a careful eye. "He's stunned," he told the young king. "Maybe a broken wing. But he will be all right."

Guinevere watched as Arthur's shoulders drooped in relief. She felt relieved, too, a wave of emotion rushing through her telling her everything was going to be all right.

And while she'd never get credit for it, she had managed to save the day.

Using magic, of all things.

She felt a pang of guilt as she headed off the field, unseen by anyone in the crowd. They were all rushing Arthur to congratulate him on his win. She watched his lips curl in a bashful grin, and she wondered if she'd been right to do what she'd done. After all, it was exactly what she always chided Mim for – using an unfair advantage to manipulate a situation to your liking. But then, if she hadn't, an innocent boy would have died. That wouldn't have been right, either.

She sighed. Ever since she'd met Arthur, things had become very confusing.

She weaved her way through the throng until she was back to where she'd started, behind the risers. Where she could end her shift and transform back to her old self. She wondered how bad of a headache she'd have when she became human again. Magic took a huge toll on her each time she cast a spell. Mim claimed it was because she didn't do it enough – like exercise, magic got easier the more you did it. It didn't cost Mim anything to shift and shift again. But Guinevere would likely be weakened for a week.

It was worth it, though. She wouldn't have changed a thing.

But before she could utter the magic words to end the transformation, she suddenly felt a hand close over her mouse body. She squeaked in surprise and tried to squirm away, but the hand was too strong. A moment later, she felt herself being lifted up into the air.

The hand opened.

And she found herself face to face with Mim.

CHAPTER SEVENTEEN
MADAM MIM

"Well, well, well, what have we here?"

Mim squinted at the little mouse, at first unsure of what she was seeing. She knew it couldn't be a regular mouse – after all, regular mice did not tend to interfere with jousting tournaments. But what else could it be? Another one of Merlin's stooges, like that ridiculous owl who had tried and failed to save his minion? She wondered how many of the forest creatures this madman had manipulated.

But then, there was something oddly familiar about this particular creature. Something about its dark brown eyes… and long thick lashes.

Mim wrinkled her nose. No. It couldn't be. Could it?

"Guinevere?" she whispered.

Suddenly the spell broke and Mim found herself cradling a rather large and heavy thirteen-year-old girl in the palm of her hand. Shocked, she leapt backwards, her arms flinging out, and the girl dropped to the ground like a stone.

"Ow!" Guinevere grunted, landing hard on her bottom.

Mim stared down at her daughter, speechless for one of the first times in her entire life. "Why, it is you!" she cried out once she'd found her voice again, even though, in hindsight, the declaration was quite obvious. "What on earth were you doing as a mouse?"

Guinevere scrambled to her feet, a guilty look flashing across her face. "Hello, Mother," she muttered, wiping the mud off her backside. She looked a little dazed. Her hand lifted to her head and she rubbed it ruefully.

Mim shook her head in disbelief. "Why, I'll be a monkey's uncle!" she cried. "You used magic! But you hate magic!"

Guinevere scowled. "Maybe I hate cheating more."

Mim giggled. She couldn't help it. Guin was just so cute when she was mad. The way her little nose wrinkled and her eyebrows furrowed…

"Stop laughing! It's not funny," Guin protested, her scowl deepening.

"No, of course not!" Mim agreed readily, trying to

swallow down her mirth. "Not funny at all. Rather – amazing, really! Simply amazing. Such a good shift, too. You got all the mouse parts just right – and that's not easy to do! I have to admit, I'm impressed. So very impressed!"

Guinevere's frown faltered. "You're not mad?"

Mim laughed. "Mad? I'm delighted! Thrilled! Sure, I wanted the fight to go differently. And I'm not pleased about losing all the gold I wagered against the lad. But you, my dear, were magnificent! Marvellous! I'm just… tearing up with pride over the whole thing."

Guinevere pursed her lips together, looking very uncomfortable. "You were *cheating*, Mother! You were using magic to make him lose."

Mim nodded, not sure why her daughter insisted on stating the obvious. "And then you used magic to make him win," she added. She laughed again. "Did you see all the confused faces on the crowd when Kay dropped his sword? It was amazing. I couldn't have done it better myself."

"It's not a joke. Arthur could have been killed!" Guinevere retorted, her voice rich with indignation. Mim felt her amusement falter a bit.

"I wasn't going to kill him!" she protested. "I was just having a little fun is all. You really need to lighten up."

"Mother, this has gone too far," Guinevere shot back, not missing a beat. "We're supposed to be fighting for justice

– to save the kingdom, not tear it apart. If we start hurting people, we'll be no better than the evil Merlin himself!"

Mim's delight at the whole event was fading fast, replaced by a feeling she didn't like at all. Not one bit. Why was Guinevere being so mean?

"You know, you seem awfully concerned about the boy you've been working to take down getting taken down," she noted, a little crossly this time. She trailed off, noticing Guinevere's face reddening. Mim's eyes widened. Oh.

"Oh, my gracious! You're in love with him!" she cried, all the pieces coming together at once. "That's what it is, isn't it! He's charmed you with his riches and feasts and pretty clothes. And now you think if you can help him, he'll make you his queen." She tsked with her tongue. "I thought better of you, my girl. I really did."

Guinevere's face had turned the colour of a ripe apple. "That's not true!" she cried. "That's not even close to true. And I don't care about any of those things, either," she added. "It's just… I don't think Arthur is like Merlin. I think he's a good person, and he's been tricked, too. Maybe if we just tell him the truth, he'll do the right thing."

Mim was laughing so hard now she was practically rolling on the ground. "The truth! You want to… tell… him…" – she could hardly get the words out through her laughter – "the truth?" She stopped laughing abruptly. "Oh, my dear girl, you are more deluded than I thought. This little adventure in the outside world was clearly too much for you. You're not acting at all like your old, sweet self." She reached out, stroking Guin's hair. "We need to get you home, and fast."

For a moment, Guinevere looked as if she wanted to argue again. Then she sighed deeply, as if exhausted. "We should *both* go home," she said. "This has all got completely out of hand. We should go home and talk everything over – figure out what should be done like two rational people. There has to be a peaceful way to convince Arthur to abdicate the throne. I'm sure if we just thought it through..."

"That sounds lovely, my dear," Mim agreed. She patted Guin's head. "And I'm absolutely in favour of all of it and can't wait to do it. I just have one tiny little task to check off my list first. Then I'll head right home. You can even start dinner, if you like! And then we can have a dance party? Just like old times."

Guin frowned, looking suspicious. "What task?" she asked. "You're not going to hurt Arthur, are you?"

"Of course not! What do you take me for? Merlin?"

"Promise me." Guinevere's eyes were diamond hard.

"I promise! I promise!" Mim cried, rolling her eyes. "On the life of my new toad, Martha the Second. And you know how much I simply adore all her beautiful warts!"

Guinevere let out a breath. "All right," she said. "Thank you."

"Anything for you, my dear." Mim gave Guin a sloppy kiss on the cheek. "Anything for you."

Guinevere opened her mouth – probably to say something else annoying – but Mim had already wasted enough time talking. She had a plan, and she was eager to carry it out.

"*Zim, zabberim, zim!*" she incanted, waving her arms and poofing herself into a brand-new magical shape. Namely that of a certain young blonde girl with big brown eyes and thick lashes. A girl who had expertly captured the king's attention. Someone he trusted. Someone he'd never suspect.

Guinevere's jaw dropped. "No!" she cried. "What are you doing?"

"I'm just going to pay a quick visit to our dear king!" Mim replied, enjoying the way Guinevere's voice sounded on her lips. "Don't worry. I'll be home in three shakes of a slug's tail, ready for our dance party!"

"Mother! What are you—" Guinevere started, looking alarmed. But she didn't get to finish her sentence. For Mim took the opportunity to snap her fingers again, and Guinevere poofed out of her sight. Off on a one-way magical trip home to their cottage in the woods, where she would be safe and sound, and, if Mim were lucky, she would start on dinner. All this magic was making Mim very hungry.

Once Guin was gone, Mim looked down at her new and improved younger self. It had been a good shift – in fact, this time only her left foot and ankle were spotted with purple. Which was easily coverable by a boot or a dress hem. No one would ever notice.

She smiled, raising her eyes to the courtyard, where the celebration was now in full swing. Let them feast and drink and believe they'd won, she thought. They would soon learn the truth.

That no one messed with the Marvellous Madam Mim.

CHAPTER EIGHTEEN
ARTHUR

Arthur looked for Guinevere after the fight was over, but she seemed to have vanished from the crowd. So had Mim, for that matter, and Arthur started to worry that perhaps the mad wizard had done something awful to his new friend in order to get back at him. He was almost positive Mim had something to do with the strange happenings during their fight – she'd been using her sorcery to try to help Kay take him down. As if the fight hadn't been hard enough on its own.

Arthur winced as he thought back to the moment he was sure he was about to die. The point of the blade scraping at his skin. The fear pounding in his heart. Everything inside of him had wanted to beg for his life. But he also hadn't wanted to shame himself in his last moments, especially not in front of the Saxons.

Now he was thankful he hadn't. After the fight ended, the Saxons were so impressed by Arthur's performance – and show of mercy – they were more eager than ever to join forces and support the new king. And the crowd was thrilled – a boy taking on a giant and winning! A feat that would surely be sung about in the taverns for years to come.

But no one was as happy as Arthur himself. He had gambled it all and come out on top. He had shown everyone he was worthy of being their king. And it would be a while, he hoped, before anyone dared challenge his rule again.

Well, except for Mim, of course. She would never give up. And Arthur knew he'd have to keep a close eye out for anything suspiciously purple in the near future.

But for now? He'd take the win.

To say he was exhausted by the day's events would have been a drastic understatement. The fight had taken both a physical and mental toll on him, and all he wanted to do was crawl into bed and rest. So while Camelot celebrated with their new Saxon friends, he decided to retreat to his chambers early and ask that supper be brought to his sollar so he could eat alone.

Though not before checking on Archimedes. Fortunately, the owl seemed much better, if in a bit of a foul mood. Probably due to his broken wing – the doctor had told him he couldn't fly for a month. A grounded owl, it seemed, was a grumpy one.

Arthur was just settling in when there was a knock on the door. He assumed it was the steward, bringing him his dinner. But instead, he was surprised to find none other than Guinevere standing outside his door, carrying a tray with a bowl of piping hot soup and a small loaf of crusty bread.

Arthur smiled, delighted to see her. "Guin!" he cried, ushering her happily into his sollar and gesturing for her to put down the soup on the table. "I was looking for you after the fight! I was getting worried when I couldn't find you."

Guinevere set down the soup. "You were worried about me? Why?"

Arthur grimaced. Right. She didn't know. He led her over to the chair by the fire, then knelt down beside her, meeting her eyes with his own. "Look," he said, "I don't want to alarm you. But the old woman sitting next to you at the fight? The one in purple?"

"Purple?" Guinevere tapped her finger to her forehead. "Ah yes. I do seem to recall a woman in purple. She was quite lovely."

"Was she?" Arthur scratched his head. Lovely was not exactly the descriptor he would use when describing Mim. "Well, she can be quite clever in hiding her true self, I suppose. But in reality, she's a very powerful wizard. She's been snooping…"

Arthur scratched his head. Well, beauty was in the eye of the beholder, he supposed. "In any case, the woman in purple is a very powerful wizard named Madam Mim. She's been snooping around the castle ever since I became king, and I think she means to take me down." He gave her a helpless look. "I was worried she might try to hurt you to get at me."

To his shock, Guinevere giggled.

"What's so funny?" he asked.

"Sorry," she said, shaking her head. "Sometimes I laugh when I'm scared. It helps… relieve the tension." She smiled at Arthur. "Thank you for warning me. I will, of course, be on guard against this powerful purple wizard."

Arthur let out a breath of relief. He was glad Guin was taking him seriously. "I'm just happy you're all right," he said. Then he grinned. "And look! So am I! I told you I'd find a way to win."

Guinevere raised an eyebrow. Arthur felt his face heat.

"All right, fine. I didn't know for sure myself. Especially when Mim started tripping me up with her magic. But it all worked out in the end! And now the peace treaty is signed, and Kay is in prison. And all is well in the kingdom."

"I am very pleased to hear that, Your Majesty," Guinevere said, bowing her head.

He laughed. "Oh please! Don't start with that whole 'Your Majesty' thing. We know each other better than that now, don't we, evil knight?" He nudged her playfully with his shoulder.

"Oh, yes," she said. "We know each other *quite* well." She giggled again.

Arthur felt his cheeks heat, though he wasn't sure why. She was certainly acting a little strange. But then, it had been a very strange day.

"Are you all right?" he asked, just in case.

But Guin only waved him off with a laugh. "Of course I am! It's been a wonderful day! Simply marvellous! And I'm so glad you were victorious against that lousy knight. In fact, I made you a very special victory soup, just for the occasion. It's my secret recipe," she added with a smile.

Arthur smiled back at her. He'd almost forgotten Guin still worked in the kitchens. He was glad they were letting her cook now instead of just sticking her with the dirty dishes. She knew so much about various herbs and plants – she would be a great addition to their staff.

"Thank you," he said, rising to his feet and walking over to the table. He leant down and made a show of smelling the soup. It smelt odd, and a little unpleasant. But then, there were a lot of foods served in the castle he was still getting used to. Back at Sir Ector's, he had only ever been allowed to eat whatever scraps were left over from his foster father and brother's feasts – only one step up from the castle hounds, really – so his palate hadn't been prepared.

"What's in it?" he asked curiously.

"Slugs," she replied with a smile. "Super slimy slugs. With some rare, delicate mushrooms found high in the hills mixed in. Very special," she added. "Fit for a king." Then she looked at him expectantly, and he realised she wanted him to take a bite.

Arthur's stomach squirmed a little as he looked down at the soup. He wasn't sure he was going to like it – he'd never been fond of mushrooms, and while admittedly he'd never tried slugs, he was pretty sure he didn't like anything slimy. But Guinevere looked so hopeful, and he knew she'd worked hard on the meal, probably spent most of the evening preparing it; he couldn't insult her by turning it down.

And so he sat down at the table, picking up his spoon. He could feel Guinevere watching him as he dipped it in the bowl and brought it to his lips. The broth had a warm, spicy flavour that turned out to be actually pretty tasty, too. He smiled, relieved he could tell her the truth.

"It's good!" he pronounced. "Thank you!"

She nodded, looking pleased as she rose from her chair. "Now if you'll excuse me, Your Maj— er, I mean, Arthur," she corrected. "I must get back to the kitchens. Please let me know if you need anything else."

Arthur nodded. "I should be fine. I'm planning to go to bed the second I finish this delicious soup. But maybe we could find some time to spend together tomorrow? To celebrate some more, once I've had a full night's sleep?"

"Oh, I would absolutely *love* that!" she cooed. "It would be absolutely marvellous."

She rose to her feet and started out of the bedroom. Arthur watched her go, feeling happy and satisfied. It had turned out to be a really good day, despite its worrying beginning. And its ending was even better – with the promise of a wonderful tomorrow. He was so glad he'd run into Guin in the forest. She'd turned out to be a truly good friend, and he no longer felt so alone, being stuck in the castle, now that she was here.

In fact, it almost made it tolerable to be king.

Guinevere was just about through the door when her dress happened to catch on a lone nail sticking out from the wall. She grunted, annoyed, and yanked on the dress's hem to free it. Arthur frowned as he caught something flash at her exposed ankle, just for a moment, before she pulled the door closed behind her.

Something... purple.

"Wait!" he cried out, alarmed. He jumped from his chair and ran to the door, yanking it open, looking down each end of the hall outside. "Guinevere? Can you, uh, come back here for a moment?"

But there was no one there. No one at all.

Arthur's heart started to stutter in. He walked back into the room in a daze, going straight to the soup and staring down at it with sudden suspicion. Could it be? But no! It had to be just a coincidence, right? That was clearly Guin. They'd had a whole conversation!

A rather strange conversation, now that he thought back to it.

Suddenly he heard a rapping at the window. At first he assumed it was Archimedes, come to congratulate him on his victory. But no, he reminded himself, the owl couldn't fly with his broken wing. Instead, it was a small yellow bird, about a quarter of the owl's size, with long thick eyelashes curtaining its brown eyes. Did birds usually have eyelashes? Arthur's head was too foggy to remember.

"Go away," he muttered. "I need to think." He stared

down at the soup again. It did smell really strange. It tasted a little strange, too, now that he thought about it. Not bad, just… different. With this unfamiliar flavour…

Tap, tap, tap.

The bird continued to peck at the window with its beak. Arthur wondered if it was hurt or something. Finally, he decided to open the window to see for himself. Maybe he could bring it down to the castle's doctor and have him look at it.

The bird flew into the room at top speed. It was carrying something in its talons, but Arthur couldn't tell what it was. He watched as it dived straight to the soup and knocked the bowl off its tray. The contents splashed onto the floor.

"What are you—?"Arthur started. But he stopped short as he realised how thick his tongue suddenly felt. As if his mouth were filled with mud. A moment later, his stomach twisted and the room began to weave in and out of focus. He grasped at his chair as he lost his balance and started to fall.

"Oh, no!" he cried. "No, no, no!"

His eyes fell on the spilt soup. Poison? Had Mim really poisoned him?

The bird was frantically flapping above him. It looked as distressed as he felt. His eyes were so heavy he could barely keep them open, and soon they fluttered closed. *Just for a moment,* he thought. *Then I'll figure out what—*

"Arthur! Stay with me, Arthur!"

He opened his eyes with effort. To his shock, the bird had disappeared.

Instead, it was Guinevere who was leaning over him, a horrified look on her face.

CHAPTER NINETEEN
GUINEVERE

Guinevere looked down at Arthur, her insides feeling as if they were being torn out bit by bit. And it wasn't just the after-effects of shapeshifting for a second time without much rest in between – though those were admittedly brutal. It was more the realisation of what her mother had done.

Turned Arthur – sweet Arthur – into a giant slimy slug.

He looked up at her, his eyestalks waggling. She resisted the urge to vomit. She'd never seen something so vile – with its writhing greyish flesh undulating across the floor, leaving a slime trail in its wake. Arthur clearly hadn't fully realised what was happening to him yet. She didn't know if that was good or bad.

"Arthur, you're under a spell," she told him, hoping she didn't sound too scared. Or angry. *Why, Mother, why? This isn't funny!* "Don't try to move."

He squinted at her with tiny black slug eyes, looking quite scared himself. Then he seemed to nod, as if remembering. He opened his mouth to speak, but only managed a soft sluglike squeal.

"Don't try to talk, either," she added. She glanced over at the spilt soup on the floor – at the slimy little slugs squirming in the broth, mixed with her mother's favourite mushrooms. Her mind flashed back to the last time she'd seen this soup. Mim had been so proud of herself. *It turns people into slugs! Isn't that silly?* At the time Guin had wondered about the practicality of such magic. Who would ever want to be a slug? Now she was starting to understand. Her stomach twisted.

"Look, I'm going to give you something to help you. It'll make you very sick, but it will get the poison out of you. Are you all right with me doing that?"

He started to nod. Then he froze, staring in horror at something behind her. At first she worried it was her mother, come back to see the fruits of her labour. But then she realised he was staring into a silver mirror, seeing his reflection for the first time.

He began to scream – a horrible slug scream. His whole

body undulated with fear. Guinevere dived towards him, placing her hand on his slimy flesh, trying to calm him.

"I know, I know!" she whispered fiercely. "It's absolutely terrifying. But you have to stay with me. Be quiet. If you scream too loud, the guards will come, and they'll take me away, thinking I did this to you. And then I won't be able to help you." Her heart pounded. *Would* she be able to help him?

She felt him surrender, his blobby body sinking back to the floor. She let out a breath of relief and removed her hand, which she used to reach down and pick up the crystal vial she'd brought into the room as a bird. It was the largest one she could carry in bird shape, and she just hoped it'd be enough.

She removed the stopper and held the vial over Arthur's head. "Open," she instructed. "It's going to taste vile, but whatever you do, don't spit it out. You need all of it to make it effective."

Arthur obediently opened his mouth. Guin tipped the bottle, and a drop of green liquid splashed onto his slug tongue. He winced, looking as if he wanted to throw up from the taste, but forced himself to swallow the medicine down. Not wanting to waste a drop, Guinevere continued to drip the potion into his mouth until the bottle was completely empty.

"I know it's horrible, but unfortunately, what happens next is going to be even worse," Guinevere apologised. She ran over and locked the door. Then she grabbed the water bucket by the hearth. She brought it over to Arthur. Just in time for him to vomit into it.

Bright purple vomit.

Oh, Mother… you promised!

But then, her mother had kept her promise, hadn't she? At least technically. Guinevere had asked her not to hurt Arthur. And she'd stuck to her word, instead doing absolutely the next worst thing. Guinevere grimaced, imagining her mother's glee as she concocted her plan. Why, she probably thought it was perfectly hilarious. In fact, she was probably on her way back to the cottage at this very moment to brag about her cleverness over dinner.

What would she think when she learnt Guinevere had interfered again? Thwarted yet another of her plans?

Guinevere shook her head, turning her attention back to slug Arthur, who was writhing on the ground. As his body twisted and turned, it began to morph new parts. First an arm. Then a leg. Then another. Until – *poof!* He was fully human again.

"Did it work?" Arthur's eyes shot back to the mirror. He let out a shrill laugh. "Oh, my heavens, I've never been so happy to see my scrawny little body in all my life."

Guinevere smiled at him, relief coursing through her. She rose to her feet. "You'll probably feel a little rough for a while," she told him. "But you're going to be all right." She reached down and took the pail, then went to the window and dumped the contents out; she wanted to dispose of any evidence. Then she turned back to Arthur. "Get some rest. I'll talk to you later." She stepped towards the door.

"Wait!" Arthur called after her, his voice anxious. "You're leaving?"

She stopped in her tracks. "Well, y-yes," she stammered, turning to face him again. "I shouldn't be here at all. It's not proper for a servant girl to be in the king's chambers, unaccompanied."

"It is if she saved my life!" Arthur shot back, not missing a beat. He struggled to sit up. "Besides, you're more than a servant. You're my friend." His eyes, large and blue and earnest, locked on her face. "Please stay with me. I don't want to be alone right now."

Guinevere's heart panged at the desperation she heard in his voice. And suddenly she felt immensely guilty about all she'd done. She'd been angry at him for lying to her back in the forest, and yet now she was doing the same – though her deception was much, much worse. He trusted her. And she was betraying him with every breath.

Maybe he wasn't meant to sit on the throne of England. But he didn't deserve this.

No. She needed to stop this. Now. She needed to walk out that door and never come back. He would be sad, of course. She'd be sad, too. But it was for the best. Nothing good could come of this dangerous game. And if he ever learned the truth – that the girl he trusted was nothing more than a liar, a part of Mim's scheme from the start... She shook her head. She couldn't bear the thought.

Better she just walk away. Even if it hurt her heart to do so.

She started towards the door again. But before she got three steps in that direction, she felt arms wrap around her, Arthur pulling her into an embrace. For a moment, she stiffened, her heart in her throat – wondering if she should pull away. But his arms were so strong. So warm. Instead, she found herself turning and melting into them, laying her head on his shoulder. She wrapped her arms around his back, embracing him fully, and pushed all the doubts and guilt and worry deep down inside.

"Thank you," Arthur murmured against her shoulder. "I don't know what I would do without you."

The guilt raged again, almost suffocating her, and she forced herself to untangle from his arms and step back to put distance between them. "I'm just glad I could help," she said, hoping he couldn't hear the tremble in her voice.

He smiled at her, such a genuine smile it broke her heart. Then his eyebrows furrowed, as if something had just occurred to him.

"I think my head's still a little foggy." He closed his eyes and opened them again. "I was so out of it, I honestly thought you came in through my window as a bird."

"A… bird?" Guinevere had hoped perhaps he had been too sick to remember that part. She tried to make herself laugh, as if it were the silliest thing in the world.

"I know." Arthur blushed. "I told you I was out of it." He looked up at her. "You came just at the right time," he mused. "If you hadn't…" His voice trailed off, as if he didn't want to say what could have happened. "How did you know to come?" he added. "And how did you happen to have the antidote on you?" His voice held confusion, but not suspicion. Which made her feel even worse.

Guinevere thought fast. "I was coming to your room to deliver your dinner," she explained. "And as for the antidote, well, I told you I dabble in herbs." It was the closest to the truth she dared come. "Something my mother taught me. I usually carry around a whole slew of lotions and potions, just in case of emergencies."

She decided to leave out the part about being zapped back home by her mother, only to find a book of potions left out on the kitchen table, open to the slug soup spell. It hadn't been hard to put two and two together.

"Madam Mim did this," Arthur murmured, half to himself. "She came in here disguised as you. I should have known something was up, though. She was acting so strange. So unlike you."

Guinevere sucked in a breath through her teeth at the mention of her mother. So Arthur was aware of Mim's ill intentions towards him. She wondered who had tipped him off. Perhaps that owl of his?

Arthur raked a hand through his hair, groaning. "This has gone too far. Mim's determined to take me down," he moaned. "I just wish I understood why. Is she angry that I'm king, for some reason? But why would she care? I wish I could understand."

Guin held her breath, realisation hitting her like a lightning strike. This was her chance to tell him the truth. The truth about his destiny. She didn't want to hurt him, and she certainly didn't want him dead or to live life as a giant slug. But he deserved to know what was really going on. How he'd been used and manipulated by an evil wizard for his own gain. It wasn't fair, what Merlin had done to him. Or what Mim would continue to try to do because of it. Perhaps if he knew the truth, he could make the right choice for himself. He could step down from the throne willingly and allow the rightful heir to take his place.

Then Mim wouldn't have any reason to target him. And he would be safe.

Maybe they could even run away together.

Two birds, flying free.

She drew in a breath. "The thing is," she said, her voice a little hoarse as she tried to form the words. "The thing is..."

Arthur's eyes were on her now. He looked a little scared. "What is it, Guin?" he whispered.

"The thing is," she replied, "what if you were never meant to be king?"

CHAPTER TWENTY
ARTHUR

Arthur stared at Guinevere, for a moment too stunned to speak.

"What are you saying?" he asked, after finally finding a somewhat wobbly version of his voice. "Of course I'm meant to be king. I pulled the sword from the stone, didn't I?"

"Yes," she agreed cautiously. "But what if it was all some kind of trick?"

"A trick?"

"You know. Like a ruse – maybe by your teacher Merlin." Guinevere's voice took on a rush of words. "Maybe he wanted a puppet on the throne of England. So he could rule behind the scenes. And he picked you – because you worship him and would do anything he says, and no one would suspect a thing."

Arthur sank back into his chair, feeling his stomach swim with nausea once again. But this time, it wasn't from poison. It was from doubt.

"No..." he whispered. "That can't be true..."

But even as he said the words, he wondered. Because even though he didn't want to admit it aloud, part of her theory made perfect sense. After all, he'd never truly understood why pulling a blade from a rock entitled him to a crown. And wouldn't it make much more sense if it wasn't some magical destiny after all, but some kind of trick?

Merlin *had* picked him, after all, out of all the boys in all the world, to educate and train. Why would he do that – why would he bother wasting so much time with a nobody like him? When he'd pulled the sword from the stone, of course, he assumed Merlin had somehow known of his destiny – even if he never told him about it – and that was why he'd been chosen.

But what if the opposite was true – what if Merlin had used him from the start, knowing full well the power he could gain over the land if he managed to trick everyone into crowning some young boy as king? Merlin had never approved of their idea to hold a tournament to determine a ruler, believing a knight of the realm would only invite more wars and violence into the land, as others had done before him. Could Merlin have decided, instead, to take matters into his own hands to avoid that fate?

But if that was the plan, why hadn't he told Arthur? Maybe because he thought Arthur wouldn't go along with any of it had he known what Merlin was orchestrating?

Suddenly a thought occurred to him. "But Merlin didn't want me to come to London to be Kay's squire," he told Guinevere. "He wanted me to stay home and continue our lessons. And if I had done that, I'd never have even run into the sword, never mind pulled it out of the stone."

"Hm." Guinevere seemed to consider this. "Perhaps he only said he didn't want you to go, to make you want to go even more. An evil wizard trick, you understand. To get you to insist on doing something you never really wanted to do in the first place." She nodded to herself. "This way he could deny he had anything to do with it. Say it was all your idea from the start."

Arthur didn't like this. Not one bit. Especially since it was starting to make far too much sense. After all, what was more likely? That he, a mere orphan boy with no noble pedigree to speak of, should be destined by the heavens to become king of all England? Or that a powerful wizard, unhappy with how things were being run and worried someone like Kay would don the crown, would take matters into his own hands?

Merlin wasn't evil, Arthur was convinced of that. But he *was* tricky. And he did, admittedly, cheat sometimes. Maybe not for selfish purposes, like Guin presumed. But maybe it was his way of saving the realm.

"Fine," he said. "But if that's the case, where is he now? He dashed off to the future weeks ago, before I ever arrived in London. If he truly wanted to rule through me, wouldn't he be ruling now?"

"Not necessarily," Guinevere said. "If he were here from the start, people might suspect his involvement. Better he stay away and bide his time until everyone accepts you as king. Then, when he does come back, no one will think anything of it."

Arthur sank into his chair, scrubbing his face with his hands. When he looked up, Guin was giving him an apologetic look.

"Sorry," she said. "This is why I didn't want to tell you."

"Do you think other people believe this, too?" he asked, his stomach churning. "Are people saying this behind my back? That I'm nothing more than an imposter king?"

She nodded slowly. Arthur groaned.

He leant back in his chair, staring up at the ceiling, which had been painted in fancy gold swirls that twirled around one another in complicated patterns. He'd never seen a painted ceiling before coming here. He hadn't even known that people painted ceilings in the first place, or why they would want to. Just one more example of how much he didn't belong here. How he should have never come here at all.

Oh, Merlin, he thought. *How could you do this to me?*

He dropped his gaze back to Guinevere. She was sitting across from him, pity swirling in her deep brown eyes. His stomach wrenched again. He thought back to their first meeting by the well. It felt like a lifetime ago after all he'd been through in recent days.

"It's funny," he murmured, half to himself. "From the very start I didn't believe I should be king. I didn't even want to be. In fact, I would have given almost anything to get rid of the crown. But now..." He shrugged. "Now I feel like I've been making a difference. Helping people. Keeping the peace. Like maybe I might be a good king after all."

"You *are* a good king," Guinevere said softly. "But that doesn't make you the right one."

Arthur felt his face crumble. He didn't want to cry, especially not in front of Guinevere, but he was afraid he couldn't help it. The past twenty-four hours had been both the most joyous and most terrible he'd probably ever experienced in his life. He'd defended his throne. He'd brought peace to the realm. And now what?

"You can just walk away," Guinevere said softly, as if she could hear his thoughts. "Leave all this behind. Live your life. Stay safe." She paused, then added. "We could go together..."

Arthur's heart wrenched at the thread of hope he heard in her voice. She really cared about him – in a way he wasn't sure anyone had ever cared about him before. And for a moment, he almost agreed. It sounded like a dream to just run away with Guin. Go back to living a simple life. The life he was likely meant to lead.

But deep down, he knew it could never be that easy. Even if he wanted to give up the throne, he couldn't exactly do it without a good explanation. No one would allow it. But he also couldn't just go tell everyone the truth – they'd assume he'd been lying from the start. They might even try to execute him for treason.

But then, if he stayed on the throne, Mim would keep trying to get to him – and at some point he was sure she would succeed. And – his head was spinning now, faster than a top – what if Guinevere was wrong about Merlin's alleged trickery? What if Arthur actually was, by some wild miracle, the true destined king of England? It seemed impossible, but he couldn't just walk away from his destiny and let England fall back into the dark ages if that were the case. Then he'd be a traitor of a different sort.

He bit his lower lip. "Look," he said to Guinevere, "before I make a move, I need to know for sure. I need proof that Merlin was behind all of this. And if he is, I need to know why he did it."

Guinevere frowned. "Isn't it obvious? He wants power."

"We don't know that for sure," Arthur replied stubbornly. "You don't know Merlin like I do. He's a good man. He may be a bit set in his ways at times, but he always has good intentions – I know he does."

Guinevere squirmed in her seat. She still looked conflicted, but there was also something else in her eyes now. A look like she truly wanted to believe him. And he found himself suddenly determined to convince her.

"If Merlin was responsible for putting me on the throne, then he would have a very good reason to do so," he added. "I need to find out what the reason is. Only then can I make a decision on what to do."

Guinevere nodded slowly. "I understand," she said after a pause. "And I'll help you in any way I can."

Arthur's heart swelled at this. "Thank you," he said. "That means a lot." He rose to his feet, stalking the room, his heavy steps eating up the distance between the walls. "First, I need to get to Merlin's tower. Maybe he's left a clue there. That's how we found out about Mim." He rubbed his chin with his hand. "I'd send

Archimedes again, but he's got a broken wing…" He pressed his lips together. "No. I need to go myself. I can't trust anyone else. Of course I'll have to find a way to sneak out of the castle."

Guinevere looked up. Her eyes sparkled. "Well, *that* I can help with."

Arthur turned to her in surprise. "Really?"

She nodded eagerly. "We can disguise you as a dishwasher and sneak you out the servants' passages." She looked up at him. "Where are we going again?"

"Sir Ector's castle in the Forest Sauvage," Arthur replied. "So not exactly nearby."

She nodded. "I know of a supply wagon that makes the journey twice a week. They bring everything right to kitchens. If we can stow away in the wagon, they'll take us right to where we need to go."

Arthur felt his heart pound with excitement. "Guinevere! You're brilliant!"

Her cheeks turned bright red. "I don't know about that," she hedged. "I mean, it may not even work."

"It'll work," Arthur declared. "I'm sure of it." He paused, then added awkwardly, "Also, you just said 'we'. Does that mean you're coming with me?" He held his breath, waiting for her reply. He knew he should tell her she didn't need to get any more mixed up in this than she already was. That he didn't want to put her in danger. But at the same time, he really didn't want to go alone.

At first she said nothing, and Arthur feared she'd been just caught up in the moment and never meant to volunteer herself for the quest. But at last, she looked up at him, her eyes shiny. "Yes. I'm coming with you. Whatever happens? We're in this together."

CHAPTER TWENTY-ONE
GUINEVERE

This is for the best. It's really for the best.

Guinevere silently repeated the mantra in her head as she led Arthur down the back stairs towards the kitchens, praying they didn't run into anyone important along the way. She'd disguised Arthur as best she could, bringing him clothes 'borrowed' from one of the stable hands, then shearing his head to his scalp. He looked a lot older with the new hairstyle, and once she'd dirtied him up a bit with some mud she'd brought in from outside, he actually looked like a servant. Maybe not surprising, since that was the role he was actually born into.

The hardest part was getting him to leave his sword and crown behind. But in the end, she convinced him it was for the best. If they were seen on the road with such treasures by bandits, they could be robbed or kidnapped and held for ransom. Or they could be called out as thieves themselves – as Guin had thought Arthur was when they first met in the woods – for possessing items clearly above their rank. She didn't need them thrown in prison before they were able to reach their destination.

She still couldn't believe she'd agreed to go with him. It was one thing to sneak him out of the castle – to keep him safe from whatever mischief her mother planned next. Quite another to agree to accompany him on his journey to the belly of the beast. Still, she couldn't help being a bit curious about the opportunity to find out more about Merlin. Was he truly the evil murderer her mother had warned her about? Or the loving mentor that Arthur adored? Guin hoped that travelling to his tower might shed some light on the man. And his true intentions.

She stole a glance at Arthur. He was so sure his mentor meant only good. Merlin was like a father figure to him. How disappointed he would be if he learnt that the man he looked up to was actually an evil mastermind out for destruction. It was going to hurt, that was for sure. At least she would be there to soften the blow. And then, maybe, he'd finally be able to walk away from it all.

She would achieve her quest – remove the wrongful ruler

from the throne – without any unnecessary violence or magic or tricks. Just the simple truth.

While her mother might not agree with her methods, she would have to accept the outcome.

"I can't believe we're doing this," Arthur whispered, shooting her an excited grin. "I never would have been able to manage it without your help."

She gave him a weak smile, trying to push down her rising guilt. What would he think if he knew the truth? Why she'd come to the castle in the first place. Why she'd befriended him. How she'd really known he was in trouble, and how she'd known how to cure him. Would he hate her for all the lies she'd told? Would he cast her out of his life forever?

She shook her head. She couldn't think like that. She just had to stay the course. She was helping him – that was the important thing. She was keeping him safe and aiding him in learning the truth. She couldn't be blamed for that.

They were halfway down the tower steps when they heard a door slam somewhere below them. Someone was coming up the stairs. They froze, looking at each other. On the narrow landing, there was no place to hide.

"Maybe it's just other servants," Arthur reasoned. But even as the words left his mouth, voices rose from below them.

"The king needs to be informed of this," said the first – a deep male voice, echoing up the stairs.

"Let's go wake him, then," the second voice urged.

Guinevere glanced over at Arthur, seeing his face had gone pure white.

"Belvidere and Gawain," he whispered. "They're coming this way. There's no possibility they won't recognise me, even with these new clothes and this hair."

Guinevere's pulse quickened. She looked up the stairs, wondering if they should make a run for it. But even if they did manage to make it back to his chambers, there would be no time for Arthur to change before the knights arrived, and his clipped hair and dirty face would cause all sorts of unfortunate questions.

"What do we do?" she whispered. The voices were getting closer.

"I don't know. Maybe I could hide my face from them?" Arthur tried to turn to face the wall, an attempt to shield himself from view. But he looked so obvious and ridiculous, Guin knew it would only catch their attention. But what other option did they have? Could she shield him somehow? But that would be obvious, too.

Unless…

Suddenly an idea came to her. She met Arthur's eyes

with her own. Her hands were trembling, but she shoved them behind her back.

"Just go with it, all right?" she asked. There was no time to explain anything.

Fortunately, he nodded. The voices were just around the corner. Guinevere stepped up to Arthur, drawing in a shaky breath, then pressed him against the wall, covering him with her body.

"What are you—?" he started to say.

But she silenced him with a kiss – just as Belvidere and Gawain rounded the corner.

"Well, well, what have we interrupted?" Gawain asked jovially.

Belvidere made a tsking noise with his tongue. "Servants! No wonder nothing gets done around here!" He rolled his eyes and kept climbing the stairs. Gawain flashed Guin and Arthur a knowing grin, then scurried off behind Belvidere. A moment later, their footsteps faded and Guin and Arthur found themselves alone again.

Guinevere stepped away from Arthur, turning her head to avoid his eyes. She couldn't believe she'd just done that! She'd never kissed anyone besides her mother before, and her stomach was doing flip-flops like a fish out of water.

"S-sorry," she stammered. "I just… I wasn't sure what else to do."

Arthur didn't reply at first, and finally she allowed herself a peek back at him. He was staring at her with awe in his eyes. She felt her cheeks burn. *Say something*, she begged him silently. *Anything!* She wondered if his lips were still buzzing from the feel of hers, like hers were from his.

"Wow," Arthur whispered at last. "That was…" He shook his head. "Wow."

"Come on!" she urged, beckoning him impatiently. Mostly to get rid of her embarrassment. "We've got to go or we'll miss the wagon."

Arthur seemed to wake from his trance. He followed her down the stairs, into the kitchens. Here, they didn't have to worry about anyone noticing them – everyone was too involved in their own tasks to pay them any heed. Just as well, Guinevere decided, for another kiss like the one on the stairs might have done her in completely.

They slipped out the back door just in time to see the supply wagon roll up. The driver jumped off his seat and began unloading his supplies.

"Once he's done, he'll go into the kitchens and get Mistress McCready to pay him for his deliveries," Guinevere explained. "That's when we'll have our chance to hide under that blanket."

"All right," Arthur agreed with a vigorous nod. "We'll just—"

But he never got a chance to finish his sentence, for at that moment, a small owl hooted loudly. She looked up to see none other than Archimedes, his wing still in a sling, staring down at them with beady eyes.

"Archimedes!" Arthur cried, his face paling. "What are you doing up there? You're not supposed to be flying, remember?"

"Pinfeathers! What are *you* doing outside the castle?" the owl demanded. "And your hair! What have you done to your hair?" He glanced from Guinevere to Arthur with suspicious eyes.

"Look, it's a very long story and I don't have time to fully explain. But I need to get back to Merlin's tower to figure some things out," Arthur explained. "Since they won't let me out of the castle, I had to come up with another way."

Archimedes seemed to consider this. "Well, then, I will come with you," he declared. "I'm sure I could help." He lifted his left wing and tried to fly towards them. But without his right wing, he lost his balance and went tumbling off the tree. Arthur had to dive to catch him before he collided with the ground.

"I'm sorry, old bird," Arthur said, looking down at Archimedes with pity in his eyes. "You need to stay here and get better. It's what Merlin would want, and you know it."

The owl ruffled his feathers. "Well, I suppose I could hang around and keep an eye on things. But don't be gone too long. The kingdom needs their king. If they find out you're missing..."

"I'll be back soon, I promise," Arthur replied. "They'll barely even know I'm missing." He leant over and gently set the owl on the ground. Archimedes waddled a few feet away, looking very disgruntled.

"Be careful," he told Arthur. "And whatever you do, don't go and get yourself killed."

"Of course," Arthur agreed, giving the owl a fond look. He turned back to the wagon, realising the driver had finished unloading his wares and had gone into the kitchen, as Guinevere had predicted. Now was their chance. He turned to Guin. "All right. Let's go."

They dived towards the wagon, throwing themselves inside of it. Arthur pulled back the tarp and crawled underneath, holding it up for Guin to follow. Once they were both hidden from view, he dropped it, covering them completely.

Guinevere could feel her heart beating madly. It was one thing to come up with this plan, quite another to carry it out. Would they get away with this? And what would Mother think when she realised Guin was gone – and Arthur along with her? A chill tripped down her spine. Maybe this was a bad idea…

But then she felt something warm on her palm. She glanced down. In the darkness under the tarp, she could barely see the outline of a hand slipping into hers. A moment later, she felt a small, comforting squeeze.

"This was a good plan," Arthur whispered.

And suddenly she didn't feel afraid any more.

CHAPTER TWENTY-TWO
ARTHUR

Travelling in the back of a wagon over bumpy roads wasn't exactly comfortable. After the first moments of adrenaline wore off, Arthur realised it was rather boring, too. To make matters worse, the driver had a penchant for singing, but not the voice for it. And his off-key, overly loud, sometimes bawdy tunes made for a very long day with very little chance to sleep.

At least Arthur had Guinevere next to him. Even if they didn't speak for fear of being discovered, it gave him some comfort to feel her warm breath on his face and know he wasn't alone. He couldn't imagine trying to do any of this without her. And he was so grateful she'd agreed to come along. This wasn't her fight, after all. But she was a good friend.

A good friend…

His hands reached involuntarily to his lips. No, he couldn't think of that any more. She'd only been trying to save him from being recognised by his knights. It went no further than that.

He reminded himself of Archimedes's words: *You don't have time for romance*. But even still, his fingers lingered a moment longer on his lips, remembering. Merlin had given him a lecture on love, and at the time he hadn't understood it one bit.

But now he thought maybe he did. If only a little…

Eventually, the wagon came to a stop. Arthur and Guin held their breaths as the driver stepped down from his seat. Arthur peeked out from under the tarp, watching him head into a small farmhouse at the edge of a great forest.

"We're here," he whispered. "That's the Forest Sauvage. I'd recognise it anywhere!"

"Quick!" Guinevere cried. "Let's slip out before he gets back!"

Arthur didn't need a second invitation. They climbed out from beneath the tarp and jumped off the wagon. Arthur almost fell as his feet hit the ground hard, his legs weakened from all that time cramped up without being used. He grabbed on to the side of the wagon for support, then shook out each leg, waking it up in turn. Beside him, Guinevere did the same.

"We made it," he said. "I can't believe we made it."

"Well, not quite yet," she hedged, looking out at the forest beyond them, worrying her lower lip with her teeth. "We still have to get through *that*."

Oh, right. In his excitement, Arthur had forgotten how dangerous the Forest Sauvage could be, filled with creatures and other nasty things that went bump in the night. He didn't have any weapons on him, either, since he'd had to leave Excalibur behind (something he was still a little bitter about).

But there was no other way to Sir Ector's castle. So through the forest it was.

"Come on," he said. "We want to get through before dark."

As they stepped under the trees, the world seemed to darken, the vast canopy of leaves above them all but blocking out the sun. It also felt colder here without the warm rays of sunshine kissing their skin. Arthur suppressed a shiver as they walked.

"I never liked this place," he remarked. "It always scared me."

"I don't know," Guinevere replied with a shrug. "I grew up here. So it's kind of like coming home."

"That's right!" Arthur exclaimed, turning to her. "I forgot you said you lived here once. What made you move, again?"

Guinevere gave an awkward shrug. "Ask my mother. It was her idea."

Arthur nodded. "It must be nice to have a mother," he remarked. "I never did. Even Sir Ector, my foster father, had already lost his wife before I came to live at his castle. But I've always imagined having a mother would be really nice."

"What happened to your parents?" Guinevere asked, suddenly sounding very curious. "Were they… killed?" She mouthed the word *killed* a little awkwardly, as if hesitant to use it.

"I don't actually know," Arthur admitted. "Sir Ector never told me – I don't know if he knows, to be honest. He found me on the castle steps, only a few days old, screaming blue murder. He took me in and allowed me to live in the castle with him and Kay. But never as a true son," he added, his voice revealing his bitterness. "More as a servant he didn't have to pay."

His mind flashed back to his foster father's face in the castle hall as Kay had come up to challenge him the day before. The man who had raised him, now plotting his demise. Arthur had always wanted to impress Sir Ector – gain his approval. And it hurt more than he wanted to admit to know the feeling was not mutual.

"I'm sorry," Guin replied. "That must have been rough."

Arthur shrugged, not wanting to be pitied. "We can't choose our birth story. But we can choose how to live the rest of our lives."

Guinevere nodded, not replying. Arthur turned to look at her. "Your mother won't be worried about you, will she?" he asked. "When she realises you've gone?" He hated the idea of worrying this poor, unknown woman.

Guinevere shrugged. "I don't know if *worried* would be the word I'd use."

Arthur could tell he was making her uncomfortable and decided to drop the subject. Still, he couldn't help a small stirring of pity for Guin, who obviously had a complicated relationship with her mother. Arthur had always assumed mothers were good and kind and loving. But maybe, as with foster fathers, this was not always the case for everyone.

He was about to try to change the subject when they heard a rustling noise in the bushes. Arthur froze in his tracks, grabbing Guinevere by the arm. She turned to look, her eyes widening as they fell upon what Arthur was already staring at across the path.

A pair of unblinking yellow eyes, shining out from the darkness.

"Don't make any sudden moves," Arthur whispered. "Maybe it'll go away."

The eyes blinked twice. Then, to Arthur's horror, they began to emerge from the bushes. As they came into the light, he realised they belonged to a long, lanky grey wolf.

A very hungry-looking long, lanky grey wolf.

The wolf lifted its head and howled, a mournful, lonely sound that made Arthur's skin crawl. This was not good. This was not good at all.

And the wolf looked right at them.

"Guin, run!" he cried. "Now!"

They burst into action, dashing down the trail as fast as their legs could carry them. For a moment, Arthur dared hope that maybe the wolf would be caught off guard and they could get far enough away before it began pursuit. But unfortunately, that didn't happen, and soon they could hear the creature behind them, gaining ground. The wolf was fast – so fast. And it became very clear to Arthur that outrunning it was not an option.

"What do we do?" Guinevere cried. She wasn't as fast as Arthur because of her long dress and slippers, and she was already falling behind.

"I don't know," Arthur replied, his heart beating fast. He looked around the forest, trying to find a big stick or rock, but saw nothing large enough to scare away a grown wolf.

"Maybe we should try to climb a—" Guinevere started,

then screamed as her foot caught under a root. Arthur watched in dismay as she careered forwards, slamming face-first into the dirt.

"Guin!" he shouted, retracing his steps to get back to her. She looked up at him with tears glistening in her brown eyes.

"I'm stuck," she confessed, tugging on her foot. It was firmly lodged in the root. Arthur got on his hands and knees, trying to pull it out. But he couldn't.

There was another howl. The wolf was getting closer. They were running out of time.

"Leave me," Guinevere told him. "Get to Merlin's tower."

"Not a chance," he said, shaking his head. "I won't leave you."

"Then he'll kill us both!"

"Maybe." He drew in a breath. "Maybe not." Scrambling to his feet, he looked down at Guin. "Lie still. I'm going to lead him away from you."

Guinevere's eyes bulged. "No!" she cried. "You can't! He'll kill you!"

"Everyone wants to kill me these days," Arthur reminded her wryly. "I'm getting kind of used to it."

"Arthur—"

"Trust me, all right? I know what I'm doing."

In truth, he had no idea what he was doing. But that didn't sound as comforting. Instead, he grabbed the largest stick he could find and waved it in the air.

"Over here, you big bad wolf!" he called out. Then he dropped the stick and started running in the opposite direction.

For a moment he worried the wolf wouldn't take the bait. But soon his ears caught more crashing sounds behind him as the wolf dived through the bushes in pursuit. He let out a breath of relief and pushed onwards, his mind racing for a plan. He couldn't outrun the wolf, that was for sure – his legs were already tiring, and he was almost completely out of breath. And he couldn't dodge the wolf like he had with Kay – it was much nimbler a creature than his foster brother in armour. He looked for trees to climb, but saw nothing with branches low enough to reach. He couldn't hide in a cave, either – the wolf would just scent him easily and follow.

So what to do? The forest was getting thicker and darker the further he ran, and he started to worry that even if he managed to lose the wolf, he'd get lost himself… forever.

Don't panic, he scolded himself. *Just think.*

What would Merlin say in a case like this? Probably something grand like *Use your wisdom, not your might.*

Which was all well and good until you tried to actually do that and still run at the same time.

Knowledge.

Wisdom.

What do I know about wolves? he asked himself. After all, he'd grown up in the Forest Sauvage and had been schooled constantly on their danger. What had Sir Ector taught him back when he was little in case he ever came face to face with such a creature?

They're as afraid of you as you are of them.

And suddenly he realised exactly what he had to do. He had to face down the wolf. Man to beast.

He had to stop running.

This was, as you can imagine, easier said than done. Because he had no idea, in reality, if Sir Ector had been right. It was one thing to boast about facing down a wolf and quite another to actually do so, all alone in the woods.

But he didn't have a choice, did he?

It took all his willpower to slam his heels into the ground. To turn around, to draw in a breath. Make his shoulders square. Lift his chin. Raise his hands menacingly in the air. Try to look two times his size.

And then he let out a roar. As loud as he could.

The wolf skidded to a stop. It stared up at him for a

moment, its eyes bulging from its head. Arthur roared again, taking a menacing step towards the creature. He knew the wolf could kill him at any moment – end this ruse. But first the wolf had to realise that, too.

And it didn't seem to get it.

Arthur roared a third time, this time charging at the wolf. The creature let out a scared whimper and started running in the other direction. Arthur chased it for a moment, feeling a thrill of excitement roll through him as he went, arms still raised, voice still roaring.

Until the wolf had disappeared completely. And he was alone once again.

He dropped his arms and sucked in huge mouthfuls of air. He'd done it! He'd actually done it.

"Arthur!"

He looked up to see Guinevere limping towards him. She had a huge smile on her face. "You did it!" she cried. "You defeated the wolf!"

Arthur felt his cheeks heat. His first instinct was to brush off her words, to protest and insist it wasn't that big of a thing. But it *was*, he suddenly realised. He, Arthur, had faced down an actual wolf and won. He *should* be proud.

And he was.

“Are you all right?” he asked Guinevere, looking down at her ankle.

“I’m fine,” she said. “It’s just a little bruised.” Her eyes levelled on him. They looked soft somehow in the dim forest light. “Thank you,” she said simply. “You saved my life.”

“You saved mine first,” he reminded her with a sheepish grin. “I guess now we’re even.”

“Perhaps so,” she agreed with a smile. “Now let’s get to Merlin’s tower.”

CHAPTER TWENTY-THREE
GUINEVERE

The rest of the trip proved much less eventful. Arthur, fortunately, still remembered the way to his foster father's keep. Soon he was leading Guinevere out of the dark forest into a golden afternoon with the magnificent castle in full view. Even better was the fact that, since Sir Ector and his son were back in London, Guin and Arthur were able to walk right into the place and head straight to the tall, crumbling tower where Merlin had stayed once upon a time.

As they climbed the old, decrepit stairs to the very top, Guinevere began to feel a growing nervousness in the pit of her stomach. They'd escaped a castle, a wolf and a dark wood. But now they were entering the inner lair of the evil wizard who'd murdered her parents. What vile monstrosities would they find inside?

Turned out, a lot of junk.

"Did… someone rob the place?" she couldn't help blurting as they walked into the room. Toppled piles of books and random papers made the place look as though it had been ransacked or torn apart by a storm. She noted a huge hole in the roof and a bucket placed underneath, now filled with rainwater. The tower had clearly seen better days.

Arthur looked around the dishevelled room. To her surprise, his lip curled in amusement. "Let's just say housekeeping isn't one of Merlin's specialties," he joked. "And he left rather in a hurry." He pointed to the hole in the ceiling, as if indicating this was how the wizard had made his exit.

"Did Merlin make you clean for him, too, like Sir Ector did?" Guinevere asked curiously, remembering what Arthur had said about his foster father.

"Merlin usually leaves the cleaning to magic," Arthur replied. "Which is… interesting… if not always effective. You should have seen the one time he tried to use magic to help me with the castle dishes!" He laughed, as if remembering the moment fondly.

Guinevere watched, curious despite herself, as Arthur

walked over to a round blue ball painted with strange brown markings and set on a stand. He spun it with his hand and it twirled around and around, the markings blurring as it went. It was still disconcerting to Guin to hear Arthur talk about Merlin. His voice took on an affectionate tone when he spoke of his teacher – as if he loved him a lot. It was clear he was some kind of father figure to him, as Mim had been a mother to her. Did he have any inkling of the darkness lurking inside this madman who had taken him under his wing?

She tried to imagine how she'd feel if the tables were turned. If Mim were the evil one, and Guin had been tricked by her treachery. The idea made her feel quite uncomfortable.

"How did you meet Merlin, anyway?" she asked, mostly to change the subject.

"Oh! It was kind of an accident," Arthur said, looking bashful all of a sudden. "I was trying to get Kay's arrow, which had gone into the woods. I accidentally fell through his ceiling just as he was having tea. And he invited me to stay." He grinned at the memory. "He told me he had been expecting someone, but he didn't know who until I dropped in – literally."

"So he didn't seek you out?" Guinevere asked, surprised. "*You* found *him*?"

"I guess so." Arthur shrugged. "He told me he wanted to be my teacher. And I was thrilled to have him. No one ever really paid me any attention before then. As I said before, I was not much more than a bother to my foster father and brother. And I was always breaking dishes in the kitchen, so the cook wasn't fond of me, either. But Merlin – he treated me like a real person. Like someone with value." He stared down at the floor. "Everything I am now, the person I've become – it's all because of him."

Guinevere nodded, not sure what to say. The Merlin described by Arthur sounded nothing like the man she'd been told to fear all her life. He sounded almost… kind. Decent. Like Arthur himself. How could a man like that murder her parents in cold blood? It didn't make any sense. She thought back to how she'd asked Mim why he'd murdered her parents. All she'd said was that he was evil. But that wasn't a real reason, was it? There had to be something else. Something Mim didn't want her to know.

But what could it be?

"So now what?" she asked, looking around the room. "Are you going to look for some writings of Merlin's? Something to prove his plan?"

"No," Arthur replied with a grin. "I'm going to try to bring him back."

"What?" Guinevere cried before she could stop herself. This was not part of the plan.

But Arthur was already shuffling through papers on a nearby table. "There's got to be a spell," he murmured. "He used a spell to send himself to Bermuda. There has to be another spell to return him home." He turned to a towering bookcase full of books. "We just have to find it."

Guinevere's heart pounded, seemingly louder and faster than when confronted by the wolf in the forest. It was one thing to search an evil wizard's lair. It was quite another to conjure up the actual evil wizard.

But she couldn't exactly say that to Arthur.

"That might be easier said than done," she reminded him instead, pulling out a book at random. It was titled *The Tome of Terrible Turnips*, which didn't seem particularly applicable to their current situation. "There are so many books in here. How will you ever be able to find the right one?"

"I'm not sure," Arthur confessed. "Especially since I can't exactly read."

"You can't?" Guinevere stared at him, astounded. She couldn't imagine life without books. It would be like life without… well, life.

"I mean, I know my ABCs, thanks to Archimedes," Arthur amended, looking a little embarrassed. "But we didn't have a chance to get much further than that. Let's just say reading wasn't a big priority in the kitchens of Sir Ector's castle. In fact, I'm not sure even Kay can read – and he's a noble knight."

Guinevere considered that this was probably true, judging from what she'd seen of the oafish lad in question. And if Arthur was never meant to be more than a squire, there would have been no practical reason to educate him. If it hadn't been for Merlin…

She shook her head. "Well, then, I don't know how this is going to work," she said. "I can read, but I'm only one person. It would take ages for me to get through all these books to find the correct spell. Even if I did know what I was looking for, which of course I don't."

She knew she was talking too fast, making too many excuses. And it hurt to see Arthur's face crumble at each one. But what other choice did she have? Undo her mother's spell, free an evil wizard from captivity, and set him loose on the world? Because that was essentially what they were talking about here.

Arthur sighed deeply, walking across the room to the window and picking up a book on its sill. "I suppose it's too much to ask for them to read themselves…"

Suddenly, to Guinevere's shock, the book seemed to leap from his hands. She watched, amazed, as it hovered in the air, then popped itself open to its first page. A moment later, a low-pitched voice rose to her ears.

"It's doing it!" Arthur cried excitedly, pointing to the book. "It's actually reading itself!"

Sure enough, the book was, indeed, reciting the words on its page. When it had finished, it turned itself to the next page and kept going.

"That's it!" Arthur exclaimed. "I completely forgot. All of Merlin's possessions are magical. He used to have this teapot that filled cups of tea on its own. And these books all packed themselves when we left his cottage for the tower! Of course they'd be able to read themselves, too! That just makes sense if you think about it!"

Guinevere watched the book, her heart pounding. Magic. This whole place was bursting with magic. And they had no idea what they were dealing with. What was she thinking, agreeing to come here? She should leave now. Before—

"I have an idea!" Arthur blurted out. "What if we commanded the books to find the spell we're looking for?"

Guinevere paled. "Do you think they'd listen?" she asked.

"They listened when I mentioned reading themselves," he reminded her. "It's worth a try, right?"

Guinevere found she couldn't argue with that. The look on his face held too much hope, mixed with desperation.

"I suppose it can't hurt," she agreed reluctantly.

Arthur nodded, looking excited. He turned to the shelf of books. "Look, um, well, I don't know if you've noticed, books, but Merlin is missing. We need to find him. Do you happen to have a spell… or something… to help us do that?"

He paused, looking at the shelf expectantly. But nothing happened. The books remained still and unread. Only the first book, which had settled onto a small table by the window, was still reciting its text.

"So much for that," Arthur muttered, sounding discouraged. He sank down in a chair by the cold, ashy hearth and put his head in his hands. "I should have known it couldn't be that easy." He sighed deeply and rubbed his face. "What am I supposed to do? Why did I even come here?"

Guinevere squeezed her eyes shut. She let out a long breath, then opened them again. "I… think you need some magic words," she said slowly. "I mean, at least to get them started…"

Arthur's head jerked up. "Of course," he said, his voice filled with excitement again. "Merlin always had magic words for each spell! Good idea, Guin!"

Guin gave him a wan smile, her insides churning. *What are you doing?* she scolded herself. *You're going to ruin everything!* After all, Mim had trapped Merlin in the future to help keep the kingdom safe. And now Guinevere was helping to bring him back?

"We just need to figure out what they are." Arthur looked down at the book that was still reading itself. A moment later, his eyes lit up and he beckoned to Guin. She stepped towards him, her knees wobbly and her hands shaking. Arthur pointed to the page, where, sure enough, a string of strange words had been illuminated in glowing golden letters.

"What do they say?" he asked, looking up at her, his blue eyes shining with hope.

She swallowed hard. *Lie!* she told herself. *Just make something up.*

But instead, the real words rose to her lips. *"Higgidis… piggidis?"* she whispered.

The room burst into life. Books started flying from the shelves so quickly, Guin was forced to duck so as not to be struck on the head. As she and Arthur watched, each book began flipping madly through its pages, faster and faster, the words blurring into one another as they read.

"It's working!" Arthur cried excitedly. "It's actually working!" Instinctively, he leapt up and threw his arms around Guinevere, locking her into an exuberant embrace. "Guin, you're like a real wizard!" he gushed happily.

"I'm not a wizard!" Guin protested before she could stop herself. She struggled out of the hug, putting her hands out in front of her as if to ward off the words. Her cheeks began to burn.

Arthur looked at her, completely confused. "I— I was just joking..." he stammered. "Sorry."

Guinevere closed her eyes, drawing in a long breath. Then she opened them again. "No, I'm sorry," she said. "It's just... well, magic scares me, if you must know."

"I understand," Arthur said, his voice softening. "I felt that way once, too. But Merlin showed me that magic can be used for good. It can help people. It can make things better."

Guinevere nodded stiffly, not trusting herself to speak. Her head felt as if it was swimming with confusion. She wanted to run from the room and never look back. But at the same time, she couldn't bear to leave Arthur's side.

The books began to move faster, words on each page lighting up one after another after another as they told their stories to the tower room. Their voices rose in a cacophony of sound until Guinevere just wanted to put her hands over her ears to block them all out.

At last, she watched as a heavy golden tome, bigger than

the rest, slipped down from the very top of the bookshelf, where it had been hidden behind a small book with a crimson cover. It flew across the room, landing on the table with a loud thump and then opening itself to a gold-leafed page. Guinevere and Arthur ran over to it and scanned the text.

"What does it say?" Arthur asked.

"It's written in Latin," Guinevere told him. "So I can't be quite sure. But I believe it says, 'How to find someone through time.'"

"That must be it!" Arthur exclaimed. "Should we—"

He was interrupted by the sound of a slamming door down below.

"What was that?" Guinevere whispered, worried.

Arthur ran to the tower door and put his ear to the wood. "Oh, no!" he exclaimed. "I think Sir Ector has returned. He must have fled the castle after they arrested Kay." He swallowed hard. "If he sees me, he could try to kill me. Like Kay wanted to. I'm sure he was the one behind the challenge in the first place. No chance Kay had enough smarts or ambition to come up with it on his own."

Guinevere gnawed on her lower lip. "What do we do?" she asked. "Should we try to get out of here?" She looked out the window. It was a long fall to the ground. Maybe she could try to find another shapeshifting spell? One that would work for both of them?

More magic. It had become a true slippery slope.

But Arthur shook his head, walking back over to the table and the spell book. "We can't leave. Not without Merlin. This is our only chance to reach him. We need to try to cast this spell, whatever it is. It's the only way."

Guinevere picked up the book and looked down at its golden words. Her heart was beating very fast. The last thing she wanted to do was try to cast a random spell without having any idea of what she was doing. Especially a spell to conjure up an evil wizard.

But then, if Arthur was right – and Sir Ector meant to kill him – Merlin might be their only hope.

"All right. Let's give it a try," she ventured. "But no promises it's going to work."

"I believe in you," Arthur said simply. And she felt a tug in her heart again.

Sorry, Mother. But I have no choice…

Drawing in a breath, she looked down at the golden words on the page. Here went nothing. *"Iter per tempus…"* she began chanting, and the golden letters started to glow on the page as she spoke them. *"Iter per tempus… tempus viator…"*

And suddenly everything went black.

CHAPTER TWENTY-FOUR
ARTHUR

Arthur opened his eyes and looked around, blinking a few times to get used to the sudden bright light that shone down on him with an intensity that was almost blinding. A moment ago, the tower had been dim, not to mention damp and chilly. Now everything was sunny and warm. He was practically sweating under his tunic and tights.

"What's happening?" he asked, trying to force his bleary eyes to focus. Something in the air smelt strangely of salt. "Did the spell work?"

"Um…" Guinevere stepped up beside him, looking quite dazed herself. She was still holding the book in her hands, but the golden letters had dimmed to black.

She blinked a few times, too, then her mouth dropped open like a fish's. "Oh..." she whispered. "Oh, no."

"What is it?" Arthur asked just as his vision began to clear. When he finally got a good look at his surroundings, he gasped out loud.

"Where are we?" he whispered.

One thing was for sure: they were definitely not in Merlin's leaky old tower any more. In fact, they were not in a tower at all, but rather outside, on the ground, standing on some kind of sandy patch of land on the shores of a vast sea.

Where were they? And how had they ended up here?

"Wait," Arthur said, a slow realisation beginning to wash over him. "Did something in that spell...?"

He trailed off, feeling embarrassed to voice his wild theory. But still, what other explanation could there be? One moment they were in one place, the next somewhere else entirely.

"Don't be alarmed," Guinevere said slowly, reaching down to scoop up a handful of sand. Arthur watched as the tiny crystals slipped through her fingers and rejoined the beach below. "But I think the spell didn't work exactly how I thought it would." She looked up, meeting Arthur's eyes with her own worried brown ones. "Instead of returning Merlin to us," she said, "I think it took us to Merlin."

Arthur stared at her, for a moment unable to speak.

The spell had taken them to Merlin? Merlin… who had been trapped in the future?

Were *they* in the future?

In Bermuda?

An unexpected thrill prickled his skin. He knew he shouldn't be happy about this accidental time travelling; it was bound to bring about even more complications than they were already facing, which admittedly were quite a few. But still! How could he not be just a little bit excited about the prospect of seeing the future with his own eyes?

Merlin had always talked lovingly about the future. All the amazing inventions humanity would develop and use in everyday life: machines that travelled faster than horses, medicine that healed like magic, and hot running water inside people's own homes to bathe in anytime they wanted, without having to jump into a freezing lake to do it. In fact, Merlin had claimed these people of the future were even able to fly from place to place using big winged inventions called planes – no shapeshifting necessary. And, even wilder, the world had actually become round!

No. The world had *always* been round, he corrected himself, remembering Merlin's words. It was just now, everyone knew it.

"This is amazing!" he cried, twirling in a circle, taking it all in. "I can't believe we're here!"

"Me neither," Guinevere agreed, though she sounded a lot less enthused. Arthur glanced at her, surprised. She looked almost frightened, wringing her hands together in front of her. On instinct, he placed a hand over hers.

"It's going to be all right," he assured her. "We're going to find Merlin. And he'll know what to do."

It was then that he spotted some kind of castle behind them. But it was unlike any castle he'd ever seen before. Three strange-looking manor houses were set in a U shape around a courtyard, each three stories high and featuring impossibly large glass windows, lined up in triple rows, all along their sides. Arthur gave a low whistle. He'd never seen so much glass in his life. And it was so smooth, too, not bubbled and rough like the glass back home.

He looked down at the courtyard, which was taken up almost entirely by a very large pond filled with the clearest crystal-blue water Arthur had ever seen. Around the pond was some kind of smooth stone perimeter – filled with strange-looking beds covered in brightly striped cloth. Each bed had a large cloth banner hanging above it, held up by a shiny metal stand, providing shade from the sun's harsh rays.

But that wasn't even the strangest part – not by far. For lying on some of these beds were people – in a horrifying state of half undress. Arthur stifled a gasp as he watched a woman wearing only two small strips of fabric saunter by them, casually carrying a wine goblet in her hand, as if it was nothing out of the ordinary to do so.

"Why, they're all practically naked!" Guinevere gasped, joining him in taking in the scene. "Have they no modesty in the future?"

"Perhaps they have different ideas about that," Arthur rationalised. "Merlin often talked about different styles, different customs," he mused. He hadn't really grasped the wizard's full meaning at the time, but now he could clearly see it for himself, on full display everywhere he looked. The world had truly changed over the years, and its people along with it. And suddenly Arthur felt the almost overwhelming desire to know everything – see everything – that this magical future had to offer.

Guinevere, on the other hand, still looked rather doubtful about the whole thing. Arthur watched as her eyes drifted from the people on the beds to something behind them. "At least the food looks nice," she observed.

Arthur turned to watch a young man dressed in a crisp white shirt and short brown trousers walk by them carrying a heaped tray full of strange-looking but heavenly-smelling food. There was some kind of flattened brown meat, Arthur noted, placed between two slices of puffy brown bread. Accompanying the meat was a tall pile of golden-coloured sticks with a splotch of thick red liquid beside them. It was all Arthur could do, as the man walked by, not to reach out and pluck one of the golden treasures from the plate to try for himself.

"Do you see Merlin anywhere?" Guinevere asked, drawing his attention away from the food.

Arthur scanned the courtyard again, taking in each person lying on a bed around the pond. For a moment, he worried he'd find Merlin in a state of similar undress as the others. But a further look told him the wizard was not among the pond dwellers.

He pressed his lips together. "No. I don't. Maybe we should ask someone?" he suggested. "Someone has to have seen him, right? I mean, let's be honest, Merlin doesn't exactly fit in here."

Neither did they, he realised suddenly, looking down at his tunic and tights and Guinevere's heavy wool dress. He wondered if they should attempt to find more appropriate attire before beginning their quest so they could blend in with the local population.

"Excuse me, did you just say *Merlin*?"

Arthur whirled around at the sound of the new voice. The man who had walked by them earlier with the tray of golden sticks was now standing behind them, his tray regrettably empty. Perched on his nose were spectacles – similar to what Merlin wore – but with dark glass obscuring his eyes. How did he see out of them?

The man looked at them curiously, his brows furrowing above his glasses. "Okay, seriously, is there some kind of Renaissance Faire going on around here that I don't know about?" he asked.

"A fair?" Guinevere asked, cocking her head in confusion, clearly not quite understanding. "What kind of fair?"

"We're just… not from around here," Arthur tried to explain, realising the man was put off by their clothing, as he had suspected. "We're from London," he added, hoping that London was still a real place in the future. And, if it was, it had a different sort of wardrobe than here.

"Yeah, I figured from your accents," the man said. "Don't worry – this place is full of Brits. You must be sweltering, though," he added, gesturing to Guinevere's dress. "We do have a gift shop on-site with lots of summery clothing and bathing suits, if you want to find something more suitable for the beach."

Gift shop. Arthur stored the words away in his mind. That must be where people received their clothing in the future. And how nice of them to give the clothing away as gifts instead of charging money like they did in the shops back home. No wonder Merlin liked the future so much! Good food, free clothes, warm weather. Why – it was almost paradise. In fact, if the entire fate of England hadn't been at stake at the moment, he might have actually thought about staying here for a while himself.

"Um, thank you?" Guinevere said. "I'll, uh, keep that in mind."

Arthur stepped forwards, trying to steer the conversation back to the missing wizard. "You asked if we mentioned Merlin. Have you seen him here? We're actually looking for him. He's been… gone for quite some time, and we're a little worried."

The man nodded, seeming relieved. "I figured someone would come for him eventually. He didn't have an ID on him, so we couldn't call anyone. He kept babbling these nonsensical words by the pool and was starting to freak out some of the guests. Probably just too much sun for the poor guy. It happens to the best of us." He stopped as if something had just occurred to him. "Wait, you're not Wart, are you?"

"I am!" Arthur exclaimed, shocked to hear his old name spoken by a stranger in the future. "I mean, that's my nickname, anyway. Merlin always called me Wart."

"I thought you might be," the man said. He gave Arthur a stern glare. "Look, I don't know what kind of fight the two of you got into, but your grandfather seems really shaken up by it. It might be nice if you forgave him for whatever it was he did. I mean, trust me, I have a grandfather, too. I know how they can be. But still. The poor old—"

"Where is he?" Arthur interrupted, starting to get impatient. "Where can we find him?"

"I have no idea," he said with a shrug. "Security took him away a few hours ago. Like I said, he was acting really strange. Mumbling to himself. Telling people he's a famous wizard – like the Merlin of the King Arthur legend or whatever."

"Wait," Arthur said, his turn to interrupt. "Did you just say *King Arthur legend*?" He glanced at Guin. She looked back at him, raising her eyebrows.

"Yeah, you know. The whole Knights Of The Round Table, Guinevere, Lancelot?" The man looked at them strangely. "I would have thought you'd be all over that kind of thing, judging from the way you're dressed." He shook his head, looking disappointed. "Kids these days. No sense of history."

"Uh, yes, sorry, yes!" Arthur barked a shaky laugh. "Of course we know all about King Arthur and his… round table," he added. Wow. Had the circular table he'd just installed back home in his meeting room somehow become legendary in the future? It seemed an odd detail for people to remember throughout the annals of time, but he was flattered nonetheless.

Also, who was Lancelot?

He realised the man was looking at him strangely. He

swallowed hard. "And, uh, yes, my… grandfather… gets, uh, confused sometimes," he added, still fake laughing. "He likes to imagine he's a time traveller from the past."

"Yes!" The man's eyes lit up. "That's right! He did say something about time travel." He snorted, giving them a rueful grin. "Between you and me, I kind of liked the old guy. He was funny. Weird, but funny." He looked out over the courtyard. "You see that man over there? His name's Joe. He should know where you can find Merlin."

"Thank you," Arthur said, feeling relief wash over him. "We'll ask him."

"Good luck," the man said. "And take care of your grandfather, won't you?"

"We will, I promise."

The man nodded and headed off in another direction. Arthur turned to Guin. "First let's go to the gift shop," he said. "We'll get clothing to fit in better. Then we won't have to deal with questions every time we talk to someone."

They headed in the direction of the 'gift shop', which turned out to be not much different from the shops back home in London – though the 'gifts' were quite different in style. Still, after a few moments of studying the others who were shopping in the store, they were able to pick out a few items of clothing that seemed more in line with what people in the future wore but weren't made of the barely-there fabric that some seemed to prefer.

Arthur grabbed a pair of brightly coloured trousers that stopped at his knees and a large shirt that Guinevere translated to read, "I survived the Bermuda Triangle." Arthur had no idea what that was, or if they had indeed survived it, but they had survived time travelling, and since there were no shirts bragging about that particular achievement, this would have to do.

Guinevere emerged from the small booth used to change clothes, looking beautiful in a long, frothy blue gown of the lightest, silkiest material Arthur had ever seen. It wrapped around her body in swaths of fabric, but left her arms uncovered. She walked up to the mirror at the end of the shop and stared at her reflection.

"I don't know," she murmured, looking doubtful. She turned to Arthur. "Do you think this is suitable?"

"I think you look lovely," he said honestly. And when Guinevere smiled, he knew he'd said the right thing. "Now come on. Let's find Merlin."

They started to head out of the shop. But before they got to the doors, a woman wearing a colourful flowered shirt suddenly stepped into their path. "Are you planning to pay for those?" she asked, looking at them angrily.

Arthur frowned, confused. "Aren't they meant to be gifts?" he asked. "This is a gift shop, yes?"

"Very funny." The woman rolled her eyes, dragging them both back to a small table in the centre of the shop, on which there sat a strange machine Arthur didn't recognise. She reached over and plucked a paper tag off each of their outfits. "The dress is thirty-nine ninety-nine," she said. "I'll throw in the shirt and shorts for an even sixty."

It took Arthur a moment to realise she was talking about money. He should have known the gifting idea was too good to be true. No future could be that perfect.

Guinevere glanced at him. "Do you have any coins?" she whispered.

Did he? Arthur reached into his satchel, feeling around. Being king, he normally had no reason to carry around gold on his person. But he had distributed coins to the poor a few days before and managed to find one leftover coin at the bottom of his bag. He pulled it out, holding it up to the woman.

"I only have this," he said apologetically. "Will it do?"

The woman stared at the coin, her eyes widening to saucers. She reached out and plucked it from Arthur's hand. "Is this gold?" she asked, looking quite astounded. Arthur watched as she bit down on it with her teeth, then stared at it again.

"Is it enough?" Arthur asked worriedly.

But the woman was ignoring him now. She had set down the coin on the table and was tapping on a small black object with a glass face in her hand. A moment later, she looked up. "Is this real?" she asked suspiciously. "It says on the Internet it's from the Middle Ages."

"Um, yes. It's very old," Guinevere agreed. "And very valuable." She glanced at Arthur. He held his breath. "It's also all we have to pay for the clothes. Is that all right?"

"Yes!" the woman replied excitedly, hastily slipping the coin in her pocket. Then she seemed to remember herself. "I mean, I suppose it'll do." She reached behind the table and handed them two hats and two pairs of the dark glass spectacles that the man had been wearing. "Take these sunglasses, too," she said hurriedly. "It's really bright out there."

Guinevere and Arthur dutifully took the hats and placed them on their heads. Arthur felt a little ridiculous in his, which fit fine, but had a strange little brim that shielded his eyes. Guin, on the other hand, looked rather lovely in her wide straw-brimmed bonnet that wasn't much different from what the serfs wore in the fields back home.

Then he tried the 'sunglasses', resting them on his nose as he'd seen the others do. Suddenly, his vision dimmed. Startled, he ripped them off his head.

"They make you go blind!" he exclaimed.

"Oh, yeah, they're a little on the dark side. But trust me, you'll thank me once you get outside. That sun is brutal today. I can't believe you've been out there without them."

"Thank you," Guinevere piped in. "We appreciate it." She grabbed her own sunglasses and began to drag Arthur out of the shop.

"Have a nice day!" the woman called out after them before turning to her next guest.

"I'm glad she took that coin," Guinevere remarked once they were outside again. "I'm not sure what else we could have offered her."

Arthur nodded, setting the sunglasses on his nose again. This time, they didn't blind him entirely, but it was as if someone had turned off a very large lamp.

"What a brilliant invention," he marvelled, taking them off for a moment to stare down at them before returning them to his face. "Those working in the fields back home could greatly benefit from something like this."

"Maybe you should invent it for them," Guinevere said with a smile. "Once you're not king, you're bound to have a lot of time on your hands. Why, you'll be able to do all sorts of interesting things with your life."

Arthur nodded, his enthusiasm deflating a bit as he was reminded of their mission. As fascinating as the future was, they weren't here as guests on a holiday. They were here to learn whether Merlin had really decided to make him king and how he could successfully abdicate the throne without managing to get his head chopped off in the process.

Guinevere caught his eye. "Come on," she said. "Let's go speak to this Joe."

They headed over to the man who had been identified as Joe. When they approached, he was tapping on one of the same rectangular glass objects the woman in the gift shop had been using.

"Excuse me," Arthur ventured. "I'm sorry to bother you. We're looking for a man named Merlin. He's old? Maybe dressed in a blue hat and robes? Do you happen to know where he is?"

The man looked up from his object, frowning for a moment. Then a flicker of recognition crossed his face. "Oh, you must mean the old dude from this morning," he said. "We brought him down to the infirmary. I think he got too much sun." He shrugged. "Not sure if he's still there."

"Where's the infirmary?" Guinevere asked.

The man pointed down a path, then turned back to tapping on his glass rectangle – conversation clearly over. Arthur really wanted to ask him what the rectangle did and why everyone seemed to be so fascinated by it, but he knew it would just make him stand out again. Instead, he turned to Guinevere.

"Come on," he said. "Let's go find him."

They dashed down the path, as directed, following the little white signs with red crosses that read 'infirmary', according to Guin. At the end of the path, they came across a small white one-storey building with the same red cross painted on its door. They glanced at each other excitedly. This must have been it.

"Come on," Arthur said, and headed through the doors.

Inside, it was also white. And really clean. In fact, it might have been the cleanest place Arthur had ever seen, and he wondered how they kept it so pristine. In the centre of the room was a woman with black hair in neat braids, sitting behind a table, wearing an outfit that was also white and clean – to match the room, Arthur assumed.

"Excuse me?" he said, walking up to the woman. "Do you have a man named Merlin here, by any chance?"

The woman looked up from yet another small black rectangle. These people of the future *really* seemed to love whatever these things were. "Merlin?" she repeated, looking a little drained. "Oh, he's here all right." She rolled her eyes. "Just follow his loud bellyaching down the hall. You can't miss him." She groaned. "And please take him with you when you leave. My migraine will thank you."

"We will," Arthur promised, though he had no idea who the migraine was or why they would thank him for retrieving his teacher. "Now where—"

"Higgidis piggidis! No, no, NO!"

Arthur's eyes lit up. "Merlin!" he cried. There was no mistaking his teacher's voice.

He started running down the corridor, fast as his feet could take him. He could feel his heart pound in excitement as they reached the door at the end. The chanting was louder here, definitely coming from the other side of the wall. Arthur grinned widely.

Merlin. We've found you at last.

CHAPTER TWENTY-FIVE
ARTHUR

"Merlin!"

Arthur yanked open the door, bursting into the room. His heart swelled as his eyes fell on his teacher, who was sitting up in a small bed and waving his hands in front of his face. Merlin was dressed oddly, in a strange, thin cotton robe printed with drawings of cute baby ducks. And his beard looked in desperate need of a brushing.

But it was him. There was no mistaking it.

"Merlin!" Arthur cried again, his heart feeling as if it would burst with joy. "Oh, Merlin. It's so good to see you!"

The old wizard looked up, his watery blue eyes lighting in recognition. "Wart?" he exclaimed, his voice filled with astonishment. "Am I dreaming? Is that really you?"

"It's really me," Arthur assured him, crossing the room and throwing his arms around his teacher, giving him a huge hug. Merlin grunted a little, clearly surprised at the unexpected gesture of affection, but he managed to pat Arthur awkwardly on the back before they parted again. Arthur smiled down at him. "It's so good to see you," he gushed. "Are you all right?"

"Oh. I'm fine." Merlin huffed, looking down at his strange attire. It was then Arthur noted he had a tube of some sort sticking out of his arm. The tube led to a small bag hanging from a pole and containing clear liquid. Merlin caught Arthur's worried look. "Don't mind that," he said quickly. "They're just trying to rehydrate me. For some reason they're convinced I've got heatstroke." He snorted. "As if I would ever allow myself to get heatstroke. Why, if I could survive a dragon blast in the middle of the Sahara, surely I can deal with the paltry sun of twenty-first century Bermuda."

Arthur bit back a laugh. It was Merlin all right. And he hadn't changed a bit. "I'm just happy you're here," he said, pulling up a chair and sitting beside the wizard. "I have so much to tell you. So much has happened since you've been gone."

"Of course it has," Merlin grumped. "I'm sure she's taken full advantage of my absence to cause as much havoc as possible." He made a disgusted face. "I should have picked a longer lasting disease," he muttered. "That would have shown her not to trifle with me!"

Arthur frowned. "Who are you talking about again?" he asked, though he had a sneaking suspicion he knew.

"Madam Mim, of course," Merlin blurted. "Try to keep up!" He squeezed his hands into fists. "I'm positive she's the one who tangled with my spell-casting skills, making it impossible for me to get back home. I can still time travel, you see. But I'm unable to pinpoint where – or when – I want to go. You can't imagine all the places I've been to since I first left you in the tower. The twentieth century, the twenty-second century – I don't recommend that one bit, by the way!" he added as an aside. He tapped his finger to his chin. "Then there was the twelfth century – that one was actually quite pleasant, if you must know; almost felt like home. But now I'm here, in the twenty-first century, where no one seems to believe a thing I say." He sighed dejectedly. "And maybe they're right. All of this has surely scrambled my noggin. And no type of hydration is going to help with that!" He stared bitterly down at the clear tube in his arm, as if blaming it for everything.

Arthur nodded dutifully, though, in truth, he had only understood about half of what the wizard was saying. But he was used to that, he supposed. And nothing could dampen his joy of being back with his teacher.

"So… you can't get back home," he tried to interpret.

"Of course I can't get back home! Haven't you been listening to a thing I've been saying?" Merlin burst out. He shook his head, his long white beard swinging from side to side. "It couldn't have been easy for Mim to do this, so I assume she had some kind of nefarious reason for doing it. Or maybe she's just still bitter that I beat her in that duel. Even though she's the one who cheated in the first place!" He waved his fist in the air. "Why, if I get my hands on her again—"

He was interrupted by a small, anxious squeak. Arthur whirled around, remembering, for the first time since he'd seen Merlin, that he hadn't come alone. Guinevere was hovering by the doorway, wringing her hands together nervously.

Merlin also seemed to notice her for the first time. "Excuse me, young lady. Do you mind? We're trying to have a private conver—" He stopped short. His eyes widened. So wide that for a moment Arthur thought they would pop out of his head.

"What's wrong, Merlin?" he asked.

"No," his teacher murmured. "It can't be…"

Guinevere flinched, almost as if she'd been struck.

She started to back away. Arthur's heart beat uncomfortably. What was going on here? Why did they look like they knew each other?

"Camile?" Merlin questioned. Then he shook his head. "No. That can't be right. Camile would be older now. You're just a child. But you look so much like her… A daughter? But then, she never had any more children after…" His face turned bright white. "You're not… You can't be…"

"This is Guinevere," Arthur blurted out, unable to stand the suspense any more. "She's my new friend. She saved my life and helped cast the spell for us to get here to find you."

"Guinevere," Merlin whispered in disbelief. Then his eyes lit up and his face broke out into a huge grin. "*Guinevere!* You're alive! And practically grown up, too!"

"Wh-what?" Guinevere stammered, still looking as if she was about to bolt from the room.

"Oh, your parents are going to be so happy when they find out," Merlin gushed, clapping his hands together with glee. "This is the best news ever!"

"You must be mistaken," Guinevere protested. "My parents are… dead." Her mouth dipped to a frown. Then something seemed to flicker across her face. Something very dark that Arthur had never seen before from his friend.

"You *know* they're dead," she added, with more force. "You..." She sucked in a breath. "*You*... killed them!"

"Wait, what?" Arthur cried. He couldn't have been more shocked if Guinevere had just accused Merlin of masquerading as a purple polka-dotted dragon. "What are you talking about, Guin?"

Guinevere turned to him. Her brown eyes flashed fire. "I'm sorry, Arthur. But you need to know the truth. Your precious Merlin killed my parents in cold blood when I was just a baby. And he tried to kill me, too!"

"No!" Arthur cried, horrified. "That's impossible! Merlin wouldn't do that!" He turned to his mentor. "Would you?" he asked, suddenly feeling a flicker of doubt.

"Of course not!" Merlin sputtered, sounding angry. "Why would I kill her parents? They're dear friends of mine." He stroked his beard. "Also, they're not dead – well, at least not back in our rightful time. So there is that, too."

Now it was Guinevere's turn to look confused. "What are you talking about? Of course they're dead," she said. But Arthur could hear a thread of doubt in her voice. Mixed with a thread of painful hope.

"Actually, King Leodegrance of the Summer Country and his wife, Camile, are very much alive," Merlin replied. "*You're* the one who is supposed to be dead."

"You're lying!" Guinevere spit out. "You have to be lying!" Her voice caught on the words. "You're trying to trick me."

Merlin shrugged. "I'm happy to prove it to you, if we can ever get out of this place. Queen Camile is just going to be beside herself with joy when she finds out. She never did have another child after you disappeared from your cradle that night. She was too distraught by losing you."

Guinevere just stared at him, not replying. Her knees trembled, and Arthur ran to grab her before they buckled out from under her.

"Guin, it's all right!" he whispered. "This is good news, right?"

Guinevere turned to him, her eyes filled with tears. "Yes… but… how can it be true? How can it possibly be true?"

"Who told you they were dead?" Arthur asked. "Was it your foster mother? Maybe she… didn't know?"

Guin's face twisted, and Arthur's heart squeezed at the pain and betrayal he saw cross her face. Whoever had told her this lie had clearly been someone she trusted. And now she was doubting everything she'd ever been told – maybe for her entire life.

Guinevere squeezed her eyes shut, then opened them again. Her shoulders drooped as if all the fight had gone out of her. Arthur watched as she bit her lower lip, then shuffled from foot to foot.

"Guin…" He placed a hand over hers, but she jerked it away. She gave Merlin one last look, then mumbled an apology and fled the room. Worried, Arthur started after her, but Merlin stopped him at the door.

"No, lad," he said gently. "It will do no good to chase her down. Let her have the time she needs to sort her thoughts. She'll come back when she's ready."

Arthur reluctantly turned back to his mentor. He knew Merlin was right, even if he didn't want him to be. He sighed deeply. "This has all turned out to be such a mess," he moaned. "Ever since the day you left. Nothing has been normal since."

Merlin frowned. "Maybe you should start at the beginning. Tell me everything that's happened since I've been away." He stroked his beard. "For example, did you ever go to that blasted tournament? What clod-headed oaf managed to win the thing? Who's our new king?"

"Well—" Arthur began.

Merlin scowled. "Oh, no. Don't tell me it was that lunkhead Kay. He's the last person on earth who should be wearing the crown. Though I'm sure Mim would love it. All the chaos he would end up causing. It would be a disaster – just as she likes it…" His voice trailed off as he caught Arthur's expression. "Well, what is it, boy? For goodness' sakes, you look like you swallowed a bee." He shook his head. "Don't leave me in suspense. Who is the king of England?"

Arthur felt his cheeks turn bright red. "It's… well, sort of, um… *me*?"

Merlin's eyebrows furrowed. He stared at Arthur for a moment, and Arthur could almost see the smoke coming from his brain.

"I, uh, pulled the sword from the stone," he added weakly.

"Well, I'll be!" Merlin suddenly let out a huge whooping cheer, startling Arthur and forcing him to take a quick step back. "*You* pulled the sword from the stone? The legendary sword Excalibur?"

"That's the one," Arthur agreed. "Evidently whoever pulls it out is meant to be king."

"Yes, of course. I know the legend. I just had no idea it was about you! Though I suppose it makes perfect sense. I always knew you were meant for greatness, of course."

"It does?" Arthur stared at Merlin, perplexed. "You did?"

"Ever since that day you crashed through my roof." The wizard grinned. "After all, why do you think I took such an interest in your education?"

"I don't know. I guess I just thought you were being nice," Arthur said. His mind was whirring with confusion and a little bit of worry. Merlin didn't seem *too* surprised about his student's very unlikely destiny. Was that because the wizard had planned it all along?

Arthur shuffled from foot to foot. "Merlin..." he began, not knowing how to bring it up.

"What is it, lad?"

"You didn't... I mean, you hadn't... just... by some means..."

"Well, spit it out, boy! What are you talking about?"

"You didn't plan this? You didn't cast a spell on the sword so only I could pull it out and it would look like a miracle?"

Merlin's eyes widened. "Why on earth would I do a thing like that?"

Arthur shrugged, squiriming a little. "I— I mean, I don't know," he stammered. "So maybe you could rule through me?"

For a moment, Merlin was speechless. He stared at Arthur, his expression unreadable. Then he leapt out of bed, ripping out the tube attached to his arm. Arthur winced, not sure that was the best way to go about it.

Merlin stalked towards Arthur. "Have you just met

me, lad?" he demanded. "You think I wanted to be king of England?"

Arthur took a small step backwards, looking a little frightened. The last time he'd seen his teacher so agitated was just before he'd blown himself to Bermuda. And Arthur *really* didn't want to have to track him down in yet another time period just to finish their conversation.

"Merlin, sit down," he begged. "It was just a theory…"

"Well, it was a very bad theory," he sputtered. "With no factual evidence to back it up." He huffed and plopped back down on the bed, looking extremely miffed. "Besides, even if I had wanted to do something like that, it wouldn't work. The magic of the sword in the stone goes deep. No mere wizard could just disenchant it on a whim to allow a person of their choosing to pull it out. Otherwise someone would have done it a long time ago."

Arthur drew in a breath, his thoughts whirling in his head. "So then… you're saying…"

"That you're the foretold king of all England?" Merlin shrugged. "It certainly appears so."

Arthur felt his heart skip a beat. Could it be? Could he really be the true king after all?

It seemed impossible. Yet what other explanation could there be? Certainly no one else would want him to be king – or have the ability to make it happen. He felt an unexpected thrill spin up his spine. He hadn't realised how much he'd been hoping for this until it actually happened.

"Of course, there's only way to find out for sure," Merlin added. "We need to consult the Internet."

CHAPTER TWENTY-SIX
ARTHUR

"The inter-net?" Arthur repeated doubtfully. "What is that? Some kind of oracle?"

"Not exactly," Merlin replied. "The Internet can't predict the future like an oracle. It can only reveal words and pictures of the past. And sometimes videos, too." He snorted. "So many videos! Though the good majority of them seem to be of cats doing silly things. For some reason people here really like their cats."

"Cats?" Arthur was so lost it wasn't funny. Merlin sighed.

"Here's the deal. Since you are from the past, the Internet can reveal your future – which is also in the past, at least at this present time," he explained. "Does that make sense?"

"Not really," Arthur replied. "And anyway, don't you already know the future?" he asked, puzzled. "You've bounced all around it! Surely you would have heard about me being king!"

"No offence, but as important as that little detail might be to you personally, it certainly is but a mere ripple in our vast universe," Merlin replied, sounding a little irritated by the question. "And besides, even I have my limitations. Remember when you first crashed through my roof? I knew you were going to be of some importance. And that I was meant to be your teacher. I just didn't know what I was teaching you for." He shrugged. "Now it's starting to all make sense. And I'm sure the Internet will be able to fill in the gaps."

Arthur nodded doubtfully. "So where is the Internet?" he asked.

Merlin swung his legs off the bed and onto the floor. Standing up, he looked around the room. "I know the nurse at the door has a computer at her desk. We'll have to borrow that." He started heading towards the room's exit with purposeful steps.

"Um, Merlin?" Arthur ventured nervously. When the wizard turned to look at him, he gestured to the duck-covered dressing gown he wore, which was, for some unfortunate and completely inexplicable reason, wide open in the back.

The wizard's cheeks turned bright pink. "Oh, right! Clothes!" He grabbed his wand off the table and waved it with a flourish. *"Bibbidi bobbidi—!"* he chanted. Then he winked at Arthur. "I learned this one from a lovely fairy godmother while stuck in 1800s France. Sweet lady, really. Though quite hung up on punctuality." He waved his wand. *"BOO!"*

There was a sudden poof, and the wizard went up in a plume of smoke. He emerged a moment later dressed in a pair of short trousers decorated with funny-looking trees and a very brightly coloured striped shirt. Which didn't exactly help him fit in. But it was better than his previous attire, so Arthur decided to let it go.

"Now," Merlin said, turning to address Arthur. "I need you to distract the nurse. Once she's gone, we'll jump on her computer and see what we can find out."

"Jump on it?" Arthur raised an eyebrow. "Won't that break it?"

"Not literally, my boy," Merlin said with a groan. "Just a figure of speech. They have a lot of those in this time period. You'll need to try to keep up."

Arthur nodded dutifully. "How am I supposed to distract her?" he asked. Then he had an idea. "What if you turn me into a mouse? Are people in the future still afraid of mice?"

"Oddly, yes," Merlin replied. "Though I've never understood why." He nodded absently. "Yes, that might actually work. Good thinking, boy." He patted Arthur on the back, and Arthur couldn't help beaming from the approval.

A moment later, Merlin was waving his wand in his direction. *"Misculus, moosculus, Mickey Mouse!"* he chanted, and suddenly there was another poof of smoke. Arthur squirmed as he felt his body collapse in on itself, just as it had so many times during their lessons. And soon he was standing on his hind legs, twitching his tiny pink nose.

Merlin clapped his hands in delight. "Huzzah! I still have it!" he declared. "Now go on, boy. Do your thing. And, uh, don't get stepped on," he added with a sheepish grin.

Arthur gave him a little mouse salute. Then he skittered out of the room and down the hall. When he reached the room with the woman at the desk, he paused only a moment, then leapt up onto her lap. She looked down, her eyes bulging from her head.

"Boo!" Arthur tried to say. It came out more like '*squeak*', but turned out to still be extremely effective. The woman leapt from her chair, screaming.

"Mouse! There's a mouse!"

Arthur felt himself go flying. He hit the ground hard

and saw stars. By the time he could see normally again, the woman was running from the building, slamming the door shut behind her.

"Not bad," Merlin remarked, walking into the room. "Not bad at all." He grinned at Arthur. "Just like old times, am I right?"

Arthur nodded, smiling through his whiskers. He had to admit, it was good to have his teacher back. Even if it did always end up leaving him animal-shaped.

He watched as the wizard walked around the table, then huddled in front of a strange little box with a glass window on the front. "Now, let's get to work," he said. "She'll be back in a few minutes with someone to deal with the rodent problem. We need to do this fast." He leant over and started tapping on a tray of buttons.

Arthur squeaked loudly, trying to get Merlin's attention again. After all, working in a kitchen most of his life, he'd seen first-hand how mice were 'dealt with', and it would likely put a damper on any possible future of him as king – or anything else, for that matter.

Merlin looked down, surprised. "Oh. Right. Sorry. You probably want to be human again, don't you?" He absently waved a hand in Arthur's direction. A moment later Arthur poofed back to his old self. He let out a breath of relief, then turned his attention to Merlin's tapping on the tray of letters.

"So is that the Internet?" he asked curiously, pressing his finger against the machine.

"It's a computer," Merlin corrected. "You access the Internet through a computer."

Arthur cocked his head. "The Internet is inside the computer?"

"No. The Internet is everywhere."

"Everywhere?" Arthur looked around, feeling bewildered. "Is it invisible?"

Merlin groaned. "Look, I'll be happy to give you an in-depth lesson on twenty-first-century technology the moment we get back home. But right now, we need to concentrate on your past— er, future."

"Sorry." Arthur leant over and placed his hands on the table, watching Merlin tap on the tray again. As he tapped, words appeared on the glass window in front of him.

"The Internet is quite miraculous," Merlin explained. "You simply type in a question, and it will spit out answers. It's as if every book in the world is inside of it, and you don't have to turn any pages to read them."

"Wow," Arthur said. "That truly is magical."

"Actually, it's scientific," Merlin corrected. He tapped on the buttons again, and something appeared on the glass. "*King Arthur destiny…*" he murmured as he tapped.

The wizard hit another button, and Arthur held his

breath as the words on the glass shifted. A moment later, a new page revealed itself.

"What does it say?" he asked anxiously. This was it. The moment of truth. The Internet was about to tell him who he really was. And once he knew, there was no going back. Suddenly he found himself wishing Guin were here. Whatever the answer, he knew she would find a way to make him feel better about it all.

Merlin cleared his throat, then started reading. "'Arthur was destined to become the once and future king and unite the land...'"

Arthur's heart leapt to his throat. Merlin kept reading, but he could no longer focus on the words.

Arthur was destined...

"So it's true?" he breathed. "I am the destined king of England?" He couldn't believe it. But there it was, spelt out clear as day on the Internet.

"The Internet never lies," Merlin assured him. "If it says you are the destined king, then you are the destined king." He scanned the window, his lips pursed. "And it seems you were a pretty legendary one, at that. In fact, it appears you even have books and major motion pictures all about you!"

"What's a motion picture?" Arthur asked.

"Oh. It's like television that's not broken up into parts," Merlin explained absently, still reading the window. "Though it appears you have a few streaming series about you, too. Too bad we don't have more time to binge them." As if that cleared anything up.

But it didn't matter, really. The point was, Arthur was king. He was the rightful king.

Merlin straightened, giving Arthur a rueful grin. "Well, my boy! It seems there's no getting out of it. It's your destiny, and you're stuck with it." He slapped him on the back. "You know, I knew from the start, with your spirit and the way you put your heart and soul into everything you did, that you'd be worth something someday." He humphed. "Archimedes didn't believe me, but I was right! It says so right there." He tapped on the glass. "King Arthur and his Knights Of The Round Table."

Arthur felt his cheeks heat, but this time with pleasure. "I need to tell Guin!" he exclaimed. "She's not going to believe it." He grinned widely, then declared, "And then I need to get back to England, before someone else tries to take over in my absence. Or Mim tries something else."

"Something else?" Merlin repeated, turning to look at him questioningly. Arthur realised he hadn't told his teacher all that had happened with the evil witch. He quickly related the main points – including the disgusting slug thing, which still gave him the shivers. When he had finished, Merlin huffed angrily.

"Ridiculous! Just ridiculous! I'm going to have a word with her when I get back! More than one, if you must know! Why, I'll make sure she never dares mess with you again."

"That would be great," Arthur said, feeling so relieved. This was exactly what he needed. Everything was going to be all right. He could feel it in his bones.

Merlin crossed the room, then crossed back, tapping his forehead with his finger. "The question is – how do we get back home? My spell book is completely scrambled. If we try to time travel, we might end up in the Jurassic era – and eaten by dinosaurs. That would really put a damper on your destiny."

Arthur didn't know what a dinosaur was, but he was pretty sure he didn't want to be eaten by one. Luckily, he did have another idea. He stepped into Merlin's path. "Guin has your book," he told him. "From your tower. It got us here. Surely it can also bring us home."

"Yes! YES!" Merlin did a little jig. "This is wonderful news! Wonderful! With my book in hand, I'll be able to reverse Mim's spell and get us all back home safe and sound!"

Arthur let out a small cheer. "And then I can get back to being king."

"Indeed, my boy, indeed. And together we can stop Madam Mim from causing any more mischief." Merlin wrinkled his nose. "Now, come! There's no time to waste! Let's get that book – and get you back to your future!"

CHAPTER TWENTY-SEVEN
GUINEVERE

Guinevere stared out at the vast sea as the sun dipped below the horizon, bruising the sky with vivid blues and purples and reds. The same sun she'd seen set a thousand times before back home. But somehow it felt different here. Now.

Everything felt different. Like she was out there, in that wild sea, unmoored, adrift. Every truth she'd ever been told in her life had become a violent wave crashing over her, threatening to drown her with doubt.

Lost in thought, she didn't hear Arthur approach. When he reached out to touch her arm, she jumped.

"Sorry," he said. "I didn't mean to startle you."

"It's all right," she said quietly, not taking her gaze off

the horizon. In truth, she was afraid if she looked at him, she'd break out into tears all over again. She felt as if she'd been crying for hours, and still her eyes were wet.

"Are you all right?" he asked softly.

She swallowed hard, pausing before answering. "I don't know," she said at last. "I mean, I feel like my whole world has been turned upside down. I don't know what to think, what to believe." She shook her head. "My parents, alive? Could it really be true?" Her voice cracked on the last bit. She couldn't help it.

But there was a bigger question in her mind. One she couldn't share with Arthur. The one that felt like a sharp knife stabbing her in the gut. Had Mim known all this time that her parents were alive? Had she lied to her face over and over again as Guinevere grew? Her foster mother's words seemed to echo in her ears. *I saved you. You would have died without me.*

All this time she had felt so grateful to her mother. But now that gratitude tasted like sawdust in her mouth. How many times had Mim called Merlin a monster?

What if it was actually Mim, not Merlin, who was the true monster?

She thought about all the time they'd spent together over the years. The singing and dance parties in their cottage. The games of cards where Mim would badly cheat and Guin would laughingly catch her at it. All the lessons Mim had patiently taught her about magic and herbs. Yes, Mim had certainly enjoyed causing mischief from time to time – but could she really have gone so far as to steal away a child from her parents?

It was almost too much to think about.

Arthur reached out, pressing his fingers against her cheek, turning her head gently – so gently – until she was looking into his deep blue eyes. She swallowed hard, powerless to turn away.

"We will find out the truth. Whatever it might be," he said firmly. "Together."

Her heart squeezed. A tear slipped down her cheek, but she didn't bother to swipe it away.

"I would like that," she murmured. It was all she could say. But at the moment, it was enough.

Arthur smiled at her. Then he turned to look out at the sea. For a moment, he said nothing. Then, "It's so pretty here," he murmured. "And so warm." It was almost as if he could sense she was at her breaking point and needed a change of subject.

"Yes," she agreed, kicking off her shoes and digging her toes into the crunchy wet sand. She wondered how Merlin was doing on his spell. He'd found her earlier and taken the book from her, promising to find a spell that would get them safely back home. He said it could take a little while and that she should enjoy the beach while he worked. And so she had, even procuring a tray of those little golden sticks, which had turned out to be delicious. "It's almost magical."

"If only I didn't have my entire destiny and the future of England waiting for me back home," Arthur joked. "I'd stay much longer. Maybe even learn how to stand on water, like them," he added, gesturing to the people out on the water riding the waves on strange long boards.

She turned to him, surprised. "So it's true?" she asked. "You're really England's king? It wasn't a trick after all?"

"I'm afraid there's no getting out of it," Arthur said, a little sheepishly.

"You're going to make a great king," she blurted out before she could stop herself. But even after she said the words, she realised she meant them. Arthur was everything a good king should be. England was lucky to have him. And Mim would just have to accept that.

A sob escaped her throat as she thought of her foster mother again. Maybe Mim had also been deceived? Maybe she truly believed what she'd told Guin all along. Because the alternative – that she'd been the one to steal Guin away from her own parents and had lied to her for her entire life – was too cruel to even consider.

But then, what about Arthur? Merlin? Mim had been so insistent that Merlin crowned Arthur because he wanted the power for himself. But was this merely another lie – another game? How could Guin know for sure?

It was too much to think about. Far too much. She forced herself to push it down deep inside to deal with later once their immediate problems were solved. When she arrived back home, she would go straight to her mother and demand to know everything – the whole truth this time. No more lies. No more deception. And if her mother wouldn't agree to this, then Guin would leave. She would find her true parents – if they were indeed alive. She would start a new life.

She realised Arthur was still watching her. "I don't like seeing you so sad, Guin," he said. "I wish there was something I could do. Or say. Or—"

On impulse, she reached down and slipped her hands into his. His skin was warm and slightly rough at the fingertips. But his hands were strong as they clasped her own. "You're here," she told him. "That's all that matters."

"I don't think I've thanked you yet," he said softly. "I mean, definitely not enough. You saved my life. You helped me rescue Merlin. I don't know what I would have done without you." He paused. "I'm lucky to have met you, Guin."

Guinevere couldn't help a small flinch at his words.

At the grateful look radiating from his eyes – a look she didn't deserve. If only he knew the truth: that their meeting was not the accident he thought it to be. That she'd purposely befriended him with the intent to bring him down. To destroy his life and his rule.

The thought tore at her heart. She hadn't known Arthur long, but in the short time they'd been together, he'd become a true friend in every sense of the word. A friend like she'd never had before. A friend like she'd probably never have again.

Which meant she could never tell him the truth. He could never know what she'd once intended to do. And from now on, she'd be the best friend a person could be. She would support him, stay loyal and true. And if anyone ever tried to hurt him again, she would be the first to stop them.

She felt his eyes on her, and she lifted her head again. He was staring at her, his hands still clasped in hers. Her breath caught in her throat as he reached up, brushing a lock of hair from her eyes.

"Guinevere," he whispered. And that was enough.

Their lips came together. Soft. Sweet. A little clumsy, too. But that was to be expected – neither one of them had much experience in the act. Guinevere felt her knees weaken. She started to sway, but Arthur held her up, his strong hands clasping her at the waist.

"Arthur," she murmured. "Oh, Arthur…"

"ARTHUR! WHERE ARE YOU, BOY?"

They broke apart, stumbling backwards to put distance between them as Merlin stomped down the beach, carrying his bag. He was dressed once more in the blue robes Arthur had described, though he seemed to have forgotten to remove his sunglasses, even though the sun now dipped below the horizon. He stumbled on a small rock and fell face-first into the sand.

"Argh!" he grumped as he tried to climb back to his feet. "Who turned out the lights?"

Arthur laughed and ran over to his teacher to take the sunglasses from his face and pocket them. Merlin looked around and huffed loudly.

"That's better," he remarked. Then he turned to the two of them, glaring with suspicion in his eyes. "Am I interrupting something?" he asked.

"No!" they both blurted out at once, then looked at one another awkwardly. Merlin rolled his eyes.

"You two are as bad as those silly squirrels," he muttered. Then he shook his head. "Now let's get going. The past won't save itself, you know."

CHAPTER TWENTY-EIGHT
ARTHUR

It was raining when Arthur, Guinevere and Merlin time travelled back to Merlin's tower. They realised this immediately, since the ceiling had so many leaks in it and all the buckets Merlin had placed to catch the water had long overflowed and flooded the floor. It took but a moment for them to be thoroughly drenched.

"Oh, dear!" Merlin exclaimed, looking over all his sopping wet books. "Thank goodness these are magically protected. Or else we'd have a disaster on our hands."

"I miss Bermuda already," Arthur moaned, looking down at his twenty-first-century garments. They were so comfortable – even when wet. He dreaded having to change back into his royal robes.

"Still, I'm glad the spell worked," Guinevere remarked, looking around the room. "I was half-afraid we'd be stuck in the future forever." She grimaced. "Not that it wasn't a nice place and all. But we have… things to do." She stared out the window, wringing her hands. Arthur wondered if she was thinking about her parents and how to find them.

"Well, I need to get back to the castle immediately," Arthur said. "Before anyone notices I'm gone." He frowned. "I wonder how long we *have* been gone, actually. Has any time passed here since we left?"

"It's tough to tell," Merlin said, "since watches have yet to be invented." He walked over to the window and peered outside. "But from the buds on the trees and the birds chirping, I'd say it's nearly spring."

"Nearly spring!" Arthur exclaimed. "But we left in the winter. It wasn't even a month after Christmas."

"Oh, dear," Merlin said. "Perhaps my spell casting is still a bit off."

"We need to get back to the castle!" Arthur cried, his heart pounding. "They must be frantic, wondering where I've been." He swallowed hard, a horrible thought occurring to him. "What if they think I'm dead? What if they've already selected a new king?"

Merlin looked at him solemnly. "That would be very bad," he said. "The number one thing to avoid when time travelling is accidentally changing history. If you're no longer king like you're meant to be, the future as we know it could spiral off into an alternate reality. Meaning everything that is meant to be, may no longer be." He paced the room, his steps eating up the distance between walls. "Oh, dear. This is all my fault. You should have just left me to rot in the future. It would have been better for everyone."

"I'd never do that," Arthur said vehemently. "You're too important to me. I'm glad we rescued you. And I'm sure we can sort everything out. We just need to get back to the castle – quickly."

"And we shall," Merlin agreed. "Just let me get packed first. Won't take a second!"

Arthur opened his mouth to tell the wizard they didn't have time for packing. But before he could get a word out, Merlin waved his wand, and the books around them came to life once again, shaking themselves off and marching towards Merlin's suitcase. Arthur had to leap aside in order not to be trampled by the parade.

"Merlin!" he cried, trying to be heard over the commotion of stomping books. "We really don't have time to—"

He was interrupted by the sound of a slamming door somewhere down below. Rushing to the window, he peered out only to see Sir Ector himself, charging up the stairs, looking sopping wet and angry. Arthur cringed. He'd almost forgotten his foster father had returned home just before they'd travelled to the future. Which was months ago, by this point.

"Quick! Hide!" Guinevere cried. "Before he sees you!"

Arthur looked around the room in a panic. "Where?" he asked.

"Behind those books!" she suggested, pointing to a towering pile in the corner that hadn't marched itself away yet. Arthur nodded and dived behind the pile, hoping it would stay put – at least for a little longer. A moment later, Guinevere joined him in the tight space.

"I say, what's going on in here? I thought I heard a ruckus!" Ector cried, barging into the room. Merlin whispered a word and the books all dropped to the floor, as if they'd never been animated at all. Ector scowled, his eyes shooting straight to Merlin.

"Marvin!" he bellowed, as usual not getting the wizard's name right. "I should have known!"

"Why, hello, Sir Ector," Merlin said gallantly. As if nothing at all was amiss. "I see you're back from London."

Ector grunted. "Of course I'm back. I've been back for two months. Ever since my fool of a son got himself arrested for treason. I tried to tell the Wart it was an honest mistake – it could have happened to anyone! – and what did he do? The lad threw me out of the castle!" He spat on the floor angrily. "Why, I raised that boy from a baby, and this is the thanks I get?"

"It's more than you deserve," Arthur muttered from behind his pile of books, soft enough so his foster father couldn't hear. Then something struck him. "But wait, I didn't throw him out of the castle," he whispered to Guin. "I mean, I definitely planned to. But I never had time to do it – before I was poisoned and you took me away."

She frowned. "That's odd. Do you think he's making it up?"

"Maybe," Arthur mused. "But to what benefit? I mean, why would Merlin care?"

Guinevere shrugged, and they turned back to the conversation. Merlin was patting Ector on the back with a comforting hand. "I'm so sorry you've had such rotten luck," he was telling the lord. "And I have no interest in adding to it now. So I'll just pick up my things and take my leave. I'll be out of your hair in no time at all."

Ector looked around the messy room, clearly dubious about the estimated time of departure.

"Using magic, of course," Merlin amended quickly.

"Oh." Ector scowled. "Well, I suppose that's all right then. Though perhaps before you take your leave, might you have a look at Kay? The boy hasn't been right in the head since the Wart freed him from prison. Not that he was a scholar to begin with, mind you. But now he seems downright dazed and confused. He keeps babbling about Wart not actually being Wart. Which of course doesn't make any sense. I'm thinking perhaps he got hit on the head a bit too hard during the fight." Ector frowned. "Though I don't remember him actually getting hit at all, now that I think about it. In fact, I still don't understand how he lost to begin with. He was doing so well..."

Arthur frowned. "Did he just say I let Kay out of prison?" he asked. "Because I definitely didn't do that!"

"No, of course not," Guin agreed, looking worried. "Maybe someone else did?"

Arthur looked up again, thankful to see Merlin ushering Ector out the door. "Let's go take a look at the boy," the wizard told the father. "It's probably nothing. He's likely just a little tired, that's all. I'm sure he's going to be just fine. Just fine indeed." He followed Ector down the stairs, closing the tower door behind him. Once they were alone, Arthur and Guinevere scrambled from their hiding spots.

Arthur ran to the window to watch Ector and Merlin approach Kay in the courtyard. "I don't understand," he murmured. "How could I have freed Kay from prison and thrown Ector out of the castle? I haven't been there in months. Maybe someone in the castle has been covering for me?"

"Covering for you," Guin replied in an uneasy voice. "Or… pretending to *be* you."

"What?" Arthur turned to her, eyebrows raised.

"You heard Sir Ector," Guin reminded him. "He said Kay keeps babbling about you not really being you." She bit her lower lip. "What if someone's pretending to be you? Someone with the power to shapeshift."

Arthur's eyes bulged from his head. "You don't think…" he began, then his voice trailed off. He was too horrified by what Guin was implying to even speak it.

"Yes," Guinevere said flatly. "You wanted to know what Madam Mim's been up to since you've been gone? Well, I think you have your answer."

CHAPTER TWENTY-NINE
GUINEVERE

Guinevere didn't consider herself a violent person. In fact, in most instances, she was very kind and gentle and good. But at the moment, it was all she could do not to punch a wall with her fist. She should have known Mim wouldn't be content to just sit around in Arthur's absence and let things play out as they were supposed to. No, she had to meddle once again.

And put herself on the throne of England.

Guin thought back to all Mim's complaints about Merlin and how he wanted the power all to himself. And yet all this time, it was *she* who had wanted the throne of England. Or maybe she hadn't planned it – maybe she suddenly decided it would be perfectly hilarious to take over, to trick everyone into thinking she was Arthur. Then she'd acted exactly the opposite of the way he would if he'd actually been there. Who knew what mischief she'd already caused in the two months she'd been in power? And who knew what was still up her sleeve?

They had to stop her. Now.

Guin sighed, frustrated. All she wanted to do was go to the Summer Country and see if what Merlin had said about her parents was true. But that would have to wait until she sorted this out. After all, it was her fault they were in this predicament to begin with – if she hadn't sneaked Arthur away from the castle, Mim would have never had the opportunity to take his place.

Her fists tightened. *Why, Mother. Why?*

"Are you all right, Guin?"

She felt Arthur come up behind her, placing a gentle hand on her back. She knew the gesture was meant to be comforting, but it only brought tears to her eyes. Arthur had been so good and kind to her from the start. If only he knew how little she deserved it. What if he learnt her true role in this thing? He'd never speak to her again.

Guin couldn't bear the thought.

"I'm just worried," she said. "What if we're too late? What if you can't get your throne back and the future spirals out of control like Merlin said? What if people are hurt? What if people die?"

"I won't let that happen," Arthur declared, sounding much braver than she'd ever heard him sound before. "We know now that I am the rightful king. And I plan to take back my throne, no matter what it takes."

He sounded so sure of himself. And for a moment, all she could think of was the boy she'd first met in the woods, who only wanted to fly away. Arthur had grown up so much since then. He'd faced his enemies and made them his friends. He'd fought a fierce battle and won – through brains instead of brawn. And he'd been willing to give it all up to travel across time and space to rescue his teacher and friend. When she looked at him now, she no longer saw a boy playing at being king, but a boy who had accepted his destiny – despite the danger it foretold.

A boy who deserved to sit on the throne.

She just hoped they weren't too late.

Merlin walked back into the tower, muttering under his breath. Guinevere looked up at him, searching his face. "What is it?" she asked.

"I'm afraid it's not good," Merlin said gravely. "According to Kay, Arthur – or someone who appears to be Arthur – is still on the throne. But he's completely changed his tune. He's refused to sign the Saxon treaty and declared them to be England's enemies, locking up their king and his men. He's raised taxes, cut food to the poor. There's massive unrest in the streets. Violence. Chaos. And it's all being done in Arthur's name."

Arthur's face paled. "This is terrible! We need to get back there. Now! Make things right. No matter what it takes."

"I agree," Merlin said. "And there's no time to waste. My poor books will have to wait a little longer, I'm afraid. This calls for faster travel – and there's no room for luggage." He waved his hands, gathering them to his side. Then he lifted his arms.

"*Higgidis… piggidis… diggidis, dundon.* Magic, carry us to London!"

And poof! They were gone.

A moment later Guinevere opened her eyes. Her lids felt heavy – as if she'd been asleep a very long time. When she blinked, clearing her vision, she looked around. "Are we here?" she asked. "Are we in London?"

Suddenly her eyes fell upon a small stone in the centre of what appeared to be a churchyard. On top of the stone sat an anvil. She scrambled to her feet, approaching it curiously.

"That was it." Arthur's voice came from behind her. "Where I pulled the sword from the stone."

She turned to watch him walk over to her and stare

down at the anvil. "It seems so long ago," he said softly. "And yet, at the same time, like yesterday."

"I still can't believe you managed to do it," Merlin remarked, coming up behind him, shaking the dust from his beard. "I only wish I had been there to see it."

"Believe me, I wish you'd been here, too," Arthur replied wryly. "Then maybe everything wouldn't have turned into such a disaster."

Merlin's face grew serious. "I know," he said softly. "And I am truly sorry for that. I let my temper get the best of me. And you didn't deserve it. You were just excited about going to a tournament. And I acted like a complete selfish buffoon." He hung his head.

Guin watched as Arthur approached his teacher, laying a hand on his arm. "It's all right," he said. "I know you were only trying to help me reach my potential. And without your teaching, I never would have lasted a day as king. So I think, maybe, we're even?" he asked, looking up at Merlin hopefully.

Merlin's face broke into a toothy smile. He reached over and pulled Arthur into a huge hug. Arthur squirmed and protested at first, but at last laughed and hugged the wizard back.

Guinevere smiled from a distance, feeling the love between the two of them, almost as if they were father and son. It made her think of Mim and their relationship. And how it could never be the same again now that she knew the truth. It hurt more than she wanted to admit.

She shook her head. There was no time for thoughts like that now. Right now they had a much more important quest: to stop Mim's mischief once and for all and get Arthur back on the throne where he belonged.

CHAPTER THIRTY
ARTHUR

Arthur stared up at the castle gates, gnawing his lower lip nervously. It was funny; for so long he'd wanted to escape these walls. Now he just wanted to get back inside. But that was easier said than done, Merlin reminded him. For if Mim really was in charge now, she wasn't going to be thrilled to see Arthur walk back through that door.

"Can't you just zap her back to her old shape?" he asked the wizard. "Make everyone see she's an imposter?"

But Merlin only shook his head. "For all her faults, Mim is a powerful wizard, and her magic is as strong as mine. I can't undo her spells. We must find another way to expose her lies to the people of Camelot."

Arthur frowned, feeling discouraged. "Well, she's not just going to admit it if we ask nicely," he countered. "And no one's going to take me at my word if she looks just like me. I'm going to have to prove I'm the real Arthur somehow." He paced back and forth, thinking hard. "But how will I do that?"

"What about the sword in the stone?" Guinevere asked suddenly.

Arthur looked up. "What about it?"

"That's how everyone knew you were king to begin with, right?" Guin reminded him. "Maybe if you pulled it again…? And Mim, well, couldn't?"

"Guin, you're a genius!" Merlin exclaimed. "That's exactly what we should do!"

"But…" Arthur scratched his head. "Couldn't Mim just magically make the sword come out of the stone on her own?"

Merlin shook his head. "The sword in the stone's magic is much older and stronger than Mim's or even mine. And just as I cannot undo Mim's spells, she cannot undo the stone's enchantment or make it work in her favour."

"Then that's what we'll do," Arthur declared, confidence rising inside of him. This could actually work. "We'll make her prove she's who says she is. And if she can't, well, then people will have to believe us."

"It's a good plan," Merlin agreed. "If you can get her to agree to go along with—"

He was interrupted by a sudden rush of people heading through the castle gates. Arthur found himself being shoved in one direction, then the next, for a moment getting separated from his friends.

"Where's everyone going?" he asked.

"It's petitioner day!" exclaimed a man rushing along with the rest. "Today's the day we get to ask the king for help."

Arthur's eyes widened. Of course! Petitioner day! The day he had once dreaded most as king. But now it could very well be the thing he needed to force Mim's hand. She'd be there in the throne room, along with half the kingdom. And if he challenged her there, in front of everyone, she couldn't very well ignore him.

"Come on," he said once he was back with his friends. "Let's go see this king!"

Guinevere took a step forwards. But to Arthur's surprise, Merlin took a step back.

"You two go ahead," the wizard said, gesturing with his hand. "I will hang behind. It might be wise not to let Mim know I'm back yet. After all, when she can't pull the sword from the stone, she's going to get angry. Very angry.

And I want to be there, in the shadows, to protect you and the people from whatever she might try to do."

"Good idea," Arthur replied, relieved at the idea of Merlin's being there to protect him. He turned to Guin. "All right. Let's do this."

CHAPTER THIRTY-ONE
GUINEVERE

Guinevere felt her knees trembling as if they were about to buckle under her as she and Arthur walked up to the castle's great hall. Arthur seemed so confident this plan would work. But he didn't know Mim like she did. And she was worried. Very worried.

They pushed their way inside the large room and looked around to gain their bearings. The place was packed with people, and everyone seemed to be yelling at once.

"What is happening?" Arthur asked, looking worried. "They all seem really angry."

Guinevere nodded, looking around at the agitated crowd. It felt as if a brawl could break out at any moment. "Maybe they sense something's wrong with their king?" she suggested, standing on her tiptoes to try to see over people's heads. She sank back to her heels, discouraged.

"We need to get to the front," Arthur said, "so we can see what's going on."

Guinevere nodded in agreement and began elbowing her away through the crowd. She got shoved back at least three times before she found people sympathetic enough to let her pass without much complaint. When she made it to the front of the room, she stopped short as her eyes fell upon the boy on the throne.

It was Arthur. Except, of course, not really. But it looked just like him. Same crown, same robes, same shock of blond hair from before he'd cut it. In fact, if she hadn't known any better, she would have been completely fooled. Like everyone in the room evidently was.

But then she caught something slightly off. A blush of violet at the king's ears.

Mim.

Mother.

Guinevere felt her knees wobble as her worst fears came true. She hadn't realised until that very moment how much she'd been hoping that she had been wrong – that it was someone else who had risen to take Arthur's place. But, of course, that was preposterous.

Who else had the power to shift into the body of another? It was always going to be Mim, and deep down, she had known it.

But still. Anger rose inside of her. She thought back to all those conversations she'd had with her mother. How offended Mim had acted when she talked about Arthur stealing the throne from its rightful ruler. Yet now she'd done the very same thing herself. And she didn't look the least bit sorry for it.

Merlin was right. Mim had been the one out for the throne all along. And Guinevere had all but helped her take it. Suddenly she felt so ashamed.

"Oh, my!" Arthur suddenly gasped beside her. "Is that…?"

He trailed off, but Guin followed his gaze and was horrified to see a small golden cage hanging next to the throne. Inside was a small owl with ruffled feathers.

"Poor Archimedes," Arthur whispered, his face pale. "I should have never left him here alone. With a broken wing and everything! If anything happens to him…"

"It won't," Guinevere promised, though in truth she had no idea what they could do about it. It was clear from all of this that Mim had fooled everyone with her ruse. She had the people; she had guards. She had knights. She had no reason at all to prove herself to anyone, least of all them.

"I'm going up there," Arthur declared. "The people deserve to know they're being deceived."

"Wait." On instinct, she grabbed his arm. He turned to her, puzzled. "Just… be careful. You don't want to make her angry." She swallowed hard, thinking. "Maybe… make it like a game instead," she added, an idea suddenly coming to her. "She's much more likely to go along with your challenge if she thinks it'll be amusing."

Arthur gave her an odd look, and she realised, too late, that she'd probably said too much. She wasn't supposed to know Mim. So how would she know about her love of games?

"Merlin told me that!" she added quickly.

"Right." Arthur scratched his head. "She does seem to like to play games, that's for sure. That's why she was so eager to duel Merlin. She thought it would be fun."

"Exactly!" Guinevere agreed, letting out a nervous breath. "Now go! I'll wait back here." The last thing she needed was for her mother to see her at Arthur's side.

Arthur smiled nervously at her, then pushed his way through the crowd towards the throne.

She watched as he approached Mim, squaring his shoulders and lifting his chin.

He looked so brave. And also, incredibly stupid. Did he have any notion how powerful Mim was? Sure, she acted like a giggling fool on the outside. But her true power ran deep. If she wanted to, she could cut Arthur down right then and there. And that would be the end of it.

Guinevere shuddered, unable to bear the thought of it.

Arthur's voice suddenly rang through the hall. "What is the meaning of this? Who is this imposter who sits on my throne?"

The rowdy court went silent immediately. Mim looked down at Arthur, a look of pure shock on her face. She hadn't expected to see him, that was for sure, and Guin allowed herself a moment of satisfaction to see her mother so unsettled. But then the shock cleared from Mim's face and her upper lip curled to a sneer.

"Well, well, what have we here?" she purred, looking Arthur up and down. "A little court jester come to play?" She grinned widely. "Oh, but you are so cute!" She turned to her court. "Look at how funny he's dressed!"

Guinevere winced, remembering they were still wearing their twenty-first-century clothes – why hadn't they changed? And why, oh, why, had she shorn his hair? In truth, he'd never looked less like a king.

But Arthur didn't falter. Instead, he leapt up onto the dais, turning to face the crowd. All eyes were now glued to him.

He cleared his throat. "My good people," he called out

to the crowd, "you have been deceived. This king who sits before you is an imposter. A wizard who practises sorcery. She has used this to shapeshift herself into looking like me, but I am your rightful king."

Mim started to laugh. Guin cringed as the squeaky sound echoed through the hall. It was Arthur's laugh, but at the same time, not. It sounded harsh, mocking, mean.

"Now, now," Mim protested. "Who's to say it's not the other way round?" She held up her hands in innocence. "Perhaps it is *you* who dabbles in sorcery. Perhaps it is *you*" – she pointed a finger at Arthur – "who has stolen *my* identity and is trying to trick these good people."

"Hmm," Arthur replied. "It seems we are at an impasse. Perhaps we should play a game to settle it all."

Mim raised an eyebrow, clearly intrigued despite herself. "A game?" she asked. "What sort of game?"

Arthur puffed out his chest, facing down his fake self. Guinevere held her breath.

"Isn't it obvious?" he asked. "We're going to play who can pull the sword from the stone."

CHAPTER THIRTY-TWO
ARTHUR

Arthur could hear the collective gasp from the crowd in the great hall. But he refused to turn around, keeping his eyes locked on the imposter before him, trying to read the expression on her face. For a moment he wondered if she was just planning to arrest him and throw away the key – or maybe even kill him outright – without giving him a chance to clear his name.

But instead, an amused smile slipped across her face. "That sounds fun!" she agreed with a giggle. She turned to the crowd, clapping her hands in delight. "What do you think? Shall we play this game?"

The crowd burst into nervous conversation – clearly conflicted about who was telling the truth. Once again,

Arthur would have to prove himself in front of his subjects. Fortunately, this time it wasn't a fight to the death. Just a simple task that had been no problem for him before.

"All right, then," Mim declared. "Off to the churchyard we go!"

The crowd poured out of the great hall and through the courtyard towards the old church down the road, eager to secure a good spot to watch the fun. Mim sauntered past Arthur, escorted by Arthur's own guards, throwing him a smug look as she passed.

Once she was gone, Guinevere appeared back at his side. "That was great!" she exclaimed. "Good work!"

"Thanks," he said, feeling his face flush with pride. "But that was the easy part. Now I have to go pull the sword from the stone again."

Guinevere placed a hand on his arm. "You can do this," she said. "And remember, you're not alone. You've got Merlin out there. And you have me, too."

His heart warmed at her words. He met her eyes with his own. "That means a lot," he said softly. "Thank you."

She reached out and slipped her hand into his. It was so warm, contrasting with his own, which felt half-frozen with fear. And when she squeezed it tight—

"Ahem! Are you lovebirds going to get on with saving

the realm anytime soon? I mean, don't let me interrupt or anything!"

They whirled around, startled. Archimedes hooted from his cage. Arthur's face broke out into a big grin. He turned to Guin.

"Can you free Archimedes?" he asked. "Mim's waiting for me."

She nodded. "I'll meet you in the churchyard." She smiled. "Go teach her a lesson!"

When Arthur arrived in the courtyard, he found Mim already holding court in front of the stone and anvil, along with what felt like half the kingdom standing around, watching eagerly. He felt an involuntary shiver spin down his spine.

When Mim saw Arthur, she clapped her hands excitedly. "There you are!" she exclaimed. "I was hoping you weren't going to chicken out!" She giggled. "Then the game would be over before it even began."

"Of course not," Arthur replied, trying to sound sure of himself. She certainly seemed confident. Did she know something he didn't? But no. Merlin assured him she couldn't manipulate the stone's magic. This was going to work.

"Sir Pellinore!" Mim cried. "Bring me Excalibur."

The old knight stepped through the crowd, carrying Arthur's sheathed sword. He made a great show of presenting it to both Arthurs as well as the crowd, and even Arthur saw there could be no doubt that this was his sword. It even had the little ding on it that it'd received during his fight with Kay. He watched as Sir Pellinore slid the sword into the anvil just as it had been on that fateful day. It slipped in easily, as if it were loose. But when Pellinore tugged on it once it was in place, it was stuck fast, just as before.

Arthur felt his confidence rise. This was going to work, he was sure of it.

"All right, then," Mim declared, circling the stone like a vulture to its prey. She looked much too comfortable for Arthur's comfort. "You say you can pull it out. Well, let's see you do it."

"You don't want to go first?" Arthur asked, rather surprised.

Mim giggled. "I'm feeling generous this evening. I'll let you have the first try."

Arthur pursed his lips. He wasn't sure why, but suddenly this was feeling a little like a trap. But how could it be? It was the same sword, he scolded himself, the same stone, the same anvil. Which meant it had the same magic. Magic Mim couldn't manipulate.

He stepped up to the stone. He could feel the eyes of half the kingdom on him, watching breathlessly. Even more breathlessly, he realised, than on the first day he'd done it, when the sky had opened up and a ray of beautiful light had shone down on him with the sound of angels singing in the air.

Of course, there was a lot more at stake this time.

Arthur looked out into the excited crowd, catching sight of Guinevere, who had now appeared at the back row. He gave her a questioning look, and she nodded, ever so slightly, causing him to let out a breath of relief. Archimedes was safe. And Merlin was somewhere nearby. He wasn't alone.

He turned back to the sword. This was it; the moment of the truth. He wrapped his hands around the hilt, then gave the blade a tug. Gently at first – the last time he'd done it, the sword had slid out like a knife from hot butter, and he didn't want to fall backwards from using too much force. But this time it didn't give as easily, and so he put more strength into the attempt, yanking on it with all his might.

The heavens did not open with holy light.

There was no sound of angelic music.

The sword did not budge.

The crowd gasped. Arthur felt his face turn red. He pulled a third time, but it was no different. The sword was stuck fast. He glanced over at Guinevere, who gave him a helpless gesture. What was going on here?

He tried again.

Still nothing.

A fifth time!

Nothing.

Nothing.

Nothing.

The sword – his precious sword – was stuck in the stone. Just as it had been all those years before he'd acquired it.

The crowd seemed to deflate. They'd been rooting for him, he realised. On some level they seemed to believe his claim. Which was good, but not enough, if he couldn't prove it to them.

"M-maybe something's wrong," he stammered. "Maybe it's been too long. Or the magic has gone, since it already worked once."

"Maybe," Mim said, stepping forwards. "But do you mind if I give it a try?"

"Go ahead," Arthur said, feeling deflated. He tried to remind himself of what Merlin had said about the stone's magic – Mim wouldn't be able to manipulate it with her own. But he was starting to feel less confident about that. What if Merlin was wrong? Or Mim's power was actually greater than they knew?

Mim grandly stepped up to the stone and anvil, making a great show of the whole thing by waving her arms in the air. She turned to her audience and bowed low, giggled a little as she straightened, and then turned, reached down, and dramatically wrapped her hands around the hilt. She drew in a breath, then pulled on the sword.

The heavens opened.

Light shone down.

Heavenly music started to play.

And the sword easily slipped from the stone.

Arthur watched, horrified, hardly able to believe his eyes. She'd done it. Somehow she'd done it. She'd pulled the sword from the stone as if she had been born to do it.

As if she were truly England's destined king.

Mim raised the sword above her head in triumph. A few people in the crowd began clapping hesitantly, still not quite sure what they'd just witnessed. Arthur began to back away, but he was quickly stopped by two guards.

Mim's eyes settled on him. Her lips curled to a smile.

"Seize this traitor," she told the guards. "And send him to the dungeon."

The guards made a move towards Arthur. He scrambled away, trying to put distance between them, but was stopped by the thick crowd behind him, who inadvertently prevented his escape. His eyes darted around the churchyard with desperation. Where was Merlin? Now would be a good time for the wizard to show himself. To save the day! To poof Arthur to safety.

But the wizard was nowhere to be seen. Instead, it was

Guin who suddenly burst from the crowd, her hair flying behind her and her eyes wild. "No!" she cried. "No, please!"

"Guin—" Arthur protested in panic. He didn't want her to be arrested, too.

But Guin ignored him, stopping just in front of Arthur-Mim and crossing her arms in front of her chest. She glowered at the wizard. If looks could kill, Arthur thought wildly, Mim would be nothing more than a puddle on the ground.

"This needs to stop, Mother!" Guin cried. "Now!"

Wait, what? Arthur did a double take.

Mother? Had she just said… *mother*?

Suddenly everything froze, just as it had that day in the great hall when Mim had first come to Arthur as Morgan le Fay. Everyone in the audience – every commoner, noble and guard – completely stuck in place. The only other person still moving, Arthur realised, was Guinevere.

Mim laughed heartily. As Arthur watched in horror, her disguise seemed to melt away, revealing her old wild-purple-haired self. She strode over to Guinevere. When she reached her, she patted her lovingly on the arm. "Oh, my sweet girl," she clucked. "There's no need to pretend any more. It's all over now. You can rest. You did your job, and you did it marvellously. Better than I could have ever dreamt!" She grinned, showing off crooked grey teeth. "I'm so proud of you, my dear. I can't even begin to explain."

"W-wait, what?" Arthur stammered. "What is she talking about, Guin?"

Guin stumbled backwards, almost tripping over a gravestone in the process. Mim cackled loudly, sheathing Excalibur and setting it on the ground. Then she turned to Arthur.

"Oh, my poor little sparrow. Did you think she was on your side this whole time? How adorable is that? She really is a good actress, isn't she? Those pretty, wide brown eyes. Those long lashes. That sweet smile. You'd never know in a million years she was working for me."

"No." Arthur shook his head vehemently. "I don't believe it. You turned me into a slug. She saved me."

"All part of the plan. You would have never left the castle with her otherwise. Which was quite considerate of you, by the way – just walking away like that and handing me the keys to the kingdom?" She grinned toothily. "Though you probably shouldn't have come back. Then I wouldn't have had to kill you."

Arthur looked from her to Guinevere, his heart feeling as if it were about to shatter in his chest. "Is this true?" he demanded, his voice cracking on the words. "Is Mim really your foster mother? Did you befriend me only to try to take me down?"

He waited with bated breath, his eyes locked on her,

begging her to deny it all. To call Mim a liar of the worst sort. To assure him she would never betray his trust. She cared about him. She'd kissed him on the beach. That had to mean something, right?

But instead of denying it, her face only crumpled. The light seemed to die in her deep brown eyes.

"Guinevere?" Arthur tried again, his voice hitching on her name. "Please… tell me the truth."

"I'm sorry," she blurted out. "Mim lied to me. She told me you weren't meant to be on the throne. That it was Merlin's evil plan to destroy England." She trailed off, staring at the ground. "I thought I was doing a good thing."

Arthur staggered backwards, as if he'd been struck by a blade. And maybe that would have been better. Maybe that wouldn't have hurt half as much as Guinevere's words. The girl he'd trusted. The girl he'd shared everything with. The girl he'd fallen in love with.

And she had betrayed him utterly.

"Oh, don't look so glum!" Mim scolded, wagging a finger at Arthur. "She really is quite fond of you. She told me so herself. But that makes no difference now. For I'm afraid you're not going to live long enough to ever see her again."

"What are you going to do with me?" he asked, trying not to despair. At the moment, he wasn't sure if he even cared. He'd lost his kingdom, and he'd lost Guinevere. What did he have left?

"Throw you in the dungeon, of course," Mim replied breezily. "Weren't you listening earlier? And then we're going to throw a marvellous party and execute you in front of the entire kingdom in the morning. Won't that be lovely?" She nodded to herself. "Why, we can even have that Saxon king of yours done at the same time! Two for one! That's bound to sell a lot of tickets. Especially if we serve slug soup. This kingdom is woefully short of slug soup, don't you think, darling?" she asked, slinging her arm around Guinevere. The girl shrugged her off, storming to the other side of the churchyard. Mim watched her go for a moment, then giggled again.

"Anyway, this has been fun! But I really must go. I have a kingdom to run into the ground. Toodles!"

She snapped her fingers, shifting herself back into Arthur's twin. Then, turning to the crowd, she waved her arms, unfreezing them. Her guards burst to life and charged towards Arthur.

"Take this imposter away," Mim crowed as the two men grabbed Arthur's arms, pinning them behind him. "Throw him in the dungeon where he belongs!"

CHAPTER THIRTY-THREE
GUINEVERE

"Did I mention how proud of you I am, my pet?" Mim asked after the sword and the stone performance, dragging Guin back to Arthur's chambers, where they could be alone. Once she'd shut and locked the door, she poofed back into her old purple self, walked over to a nearby chair, kicked off her boots, and placed them on the table. The sweaty shoe smell made Guinevere's stomach turn. Which was quite a feat, considering how nauseated Guin already was from what had just transpired in the churchyard.

Her mind flashed back to Arthur's face. The look of betrayal deep in his blue eyes. The way he had gazed at her – as if she were some kind of monster. But then, was he really wrong? Because of her, he was about to lose everything – including his life. What monster could do worse than that?

"This is what you were planning from the start, wasn't it, Mother?" she accused, her voice still shaky as she planted her hands on her hips. "Merlin never wanted the throne to begin with. It was you all along. You wanted the power for yourself."

"Power? Don't be silly, my pet. Since when have I ever cared about power?" Mim spit out dismissively. "I *much* prefer chaos! Sweet, beautiful chaos! And thanks to you, I have it in spades! Arthur was so stuck on his law and order, and peace, and rules, and juries of his peers – such nonsense! So boring! But now! Now everything is so pleasantly unpleasant! And who knows what fun will happen next? Something truly gruesome and grim, if we're lucky! And I'll have a front-row seat to it all." She beamed at Guin. "And I couldn't have done it without you! Why, my dear, whatever can I do to repay you? Do you want a pony? I remember when you were little, all you wanted was a cute little polka-dotted pony."

"I don't want a pony," Guinevere snapped. "I want the truth. You've been lying to me my entire life, haven't you? Not just about this, but about everything. Even my parents!"

"Your parents?" Mim's smile faltered. "What about your parents?"

Guinevere clamped her mouth shut, realising perhaps she'd said too much. The only way she could have known about her parents was through Merlin, and Mim didn't know Merlin was back. If Guin had any hope for Arthur to be saved, she had to keep it that way. The truth about her parents would have to wait – Arthur's life depended on it.

"Nothing! It doesn't matter! Just stop these games! Let Arthur be king like he's meant to be!"

Mim laughed – actually laughed. "Oh! You're so cute when you're angry!" She reached out and tweaked Guin's cheek, as if she were a baby. "But I promise you, I'm not as terrible as you seem to think. Maybe I *did* make up the whole Merlin-putting-Arthur-on-the-throne thing. But that doesn't mean he's the destined king of legends, either. Why, in fact, he's nothing more than a random boy who happened to be in the wrong place at the right time."

"What?" Guinevere frowned, suddenly uneasy. "What are you talking about? Only the rightful king could pull the sword from the stone." But even as she said the words, she wondered. Arthur *hadn't* been able to pull the sword from the stone a second time. Which meant something wasn't right.

"The *real* sword in the stone, perhaps," Mim agreed cheerfully. "But I swapped that out ages ago. After all, we couldn't just have *anyone* become king of England. It's far too important of a job." Her eyes rested on Guin, bright and shiny. She looked far too pleased with herself. "I needed someone completely unqualified. Someone I could easily control. Someone like your dear sweet Arthur." She cackled.

So that's how she'd done it. Mim couldn't overpower the magic in the stone, so she'd replaced it entirely with a stone of her own. One with her own magic at its heart.

Guin remembered how angry she'd been when Mim had first told her about Merlin's alleged trickery. So indignant that anyone would try to twist the strands of fate to their favour. But it hadn't been Merlin. It had been Mim from the start.

"I don't understand," she said, her voice quavering. "If you somehow made Arthur king in the first place, why did you want to take him down?"

"Oh." Mim's mouth dipped to a frown. "Well, that was a bit of a miscalculation, you see. I had no idea at the time Arthur was Merlin's protégé and that he would have all sorts of ridiculous ideas in his head because of it. Of course, by then, it was far too late to pick someone else, so I had to get creative."

Guinevere squeezed her hands into fists. "Creative? You tried to kill him!"

"I did nothing of the sort!" Mim blustered, looking offended. "He could have happily lived out his life as a giant slug. Slugs can live about six years, you know.

And they can have up to twenty-seven thousand teeth! Imagine all the lovely dinners you could chew up with those. Why, it would have been a quite pleasant existence for the lad, if you ask me! He should have been thanking me for the privilege!"

"Mother—"

"But evidently *you* couldn't accept that. So *you* took him away from the castle. Not me! Which left a glaring vacancy on the throne of England. I mean, what was I supposed to do if not waltz into the place and stand in for him to keep things going in his absence? In fact, no one batted an eye. Even when I ripped up that ridiculous treaty with the Saxons." She giggled, then sighed. "Of course I was worried at first that you wouldn't come back, either. I would have missed you dreadfully, you know. No one to play cards with or dance with. It would have been so sad. But now you're back! And everything is as it should be. Or will be, anyway, once we rid ourselves of that pesky little sparrow for good."

Guinevere drew in a shaky breath, her heart aching in her chest. This was all her fault. And Arthur would never forgive her for it. Why, oh, why hadn't she told him the truth about who she was from the start? Or at least once she realised her mother might be up to no good. It would have been hard for him to take, but at least the words coming from her own mouth could be seen as a confession, rather than a betrayal. Instead, she'd kept silent, too afraid of what he might think, hoping her dark secret would stay buried forever.

But secrets always came out in the end. She should have known that.

"So about that pony!" Mim added cheerfully. "Purple spots or pink?"

"I told you – I don't want a pony!" Guin shot back, her voice cracking on the words. "I don't want anything from you ever again!"

"Oh, fine!" Mim rolled her eyes. "Be glum and gloomy if you must! But I won't let you rain on my parade! I'm still your mother! And I'm grounding you until your attitude improves!"

"What?" Guinevere startled. "What do you mean, grounding me?"

Mim raised her hand in Guin's direction and muttered something under her breath. Guin felt a tug inside of her, like something was being yanked out. She clutched her stomach, confused.

"What are you doing?" she demanded.

"It's for your own good," Mim declared, standing on her tiptoes to kiss Guinevere's cheek. "Goodbye, my darling. I love you, and I'll see you soon."

And with that, she flounced towards the door, stepped out, and slammed it shut behind her.

A moment later Guin heard a loud click.

Mim had locked her in.

CHAPTER THIRTY-FOUR
GUINEVERE

Guinevere looked around the room, her heart pounding. For a moment, she felt paralysed in place. Then she sprang into action, running to the window – the same window she'd come through as a bird to rescue Arthur from life as a slug. Now her only possible escape.

Did Mim really think she could keep her here? That Guin wouldn't just shapeshift and fly away? The wizard might have won the battle, but as long as Guinevere had breath in her body, she would not concede the war. She would not let Arthur suffer or die on her account. She'd saved him twice.

Third time would have to be the charm.

She drew in a breath, reaching inside of herself to draw

up the magic she needed for a shapeshifting spell. But to her surprise, she couldn't find it. It was as if there was a well inside of her, and it had been thoroughly depleted.

Panic flooded her. No. That wasn't possible. She tried again.

Nothing.

It was then that she remembered the tug she'd felt just before Mim left. The feeling of something leaving her body. Had it been her reserves of magic? Had Mim stolen them out from under her?

And without magic, what could she do?

She looked out the window again, trying to fight the sinking sensation in her stomach. She couldn't fly, but maybe she could climb down somehow. The roof was steep, but if she took some of the blankets from the bed, she could tie them together and make a rope…

It didn't seem like a good idea. But it was the only one she had.

She ran to the bed and grabbed the blankets; she twisted each one and tied them at their ends, then snaked them out the window. The makeshift rope grew longer as she worked, but soon she was out of blankets – and the ground was still too far from the end of the rope for comfort. If she tried to jump, she'd likely break her bones.

But what choice did she have? She couldn't stay up here and simply wait around for Arthur to be killed by Mim.

Oh, Arthur, she thought. *I'm so sorry.*

She closed her eyes, trying to gather her courage. She thought of Arthur facing that wolf, deep in the woods of the Forest Sauvage. He'd been afraid, too. But he'd faced his fears. To save her.

Now it was her turn to do the same.

She opened her eyes, tied up her dress to her thighs, and started to climb out the window. But just as she was about to swing her leg over the sill, she felt a giant shove in the opposite direction, sending her barrelling back into the room.

"Argh!" she cried as she hit the floor hard, seeing stars. "What are you doing?"

A new voice rose into the room. "I should probably be asking you the same thing."

Guinevere looked up, heart stuttering. A towering shape stood silhouetted in the light streaming in from the window. For a split second, she thought it was Mim again, foiling her escape plan. But then she realised the shape was too tall, too narrow, too pointy-hatted to be her.

"Merlin!" she cried, her voice croaking with relief.

All her life, Guin had been deathly afraid of the wizard. Yet now he was the most welcome sight in the world.

She collapsed on the floor, breathing heavily and telling herself everything would be all right: Merlin was here.

Merlin stepped further into the room, looking down at her with a grumpy look in his eyes. "What in heaven's name did you think you were doing?" he demanded gruffly. "You could have fallen to your death, for goodness' sake. Not very wise, I must say."

She hung her head. "I know," she said. "But I didn't know what else to do. Mim locked me in, and I had to get out to help Arthur."

She watched as Archimedes flew through the window, hooting at her angrily. "Help Arthur?" he repeated scornfully. "Why, from what I understand, you're the reason he's in this mess to begin with! The poor lad! Why, Merlin should have left you in the twenty-first century! Or the twenty-second – which, by all accounts, is far worse!"

"Now, Archimedes," Merlin scolded. "Give the poor girl a break. We all make mistakes." He reached down and held out a hand. Guinevere took it, and he pulled her to her feet, then walked her over to a nearby chair and helped her settle into it. Waving his hand, he conjured up a steaming pot of tea, complete with a little sugar dish, on the table beside her.

Guinevere looked at the wizard gratefully. She couldn't believe she'd once thought him evil. Instead, he was kind and good. Perhaps better than she deserved.

"He's right," she said, giving Archimedes a rueful look. "I've made mistakes. I won't deny that. But you have to understand why." She sighed. "I grew up with Mim. And my whole life, she told me that *you* were the evil one. That you killed my parents and tried to kill me."

Merlin huffed. "That's the most ridiculous thing I ever heard! Whyever would I want something like that? Your parents are lovely people. Why, your mother once knitted me the nicest jumper you ever did see. And you certainly don't kill people who knit you nice jumpers."

"I suppose not," Guin agreed. "But I didn't know that at the time. And so when she told me I was England's only hope to save the realm, I thought I was doing something good and just." She hung her head. "It wasn't until I met Arthur and saw what a good person he is that I realised I might be fighting for the wrong side."

"Brilliant conclusion," Archimedes hooted. "Too bad you didn't think of it sooner."

"Now, now, Archimedes," Merlin scolded the owl again. "Let's not be rude. This girl clearly has seen the light." He peered at her with watery but sharp blue eyes. "Why, I think she cares for the boy. And I can only assume she wants to help us set things right."

"I *do* care about Arthur," Guin admitted. "And I don't want anything bad to happen to him. I also don't want anything to happen to England. I'm prepared to do whatever I can to help – even if it costs me my own life," she added bravely.

"Well, hopefully it won't come to that," Merlin replied. "But I do admire your courage. And your affection for our boy. Love is a powerful thing, you know. Perhaps the most powerful force in the universe."

Love. Guinevere startled on the word. Did she love Arthur? She wasn't even sure she understood the feeling. The only person she thought she'd ever loved before was Mim. And look how that had turned out.

But Arthur – that feeling was different. So different. Maybe it was love. Just a different sort.

"So what do we do?" she asked. "How do we rescue Arthur?"

To her surprise, Merlin shook his head. "We don't."

"What?" Guinevere cried before she could stop herself. "He's in prison. Mim's sentenced him to death for treason. He's to be killed in the morning!"

"Yes, I am well aware," Merlin said, pacing the room. "But if we simply go rescue him, we'll be right back exactly where we started. Otherwise I would have saved him in the churchyard. But it wouldn't have done any good."

"Except, of course, Arthur wouldn't be in prison," she ventured. "So, that'd be good, right?"

"Yes, yes, of course. But don't worry. It's only temporary. And I promise you, that sorceress won't be able to harm a hair on his head," Merlin assured her impatiently. "But in the meantime, we must find a way to expose Mim's treachery to the people. That's the only way to be rid of her for good."

"How do we do that?"

Archimedes hooted. "He was hoping you'd know. That's why we're here."

"Me?" She blinked, surprised.

Merlin nodded vigorously. "After all, you grew up with the woman. You know her better than anyone else. If anyone knows a weakness, it would be you."

She frowned. That made sense, of course. But what was Mim's weakness? She'd never thought about that before. Mim had always seemed so strong. So powerful.

"Is there something she cares about?" Merlin pressed. "Something that would upset her to lose. Or startle her. Or scare her, even."

"I'm… not sure," Guinevere mumbled, hating the look of disappointment that followed her words. Archimedes huffed and fluffed his feathers.

"I told you this was a mistake," he muttered.

"No!" Guin cried. "I can help. I'm sure I can. Just…" She thought hard, fast. "Why don't I go back to Mim's cottage?" she suggested, her words coming in a rush. "She might have left something there. Something we can use. She has diaries, too. She's always kept them in her room. Maybe there's some clue there."

Merlin stroked his beard. "Yes," he agreed. "That sounds very practical. Except for the fact that the cottage is quite far away. Sure, I can zap you to the Forest Sauvage, but it will take you a very long time to get back again. Time we don't have."

"Actually, it won't," Guinevere corrected. "Mim poofed our cottage to the outskirts of town just before Arthur became king. Now it's not far at all." She thought for a moment. "Do you know where the well is just outside of town? If you can get me there, I can make it the rest of the way on my own."

"I can certainly do that," Merlin agreed, looking relieved. "And while you're gone, I will go see the boy. He's got to be terrified at this point, and I don't want him to think we've abandoned him."

"And what about me?" Archimedes asked.

Merlin smiled. "Don't worry. I have an important errand for you," he told the bird. "But first, let's get our girl on her way." He waved his hand, reciting the magic words. Guinevere drew in a breath, preparing herself for another teleportation. She hoped this one wouldn't leave her with a huge headache. Still, she supposed, even that would be better than climbing down a tower holding on to nothing but blankets.

"Good luck!" Archimedes chirped just as Merlin was about to finish his spell. "Don't fail us!"

I won't, she thought as she poofed into thin air. And she meant it, too. Maybe more than anything else in her life. This was her one chance to make things right.

She wasn't about to waste it.

CHAPTER THIRTY-FIVE
ARTHUR

Arthur paced his small dungeon cell, his stomach churning with unease. He'd lost track of how long he'd been stuck here – there were no windows to give him any clues. The place smelt like overripe fruit, and there was nowhere to sit down except the cold hard floor. There wasn't even a bed, just a thin pile of straw in the corner, probably covered in fleas.

This was not good. Not good at all.

Oh, Merlin, he thought. *Where are you? Why didn't you save me like you promised?*

He'd been so sure the wizard would appear as the guards dragged him away, to make a dramatic rescue and take him somewhere safe. But the wizard never appeared. Arthur hoped nothing had happened to him.

His heart squeezed as his mind flashed back to the scene in the churchyard. The moment he hadn't been able to get out of his head. When he'd learnt the truth about Guin and her mother. What she'd been sent to do, under the guise of friendship.

She hadn't even tried to deny it.

His stomach heaved. He was close to throwing up, his mind torturing him with the memory of that Bermuda beach in the future, of Guin's lips brushing against his and him feeling as if he would live forever.

But no. It had all been a lie. Every sweet look, every embrace. A vile lie to help take him down so an evil wizard could ascend the throne in his place.

So Mim could pull the sword from the stone.

How had she done it? There was only one way he could think of: she had to have replaced the real stone with her own. One that her magic could control. But how had she known to do it in time for the challenge? And why did it appear exactly as it had the day he'd pulled out the sword the first time?

Not that it mattered how she'd done it. Just that she had.

Leaving Arthur looking like a liar in front of the kingdom.

He sank to the ground, no longer caring about the cold floor. He scrubbed his face with his hands. "What am I to do?" he wailed.

"Who's there?" asked a gruff voice from the next cell. Arthur lifted his head blearily. It sounded vaguely familiar.

"It's me, Arthur," he said. "Who are you?"

"Arthur?" Suddenly there was a man on the other side of the bars. Arthur gasped to realise it was none other than Baldomar, the Saxon king. "Why are you down here with the rest of us?" he scoffed, his voice filled with scorn. "Aren't you busy breaking your word and treaties?"

"That wasn't me," Arthur cried. "I'd never do that." He sighed. "It's kind of a long story. Let's just say I might have won the battle with Kay, but I have lost the war for my crown."

"As have I, lad," King Baldomar replied, pacing his small cell. "I'm told they're to execute me tomorrow. Which is fine, I suppose. I don't want to go home anyway. They'd never accept me after how I've failed them."

"You didn't fail them," Arthur protested. "I did." He closed his eyes. "And I'm sorry."

"So that's it?" King Baldomar asked. "You're sorry? You're done? You're content to die like me tomorrow?"

"No, of course not," Arthur said, feeling suddenly ashamed. He scrambled to his feet. "I don't plan to die," he assured him. "Merlin will save me." He paused, then added, "He will save *us*."

"Merlin? Is he one of your knights?"

"He's a wizard, actually. And very powerful," came a new voice from behind Arthur. Arthur whirled around to find a man dressed in ragged beggar's robes, stooped over a cane. Arthur frowned, confused. Then he caught a flash of sparkling blue under the robe's hood: eyes he'd recognise anywhere.

He ran to the front of his cell, grasping the bars with his hands. "Merlin!" he cried. "Where have you been?"

"Shh!" the wizard scolded. "Do you want to wake the whole prison? I'm in disguise, in case you didn't notice."

"Sorry," Arthur whispered. But his heart soared. Finally, he was here! Arthur had never been so happy to see someone in his entire life. "You've come to rescue us, right?" he asked, gesturing to the Saxon king. His heart beat fast.

But to his surprise, the wizard only shook his head.

Arthur's heart stuttered. "You mean you can only rescue *me*?" he asked, tossing an apologetic look at the Saxon king.

"Actually, I can't rescue anyone. At least not at the moment."

"What?" Arthur let go of the bars. "What do you mean

you can't rescue anyone? Turn me into a mouse, like you did in Bermuda! Or a squirrel or a bird, even! Just something small enough to let me slip through these bars and escape. It'll be easy!" he added, hating the desperation he heard in his voice. "Just use your magic."

"Sorry. I suppose I misspoke," Merlin said, clearing his throat. "Yes, I *could* stage a magical rescue – I certainly have the powers to do so. But I'm choosing not to."

"*This* is your big hero?" The Saxon king raised an eyebrow.

"I don't understand," Arthur said, ignoring him. "Don't you care that I'm about to die?"

"Of course I do!" Merlin huffed, looking a bit offended. "And I'd never let anything happen to you – you must know that. You just need to have a little patience. After all, a magical rescue now will solve nothing. You'll just be arrested again, and we'll be back where we started. Even if you did manage to escape somehow, you'd never be able to take back the throne. Which means Mim would remain in power – and that would be a disaster of epic proportions. No." Merlin shook his head, his beard waving from side to side. "We must be smart about this. We can't act rashly. The magic will help when the time is right – and no sooner."

Arthur took a step backwards, feeling defeated. He didn't

want to admit Merlin was right, but his words made an unfortunate amount of sense.

"So what's the plan?" he asked.

"Well," Merlin said, "first we need Guinevere to return. And then—"

"Guinevere?" Arthur interrupted. "You can't trust her! She betrayed me! She was on Mim's side from the start."

"From the start, yes," Merlin agreed amicably. "But I have reason to believe she's changed."

"Bah," Arthur spit out, pacing his cell. He didn't want to admit to Merlin how much Guinevere had hurt him. He was sure the wizard could never understand. "I don't want her help!"

"If you want to live, you do," Merlin scolded. "Didn't you learn anything from our lesson?"

Arthur sighed, leaning against the side of his cell, the fight going out of him. "Which one?" he asked, feeling exhausted.

Merlin rolled his eyes. "The one about love, of course! How love is the most powerful force on earth."

"Love?" Arthur glanced over at the wizard, his heart thudding. "What about love?"

Even as he asked, his mind flashed back to the lesson in question: the time Merlin had turned them into squirrels, and he'd met a red-headed girl squirrel who'd started chasing him around the tree. At first, he'd found her incredibly irritating. But in the end, she'd saved his life.

Because she loved him.

That love business is a powerful thing, Merlin had said.

Arthur's head shot up. "Does… Guinevere love me?" he asked, his voice hoarse.

Merlin burst out laughing. "Of course she does, silly boy! You'd have to be blind not to see it."

"Wow," he said, feeling his head spin. "I had no idea."

"Guinevere made some mistakes, yes. But she's always had good intentions. And she truly does want to help. Which is lucky for us, since she's the only one in the right position to do so." He shook his head.

Arthur sighed. "This is all such a mess. Sometimes I wish I never pulled the sword from the stone to begin with. Then none of this would have happened."

"And then some clod like Kay would have been our king after the tournament," Merlin reminded him. "That wouldn't have been ideal, either, if you think about it." He brushed a spider off his beard. "If only we had democracy. But I suppose that won't be introduced here for hundreds of years."

"De-mah-cracy?" Arthur repeated doubtfully. "What's that?"

"Oh." Merlin waved a hand. "It's a government they have in the future. People get to choose their leaders by voting for them. It's more civilised than a tournament. And much smarter than just letting someone pull a blade from a stone."

Arthur considered this for a moment. "That does sound—"

But his words were interrupted by the banging of a door. The guards were on their way back. Merlin waved a hand.

"I have to go! I'll see you tomorrow. And be ready for anything!"

And with that, he poofed out of the room, leaving only a cloud of smoke behind. A moment later, the guards stepped into the room, looking around suspiciously.

"I thought I heard talking," one of them said.

"Yes, I was speaking to my friend King Baldomar," Arthur assured them.

"We were having a lovely conversation on the joys of love," the king added cheerfully. He beamed at the guards. "Has either of you two ever been in love?"

The guards looked at one another and grunted, then stormed out of the room again. Arthur glanced over at King Baldomar and smiled. He smiled back.

"You think this plan of Merlin's will work?" Baldomar asked.

"I hope so," Arthur replied. "Because it's the only chance we've got."

CHAPTER THIRTY-SIX
GUINEVERE

Guinevere looked around. Her head was spinning, and she felt a little sick to her stomach. But she was no longer trapped in a tower, so there was that. Merlin's magic had worked. She was at the well, not too far from her mother's cottage.

Her eyes fell upon the stone well in question, and she felt her heart ache a little. She thought back to the last time she'd drawn water from this well, when she'd been talking to a very nice boy she'd just met about becoming a bird. If only she'd known at that moment all that was in store for the two of them. She wondered if she wouldn't have just turned them both into birds right then and there and convinced Arthur to fly away forever.

Oh, Arthur, she thought. *I hope someday you can forgive me.*

She shook her head. There was no time for these thoughts. Arthur was depending on her, and she couldn't let him down. She took off down the path, fast as her legs would carry her, until she arrived at the cottage and burst through the door as she had so often done in the past, when she'd greet her mother with a cheery smile. Not a care in the world.

Of course, today, Mim was not at her favourite table, playing her favourite game of cards. The cards were still there, but they were covered in a thick layer of dust. So was everything else in the place. It was clear Mim hadn't been here in months. But then, why would she come back to these humble surroundings? She had a castle now. She'd stolen a kingdom.

Guin looked around the cottage, feeling an unexpected ache in her throat. Memories came flooding back, uninvited, of all the nights she'd spent playing games at the same table, laughing as Mim would try to use magic to cheat. Or the times they'd clear the table away to create a dance floor. Or curl up by the fire and tell stories. The two of them against the world.

But it had been nothing more than a lie.

Guin shook her head. She couldn't think of that now. It hurt too much and would only prove a distraction.

And she couldn't afford to be distracted – not while Arthur was in danger.

She forced herself to turn away from their game table and all the memories it contained. Instead, she headed back to Mim's bedroom, where she kept her diaries hidden away. Mim had never liked Guin coming back to her room, saying she needed her private space. But there was no one to stop Guin now.

The bedroom was messy and also covered in dust. There were bookcases rising high, not unlike Merlin's in his tower, filled with books and vials and beakers, potions and herbs. Guin supposed whether you were a bad wizard or a good one, you used the same supplies.

She located the shelf with the diaries easily enough, grabbing one at random and paging through it. The book was filled with rants and raves and prophecies and recipes for disturbing-sounding diseases, all scrawled in messy handwriting across the pages without regard for margins. There were drawings, too: sick and twisted figures and animals with too many heads or legs.

Guin set the book down, feeling sick to her stomach. How had she not seen the signs? How had she not known her mother's mind? Mim had always been a bit odd, almost childlike in her naughty behaviour. But in a harmless, fun way. Guinevere had no idea how deep her foster mother's madness truly ran.

She didn't want to read any more, but she knew she had no choice. Arthur needed her to find something – anything – to help him. And so she forced herself to pick up another book, then another. The diaries were not filed by date, and even inside, they were not always in any obvious order. There were scraps of spells, purple doodles, bad poetry. But here and there she found actual entries – some of them distinctly about her.

One caused her breath to catch in her throat.

Those fools! They have no idea what they've lost. She is a treasure. A true princess of the Summer Country, born of fae blood with all the gifts it entails. And now she is mine! All mine – to mould as I wish. Why, she will become the most powerful wizard in the world under my tutelage.

Guinevere drew in a breath. And there it was. The proof she'd been dreading all along. Mim had stolen her away, just as Merlin said. She had purposely taken Guin from a loving family, making them think she was dead. All for her own selfish purposes.

Anger rose inside of her, her blood feeling as if it were boiling under her skin. She thought of all the stories she'd been told. Mim always played the role of hero, defeating Merlin and saving Guin's life.

It was too much. Far too much. All she wanted to do was collapse into tears. To surrender to the grief and curl into bed and fall into a deep sleep and never wake up. But instead she forced herself to open yet another book. Turn to yet another page. And another…

Guinevere hurt her arm today, falling from a tree. She screamed so loudly, I thought at first she had broken her neck! I was so worried…

Guinevere keeps asking to go to town with me. She wants to meet other children her own age. But of course I can't risk it – what if someone recognised her? They'd try to take her away from me forever! Maybe I can conjure up some magical children for her to play with…

Guinevere continues to be afraid of magic. I don't understand it. She would be the most amazing wizard if she just gave it a try. But I won't try to push her too much. She has to want it.

Page after page about Guin. But little she could use to help Arthur. In fact, Mim spoke practically nothing of herself as she rambled on about her daughter. She didn't reveal any weaknesses. She didn't confess any fears. In fact, Mim didn't seem to care about anything at all.

Well, except me, Guin supposed, finding yet another entry. Somehow, despite the sick and twisted origin of their relationship, Mim *did* seem to care about her.

She turned to the last page of the diary.

I can't believe it. I sent Guinevere in to help me get Arthur off the throne and what has she done? She's gone and fallen in love with the boy! In fact, she's sided with him and that blasted Merlin, over her dear sweet mother. After all we've been through together. After all I sacrificed for her. Doesn't that mean anything to her at all? What happened to me and her against the world?

Guin bit her lower lip, her mind suddenly churning. This was it. This was exactly it. Her mother's one weakness. The one thing that might be strong enough to take her down.

But would it work?

She set down the book and rose to her feet. She had to find Merlin. *Now.*

CHAPTER THIRTY-SEVEN
ARTHUR

Arthur awoke in his cell the next morning, his muscles aching from sleeping on the small, flea-ridden pile of hay the dungeon considered a bed. He hadn't slept well, to say the least, though it turned out the cold, hard stone floor of his cell had been the least of his problems. Rather, it was his mind that had kept him awake, refusing to settle, replaying over and over what was meant to happen that day.

Namely, his execution.

He'd tried to stay optimistic. Merlin had sworn he had a plan – and Arthur did believe him. The problem was, that plan appeared to hinge largely on the girl responsible for his being in this situation in the first place. Merlin seemed to think Guinevere had changed, but what if she was still playing her games – still secretly on Mim's side? Wouldn't that be the best trick of all? To convince them that she would help save Arthur, only to undermine them completely and carry out her mother's wishes in the end?

But no, Merlin had insisted she was on their side now. That she had been deceived, but now she knew the truth. That she loved Arthur, and she would do whatever it took to keep him safe.

Arthur wanted to believe it. In fact, there was nothing he wanted to believe more. Because, he realised, he loved her, too. Her smile, her laugh, the way her brown eyes sparkled. Surely all that couldn't have been faked, right? If so, she was the best actor of them all.

And Arthur, the biggest fool.

The jailer approached his cell, rapping on the bars with a metal pole. "Get up, Your Majesty," he jeered. "It's time." Then he approached the Saxon king in the next cell. "You too, barbarian."

Arthur rose to his feet, feeling his heartbeat quicken. He stole a glance at King Baldomar, who shrugged and gave him a hopeful look. The jailer unlocked the cell doors and opened them wide. Four soldiers stepped up behind him, ready to escort their prisoners aboveground.

To their awaiting deaths.

They were chained together, then led upstairs, through

the castle keep, and into the courtyard outside. A stage had been set up since Arthur had last walked through it, and on top were matching pyres of wood.

A crowd had already gathered around the stage, watching the scene with nervous eyes. He could tell they were still unsure about what was going on. And they didn't like it one bit. Arthur even noted Mistress Mabel near the back, cradling Helen of Troy. When she caught sight of him, she gave him a worried look, her face torn with confusion.

The guards roughly led him onto the stage and tied him to the pile of sticks. He glanced over at King Baldomar, who was not faring much better on his pyre. The king wore a look of grim determination, showing not even a hint of fear. Arthur had no idea what his own face looked like at the moment, but he could guess it wasn't so noble or brave. Though who could blame him? He wasn't a warrior, used to hard battles like the king. He was a just a boy.

A boy who would soon be dead if Merlin and Guinevere didn't come through.

The crowd hushed as Mim stepped out from the castle far above, standing high on a balcony, overlooking the scene below. She was wearing robes of purple with ermine trim and a crown that she must have commissioned herself – for it fit her Arthur-shaped head perfectly. She surveyed the courtyard, her gaze roving over Arthur's subjects, a mischievous look in her eyes. She was enjoying the spectacle, that was for sure.

Arthur, meanwhile, searched the crowd, looking for Merlin. Or Archimedes. Or Guinevere, even. Someone – anyone – to give him a hint that this grand rescue was actually about to happen. But he saw no familiar faces at all. Where were they? Were they hiding nearby? Did they have a plan?

"Good morning, my lovelies," Mim called out from her balcony in a perfect replica of Arthur's voice. Though somehow she made it sound stronger and more in control than his typically childish squeaks. "So nice to see you up so early. Are you ready to watch us execute two traitors who conspired against England and planned to turn it over to our enemies?" She clapped her hands in glee. "Won't that be so much fun?"

Arthur could see King Baldomar roll his eyes at this. He couldn't blame him. The bigger question was, how could the crowd actually believe this was him? He'd never talk like that!

And she wasn't finished, either. "This naughty boy," she added, gesturing to Arthur below, "is accused of using sorcery to take on my appearance and try to trick you into believing he was me. But now we know the truth.

The sword in the stone proved it once again in front of everyone, revealing his deception!"

King Baldomar scowled at the crowd. "This boy here in front of you has more strength of character in his little finger than the lot of you do together. And you are all fools if you need a silly sword pulled from a stone to see his worth."

Arthur felt a swell of pride at the king's words. Not that they would do any good, but it was nice to hear them, anyway. And Baldomar was right, too, he realised. Whether the sword in the stone was a true miracle or just a trick, it should not be the only benchmark to one becoming king. A king should have to earn his place by his actions and the love of his people, not through some silly divine intervention that could be easily falsified by magic.

He scanned the crowd again, biting his lower lip. Speaking of magic, where was Merlin? He was certainly taking his time. Whatever rescue he had planned, he'd better hurry up about it, or there would be no one left to rescue.

"Kill them!" cried someone in the crowd. "Light them up!"

Mim smiled like a cat who had just eaten a mouse. "Very well," she said. "If you insist." She clapped her hands. A moment later, a man stepped onto the stage, wearing an executioner's hood to hide his face. He carried a lit torch.

Arthur cringed as he stepped closer to the two pyres. Whom would he light up first? Arthur didn't exactly want to volunteer for the honour – but he also wasn't eager for a front-row ticket to his new friend's murder.

He turned to the crowd. "Please!" he begged. "You're being deceived. Even if you don't care to save my life, please try to save your own. She will tear England apart if you let her. Don't be fooled by her treachery."

Mim yawned. "This is boring," she jeered. "Let's get on with the show!" She motioned to the executioner. He stepped closer to the pyres. The smoke from his torch tickled Arthur's nose, and he fought the urge to sneeze. He didn't have much time left.

Come on, Merlin!

"Wait!" A voice rang out from the crowd. For a second, Arthur thought it must be Merlin. But instead, it was Guinevere who stepped out from the throng. She scrambled up onto the stage, her face filled with defiance and not a hint of fear.

Arthur looked up towards Mim, just in time to see her face turn white. "What are you doing?" she demanded. "I mean – who is this girl?" she corrected quickly. "Get her off the stage!"

"You know very well who I am," Guinevere replied, planting her hands on her hips. "I am the girl who conspired with this boy to take you down. I am here now to turn myself in. I am as guilty as they are and should be made to pay for my crimes in the same manner."

"Guin!" Arthur cried, horrified. "What are you doing?"

But Guin ignored him and marched over to the pyre. She climbed up onto it, behind Arthur, and pressed her back against the wood. The crowd rumbled nervously, not sure what was going on. Mim's face had turned a peculiar shade of purple. She raised her hands and flung them out towards the audience. For a moment, everyone froze in place. But then, just as quickly, they stuttered to life again. As if the spell had fizzled.

Or someone had broken it.

Arthur gasped. Was Merlin here?

Mim scowled. She tried to freeze the crowd again. But they unfroze just as easily. A hum began to rise from the courtyard. The people were starting to catch on that something was happening to them, and they didn't like it.

The executioner stepped up to the pyre, raising his torch.

"No!" Mim cried. "Stop! I order you to stop!"

"Goodbye, Mother," Guinevere said simply, meeting her mother's eyes with her own. "I hope this has been fun for you. That's what you wanted, right? A little fun?"

"Guinevere! Step away from there! Stop it – you monster – don't burn her!"

The executioner ignored her, lowering his torch. As the flames licked at the wood, his cloak slipped a bit from his face. Arthur gasped.

It was Merlin!

"No!" Mim's voice took on a desperate tone. She waved her hands at the pyre, but whatever magic she was trying to do clearly wasn't working against Merlin's own. "Stop this! Now!"

Smoke began to rise in the air. Guin started to cough. Arthur's eyes stung. Whatever was supposed to happen had better happen soon, or—

"ROAR!"

Arthur looked up, squinting to see through the smoke. When his eyes fell to the balcony, he realised the fake King Arthur had disappeared.

And in his place? A giant purple dragon.

CHAPTER THIRTY-EIGHT
GUINEVERE

The crowd gasped, their eyes on the dragon. Guinevere smiled to herself even as tears slipped down her cheeks from the smoky air. It had worked! Mim had taken the bait, as Guinevere had hoped she would. To save Guinevere – the one thing she cared about in this world – she had given herself away.

A moment later, Guin found herself flying through the air, having been scooped up in Mim's new claws. The dragon deposited her safely on the balcony above, then peered at her with angry eyes.

"Why would you do that?" she asked, her voice filled with confusion and hurt. For a moment, Guin almost felt bad. But then she looked down at the scene below, reminding herself what this woman had done.

"Because, Mother, this isn't right. This isn't fun and games any more. This is someone's life. And maybe you don't care about Arthur. But I do. I care about him. And if you ever cared at all about me, you'll stop this game right now." She swallowed hard. "If you do, I'll ask Arthur to show mercy."

For a moment, Mim said nothing. And Guin dared to hope that maybe, on some level, she'd agree. But then her gaze dropped to the scene below – Merlin had freed Arthur and the Saxon king from their pyres and was now directing the people to pass buckets of water up to the stage to put out the fires.

Mim's dragon face twisted in rage. "No!" she growled. "Because then that cheating wizard will win again. I cannot stand for that! Not after the last time."

"Mother," Guin pleaded. "Who cares about—"

But she was too late. Mim turned on the spot – graceful, actually, for her gigantean size. Then, as Guinevere watched in horror, she dive-bombed towards the ground below, releasing purple flames from her mouth.

"Arthur!" Guinevere called in panic. "Look out!"

Arthur looked up just in time to see the flames barrelling towards him. He dived to the left, but it wasn't enough to avoid the fire. At the last instant, Merlin leapt in front of him, shapeshifting into a giant salamander and shielding his pupil. The flames bounced harmlessly off his slimy back, causing Mim to roar again in fury. Guinevere gripped the railing of the balcony, her knuckles turning white. She wanted to help, but what could she do from up here? Her mother wasn't just going to give up without a fight.

It was then that she noticed the sword, Excalibur – the one Arthur had been wearing the day they'd met. The one he'd pulled from the stone. Mim must have left it behind when she shapeshifted into a dragon, which gave Guinevere an idea.

It might have all been a trick – but it was a real sword. Maybe it would still be of some use.

"Arthur!" she called down to him. As he looked up, she tossed the sword off the balcony. He ran to catch it, grabbing it easily as it fell to the earth. Then he ripped it from its sheath just as Mim dived towards him for another attack. As Guin watched, breathless, he launched Excalibur at the dragon with all his might. The throw was a bit wobbly, but it did the trick, knocking Madam Mim backwards with its force and breaking her spell.

Mim screamed, falling out of her shapeshifted form. She crashed to the ground, her old purple-haired body tumbling over itself three times before settling. Before she could sit up on her own, King Baldomar stalked over to her, grabbed her by the scruff of the neck, and yanked her to her feet.

Merlin turned to the crowd.

"As you can see, this is not your King Arthur," he announced, perhaps unnecessarily, as it was pretty obvious at this point. "May I introduce you to Madam Mim. She's the one who's the true traitor to the realm."

The crowd booed loudly, looking relieved to finally have some evidence in Arthur's favour. A few threw pieces of rotted fruit at Mim's head. Mim glowered at Merlin as apple juice streamed down her rosy cheeks.

"I was just having some fun," she muttered.

"Your days of *fun* are over, sorceress," came a new voice. "I shall personally see to that."

Guinevere's eyes shifted to the crowd, trying to find the source of the voice. A moment later, a strange woman pushed her way through the throng and stepped up onto the stage. She was dressed in silver robes, and her hair fell down her back in tangles of golden curls. She looked strangely familiar, though Guin was also pretty sure she'd never seen her before.

At least not for a very, very long time.

"You, madam, are under arrest for kidnapping a royal princess of the Summer Country," the woman stated.

She clapped her hands, and a squadron of guards appeared in line behind her. But she did not take her eyes off Mim. "You will be tried for treason and be made to answer for your crimes against my country." She turned to King Baldomar. "And for those against yours, as well, sir, if you agree."

The Saxon king bowed his head in her direction. "I thank you for that. Any allies of Arthur's are allies of ours."

"Indeed," Arthur said, patting the king on the back. "We are all in agreement on this matter. Now go and free your men from the dungeons. They have suffered enough."

King Baldomar gave him a grateful look and headed towards the dungeons. Guinevere watched him go for a moment, then turned back to the woman standing before her. She felt her knees wobble. She stared at the woman, tears streaming down her cheeks. "Mother?" she called out in a hesitant voice. "Is that… you?"

The woman's eyes lifted to the balcony. Her jaw dropped. Her hands trembled.

"Guinevere?" She said it as a whisper, but Guin could hear her as well as if she'd been shouting. "Oh, my darling girl!"

Suddenly, Guin felt herself floating; Merlin had created a magical bubble that picked her up and pulled her gently to the ground. Her feet had barely touched down when she found herself running towards her mother, throwing her arms around her, and squeezing her tight. Her mother squeezed her back just as hard. And Guin felt for a moment as if her heart would burst.

"Oh, sweet girl," her mother murmured, stroking her hair. "I'm so sorry for all you've been through. When Archimedes came and told me, I almost couldn't believe it." She shook her head. "All these years… I thought you were dead."

"I thought you were, too," Guin sniffled. "I—"

"Guinevere!" Mim's voice cut through the air like a knife. Guin turned to see the old wizard on her knees, her hands tied behind her back, surrounded by guards. She gave Guin a pleading look.

"Guinevere," she moaned. "Don't let them do this to me!"

Guinevere took a step towards her, looking down at her with steely eyes. She wanted to be angry, furious at what this woman had done. Instead, she just felt horribly sad.

"Please! Don't turn your back on me now!" Mim begged. "It's you and me against the world, remember?"

"There was a time I believed that," Guinevere said softly. "But it was never really true, was it? You were always only out for yourself and I was just your useful pawn. You claim you care about me – yet you stole my entire life away. How can I forgive you for something like that?"

Her voice choked on the words. Mim had been everything to her for so long. But everything had been a lie from the start. Yet another stupid game. With the highest stakes of all.

Mim's face crumbled. Fat tears slid down her cheeks. Guinevere couldn't remember a time she looked so pathetic. So weak. Even when she'd had that dreaded disease, she'd had a spark left in her eyes. Now Guin saw nothing at all.

Then Mim scowled at her, her bravado seeming to return. "You stupid girl!" she growled. "You never were any fun!" She started laughing hysterically. "Not any fun at all!" She kept giggling as the guards began to drag her away.

Guinevere sighed. "Maybe not," she murmured, half to herself. "But at least now I know who I am. And where I'm meant to be."

CHAPTER THIRTY-NINE
ARTHUR

"How do you feel?" Merlin asked as Arthur shoved a big hunk of meat into his mouth at the dining table about an hour later. He couldn't remember the last time he'd had a proper meal. Luckily, the castle cook, Mistress McCready, had been more than happy to throw out all the slug soup Mim had asked her to make and whip up a hearty meal fit for a king.

"Much better now," Arthur said after swallowing down his bite. Merlin wasn't a fan of people speaking with their mouths full. Evidently it was considered 'rude' in the future. "Now that I've had a..." He paused, trying to remember. "What was that waterfall thing you rigged up so I could wash indoors?"

"A shower," Merlin replied with a smile. "A truly remarkable invention of the future."

"Agreed," Arthur said. "I might even be willing to take one of those twice a year."

Merlin sighed. "Or twice a week?" he tried.

"Let's not be ridiculous," Arthur teased. Then he sobered. "So is everything all right? Have they taken Mim away?"

"Guinevere's people left about an hour ago," Merlin said. "With Mim as their… invited guest. Let's just say I don't think we'll have to deal with her for the foreseeable future."

"Thank goodness for that," Arthur declared. "I've had enough purple for a lifetime, thank you very much."

"Agreed," Merlin said. "I'm about ready for things to go back to a nice, boring old—"

He was interrupted by a door opening at the far end of the hall. Arthur looked up to see none other than Guin stepping through, looking at him hesitantly. She was wearing a pale blue silk dress much in the style of her mother's – the proper attire of a princess, he supposed. He just hoped it wasn't too itchy.

"Guinevere," he said, his voice hitching on her name.

"Arthur…"

Merlin raised his eyebrows. Then, without a word, he

snapped his fingers and poofed away in a cloud of smoke. Arthur couldn't help a small smile. The wizard knew when it was time to make an exit.

Guinevere stepped up to the table. Her eyes lowered to the ground. "Hello," she said in a soft voice.

"Hello," he returned, feeling nervous all of a sudden. "I thought maybe you had left with your mother."

She shook her head. "I told her I'd join her soon. But I had some… unfinished business first." Her cheeks turned bright red. "Oh, Arthur," she murmured, looking up at him, her big brown eyes meeting his. He felt his heart pang at the look on her face. "I'm so sorry."

Arthur rose from the table and walked around it until they were face to face. Then he reached out, grabbed her hands, and pulled her closer to him. He threw his arms around her and squeezed her tight. She was stiff at first, but eventually seemed to melt into his embrace. He pulled away and smiled at her.

"Thank you," he said simply.

She shook her head, dropping her gaze. "You shouldn't thank me. This is all my—"

He stopped her words with a kiss, pressing his lips against hers. She reacted with shock at first, then kissed him back. Softly, sweetly. It was perhaps the best moment in the world.

Vanquishing evil was amazing. But kissing Guinevere – well, that was something else entirely.

"You did nothing wrong," he told her when they parted. "You were lied to. Deceived. But when you learnt the truth, you tried to make things better. You *did* make things better! I wouldn't be alive if it wasn't for you. You're a hero, Guin. As much a hero as any knight of the round table."

Her cheeks coloured, and a small smile slipped across her mouth. "I am rather heroic, aren't I?" she joked. Arthur laughed and hugged her again. At that moment, he didn't want to ever let her go.

When they did eventually pull apart, Guinevere gazed upon him with loving eyes. "So how does it feel to be king again?" she asked.

Arthur pressed his lips together. "Funny you should ask."

She cocked her head in question. "What do you mean?"

"I've been doing a lot of thinking," he confessed. "And Mim and even Kay were actually right about one thing. Why should we let some magic sword decide who should be king? The people deserve to choose the ruler they want. Like they do in the twenty-first century." He tapped his head, trying to remember the word. "Merlin called it a democracy. Where people vote for their leaders."

"And you want people to do that?"

"Yes," Arthur said, the idea growing stronger as he thought about it. "We will hold a vote. And every man, woman and child of London will be able to choose the leader they want. Then whoever gets the most votes will be king. Or queen," he added hastily, catching Guin's look.

She smiled at him. "That sounds great, Arthur," she said. "And I know just who will have my vote."

CHAPTER FORTY
ARTHUR

Two Weeks Later

The sun was shining high in the sky by the time Arthur awoke. He'd been up long into the night putting the finishing touches on the voting booths he and Merlin had created. He hadn't realised how exhausted he was until his head hit the pillow and he passed out immediately. And he didn't wake up until he felt Merlin shake him.

"Come on, boy! Are you going to sleep all day?" the wizard grumped, looking displeased. "You have an election to run!"

Arthur stretched his hands over his head, no longer tired. An election! He'd almost forgotten about that!

"Has anyone cast a ballot?" he asked, trying to remember the terms he'd gone over with his teacher.

"Has anyone cast a ballot?" Merlin looked at him incredulously. "You might as well ask me if anyone has not cast a ballot! Half the kingdom has turned out for this election! And they all seem extremely eager to choose their next ruler."

"I wonder who it will end up being," Arthur mused, slipping out of bed and grabbing a tunic and a pair of tights from his wardrobe. "Most likely one of those fancy knights. Sir Morien, Sir Gawain – he's very popular with the people. Maybe even Sir Pellinore – he's old, but smart. Just hopefully not Kay." He made a face. "Surely the people are smarter than that, right?"

Merlin smiled mysteriously. "I guess we'll have to wait and see…" he said.

Arthur nodded. But deep inside he was still nervous about the whole thing. After all, leaving the kingdom's leadership up to the people had never been done before. Who knew what would come of it?

He thought back to when he'd introduced the idea to the people.

"We need to find a proper English king," he'd told them. "Not from some perceived destiny or a jousting tournament. The king needs to be fair and wise and true to his people. He needs to want what's best for them, not just glory for himself. He needs to understand that might does not always equal right. The biggest sword does not give you the right to rule. Instead, we need the biggest heart."

"So who are you appointing?" a woman from the crowd had asked. "Who's to be our next king?"

"We will all decide that together," Arthur declared.

The crowd went wild with this idea. Of course they'd never heard anything like it. *Thank you, twenty-first century*, Arthur thought with a small smile. *Thank you, Merlin.*

They'd spent the next two weeks getting ready for the vote. Merlin was a great help, poofing himself from town to town, creating magical voting booths that would tally up their own results and send them straight to London. Meanwhile Archimedes worked to educate the people on how to use letters to spell out their favourite candidate's name – to help those who could not read or write themselves. Arthur took a few lessons himself – so he could recognise the winner's name when it came time for him to give the results. Guinevere helped with this and promised when the vote was all over she would teach him to read properly.

Once dressed, he headed out of his chambers with Merlin and down the stairs to the great hall. There, Guinevere and Archimedes were waiting for them.

Guinevere had dressed in the same simple yet elegant blue dress she'd worn to the Saxon banquet, and her hair was done up in a new set of complicated braids. She smiled as she saw Arthur, stepping up to give him a hug. He hugged her back, his heart full.

"I voted!" she told him, pulling away from the embrace. "It was very exciting."

"I suppose I need to vote myself," he said thoughtfully. "Who did you vote for?"

She smiled mysteriously. "You're not supposed to tell who you voted for. Merlin said."

"Oh." He blushed. "Well, then I guess I won't tell you who *I'm* voting for, either."

Guinevere stuck her nose in the air playfully. "That's good, because I don't even want to know!"

In truth, there was only one person Arthur could think of voting for, and that was Merlin. He was the smartest man Arthur had ever met, and he believed in peace and education over war and chaos. What better person to lead the realm into a new era of prosperity and goodwill?

He walked out of the castle and into the courtyard, where the voting booths had been set up.

There was still a long line of townsfolk waiting to cast their ballots, but the guards escorted Arthur to the front of the line, and no one seemed to mind. He guessed he might as well take advantage of his kingly privileges while he had them!

After casting his vote for Merlin, carefully spelling out the wizard's name the way Guin had taught him, he headed back out into the courtyard. He could feel a few people in line watching him, and he smiled and waved at them and wished them luck.

"Everything all right?" Guinevere asked, approaching him. "Did you vote?"

"I did and yes," he responded. Then he looked around the courtyard. "Though I have to admit, I'm going to miss this place."

"You're doing the right thing," she assured him. "I'm proud of you for leaving it up to the people."

Archimedes flew down from the turrets. "I hear the first results are starting to come in," he said. He looked a little tired, and Arthur knew it was past his bedtime.

"And…?" he asked, curious. "Who's in the lead?"

"They won't say until everyone's voted," the owl explained. "But it shouldn't be much longer now."

Arthur nodded, feeling a little impatient. Guinevere caught his look. "Let's go take a walk somewhere," she suggested. "Get your mind off things. We'll return when they're ready to announce the results."

And so they did. For Arthur was no longer confined

within the castle walls. He could go where he wanted, when he wanted – a freedom he'd never truly had before.

It was a feeling he'd grown to like quite a bit.

They wandered down the winding river, watching the farmers and fishermen and washerwomen go about their daily tasks. They strode down a forest path until they reached the well where they had first met.

"Remember when you wanted to be a bird?" Guinevere teased. "And fly far, far away?"

"I'm glad I didn't," he admitted. "There's so much right here." Then he glanced shyly at her. "When are you leaving?" he asked. She'd stayed longer than she'd planned to already, wanting to help him set up the election before she returned to her old home.

"Right after they announce the winner," she said. "I'm excited, but nervous. I hope my family likes me."

"How can they not?" Arthur cried indignantly, his heart squeezing at the happiness he saw on her face. Guinevere deserved this – the life she had always been meant to lead. "I'll miss you," he added. "So much."

Guinevere looked up at him with veiled eyes. "I'll miss you, too," she said softly. "But don't worry. I promise to come back soon. Merlin's actually offered to teach me some magic. He thinks I have the makings of a great wizard."

"If Merlin thinks so, then it must be true," Arthur declared. "He's an expert at seeing potential."

Guinevere grinned. "I think I finally understand what you see in him. He's actually pretty great."

"He's the best," Arthur agreed. "Even if he is a little grumpy at times."

Eventually they headed back to the castle, though they took a little more time than perhaps was strictly necessary. When they finally reached the gates, Merlin met them, his eyes alight with excitement.

"It's time!" he cried. "The results are in. Come, come! They're waiting for you to announce them."

Arthur wondered why they needed him for this, but dutifully followed Merlin into the courtyard, where everyone was waiting. The place was packed, and it felt as if the whole town had turned out to hear the election results. Arthur climbed onto the same stage that had once been meant to be his funeral pyre and looked down at the crowd below. Everyone looked anxious and hopeful, and he felt a thrill of excitement race through him.

"Thank you for voting," he told the crowd as Sir Pellinore walked the envelope with the results to him. "You should be proud that you had a part in selecting the new ruler to lead us into the future." He smiled. "And now, I won't keep you in suspense any more."

He tore open the envelope. The crowd collectively seemed to hold their breaths.

He unfolded the paper.

Looked down at it.

Squinted and did a double take.

"Wait, what?" He looked up. "There must be some mistake!"

Guinevere grabbed the paper from his hands, scanning it with her eyes. A slow smile spread across her face. "I don't think so," she said. "I think this is exactly right."

Arthur felt like he was about to fall over. He looked out over the faces of the people in front of him. Their hopeful eyes, their big smiles.

"You— you want *me* to be your king?" he stammered, looking down at the paper one more time as if he expected the name to change without warning. "You voted for me?"

The crowd erupted into cheers. Guinevere bounced up and down. Merlin grinned a wide, toothy grin, and Archimedes slapped Arthur on the back with his wing.

"They want you, lad," Merlin declared. "Not because of some miracle or some feat of strength. But because you have proved to them that you are a kind, fair, capable leader. They believe you are the one who will take them from the darkness and bring them into the light."

Arthur felt too stunned to speak. He glanced at Guinevere. Her smile could have lit up the moon. "Did you know about this?" he asked incredulously.

"Of course I did," she said with a smile. "The Internet said so, right?"

Arthur shook his head, still having a hard time believing it all. But the people had spoken. They wanted him as king.

"So what do you say?" Merlin asked, raising a bushy eyebrow. "Do you want the job or what?"

Arthur forced his head to bob up and down. "I want it," he said. "I would be proud to be their king. As long as you stick around," he added, gesturing to Merlin. "After all, a good king needs a good education."

Merlin nodded approvingly. "I'm glad you recognise that. And I'm happy to do it. After all my travelling, I could use a place to hang my hat for a while. Might as well be here in Camelot."

Arthur smiled, then turned back to the crowd. "Then I accept your offer. And I only hope I prove worthy of your faith in me."

The crowd cheered. People began to dance, and musicians took up a lively tune. Soon everyone was celebrating together. Arthur even spotted a few Saxons in the crowd, dancing and laughing with the rest.

A smile crossed his face. His people. His kingdom. For now and always.

He might not have been some miracle king, but the people didn't care about that. They cared about him. As much as he had grown to care about them.

And for the first time in his life, his true destiny was set in stone.

Mari Mancusi is an Emmy Award–winning former TV news producer and author of more than two dozen sci-fi/fantasy books for kids, teens and adults. Her award-winning series have been translated around the world and have been placed on several US state school reading lists. In addition to writing, Mari is an avid cosplayer, gamer, Disney fan and world traveller. She lives in Austin, Texas, with her husband, daughter and two dogs. She can be found online at www.marimancusi.com or on TikTok under @marimancusi8.

ALSO AVAILABLE IN THE TWISTED TALES SERIES

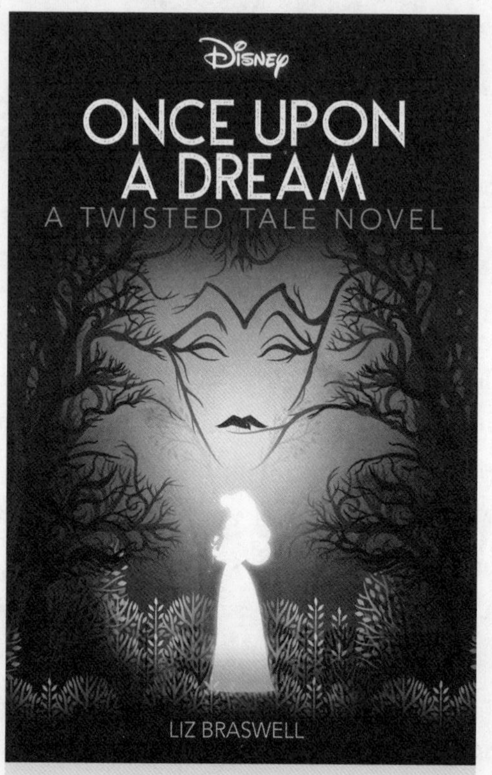

WHAT IF THE SLEEPING BEAUTY NEVER WOKE UP?

The handsome prince is poised to kiss the beautiful sleeping princess and live happily ever after, but as soon as his lips touch hers he too falls fast asleep. It is clear that this tale is far from over.

Now, Princess Aurora must escape from a dangerous and magical land created from her very own dreams.

With Maleficent's agents following her every move, Aurora needs to discover who her true friends are and, most importantly, who she really is.

ALSO AVAILABLE IN THE TWISTED TALES SERIES:

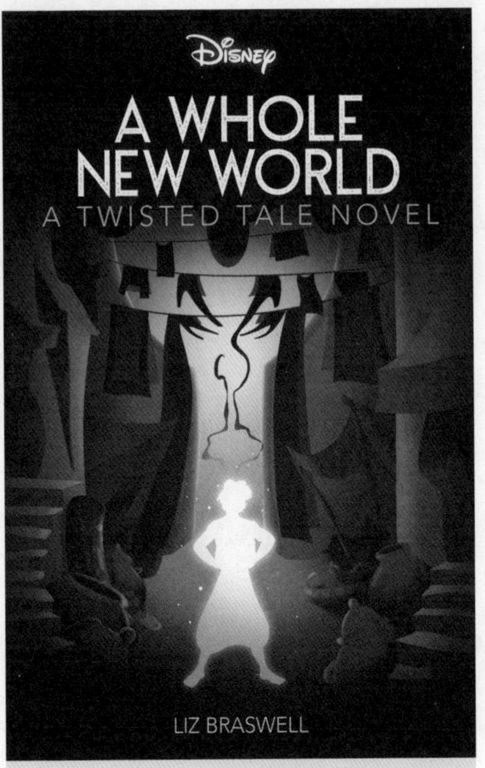

WHAT IF ALADDIN HAD NEVER FOUND THE LAMP?

Aladdin is a Street Rat just trying to survive in a harsh city, while Jasmine is a beautiful princess about to enter an arranged marriage. Their worlds collide when the sultan's trusted adviser suddenly rises to power and, with the help of a mysterious lamp, attempts to gain control over love and death.

Together, Aladdin and Jasmine must unite to stop power-hungry Jafar tearing the kingdom apart in this story of love, power and one moment that changes everything.

ALSO AVAILABLE IN THE TWISTED TALES SERIES:

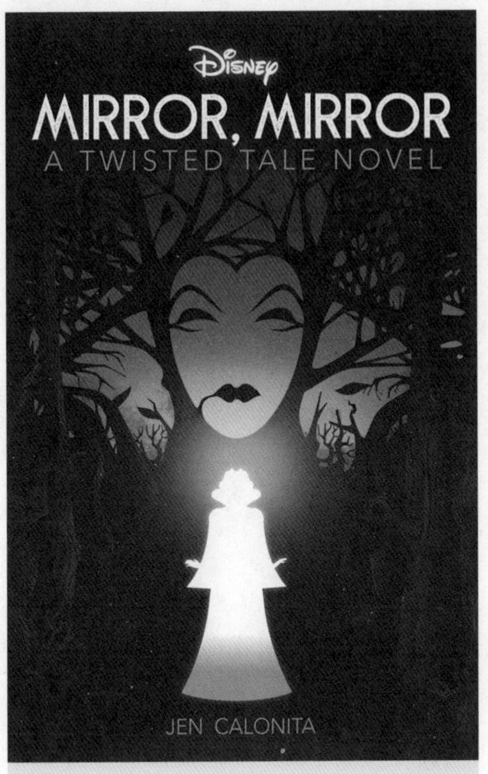

WHAT IF THE EVIL QUEEN POISONED THE PRINCE?

Following her beloved mother's death, the kingdom falls to Snow White's stepmother, known as the Evil Queen.

At first, Snow keeps her head down, hoping to make the best of things. However, when new information about her parents comes to light, and a plot to kill her goes wrong, Snow embarks on a journey to stop the Evil Queen and take back her kingdom.

Can Snow defeat an enemy who will stop at nothing to retain her power... including going after the ones Snow loves?

ALSO AVAILABLE IN THE TWISTED TALES SERIES:

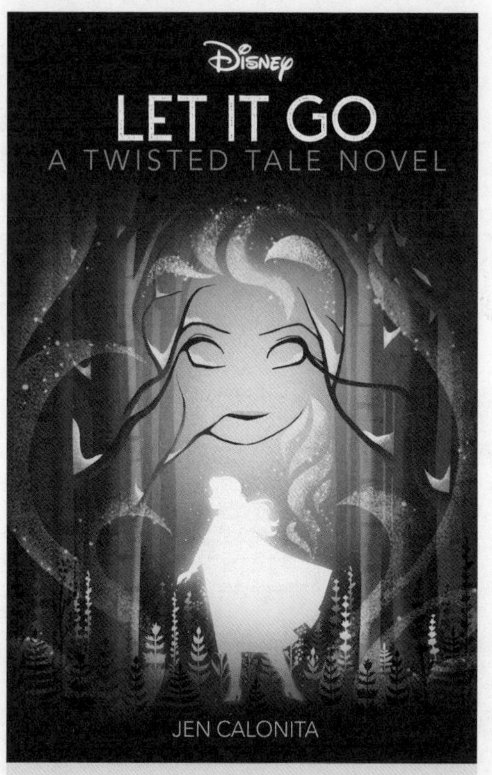

WHAT IF ANNA AND ELSA NEVER KNEW EACH OTHER?

Following the unexpected death of her parents, Elsa finds herself the sole ruler of Arendelle and mysterious powers begin to reveal themselves.

Elsa starts to remember fragments of her childhood that seem to have been erased – fragments that include a familiar-looking girl.

Determined to fill the void she has always felt, Elsa must take a harrowing journey across her icy kingdom to undo a terrible curse… and find the missing Princess of Arendelle.

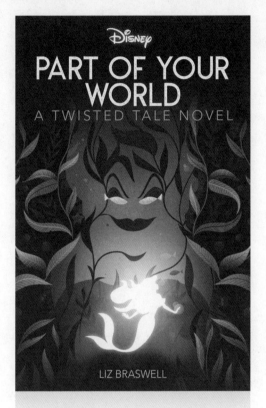